THE BIG BOOK OF
Swashbuckling Adventure

THE BIG BOOK OF
Swashbuckling Adventure

CLASSIC TALES OF DASHING HEROES, DASTARDLY VILLAINS, AND DARING ESCAPES

SELECTED AND INTRODUCED BY
LAWRENCE ELLSWORTH

PEGASUS BOOKS
NEW YORK LONDON

THE BIG BOOK OF SWASHBUCKLING ADVENTURE

Pegasus Books LLC
80 Broad Street, 5th Floor
New York, NY 10004

First Pegasus Books edition December 2014

Interior design by Maria Fernandez

Library of Congress Cataloging-in-Publication Data is available.

ISBN: 978-1-60598-650-0

10 9 8 7 6 5 4 3 2 1

Printed in the United States of America
Distributed by W. W. Norton & Company

Dedicated to my younger children,
Sanderson Ellsworth Ettridge and Honor Ellsworth Ettridge,
who had to put up with me as I compiled it. Some day they'll forgive me.

Contents

Introduction

LAWRENCE ELLSWORTH

The word "swashbuckler" conjures up an indelible image: a hero who's a bit of a rogue but has his own code of honor, an adventurer with laughter on his lips and a flashing sword in his hand. This larger-than-life figure is regularly declared passé, but the swashbuckler is too appealing to ever really die. Who wouldn't want to face deadly danger with confidence and élan? Who can deny the thrill of clashing blades, hairbreadth escapes, and daring rescues, of facing vile treachery with dauntless courage and passionate devotion?

Sign me up, please.

The swashbuckler tradition was born out of legends like those of the Knights of the Round Table and of Robin Hood, revived in the early 19th century by Romantic movement authors such as Sir Walter Scott. The genre really caught hold with the publication of Alexandre Dumas' *The Three Musketeers* in 1844, and for the next century it was arguably the world's leading form of adventure fiction, challenged only by the American Western.

Swashbucklers at first were nearly all gentlemen, usually down on their luck or dishonored, but nonetheless born to rank or nobility. A darker strain joined the genre following the publication of Robert Louis Stevenson's *Treasure Island* in 1883, which added pirates and buccaneers into the mix—for though they were the villains in Stevenson's novel, the fiercely independent freebooters of the great age of piracy were attractive enough in their own right to inject a new jolt of energy into popular tales of historical adventure. The articles and illustrations of Howard Pyle, starting in 1887, were particularly influential, establishing the colorful image of the Caribbean pirates that we still recognize today.

In 1906 the popularity of Alfred Noyes' poem "The Highwayman" brought the masked outlaw to the fore, a character type that was crossed with Baroness Orczy's *The Scarlet Pimpernel* (1905) by Johnston McCulley in 1919 to create the leading swashbuckler of the 20th century, the aristocratic bandit Zorro.

The action and visual flair of the swashbucklers were perfect for the movie screen, and Hollywood brought them to life with brio and panache, starting most successfully with lavish productions of *The Mark of Zorro* (1920) and *The Three Musketeers* (1921), both starring Douglas Fairbanks, Sr. The 1920s through 1940s were the heyday of the Hollywood swashbuckler, but they continue to find favor with moviegoers right up to the present, notably in the recent *Pirates of the Caribbean* series. In fact, in the century from 1911 to 2011, *The Three Musketeers* alone was filmed more than two dozen times.

The popularity of historical swashbuckler stories declined in the nuclear-haunted 1950s, but the genre revived in the late 1960s with the success of paperback reprints from the adventure pulps of twenty to thirty years earlier. Most popular were the fantastic adventures of Edgar Rice Burroughs, author of the John Carter of Mars series, and Robert E. Howard, the creator of Conan the Barbarian. These, along with the rising influence of J.R.R. Tolkien's *Lord of the Rings* books, ensured the swashbuckler's continued pre-eminence, albeit in a setting of fantasy rather than history.

In today's bookstores the Fantasy shelves bulge with tales of dashing swordsmen and (increasingly) swords*women*, testament to the continued appeal of a bold story clearly told, featuring a rogue maintaining his or her personal integrity in the face of death and dishonor. And if that sounds appealing to you, then this is your book.

Fantasy collections are common these days, so this anthology is dedicated to the swashbuckler's roots: historical adventures by the masters of the genre. Most of these stories have been out of print for decades; some have never before been collected in book form. All are top-notch entertainment.

So, ready for some action?
En garde!

THE BIG BOOK OF
Swashbuckling Adventure

About Rafael Sabatini

In the nineteenth century Alexandre Dumas *père* was the undisputed king of historical adventure, but in the twentieth century that crown was worn by Rafael Sabatini (1875-1950). Born in Italy, the (possibly illegitimate) child of two opera singers—one Italian, one English—Sabatini was raised and schooled in Britain, Italy, and Switzerland, and was fluent in at least five languages. Settling in England in the early 1890s, by 1899 he was selling short stories to British magazines, and in 1902 published *The Suitors of Yvonne*, the first of thirty-one historical novels, pretty much all of which can be classified as swashbucklers. Indeed, in the early twentieth century the name Sabatini practically defined the genre.

He was a modestly successful novelist for twenty years before he had a hit with *Scaramouche* (1921), a huge international bestseller that was followed in the next year by *Captain Blood*, an even bigger one. For the rest of the boom years of the 1920s his novels, including re-releases like *The Sea Hawk* (1915), sold hundreds of thousands of copies. With the Great Depression his sales decreased markedly, but his fame was still such that he weathered the storm better than most. It was only when the events of World War II began to make the conflicts of the past pale in comparison that his star began to set.

Here, however, is a tale from early in his career, proving that he had an assured style and strong command of dialogue from the very beginning. As always, Sabatini's characters prefer direct action to delegation, which sometimes led him to put swords into unlikely hands—as in this story from *Everybody's Magazine* of February, 1900.

Sword and Mitre

RAFAEL SABATINI

The Marquis de Castelroc stood smiling before me, and in his outstretched hand he held the appointment which, unsolicited, and even against my wishes, he had obtained for me in Lorraine.

For some moments I remained dumbfounded by what I accounted a liberty which he had no right to take, and yet, imagining that feelings of kindly interest had dictated it, I had not the heart to appear resentful.

At length I broke the painful silence. "*Monsieur* is extremely kind," I murmured, bowing, "but as I told you a week ago, when first you suggested this appointment to me, I cannot and will not accept it; nor can I fathom your motives for thus pressing it upon me."

The smile faded from his handsome, *roué* face, and the hard lines which characterized his mouth when in repose reappeared.

"You refuse it?" he inquired, and his voice had lost all that persuasive gentleness of a moment ago.

"I regret that I cannot accept it," I replied.

He dropped the parchment onto the table, and going over to the fireplace, leaned his elbow on the overmantel. With his gaze fixed upon the ormolu clock, he appeared lost in thoughts of no pleasant character, to judge by the expression of his face.

I endured the ensuing silence for some moments; then, growing weary, and remembering a pair of bright eyes that were watching for my arrival in the Rue du Bac, I coughed to remind him of my presence.

He started at the sound; then turning, came slowly across to where I stood. Leaning lightly against the *secrétaire* of carved oak, and laying a shapely hand, all ablaze with jewels, upon my shoulder, he gazed intently at me for a moment with those uncanny eyes of his.

"You are still a very young man, M. de Bleville," he began.

"Pardon me," I interrupted impatiently, "but I was twenty-four last birthday."

"A great age," he sneered lightly; then quickly changing his tone as if he feared to offend me, "I speak comparatively," he continued. "You are young when compared with me, who am old enough to be your father. Youth, *mon cher vicomte*, is rash, and often does not recognize those things which would revert to its own advantage. Now, I mean you well."

"I doubt it not, *monsieur*."

"I mean you well, and take more interest in you than you think. I have noticed that you are growing pale of late; the air of Paris does not agree with you, and a change would benefit you vastly."

"I thank you, but I am feeling passing well," I answered with some warmth.

"Still," he persisted, puckering his brows, "not so well as a young man of your years should do. Lorraine is a particularly healthy country. You will take the appointment."

"A plague on the appointment!" I exclaimed, unable longer to restrain the anger which his impertinence excited. "I do not want it! Do you not understand me, sir? *Nôtre Dame!* But your persistence grows wearisome. Permit me to bid you good night; I have pressing matters to attend."

So saying, I reached out for my hat which lay on the table beside the lighted tapers. But he caught my arm in his hand with a grip that made me wince.

"Not yet, *vicomte!*" he cried huskily. "I take too great an interest in you to let you go thus. We must understand each other first."

His pale face had an evil scowl, and his voice a ring of mockery little to my taste.

"Your life is in danger, *monsieur*," he said presently, "and if you persist in your determination to remain in Paris, evil will befall you."

"And from whom, pray?" I inquired haughtily.

"My Lord Cardinal."

"Richelieu!" I gasped, and I know that I paled, although I strove not to do so.

He bent over until his lips were on a level with my ear. "Who killed Beausire?" he whispered suddenly.

I recoiled as if he had struck me. Then, in an access of fury, I sprang upon him, and seizing him by the costly lace about his throat, I shook him viciously in my grasp.

"What do you know?" I cried. "Answer me, sir, or I will strangle you. What do you know? Confess!"

With an effort he wrenched himself free, and flung me back against the wall. "Enough to hang you," he snarled, panting for breath. "Keep your distance, you young dog, and listen to me, or it will be the worse for you."

Limp and mute, I remained where I was.

"You may not know me well, Bleville"— he spoke now in calm and deliberate accents—"but those who do will tell you that I am a dangerous man to thwart. Your presence in Paris is distasteful to me. I have determined that you shall quit it, and go you shall—either to Lorraine or the Bastille, as you choose."

"I choose neither, sir," I answered defiantly.

He shrugged his shoulders. "There is no third course open for you, unless, indeed, it be Montfaucon and the hangman. Come, be reasonable; take this appointment and go to Lorraine to recruit your health. Remember, *vicomte*, the cardinal has not forgotten his nephew's death, and it will go hard with you if I but whisper your name in his ear."

"You cannot substantiate your calumny!" I exclaimed.

"Ho, ho! Calumny, eh?" he jeered.

"Yes, calumny," I repeated, thinking to have found a loophole.

But my hopes were soon dashed. "Pish!" he said. "But I have proofs, boy; written proofs. I have a letter which Beausire wrote to his wife on the morning of his death, wherein he told her that he was going to St. Germain to a rendezvous with de Bleville."

"And why," I inquired suspiciously, "if such be the case, why was this letter not shown to Monseigneur de Richelieu by the widow?"

"Because it contained a request that if he fell, no disclosures should be made. The widow was forced to respect his last wishes. But she died last week, as you may possibly be aware. She was my sister, as you may also know, and after her death I found this letter among other treasured papers.

"What do you say now? Will you accept the appointment?"

"It was an honorable duel," I murmured sullenly.

He laughed. "You can explain that to his eminence," he answered derisively, "if you think it will weigh with him."

I knew full well that it would not; for, besides the royal edicts which forbade dueling—and in virtue of which we had gone to St. Germain to fight without seconds, trusting to each other's honor, so that there might be no witnesses, and so that the survivor might not be pestered with the law—Beausire was the cardinal's nephew.

Again Castelroc repeated that monotonous question, "Will you accept the appointment?"

For an instant I wavered, and had it not been for the memory of Mlle. de la Haudraye, who, at that very moment would, I knew, be waiting for me in the Rue du Bac, I believe I should have ended by assenting. As it was, I could not leave Paris then. It was but the night before that I had tasted of the cup of life's happiness, when she had promised to become the Vicomtesse de Bleville, and I would make a desperate stand before the cup was dragged from my lips.

"Would you vouchsafe to tell me why you desire my absence?" I inquired at length.

"Because your presence annoys me," he answered surlily.

"That is no explanation, *monsieur*. I must have a reason."

"And, by Heaven, you shall!" he retorted furiously. "Listen, sir. There is a certain lady in Paris whom I love and whom I desire to wed; but I may not do so while you are by."

The absurdity of his explanation was such that I could not withhold a laugh. "I do not understand how my presence can affect your *affaires du cœur*."

"No more do I! *Mort de ma vie*, I do not!" he answered vehemently. "But women are strange things, and this one has the bad taste to prefer you to me."

"And you think," I answered banteringly, not because I believed his preposterous tale, but because I desired to humor his mendacity, "that if I were absent, if this amorous maid's heart were no longer set aflame by the sight of my beauty, she might turn kindly to you?"

"You have said it!" he cried bitterly. "For you are young and rich, and she would marry you for your money alone, whereas I am not so young, and far from wealthy."

I looked at the richness of his apparel, and of the room wherein we stood, and smiled. "But, M. de Castelroc," I exclaimed, "how can I be guilty of all this? I do not seek to wed the maid."

He looked at me in blank astonishment. "You do not seek to wed Mlle. de la Haudraye?" he muttered.

"Who?" I thundered, starting forward.

"Mlle. de la Haudraye."

For a moment I stared at him; then, stimulated by anger and scorn, I burst into a long, loud laugh.

"It amuses you?" he said icily.

"*Par Dieu!* In truth it does! Imagine the presumption of a man of your years and reputation, aspiring to the hand of such a woman as Mlle. de la Haudraye! *Mon Dieu*, 'tis passing droll!" And with my hands on my sides I gave unrestrained vent to my hilarity, forgetful for the moment of the cardinal and the dungeon yawning at my feet.

But Castelroc sobered me suddenly by picking up that plaguey parchment. "When you have had your laugh, you young fool, perhaps you will reconsider the advisability of accepting this document," he snarled, white with passion.

"May the devil take you and your document," I answered, picking up my hat. "Do what you please. I remain in Paris."

"I will give you twenty-four hours to deliberate," he cried.

"My mind will be unaltered in twenty-four years."

"Then, *mon Dieu*, I will go at once."

He touched a bell that stood upon the table. "My hat and cloak, Guitant," he said to the servant who answered his summons, "and order my carriage. I am going to the Palais Cardinal."

"And I to the Rue du Bac," I cried, as the door closed upon the lackey. "To the Rue du Bac, to tell Mlle. de la Haudraye what manner of man you are, and what you are about to do. Now, master *mouchard*!" I exclaimed triumphantly, "if you imagine that your suit will prosper after that; if you imagine that the Comte de la Haudraye will permit his daughter to wed one of the cardinal's spies, you are a greater fool that I hold you for."

It was a rash speech, but for the life of me I could not have withheld it.

"You shall not go!" he roared, turning livid. "You shall not leave here but to go to the Bastille." Then raising his voice: "Ho, there, someone! *À moi!*"

My sword was out in a trice, and I rushed wildly at him, for his threat had frightened me, and I saw that my rashness was like to cost me dear.

He drew as I sprang forward, and was barely in time to parry a stroke that threatened to end his intriguing for all time. Before I could disengage my arms were seized from behind, and, struggling madly, I was held there at his mercy.

But he only laughed and, sheathing his sword, said the cardinal would deal with me. I was flung rudely down, and while one servant pinned me to the ground, another fetched a rope wherewith they bound me firmly, hand and foot. Then Castelroc rolled me over and struck me on the face.

I opened my mouth to tell him in fitting terms what I thought of this act, when, quick as lightning, he gagged me with a *poire d'angoisse*; then, with a parting gibe, he strode away and, locking the door after him, left me there, stretched upon the ground, powerless, inert, and mute.

II

For perhaps ten minutes I lay where I had been thrown, too stunned by the rude manner in which I had been handled to indulge in active thought. I did not think—at least not coherently; I was content to lie, like the human log they had made me, with a dull sense of anger at my defeat and powerlessness, and with a dismal feeling of despair.

Presently, however, I revived somewhat. The ticking of the ormolu clock was irritating to me, and I felt a burning desire to dash it from its shelf and silence it. But as I gazed upon the ornament I turned my thoughts to the time it measured, and in spirit I followed the Marquis de Castelroc to the Palais Cardinal.

"Even now," I thought, "he will be there; say he is kept waiting five minutes, it will be half past eight before he has speech of the cardinal, another five minutes to relate his story, and ten minutes for his return, accompanied by an officer of Richelieu's guards or of the *Mousquetaires*. By a quarter to nine I shall be arrested; by nine o'clock I shall be in the Châtelet, and by tomorrow in the Bastille."

I shuddered and groaned alternately for the next minute—and groaning with a choke-pear in one's mouth is not easily accomplished.

Next I remembered that I had my own rash tongue to thank for the ropes about me. Had I held my peace I might have been left free to proceed to the Rue du Bac, and warn Adeline and her father of what was about to take place. I could have gone calmly to the Bastille afterward, reassured by the vows which I knew my lady would utter, and—I thought—fulfill, to wait for me. She might have to wait a few years, but even the Cardinal de Richelieu could not live forever; he was already old and, in the end, I should be released, and we might still be happy.

But to disappear in this fashion, as if the earth had consumed me—it was dreadful! She would not know that it had been Castelroc's handiwork, and after she had mourned me for a few weeks, with that villain at hand to console her, who could say what might happen?

Women, I told myself, were fickle things, and many had an unhealthy fancy for a profligate, especially when, like Castelroc,

he chanced to be courtly, handsome, and gifted with a persuasive tongue.

As these thoughts paraded themselves tormentingly before my brain, I was nigh upon becoming mad with anger. In a paroxysm of rage I writhed like a wounded snake upon the polished floor, and rolled myself over and over, until I had almost broken my pinioned arms.

I paused at length in my futile struggles and lay panting on my back, staring stupidly at the hands of the timepiece, which now pointed to half past eight. In another quarter of an hour Castelroc would return.

Oh, if I could only have that quarter of an hour free, so that I might yet go to the Rue du Bac!

Then the thought of escape presented itself, and I was astonished that it had not occurred to me before. The next instant, however, I laughed inwardly—the choke-pear prevented me from laughing aloud—as I remembered how impossible it was. But I set myself to think.

If only I could release my hands! But how? I looked about. My sword lay on the ground, but I could devise no means of employing it.

Then my eyes alighted on the tapers that had been left burning, and my heart almost ceased to beat at the idea they suggested.

I glanced at the clock. It was already twenty-five minutes to nine. If only I had time. And at the thought I fell to cursing myself for not having acted sooner.

In ten minutes Castelroc would be back. Yes, but that was if he gained immediate audience. What if the cardinal kept him waiting? He might spend a half hour, an hour, or even two hours in the antechamber. Richelieu was not particular, and he had tried the patience of better men than Castelroc in this fashion.

Still, fortune favors fools and rogues as well as brave men, so it would not do to build my hopes upon a moonbeam. Of ten minutes I was certain, and what a desperate man could do in ten minutes, I would do.

With the agility of a reptile I wriggled across the room, and having turned myself upon my face, I contrived to kneel. Next, with my chin upon the table, I strove to raise the weight of my body.

I had almost succeeded when of a sudden my feet slipped and I fell heavily to the ground, dragging the table with me. Two of the tapers spluttered and went out, but the third, fortunately, still burned upon the floor.

With a wildly thumping heart I lay there listening, wondering if the noise of my fall had attracted attention. But as all remained quiet I crawled over to the lighted taper, and having gained my knees, I bent over it backward, holding the rope that bound my wrists in the flame, heedless of the searing of my flesh.

In half a minute my hands were free, although severely cut and scorched. To draw the gag from my mouth, and cut the cords at my ankles with my dagger, was the work of an instant.

Then, having righted the candle and recovered my sword, I made stealthily across the room to the window.

It wanted but twenty minutes to nine. I had but five minutes more.

III

I opened the window and looked out. It was a fine night, and clear enough, although the moon had not yet risen, for which I was thankful.

Pausing for a moment to inhale a deep, invigorating breath of the pure April air, I glanced about me for a means of escape, but groaned as I beheld the street pavement a good forty feet beneath, and nothing that might assist me to climb down, as I had hoped.

I wasted a full minute in cursing my ill fortune, as I realized that, after all, there was nothing for it but to submit to the inevitable and remain.

Only three minutes left! The thought acted on me like a dagger prod, and served to quicken my tumultuous thoughts. I turned wildly this way and that, and at last my eyes fastened upon the sloping roof of the adjoining house, not more than twelve feet below the window whereat I stood, but quite three feet away to the left.

For a moment I thought of jumping it; but the peril was too great. I would of a certainty have been dashed to pieces. Then a bright thought occurred to me, and I rushed back for my cloak, which lay in the room.

An iron stanchion protruded from the wall, a little to the left and some two feet below the window. I know not what it did there, nor for the moment did I care. It was already a quarter to nine.

Reaching out, I tied with trembling hands a corner of my cloak to that most apropos of stanchions. Even as I completed the task, a carriage came rumbling down the street; I felt myself grow cold with apprehension. Could this be Castelroc?

I went near to dropping from my perch on the window sill at the thought. But the coach passed on, and I took its advent as a good omen. I would cheat the dog yet! Verily, I laughed as I lowered myself gently from the window.

For a moment I clung to the sill, suspended in mid-air; then, moving my right leg across, I got astride of the stanchion, wondering for the first time if it would bear my weight, and sweating with fear at the thought.

But the iron was stout and firmly planted. Presently I was sliding slowly down my cloak, until there was perhaps a yard of it above my head. Next, taking a firm hold, I set myself to swing backward and forward, until at length the roof of the adjoining house was immediately below my feet.

Twice might I have loosened my hold and dropped with safety, but a miserable fright made me hesitate each time until it was too late. The third time, however, realizing that the strain was beginning to tell upon my arms, and that I might not have strength enough to swing across again, I commended my soul to God and let go.

Down I came with a crash upon the tiles, and it is a miracle that I did not slide over the edge of the sloping roof, plunging into eternity. I did, indeed, slip for a foot or so; but in wild terror I clawed the roof like a cat, and caught myself betimes.

Panting and covered with perspiration, I lay there for a minute or two to regain my breath and steady my shaken nerves, gazing at my still dangling cloak and at the lighted window above, and marveling greatly that I had had the daring to undertake so desperate a journey.

Castelroc had not yet returned, so I concluded that the cardinal had kept him waiting. Still, he might appear at any moment, and I was too near my prison to feel safe as yet. So picking myself carefully up, I crawled along on hands and knees for a while, until presently, growing bolder with experience, I rose to my feet and hurried as rapidly as I dared along that elevated highway.

For some five minutes I pushed steadily onward, with naught save a stray cat or two to keep me company. Albeit the road was passing new to me, and vastly interesting, I began to weary of it, and paused to think how I might descend to the more usual walks of men.

I had reached the corner of the Rue Trecart by then, and looking about me, I saw an attic window conveniently situated on one of the roofs to my left. Turning, I wended my steps in that direction, and with infinite pains I crawled down until I stood beside it. The window was fastened; but it was an easy matter to put my foot through it, and afterward my arm, and thus gain admittance.

I stood for a moment in a small, unfurnished room, to listen if there might be anyone on hand to resent my intrusion. Hearing naught, I went forward, opened the door, passed out onto the landing, and in the dark felt my way stealthily down the stairs.

I had reached the first floor and was debating whether I should go boldly down and quit the house in a rational manner by the street door, when suddenly, hearing male voices and a certain raucous laughter, suggestive of the bottle, I deemed it best to risk no meeting that might be avoided.

I applied my ear to the keyhole of the door by which I stood. As all remained still, I turned the handle and entered.

There was nobody in the room, which I could just discern was tastefully furnished and contained a bed; so, closing the door after me, I stole across to the window, which opened onto a wooden balcony.

As I reached it my attention was arrested by the clash of steel below. "What," I thought, "brawling at this hour, and in the very streets of Paris, in spite of the edicts?" Softly I opened the window and stepped out onto the balcony. The sight which met my eyes filled me with astonishment and anger.

A tall, well-built cavalier, with his back against the wall immediately beneath me, the crown of his hat almost on a level with the balcony, which was not more than six feet from the ground, stood defending himself with masterly dexterity against the onslaught of three evil-looking knaves.

If these men had no respect for the laws of the king, they might at least have some for the laws of chivalry. I did not hesitate a moment what to do, and forgot my own affairs utterly. Drawing my sword, I vaulted over the low wooden railings and, like the warrior St. Michael from heaven to do battle for the right, I dropped, with a yell, into their astonished midst.

IV

Nôtre Dame! How those three ruffians stared at my unexpected and inexplicable advent! And I, having seen what manner of men they were, felt no compunction at profiting from their surprise to run my sword through the nearest of them, from breast to back. He uttered a sharp cry, dropped his rapier, clawed the air for a moment; then, falling in a heap upon the ground, lay still.

With a shout of rage another one sprang at me before I could release my sword. The lunge he directed upon me would assuredly have sent me from the world unshriven, had not the cavalier interposed his blade and turned the murderous stroke aside. The next moment, however, he had to defend his own skin from the third ruffian, who sought to take the same advantage of him that his fellow had endeavored to take of me.

But the respite had permitted me to regain my sword, and I now engaged my assailant across the body of his fallen comrade, and kept him busy, albeit the light was bad. As I had expected, he was but a sorry swordsman, and his parries reminded one of a windmill. Nevertheless, he kept up a vigorous cut-and-thrust play of the old Italian school, which, although soon reckoned with in daylight, is mighty discomposing in the dark, and on a slippery ground, with a body at your feet to stumble over if you lunge too far.

During the first few passes I laughed at his labors, and asked him banteringly

if he were wielding a battle-axe; but presently, when I had been forced to turn my sword into a buckler three or four times, I recognized that the season was ill-timed for jesting. If only I could catch that busy arm of his quiet for a second, I knew I should have him.

Presently he essayed a direct thrust, thinking to force my guard, but I caught his point, and with a sharp *riposte*, which ended in an engage in *tierce*, I brought his play to a standstill at last. The opportunity was not to be wasted; so, with a quick one-two stroke, I sent my point round under his elbow, and while he went fumbling away to the right for my blade, it was grating against his ribs on the left.

The man uttered no sound. He fell heavily across his companion's body. Then, raising himself by a stupendous effort, he fastened one arm around my leg, and attempted to shorten his sword. The exertion soon overcame him, however, and as I kicked my leg free, he sank down in a swoon.

The whole affair had not lasted two minutes. The cavalier was still at work with his opponent; but when, turning, I advanced to his aid, the remaining ruffian sprang back, and setting off at a mad gallop down the street was soon lost to our eyes and ears alike.

"I am deeply indebted to you, *monsieur*," said the cavalier in a curiously muffled voice, as he held out his left hand to me. "My right hand is bleeding slightly," he explained.

I took the proffered hand and, in answering him, I looked up at his face and saw he wore a mask. "I am happy to have been of service to so valiant a gentleman," I said, bowing. "But how came you, if I may inquire, into such company?"

"I was decoyed hither," he answered with a bitter laugh. "I was bidden come alone, and I was foolish enough to accept the invitation."

Whereat, thinking that possibly there was some jealous lady in the matter, and knowing how such affairs are managed, I inquired no further.

"Had it not been for your timely arrival," my companion added, "there would have been an end of me by now. But whither are you bent?" he inquired suddenly.

"To the Rue du Bac," I answered, as my own forgotten affairs came back to my mind.

"Then I will take you there in my carriage; it is waiting not many yards from here. I can thus make up to you for the time that you have lost on my behalf. But let us see these knaves first."

We turned the two fellows over. One of them was but slightly wounded; but the other one—the first to fall—was quite dead. We dragged them under the balcony, and propped them against the wall. "I will send someone to attend to them," said my companion. "Come, it is not safe to linger. The patrol may pass at any moment."

With that he linked his arm in mine and drew me away from the spot. And as we went he fell to thanking me again, and ended by praising my swordsmanship— albeit he had seen but little of it himself— and saying that it was an accomplishment one should be thankful for. "And yet, *monsieur*," I exclaimed, "although I am thankful enough tonight, since it has afforded me the opportunity of serving you, yet am I at this very moment in grievous trouble, thanks to my rapier play."

"Ah!" he murmured, with a show of interest. "And if I am not impertinent, what is this trouble? I may be able to assist you—who knows?"

I required no second invitation, for youth is ever ready with its confidences, and as we walked along, I began my narrative. When I spoke of Castelroc as a spy of Richelieu's, he stopped abruptly. "The Marquis de Castelroc is no spy of the cardinal's," he said coldly.

"Ah, pardon! I have offended you, *monsieur!*" I exclaimed. "Castelroc is a friend of yours."

"God forbid!" he ejaculated.

"But you know him?"

"Yes, for the greatest rogue unhanged. But pursue your tale. You interest me."

V

Briefly I told my story down to the point where I had sprung from the balcony to his assistance. "The dastard!" he muttered, then quickly added: "*Hélas*, my poor friend, your case is indeed grave; but if you were to seek audience of the cardinal and explain to him—*qui sait?*—he might forgive. The affair is old and probably forgotten. Moreover, you appear to have been forced into this duel with Beausire, and, *ma foi*, I fail to see how a gentleman could have done otherwise than fight under such circumstances."

"Aye, *monsieur*," I answered, shaking my head, "but the cardinal will not trouble to inquire. His edicts forbid dueling. That is sufficient. But if more were needed—Beausire was his nephew."

"You misjudge him."

"Nay, *monsieur*, I do not. I recognize in his eminence a great and just man, too just to err on the side of mercy."

At that juncture we turned the corner and walked full into a patrol coming in the opposite direction. My companion surprised me by bidding the sergeant go attend to the wounded man we had left behind. "Has there been a duel?" the fellow inquired.

"Possibly," answered the cavalier with great composure.

The sergeant eyed us suspiciously for a moment, then bade us return with him. "We have business elsewhere, and the affair does not concern us," answered my companion.

"I know not that—" the other began, when suddenly:

"Peace, fool!" the cavalier muttered, and drawing forth his right hand, which he had said was wounded, and hitherto kept carefully hidden under his cloak, he held it up.

I knew not what magic was in those fingers, but at the sight of them the sergeant fell back with a cry of dismay; then, recovering himself, he bowed low before us and bade us pass.

A moment later, and before I could master my surprise at what I had witnessed, we entered a carriage that stood waiting hard by. "Palais Cardinal?" said my companion.

"No, no!" I exclaimed, making for the door; but the coach was already in motion. I turned to expostulate with my companion. He had removed his mask, and a wild panic seized me as, by the light of a street lamp, I recognized—*the cardinal!*

"Well, my young friend," he laughed, "you are in luck tonight; and since you have caught Richelieu breaking his own edicts, you have a right to expect that he will not judge you over-harshly, and that for once this 'great and just man' *will* err on the side of mercy."

"Your eminence!" I cried.

He raised his hand, upon which I now beheld the sacred amethyst which had subjugated the sergeant. "Say no more," he said, "you owe me nothing, while I owe you my life. As for this Castelroc, I am sorry to keep you from Mlle. de la Haudraye for a few moments longer; but I shall be grateful if you will afford me the amusement of beholding his face when we walk in, arm in arm, to grant him the audience for which he is, no doubt, still waiting. I know the gentleman of old; he was involved in a Gascon plot last winter, and had a finger in one of Anne of Austria's tasty pies a few weeks ago. I have been lately thinking of finding him a change of lodging, and your story has decided me. I do not think a sojourn in the Bastille would be amiss, do you?"

I confessed with a laugh that I did not, and a few minutes later Richelieu's fancy for studying facial expressions found ample entertainment in the countenance of the *marquis.*

As ten was striking—so quickly did it all occur—Castelroc and I left the Palais Cardinal in separate carriages, he going to the Bastille with a mounted escort, and I—at last—to the Rue du Bac.

About Anthony Hope

Sir Anthony Hope Hawkins (1863-1933) wrote some thirty-two books, mostly novels, many of them best-sellers that were adapted to stage and screen. Today he is remembered only for his swashbuckler *The Prisoner of Zenda* (1894) and its sequel, *Rupert of Hentzau* (1898). They were set in the fictional principality of Ruritania, and were so popular that they spawned a host of imitations known as "Ruritanian romances."

A *littéraire* at Oxford, Hawkins took a first in Classics at Balliol College, then a law degree. He settled into work as a barrister in the City in London, but time weighed heavily on his hands and he turned to writing, publishing under the name "Anthony Hope." His first literary success, *The Dolly Dialogues* (1894), established the pattern for most of his novels, wry commentaries on London society that mixed romance with politics. His second success was *The Prisoner of Zenda*, a rollicking adventure in a very different mode. Tastes have changed, and nowadays Hope's Edwardian comedies of manners are largely forgotten, but *The Prisoner of Zenda*, with its iconic dash, flair, excitement, and humor, lives on.

You may have read *Zenda* or seen one of its movie adaptations; you may even have read the sequel, *Rupert of Hentzau*, as it is sometimes published these days together with *Zenda*. But odds are you don't know *The Heart of Princess Osra* (1896), Hope's collection of short stories set in Ruritania about a century and a half before the events of *Zenda* and *Rupert*. *Osra* is a mixed bag: some romances, some character pieces, some comic vignettes—and a few rip-roaring swashbucklers, like the story that follows.

The Sin of the Bishop of Modenstein

ANTHONY HOPE

In the days of Rudolf III there stood on the hill opposite the Castle of Zenda, and on the other side of the valley in which the town lies, on the site where the *château* of Tarlenheim now is situated, a fine and strong castle belonging to Count Nikolas of Festenburg. He was a noble of very old and high family, and had great estates; his house being, indeed, second only to the Royal House in rank and reputation. He himself was a young man of great accomplishments, of a domineering temper, and of much ambition; and he had gained distinction in the wars that marked the closing years of the reign of King Henry the Lion. With King Rudolf he was not on terms of cordial friendship, for he despised the King's easy manners and carelessness of dignity, while the King had no love for a gentleman whose one object seemed to be to surpass and outshine him in the eyes of his people, and who never rested from extending and fortifying his castle until it threatened to surpass Zenda itself both in strength and magnificence. Moreover Nikolas, although maintaining a state ample and suitable to his rank, was yet careful and prudent, while Rudolf spent all that he received and more besides, so that the Count grew richer and the King poorer. But in spite of these causes of difference, the Count was received at Court with apparent graciousness, and no open outburst of enmity had yet occurred, the pair being, on the contrary, often together, and sharing their sports and pastimes with one another.

Now most of these diversions were harmless, or indeed, becoming and proper, but there was one among them full of danger to a man of hot head and ungoverned impulse such as King Rudolf was. And this one was dicing, in which the King took great delight, and in which the Count Nikolas was very ready to encourage him. The King, who was generous and hated to win from poor men or those who might be playing beyond their means in order to give him pleasure, was delighted to find an opponent whose purse was as long or longer than his own, and thus gradually came to pass many evenings with the dice-boxes in Nikolas's company. And the more evenings he passed the deeper he fell into the Count's debt; for the King drank wine, while the Count was content with small beer, and when the King was losing he doubled his stakes, whereas the Count took in sail if the wind seemed adverse. Thus always and steadily the debt grew, till at last Rudolf dared not reckon how large it had become, nor did he dare to disclose it to his advisers. For there were great public burdens already imposed by reason of King Henry's wars, and the citizens of Strelsau were not in a mood to bear fresh exaction, nor to give their hard earnings for the payment of the King's gambling debts; in fine, although they loved the Elphbergs well enough, they loved their money more. Thus the King had no resource except in his private possessions, and these were of no great value, saving the castle and estate of Zenda.

At length, when they had sat late one night and the throws had gone all evening against the King and for Nikolas, the King flung himself back in his chair, drained his glass, and said impatiently, "I am weary of the game! Come, my lord, let us end it."

"I would not urge you, sire, a moment beyond what you desire. I play but for your pleasure."

"Then my pleasure has been your profit," said the King with a vexed laugh, "for I believe I am stripped of my last crown. What is my debt?"

The Count, who had the whole sum reckoned on his tablets, took them out, and showed the King the amount of the debt.

"I cannot pay it," said Rudolf. "I would play you again, to double the debt or wipe it out, but I have nothing of value enough to stake."

The desire which had been nursed for long in the Count's heart now saw the moment of its possible realization. He leant over the table and, smoothing his beard with his hand, said gently, "The amount is no more than half the value of your Majesty's castle and demesne of Zenda."

The King started and forced a laugh. "Aye, Zenda spoils the prospect from Festenburg, does it?" said he. "But I will not risk Zenda. An Elphberg without Zenda would seem like a man robbed of his wife. We have had it since we have had anything or been anything. I should not seem King without it."

"As you will, sire. Then the debt stands?" He looked full and keenly into the King's eyes, asking without words, *How will you pay it?* And adding without words, *Paid it must be.* And the King read the unspoken words in the eyes of Count Nikolas.

The King took up his glass, but finding it empty flung it angrily on the floor, where it shivered into fragments at Count Nikolas's feet; and he shifted in his chair and cursed softly under his breath. Nikolas sat with the dice-box in his hand and a smile on his lips; for he knew that the King could not pay, and therefore must play, and he was in the vein, and did not doubt of winning from the King Zenda and its demesne. Then he would be the greatest lord in the kingdom, and hold for his own a kingdom within the kingdom, and the two strongest places in all the land. And a greater prize might then dangle in reach of his grasp.

"The devil spurs and I gallop," said the King at last. And he took up the dice-box and rattled it.

"Fortune will smile on you this time, sire, and I shall not grieve at it," said Count Nikolas with a courteous smile.

"Curses on her!" cried the King. "Come, my lord, a quick ending to it! One throw, and I am a free man, or you are master of my castle."

"One throw let it be, sire, for it grows late," assented Nikolas with a careless air; and they both raised the boxes and rattled the dice inside them. The King threw: his throw was a six and a five, and a sudden gleam of hope lit up his eyes; he leant forward in his chair, gripping the elbows of it with his hands; his cheeks flushed and his breath came quickly.

With a bow Count Nikolas raised his hand and threw. The dice fell and rolled upon the table. The King sank back; and the Count said with a smile of apology and a shrug of his shoulders, "Indeed I am ashamed. For I cannot be denied tonight."

For Count Nikolas of Festenburg had thrown sixes, and thereby won from the King the castle and demesne of Zenda.

He rose from his chair and, having buckled on his sword that had lain on the table by him, and taking his hat in his hand, stood looking down on the King with a malicious smile on his face. And he said with a look that had more mockery that respect in it, "Have I your Majesty's leave to withdraw? For ere day dawn, I have matters to transact in Strelsau, and I would be at my castle of Zenda tonight."

Then King Rudolf took a sheet of paper and wrote an order that the castle, and all that was in it, and all the demesne should be surrendered to Count Nikolas of Festenburg on his demand, and he gave the paper to Nikolas. Then he rose up and held out his hand, which Nikolas kissed, smiling covertly, and the King said with grace and dignity, "Cousin, my castle has found a more worthy master. God give you joy of it."

And he motioned with his hand to be left alone. Then, when the Count had gone, he sat down in his chair again, and remained there till it was full day, neither moving nor yet sleeping. There he was found by his gentlemen when they came to dress him, but none asked him what had passed.

Count Nikolas, now Lord of Zenda, did not so waste time, and the matters that he had spoken of did not keep him long in Strelsau; but in the early morning he rode out, the paper which the King had written in his belt.

First he rode with all speed to his own house of Festenburg, and there he gathered together all his followers, servants, foresters, and armed retainers, and he told them that they were to ride with him to Zenda, for that Zenda was now his and not the King's. At this they were greatly astonished, but they ate the fine dinner and drank the wine which he provided, and in the evening they rode down the hill very merry, and trotted, nearly a hundred strong, through the town, making a great noise, so that they disturbed the Bishop of Modenstein, who was lying that night at the inn in the course of a journey from his See to the Capital; but nobody could tell the Bishop why they rode to Zenda, and presently the Bishop, being wearied with traveling, went to his bed.

Now King Rudolf, in his chagrin and dismay, had himself forgotten, or had at least neglected to warn the Count of Festenburg, that his sister Princess Osra was residing at the castle of Zenda; for it was her favorite resort, and she often retired from the Court and spent many days there alone. There she was now with two of her ladies, a small retinue of servants, and no more than half a dozen Guards; and when Count Nikolas came to the gate, it being then after nine, she had gone to her own chamber, and sat before the mirror, dressed in a loose white gown, with her ruddy hair unbound and floating over her shoulders. She was reading an old story book, containing tales of Helen of Troy, of Cleopatra, of Berenice, and other lovely ladies, very elegantly related and embellished with fine pictures.

And the Princess, being very much absorbed in the stories, did not hear nor notice the arrival of the Count's company, but continued to read, while Nikolas roused the watchmen, and the bridge was let down, and the steward summoned. Then Nikolas took the steward aside and showed him the King's order, bearing the King's seal, and the steward, although both greatly astonished and greatly grieved, could not deny the letter or the seal, but declared himself ready to obey and to surrender the castle; and the sergeant in command of the Guard said the same; but, they added, since the Princess was in the castle, they must inform her of the matter and take her commands.

"Aye, do," said Nikolas, sitting down in the great hall. "Tell her not to be disturbed, but to give me the honor of being her host for as long as she will, and say that I will wait on her, if it be her pleasure."

But he smiled to think of the anger and scorn with which Osra would receive the tidings when the steward delivered them to her.

In this respect the event did not fall short of his expectations, for she was so indignant and aghast that, thinking of nothing but the tidings, she flung away the book and cried, "Send the Count here to me," and stood waiting for him there in her chamber, in her white gown and with her hair unbound and flowing down over her shoulders. And when he came she cried, "What is this, my lord?" and listened to his story with parted lips and flashing eyes, and thus read the King's letter and saw the King's seal. And her eyes filled with tears, but she dashed them away with her hand.

Then the Count said, bowing to her as mockingly as he had bowed to her brother, "It is the fortune of the dice, madame."

"Yes, my lord, as you play the game," said she.

His eyes were fixed on her, and it seemed to him that she was more beautiful in her white gown and with her hair unbound over her shoulders, than he had ever felt her to be before, and he eyed her closely. Suddenly she looked at him, and for a moment he averted his eyes; but he looked again and her eyes met his.

For several moments she stood rigid and motionless. Then she said, "My lord, the King has lost the castle of Zenda, which is the home and cradle of our House. It was scarcely the King's alone to lose. Have I no title in it?"

"It was the King's, madame, and now it is mine," smiled Nikolas.

"Well, then, it is yours," said she, and taking a step towards him, she said, "Have you a mind to venture it again, my lord?"

"I would venture it only against a great stake," said he, smiling still, while his eyes were fixed on her face and marked every change in the color of her cheeks.

"I can play dice as well as the King," she cried. "Are we not all gamblers, we Elphbergs?" And she laughed bitterly.

"But what would your stake be?" he asked sneeringly.

Princess Osra's face was now very pale, but her voice did not tremble and she did not flinch; for the honor of her House and of the throne was as sacred to her as her salvation, and more than her happiness.

"A stake, my lord," said she, "that many gentlemen have thought above any castle in preciousness."

"Of what do you speak?" he asked, and his voice quivered a little, as a man's does in excitement. "For, pardon me, madame, but what have you of such value?"

"I have what the poorest girl has, and it is of the value that it pleased God to make it and pleases men to think it," said Osra. "And all of it I will stake against the King's castle of Zenda and its demesne."

Count Nikolas's eyes flashed and he drew nearer to her; he took his dice-box from his pocket, and he held it up before her, and he whispered in an eager hoarse voice, "Name this great stake, madame; what is it?"

"It is myself, my lord," said Princess Osra.

"Yourself?" he cried wondering, though he had half guessed.

"Aye. To be the Lord of Zenda is much. Is it not more to be husband to the King's sister?"

"It is more," said he, "when the King's sister is the Princess Osra." And he looked at her now with open admiration.

But she did not heed his glance, but with a face pale as death she seized a small table and drew it between them and cried, "Throw then, my lord! We know the stakes."

"If you win, Zenda is yours. If I win, you are mine."

"Yes, I and Zenda also," said she. "Throw, my lord!"

"Shall we throw thrice, madame, or once, or how often?"

"Thrice, my lord," she answered, tossing back her hair behind her neck, and holding one hand to her side. "Throw first," she added.

The Count rattled the box; and the throw was seven. Osra took the box from him, looked keenly and defiantly in his eyes, and threw.

"Fortune is with you, madame," said he, biting his lips. "For a five and a four make nine, or I err greatly."

He took the box from her; his hand shook, but hers was firm and steady; and again he threw.

"Ah, it is but five," said he impatiently, and a frown settled on his brow.

"It is enough, my lord," said Osra; and pointed to the dice that she had thrown, a three and a one.

The Count's eyes gleamed again; he sprang towards her and was about to seize the box. But he checked himself suddenly and bowed, saying, "Throw first this time, I pray you, madame, if it be not disagreeable to you."

"I do not care which way it is," said Osra, and she shook and made her third cast. When she lifted the box, the face of the dice showed seven. A smile broadened on the Count's lips, for he thought surely he could beat seven, he that had beaten eleven and thereby won the castle of Zenda, which now he staked against the Princess Osra. But his eyes were very keenly and attentively on her, and he held the box poised, shoulder-high, in his right hand.

Then a sudden faintness and sickness seized on the Princess, and the composure that had hitherto upheld her failed; she could not meet his glance, nor could she bear to see the fall of the dice; but she turned away her head before he threw, and stood thus with averted face. But he kept attentive eyes on her, and drew very near to the table so that he stood right over it. And the Princess Osra caught sight of her own face in the mirror, and started to see herself pallid and ghastly, and her features drawn as though she were suffering some great pain. Yet she uttered no sound.

The dice rattled in the box; they rattled on the table; there was a pause while a man might quickly count a dozen; and then Count Nikolas of Festenburg cried out in a voice that trembled and tripped over the words: "Eight, eight, eight!"

But before the last of the words had left his shaking lips, the Princess Osra faced round on him like lightning. She raised her hand so that the loose white sleeve fell back from her rounded arm, and her eyes flashed, and her lips curled as she outstretched her arm at him and cried:

"Foul play!"

For, as she watched her own pale face in the mirror—the mirror which Count Nikolas had not heeded—she had seen him throw, she had seen him stand for an instant over the dice he had thrown with gloomy and maddened face; and then she had seen a slight swift movement of his left hand, as his fingers deftly darted down and touched one of the dice and turned it. And all this she had seen before he cried eight.

Therefore now she turned on him and cried, "Foul play!" And before he could speak, she darted by him towards the door.

But he sprang forward and caught her by the arm above the wrist and gripped her, and his fingers bit into the flesh of her arm as he gasped, "You lie! Where are you going?"

But her voice rang out clear and loud in answer, "I am going to tell the world that Zenda is ours again, and I am going to publish in every city in the kingdom that Count Nikolas of Festenburg is a common cheat and rogue, and should be whipped at the cart's tail through the streets of Strelsau. For I saw you in the mirror, my lord, I saw you in the mirror!" And she ended with a wild laugh that echoed through the room.

Still he gripped her arm, and she did not flinch; for an instant he looked full in her eyes; covetousness, and desire, and shame, came all together upon him and overmastered him, and he hissed between set teeth, "You shan't! By God, you shan't!"

"Aye, but I will, my lord," said Osra. "It is a fine tale for the King and for your friends in Strelsau."

An instant longer he held her where she was; and he gasped and licked his lips. Then he suddenly dragged her with him towards a couch; seizing up a coverlet that lay on the couch he flung it around her, and he folded it tight about her, and he drew it close over her face. She could not cry out nor move. He lifted her up and swung her over his shoulder and, opening the door of the room, dashed down the stairs towards the great hall.

In the great hall were six of the King's Guard and some of the servants of the castle, and many of the people who had come with Count Nikolas; they all sprang to their feet when they saw him. He took no heed of them, but rushed at a run through the hall, out under the portcullis and across the bridge, which had not been raised since he entered. There at the end of the bridge a lackey held his horse; and he leapt on his horse, setting one hand on the saddle, still holding Osra; and then he cried aloud, "My men follow me! To Festenburg!"

And all his men ran out, the King's Guard doing nothing to hinder them, and jumping on their horses and setting them at a gallop, hurried after the Count. He, riding furiously, turned towards the town of Zenda; the whole company swept down the hill and, reaching the town, clattered and dashed through it at full gallop, neither drawing rein nor turning to right or left.

And again they roused the Bishop of Modenstein, and he turned in his bed, wondering what the rush of mounted men meant. But they, galloping still, climbed the opposite hill and came to the castle of Festenburg with their horses spent and foundered. In they all crowded, close on

one another's heels; the bridge was drawn up; and there in the entrance they stood looking at one another, asking mutely what their master had done, and who was the lady whom he carried wrapped in the coverlet.

But he ran on till he reached the stairs, and he climbed them, and entering a room in the gate-tower, looking over the moat, he laid the Princess Osra on a couch, and standing over her he smote one hand upon the other, and he swore loudly: "Now, as God lives, Zenda I will have, and her I will have, and it shall be her husband whom she must, if she will, proclaim a cheat in Strelsau!"

Then he bent down and lifted the coverlet from her face. But she did not stir nor speak, nor open her eyes. For she had fallen into a swoon as they rode, and did not know what had befallen her; nor where she had been brought, nor that she was now in the castle of Festenburg, and in the power of a desperate man. Thus she lay still and white, while Count Nikolas stood over her and bit his nails in rage. And it was then just on midnight.

On being disturbed for the third time, the Bishop of Modenstein, whose temper was hot and cost him continual prayers and penances from the mastery it strove to win over him, was very impatient; and since he was at once angry and half asleep, it was long before he could or would understand the monstrous news with which his terrified host came trembling and quaking to his bedside in the dead of the night. A servant-girl, stammered the frightened fellow, had run down half dressed and panting from the castle of Zenda, and declared that whether they chose to believe her or not—and, indeed, she could hardly believe such a thing herself, although she had seen it with her own eyes from her own window—yet Count Nikolas of Festenburg had come to the castle that evening, had spoken with Princess Osra, and now (they might call her a liar if they chose) had carried off the Princess with him on his horse to Festenburg, alive or dead none knew, and the menservants were amazed and terrified, and the soldiers were at their wits' end, talking big and threatening to bring ten thousand men from Strelsau and to leave not one stone upon another at Festenburg and what not. But all the while and for all their big talk nothing was done; and the Princess was at Festenburg, alive or dead or in what strait none knew. And, finally, nobody but one poor servant-girl had had the wit to run down and rouse the town.

The Bishop of Modenstein sat up in his bed and he fairly roared at the innkeeper, "Are there no men, then, who can fight in the town, fool?"

"None, none, my lord—not against the Count. Count Nikolas is a terrible man. Please God, he has not killed the Princess by now."

"Saddle my horse," said the Bishop, "and be quick with it."

And he leapt out of bed with sparkling eyes. For the Bishop was a young man, but a little turned of thirty, and he was a noble of the House of Hentzau. Now some of the Hentzaus (of whom history tells us of many) have been good, and some have been bad; and the good fear God, while the bad do not; but neither the good nor the bad fear anything in the world besides. Hence, for good or ill, they do great deeds and risk their lives as another man risks a penny. So the Bishop, leaving his bed, dressed himself in breeches and boots, and set a black hat with a violet feather on his head, and, staying to put on nothing else but his shirt and his cloak over it, in ten minutes was on his horse at the door of the inn. For a moment he looked at a straggling crowd that had gathered there; then with a toss of his head and a curl of his lip he told them what he thought of them, saying openly that he thanked heaven they were not of his diocese, and in an instant he was galloping through the streets of the town towards the castle of Festenburg, with his sword by his side and a brace of pistols in the holsters of the saddle.

Thus he left the gossipers and vaporers behind, and rode alone as he was up the hill, his blood leaping and his heart beating quick; for as he went, he said to himself, "It is not often a Churchman has a chance like this."

On the stroke of half-past twelve he came to the bridge of the castle moat, and the bridge was up. But the Bishop shouted, and the watchman came out and stood in the gateway across the moat, and the night being fine and clear, he presented an excellent aim.

"My pistol is straight at your head," cried the Bishop, "let down the bridge. I am Frederick of Hentzau; that is, I am the Bishop of Modenstein, and I charge you, if you are a dutiful son of the Church, to obey me. The pistol is full at your head."

The watchman knew the Bishop, but also knew the Count his master. "I dare not let down the bridge without an order from my lord," he faltered.

"Then before you can turn round, you're a dead man," said the Bishop.

"Will you hold me harmless with my lord if I let it down?"

"Aye, he shall not hurt you. But if you do not immediately let it down, I'll shoot you first and refuse you a Christian burial afterwards. Come, down with it."

So the watchman, fearing that, if he refused, the Bishop would spare neither body nor soul, but would destroy the one and damn the other, let down the bridge, and the Bishop, leaping from his horse, ran across with his drawn sword in one hand and a pistol in the other.

Walking into the hall, he found a great company of Count Nikolas's men, drinking with one another, but talking uneasily and seeming alarmed. And the Bishop raised the hand that held the sword above his head in the attitude of benediction, saying, "Peace be with you!"

Most of them knew him by his face, and all knew him as soon as a comrade whispered his name, and they sprang to their feet, uncovering their heads and bowing. And he said, "Where is your master the Count?"

"The Count is upstairs, my lord," they answered. "You cannot see him now."

"Nay, but I will see him," said the Bishop.

"We are ordered to let none pass," said they, and although their manner was full of respect, they spread themselves across the hall, and thus barred the way to the staircase that rose in the corner of the hall.

But the Bishop faced them in great anger, crying, "Do you think I do not know what has been done? Are you all, then, parties in this treachery? Do you all want to swing from the turrets of the castle when the King comes with a thousand men from Strelsau?"

At this they looked at him and at one another with great uneasiness; for they knew that the King had no mercy when he was roused, and that he loved his sister above everybody in the world. And the

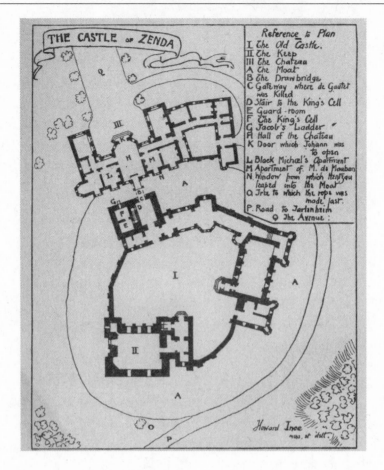

Reference to Plan

I The Old Castle.
II The Keep
III The Chateau
A The Moat
B The Drawbridge
C Gateway where de Gautet was Killed
D Stair to the King's Cell
E Guard-room
F The King's Cell
G Jacob's Ladder
H Hall of the Chateau
K Door which Johann was to open
L Black Michael's Apartment
M Apartment of M. de Mauban
N Window from which Hentzau leaped into the Moat
O Tree to which the rope was made fast.
P Road to Tarlenheim
Q The Avenue

THE CASTLE of ZENDA

Bishop stepped up close to their rank. Then one of them drew his sword halfway from its scabbard. But the Bishop, perceiving this, cried, "Do you all do violence to a lady, and dare to lay hands on the King's sister? Aye, and here is a fellow that would strike a Bishop of God's Church!" And he caught the fellow a buffet with the flat of his sword that knocked him down. "Let me pass, you rogues," said the Bishop. "Do you think you can stop a Hentzau?"

"Let us go and tell the Count that my lord the Bishop is here," cried the house-steward, thinking that he had found a way out of the difficulty; for they dared neither to touch the Bishop nor yet to let him through; and the steward turned to run towards the staircase. But the Bishop sprang after him, quick as an arrow, and, dropping the pistol from his left hand, caught him by the shoulder and hurled him back. "I want no announcing," he said. "The Church is free to enter everywhere."

And he burst through them at the point of the sword, reckless now what might befall him so that he made his way through. But they did not venture to cut him down; for they knew that nothing but death would stop him, and for their very souls' sake they dared not kill him. So he, kicking one and pushing another and laying about him with the flat of his sword and with his free hand, and reminding them all the while of their duty to the Church and of his sacred character, at last made his way through and stood alone, unhurt, at the foot of the staircase, while they cowed by the walls or looked at him in stupid helplessness and bewilderment. And the Bishop swiftly mounted the stairs.

At this instant in the room in the gate-tower of the castle overlooking the moat there had fallen a moment of dead silence. Here Count Nikolas raised the Princess, set her on a couch, and waited till her faintness and fright were gone. Then he had come near to her, and in brief harsh tones told her his mind. For him, indeed, the dice were now cast; in his fury and fear he had dared all. He was calm now, with the calmness of a man at a great turn of fate. That room, he told her, she should never leave alive, save as his promised wife, sworn and held to secrecy and silence by the force of that bond and of her

oath. If he killed her he must die, whether by his own hand or the King's mattered little. But he would die for a great cause and in a great venture. "I shall not be called a cheating gamester, madame," said he, a smile on his pale face. "I choose death sooner than disgrace. Such is my choice. What is yours? It stands between death and silence; and no man but your husband will dare to trust your silence."

"You do not dare to kill me," said she defiantly.

"Madame, I dare do nothing else. They may write 'murderer' on my tomb; they shall not throw 'cheat' in my living face."

"I will not be silent," cried Osra, springing to her feet. "And rather than be your wife I would die a thousand times. For a cheat you are—a cheat—a cheat!" Her voice rose, till he feared that she would be heard, if anyone chanced to listen, even from so far off as the hall. Yet he made no more effort, seeking to move her by an appeal to which women are not wont to be insensible.

"A cheat, yes!" said he. "I, Nikolas of Festenburg, am a cheat. I say it, though no other man shall while I live to hear him. But to gain what stake?"

"Why, my brother's castle of Zenda."

"I swear to you it was not," he cried, coming nearer to her. "I did not fear losing on the cast, but I could not endure not to win. Not my stake, madame, but yours lured me to my foul play. Have you your face, and yet do not know to what it drives men?"

"If I have a fair face, it should inspire fair deeds," said she. "Do not touch me, sir, do not touch me. I loathe breathing the same air with you, or so much as seeing your face. Aye, and I can die. Even the women of our House know how to die."

At her scorn and contempt a great rage came upon him, and he gripped the hilt of his sword, and drew it from the scabbard. But she stood still, facing him with calm eyes. Her lips moved for a moment in prayer, but she did not shrink.

"I pray you," said he in trembling speech, mastering himself for an instant, "I pray you!" But he could say no more.

"I will cry your cheating in all Strelsau," said she.

"Then commend your soul to God. For in one minute you shall die."

Still she stood motionless; and he began to come near to her, his sword now drawn in his hand. Having come within the distance from which he could strike her, he paused and gazed into her eyes. She answered him with a smile. Then there was for an instant an utter stillness in the room; and in that instant the Bishop of Modenstein set his foot on the staircase and came running up. On a sudden Osra heard the step, and a gleam flashed in her eye. The Count heard it also, and his sword was arrested in its stroke. A smile came on his face. He was glad at the coming of someone whom he might kill in a fight; for it turned him sick to butcher her unresisting. Yet he dared not let her go, to cry his cheating in the streets of Strelsau.

The steps came nearer. He dropped his sword on the floor and sprang upon her. A shriek rang out, but he pressed his hand on her mouth and seized her in his arms. She had no strength to resist, and he carried her swiftly across the room to a door in the wall. He pulled the door open—it was very heavy and massive—and he flung her down roughly on the stone floor of a little chamber, square and lofty, having but one small window high up, through which the moonlight scarcely pierced. She fell with a moan of pain. Unheeding, he turned on his heel and shut the door.

And, as he turned, he heard a man throw himself against the door of the room. It also was strong, and twice the man hurled himself with all his force against it. At last it strained and gave way; and the Bishop of Modenstein burst into the room breathless. And he saw no trace of the Princess's presence, but only Count Nikolas standing sword in hand in front of the door in the wall with a sneering smile on his face.

The Bishop of Modenstein never loved to speak afterwards of what followed, saying always that he rather deplored than gloried in it, and that when a man of sacred profession was forced to use the weapons of this world it was a matter of grief to him, not vaunting. But the King compelled him by urgent requests to describe the whole affair, while the Princess was never weary of telling all that she knew, or of blessing all bishops for the sake of the Bishop of Modenstein. Yet the Bishop blamed himself; perhaps, if the truth were known, not for the necessity that drove him to do what he did, as much as for a secret and ashamed joy which he detected in himself.

For certainly, as he burst into the room now, there was no sign of reluctance or unwillingness in his face; he took off his feathered hat, bowed politely to the Count, and resting the point of his sword on the floor, asked, "My lord, where is the Princess?"

"What do you want here, and who are you?" cried the Count with a blasphemous oath.

"When we were boys together, you knew Frederick of Hentzau. Do you not now know the Bishop of Modenstein?"

"Bishop! This is no place for bishops. Get back to your prayers, my lord."

"It wants some time yet before matins," answered the Bishop. "My lord, where is the Princess?"

"What do you want with her?"

"I am here to escort her wherever it may be her pleasure to go."

He spoke confidently, but he was in his heart alarmed and uneasy because he had not found the Princess.

"I do not know where she is," said Nikolas of Festenburg.

"My lord, you lie," said the Bishop of Modenstein.

The Count had wanted nothing but an excuse for attacking the intruder. He had it now, and an angry flush mounted in his cheeks as he walked across to where the Bishop stood.

Shifting his sword, which he had picked up again, to his left hand, he struck the Bishop on the face with his gloved hand. The Bishop smiled and turned the other cheek to Count Nikolas, who struck again with all his force, so that he reeled back, catching hold of the open door to avoid falling, and the blood started dull red under the skin of his face. But he still smiled, and bowed, saying, "I find nothing about the third blow in Holy Scripture."

At this instant the Princess Osra, who had been half stunned by the violence with which Nikolas had thrown her on the floor, came to her full senses and, hearing the Bishop's voice, she cried out loudly for help. He, hearing her, darted in an instant across the room, and was at the door of the little chamber before the Count could stop him. He pulled the door open and Osra sprang out to him, saying, "Save me! Save me!"

"You are safe, madame, have no fear," answered the Bishop. And turning to the Count, he continued, "Let us go outside, my lord, and discuss this matter. Our dispute will disturb and perhaps alarm the Princess."

And a man might have read the purpose in his eyes, though his manner and words were gentle; for he had sworn in his heart that the Count should not escape.

But the Count cared as little for the presence of the Princess as he had for her dignity, her honor, or her life; and now that she was no longer wholly at his mercy, but there was a new chance that she might escape, his rage and the fear of exposure lashed him to fury. Without more talking, he made at the Bishop, crying, "You first, and then her! I'll be rid of the pair of you!"

The Bishop faced him, smiling, standing between Princess Osra and his assault, while she shrank back a little, sheltering herself behind the heavy door. For although she had been ready to die without fear, yet the sight of men fighting frightened her, and she veiled her face with her hands, and waited in dread to hear the sound of their swords clashing.

But the Bishop looked very happy and, setting his hat on his head with a jaunty air, he stood on guard. For ten years or more he had not used his sword, but the secret of its mastery seemed to revive, fresh and clear in his mind, and let his soul say what it would, his body rejoiced to be at the exercise again, so that his blood kindled and his eyes gleamed in the glee of strife. Thus he stepped forward, guarding himself, and thus he met the Count's impetuous onset; he neither flinched nor gave back, but finding himself holding his own, he pressed on and on, not violently attacking and yet never resting, and turning every thrust with a wrist of iron. And while Osra now gazed with wide eyes and close-held breath, and Count Nikolas muttered oaths and grew more furious, the Bishop seemed as gay as when he talked to the King, more gaily, may be, than bishops should. Again his eye danced as in the days when he had been called the wildest of the Hentzaus. And still he drove Count Nikolas back and back.

Now behind the Count was a window, which he himself had caused to be enlarged and made low and wide, in order that he might look from it over the surrounding country; in time of war it was covered with a close and strong iron grating. But now the grating was off and the window open, and beneath the window was a fall of fifty feet or hard upon it into the moat below. The Count, looking into the Bishop's face, and seeing him smile, suddenly recollected the window, and fancied it was the Bishop's design to drive him on to it so that he could give back no more; and, since he knew by now that the Bishop was his master with the sword, a despairing rage settled upon him; determining to die swiftly, since die he must, he rushed forward, making a desperate lunge at his enemy. But the Bishop parried the lunge and, always seeming to be about to run the Count through the body, again forced him to retreat till his back was close to the opening of the window. Here Nikolas stood, his eyes glaring like a madman's; then a sudden devilish smile spread over his face.

"Will you yield yourself, my lord?" cried the Bishop, putting a restraint on the wicked impulse to kill the man, and lowering his point for an instant.

In that short moment the Count made his last throw; for all at once, as it seemed, and almost in one motion, he thrust and wounded the Bishop in the left side of his body, high in the chest near the shoulder, and, though the wound was slight, the blood flowed freely; then drawing back his sword, he seized it by the blade halfway up and flung it like a javelin at the Princess, who stood still by the door, breathlessly watching the fight. By an ace it missed her head, and it pinned a tress of her hair to the door and quivered deep-set in the wood of the door.

When the Bishop of Modenstein saw this, hesitation and mercy passed out of his heart, and though the man had now no weapon, he thought of sparing him no more than he would have spared any cruel and savage beast, but he drove his sword into his body, and the Count, not being able to endure the thrust without flinching, against his own will gave back before it. Then came from his lips a loud cry of dismay and despair; for at the same moment that the sword was in him he, staggering back, fell wounded to death through the open window.

The Bishop looked out after him, and Princess Osra heard the sound of a great splash in the water of the moat below; for very horror she sank back against the door, seeming to be held up more by the sword that had pinned her hair than by her own strength. Then came up through the window, from which the Bishop still looked with a strange smile, the clatter of a hundred feet, running to the gate of the castle. The bridge was let down; the confused sounds of many men talking, of whispers, of shouts, and of cries of horror, mounted up through the air. For the Count's men in the hall also had heard the splash and run out to see what it was, and there they beheld the body of their master, dead in the moat; their eyes were wide open, and they could hardly lay their tongues to the words as they pointed to the body and whispered to one another, very low: "The Bishop has killed him—the Bishop has killed him."

But the Bishop saw them from the window, and leant out, crying, "Yes, I have killed him. So perish all such villains!"

When they looked up, and saw in the moonlight the Bishop's face, they were amazed. But he hastily drew his head in, so that they might not see him anymore. For he knew that his face had been fierce, and exultant, and joyful.

Then, dropping his sword, he ran across to the Princess; he drew the Count's sword, which was wet with his own blood, out of the door, releasing the Princess's hair; and, seeing that she was very faint, he put his arm about her, and led her to the couch; she sank upon it, trembling and white as her white gown, and murmuring, "Fearful, fearful!" And she clutched his arm, and for a long while she would not let him go; and her eyes were fixed on the Count's sword that lay on the floor by the entrance of the little room.

"Courage, madame," said the Bishop softly. "All danger is past. The villain is dead, and you are with the most devoted of your servants."

"Yes, yes," she said, and pressed his arm and shivered. "Is he really dead?"

"He is dead. God have mercy on him," said the Bishop.

"And you killed him?"

"I killed him. If it were a sin, pray God forgive me!"

Up through the window still came the noise of voices and the stir of men moving; for they were recovering the body of the Count from the moat; yet neither Osra nor the Bishop noticed any longer what was passing; he was intent on her, and she seemed hardly yet herself; but suddenly, before he could interpose, she threw herself off the couch and onto her knees in front of him, and, seizing hold of his hand, she kissed first the Episcopal ring that he wore and then his hand. For he was both Bishop and a gallant gentleman, and a kiss she gave him for each; and after she had kissed his hand, she held it in both of hers and as though for safety's sake she clung to it.

But he raised her hastily, crying to her not to kneel before him, and, throwing away his hat, he knelt before her, kissing her hands many times. She seemed now recovered from her bewilderment and terror; for as she looked down on him kneeling, she was halfway between tears and smiles, and with curving lips but wet shining eyes, she said very softly, "Ah, my lord, who made a bishop of you?"

And her cheeks grew in an instant from dead white into sudden red, and her hand moved over his head as if she would fain have touched him with it. And she bent down ever so little towards him. Yet, perhaps, it was nothing; any lady, who had seen how he bore himself, and knew that it was in her cause, for her honor and life, might well have done the same.

The Bishop of Modenstein made no immediate answer; his head was still bowed over her hand, and after a while he kissed her hand again; and he felt her hand press his. Then, suddenly, as though in alarm, she drew her hand away, and he let it go easily. Then he raised his eyes and met the glance of hers, and he smiled; and Osra also smiled. For an instant they were thus. Then the Bishop rose to his feet, and he stood before her with bent head and eyes that sought the ground in becoming humility.

"It is by God's infinite goodness and divine permission that I hold my sacred office," said he. "I would that I were more worthy of it! But today I have taken pleasure in the killing of a man."

"And in the saving of a lady, sir," she added softly, "who will ever count you among her dearest friends and the most gallant of her defenders. Is God angry at such a deed as that?"

"May He forgive us all our sins," said the Bishop gravely; but what other sins he had in his mind he did not say, nor did the Princess ask him.

Then he gave her his arm, and they two walked together down the stairs into the hall; the Bishop, having forgotten both his hat and his sword, was bare-headed and had no weapon in his hand. The Count's men were all collected in the hall, being crowded round a table that stood by the wall; for on the table lay the body of Count Nikolas of Festenburg, and it was covered with a horse-cloth that one of the servants had thrown over it. But when the men saw the Princess and the Bishop, they made way for them and stood aside, bowing low as they passed.

"You bow now," said Osra, "but before, none of you would lift a finger for me. To my lord the Bishop alone do I owe my life; and he is a Churchman, while you were free to fight for me. For my part, I do not envy your wives such husbands." And with a most scornful air she passed between their ranks, taking great and ostentatious care not to touch one of them even with the hem of her gown. At this they grew red and shuffled on their feet; and one or two swore under their breath, and thanked God their wives were not such shrews, being indeed very much ashamed of themselves, and very uneasy at thinking what these same wives of theirs would say to them when the thing became known.

But Osra and the Bishop passed over the bridge, and he set her on his horse. The summer morning had just dawned, clear and fair, so that the sun caught her ruddy hair as she mounted in her white gown. But the Bishop took the bridle of the horse and led it at a foot's pace down the hill and into the town.

Now by this time the news of what had chanced had run all through the town, and the people were out in the streets, gossiping and guessing. And when they saw the Princess Osra safe and sound and smiling, and the Bishop in his shirt—for he had given his cloak to her—leading the horse, they broke into great cheering. The men cheered the Princess, while the women thrust themselves to the front rank of the crowd and blessed the Bishop of Modenstein. But he walked with his head down and his eyes on the ground, and would not look up, even when the women cried out in great fear and admiration on seeing that his shirt was stained with his blood and with the blood of Nikolas of Festenburg that had spurted out upon it.

But one thing the Princess heard, which sent her cheeks red again; for a buxom girl glanced merrily at her, and made bold to say in a tone that the Princess could not but hear, "By the Saints, here's waste! If he were not a Churchman, now!" And her laughing eye traveled from the Princess to him, and back to the Princess again.

"Shall we go a little faster?" whispered Osra, bending down to the Bishop. But the girl only thought that she whispered something else, and laughed the more.

At last they passed the town, and with a great crowd still following them, came to the castle of Zenda. At the gate of it the Bishop stopped and aided the Princess to alight. Again he knelt and kissed her hand, saying only, "Madame, farewell!"

"Farewell, my lord," said Osra softly; and she went hastily into the castle, while the Bishop returned to his inn in the town, and though the people stood round

the inn the best part of the day, calling and watching for him, he would not show himself.

In the evening of that day the King, having heard the tidings of the crime of Count Nikolas, came in furious haste with a troop of horse from Strelsau. And when he heard how Osra had played at dice with the Count, and staking herself against the castle of Zenda had won it back, he was ashamed, and swore an oath that he would play dice no more, which oath he faithfully observed. But in the morning of the next day he went to Festenburg, where he flogged soundly every man who had not run away before his coming; and all the possessions of Count Nikolas he confiscated, and he pulled down the Castle of Festenburg, and filled up the moat that had run round its walls.

Then he sent for the Bishop of Modenstein, and thanked him, offering to him all the demesne of Count Nikolas; but the Bishop would not accept it, nor any mark of the King's favor, not even the Order of the Red Rose. Therefore the King granted the ground on which Festenburg had stood, and all the lands belonging to it, to Francis of Tarlenheim, brother-in-law to the wife of Prince Henry, who built the *château* which now stands there and belongs to the same family to this day.

But the Bishop of Modenstein, having been entertained by the King with great splendor for two days, would not stay longer, but set out to pursue his journey, clad now in his ecclesiastical garments. And Princess Osra sat by her window, leaning her head on her hand, and watching him till the trees of the forest hid him; and once, when he was on the edge of the forest, he turned his face for an instant and looked back at her where she sat watching in the window. Thus he went to Strelsau; and when he was come there, he sent immediately for his confessor, and the confessor, having heard him, laid upon him a severe penance, which he performed with great zeal, exactness, and contrition. But whether the penance were for killing Count Nikolas of Festenburg (which in a layman, at least, would have seemed but a venial sin), or for what else, who shall say?

About H. Bedford-Jones

You can't have an anthology of historical swashbucklers without a few stories drawn from American pulp magazines of the early 20th century, where they burgeoned and throve. It's more than appropriate that our first pulp swashbuckler is a tale by Henry Bedford-Jones. Beside Max Brand and Erle Stanley Gardner, HB-J was one of the most popular and prolific writers of the pulp fiction era—and though like Brand and Gardner he wrote plenty of Westerns, detective stories, and contemporary thrillers, it was in the realm of historical adventure that Bedford-Jones really shone. You could always depend on an HB-J historical to have engaging characters, be well-researched, and move at a pace that never flagged. It was said of Bedford-Jones that whenever two or more men had fought throughout history, he knew about all about the circumstances and how the men were armed.

Bedford-Jones was born in Ontario, Canada, in 1887, and moved with his family to Michigan when he was one year old, later living in Chicago and California. He began his career as a journalist, switched to writing fiction for the pulps in 1909, and wrote constantly until his death forty years later. He wrote 195 novels, 29 of which received book publication, and over 1100 shorter pieces. A number of his swashbucklers were published in hardcover during the 1920s, boom years for book publishers, and the era when Rafael Sabatini's historicals were at the height of their popularity. Bedford-Jones was a devotee of Dumas' *The Three Musketeers*, and some of his best novels from that period were pastiches featuring d'Artagnan or Cyrano de Bergerac.

Bedford-Jones was also an aficionado of the age of piracy, as you'll find in the following tale, which is based very loosely on the career of Edward "Ned" Low, a real pirate of the 1720s who flew a black flag sporting a crimson skeleton. HB-J has fictionalized the real Low's background to create a very engaging piratical rogue indeed in this novelette, which first appeared in the *Adventure* pulp of December 20th, 1922.

Pirates' Gold

H. BEDFORD-JONES

DECEMBER
20th
1922
25c

PUBLISHED
THREE TIMES A MONTH

Adventure

It was past six bells and growing on to noon, and I was a homesick man as I stood on the quay below London Bridge and watched the *King Sagamore* swinging on her hawser out in the tideway. For she was Virginia-owned, and I, George Roberts of Virginia, knew her well, so that the sight of her was like a touch of home to me.

Also, I had a vile headache, and my memory of the previous night's events was very hazy. I had met a number of other captains, and I think some shipowners, at the Royal Arms, though I could remember only Ned Low and the dark man, Russel, because I liked the one and disliked the other. I seemed to remember that Low had promised his interest to try to get me a ship, or else a chief mate's berth, but I could recall little of what he had said, except that he told some gorgeous yarns of the Guinea trade.

"Good morning, Captain Roberts!" came a voice, and I turned to see Russel himself approaching.

I greeted him without pleasure, for there was a sneer in his eyes, and I did not like his gold-laced hat and jeweled fingers, or the look in his dark face.

"You seem mighty busy," he went on, his heavy-lidded gaze searching me. "The cap'n put you under the table, I hear! Well, what think you of the *King Sagamore*?"

"Out of trim," I responded. "She's down by the head, or I'm a Dutchman!"

"Oh!" said Russel, eying me. "But you're a Virginian, sir—and a seaman to boot! I never heard of seamen coming from Virginia or the other colonies."

This angered me, as it also puzzled me. Why on earth the man should want to pick a quarrel, I could not see. But, knocking out my pipe and smiling, I obliged him swiftly. "Plenty you never heard of, I imagine! Particularly here in England."

"Eh?" He bent his black brows upon me, scowling. "How mean you?" he added.

"Why, just this: what was your name before you made it Russel?"

At that, his white teeth showed. He clapped hand to belt as if feeling for a pistol, and I laughed at him.

"Aye, try it with a Virginian!" I told him, and chuckled again. "Think you're on the high seas, my bucko? Russel, forsooth! If you're not a Portugee, I don't know my business! Aye, snarl all you please—and ladies' rings to your fingers. You cursed fool, don't you know they hang pirates in London town? How long since you were on the Account, as the gentry of that profession term it?"

That reached him between wind and water, as it were. I really meant to taunt him into action, since I wanted to feel my fist in his dark face; but I went too far. His hands dropped. He stood motionless, his eyes eating into me, and they became bloodshot.

"On the Account!" he repeated the phrase, a thickness in his voice. "You speak glibly of it! Perhaps you've been on the Account yourself, my fine Virginia sailor?"

"Why, perhaps I have," said I cheerfully. "And what of it?"

He looked at me for another moment, then turned on his heel and strode away very swiftly, as one who goes of set purpose. I looked after him, frowning. He had been at the tavern with Captain Low the previous night. Ned Low was an engaging rascal of the sort that men love, had been master of a Guineaman, and had traded at the Indies. Russel was of a very different stripe; a sinister man, certainly no Englishman, and I wondered that Ned Low would keep company with him.

However, I dismissed the matter, filled my pipe afresh and turned to watch the ship out in the stream. She was making ready to sail, and to a seaman's eye she presented some uncommonly interesting aspects.

That homesick feeling grew on me as I looked. My first voyage had been made in her, under old Andrew Scott—a cold and hard master he was, too! Anyone who had sailed with Scott had tales to brag of. But Cap'n Scott was dead and gone these two years, thanks to a drinking bout with Sandy Fisher aboard the *Margaret* at Barbados; for Sandy craftily mixed some rare claret in the rum, and Cap'n Scott never rose from under the table.

Well, Scott was dead, and here was I a captain, and yonder the old *King Sagamore*! Heartily did I wish that I were commanding her or at least aboard of her, since I was down to my last guinea, with no hope of a ship except I took out a slaver, for which I had no stomach.

Gossip along the quay told me that she was bound for Virginia, but I doubted this. She was in ballast, and no ship went to Virginia in ballast these days. Also she had bent a new suit of canvas and was fresh-varnished; and I, knowing how stingy were her owners, realized that this was something like a miracle.

What was more, I perceived a feather-bed being put aboard her from the lighter alongside. A feather-bed, indeed! No wonder all the Thames boatmen jeered her as they passed, and the crew of a fishing-lugger tied at the quay began to bawl comments which set the river in a roar of laughter. I wondered who was going to use that feather-bed.

One cannot deny that the *King Sagamore* has a certain roll to her in the best of seas; an uneasy and fretful roll, as if endeavoring to shake loose of the bloodstains that have sunk into her teak. Even old Cap'n Scott had groaned and left the deck at times.

Just now I heard a voice calling out, "There 'e be, sir! That's 'im a-smoking of the 'bacca!"

I glanced about, to see a quay loafer pointing me out to a gentleman approaching rapidly. I faced about to meet this stranger in some surprise.

He was a man in a hurry; a small fellow of forty-odd, wizened and thin in the cheeks, his eyes very sparkling. From his heaving chest and awry wig, he had lately been running. As he strode up to me he produced a snuff-box with a great air of grandeur.

"Your pardon, sir," he addressed me, his words rapid and with authority. "You are Captain Roberts, the Virginian?"

"I am," was my response.

"My name is Dennis Langton, merchant and goldsmith, living at the Wheatsheaf in Lombard Street. I had word this morning from Low that you'd be sailing with us."

He rattled this all out in a breath. Then he flung a glance over his shoulder and suddenly thrust the snuff-box at me.

"Here, take this and fetch it aboard wi' you—move sharp now! Tell Ned that I'll come aboard as he drops downstream. Give it to him and no other. With you this side of Gravesend—Devil sink me! The dogs have caught the trail—hide it, lad—"

Leaving the snuff-box hidden in my fist, the spry little man darted away from me and ran for cover like a hunted rabbit. I gaped after him, thinking him a madman until the burst of shouts went up from the running men.

"Stop, thief!" went up the yells, shrill and sharp with the hunting fever. "Escape! Trip him up—'scape! 'Prentices out—stop, thief—king's name! Pirate and thief—"

Upon and past me swept a shrilling throng in a mad rush, two constables in the lead. Langton vanished in among the buildings, and they after him, and the chorus of yells was swiftly drowned in the noise of the city.

I stood there staring after the rout, until the whimsicality of it all drew a laugh from me. The swift change from the pompous manner and address to the wild flight was ludicrous. The incident was strange and unreal—a merchant of Lombard Street pursued as thief and pirate!

Pirate! Dennis Langton! Suddenly the name flashed across my consciousness and startled me. Three years previously, or rather four, since it was early in 1720, I was mate aboard the ship *Susannah*, owned by a merchant of Southwark Side, near London. There had been much talk aboard her of how she had fallen prey to a brace of pirates near Madeira last voyage and had later escaped. Spriggs was one of the rovers, the same who was lately hanged at Tyburn and still hangs there.

And the other one—now the name came back to me clear enough! Langton, and none other; Dennis Langton, a soft-spoken man, who was reputed to have murdered many with his own hand.

Could the pirate Langton be the same man as this merchant and goldsmith? Most unlikely, and yet all things are possible in this world!

Now came suspicion that he had stolen the snuff-box which he forced on me, and that I might be taken for a thief. This vanished when I opened my hand. The box was a small one of black wood, absolutely worthless. Nor had the little man the look of a cutpurse.

And what was it he had said about Captain Low? A message for Low, too. And what was that about my shipping with Low? I felt bewildered.

Thrusting the snuff-box into my pocket, I drew again on my pipe, frowning over this singular incident. I was still turning it over in my mind perplexedly, when there arose a new and more singular matter which drove it completely out of my head; and no wonder!

Hearing my name called, I looked around to see Captain Low himself coming toward me, bravely puffing at a pipe and laughing to himself over some inward joke. "Ha, Roberts! A fine morning to you, George! Damn me, but we had a pretty rouse last night! Why are you standing here thus idle in the market place?"

"Why, for lack of work!" Smiling, I gave him a grip of the hand. "It seems to me that you said something about looking you up today—but I confess that last rum punch we brewed put a stopper on my brain! Sink me if I can remember a thing."

"What!" Low gave me a singular yet whimsical look. "Come, lad! You don't mean to say that you can't remember our discussion?"

"Not a thing," I said ruefully. "I've lost even the name of your ship, Ned!"

He broke into a roar of laughter, dropped his pipe and smashed it, roared again, then clapped me heartily on the shoulder and swung me about. "There she lies, Roberts. Damn me, this is a creamy jest! Wow! Wait until I tell John Russel about this! And you entered with me as chief mate, too! Oh, lad, ha' pity on me! Yonder's the *King Sagamore* with poor Gunner Basil loading the last aboard; and me sleeping abed all morning thinking you stood on her deck!"

"Good Lord!" I stammered. "D'you mean to say that I, George Roberts, shipped as chief mate with you—"

He fell to roaring again with laughter, and I chimed in, helpless to withstand it. We stood there like two fools, holding our sides and sending up shouts of mirth that drew curious folk about to stare and wonder if we were loose from Bedlam.

At length I came out of the fit of laughter, and we walked apart down the quay, discussing matters. When I told Low how I had been homesick for the *King Sagamore*, he began to bellow again.

His news struck me with incredulity, but a glad man I was for the carouse of the night before, since I appeared to have landed a good berth with a man I liked. Ned Low was fully as tall as I, and even wider in the shoulder; a lean man, his face brown and hard as if carven from mahogany, but ever ready to slip into the cheeriest laughter man ever heard. He had a whimsical touch about him, and I think had run away from Oxford for love of the sea, since he could quote the classics by the hour and spoke sometimes of Magdalen Towers.

Well, he speedily made it clear to me that I was signed with him, and that he had all morning supposed me to be aboard, at which we laughed again.

"Russel came back and dragged me from table just as I was sitting down to breakfast with word that you were standing on the quay like a man in a dream," he concluded with a final chuckle. "So I came along to see—"

"Russel!" I said, and frowned. "Does he sail with us?"

"Aye." Low took my arm frankly and turned me eye to eye with him. "Listen, Roberts! We've scant time to talk—I must get aboard and see to things. But you're a man after my own heart; I drank you under the table last night to make certain, since rum brings out the worst of a man!

"I know you and Russel must fall out. That's as it should be; but look out that Russel doesn't slip a knife into you. Understand? I have to take him as second mate, willy-nilly, and as we explained last night—Well, run along and get your things, and don't miss the tide on your life! I must aboard."

He turned, calling to a wherry just leaving the landing-stairs and made her with a swift run and a leap. I marveled at his cat-like agility, responded to his wave of the hand, and turned to seek my own clothes at the Hare and Hounds, fortunately close by.

For all that I was a happy-go-lucky young devil this morning's affair left me in somewhat of a daze. Or perhaps the rum punch contributed to that effect. However, I was gradually coming to an understanding of things. Russel had come up to me in an evil humor, thinking that I was shirking my duty by loafing ashore; which would well account for his attitude.

Not until I had nearly reached my lodgings did I recall that extraordinary meeting with the man Dennis Langton, and clapped hand to pocket with an exclamation. I had clear forgotten to speak of him to Ned Low!

However, no matter now. It was evident that he must have seen Low that morning, or have heard from him that I was in charge of the ship.

I packed my trunk and stepped into the ordinary to pay off my landlord. Just then a number of men came crowding in with much high talk, amid which I caught the name of Langton. At that I turned and listened, while the landlord gaped likewise.

"And to think that Langton has all this while been a merchant in Lombard Street!" cried one man with a volley of oaths. "A pretty pass we're coming to in London town!"

"They say," chimed in another, "that he has already sold out his business and was in shape to skip the city—"

"All by accident he was betrayed," spoke up another, a latecomer. "You've not heard? Zounds, a ripping story! In Lombard Street itself, only this morning, gentlemen! He came face to face with a shipman whom he'd plundered years ago, was recognized, dodged the hue and cry and broke clear away. Now the constables are searching the city for him, and the waterside as well. A pirate at loose—zounds!"

I paid my score, engaged a man to carry down the trunk and went my way somewhat thoughtfully.

This Dennis Langton, known for a pirate, was a friend of Low and was hoping to get aboard the *King Sagamore*. I was going as mate aboard that ship. So was John Russel; and my words had stung Russel that morning. Russel, like Langton, had been on the Account, as those who take to piracy term the profession.

What about Ned Low? He was one of them; no use shirking the fact. This fine Virginia ship was going a-sailing on a mighty queer cruise, in ballast at that!

And what about me, George Roberts of Virginia?

Why, that was simple enough! Duty lay clear and straight before me—inform the authorities, have everyone aboard the *King Sagamore* laid by the heels, and become a popular hero! The ship would be saved to its owners and everybody happy.

Against this there balanced Ned Low's frank and keen blue eyes, the clap of his hand on my shoulder, the comradely liking I bore him. Aye, because I liked him I laughed at duty! Besides, I was never a great hand at informing. If I want a thing done, I go do it; this running to catch-poles and constables is not to my mind.

So we came down again to the quay, and as I pocketed my pipe my hand touched the black snuff-box. I drew out the thing and looked at it, pressed the catch and opened it. Inside there was no snuff, but a folded, bone-hard bit of vellum. I put the thing away once more.

"Let sleeping dogs lie!" I reflected. "Dennis Langton may be caught. If he's been posing as a merchant here in London, he'll be well known and should be caught in an hour's time. That may simplify matters a bit.

"As for Ned Low, I trust him more than a little, and he should have sense enough to know that I'm not going on the Account. Perhaps that's not his own intention, either! I may be wronging him."

I called a wherry and was taken out toward the ship. As we approached her I fell to laughing again; for I had not the least notion whither she was bound or on what errand. And I remembered that feather-bed going aboard, so that the whole affair struck me afresh with such whimsical humor that I could not refrain from laughing.

Captain Low looked over the rail as we drew near, and he caught the infection and began to roar again with mirth, and was still grinning as I came over the side. "Welcome!" he cried, and struck hands again, a hearty grip. "What's so merry?"

"Why, I can't remember where we are bound for," I said. "Guinea or the plantations?"

"It wasn't mentioned," and Low chuckled. "The Verde Islands, if you want to know, and then Barbados or elsewhere."

"Then we stow salt at the islands, do we?"

Low glanced around, saw that we were alone and gave me a straight look. "Nay, Roberts—we stow gold! Art satisfied? And not on the Account neither."

I nodded, and once again forgot about Dennis Langton's message.

II

After stowing my duffel away in one of the stern cabins I came on deck again and inspected things. Captain Low had everything shipshape, and now there was little to do save to await the tide. Russel had not come aboard as yet, either.

Truly a sweet ship was the *King Saga-more*! Built originally for the India trade, she had much of the black teak in her making, and this was ever kept oiled and waxed, in neat contrast to her white deck and varnished spars and the new canvas stowed aloft. At her bow the torso of a feathered savage was set for figurehead;

glass eyes the sagamore had in his painted visage, and I have heard said that the evil eye was entered into him.

The men were clumped in groups forward. And to my disgust one of them was standing on the rail, exhorting several around him with a voice of wild fervor; a tall, thin man, hair flying in the wind, cheeks like yellow parchment and a godly eye. Gunner Basil was this, who had a true preaching whine to his Puritan voice.

"No place for you, gunner!" I said when I understood who he was. "Get you aft!"

He rolled his eyes at me and shook his head. "Nay, nay, sir! It is time that one officer of this ungodly heathen vessel should be able to think for the souls o' these poor men!"

"Your argument may be sound, gunner," I said, "but you had best learn that your place is to obey first and argue later."

With which I clipped him under the ear and took his place at the rail. "Douse him with a bucket, lads," I said to the men, "and look alive! Where's the bosun? Ah! Damn me if it isn't Bosun Pilcher out of the *Merry Thought!* Bose, remember our voyage in the Guineaman, do you? Glad to find you here, old friend. Watches made up, are they? All taut?"

"Aye, sir, all taut," and Pilcher grinned. A savage brown fellow he was, with golden earrings dangling against his cheeks; short and squat, powerful of build, he was worth a dozen men in a pinch.

"What are these preachers we have aboard, bose?" I demanded, looking at the men who stood about. A long-haired lot, with sanctimonious faces and rolling eyes.

"Puritans," said Pilcher, and spat over the rail. "Damned if they ain't, sir! It was Mr. Langton shipped the lot. I said 'twas no luck to let a crew be shipped by a Lombard Street merchant, nor is it. Not an oath all mornin', and us a-working like blacks!"

The crew shipped by Langton! I whistled at that. Obviously no one aboard knew anything about Langton's adventures of the morning. Leaving my perch, I took Pilcher's arm and led him forward into the bows, where we might have a quiet word.

"What's this, bose?" I asked. "Say no word of it, but the merchant Langton is being hunted through the city for a pirate. Russel has been on the Account, or I'm a liar! And I'm not so sure about the master—"

"Cap'n Low is the bloodiest of the lot," said Pilcher gloomily. "I'm not s'prised to hear about Langton; not me! Low was piratin' around Madagascar last year. Oh, I'm a wise man, I am! But nobody aboard knows it, d'ye mind, sir! If 'twas not for what we've got stowed aft I'd ha' jumped ship."

"Eh?" I stared at him. "What's stowed aft, then?" I asked.

He gave me a grin. "Oh, you don't know, sir? Well, I'll not tell ye. Why Langton went and shipped these here psalm-whining fish I don't know, but that bleedin' Gunner Basil ain't the soapy fool he looks nor acts, Mr. Roberts! You and me are honest men, and the score up for'ard are honest fools; but Gunner Basil ain't one or t'other. D'ye know where I heard tell of him? Far and away it was, last v'yage—"

We leaned against the rail, filled and lighted our pipes, and Bosun Pilcher told me what he knew about our zealous gunner. It was worth the telling.

"D'ye mind, sir, last v'yage 'twas in a Bristol brigantine, to Madeira and the Verde Islands, and back with wine and salt, and a weary time it was, for she leaked like a sieve all the while. We hove out o' Funchal and made for the Isle o' Sal to take our salt aboard, that was in the making; and got safe into the north end of Palmera Roads, and anchored with the palm-trees east-and-by-north, in that spot o' clear sand bottom, five fathom.

"A man came off to us, a white man, marooned there, he had been, by a Frenchman named Maring or some such name, a pirate it was. He told us of a great fight there had been aboard o' the Frenchy six months back, and how there was a famous gunner aboard of her, a gunner by the name o' Basil, full of all pirate learning and a very law-shark for all them that were on the Account. And he said the Frenchy had shot off the lobe of this gunner's ear with a pistol and had set him ashore, all from some dispute over a woman.

"And sink me if this here preacher ain't the identical scoundrel, sir! You look at his ear, and there it be.

"Well, and that's not the whole of it, neither. This chap told us a long story, which I disremember in the main; but 'twas all about this here Gunner Basil and some wild tale that lay along of he. D'ye mind the pirate Avery? Gunner Basil had sailed with him, and talked in his cups about Avery's treasure that lay buried at one of the Verde Islands; he knew where the place was, and there be not another living man knew of it, and he was all for going after it. A wild tale enough!"

"Wild, but it might hold truth," I commented. "Avery burned down one of the towns in those islands, and cruised about there. However, what matter to us? This Gunner Basil, you think, is pretending to be a preaching Puritan just now?"

"Aye, to save his neck, belike." Pilcher shook his earrings. "Folks do call me a pirate because I wear hoops, and have a roll to my legs on dry land, and have use for an honest oath or two; but zounds! You know me, Master Roberts. I had liefer be me than this cutthroat devil of a Gunner Basil, with his Scripture and Psalms and whine!"

I had to laugh at this, which was true enough. Bosun Pilcher had the looks of a pirate and the life of an honest man; a wife and six children in Jamestown, and a sober, careful record. Gunner Basil, on the other hand, with all the earmarks of a fanatical blue-nosed Puritan, was by repute a devil on the leash.

"Well, bose," I said, knocking out my pipe, "keep a close tongue and wait for what turns up. You'd best look over the capstan and hawse and be ready to up anchor. Tide's almost at the turn, and I see a boat yonder with Mr. Russel coming aboard."

I turned and started aft, having now remembered something mighty important. As I went I encountered Gunner Basil, who touched his forelock to me as I passed and made no comment on my lesson in obedience. Russel's boat was hailing us, and at the break of the poop I found Captain Low waiting for me. I was up the ladder and had him by the arm, fumbling in my pocket.

"Ha, cap'n! I met a friend of yours ashore, and he charged me with word for you—"

Before I could say more, Russel was over the rail and leaping up to us, his dark face all ablaze with fury and excitement. "The word's out after Dennis!" he cried, but low-voiced that the men might not hear. "Devil's luck, Ned, devil's luck! Some fool recognized him this morning; put the catchpoles after him! Zounds,

if we don't get up the hook and into the Channel they'll twig the whole affair! Up and away, I tell you!"

Ned Low flung a glance at the after companion. His eyes were suddenly stricken. "Damn me, this is bad news!" he murmured. "And at the last minute!"

"Up and away!" snarled Russel, still panting.

"No, no, I'll not run and leave him!" exclaimed Low warmly.

But I intervened. "Langton isn't nabbed, and won't be," I said, coolly enough, while they stared at me. "I met him ashore, and he had time to give me a message for you, cap'n, before the constables set him running afresh. Said for you to drop downstream with the tide, and he'd come aboard—this side of Gravesend, most likely."

"Good!" cried Low. He snapped erect as if this news had put fresh life into him, and his smile leaped out once more. "Trust Dennis to come clear! Mr. Russel, be ready to shake out those topsails in five minutes; the tide's nearly at the turn. Mr. Roberts, take charge for'ard and see the anchor's well stowed."

Russel gave me one look that was like a stab; then his white teeth flashed in a laugh. "So you know Langton, Mr. Roberts!" he said, and nodded. "Good enough. We'll pull together after all."

Oddly, it seemed that his ill will toward me had vanished; this was all seeming, however, because he thought that I was a friend of Langton, and bore this latter some well-founded fear. He was soon enough snarling again.

I went forward while the bosun's whistle shrilled and the men jumped to stations. Everything was shipshape; the men began to stamp about the windlass, capstan bars of dark teak all ashine in the sun, pawls clinking as the ship walked up on her hook, and the canvas aloft beginning to loose. A sweet ship was the *King Sagamore*! Every little detail of her was sweet and natty. Even the fife-rail was of red teak, and the belaying pins of black, heavy as iron.

Now she leaned over to wind and tide and began to slip through the water, while Cap'n Low himself conned her through the river traffic; six bells was struck from the brass bell, and I minded the cabin-boy struck them; a slim lad, a guttersnipe of the town, his face pinched and marked with deviltry beyond the ken of most men.

And I noted an odd enough thing. Shoving on the black capstan bars of teak, or hauling on the lines, there was no singing from those men of ours. Instead, not a sound from them until we were bracing the yards a bit, and then one long-nosed rascal began to chant out a psalm, in which they all joined. Damn me, but I can still hear the roar of mirth that went up as a barge passed us and caught the words!

I sent the gunner down to see that all the ports were closed; she carried four guns to a side and six patteroes—a well-armed jade! Or, should I say, warrior? The matter of sex is all a jumble when it comes to the *King Sagamore*. Pocahontas would have been a better name for her.

This psalm-singing was too much for me, however. "Belay that singing!" I ordered at length. "Bose, pipe 'em the old bowline! Join in, you Newgate rascals, or you'll taste trouble!"

So presently Pilcher led them, and the voice of Gunner Basil boomed up the words from below, and the rascals stamped the deck to a right tune:

"Oh, haul upon the bowline, the
    fore and maintop bowline!
"Oh, haul upon the bowline—the
    bowline, *haul!*"

And so we had everything snugged down for the present, and I joined Cap'n Low on the quarterdeck, while Russel and the gunner stood at the rail, watching the riverbanks slide past us.

Now I went up to Low, who stood at the wheel, and spoke to him softly. "Ned, I said nothing of it before Russel, but Dennis Langton gave me more than a word for you. Hold out your hand and take the little box."

He dropped a hand to his side, and I put the little black snuff-box into it; and, not taking his eyes from the water ahead, he nodded. "Good, Roberts!" he said quietly. "So Dennis is playing fair with us, eh? Fine. Ah! Look there, behind those fishing-smacks—is that a boat? Here, take my glass."

I took the spyglass from his pocket and leveled it. "Aye! Two oarsmen and Langton himself in the stern. Now they've seen us—"

"Stand by with a line, Russel!" cried out Low. "Roberts, stand by those braces and be ready. We'll pick him up on the jump."

Pick him up we did, nigh swamping the wherry in the attempt. Langton came up and over the rail, nimble as a cat; but he had not been on the escape for nothing, since his clothes were torn and muddied and his wig clean gone, leaving him bald and shiny.

Nor was this all; for no sooner was he on deck than he staggered and collapsed into the arms of Russel with a choked cry, and I glimpsed a smear of blood across the mate's shoulder.

Ned Low saw it too, for he turned to me with a quiet word. "*Habet!* Lead in the lungs, and that's one of us gone to Hell. Crack on all sail, Mr. Roberts! I leave the deck to you. Get us out o' this cursed water and to sea before they send a man-o'-war to stop us. This is a sad business—the poor girl!"

What he meant by this last I had no idea, for I was already calling all hands, and Pilcher piped the men to the weather braces and aloft on the instant. Russel and Ned Low carried the figure of Langton to the quarterdeck, and I saw nothing more of them for the time, being mighty busy alow and aloft. Gunner Basil I sent to the helm, needing a good man there if we were to race out of the river. The sails were loosed already, and the men piping down from aloft.

"Haul aboard! Get your tack well down, bose! Tend braces, you lads—set taut! Sheet home—sheet home and hoist away, there! Lead along and man the flying-jib halyards—clear away the down-haul—hoist! All hands main braces—"

So it went, with Pilcher's pipe whistling shrill and the canvas fluttering out. Much to my surprise I perceived that these long-nosed dissenters forward were good enough seamen; and in no long time we were bowling away for dear life, our new canvas straining in the wind and Gunner Basil handling helm in sweet fashion.

Then, with all clear, I turned to the quarterdeck—and stood thunderstruck.

Russel, sitting under the weather rail, held the head of Dennis Langton in his arms, while Ned Low knelt beside and talked to Langton, who was coughing blood. The man had a bullet through the body, and it needed no surgeon to know that his hours were numbered. It was not this, however, that held me transfixed, but the person kneeling over Langton's hand; for this was a woman!

She had come from the after cabins obviously; a straight, slim slip of a thing all yellow golden hair and sober gray gown and long hands. Her face I could not see, but judged that she was young.

A flutter aloft caused me to look at the helmsman. Gunner Basil was staring at the scene, and being down the wind was probably hearing their words. With an angry shout I leaped to the wheel, shoved him away and ordered him to take charge forward. He went, but with a sour snarl in his yellow parchment face.

Indeed, standing in the wheel-box I found that the wind brought me snatches of talk from the group. The girl was sobbing, and Dennis Langton was speaking to her between his terrible coughs. The words reached me clearly.

Even as I listened, even as I felt the ship with the wheel and held her in the wind, even as I watched shore and opening river-mouth, I was aware of Gunner Basil and that devil-eyed little cabin-boy, talking together near the foot of the main; and I wondered vaguely of what they were speaking.

"Keep it, Polly!" came Langton's gasping voice. "All for you—swear—promise me!"

The girl sobbed out something. Without looking at him I was aware that Langton's head lifted, and his eyes leaped to Ned Low.

"Ned, Ned! You'll not take it from her? Aye, you were always on the level—met on the level with us, parted on the square—ho there, Tyler! Out sword, Tyler; run the knave through! Damn your eyes, Tyler, you missed him! Netting's up and we can't board—"

For a moment he raved, then fell suddenly silent, gasping and sobbing for breath, coughing up the black blood. I stole a glance, and his face was white as beech-ash.

"Call Russel, Ned!" came his voice again. "Where's Russel; John Lopez that was, John Russel that is now?"

"I'm here, Dennis," said the dark mate, bending over so that Langton knew him.

"Swear to me, then," gasped the latter. "Swear you'll give my share to Polly—swear you'll be true to her, not cheat her—swear!"

"Aye," said Russel, whose real name seemed to be Lopez. "I swear it, Dennis, and the cap'n to witness!"

"Swear it, Ned!" cried out Langton, looking up.

Ned Low, his face set and mournful, inclined his head. "I'll be true to you and her, Dennis, and will protect her, so help me! I swear it by the oath that you and I know—the oath of the book and compass and word!"

"Where's Roberts, the Virginian?" Langton's head lifted. "Call him! Good man, Roberts; true man—stand by him, Ned! I liked that man. Call him—swear him—"

Ned Low strode over to me. "Give me the helm, and go to him. Quick, man, before he passes!"

I obeyed. Although I was in the dark as to this oath, it appeared honest enough and would soothe the passing of a dying man.

As I knelt before Langton, recognition came into his eyes, fighting the fear of death that was filling him. "Swear, Virginian!" he panted out. "Stand wi' Polly—her share—"

"I swear, Dennis Langton," was my response.

His head dropped back, and a cry came from the girl's throat—then, with a furious and frightful effort, Dennis Langton swept Polly aside, wrenched himself to his feet, swayed there and shook his fist toward London. Laughter and blood came from his lips, and one last wild cry.

"Cheated you, Jack Ketch—cheated you first and last, Tyburn Tree! Sink me to Hell if I haven't the laugh o' you after all! Zounds!"

He rattled on the word, and died, and pitched forward with a laugh terrible on his lips. Thus passed the first of our company aboard the *King Sagamore*; and as I watched Russel take the weeping girl to the companionway I wondered to what oath I had sworn myself, in the hand of a dying pirate!

III

While we pitched and rolled down-Channel that night I was below with Ned Low, seeing that Dennis Langton was properly sewed up for burial. Gunner Basil brought a shot for his feet and then, touching his forelock, respectfully enough addressed us; in the light of the swinging lantern his parchmenty face looked more yellow and wolfish than ever.

"Beg pardon, masters, but who's a-goin' to say the prayer over him?" he asked.

"I am." Ned Low glanced up. "Why?"

"It ain't fittin', sir," protested the gunner with an air of earnest, stubborn conviction. His pale, deadly eyes were fastened upon Low. "He died in sin, most like, but it ain't fittin' for you to say no prayer, sir. It's the spirit movin' me to protest."

Ned Low straightened up. "Now, sink me! I'm master o' this ship—"

"We that has a higher hope don't hold wi' no blasphemy; beg pardon, master, what be you but an ungodly, unregenerate sinner? Blasphemy it is, no less. More'n one of us aboard ha' heard tell o' 'Bloody Ned,' cap'n. Tha' ain't here nor there; but when it comes to sayin' prayers, I speaks up! It's the spirit movin' in me—"

Bloody Ned! Well, there it was, like a slap in the face. I had heard of Bloody Ned, too, but had not connected the name with my good friend Captain Ned Low.

For a moment I thought Ned would strike the man down. Eyes clenched with eyes, and in the obscurity behind Gunner Basil I perceived more than one dark figure lurking. Then in time I recalled the tale that Bosun Pilcher had told me, and pushed forward with a nudge in Low's ribs.

"What's all this?" I demanded. "This is fine talk from you, Basil, who were on the Account with Avery and served as his gunner! And what about that French pirate you sailed with—the one who pistoled you and marooned you after the big fight, eh?"

There was dead silence, broken only by the groan of stanchions and the creak of blocks. My knowledge of his past took Gunner Basil all aback; he gaped at me from a livid and stricken face. Ned Low uttered a soft oath of astonishment. A murmur began to rise from the listening men.

I struck again while the iron was hot. "A prayer would come with ill grace from you, gunner—as lief from Bloody Ned as from Avery's gunner, if I'm the victim! Who was it nicked the lobe off that ear of yours with a pistol ball, eh?"

Gunner Basil staggered again at that thrust. I felt a swift stab of fear as I met those pale eyes of his; then he began to shake his long head and whine. "When a man repenteth him of the evil and turns to godliness, the scornful make mock of him! Aye, sir, you ha' the right of it; a sinful man I ha' been, and taken part wi' men o' blood. And now that regeneration ha' come upon me, by the works o' the blessed Tom Deveney o' Houndsditch—"

"Regeneration your eye, ye damned lousy swab of a liar!" broke in a roar, and Bosun Pilcher lurched forward. "Who was it a-throwin' oaths so free and fine but a half-hour ago? You, ye scabby sojer, thinkin' no one was by to hear! Now out knife if ye dare, and I'll show ye summat—"

It looked like blows and hot breath, for Pilcher had hand on knife and Gunner Basil was clutching under his arm; but Ned Low stepped forward and stood between the two men and reasserted his command. "Damn me, d'ye think we're on the Account, to settle quarrels wi' the steel!" he cried out. "Out o' this, bose! You, gunner, give me no more of your sanctimonious lip, d'ye hear? You'll taste a dozen of the cat next time. Get this boy made ready, and five bells in morning watch call all hands for burial. Mr. Roberts, it's hard on eight bells—you'd better step up and stand by to take the deck from Mr. Russel."

"From Portugee Lopez, ye mean," shot a voice from out of the shadows. "Lopez, the bloody pirate what scuppered three Deal craft last year!"

"Who was that?" napped Ned Low, hand dropping to belt. "Out of the dark, you rat! Who was it?"

None answered him, however, and the darkness proved empty to the swing of a lantern. So I went on deck again, wondering not a little. That voice had held an odd twang, not unlike the tones of the impish cabin-boy, but that was impossible. The child stood in deadly fear of us all and was seasick to boot.

With a fair wind, ballast trimmed anew and one of our brawny dissenters at the helm, we bore down-Channel into the darkness; while I, after lighting my pipe in the lee of the pilot-house, reflected a while upon my situation. It might have been worse, what I knew of it, and it might assuredly have been bettered. Certain outstanding things looked dark.

One certainty was that in London town I had run foul of three fine rogues, and like a blockhead had been hooked. Langton's end spoke for itself. Russel, or Portuguese Lopez, obviously had something of a reputation as a pirate. Of Bloody Ned I had heard and was grieved to find it was my own Ned Low, the man whom I so liked. As to the girl Polly, I had not seen or heard of her again, but she seemed to be some relation to Langton.

Why had these men outfitted and chartered—as they must have done—the *King Sagamore*? To get gold from the Cape Verde islands, Ned Low had said.

All very fine; but how? There was the puzzler. They had not meant to run away with her and go on the Account.

Langton in his capacity as a city merchant had probably given bonds for her, and he had most certainly picked the crew himself. These men were godly rogues, and I did not like them in the least—but they were honest men. Langton would never have picked such a crew to ship as pirates.

Then again there was the question of Gunner Basil. Captain Low had been utterly astounded at learning the gunner's record; he had known nothing of it. Ergo, Dennis Langton had known nothing of it and had shipped the gunner at face value.

But why the devil had Gunner Basil shipped aboard us? I took no stock in his "regeneration"—one look in the man's eyes clapped a stopper on all that. He could fool the men up forward, but he could not fool me, much less Bosun Pilcher.

And what was that oath I had taken? It disquieted me.

⚊

I had reached this point, and two bells had just been struck, when the tall figure of Ned Low approached. He glanced at the compass, lighted his pipe, then took my arm and led me to the lee rail, where we could speak without being overheard.

"Roberts, I've been talking with John Russel, and I'm worried," he said frankly and bluntly. "This morning, standing on the quay, you as good as told Russel you'd been on the Account yourself. Tonight you flashed some information on Gunner Basil that staggered him—and me with him. How came you to know it, lad? If you've lied to me, then let's have it out sharp and quick, and reach an understanding."

This was a stiff jolt, and I let him know it. "About Russel, that was said in jest, to taunt him. As to the rest, Ned—well, I learned tonight that you are Bloody Ned. It grieved me, but I didn't come running and whining to ask if the news was true. Zounds! If I'm such a fool that I can't read a man's eye for true or false, it's a queer thing. And I'll stick by my guns, swing me if I don't!"

Low caught my hand and gripped it hard. "Spoken like a man, George Roberts!" he said warmly. "Aye, and with a bitter back to the words that I deserve! Your pardon, lad. We'll have a meeting in the cabin tomorrow morning after breakfast, all four of us, and you'll know then why I'm anxious."

"Who's the fourth, then?" I asked.

"Polly Langton, niece and heir of poor Dennis. That was a stiff loss to us, George! Dennis had a head worth any two going."

"He'd not much when he shipped our gunner," I said acidly.

Ned Low whistled. "Perchance. But the scoundrel may ha' told truth after all, lad; there's a chance of that, d'ye mind! Men have reformed ere this, and will again. Why, look at me, myself!"

He was silent for a moment, then took me across the deck again and under the weather rail, where we sat down in comfort. I think he had been much moved by my challenging answer to his doubts; at least he spoke with a refinement and feeling in his voice that I had not previously heard.

"Roberts, y'have never seen or heard, I suppose, of a man calling himself Trunnel Toby, having a long face like a horse, and sad eyes, and a gold ring in his nostrils, and the likeness of a bleeding heart tattooed upon his breast, just above his own heart?"

"Not I," was my answer.

"I have sought that man going on five years," said Ned Low. "Once I knew that his ship lay in Carlisle Bay, and I sighted her plain; but there was a gale blowing, and we were short of men, and before we could hand the small sails and luff for the bay we were driven past, and the gale held us, and when I came back again he was gone. Oh, but I ha' tried with heart and soul to find that man, all up and down the dark bowl of the sea!

"And once I was within an hour of him. At Madagascar that was; aye, missed him by a scant sixty minutes, though I caught three of his men left behind, and hanged them! He had heard of Bloody Ned, and he ran for it. And off the Zanzibar coast I met a ship that had spoke him two days before, and north we ran and passed him in a hurricane, and he came over to the Brazils for fear o' me. Now and again, and every way, I found men who had sailed with him, men who had partnered or traded with him, and I hanged them all as I came on them.

"But I never found Trunnel Toby, and ha' lost hope of finding the man now, so I am off to recoup my wasted fortune again, and search some more. The last o' my guineas are in this ship, Roberts; and a big sum from poor Langton, and a share from John Russel. And I am afraid to ask Gunner Basil if he knew the man, for if he did I would hang him, and we have need of a gunner aboard. Besides the man may have reformed, as he says; I'd put it past no man to turn righteous.

"For look you, George! There is a reason behind all of us. Aye, there's a reason back of each man who dares this wine-dark sea and listens to the rigging as it sings the slumbering song o' night up above! Lord knows I've earned the name of Bloody Ned, earned it with hangings of men alow and aloft—but all of them men who had known Trunnel Toby, d'ye mind that!

"And I've naught to repent of at all, either. I've touched no man's life but for this cause; I've touched no man's money but mine own, honestly made.

"And poor Langton, to whom that gunner laid his tongue, had become an honest man. D'ye know why, George? Because of the girl down below, his niece Polly; and she's a rare lass, I tell you! Bred of the Devon blood, she is, and can hand sail with any man or read the card or steer by the wind. So when I came and said that I was for the gold and had given up the search for Trunnel Toby until we had the guineas again, Langton knew it was an honest word and came in with me; and John Russel made up the sum we lacked, and we bought this ship, George."

"Bought her!" I said in some wonder, for that would have taken round money.

"Aye, just so. A company venture for the gold. We'll have it again soon enough, and then I'll buy out the other shares and keep the *King Sagamore* and go again after Trunnel Toby. Sure y'have never heard of the man?"

"Never," I said. "But there's Bosun Pilcher come to look at the helm; call him, for many a thing he has heard and seen, and an honest man to boot."

Ned Low lifted his voice, and the dark shadow of bose detached itself from the pilot-box and came over to us on the sloping deck. So there Ned Low asked his question again, and described the man he sought.

Bose turned the quid in his mouth and chewed upon it and spat over the stern rail, and then made careful answer. "Why, sir, there be many a man wi' face like a horse, and one or two aboard here, but not that man. Seems like I've heard tell of he, too; let's see now—was it aboard the *Merry Thought*? No, 'twas not; yet 'twas not so long ago—

"Ha! Damn my eyes, sir, if 'twas not two v'yages back, on the *Picket* brigantine, wi' Cap'n Baxter out o' Bristol town! I mind it well enough now. We were lying at Lisbon, and a supra-cargo there was tellin' me of such a man, bleedin' heart and all! Mate on a London trading-brig, he was, and had got into trouble wi' the Portugee folk, and had skipped between two days. That's where I heard the name, and more'n that I can't bring to mind."

"Then let it pass," said Ned Low, sinking back against the rail.

"Aye, sir," said bose. "Four bells it is, sir."

"Make it so, bose," I told him, and he went off into the darkness.

The brazen tinkle of the bell had died away before Ned Low spoke again. "And what think you, George," he said, "of sailing mate with Bloody Ned?"

I laughed a little at that. "What else but your own words, Ned? We're not on the Account, but for honest gold, you say; and enough said. There's a reason behind every man sails up the sea, you say; and enough said. For the rest, I like you, I have

two fists, and if I go to the devil it's my own fault and no other man's leading."

"Well said, George. What reason is behind you?"

"Ruined fortunes, a girl who jilted me, and lack of ties to keep me ashore. Those in the first place. In the latter place, love of good ships, work to do and strength to do it with, and knowledge of my profession. For I hold the sea to be a profession, Ned, in despite of all men! I sailed a small sloop with two boys from the Azores to Barbados once to prove the fact. What was more, I built the sloop before sailing her."

"You're a philosopher, George, and damn me if I don't wish I might be one too!" he responded, and sighed. "Work to do, and strength and knowledge to do it with! What more could any man ask of fortune? But my work's undone as yet, and when done it's only a man hanged after all, and small joy of it to me!"

With this he rose, and was gone down below.

I wondered much about his words and his curious tale of Trunnel Toby, and what reason must lie behind his strange pursuit of that creature up and down the waters of the earth. Reason in plenty there must be, but I could not evoke it from his words. It began to appear, however, that he was not the black pirate he was painted, and this was something to cheer me.

So the night wore through, and the wind held fair, sweeping us steadily to the southward on our course, and with the dawn or a little while after we gathered all hands in the waist. Now all the world was shut away from us. We aboard the *King Sagamore*, bounded by those walls of English oak and India teak, were in a little world apart, devils and angels and men together. There was the dead man, shrouded decently; and by him Ned Low, book in hand, and dark, quick-eyed Russel, dirk and pistol in belt, and Gunner Basil, pale, terrible eyes flaming and stabbing about. Little love those pale eyes bore me, either!

There, too, Bosun Pilcher, gold earrings bobbing beside savage brown cheeks, and back of him the men, making a full score of us, all told. Some I had come to know by this time. Dickon the cabin-boy, gray with the sickness and mouthing vile oaths; Simon Blake and Ezra Blake his brother, gaunt, hard-jawed fellows who could prate psalms by the hour; and Philip the cook, a black man who was very joyful about his work and always grinning. Humphrey Stave was chips and sailmaker, a bent gnarled figure with deep eyes behind spectacles, and a bit deaf; Stave was the only other man forward who was not a man of religion and godliness, so that he companioned much with Pilcher.

The others were all hard men, devout enough and good seamen, but given to exhorting each other with prayer and advice. Dennis Langton had picked them for this very reason, having no mind to ship pirates on this voyage.

Nonetheless, he had made a mistake. One of the men, Thomas Winter, was long in the face, a real horse's face indeed, seeming but little short of a half-wit, nor ever raised his eyes to meet those of another man.

Well, we buried poor Dennis Langton there, sliding him off into the rolling seas; and after reading the proper service Ned Low softly asked the gunner to speak a prayer. Gunner Basil did so, praying a good ten minutes in a long, whining singsong, the other knaves all joining in with their nasal "Amen" when the spirit moved.

Then breakfast, and then to the cabin for the promised meeting, while Gunner Basil held the deck. And in this meeting I had sight of Polly Langton and likewise got a bid from fortune.

IV

We gathered in the stern cabin, and the new sunlight streamed down through the small skylight above and illumined the cabin with a glory of radiance as the ship rolled. Between stern window and skylight we had plenty of light.

The cabin was not ornate. It was our mess cabin aft, and was meant for use, not for ornament. Along the stern wall under the window ran a long file of muskets, locked in their rack by an iron bar and padlock. A locker for charts, another for instruments; a huge cupboard that held dishes and wine and other things; table and chairs and iron lantern slung in gimbals—this was all. Under the table was a trap leading to the lazaret below.

With the traces of grief gone from her cheeks Polly Langton sat down, and we after her. For lack of mourning she wore here a gray gown; a kerchief about her throat fastened by a gold brooch; and what a head was this rising above! All a glory of yellow gold hair, and a red-cheeked, west-country face that was filled with sweetness and ability, browned by the sun and air, with skin delicately textured as any court lady's!

Yet the splendor of her face lay in the eyes; gray with golden flecks were they, level and meeting a man's gaze fair and unafraid; deliberate eyes, not to be hurried or overborne. Through these windows one perceived the fine woman's soul within, shrinking a little, yet meeting the issues of fate with a certain cool poise that was almost disdain. Could this girl ever be waked into hot passionate anger or emotion, I thought, she would stop at nothing!

Painted and powdered, patched and gowned, Polly Langton might have been no beauty; but in her simplicity she was beautiful enough. I did not miss the grip that was in Russel's eyes as he watched her; nor did she; for she gave him a slow look that made him change countenance.

Ned Low, when we were seated, put on the table before him that little black snuff-box which I had brought him from Langton. Then Russel spoke up, civilly but with a thrust to his words. "One minute, cap'n! This is secret company business. Why does George Roberts sit with us?"

"At my bidding," and Ned Low smiled a little, taking no offense. "He is my friend, and I trust him to the full. Also I propose that he is to have a full third of my share of the gold when recovered—"

"I want no gifts, Ned," I intervened.

"No gift at all, George Roberts," he returned, a somber look in his eyes. "We don't know what lies ahead of us, but I think you are going to be a great man in this enterprise, and here you, a captain like myself, are serving as mate. Zounds, man! Was it not agreed between us that first night we met?"

"As to that I can't say," was my response, and Ned uttered a laugh.

"It's a company matter," spoke up Russel, an ugly note in his voice. "Put it to the vote, I say!"

"It's no company matter what I do with my own," snapped Low angrily, a dark color rising in his cheeks. "But the deciding voice lies with Miss Polly, and I put the vote. What say you, madam?"

All this while the girl had been looking at me with appraising eyes. Now she leaned back in her chair and spoke as if she had no interest in the affair. "I agree," she said quietly, "though it is your own business, as you say."

So Russel sat back and bit his lip.

"Now," began Ned Low, "let us inform Captain Roberts of our quest. You've heard of the pirate Franklin, George? Some time since, I was in company with him when he took a huge amount of moidores out of a Portugee Indiaman from Goa."

He broke off, for the girl was holding his eye. He flushed a trifle once more.

"Then it is true," she asked coolly, "that you and Mr. Russel were on the Account, as they call it?"

"That is true," said Ned. "It is also true that I would touch no penny of the loot, my lady. Then I had no use for it. Now I have use. Captain Franklin buried a great share of the gold, which he swore belonged to me, on one of the Verde Islands. He and I alone knew the place. It is this gold that we go to recover.

"According to the agreement, a third share goes to me, another to John Russel, another to Mistress Langton here. Out of my share, a third goes to Captain Roberts. This is understood and agreed?"

A nod came from the other two. But now Polly Langton spoke up—cool and well-considered words; and her speech must have come as a tremendous shock to each one of us.

"Since Captain Roberts is a friend of yours, Captain Low, and is to share in your proceeds, he is evidently tarred with the same brush as you and Mr. Russel! By your own word you are pirates. How my poor uncle came to his death I know not, but I think it was through entering into this scheme of yours.

"Shame on you! He was an honest city merchant, and you bloody men tangled him in your ruthless wiles! Had it not been for you we would still be living in Lombard Street, and happy there."

She paused, coldly deliberate. Ned Low was staring at her like a man thunderstruck. John Russel was all agape, but harsh amusement was rising in his eyes. Before it could break out she was calmly continuing her speech.

"I promised my uncle to take this gold if we got it. What I do with my share is another matter. I may be penniless, but beyond taking out what my poor uncle put into this venture, I'll not turn this bloody coin to my own use.

"Very well, then. I want it understood that I'm a full third partner in this enterprise, and intend to remain so. I'm not to be put in a corner and disregarded because I am a woman. My uncle picked a good crew for this voyage; if you gentlemen think you can run away with this ship or go pirating, you'll discover otherwise.

We are here for a certain purpose, and none other."

Now her voice softened—perhaps from what she read in the eyes of Ned Low. "Indeed, I do not mean to speak like a shrew, but there's the fact. You're pirates. I am a woman, but I have some ability at sea. The crew are honest men. I think you mean me well, and will respect the oath you gave my poor uncle; but I want to have things understood. Already the men are whispering that you intend running away with the ship. Be careful! That's all. I am through, Captain Low."

There was a space of silence while we stared at her. It was easy to perceive that Dennis Langton had kept her ignorant of his past. She thought him a good, honest merchant, not knowing that he had buccaneered with the worst of them, had partnered with the infamous Spriggs. She was acting upon genuine belief, deeming the rest of us mighty insecure men.

Russel uttered a laugh and began to speak, a sneer in his heavy eyes. Ned Low turned to him, face set and cold, and uttered three words: "Be silent, John!"

Russel checked himself, shrugged and leaned back grinning. Thus the matter passed; Ned was trying to keep from the poor girl the knowledge of what her uncle had been, was trying to leave her memory of him unsoiled. Yet he was a fool for his pains. She was bound to learn the truth eventually.

"Since I haven't known you or your friends three days, Miss Polly," I said easily, "you can't charge me with their crimes. My record is clear for all men to read, and if you'll go out to Virginia you'll find that it's not a bad record, either. And as to Captain Low, I believe you'll find that he's—"

"Stow it, George!" snapped Low.

I obeyed, for he was angry.

He looked across the table at the girl, and she at him, though her gaze had softened a bit. Very handsome he was, and too proud to take notice of her words. He opened the black snuff-box that lay before him and took out the hard, folded bit of vellum, all the while keeping his eyes on the girl. And then he spoke to her briefly.

"Dear lady, you have naught to fear from us, upon my honor! Now let us to business. I propose to lay this little chart before you—Franklin himself made it— and then destroy the thing. We shall keep the position of the moidores in our own minds. If by any chance of the sea we do not reach the Verde Islands, then whichever one of us can first come to the spot is at liberty to take the gold."

There was a little silence while he opened up the vellum. It was not easy, for the whitish skin was hard and dry and promised to crack at the folds. As he opened it slowly, I saw that on one side of it was writing, and that over the ink there had been wax laid on and polished, keeping the ink waterproof.

Then abruptly the voice of the girl leaped at us. Soft it was, but uttered in broad Devon that betrayed her apprehension and fear. "Quick! Catch mun—look to door!"

She said afterward that the door-catch had moved slightly. Russel saw it, for he was out of his chair, silent and with a stealthy agility that amazed me, and in two steps was at the door. He opened it. There came a terrific crash as a tray dropped to the floor, and we saw Dickon the cabin-boy outside.

Russel had him by the shoulder, and heaved him inside and swore at the ale that spattered his feet.

"What means this, lad?" demanded Ned Low angrily. "Who bade you listen at doors?"

The little imp was no whit in awe or frightened; he faced us in sullen defiance. He could not have seen fifteen years, yet the debased evil of his features would have done credit to any pirate, and he glowered at us with all the hatred of a man for men. "It bain't so," he said stoutly. "I weren't a-listening, Master Low! Cook Philip sent me wi' breakfast for mistress—and now look at un! Pewter bent, ale gone—"

Russel gave him a hearty cuffing and threw him out into the passage. As the boy picked himself up I saw the look he flung at Russel—a deadly, vicious look such as comes from the eyes of a disturbed and angry snake. Then Russel slammed the door shut and came back to his chair.

"I was mistaken," spoke up Polly contritely. "I thought perhaps someone was listening—I'm sorry if little Dickon suffered for my error."

"He's not hurt," said Russel. "Now, Ned, out with it! Which one of the islands is it?"

"St. Vincent," answered Captain Low, holding the vellum spread out under his fingers. "You know it?"

"I've not landed there," said Russel.

"Franklin has it marked 16° 49′ north latitude by 7° 6′ west longitude from the Cape de Verde," went on Ned Low, "but I think he's off a point or two. George, get out the charts, will you? We'll show Miss Polly just where we're going."

I got out the proper chart, by which time the others were ready to relinquish the bit of vellum to me, though Russel watched me keenly while I handled it. Upon it was rudely scratched the outline of St. Vincent, one of several uninhabited and rocky islands to the northwest of the Cape Verde group. On the northeast tip of the island was marked a cross, with the bearings below.

I uttered an exclamation. "Upon my word, gentlemen! I remember this place; I was there for turtle while we were making sail at the Isle de Sal! Aye, the very spot— and we had best lay up the ship in the cove at the north side of the island, which is the closest."

"It is ill spoke of on the chart," said Russel, looking up.

"Aye, for the trades blow square into it," I assented. "But a ship may be towed out by boats during the morning calm. I've seen the St. Nicholas men do it often. And the bay is so smooth that you may lay a ship ashore without the least damage."

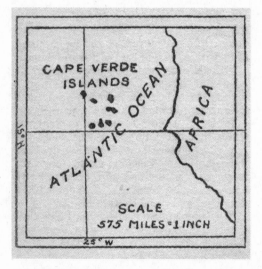

"Memorize these bearings, George," said Ned Low. "We must destroy the thing."

That was an easy matter, the more so that I knew the exact spot. The northeast side of the island, unlike the rest, is low and sandy. A cable-length off the shore at low tide is a round, smooth rock that rises like a broken column out of the water to the height of ten feet; Franklin had marked it "Tower Rock," and there could be no mistake. Bearing from this due west a quarter-mile were a group of dragon-trees.

Now I recalled these trees quite clearly, since they were the only group of this species which had escaped destruction, and I was interested in their singular nature and had even visited them, getting some of the gum. Half a cable-length to the west-and-by-north of these trees was a large boulder jutting out of the sand, and the gold was buried on the north side of that boulder.

So said the vellum, and you may judge of my interest in the matter, and of how the others were interested to hear me tell of the place as I knew it, though I did not recall that boulder. Franklin had been a few points amiss on his bearings of the island, but that was nothing. He certainly was not astray on his local features.

"Do you think," Polly Langton asked me, a sparkle in her eyes, "that anyone might have come there and found the treasure?"

"Not unless he were looking for it," I told her. "No one comes to that island except for turtle, or to shoot wild goats, or to fish. The black island men from St.

Nicholas come there often, but they make no stay. There is fresh water in a large bay on the northwest side of the island— Porto Grande it is called."

"Aye, it is marked." Ned Low rolled up the big chart. "Russel," he went on, "have you finished with the bearings? And you, George? And you, Miss Polly?"

We had it all in our heads, well enough. So Captain Low struck a light, and presently the white vellum curled and crumpled and became a black ash on the table.

Then Low looked up at us, and laughed in his gay manner. "And now, comrades, a sneaker to our good luck and fortune!"

He brought wine and flagons from the cupboard, and we pledged Franklin's gold, the girl with a flash to her eye and color to her cheek. Then, since Polly Langton had not yet broken her fast, I went to hasten Dickon with his second tray, and so took charge of the deck. And this ended our conference.

We had now no further talk among ourselves of the gold, for it was a dangerous matter, and would keep well enough until we arrived at the spot. With the next morning indeed foul weather came upon us; not contrary, but heavy gales that swept us on our course yet kept all hands on the jump. Day after day they continued unabated, and the *King Sagamore*, for all her battering and straining, leaked no more water than could be got rid of in an hour's pumping of mornings.

During those days we were too busy to have much time for mischief, which in the light of after events I think was most fortunate. There was indeed some preaching and ranting up forward, but since it gave the men an outlet we made no objection, even when Gunner Basil made longwinded discourses of a Sabbath.

What with the ship's roll, few of us were not seasick at times, and I saw little of Polly Langton these days. What little I did see, however, woke in me admiration for her bearing and character and spirit. I think she had ceased to class me with pirates, for she was smiling and merry when we met, and sometimes took the wheel during my watch on deck, fighting it with the skill of any man among us.

Dickon the cabin-boy was quite sick during this period, which was another fortunate thing in my opinion. We replaced him for the time with Thomas Winter, the long-faced half-wit of whom I have spoken. A curious man was that, who seldom spoke, never met the level look of an eye, and mingled not at all with the other men. He had been long at sea; his hands and forearms were much tattooed; yet none could get him to speak of his goings and comings. He had a vacancy in his aspect that surely belied his wits.

This fellow Winter, also, seemed to be taken with strange spells. One day at noon we had a fleeting glimpse of the sun, and after shooting it with Low I hastily left the deck and jumped below to make calculations and verify our reckoning. As I came into the cabin I found Gunner Basil there, and the man Thomas Winter was speaking to him. I had chance to hear only a few words, but those were spoken in a new voice to me—a sane and sound and bellowing voice.

"Why, damn your eyes!" Winter was roaring at the gunner. "Who are you to tell me what to do, you whelp of Satan? You stow your jaw, blast you! I'm the one—"

He broke off at sight of me and cringed. I was the more astonished, for Gunner Basil seemed to be taking his oaths with shame-faced manner.

"What's this?" I broke in upon them. "Winter, was that you I heard? What d'ye mean?"

"Pardon, sir," he mumbled. "They roarin' winds do fetch gusty words out o' me at times, sir, and all o' seven devils a-perched up aloft!"

He shambled away out of the cabin. Gunner Basil looked at me, wagged his head sorrowfully and tapped his skull. He let out his nasal whine. "Bear with him, sir; bear with him! The poor afflicted fellow deserves the patience of all men. If he is a bit daft, he is also a good seaman— can hold her by the wind wi' never a flutter o' canvas from hour to hour!"

With an impatient word I settled down to my figures. Afterward I remembered again the complete change of voice and language which had been effected in the daft man, and how he had cringed at sight of me. This wakened my pity, and I thought no more of the incident.

V

Fair weather came back to us as suddenly as it had departed, and found us well advanced on our course, though much strained and battered about. Within two days all our sick were recovered, and we fell to work overhauling the rigging as we sailed, for the new cordage had stretched abominably and must be re-pitched into the bargain.

Hardly had we come into clear skies, however, then trouble let loose aft, as if it had been waiting for fine weather before breaking.

We were heeling smartly along under a spanking breeze out of the northeast-and-by-east, everything drawing well, and four bells of the afternoon had just struck. Old Humphrey Stave was seated by the for'ard water-butt, working with palm and needle at a spare topsail when the bosun appeared and talked for a little with his crony. Then Pilcher came aft, touched his forelock, begged some tobacco from me and fell into talk. He had something at the back of his mind, but was slow in reaching it.

"Cook be heatin' of some pitch in the galley," he observed, "when you're ready to get that for'ard rigging painted, sir."

Simon Blake was at the wheel. "When it's ready," I said, "send a man aft to relieve Simon here, and let him and Ezra Blake take up the buckets. They're good careful men, and I don't want the deck spattered."

"Aye, sir." Pilcher shook his earrings, then gave me a queer look. "There be some wild talk for'ard, sir," he went on.

"What about, bose?"

"That you've been on the Account, sir, and I give the lie to it. But that bain't all. I don't like them there godly men, nor they me; but I've heard whispers. They do say as you and Mr. Russel and Mr. Low ain't doin' right by the lass, and that she's mortal afraid o' you gentlemen. Then there's summat about Mr. Russel bein' one Portugee Lopez, and it bain't no secret that Mr. Low is Bloody Ned—"

"Who's doing this talk?" I demanded, frowning. We were beyond earshot of the helmsman.

"That I don't know, sir; just driftin', it is. These godly scum for'ard seem to think they'll be made to turn pirate."

"We'll work it out of 'em," I said cheerfully. "Run along and attend to that pitch, now."

He swung forward. Barely had he gone when from below came Polly Langton and Captain Low. They flung me a bare nod, then resumed some talk they had started below decks, and I saw that the girl was flushed and earnest, while poor Ned Low was cold and set and hard in the face. They paused by the windward rail, so that their words came to me and to Simon Blake, at the wheel.

"And have you no shame for it?" demanded the girl hotly.

"Shame?" Ned uttered a curt, bitter laugh. "By the Lord Harry, no! If I'd hanged twice a hundred men, and knew that twice that number would yet die to my hand, I'd go on to the end and be proud of it!"

"I am sorry to hear such words on your lips," and she spoke gravely, her anger held down. "I had thought you a gentleman, and I find you glorying in your bloody deeds, in your piracies and murders! Go on to the end, you say. Do you dare admit that your share of this enterprise is to be used in the same fashion—that if the venture succeeds, if you buy out this ship from our company, you go on the Account once more?"

I cursed under my breath, for Simon Blake was drinking all this in, as his dour face testified; yet I dared not intervene.

"Aye," said Ned Low. "I'll not lie to you, Miss Polly."

"Oh, shame on you!" she cried out. "To think that you and your precious friends so inveigled my poor uncle! You and they, to take his money and use it for more piracy and murder—how do I know you and they will respect that oath to my uncle?"

"Why, take us on trust!" Ned broke into a laugh, half-vexed, half of whimsical exasperation. "As for my friends, I care not and know not what they'll do with their share. My share puts Bloody Ned on his feet again, madam, and that's my own affair."

She gave him a long look, eyes angry, bosom heaving. "Then I am minded to draw out of this venture, sir."

"You can't." Low turned on her, pressed beyond endurance. "This is a company matter, my girl—don't try to make trouble! There's more behind it all than you know. There's more hangs on it than you know. We'll see you safe in London again with your share; and beyond that—have a care! This gold o' Franklin's belongs to all of us, mind, not you alone."

Now, whether she had meant her threat I know not, but Simon Blake caught his breath sharply, and his face was set in grim lines. But the girl laughed out right merrily under the angry gaze of Ned Low—perhaps she had only meant to tease him, after all. Then she turned and went below without more speech, while Ned fell to pacing the quarterdeck.

It was a moment after this that Thomas Winter, who was in my watch, came shambling aft to relieve Simon Blake from his trick. A few words passed between them. I stepped up, and Winter repeated the order to go for'ard and tar the lines. Blake nodded assent and obeyed.

I followed forward, as Simon and Ezra Blake secured their buckets and brushes, and came to a pause beside the water-butt, where Humphrey Stave sat and sewed.

"Do those buntlines and the forelift first," I told them, "then work in along the yards from each side, and do the shrouds as you come down. Simon, overhaul that loose foot-rope at the strap, on the foreyard; tighten it up and watch your seizing."

"Aye, sir," responded Simon, passing the lanyard of his bucket about his neck.

The two men mounted, and a moment later I turned to find Ned Low at my elbow. He gave me a whimsical glance, and chuckled softly. "Caught the bastard, and no mistake, eh? You heard?"

I nodded. "Aye, Ned. So did Blake, at the helm. The men for'ard are talking already about things."

"Oh, trice up a couple and give 'em a dozen apiece," he said carelessly, "and there'll be no more gossip. Somebody's been talking to the lass, though, and I don't like it. John Russel has his eye on her. You watch sharp, lad.

"Well, Humphrey Stave, how goes it with the palm? Man, that's as neat a patch as ever I saw laid!"

Old Humphrey squinted up over his spectacles. "Aye, master, and thankee! You'm be good judge of un, sir."

For a moment Low stood glancing around the deck. What he saw in that swift, eagle-like glance of his, I never knew. But suddenly his hand fell on my arm, and his voice sounded in my ear. Ah, the urgency, the repressed fury of that voice!

"Quick, for the love of Heaven! Loaded pistols in the chart locker. Get Russel and the gunner. Don't run aft, now—easy does it—"

My blood jumped. I turned and walked aft, seeking as I did so what had caused his abrupt alarm and caution. Except that most of the port watch were on deck sunning themselves, I could see nothing out of the ordinary. The men seemed to eye me hard as I passed aft, but that might have been imagination. The quarterdeck was empty, save for the long figure of Thomas Winter at the helm.

Once at the companionway I was down the ladder with a leap, and darted aft to the cabin. Russel was doubled up in my cabin; I paused to fling open the door. "John! Up and arm—quick, man!"

He had his own arms, and usually wore them, so I darted on into the main cabin and in the chart locker came upon two pistols, loaded and primed. I ran back, found Russel sitting on the edge of his bunk and blinking at me, and swore at him. "On deck! Swift about it!"

I ran on down the passage and came to the companion ladder. As I started up it, something flew out of the darkness below—a knife, that whanged into the wood beyond my ear with a vicious song. Who flung it I could not see and dared not pause to ask, for I was in fear of what might be happening forward.

Up the ladder and to the deck again, and just in time to see it happen!

—

They thought me gone below, of course, thought Ned Low alone there among them, the dogs! As my head came up, I saw the thing fall—saw the bucket, heavy with pitch, leave the hand of Simon Blake and go hurtling down from the topsail yard. Low did not see it, but he saw Bosun Pilcher gape upward and heard Pilcher cry out and leap aside blindly.

There was a terrible dull sound, and old Humphrey Stave threw out his arms and bent forward across his sail with his skull stove in. Another and more frightful cry burst from Pilcher; I saw the bosun lean back, saw his arm curl and straighten, saw his knife go flaming up through the air. "Take it, ye damned murderer of old men!" he yelled out, and Simon Blake took it fair in the throat, and pitched off the yard clear of the ship's side.

Now there was a heave of men over Pilcher; and I, running forward, saw Ezra Blake lean over from the futtock shrouds and drop his own heavy bucket toward

Ned Low. The latter, warned by my shout, leaped aside once more and the bucket missed. I flung up one pistol and shot the treacherous hound, and he fell straight at the foot of the foremast, where men were tearing cutlasses from the rack.

Then Ned Low was into them with both hands, and as one man swung at him with a blade I fired again and that man fell. All this, and the body of Ezra dropping among them, and the sight of me running forward, with John Russel behind me and the gunner also on deck, gave them pause.

Pilcher broke loose and stood beside the captain, and I joined them. Then came Russel leaping like a hound across the deck with a pistol in one hand and knife in the other, and a wild grin upon his dark face. Behind him came Gunner Basil, long hair flying, pale eyes darting about.

"Up with those cutlasses again, ye dogs!" shouted Low, and they obeyed sullenly. "So it's mutiny, is it—murder and mutiny, ye swine of righteousness! You there about the arms rack, stand fast!"

Four of the men there were, still half-determined to fly at us, and Low held out his hand toward them. "Gunner Basil! Trice up those four devils. Bose, pipe all hands and give those rascals two dozen."

One of the other men stepped forward defiantly and stretched his arm at Pilcher.

"There's the man o' blood, cap'n!" he shrilled forth. "Flung his knife, he did, and murdered poor Simon Blake, as godly a man as ever walked—"

"After Blake tried to stave in my head, eh?" said Low, pale with fury. "After he'd murdered poor chips, eh?"

"It was an accident!" cried out the man. "I seen his lanyard break and—"

"You lie," said I angrily. "I saw him fling the bucket. You liar, go and join those four scoundrels and take a dozen yourself for your lies!"

"Approved," added Ned Low curtly. "Bind these five men, you dogs, and do it swift! Where's the gunner?"

"Here I be, sir." Gunner Basil came to the front. He gave an order, and for a moment I thought there would be open mutiny. Then as John Russel grinned and lifted pistol the men obeyed. The five about the mast were bound.

"Now, men," said Low sternly. "I want an explanation of this. Pick your spokesman and send him aft to me as soon as the lashing is over."

He turned and walked aft. Then came Polly Langton running, and joined Pilcher, who was holding the head of poor old Humphrey Stave in his arms, tears coursing down his savage brown cheeks.

Humphrey blinked up out of the blood, and saw the girl there, white and feared. "Oh, minny, minny!" cried the dying man. "Here's your lad Humphrey coom home again! Oh, minny, I ha' cried for 'ee! Home from sea, minny, wi' presents for 'ee—"

His head sagged over, and that was all save that Pilcher broke into a storm of sobbing and wild cursing grief.

Then the girl's voice thrust in. "What—what is all this?" She saw the five men being led aft to the main. "What have those men done? I heard shots—"

"Murder and mutiny, lass," said John Russel, smirking at her. "But for George Roberts here they had murdered Ned Low and taken the ship."

"Aye, and they killed poor old Humphrey," I added. "Bose, go and do your duty, man."

Tears unwiped, Pilcher leaped up and ran aft for his lash. White-faced, the girl stared about, saw the five being triced up and knew the purpose of it. I called to the other men about us, and at my order they laid out old Humphrey and Ezra Blake. Simon was gone into the deep already. The other man whom I had shot was but wounded across the scalp.

"Take charge here, John," I said to Russel. "I must see to a matter below."

I went aft, passing Ned Low, who stood white and stern at the rail of the quarterdeck, his eyes glittering fiercely. How far this mutiny extended we could not tell, of course; whether all the crew were in it, or only the two Blakes. Perhaps indeed Simon Blake had merely seized the chance to kill the captain without premeditation.

Going below, I looked along the ladder for that knife which had so narrowly missed my head. The knife was gone, and I swore roundly to myself over the fact. Either Gunner Basil or Russel had flung it, I felt convinced, and I suspected the former.

As I looked, Dickon the cabin-boy came sleepily to the foot of the ladder, rubbing his eyes. "What be the fuss, sir?" he asked. "I was asleep down yonder—"

"Get up and see," I responded. "And let the flogging of better men keep you from evil courses, younker! Up with you."

He went to the deck above, and I after him. And there I saw a thing that was bad for discipline.

Pilcher had begun laying on the lash, and the first man under his whip was bloody, for the bosun was in savage mind. But Polly Langton had stopped him and now was standing by, looking aft at Ned Low and demanding that the men be given fair trial. Poor lass! She little dreamed what her intervention was going to mean in the end!

"Dear girl," replied Ned softly enough, yet with steel in his voice, "these men ha' tried to murder me and take the ship. They ha' done murder already. They're getting off light with two dozen, lass. Stand aside, and interfere not!"

"I'll not have it!" she stormed back at him. "You bloody-minded pirates, this is past endurance! These poor men—"

"Bose!" Now the voice of Ned Low thundered out like a trumpet across the deck. "Lay on, I bid ye!"

Pilcher shook his earrings, and the cat swung, and the man under it screamed out.

At this, Polly Langton turned about, and held out an arm to the men who watched the scene. "Help me stop it!" she cried wildly enough. "Take the ship from these pirates, these murderous brutes— come, men! Stand by me; don't let your comrades be lashed like dogs—"

Well, the words died on her lips as she saw the uselessness of it. John Russel, all agrin until his teeth flashed white in the sun, stood to one side, and the hearts of the men sickened in them under his look. So Polly knew that her plea was futile, and with a little groan that hurt my soul she turned again to Ned Low.

"Well do they call you Bloody Ned!" she said in a slow and deliberate voice that carried far. "Never dare to speak to me again, you or your friends—I wash my hands of you and your filthy gold and all your doings! Go on; do your worst to these helpless men, but never speak to me, I command you!"

With this she bent her head and, tears on her cheeks, went aft and so below. While Bosun Pilcher, tears likewise

on his own cheeks but from different cause, brought down the cat with all his brawn in the blow, so that the hurt man screamed again.

Presently it was done, Gunner Basil standing by and counting the blows to each man. Then, the groaning dogs staggering forward, Ned Low summoned the spokesman from the other men. All this while Thomas Winter had stuck to the wheel, wagging his long face vacantly but keeping the ship close to her course.

The spokesman came aft. A young, hard-faced fellow he was, by name David Spry, and he poured forth a long and whining plea, full of pious sentiments. The gist of it was that none of the men had intended mutiny; that they believed Bosun Pilcher had murdered Simon Blake and had so acted; that they were repentant and heartily sorry for their misdoing, and humbly begged forgiveness. All in all it was a moving and earnest plea, full of arrant hypocrisy and a lie from start to finish. Ned Low told the man as much.

"What's got into you godly rogues I don't know," he concluded. "But I know who's master o' this ship, and you'll know it, every man of you! Go for'ard. All hands stand by to bury the dead at two bells in the next watch. That's all."

David Spry went forward, and we shifted the men about so that the watches were again balanced. But Bosun Pilcher sat up in the forechains and cried like a baby over the passing of old Humphrey.

That evening, after the dead were gone and it was again my watch, Ned Low came up to me as I was having the lights filled and placed. We were alone upon the quarterdeck save for the man at the helm, and we were out of hearing.

"George," said Low, quietly, "what the devil can I do with her? She won't join us at mess, won't so much as speak to any of us aft. Her attitude has already had an effect on the men. Damn me, I can't take a girl by the neck and throttle her!"

"If you did, Ned—" and I checked myself.

A low laugh came from him. "Oh, aye! You'd be at my throat. Well, lad, much joy to you of the vixen if you win her. An honest lass, with the courage of her convictions—but oh, good Lord!"

The words came from him in a groan. "Five years ago this night I was a man in hell, George. Look ye, now! I'm suspicious of this Gunner Basil. Philip, the cook, came to me tonight and, says he, Basil and our half-wit Winter met outside the galley, and Winter drew a knife on the gunner cursing him most vile.

"'Now see what you've done, you bastard!' says Winter. 'For tuppence I'd cut the rotten heart out of you for not waiting, you dog, you!'

"That's strange talk for a daft man, George. And the cook says that Gunner Basil was in mortal fear. This Winter may be harmless, but like most daft men he may have dangerous spells."

"I don't doubt it," I answered, and told him of that day when I had come on Thomas Winter down in the cabin. "Excitement seems to send the poor madman's wits flying. But what's all this got to do with five years ago tonight, Ned?"

"I don't know," said he shortly enough. For a moment he laid his arm across my shoulders. "Oh, lad," he said softly, "don't you see that the lass is raising hell with those honest fools up for'ard—and herself all honest, too?"

"Aye," I told him. "But how to prevent it?"

"Ask the stars, George," and he draw away with a laugh. "Damn me if I know! Good night."

VI

All this while I had not seen a great deal of John Russel. The little we saw of each other, however, intensified the feelings that had arisen between us that morning on the quay below London Bridge. I heartily detested his smooth, sneering ways, and I think he was unable to puzzle me out—had not the honesty to take me for what I was, yet could not quite fathom me for a knave like himself. Ned Low, I felt certain, distrusted the man on general principles.

Fools that we were! We might better have directed our suspicions elsewhere, had we known it—but how were we to know it? Thus moves life itself, toward some vain objective, only to find itself suddenly directed toward othersome. For now, looking back at it all, I really believe that Russel was square enough in his intent toward the rest of us; but our mutual dislike ripened into distrust, and the distrust rotted into maggots of hatred, all quickly and suddenly.

It happened one day when the wind was fitful and changing, and the air heavy with brooding storm, so that all hands were kept bracing about the yards and men's tempers were apt to fly out at nothing. Not that I make any excuse of this for my own part, since through several days Russel and I had been approaching a crisis.

This came about in some degree through the attitude of Polly Langton. Ever since that day Humphrey Stave was slain she had kept to her word and held no intercourse with any of us aft. Her meals were served in her own tiny box of a cabin, and she treated us with a stony silence as if we did not exist. When she walked the deck, it was forward; and often she talked with the men, and sometimes would relent a little when I saluted her, though she spoke not.

Because I perceived that she thus softened a little toward me, her manner irked me not at all; but John Russel it infuriated. I observed that after some meeting with her he would walk the decks like a devil incarnate, raging among the men; and once he beat David Spry so furiously with a belaying-pin that the seaman bore the marks of it a fortnight.

Not that he had cause, either. The men were tamed, were obedient and lively and had given no further sign of any trouble.

Between me and John Russel, however, the hot tropic sun quickened ill-feeling. On the morning in question we had a sharp exchange of words when watches were changed. Having lost three men, we were short in each watch; added to which, one of the men was ill with the ague, passing from a quotidian into a tertian, and being too weak to move. So Russel desired to shift Bosun Pilcher out of my watch into his own, which offer I very bluntly refused. We nearly came to blows over it, yet did not.

At eight bells in the afternoon I turned over the deck to him and went below at once to get some sleep; storm was brewing and the heaviness of the air had given me a headache. As I came below I met Dickon in the passage and ordered him to fetch me a mug of ale into the main cabin. There I sat down to the table to pick our course on the chart, as we were getting close to the islands and had need of care.

Hearing someone enter, I spoke over my shoulder without looking up, thinking it Dickon. "We're past the Canaries, and I would we had some of that wine aboard! Go you and tell Philip to get a fresh butt brought up for'ard, for the water in that is foul, and to have it well lashed in place at once."

"Damn your impudence!" said the voice of Russel. "Run your own errands, you cursed Virginian."

I turned to see Russel at the cupboard, pouring a cup of wine. "Hark 'ee, Russel or Lopez," I told him, "a little more civility, if you please! I took you for Dickon—"

"Devil sink you and your takings!" he broke in with sudden access of fury, turning at me and snarling like a wolf.

Just then Ned Low came into the cabin, and Russel gulped at his wine. Ned perceived nothing amiss, but came and glanced at the chart and chuckled merrily.

"Ha, good and well done, George! By the Lord Harry, we've a record to boast of this voyage—hardly a ship spoke, not a head wind nor a calm, and a course fair and straight as an arrow to the islands! Gunner's on deck, John? I must speak with him."

He passed out and was gone. Russel looked after him with a dark sneer. "Aye, you'll speak wi' Gunner Basil once too often!" he growled. "I've warned you against that pale-eyed devil, you poor fool of a gentleman, you—"

"Keep your tongue off Low," I snapped.

He whipped out an oath, and I saw murder in his eyes; his hand dived down to the pistol in his belt. At that I was out of the chair and at him and knocked the pistol into the corner.

His fist took me under the ear and smashed me against the wall. As I rose I caught sight of Dickon, ale-mug in hand, standing in the doorway and staring out of his evil eyes. Then Russel was atop me, and his knife was out; but I met him with a blow from the shoulder that tapped the claret, and got out from the wall. He came on, cursing and letting drive with the knife, but I evaded him and got home another blow.

Then sanity began to crowd into my brain. "Let be, you fool!" I cried out, parrying his stroke. "More of this and we'll all find ourselves—"

He stopped short in his stride like a man paralyzed, and for an instant I thought that my words had checked him. It was not my words or my fist, however. He stood there with the knife held out toward me, so that it dropped and tinkled on the floor. His eyes widened on me and his mouth opened, but no words came forth.

Then a bubble of red froth broke on his lips; he dropped to his knees and rolled down on the floor, and I saw the haft of a knife sticking out from his back.

Even while I stared at him in blank horror and wonder I caught the shrill voice of that devil's spawn Dickon from the companionway. "Ahoy, cap'n!" it cried out. "Cap'n Low! The mate ha' killed Mr. Russel, cap'n!"

John Russel, dying, heard that lifting, piercing cry. He heaved upward, raised himself to one elbow, wrenched up his head, and looked at me. A ghastly, twisted smile curled his lips as he slobbered the blood from his pierced lungs. He tried to speak, and could not—then sudden words burst from him.

"Now 'ware of them, Roberts, or you're snared! Tell Low—that the man—man Thomas Winter—"

He strangled on his own life-stream, and died on the word.

Now came Ned Low running, with the imp Dickon pointing and crying at his heels, and behind them Gunner Basil and the bosun. Some of the men were following; but Captain Low sent back an angry shout that checked them and ordered Pilcher back to keep the deck. The bosun obeyed with an ill grace and waved his hand to me before he went. Ned Low came on into the cabin.

"I seen it done, cap'n!" shrilled that little devil Dickon, pointing at me. "Took un in the back, 'e did—"

"You little liar!" I burst forth angrily. "It was you flung that knife—"

I started for him; but Gunner Basil whipped out a pistol at me, and I checked myself. A dying man does not waste words.

John Russel had spent his last breath in warning me, and those pale, murderous eyes of the gunner's told me who was back of this snare. I think Gunner Basil would have pistoled me then, had not Ned Low knocked up his weapon.

"What in the devil's name is all this!" he cried out. "Dickon, stow your jaw! George, what happened?"

"Why, Russel and I were fighting," I said bluntly. "In the midst of it Dickon there threw a knife and struck Russel in the back. That's all."

"A black lie!" screamed the boy, flying into a fury of rage. "It was you stabbed un as 'e leaned over the table—never give un a chance! And—"

"Do not cast the stain o' murder on the innocent boy, Mr. Roberts!" spoke out Gunner Basil in his best preaching manner. "A sanctified vessel is the lad—"

I plunged at him, but Ned Low caught my arm and flung me back. He turned a cold face to the gunner and ordered him on deck. "It's your watch, and see that you keep it," he finished. "This is none of your affair. I want no more words from you, mind that!"

Basil looked him in the eye, and dropped his gaze. "Aye, sir," he said, and departed to the deck meekly enough.

Ned Low took a step forward, leaned over the body of Russel and pulled forth the knife. He rose up and gave Dickon a keen glance. "Dickon," he said in a kindly tone, "keep this matter to yourself. You understand?"

The little devil was no more astounded than I was, and could only stare and mumble something about Portugee Lopez. Ned Low nodded thoughtfully. "True, Dickon. The man was pirate and outlaw. Tell the bosun to bring two hands here and remove the body. And no talking, mind."

The imp gave me one exultant, diabolical grin, and departed. No sooner was he gone, however, than Ned Low turned to me, a blaze of eager vehemence in his face. "George, never mind talking!" he burst out softly. "Forgive me, lad. Don't ye see, the little fiend is not alone? Gunner's with him, and more besides. When the call came cook Philip was just yammering to me about some trouble for'ard, and there's a gale breaking within the hour and the sails to be handed. Let this matter pass for the moment; we'll make the boy confess his lie later on."

"You're right," I assented. "And, Ned! When Russel died he was trying to tell me something. He heard the boy shouting at you and warned me of a trap. He tried to send you some message about the man Winter but could not get it out."

Low's eyes narrowed speculatively. "Winter! That proves my point; John had guessed the trouble for'ard—thought the daft man was in it, eh? John was no fool in such things. Well, slip a pistol into your pocket from the locker, George, and take the deck.

"Or, stay! You're weary. Go sleep, and bar your door; there's deviltry afoot somewhere. I'll take this watch. We can't trust Gunner Basil."

I nodded and went to my own cabin. There came a tramp of feet as a number of men descended the ladder; also I heard Polly Langton's voice and knew that the girl was aroused by the noise. Like a coward I flung myself on my bunk and left Ned Low to do the explaining to the lass.

After perhaps an hour of sleep I wakened as the *King Sagamore* keeled over almost on her beam ends—wakened to the trampling of feet, the shouts of men, the pipe calling all hands. Getting hurriedly on deck, I found that the blow had come.

Except for a rag of sail forward we were stripped to meet it. The first blast of the wind had sent us over; now there was peace for a moment. The ship righted, fell away; and then the main fury of the storm drove down. Through the darkness the huge masses of cloud to windward were lightning-shot, sending an eerie glare across the waters.

Now we beheld it coming—a white line of spray and spindrift, racing down from the horizon under the glare of lightning. I was busy amidships, getting everything lashed down anew; when the keen, cold blast of wind smote us I sang out to all hands to hold on, and we leaped to the lifelines. Then we were smothered under water and spray.

Two of our men must have gone at that minute, for we never afterward saw them.

⌒

A poorer ship than the *King Sagamore* would never have risen out of that welter, for she laid over while three heavy seas swept her. Then she began to rise; the scrap of sail forward caught and held; she answered her helm and came before the wind, and we were off.

That night the loss of those two men was felt badly, for every hand was needed; and to add to our troubles the ship was making water, a butt having been loosened somewhere forward and the leak hard to get at. Nonetheless we counted ourselves lucky all told; particularly in this, that the gale was driving us fair on our course, and we might look to raise the islands in two days or less.

Now of the company that had left London, twenty all told besides Polly Langton, we had lost six. Aft, there remained captain, mate and gunner, and we took the bosun into our company as second mate. Forward were Dickon, Philip the cook, Thomas Winter, and seven of the sons of righteousness who were led by David Spry; ten in all. It was by no means a large ship's company, but we could take on a few hands at the islands, for the Cape Verde men are glad to ship.

So night wore into dawn again, and ever we fled south and south with the storm roaring at our heels, the *King Sagamore* picked up and hurled forward with a hissing rush by every mountain-wave. With daybreak the leak began to show so bad that I resolved to take it in hand myself, for it was beneath a timber near the well on the larboard side.

Ordering Thomas Winter down into the hold with a lantern, I followed with David Spry to help me. We got the timber cut away about the trunnel, which remained fast in the plank; the butt had started indeed, and the water shot in the full breadth of the fourteen-inch plank.

When we had somewhat checked the force of the stream with oakum we moused the trunnel, took two clove hitches about it and lashed the trunnel to a bar, just as a port is lashed. I had brought along two rollers, or screws, such as we use in Virginia to roll tobacco hogsheads; these I screwed fast at each corner of the plank and then lashed them into the bar. All this took time and energy; and, having done most of the work myself, I was half-drowned and aching in every muscle of my arms when we finished.

"Now, David Spry," I said, "fetch that calking mallet and drive the oakum tight. Lay more oakum on; and you, Winter, get us a chock of wood. We'll nail battens over that, and I'll guarantee she won't weep."

"Aye, sir," said David Spry, picking the mallet out of the water. "She'll not weep a drop."

Thomas Winter held up the lantern high. I was leaning against a beam for support. In the yellow light that half-witted face of Winter's altered suddenly to a look of such wild ferocity that I was for the moment paralyzed.

"She'll not weep, David Spry!" he cried out in a bellowing voice. "Strike, lad!"

The seaman struck—not at the seam, but at me.

The mallet caught me above the ear and drove my head against the oak. So sudden, so unexpected and bitter, was the assault, that before I knew what was happening I was dazed and reeling under the blow. I went down into the knee-deep water, and Spry flung himself down on top of me, fetching me another crack that knocked the sense out of me.

So there was I, taken like a pole-axed bull.

When I wakened again, it was to hear my name called. I found myself lying in darkness, but on dry planks. When I moved there echoed from the blackness a rattle of chains, and I found my wrists and ankles in irons. By the surge and heave of the deck, the groaning of beams and the creak of the rudder-irons nearby

I perceived that I was lying in the lazaret aft, down in the run of the ship.

"George!" came a voice again to me. "George Roberts!"

"Hello, Ned!" I answered. "Is that you?"

"Aye," he replied as his foot touched mine. "Art hurt?"

"Naught worse than a lump or two over the ear. You're not taken likewise?"

"Taken without a blow, lad!" His voice was bitter. "They called me down, said that you needed me—and clapped a tarpaulin over my head as I came. Damn me! That half-wit Winter has the strength o' ten men! Well, here I am, and here you are."

I was slow to speak, stunned by the realization of it. Mutiny at such a moment was madness—or so it seemed. Whom had they, except Gunner Basil, to manage the ship? And he was no navigator.

"I'd give a thousand pound," said Ned Low, "to know what it was John Russel tried to say about that devil Winter!"

"You don't think it's he who has taken the ship?" I demanded.

"No, no!" Ned Low laughed a little. "This is Polly Langton's doing, George."

VII

The passage of time was nothing to us as we lay in the pitch darkness amid the powder and the cabin stores. Indeed, we lay there the whole day unheeded, all hands being busy above; but the day seemed like weeks to us.

Ned Low had heard some smattering of talk while he and I were being chained in the lazaret; enough to show him that the mutiny had come about through Polly Langton. He had heard Spry swearing that they would stand by the lass and see us hanged for the pirates we were, which indeed appeared proof positive. Yet she was no navigator, though a good seaman in all else, so how could she hope to bring the ship to any port?

"Ned," I asked during the weary wait, "d'you mind that little black box I brought aboard from Langton? You've never said how it was he had the chart."

"I had left it with him to compare with a paper he had in Franklin's writing," said Ned Low. "Poor Langton! Little he guessed what was up this cruise!"

"Well," I said, "for one, I'm not so sure about Polly's being the chief mutineer. That devilish little wastrel Dickon has more infernal brain than we credited him with. I think now 'twas he tried to get me with his knife that day Humphrey Stave was killed. And Gunner Basil is a bad one for certain, though he may be holding to his pious pose. But where's Bosun Pilcher? He'll not turn against us."

"He was on deck when they nabbed me," came Low's voice. "Aye, he's true, and so is black Philip. But that cursed Thomas Winter! I'd like to know what John Russel had to say about the dog."

"Ned," I said after a long space of silence, "tell me about your chase after this Trunnel Toby. And that day Humphrey Stave was killed, you remember? You said how five years ago that night something had happened. What is it all, Ned? What reason lay behind you and the wine-dark sea?"

"Oh ho! Art quoting Homer to me, eh?" Ned Low's laugh rang bitter, but ended in a soft word. "George, sometimes I think the waves are weary with weeping—but pshaw! Five years ago I had everything in life, George; university honors, a home and family, and the promise of a girl I loved."

These words had tumbled out of him, as it were; jerkily to the flitting of his thought. Now for a little while he was silent, and finally spoke. His voice was hoarse, whether from the thirst that we had or from the tumult of his spirit, I know not.

"Why, George, that is a lengthy recital, and I am no teller of tales; but since we have a quiet watch below, shall out with the yarn and appease your curiosity—"

"It is no such thing," I broke in. "It is interest and friendliness, and you know it!"

"Aye, and your pardon, lad," he answered and sighed. "I have grown cynical of men, George, and belief comes hard to my lips; but my heart is sound enough and loves you. You've never been in the west country, by Wrexham and Marchwiel and the Brondeg Hills, and Wat's Dike, along the Welsh border?"

"No nearer than London town," I responded.

"Then take my word for it, no lovelier country may be found, George! My father was a magistrate and a knight, and of latter years had grown wealthy through his shares in the Company of Hudson's Bay. And one day he gave sentence to a poacher for killing a hare. A seaman it was, who had wandered riotously up from Bristol, spending guineas by the way. Guineas gone, the seaman headed for Bristol again, trapping the hedges for meals, and so fell foul of the law and was taken. My father sentenced him to transportation.

"Even the man's name was not known. He was a man with a long face, they say, and melancholy eyes and a voice like a roaring wind when he flung out curses; a gold ring fast in his nostrils, and over his heart was tattooed a crimson bleeding heart. That, and the name he went by, was all the picture I could gain of him.

"Well, into jail he was clapped, cursing and swearing bitter vengeance upon my father, who had sentenced him. Two days later came travelers, shipmen going to Bristol, and they heard of the man and viewed him as he lay in jail. They recognized him for one Trunnel Toby, a man famed for foul deeds and piracies. Word of it came to London, and he was sent for to be hanged at Tyburn as a notable example to other pirates.

"So they took him away, chained him like a beast. How he did it I know not, but he slew both his guards and escaped clear away. And on a Sunday night he came, bringing other rogues with him, to Ravenscroft Hall where my father lived."

Now the hoarseness gained upon Ned Low, so that for a little while he sat in silence, and I could hear his dry mouth working. I had by this time caught the drift of what was afoot, and guessed whither his tale led. The telling of it would ease his heart, so I kept still and let him go his own gait.

He resumed presently, speaking soft and low. "There was a lass I loved, George, and since my parents were lonely, often she would come to the hall and spend a day or two. She was spending that Sunday so when this foul Trunnel Toby and his mates arrived. They picked their time, knowing that few of the servants would be about.

"Well, they broke in and slew like dogs gone mad in Summer's heat! They slew and robbed, plundering Ravenscroft as they would ha' plundered any ship on the high seas. Two of the dogs fell under my father's steel ere they pistoled him—Toby himself fired the shot, and that same bullet slew my mother. The dear lass they murdered likewise, and fled with their booty, having horses in waiting.

"And the devils got clear away, George; clear away! They had a ship waiting by Bristol, and Trunnel Toby was captain of her.

"To this I was called home from Oxford. One of the two whom my father slew lived long enough to tell who and why, and then died. For a fortnight I was like a man out of his wits, and then I fell to work. I raised what money I could, sold off what lands were free and went to London.

"There I bought a stout sloop, armed her and manned her with the scurviest knaves could be picked up. There was a devil in me then, lad; for all I was just turned twenty-one I made those knaves fear me most bitterly. So we put to sea, and since that day I have never lessened in the search for Trunnel Toby.

"A year, and I was captaining my own ship, a fine, fast ship that we took from a French rover off Brazil. They had little ease who sailed with me, I promise you! We were on the Account sure enough, but we molested no innocent trader, George—only hunted up and down the seas whatever ship Trunnel Toby might be in.

"He heard of it, and others heard of it, for I hanged every man that had sailed with him or shared with him. More than once, as I have told you, I came close to him, but the hound was wary. I made the seas so hot for him that men were afraid to ship under him, and he was forced to take lesser berths. Always he fled from me; for he knew why I was after him, although no one else knew the reason, and he was afraid to face me.

"Ah, but he is a man of blood past reckoning! A fiend in human form, George; I've heard how he has dealt with captive men and women, so that your blood would freeze to imagine it.

"And he's no coward, either. Only last year with some small boats he boarded a Portuguese Indiaman in the very harbor o' Funchal, slew every soul aboard her and with the remnants of his men worked her out from under the shore guns. I was there a week later and heard the tale, and tracked him to the African coast.

"Indeed, I found the ship in the Guinea River, up a bit from the English factory at Sierra Leone, and I took her. Every man aboard her I hanged, but Trunnel Toby himself got ashore and fled among the blacks up the river. There I lost him, for I pursued with boats and discovered that he had doubled back to the coast again and escaped me in a ship bound for Virginia with slaves. And since then I have been able to obtain not the slightest trace of him.

"Most like he is in Virginia now. With my share of Franklin's gold I'll buy this ship and start out anew, and I think I'll find him in Virginia, for he's poor and without followers, and even the brethren of the coast are afraid to sail with him for fear I'll trace them down and hang them. And that's the reason behind me, George Roberts."

"You've told it to Polly Langton?" I demanded.

"The Lord forbid!" exclaimed his voice, startled. "I've told it to none save you."

"Then no wonder she deems you a common pirate," I said thoughtfully.

"I forbid you to mention it, George."

"Oh, I'll not! I thank you for the confidence, Ned Low, and if it's ever in my power to aid you, count on me. Here we are chained up like felons, and what's to come of it?"

He made no answer to this. Presently, for all my pondering on that sad story of his and the wreck which had been made of his life, I fell asleep from utter weariness.

⁓

It was after night when I wakened, for the trap to the cabin above was open, and David Spry was coming down with a lantern and food and mugs of ale. Ned Low was asleep, and Spry stirred him with his foot until he sat up, then gave us the food and ale and watched us make way with it. His dour, gloomy face was saturnine.

"Wind be falling," he announced, "and we're like to raise the islands tomorrow."

Ned Low glanced up at him. "You'll raise nothing but the coast of Hell, you mutinous dog!"

"Aye, by your guidance." David Spry grinned, and then sobered. He sat him down on an ale-keg and regarded us while he played with his knife in one hand. "Harkee, masters! The ship's ours. Mistress Polly be in command of she, and Thomas Winter the cap'n—"

"Winter!" I said, choking on my ale. "Are you mad?"

"Nay, un can navigate right well," said David Spry, and grinned again. "Now, Master Winter bain't a man of God, not he! Nor Gunner Basil neither, for all his pretended repentance; for did we not hear un swearing great oaths? Aye. Nor Bose Pilcher neither. And they all say to hang the two of ye and take the ship. We'll not abide this, masters."

We listened to him in stark amazement. He was in deadly earnest, and we realized that he was speaking for the hands forward no less than for himself. But Pilcher—

"Need not call us mutineers, masters," he went on. "We'm be honest men. You be rogues and scoundrels belike; and for the lady up above we've took the ship over, and to save the blood of honest men from your hands. Ye unregenerate sons o' Belial, take shame to yourselves!

We'm be honest British men and sail not wi' murderers and pirates and suchlike."

"Yet you're going to murder us," put in Ned Low.

"Not us, master. Set un ashore, maybe." The man rose and took our mugs. "Think o' your sins now, do 'ee spend the night at prayer. It won't hurt ye none."

He climbed up again through the trap, which he left open, perhaps for convenience. We remained in the darkness.

Presently I heard Ned Low chuckle. "George, sink me if this isn't the richest joke ever perpetrated! Here that lass has taken my own ship from me, Bloody Ned—and is mistress of the ship herself!"

"The joke will end as it began—with death," I said broodingly. "These long-noses have seen through Gunner Basil at last, it appears—that's one good thing! But what d'ye think about Thomas Winter, eh? Who dreamed that the lout could navigate—or is he lying to the others about his ability?"

A whistle broke from Ned Low. "Damn me, George, I'd give a thousand pound to know what it was John Russel—"

"Make it five thousand," I said, "and Russel might come back from Hell to tell you."

He laughed at that. "I doubt it. So those devils are figuring on hanging us, eh? I'm surprised that the bosun is with 'em."

"He's not," I said. "I know Pilcher, Ned, and he's a true man. But listen! There's a light above—"

Through the open trap we saw a light in the cabin above. It darted down, a square of radiance, and with the roll of the ship illumined our prison-chamber by flashes, now here, now there. Both Ned Low and I were ironed wrist and ankle, and chains ran from the irons to ring-bolts in the deck, so that we had freedom of movement but no liberty. Between us was a small keg of excellent port, laid aboard for cabin use; and I knew we would not die of thirst or suffer from it again.

Now a voice came to us from the cabin. The words we could not catch, although by the tone it was the voice of Gunner Basil. Right after it came the clear, high tones of Polly Langton. "Nay, I will not! I am weary, I tell you, and shall do no talking until tomorrow. Let the two men lie in peace—look to it, gunner; and you, bosun! If harm comes to them you both hang, I swear it! Time enough tomorrow for a talk."

Pilcher made roaring response, perhaps in order that we might hear. "But, mistress! The men want to know if you be with 'em or no! It's for your sake we have taken the ship—"

"You and the gunner and that man Winter can talk with me at eight bells in the morning, and not before," came her response, and after this, nothing. Presently the light vanished from above.

A bowl or porringer in which some food had been fetched remained with us. I took this and set it under the spigot of the keg and drew some port. After drinking I passed it along to Ned Low. "I have a pipe but no tobacco, Ned—"

"Here's 'bacca and a tinder-box."

Neither of us spoke until I had managed, with some trouble, to get the good brown weed alight and had passed the pipe to Ned Low. "Did you get the catch in her voice, Ned?" I asked. "And she's sparring for time, d'ye mind! Come, Ned, things are not quite so obvious as we thought. The lass is having hard work of it somehow."

"Bah! Nothing of the sort," growled he. "The jade has come to realize that neither she nor Winter can navigate, that's all. She's afraid. By morning, George, they'll make us an offer if we'll navigate for 'em. Wait and see!"

I was not so sure about this, and events proved my doubts well founded.

"Who keeps the keys of these irons, Ned?" I asked suddenly.

He laughed harshly. "The gunner. There's a spare set o' keys in the chart locker, but small use they are to us here."

By the movements of the ship we soon perceived that the sea was going down, but the night wore away intolerably for us, and the thought of being thus chained like slaves for any longer time was past endurance.

We had worse than thoughts to torment us, however—worse even than the rats which scurried about and over us until movement frightened them. It was, I think, with the midnight change of watches when the filtered rays of a tiny iron lantern came about the ladder, and then a sound of maudlin cursing and swearing. Down the ladder tumbled the boy Dickon, by some miracle preserving the lantern unhurt as he fell, and picked himself up with more oaths. He was, to put it bluntly, drunk as a lord.

He set the lantern on the ladder and turned to us, cursing and reviling us with the tongue of an arrant pirate. A vast change had come about in him; he had knotted a red kerchief about his head, wore a shirt looted from my bag, and had donned my sea-boots which came nearly to his knees. About his waist were belted pistols, though unloaded, and in his hand he held a deadly little gimlet dirk—a round-handled weapon, the blade protruding from the fingers of his clenched fist.

"Pirates, is it?" he maundered, coming toward us. "Sink me, but I ha' been cabin boy to Avery, and this is a poor pack o' thieves and woolsack rogues—there, ye lousy dogs! Wake up and give tongue. An I had my way ye'd walk the plank come sunup; aye, and if the old gunner had his way too!"

With this he fetched me a kick and stood regarding us drunkenly, the devil in his face. Cabin boy with Avery, indeed!

Avery had died before the young rascal was breeched.

"Stare at me, dogs!" He leered at us as he spoke. "Aye, damn ye for cowardly curs! Silly old Langton never dreamed 'twas all cut and dried, eh? Nor you, called Bloody Ned—I'll blood ye, and a pox take ye—"

With this he leaned forward and jabbed that little dirk of his into the calf of Ned's leg. The same instant my foot took him in the waist, all my weight back of it.

"*Woof!*" The air burst out of him; he went back head-first among the boxes, dropping the dirk as he fell. Groaning, holding his hands to his middle, he rose up; then Ned flung the pewter porringer at him and caught him across the eyes. A howl broke from the imp. Catching up the lantern, he scrambled back whence he had come, and his groans died out overhead.

"Sickened him, and well done too!" said Ned, laughing.

He leaned forward, and with his foot raked in the dirk. "Here's the first symptom of hope we've had, George— aye, I have it. A good little weapon."

"Did the pup hurt you?"

"A scratch. He'd have murdered us if he'd been let alone. Did ye mark what he said about Langton, George? 'All cut and dried,' quoth he!"

I recalled now how Dickon and Gunner Basil had been thick from the very start. It was clear enough that they had fooled Dennis Langton into shipping them; yet we vainly sought a reason until I recalled the tale Pilcher had told me and laid it before Ned Low, with some further details that I had forgotten when I first confronted Basil.

"That must be the right of it, Ned!" I concluded. "Gunner Basil served under Avery, d'ye mind? And this talk about knowing where Avery's gold was hid— d'you think it's the same gold we're after?"

"It's not," said Ned stoutly. "I was at the taking of this hoard; none but Franklin and I knew where it was hid. It may well be, however, that Avery buried some other gold about the islands, and that the gunner knew of it. Avery's been dead long years. Yet I don't like the smell of it at all, George; to me it looks like a plan ready laid. All cut and dried, said he! I'd give a thousand pound if I knew what it was John Russel wanted to say about Winter—"

"Hist, below!" came a sudden low voice.

We fell silent.

"Below, cap'n! Art well?"

"Aye," responded Ned Low. "Who's there?"

"Me—Philip! What can I do for you, master?"

Lord, but how my heart leaped at those words! The black cook!

"Get the keys from the chart locker and loose us from the irons!" snapped Ned swiftly.

Hope thrilled in his voice, and I felt eagerness surge through me. Philip was a true man, and—

A curse, a shrill cry, the sound of trampling feet came to us, and the voice of Gunner Basil poured forth furious oaths. He had come upon Philip, had discovered him aft, and now drove him forward with blows and beery revilings; evidently a cask had been broached forward. And so our hopes died even more swiftly than they had arisen. All became silent up above.

"Well," quoth Ned philosophically, "better luck next time, lad! And at least I have the little dirk."

It was small consolation, to me at least.

VIII

With the morning, suddenly and most terribly, there was laid open before us the whole book of villainy which those above were writing. No, not the whole book, either; one page of it was still hidden from us!

David Spry came down to us again, left us food and ale and went his way without saying a word, hurriedly. A little while afterward voices came to us through the trap, which remained open.

The first voice which reached us was that of Spry himself. "I am come to speak

for them for'ard," he said. "The bosun is a child o' darkness, and we who be honest men will ha' naught to do with his decisions. I say to your face, Gunner Basil, that we ha' doubt of your regenerate state; and I demand to be heard among ye."

The gunner's whine rose, but with an ugly note to it. "I accept the burden which be laid upon me; aye, the burden o' doubt and mistrust! For my sins—"

"Stow it," commanded a new voice curtly and with irritated contempt. "Stow it, ye swab! As for you, David Spry, ye are dead right, lad. Aye, sit among us, and be welcome."

Light came filtering down to us through the open trap. I stared at Ned Low, and he at me, with open wonder and astonishment. What voice was this? It was new to us; we could not place it.

Then even as we stared came the answer to our wondering. Polly Langton's voice floated to us. "Well, Thomas Winter? Where is the bosun?"

"On deck," returned Winter. "One of us must keep the deck, miss. Will ye sit?"

From Ned Low broke a low ejaculation. Winter, indeed! There was no daft vacancy in this voice; it was the full-throated growl of a seaman, as different from the man's usual tones as day from night.

The sickening conviction broke upon me full force. "Ned, it was a plot from the very start!" I said softly with an oath at my own past blindness. "He and the gunner and Dickon, perhaps others! The man was no half-wit at all."

"We're a trifle late discovering the matter," and Ned Low smiled whimsically.

"Now let us have an understanding once and for all." Polly Langton spoke up coolly, quiet command in her voice, and I could imagine her level eyes sweeping from man to man. "You have taken this ship from her officers and owners, claiming to do it on my behalf, but without any orders or bidding of mine. Thus far I have consented to the matter, for the ship was in storm and distress. Now speak out your purposes flatly. What mean you to do?"

There was a moment of silence. Ned Low looked at me and made a grimace; here was a morsel of news indeed! We thought that the lass had been a party to our captivity, but now the matter appeared otherwise. As for me I felt a glow of warmth and joy, since it had been hard for me to lose faith in her.

"Mistress," began Gunner Basil, "it be in the purposes of Providence—"

"Stow it!" commanded Thomas Winter. "David Spry, do ye answer the lady."

There was something grim, something significant, in the way this man spoke to Gunner Basil. I remembered how I had overheard him addressing the gunner formerly in the cabin, and instinctively I began to feel a cold chill at the thought of the man. Gunner Basil was no baby, but a murderous scoundrel himself; yet the gunner obviously stood in blank fear of this man Winter, whom we had accounted a daft person!

Ned Low must have felt something of the same sense, for he murmured to me, "Mark, 'tis Winter who gives orders! Winter who captains the ship! Winter who navigates her—"

"Why, mistress," broke in the cold voice of David Spry from the cabin above, "we be honest men—some of us at least. Do 'ee mind how, that day Simon and Ezra Blake were murdered, and men lashed, ye cried to us to stand by 'ee against they pirates and bloody rogues? Well, we ha' done so, and that be all."

"All, you say?" spoke out the girl. "What say you, Winter? And you, gunner?"

"Aye," they answered together.

"And what is your purpose now, David Spry?" she demanded. "Do you know why we sail to the Verde Islands?"

"Aye, mistress," he responded. "We ha' heard talk o' gold. We stand with 'ee, I say, and we be honest men. We want no gold but our pay. We'll not see they pirates do no more robbery an' murder, nor take the gold from 'ee, mistress. We'll ha' no more to do wi' they sons o' Belial an' darkness! Do 'ee say the word now, and we stand with 'ee."

"Oh!" said the girl's voice. "What say you to that, Winter? And you, gunner?"

"Aye," they answered again.

Then her voice leaped out at them. "Very well. If you be minded to obey me, Winter, go above and take the deck, and send Bosun Pilcher down here."

Ned Low gave me a shove with his foot, and grinned admiringly. I awaited the answer. It came with a scrape of feet, and the heavy tread of Thomas Winter leaving the cabin.

Immediately afterward the girl spoke, but softly, so that we could hardly hear her. "Gunner, what and who is that man? Since the day we left the Thames, he has been known to all aboard as a man of poor sense, no better than a fool. Now he is lucid, and you obey him, and he navigates the ship!"

"Why, mistress, 'tis the dispensation o' Providence!" replied Gunner Basil in oily tones. "I know him no more than you, but praise be, in the hour o' need he has been lifted up as a horn o' salvation to us! What 'ud we ha' done, else, for a navigator, mistress? If it be not a plain case o' Providence, I know naught!"

Now Pilcher evidently made his appearance, for Polly Langton addressed him bluntly. "Bose, these other men have declared that they have taken the ship on my behalf, will stand by me and take my orders. What say you?"

"I say now, as I said afore," said Pilcher, "that Cap'n Roberts be no pirate! But as for standing by 'ee, mistress, I say aye to that. What's done is done. I obey."

"Very well; then we are agreed," said the girl. "These are my orders! First, that we complete our voyage and get that for which we have come. Second, that the treasure be divided among those to whom it belongs—me, and Cap'n Low, and Mr. Roberts. Third, that these two gentlemen be kept confined until the division is made, then be given their shares and free passage ashore at the first port we make. Now, lads, speak out! Yes or no?"

"That's fair, mistress," said David Spry. "I agree."

"As righteous men," said Gunner Basil, "we ought to hand they over to the law; but I yeasay your orders, mistress. Aye."

"And you, bose?" she asked.

"Aye," said Pilcher.

"Very well. See that it be so done. Who among you elected Winter captain?"

"It was agreement, miss," said David Spry. "He could navigate."

"Very well. It is understood."

The sound of feet and the scrape of chairs told us that the conference was over. I was about to speak when Ned Low, his head cocked on one side, made a gesture of caution.

I waited. A moment afterward we caught a soft sound of laughter and the voice of Gunner Basil—shorn of its whine. "Ha, Dickon! Here's a mug o' wine, ye devil's imp! Now run and tell our cap'n, blast his soul, to step down here and finish the bottle with me. Move, ye damned pup!"

A mocking retort from Dickon, and the boy fled on his errand. I sat motionless and stared at Ned Low. We waited expectantly, and were soon rewarded. Winter's heavy tread jarred the deck, and Gunner Basil greeted him with another laugh and an invitation.

"I ha' no time to drink, ye black dog," responded Winter's suddenly masterful voice. "It went well?"

"Aye," said the gunner. "She's after the gold, right enough."

"Good! Then we'll not have to squeeze the location out of her," said Winter. "Play it fine and slip not, or I'll carve the heart out of your carcass, d'ye mind that?"

"But, lad!" cried the gunner. "When this be done, will ye not run to the other island and pick up that gold I told ye of? The gold that Avery buried, his own share it was! No man alive but me knows the place, now that Cap'n Avery be burnin' in Hell! What say?"

"Like enough," answered Winter indifferently, as if postponing a matter on which he were none too eager. "But, mind ye, we have to make the rendezvous first, lad! We ha' not enough hands to work ship, and will have less. Obey the lass, mind ye! Let her put her gold aboard afore we act. And take good care o' Cap'n Low now; good care! I'll carry him along of us to the rendezvous. There's yet a fortnight

afore the *Rose Pink* can be looked for; so, Gunner Basil, bide patient. If ye spoil my work, I'll spread-eagle ye!"

Now both men apparently left the cabin. I drew a long breath and met the gaze of Ned Low, for the moment wordless. But it seemed as if new life had come into him; as if these staggering disclosures had invigorated and heartened him. All the old reckless gaiety back in his eyes, he gave me a grin of sheer, delighted amusement.

"Ha, George! Now we have the right of it, now we have the whole scheme unfolded, sink me else! Damn me, but the rogues were smart! D'ye see, George, they were stranded in London town most likely or else were waiting for word from their friends. So they shipped aboard us and made a rendezvous with the *Rose Pink* at one of the islands—"

"Whose ship is she?" I demanded. "Who's this devil Winter, anyhow?"

"Damn me if I can figure it, George! The *Rose Pink* is a right good ship o' twenty-two guns; Spriggs had her, but sold her to a Frenchman before he was taken and hanged. Whose she is now, I know not."

"Perhaps Winter knew all along of our errand," I mused.

"Not so. More likely he and the gunner and Dickon shipped with us, meaning to betray us as a prize to the *Rose Pink*; they did not look for so quick a passage as we made, which explains why a fortnight still lacks to the time appointed. Ye see how they ha' made use of these honest fools for'ard? On the way they learned o' what we were after, and Winter is handling the matter so Polly Langton will uncover the gold for him. Cursed clever rogue, ain't he?"

"Too cursed clever for us, Ned. We'd better acquaint the lass with the truth—"

"Tut, tut! She'd never believe us; it would be taken as a ruse to get clear of our irons, lad. Make no mistake, George, the devil is loose aboard here! Bose Pilcher knows it. You heard how meek he spoke, assenting to all that was said! Take cue from him, George, and bide patient."

Ned Low was aroused now and no mistake, and I began to see the man of energy below that gay and almost insouciant exterior. There was a bite to his words. I verily believe he was enjoying himself, was scenting the battle. Perhaps indeed he had some prescience of that which was to come.

"Damn it, I don't intend to stay in this hole a fortnight!" I cried angrily.

"We'll not. Philip will be back when he gets a chance—perhaps when watches are changed and Polly takes the deck. Trust the black man, George!"

"But what the devil can we do even if free?" I demanded. "We've no arms."

Ned Low laughed out at this. "Ha, George—what'll we do? It'll be a sweet play, I'll warrant you! Mind now, have patience! Leave the business to me."

His tone of confidence irritated me. "You're God-damned cocksure about it, Ned. What'll you do then? Out with it!"

"Why, hide honor under necessity, as Falstaff has it!" He chuckled again. "When needs must, lad, I can play the pirate very well, I do assure you! Ha' faith, and wait."

"I'm no pirate," I said sulkily, "and shan't go on the Account for any man."

He laughed at that, then drew a dismal sigh. "Heigh ho! Times aren't what they were, George, even in the good old days when Kidd and Avery were in their prime! If we'd lived a fewscore years ago! What ruffling, bold times they were, eh? Sink me if there's any romance at sea these days! Ships in the new fore-and-aft style, all the galleons rotted out, and the brave buccaneers degenerated into rascally thieves who'd slit your weasand for a shilling rather than risk a fight for a thousand pound!

"Well, a few hours more and Bloody Ned will be walking his own deck again—then hey for villainy! I'll slit weasands my own sweet self, and a kerchief about the head will vastly transform you, George; should take to earrings, like the bosun."

Realizing that he was only playing on my ill humor, I made no response to this.

⌐⌐

The hours dragged past most unbearably, for it was stifling hot down in the lazaret; we both waited impatiently for noon to arrive, but it came on leaden wings. At length we heard cries and the stamping of feet on deck, though what had happened we did not learn at once.

A little later Dickon came into the cabin and began to arrange it for the meals of those who were now aft. The little imp had either forgotten the loss of his dirk or else dared not mention it. Instead of closing the trap, over which he moved the table, he began to shy oaths and hard biscuit down at us. In the midst of this he gave us news. "A pox on ye, dogs! Tomorrow morning we'll have the hanging of ye," he shrilled most venomously. "We've raised the land, and by night we'll be hook down. Tomorrow we'll string ye up to a merry tune!"

His head vanished from the opening, and we heard Gunner Basil's voice. "Ha, Dickon! Make no talk of hanging where the lady can hear, ye imp o' Satan! Out with ye now and bear dinner. Here's Pilcher, what's second mate now, to eat wi' me. Ho, Pilcher! Be it true that land yonder be the islands, hey? What says cap'n?"

"Cap'n be ciphering and changing course to make the right island," said Pilcher's voice. "Harkee, gunner! I ha' heard tales of ye afore this, man. Mark, I said no word this morning afore the lass—but I know well enough that you, and the cap'n likewise, aren't no chickens.

What's i' the wind, man? Are ye for the Account? If so, here's my hand on it!"

The two men fell into low-pitched talk, little of which we could overhear, until the half-convinced tones of Gunner Basil lifted in argument. "Do 'ee listen, Pilcher! There be an article to which all the company, like all companies on the Account, be sworn; and that is not to force no married man to join us; d'ye see? I ha' heard that you be married, Pilcher. The cap'n might be glad of ye, for you know they coasts o' Virginia, whither we'll be bound; but if ye be joining from fear—"

I listened in no little amusement while Bosun Pilcher swore by teeth and toenails that he was not married, hated women as the Devil hates holy water, and desired to go upon the Account of his free will. He convinced Gunner Basil too, and only a master-liar could have done that thing, especially as the two men disliked each other.

It was obvious that Pilcher was trying to get into the confidence of the rogues and was stopping at nothing to do it. We heard no more, for the gunner discovered the open trap under the table, and with an oath slammed it shut; but we had caught enough to be of great heart to us.

About an hour afterward the trap was hauled open again. That imp Dickon had secured some rock ballast and now began to heave the lumps of stone at us with many foul curses; he would assuredly have worked us some damage had not Thomas Winter come into the cabin and kicked him out. With Winter was David Spry.

Both of them were in huge glee, and no wonder! For by some miracle, since Ned Low was not at all sure of having run out his easting, the island which had been sighted was none other than St. Vincent itself, the very one for which we were bound. The two men discussed this, from which we learned that before sunset the ship would be anchored, then entered up the log and departed again.

"I'll lay you two to one, George," quoth Ned exultantly, "that they'll go after the gold—take the boats and go—this very night! If they do, we're free."

I would not take his bet, however. Unless we were freed before Polly Langton left the ship I feared that the imp Dickon would pistol us where we lay. And such indeed was his intent, for the lad was bloody-hearted as Winter himself.

IX

Notwithstanding our hopes of the black cook, Philip, we saw nothing of him then, until later in the afternoon, when by the stamping and singing above and by the change of motion in the ship, we understood that all hands were at the braces and the *King Sagamore* was beyond doubt heading up for the harbor.

"They'll pick the northeast haven, that being closest to the treasure," said Ned Low coolly. "Is it rocky about there, George?"

"No; all sand-hills, and two long spits of sand protect the cove," I told him. "Indeed they might go across the end of the island to get the gold, since it cannot be a mile and a half or two—"

"Not they!" And Ned laughed heartily. "They'll row ten mile to avoid walking one. Wait and see!"

"If Philip uses that woolly head of his," I observed, "he'll come aft, get the keys, and free us the minute the anchor goes down. All hands will be busy up above for a spell."

The anchor did not go down in a hurry, however, for the ship tacked about more than once before she was in shape to make the entrance to the bight. Gradually she came to an even keel, we could hear the thunderous roar of Thomas Winter as he bellowed orders, and presently we were at rest.

Our voyage was done.

Almost at once we were aware of a soft-footed scurrying up above in the cabin. I was minded to call out, but Ned Low restrained me; excitement was upon both of us at thought of Philip there, getting the keys and coming down to let us free.

Philip it was, but in mighty fear, since he had no legitimate business aft. We heard a sudden ejaculation burst from him; then like a blow the voice of David Spry reached down to us.

"What be doin' here, ye black man? Ha, in the cap'n's chests—"

A cry broke from Philip, then the furious thud of a blow. Spry uttered a shout, which must have passed unheard on deck. The two men now began fighting across the cabin, and in the midst of this something fell between me and Ned Low, tinkling on the boards.

"The keys!" cried Ned eagerly. "Grab them, George—"

I found them and closed my fist on the precious things.

Up above the two struggling men came to the deck with a crash, and their legs showed in the opening of the trap. From Philip a choked cry of despair and fear rang out; a moment they lay fighting there at the opening, then came gradually through, and at length fell precipitately, crashing down atop of us headlong.

I saved them from broken necks, but at the cost of being knocked well-nigh senseless. When I had writhed clear, so far as the length of my chains permitted, I saw David Spry kneeling on the chest of the black and whipping out his sheath-knife.

"Enough o' that, Spry!" commanded Ned Low.

Spry looked about and found that gimlet-dirk at his back. He was paralyzed.

"Drop the knife, now! George, George, throttle him, lad!"

Even as the fellow raised a wild yell in his throat, I lunged forward and got him with both hands, dragging him to the deck with me. Now he was beyond reach of the dirk, and knew it, fighting furiously to get at me; while black Philip, twisting to his knees, added his strength to mine.

With never a sound out of him, David Spry fought on until he was black in the face as Philip and then suddenly collapsed.

"Quick, George! Give Philip the keys. Now, cook, loose my wrists, then get back up to the cabin and make all straight, and get for'ard," commanded Ned swiftly. "Look alive, lad; look alive! Not a minute to lose. We'll take care of all here."

Under the spur of his tongue Philip fumbled about for the keys, where they had dropped out of my hand. Panting like a blown horse, he found them and worked at the ironed wrists of Ned Low until a sharp word broke from the latter.

"Done! Enough, lad—up with ye! Leave all to us. Wait for word from us. Quick now!"

Obeying in his blind fashion, Philip leaped for the ladder, planted a final kick in the ribs of the senseless seaman, and made the best of his way above.

When he had freed his ankles Ned Low knelt before me and worked on my irons with the keys. Blessed relief! In another moment my wrists were free, and I was rubbing at the torn skin, while Ned freed my ankles likewise.

"Now," I said grimly, "there'll be a reckoning alow and aloft—"

"Softly, softly!" said Ned, and laughed quietly in his throat. "First give me a hand with this godly rogue—thus! Good. Now strip the shirt from him and truss that jaw of his all shipshape."

In no long time we had Spry ironed in Ned Low's place, and so well gagged that nothing but a stifled moan could come from him. He would not soon recover his senses, however.

"Give us a sneaker of that port, lad," said Ned, handing me the bent pewter bowl. "Aye, a good one! Now look 'ee, George, be not hasty to wrath, as Master Spry might say. They'll not miss this rascal, what with the excitement and all. They'll leave an anchor-watch and turn in all hands soon enough."

A few swallows of wine made us both sense our freedom more acutely.

"You'll try and take the ship tonight, then?" I asked.

Ned Low grinned. He was getting my pipe alight, and had trouble with the tinder; but at length he got it drawing, and shook his head. "Not a bit of it, George! Mind, now! We have the run of the ship here below, if we want it. We've all the cabin stores here to hand. Let's

eat, drink, and be merry, lad! Let's have a sound night's sleep, keeping alternate watch lest anyone comes down, and be ready for the morrow.

"Figure it out for yourself," he went on with an eager earnestness. "They'll take the longboat to row around the point o' the island after that gold, and they'll go at the break o' day. Who'll go? Polly, for one; Thomas Winter, for another. Winter will take the six honest lads from up for'ard to row the boat. He'll leave Gunner Basil here to keep the ship with Pilcher. Take the ship while he's gone, George, and when he comes back we'll have the dog at our mercy! Eh?"

There was sense to this; I was forced to admit it, though somewhat against my will, for further waiting was both dangerous and irksome.

"If things go as you expect," I said, "that's the best plan. Agreed! Then let's get some food broken out before the light fails. Lord, but it's great to be free to stretch again! What if Dickon comes down here, Ned?"

"Clap him in irons." Ned Low grinned. "I'll hang that little bastard, George! I'd sooner fling him overboard, but he'd not drown, mark me! Well, I'll not hang him either, for he's only a lad. Wait and see, George; the rascal may yet hang himself."

"And so save Jack Ketch a job," I said. "All right, Ned! I agree. Now to dine."

We were not disturbed again all that evening, for it appeared that owing to the heat and the calm of the day dinner was served on deck. We ate our fill, luxuriated in our freedom and let our captive snore. From the silence above, all hands were sleeping.

Ned Low had curled up and gone to sleep, and I, on watch, was beginning to nod, when a slight noise sounded above, and then came the voice of Polly Langton softly.

"Are you there, Mr. Low—Mr. Roberts?"

I touched Low's face, and he sat up.

"Aye, mistress!" I responded. "And we are like to stay here a while, thanks to you!"

"Oh, you must not—you don't understand!" There was a break in her voice. "If I had done anything else they would not have obeyed me! Don't you see, I had to act as I have done, in order to keep where I am? When we get back with the treasure, I shall have you released at once, and then—"

"You've been badly fooled, Miss Polly!" I spoke out, throwing off Ned's warning hand. "Winter and the gunner have a rendezvous at one of the islands with a pirate ship; they are using you to get the gold, then they mean to take this ship and join their comrades. Go with them and bring back the gold, and trust all to us. Make them take the bosun with you, and do you have a talk with Pilcher, for he knows the whole game. He can give you proof enough of everything. But be careful! Don't let Winter suspect that you know—"

"Ah—I hear someone—I dare not stay!"

She was gone again, and what effect my words had upon her we could not tell. Although we listened for a while we could hear nothing.

Finally Ned Low whispered to me. "Why the devil did you tell her to take Pilcher?"

"We don't need him," I responded. "She may."

"True enough," mused Ned Low. "Sink me if I don't believe her, George! Aye. She's handled things well enough, all considered. She's none of your patched and powdered fools who cry, 'La, la!' and fly into hysterics at the sight o' blood; but an honest Devon lass, with hard good sense and sober wits. George, I take back all my harsh words and thoughts about her!"

"Then go to sleep again," I bade him. He obeyed, laughing softly to himself.

⁓

The remainder of the night passed quietly. David Spry came to himself and tried to shake off his irons, but soon relapsed into immobility. The more I thought about Polly Langton's words to us the more I admired the girl's good sense in acting just as she had done. I could see now, in the light of those few sentences from her lips, that she had done the best possible thing for all of us.

She had of course played into Winter's hand without knowing it. Those poor "honest fools" up forward, panicky over being led astray by bloody pirates and murderers—as they considered me and Ned—had undoubtedly been prodded and urged all along, ever since we weighed anchor, by Winter and the gunner; in dealing with those fanatics the girl had been walking in slippery places and was aware of it. So all in all I felt greatly heartened by her few words; and when I waked Ned and laid myself down to sleep it was with the feeling that we owed a large debt to Polly Langton.

Morning came at last. Even before the first break of day, we were roused by the activity overhead. Obviously Winter intended to be off and away with the light, and our only fear was that he would visit us to make sure of our safety. As we later learned, we had been placed in the keeping of David Spry, and all hands were too filled with thoughts of gold to waste worry over what had become of Spry. Even Winter could not be blamed for supposing his prisoners well ironed and stowed; for he, playing a deep and desperate game—deeper even than we yet knew—was that morning on the verge of success, with the gold all but his.

Ned and I broke our fast very pleasantly; and though poor Spry's eyes besought us to have pity on him we dared not loosen his gag, promising to take care of him after a bit. Nor did we have any particular desire to ease his lot, since he had certainly made ours hard enough when he had the mastery.

The stern window of the cabin above was open. We heard the men embark as soon as there was light enough to pilot the boat from the harbor. Water and provisions were placed aboard the boat, and the deep voice of Thomas Winter penetrated to us with his final orders. Then at length silence ensued, and we knew the boat had departed.

"Now, George!" Ned Low drew a deep breath, and then laughed out gaily. "The question remains as to how many went along! Be quiet a while, lad. Give 'em a chance to get out o' the harbor. Beshrew me if I don't pistol that cursed Gunner Basil, and we do not want them to hear the shot."

"First get your pistol," I reminded him dryly.

He caught my arm. Steps sounded above, and immediately after, the voice of Gunner Basil himself, evidently addressing that imp Dickon. "What's that ye want, Dickon lad—wine? Well, well, fill your cursed skin if ye will! Hast deserved it, ye limb o' Satan! Here, pour me a stoup likewise; I'll wash my mouth clean o' that God-damned sanctimonious talk. This time tomorrow, lad, we'll ha' the gold aboard, and hey for the Indies!"

"Here's luck, damn yer eyes!" shrilled the boy's voice.

"Sweet lad!" murmured Ned Low.

Now Dickon vomited a volley of oaths, demanding to know why he had not been taken along with the others.

"The black scum of a cook must go," he swore roundly, "and that dog Pilcher, and they six godly fools from for'ard; eight sons o' dogs at the oars, wi' the cap'n and his lass in the starn—and me left here! Damn their eyes, I hope the God-damned boat sinks with all hands!"

Gunner Basil fell a-laughing at these oaths and valorous wishes. "You and me, younker," he responded, "got to stick here idle while they work. Aye, the cap'n knows Gunner Basil can lay a gun! Guzzle away, ye varlet, and I'll go set me a fishline for'ard. There be mighty fish in these waters."

For a while there was silence. Ned and I conferred together, being in no haste, and were delighted by the news we had gained. Those two were alone on board, which made things so much easier for us. Basil alone was sufficient to guard the ship, and Winter had wanted all the hands possible along to work out the treasure, as well as to row the longboat, which was a heavy craft.

All of a sudden we heard a satanic chuckle from above, and then the head of Dickon appeared in the trap. The boy was half-drunk, and I looked up to see a pistol in his hand. Staring down into the darkness, he could for the moment see no details.

"Now, ye dogs!" he shrilled at us in maudlin tones. "Now ye have it, Bloody Ned! I'll bleed the both of ye, blast yer damned souls!"

Ned and I must have realized at the same instant that the little devil was run amuck. We sprang up together, but collapsed and fell back. He, weaving the pistol about in his unsteady hand, uttered a wild laugh and more curses. "I'll bleed ye, ye dogs!" he went on. "I'll show ye who's the best pirate aboard this damned ship, damn ye! Take that! And there's more for ye where it come from—"

The roar of the pistol, volleying smoke and flame into our very faces, proved his words. Only that collision with Ned had saved my life, for the thing bellowed not a yard above my head. I was already heaving for the ladder again, and this time made it, and was up at the murderous little wretch while he still peered through the smoke.

He uttered a strangled cry and rolled aside, but I was through the trap and had him. And how the drunken rascal fought me! He gouged and bit with the venom of a very fury, until I got hold of his fallen pistol and slashed him over the head with the barrel. That laid him quiet at last, knocking the senses out of him.

I rose, and then found that Ned had not followed me. "Ned!" I cried. "Ned! You're not hit, lad?"

His head rose through the trap, a grim look in his face. "The bullet slew David Spry," he said, and came to his feet, looking down at the boy. "Sink me, but I could hang this little murderer—"

"No time," I broke in. "That shot will fetch the gunner, Ned! Get your pistols!"

"Right!" he cried, and whirled about.

Even as he started toward the lockers, Gunner Basil came running down the passage with a shout to Dickon. There was nothing else to do; I went for him with the empty pistol, and he stopped short in the doorway, his pale eyes popping at sight of me and Ned. His hand flew to the pistol in his belt, but I was ahead of him, and sent him staggering with one shrewd blow in the face.

He tried to run for it, with me at his heels, and got to the companionway. Then as he started up for the deck I had him by the leg. He drew his pistol and fired down, and the bullet actually nicked my cheek and cut the skin of my shoulder, so that he pulled free of me.

Nonetheless I got him, for I reached the deck only a step behind him and gripped his shirt, and he whirled at me with knife up. I caught his wrist and we went to the deck together, while Ned Low seized the pistol I had dropped and waited with butt reversed. His chance came as we rolled into the scuppers, and under the smash Gunner Basil relaxed in my grip.

I rose, panting, and regarded the man. His face was smeared with blood, and though the eyes were closed that yellowy parchment face was evil to see.

Ned Low touched my arm. "Get a coil o' light line for'ard, George. We'll tie up him and the boy."

Breathing heavily, yet mighty rejoiced to be free, I went forward and got the line. There I paused to glance around, and the pause cost us dear in the end. The *King Sagamore* lay in the quiet, landlocked bay, with nothing in sight but the long sandspits to seaward and the sandhills around. We were but a cable-length from the shore.

A sudden shout from Ned Low roused me. I caught sight of Dickon, just risen from the companionway, and Ned leaping at him. The boy ran like a hare, evaded Ned and got to the rail. With one clean plunge he was overboard.

Ned jumped to the fire-rail, caught out two of the teak pins and flung one. It drove within a foot of Dickon's head as he came up and struck out for shore. The little fiend twisted his head and looked up at us. "I'll bleed ye yet, ye dogs!" he screamed shrilly.

Angered, Ned loosed another pin, but Dickon saw it coming and dived. Escaping it, he came up again and struck out for shore. Then I perceived something else, and flung a shout at him: "Quick, boy! Sharks astern!"

True enough; a black fin was cleaving the water, and another after it. Dickon redoubled his efforts, and made so great a splashing that he got into the shoal water safe, and a moment later staggered up on the sand. He paused there only to shake his fist at us, then turned about and ran across the sand, and presently was gone over the nearest hill.

Ned Low and I bound Gunner Basil hand and foot, gagged him and lashed him to the foot of the mainmast. The ship was ours again.

"And what about Dickon, Ned?" I demanded.

He shrugged, reading my thought. "The chances are ten to one, George, that he'll not find Winter and the men. And if he does, what of it? We have the ship."

X

In the course of the day Ned Low and I got David Spry decently buried and reoccupied our own cabins. Likewise we noosed a huge turtle swimming alongside, for the season was just beginning and the island waters were thick with the creatures, and we dined famously.

We laid out loaded muskets and pistols with which to receive Winter when he came, and all the while the pale eyes of Gunner Basil watched us. We left him bound and gagged all day, then fed and watered him and took him below, ironing him where we had lain. He had not a word to say.

It was late in the afternoon when we descried a boat, under sail, coming up the bay. The glass showed it to be one of the island boats, with four black islanders aboard; at sight of us they were fearful, but I stood in the shrouds and signaled them, so that they came on and rowed alongside. I could speak their tongue to some extent, and when they came aboard we had a conference.

They were simple fellows, come hither after turtle. I told them that our men had mutinied and gone off in a boat but would return, and that we wanted a dozen islanders to ship aboard us as far as Lisbon. They were suspicious until I gave them what money we had and told them my name, and that I had visited their island of San Nicholas more than once.

"Your governor knows me," I told them, "also Senhor Gonsalvo, the former governor. They will tell you that I am an honest man of my word. How soon can you get the men here?"

They talked together, and decided to return at once to San Nicholas, saying that they could be back the day after tomorrow in the morning, barring bad weather. Ned Low made me a sign of delighted assent, and so we agreed upon it. Before sunset the blacks were rowing out of the bay, and so departed.

Although Ned and I kept watch and watch that night, we saw no signs of Winter coming back. Sunrise was at hand, we were getting breakfast in the galley, when Ned stepped to the rail, then called me and ran aft for the glass. Sure enough, there was a blot out between the sandspits.

When we had inspected that blot through the glass we stood staring one at the other in blank amazement. For the tube showed us that this was the longboat indeed, with a figure stooped aft, bailing the water out of her, which we took to be that of Polly Langton; only two others were aboard her, and these at the oars— cook Philip and Bosun Pilcher. They were rowing her slowly and wearily, as men who had been long hours at the task, and the boat was low in the water.

"Stove in, George," said Ned Low, wrinkling up his eyes perplexedly. "Now what's it mean, I wonder? Where's Winter and the other six?"

So slowly did they come on that it was after sunrise when they drew near, and Polly waved to us. The two men were too exhausted to wave, although we caught a faint grin from Philip and saw the bosun nod his head to us as the faces strained upward. The boat was half-filled with water, and we saw that she was badly stove in the bows.

In fact, so weary were all three of them that they hardly made any comment upon finding us two alone there and the ship ours. The two men crawled over the rail and sank down, gasping for breath. Polly leaned against the rail and looked at us with a tremulous smile upon her lips. Her hair was fallen about her cheeks, and she was very lovely.

"Where's Winter?" I asked.

She nodded toward the sandhills. "Coming. We ha' been rowing most o' the night—"

"Rest then," said Ned. "Come, George! I'll be cook. You bring ale."

I fetched some ale, and Ned produced biscuit and turtle-steak. We asked no questions, but waited, and when she had eaten a little the girl suddenly looked up at us. "Gentlemen, I ask your pardon, for—for everything," she faltered. "I ha' learned the truth—"

Ned took her hand and smoothed it, looking into her eyes. "Dear lass," he said gravely, "why speak so? Sure, we owe our lives to your wit and good sense. Had you not taken the head of things—"

Her eyes widened and came to me. "But—but they used me as a tool!" she said. "Bose Pilcher has told me all, as you told me last night, Mr. Roberts! It is all true about that man Winter—"

"Does he suspect that you know?" I demanded.

"No, no! He was glad enough when I offered to come back in the boat and bail her—"

"Then where's the gold?"

Ned broke out in a laugh. "Come, lass, forget all else and tell us what's happened?"

"Aye, he has the gold," she said, color coming into her cheeks. "We found it just where the directions said. But in coming ashore we ran on a sunken rock that hurt the boat; to fetch back the gold in her was impossible. So Winter remained to bundle it into canvas and carry it across the headland to the bay here. He was too excited over the gold to protest my departure, and sent Pilcher and cook Philip with me. He is sure that bose has joined in his schemes, you see. He'll be here sometime today."

"Good!" cried Ned joyfully. "You lads, get for'ard and sleep while you can. First, however, help get the boat hauled in, and I'll go to work on her. Canvas and pitch will make her tight enough to use in a pinch."

When the boat was hauled aboard Pilcher and the cook stumbled off to sleep, and Ned fell to his task, whistling blithely.

I got a spare sail rigged aft for a sun-shelter and remained talking with Polly Langton, who refused to go below. She was much concerned to have matters set right between her and us—but no more anxious on this head than was I myself.

From Pilcher, I discovered, she had gained a very accurate understanding of the whole situation—including her worthy uncle's past history, since the bosun had held back nothing. However it must have shocked her, she was now facing too stern realities to spend much thought on the past.

Now I went over with her the varied details of the voyage, pointing out how this and that had come about; and, having the perspective of distance and an awakened mind, Polly could clearly enough discern the right and wrong of things. Of Ned Low I could say very little, but I told enough to make her see that he was not altogether the bloody pirate he had been named.

In an hour we were talking and laughing together as friendly as ever or perhaps more so, and there came up mention of her native Devon. At that she cried out bitterly, "Oh, if we could only get away from here before the men come back! I want none of that gold. I would it were all at the bottom of the sea! And I am afraid of Winter. If you had heard and seen him when they brought the gold up out of the hole you'd have thought he was more devil than man! Can't we work the ship out now, at once?"

"It might be done," I said, casting an eye at the bay. "There's a light air off the land—oh, Ned! Ned!"

Ned Low had finished his work on the boat and came at my call, pipe in one hand and mug of ale in the other. Very merry and laughing he was, too.

"Ned, the lass fears Winter. And I am none so sure that it were wise to lie here all today and tonight. He took a brace of muskets with him, and pistols. What d'ye say to letting the gold go hang, slipping the hawser, and—"

"Not by a good deal!" exclaimed Ned coolly. He regarded Polly with a smile, his brown face very frank and cheerful to see. "I don't blame ye, Polly, for wanting to be rid of it all and away from here; but, lass, gold is mighty useful in the world. Once away from the *King Sagamore*, once back in London or Devon or where ye will, a few thousand guineas is a mighty fine thing wherewith to fight the world, the flesh and the devil! If the clergy had each a pocketful o' money there'd be less talk of Hell and more of Heaven—I'll wager ye never heard a bishop talk of Hell, now! Nor ever will. We see the world quite different through gold spectacles, lass—"

"A brave dissertation, Ned," I broke in dryly, "but come to the point!"

He pointed overside with his pipe, to where several large black fins were slowly cleaving the water. "There y'are—come to pick the leavings of our turtle! What better guard could we have against Winter tonight, George? Without a boat he can't reach us, and a musket-ball or two will do us no harm. So fear not; we are safe from him and all others!

"As for the gold, I mean to have it from him; that's one reason for not leaving.

The second is like unto it—I'll not leave him wi' that gold in his paws, d'ye mind? I need the gold, and I'll not see him rewarded with it. Nay, leave him ashore for a day or so without fresh water or food or strong liquor, and hear how the dog'll whine to us! We'll give him bread for gold, and when the last red round piece is down below I'll slip the cable and set our black island men to the braces and leave Thomas Winter here to think on his sins.

"For your sake, lass," he continued, "I'll not try to hang him, since that might make or lead to trouble. We'll leave him marooned and be content wi' the gold."

⌒

Leaving him to argue the matter with Polly, I took his mug and went forward to get some ale. While I was there, Pilcher came yawning on deck. I paused for some talk with him, and he told me what had finally and terribly convinced the girl. Under the jubilant excitement of finding the gold Winter had momentarily flung off his mask, telling the lass that he meant to have her as well as the gold; he had charged Pilcher to watch her closely and to lock her into her cabin on reaching the ship.

What Winter had said to Polly Langton was enough to set any man's blood to boiling. Then and there I changed my mind about leaving the bay.

"Bose, who's this fellow Winter?" I demanded. "He's no riffling jack playing in luck. There must be a name to him that men would know."

"Aye, sire, but I could never come at it." Pilcher shook his gold earrings. "Gunner Basil knows him, I be certain; no one else. Where be gunner and Dickon, sir?"

I told him of Dickon's escape. "Gunner's ironed down below. You must have deceived them all finely, bose! Winter really thought you'd go on the Account with him, eh?"

"Gunner be an old fool," Pilcher grinned at me. "Yet there's murder in the heart of un, mark that! The tales he's poured into me would shiver your soul, Mr. Roberts! If he be not a liar he ha' seen and done such things as 'ud melt a Turk!"

"Go down and talk to him," I suggested. "Perhaps you can get something out of him about Winter. That man's a pirate, a known man, I'm certain of it."

"Be going to hang un, sir?"

"Aye. You might get the line and block ready now, too."

I went aft with the ale and informed Ned and Polly bluntly that I was for staying until the men returned. Then Ned Low saw what the bosun was doing at the main and questioned me about it. "Making ready for Winter," I said. "The man hangs."

"Why so changed?" said Ned, laughing. "Would you jeopardize us all?"

"He insulted the lass here," I said. "Make no more talk about it now."

Polly Langton looked at me, and the color came into her face. We must have looked mighty humorous, for Ned Low began to laugh again and went forward. When he was gone, the little lass spoke softly. "You must not bear him such ill, Mr. Roberts—"

"No protests, if you please!" I told her frankly. "Pilcher told me what was said, and I'll give that rascal what he deserves if it kills me! But it won't. Before we leave here the rogue hangs."

She looked troubled, but made no more mention of the matter.

All this while we were keeping a sharp eye upon the sand-hills, but in vain; and since Winter and the six men could not come near the little bay without being seen, we were safe in taking our ease.

After a little Philip appeared and came aft. We were prompt to thank him for his loyalty, and for those keys which had near cost him his life to obtain. The Negro was delighted with our words of praise, and Ned promised him more substantial reward later, when occasion offered.

I had never seen Ned so full of good spirits as this morning. Polly began to take all in jest his announced purpose of buying out her share of the ship and going forth once more on the Account, and small wonder; no man ever looked less like a pirate than Ned Low that morning. Even when he stated that he would transship her at Lisbon she thought him joking.

So came noon, and Philip brewed us a mighty stew of green turtle in the regular island style, which we hugely enjoyed. Pilcher had held some conversation with Gunner Basil, but it was all one-sided. He reported that the gunner would utter nothing save oaths, and those unfit for repetition.

We had just lighted our pipes, and cook Philip was clearing away the meal from the shelter aft, when Polly Langton looked up and changed countenance suddenly.

I followed her gaze, and came to my feet. "Stand by, Ned! Here they are."

We stood at the rail, watching the seven bowed men coming over the crest of the sand toward the bay. Seven? No, there was one more following them; eight in all, and the eighth was the cabin boy Dickon.

XI

Foremost of the eight came Thomas Winter. He and the six men after him had flung away their arms, even to pistols; they bore each of them a rude canvas sack, some on shoulders, others in arms, and by their weariness under that dragging weight of wealth we knew how great was the treasure they had unearthed.

Dickon alone carried no burden. "Dickon has told them his tale—yet they come!" exclaimed Ned Low, watching the scene with frowning perplexity.

We shared his uneasy wonder, all of us. We had expected anything but this open coming. It could not be doubted that Winter now knew we held the ship, and he probably thought the gunner dead; he could have had little hope of Pilcher and the cook having subdued us. Yet he came on openly, the six men behind him, bringing their golden treasure down to the shore of the bay! And all unarmed, too, except for knives.

"I looked for them to attack us tonight somehow," I observed, "but not for such a coming. Watch out for tricks, Ned!"

"Yes, yes!" added Polly earnestly. "Don't let him trick you!"

"Fear not," said Ned Low quietly. "I want but that gold of him, and he can have the island! And let him try his tricks, now that we know him for what he is."

The eight came filing down to the sandy shore of the bay, a scant cable's length from us. "Way enough, lads!" cried Thomas Winter, dumping his load into the sand. In the hot stillness of the bay, with not a breath stirring aloft, each sound reached us plainly; the hot panting of the men, as one by one they added their burdens to the pile; the oaths and curses of Dickon, toiling in their wake; the dull sound of clinking metal as the pile of gold grew complete. More than one of the godly rogues vented himself of profane words as shoulders and arms were rubbed.

"Gold makes a change, even as I told you, in men," commented Ned Low. "Mark those rascals, George! A day or so ago they were pious, regenerate dogs— and now look at the flame in their faces, the passion in them!"

"More like thirst," commented the girl practically. "The water in the boat's cask was foul. And they have thrown away even the provisions in order to carry the gold."

That was true. The group of men stood there staring at us, and even in the face of Winter we could read the hopeless despondency of a beaten man. They had neither water, food, nor arms. We, who held the ship, held everything.

At length Winter came down to the water's edge and hailed us. "Ahoy! Pilcher, are you there, bosun?"

"Aye," roared back bose. "Here and with the captain, ye damned dog!"

Winter stared at us from his long face. "I hadn't thought ye'd go back on us, bose," said he, and shook his head. "Be you with 'em too, Miss Polly?"

She would not answer him. Ned Low made laughing response. "Come aboard, Thomas Winter! Come aboard, with the men. Swim, lads, swim! The ale is warm, but hearty; and here's fine fresh turtle, and fish for the taking! Come aboard, lads, and never mind the sharks."

The other men and Dickon were by now sprawled in the sand in various attitudes of despair. But Thomas Winter stood and stared at us. "Master Low, ye'd never see us starve an' die o' thirst?" he cried.

"Aye, and with a good heart!" said Ned cheerfully. "There's water to the south end of the island, lads. Take up your gold and go for it."

Sullen curses from the men showed how his words bit, and how they themselves had changed from their former godliness.

Ned Low laughed at them. "Come, come, regenerate hearts!" he derided. "Shall I have up Gunner Basil out of his irons to give you some godly exhortation?"

"Master, we be poor, unlucky men," returned Thomas Winter mournfully. "There be no gettin' around it; you ha' beat us. We ha' throwed the main, and you ha' beat us despite all. Will ye not ha' mercy on us?"

"Not I," said Ned Low blithely. "What about your rendezvous with the *Rose Pink*, Master Winter? Do you still think to pick her up, and carry these good honest lads off to a life o' piracy?"

I watched the men at this, hoping to find that this was news to them; but they, clustered about Dickon, merely glared at us. Evidently they had thrown off all restraint. The very sight and sound of the gold had corroded their souls.

Thomas Winter only wagged his long head and wiped sweat from his brow. "You ha' beat us," he said again. "We ha' no water, no food, and will die like dogs out here i' the hot sun. Take us aboard, master, even if it be in irons!"

"Not I," quoth Ned Low, tamping tobacco into his pipe. "I want ye not. You have gold there in plenty. Eat it, drink it! Make a canopy of it to shade yourselves from the sun! We'll be gone from here tomorrow morning, and ye can enjoy the gold to the full."

A sudden transport of rage shook Winter. "Gizzard and guts! Will ye have no mercy, damn ye?" he roared out.

"Should have thought of that yesterday," I broke in, and he stared at me as if he had never seen me before. "You dog, Winter! I'll see you hanged for what you said to the lass. Mind that! I'll see that the island men know you for pirates, and the first king's ship we speak will come to take you off."

"Master Roberts, you'll never do that?" he returned, as if struck aghast by the possibility. "We didn't do no harm to you, sir—only put ye in the bilboes, so to speak, for a day or two. We be main sorry for all we ha' done, masters; aye, we be main sorry! We be naught but poor sailormen, masters. Ye'd not bear malice against us? And now you ha' the ship and all's well, you'd never go off and maroon us here?"

"Aye," said Ned imperturbably. "Like the dogs you are!"

"Do 'ee speak to un for us, mistress!" Brazenly Winter addressed himself to Polly. "After all, mistress, we be Englishmen! Maybe we ha' been tempted; aye, it's true enough, the yellow gold tempted us, mistress! But we be not all bad. Do 'ee speak a word to cap'n, and he'll hear it. We'll work ship good and faithful, we will. Aye, he can have us in irons for the mutineers we be, so he don't leave good men here to die o' thirst! Do 'ee speak a word to un, do now!"

Polly stood and looked at him, her eyes inflexible. Ned Low laughed again. "She'll not speak the word, Winter, nor would I listen. Ye'll set no foot on this ship again."

Thomas Winter stood desolate, with head hanging, for a long moment. Then he heaved a great sigh and looked up. "It be main hard on us, masters!" he said slowly. "Will ye make no terms?"

"Not with you, Winter," answered Ned, who by this time had his pipe alight and stood puffing calmly. "I'll take the men aboard and will hand them over for trial; that's their wages if they want to come."

"Where be David Spry, cap'n?" spoke out one of the men.

"Dead," I responded. "Murdered by Dickon, there—"

"A foul lie, mates!" screeched young Dickon. "Spry were murdered like poor

Mr. Russel—knifed un in the back, Master Roberts did! Don't believe un! It's but to murder us he wants us aboard!"

I disdained to answer this. Among the men there arose a violent altercation. Some were for accepting Ned's terms, anxious to get away from the island at any cost; others called Ned and me bloody murderers and would not allow it.

Then one of the men leaped up hotly. "We all stick or we all go!" he cried out. "Who says stick?"

He and three others voted to stay. Two of the men cried that they would come aboard, and he turned on them angrily. "No, ye don't!" he cried. "All or none it is. We stick with 'ee, Winter!"

Ned frowned at this, for I think he had counted on some of the men helping to work ship, and this attitude of theirs rather took him aback.

Winter, who had listened to them in silence, now faced us again and spoke. "You ha' the whip hand of us, master," he said resignedly. "But if ye will have no pity on us, will ye not barter us even for the gold? Give us biscuit and some rum, and water enough to last until we ha' found the springs, and set a price on it!"

Now I perceived by the light in Ned's eyes that it was for this he had been waiting all the time, for he was intent upon getting that gold aboard. One of the men cried out for shoes, since the sand blistered their bare feet, and another for hats.

"It might be done, lads," rejoined Ned Low, not too eagerly. "Ye have seven bags o' gold there. For the top four of those bags I'll set ashore all the things ye desire; and for the bottom three bags I'll leave the longboat behind when we sail i' the morning. What say ye to that?"

"The boat's stove!" said Winter.

"Aye, but I've patched her, and ye can clap another patch over. What say ye now?"

Winter turned and stepped back to the men. There was a hoarse discussion for and against the offer, since certain of the men had no mind to hand over all the gold. Winter, however, argued with them at length, showing them the hopelessness of their condition.

Polly and I came back under the awning of sail, and Ned joined us. "Winter has enough sense to know he's beaten," he observed complacently.

"Be careful of him," said Polly slowly. "Be careful! Let the gold go and put to sea now, or he'll play us some trick yet."

"Not he," and Ned chuckled heartily. "Hark to 'em arguing about it! Why, lass, they haven't so much as a pistol among 'em! It'd be a sin and shame to leave all that gold behind; your gold, that your uncle died to leave you his share of, honestly bought; and the gold poor John Russel died for, and his share ours too! Eh, George? Why so solemn?"

"Gold gets paid for," I said. "Oh, I'll be glad o' my share, Ned—but gold gets paid for. Some pays in work and sweat and gets little, like I've done these years at sea; but I've got better things than gold. Some pays in roguery and gets much, and think it the biggest thing in life; but the gold decays on 'em, and they find it's not so big after all."

"Gold don't decay," said Ned briskly, and clapped me on the shoulder. "Ha, George, so art still a philosopher, eh?"

"And I think George has the right of it," said Polly, then blushed red. "I mean Mr. Roberts—"

"Na, nay!" said Ned, laughing. "It's George and Ned and Polly among us three, lass, why not? Aren't we friends and comrades together? If we be free and easy, it's all in good comradeship."

"What about Dickon?" I demanded. "You'd not take him aboard, even if the men come?"

"No. I had meant to leave him out of the offer," said Ned, and knit his brows. "I want those two men if they'll come; we'll have need of them. We must work the ship around to the south end of the island and take on fresh water, too. We'll need those men, George. But Dickon stays here, the foul little beast! Gunner Basil we'll take with us—"

"Ahoy, cap'n!" called out the deep voice of Winter.

We went to the rail, and found him ankle-deep in water, staring at the ship.

"Agreed, cap'n," he called, "on one condition—that ye let Gunner Basil come free to us. He knows where there be more gold. We can get it i' the boat and join the *Rose Pink* if we ha' no bad luck. That's our best offer, cap'n, and I ha' sweat makin' them agree to it."

"Done with you, Winter," said Ned Low promptly. "Now listen well! Those men o' yours shall retire a hundred feet to the top o' that little sand-hill. You wait for us where you are. At the first sign o' treachery, you'll be shot, and those men with you. Understand that, do you?"

"Aye, sir; but why talk so?" Winter looked astonished. "I be not treacherous, master! It's mortal good o' you, says I, to be so main kind to us—wi' boat and all! Bain't that so, lads? Come, lads, gi' the master three cheers!"

Not they; the six men were again vehemently discussing Winter's offer to them, two begging to be let go aboard the ship, the other four dissenting violently. Dickon took no share in that talk, but sat chewing on a stick to ease his thirst, glowering savagely at the ship.

"You're going to make the barter now, Ned?" I asked.

He nodded, beaming gaily. "Aye, lad! Get the gold aboard and stowed. Then by morning most like all six of those rogues will beg to be took away on my terms. We ha' the sharks for watchdogs, mind ye! It's all safe enough. Wait now, and you'll see; I'll take no chance of that dog tricking me."

Under his assuring confidence, Polly's uneasy look vanished, and I gave over all protest. Indeed, the thought of that gold coming aboard us had a sort of necromancy that bewitched us all with its wizard light.

We turned to in the waist and got the boat into the water. Winter sang out to know when we would release Gunner Basil, and Ned told him in the morning before we sailed; with which Winter had to content himself, taking our word on the matter.

Finding that the boat was well patched and worthy, we got into her some bags of biscuit and other stores, with rum and a breaker of water and everything that could be useful to the rascals save firearms. Winter anxiously demanded if we would leave the boat in the morning likewise, to which Ned assented.

"Boat and gunner together, Winter! Now get your men up the hill."

Ned turned to us. "George, you and the bosun take pistols and row the boat ashore. Philip, you stop here at the rail wi' the muskets handy, and let fly if you see anything amiss."

His scheme was safe enough, it appeared. Pilcher and I got down into the boat, put out an oar each with pistols at our feet, while Ned sat in the stern with two more pistols, so if need were our pistols could account for six of the rascals. Meantime Dickon and the six men had retired as commanded to the crest of a little sand-hill a hundred feet back from the water.

"Give way!" said Ned, seating himself. He looked up and waved a hand laughingly. "Fare you well, Polly! We'll bring you gold when we come again."

"Be careful!" she warned once more.

We headed the boat for the shore and heaved her slowly through the water. Presently her nose scraped. Thomas Winter caught her by the bow, and as Pilcher and I stepped out, gave a tremendous pull that brought her a quarter-length up on the sand.

"Now," said Ned Low, cocking his pistol, "watch yourself, you dog! Take out the stuff and throw in the gold. Pistols, George, and watch him!"

Thomas Winter, his long horse-face adrip with sweat, gave us a reproachful look. "Can 'ee not see when a man be playin' fair?" he said, and stooped over his task.

Indeed it seemed a bit ridiculous that three of us should wait there with our pistols in hand while one man labored. Winter put his giant strength to work with a will and heaved the stuff ashore until at length he had the boat cleared. Then, wiping his brow, he dropped in the sand for a brief rest.

At this instant we caught a cry from the men on the sand-hill. "Ho, master! Ho, cap'n! Wilt take me and Jeff aboard?"

"Aye, that we will!" sang out Ned Low, who still sat in the boat's stern.

We heard a cry from Polly. Among the men on the hill arose something of a scuffle. Two of them were trying to break away, the others were restraining them. Winter paid no heed to this, but lay panting, his eyes closed.

Then the two men got free and began to run, the others hot after them as they leaped down the hillock. The two struck at their pursuers, who followed at their heels, cursing and struggling.

Ned Low heaved up his pistol. "Let 'em go, you rascals!" he cried.

At that Thomas Winter heaved himself up and looked. Then his stentorian voice roared. "Stand back, ye villains! Back, or I'll break your blasted heads—"

The two foremost came running to us, the others still at their heels. Ned hesitated to fire, as did Pilcher and I. From the ship Philip let fly with a musket, the ball going high.

A cry broke from one of the men running to us. "Don't let un stop us, cap'n! We'm coming—"

Winter roared at them again, but the rout of men came rushing at us. At a little distance Dickon and the four pursuers paused. The other two came panting up and dropped on their knees beside the boat. "Wilt take us, cap'n?" they begged together.

"Aye, but you'll stay in irons until we sail," said Ned Low, then looked up at the others. "In with you, lads. You there, stand back! Back!"

Sullenly the others began to obey, while Winter roared at them again. One of the men clambered into the boat—and then went sprawling atop of Ned. The other was up and at me before I realized his intent. Winter whirled and flung himself at Pilcher.

And the others came bursting at us.

XII

I cut a sorry figure in this mishap, for my pistol went off in the air, and I was on my face in the sand with two men plunging on me. Ned Low blew out the life of his assailant, but could not get rid of the body before another was on him. As for the bosun, he went down like an ox under the fist of Winter, and stayed down.

And cook Philip dared not fire for fear of hitting us.

A cruel trap it was, well sprung and full of guile, and we were in truth snared in our own folly. I was bound hand and foot and left lying, but wrenched myself about so that I could see what was happening. All this took place, not as I give it here, but so swiftly that it were hard to realize at once.

Ned Low was struggling both with dead and living, trying to get his other pistol free, in the stern of the boat. She had careened as the load was taken out of her, and now Thomas Winter, an ugly grin showing his fangs, leaned forward and bore down on her with his weight. As she gave, Ned Low and his assailant were tumbled into the water.

"That takes the bite out of his pistol!" quoth Winter. "At him, lads—and alive, mind ye! Any man uses his knife, I'll spread-eagle!"

Why he was so anxious to take Ned alive was by no means clear, and it came very near to costing him all that he had gained. For Ned was on his feet, knife in hand and standing waist-deep in water; twice, with knife and fist, he broke clear of the men and was trying to swim for it to the ship, taking the chance of sharks. He could not get away, however.

At length one of the men got a grip on his knife-arm, and the others piled in. All went down in a turmoil of water and spray, and they haled Ned ashore with a man hanging to either arm, and so bound him.

Winter turned, shot out a long arm and seized Dickon by the shoulder. "Boy, bide ye here and watch un, and if ye murder un I'll flay the hide off thy back!" he said, in so deadly a voice that the boy shrank back.

Then, loosing Dickon, Winter roared at the men, "Pile in, lads; pile in! To the ship, afore they lay a gun on us!"

He shoved out the boat and leaped in, the five remaining men after him. There were only two oars in the boat, but with two men to an oar they sent her through the water. From the *King Sagamore* began to bang muskets; both Polly and the black cook were firing from the rail, but quite failed to stop the boat. Two of the men were wounded, and no other damage was done.

A groan broke from Ned Low as the boat swept in under the ship's side and the men began to go up. Dickon, who had picked up one of Pilcher's fallen pistols, echoed the groan in a demoniac chuckle.

Not quite so easily done, however! The first man over the rail went back to feed the sharks, with a ball through him. Winter and the others piled aboard and beat the black cook down; we could hear Winter roaring at them not to kill him, for they would have need of every man to work the ship.

Polly had fled to the quarterdeck with a pistol, and now Winter ran at her. She would have killed him then, with luck; but the priming flashed in the pan, Winter tore away the weapon and picked her up and took her below. A moment later he reappeared, having locked her in a cabin.

Upon that, having secured the ship, the men began to go over her like famished wolves. Gunner Basil was found and let loose. The ale-cask was broached and our turtle was made way with; one and all were so keen for food and drink that they forgot all else.

Dickon stood on the shore and bawled curses at them unheeded. So he turned to the pile of stuff we had brought ashore, broke out some biscuit, opened the rum and the water and began to get himself into a fine condition of drunkenness.

Ned and I looked one at the other, but I could not reproach him. "You were right, George," he said, and swore bitterly.

That was all, but it showed how keen was his self-blame for what had happened.

After a little Dickon came to his feet, staggering, for the rum had shot to an empty stomach and he was drunk. Plucking out his knife, he made his uncertain way to the form of Bosun Pilcher, who lay as Winter had stretched him out. Squatting down, he began with deliberate deviltry to cut the gold earrings from the ears of the bosun.

Naturally enough this treatment revived Pilcher, who sat up cursing. Dickon hiccupped, fell away and retreated. I cried out to Pilcher to kill the young devil and free us, but as bose came to his feet Dickon picked up his pistol and let fly. Pilcher reeled to the shot, and a staining smear of red leaped out across his face; turning around, not knowing what had happened, Pilcher ran for it. Dickon

with the second loaded pistol staggered after him and fired again, but missed.

The bosun disappeared over the crest of the sand-hills, whether dying or dead we knew not, and Dickon came back again muttering oaths. A roar of maudlin approbation came from the men watching at the ship's rail. He shook his fist at them and returned to his rum.

With all these things the afternoon was passing quicker than we knew; but to me and Ned Low, lying there on the open sand, the time dragged like an eternity. Dickon gave no heed to us, but sat maundering over the pistols, trying to recharge them with futile fingers until his potations and the hot sun sent him fast asleep. The pile of goods we had fetched ashore lay where Winter had flung them. Beyond the pile of canvas-sacked gold lay gray and hideous, at least to my eyes; since for this gold had Polly's liberty and our own lives been bartered. The men aboard ship were still drinking and feasting.

The sun was fast westering when Ned Low turned a white, strained face to me. "I ha' almost got it, but not quite," he said in a low voice. "When I roll over, see can you put your fingers on the cord."

A chorus of drunken song lifted to us as he wrenched about in the sand and got his back to mine. Of Pilcher we had seen nothing. Either the bosun was dead or lying hurt and unconscious like a wounded animal.

Instinctive hope rises in all of us. Now as I fumbled with blind fingers for the cords at Ned's wrists I perceived Dickon asleep in the sunlight of the dying afternoon, saw the pistols at his feet, realized that we might yet have a desperate chance to win. And as the thought came to me I heard the rattle and clatter of men getting into a boat, and turned my eyes to the bay to see the longboat shoved off from the ship and sent toward us by half-drunken oarsmen, with Winter in the stern.

"Give way, ye dogs!" came his voice. "Lively does it!"

"No time to lose, lad," said Ned coolly. "I've been all afternoon working 'em loose."

"There y'are then."

I could not see him as I lay, but I heard him curse softly. His hands were too stiff and bloodless for his fingers to work on his bound feet. Meantime the longboat was coming in to the shore, Winter standing in the stern and roaring at his rowers to lay back. Drunk as they were, they brought him in with a rush.

He leaped out of the boat and was at us—just as Ned Low rose up free. For a long moment the two men looked at each other; behind Winter, the four men tumbled ashore and stood gaping, too fuddled to know what was going on. But I, looking up at Winter, perceived that he seemed cold sober. Behind Ned, Dickon was stirring and staggering to his feet, wakened by the voices. Winter and Ned Low stood motionless, a grin upon the horse-face of Winter, who realized that Ned's feet would scarce bear him as yet.

"Why, here's Bloody Ned the pirate!" said he, and guffawed.

I had never before known, as I knew now upon looking up at him, the indescribable villainy of the man's face; perhaps he had never before let himself go free of restraint. Now, with the mask off, the furious and inhuman cruelty of him was all evident.

"I'll fight 'ee bare-handed, Bloody Ned!" he went on. "Dost remember the fight ye had wi' Francis Spriggs on his own quarterdeck, eh?"

Ned started. "Zounds! How in the devil's name d'ye know of that, Winter?"

"I heard tell on it." Winter took a step forward, his huge hands clenching and opening again at his sides. His mirth vanished. He showed his yellowed fangs in a snarl, as does a dog to frighten an adversary. "Fight, ye bruiser! I ha' looked a long while to get my fingers around that windpipe o' thine; gizzard and guts, but I'll tear it out afore I finish 'ee!"

A spasm of ferocity crossed his face. He lunged forward and dealt a powerful blow with his fist.

Ned avoided it, stumbled a little on his numbed feet, evaded the huge Winter and so came around in front of me. There he faced about and put up his hands, and for a moment I saw the old reckless gaiety in his face. "Fall to, ye bastard!" he called out—and then drove in a right-hander that rocked Winter's head on his big shoulders.

Now they fell to in all truth. Ned's recklessness vanished; before half a minute was gone he knew that Winter was coming in to tear the throat out of him, literally. After the first few blows all Winter tried to do was to grab with those steel-hook fingers of his. Once he got a grip on Ned's shoulder, and nothing but a full-weight smash on the point of his chin loosened it.

As he came, Winter began to curse. It was no ordinary cursing, but the foulest outpouring of rottenness that could be spawned in tavern or forecastle. That volley of filth drove Ned white with sheer fury, for there was a venomous madness in it that burned. As for me, I wondered what reason there could be back of it, for Winter's rage was no ordinary battle-anger.

"If you want it, take it, you dog!" panted Ned suddenly. He opened his arms and let Winter come into a clinch. Both men gasped under the impact, then Winter set himself and made as if he would tear Ned Low asunder.

Instead Ned sent him headlong over the hip in west-country fashion, and when he rolled over and leaped upright, half of Winter's shirt was torn away. And over

his heart there was tattooed a crimson, bleeding heart!

I saw it, and Ned saw it in the same instant. Ned Low took a step backward, and his face was ashen. For a moment he stood powerless, absolutely paralyzed by the realization of whom he faced.

Winter grinned and snarled, and then cursed him anew. "Aye, it's Trunnel Toby!" he roared out furiously. "Trunnel Toby it be, ye spawn o' hell, who have chased me these five year! And now it be Trunnel Toby a-chasing of you—"

Ned seemed to shiver. Then a frightful cry broke from his lips, and he hurled himself forward, and the other came to meet him. No less was the hatred of the hunted than that of the hunter.

But now Ned Low was a very flame of fire. Not a word came from his lips, and his face was a gray mask; his arms wrought upon Winter like the rods of an engine, and all the brute power of the other man was helpless before him. It was an awful thing upon which we stared in that moment—a man taking bitter and utter vengeance for such wrongs as few men have suffered.

For Ned Low was taking vengeance in red and running measure. He moved about Winter like a dancing corposant, and left the fiery mark of his fists wherever he touched. Not once could Winter reach him. He drove in without mercy or pity, until Winter was backing helplessly before him, roaring in fury yet unable to fight back.

Then Ned began to utter sharp, panting words. "Take that—for the girl—ye murderer! And that—and that—for the old man—for the two ye killed—wi' one bullet—and that—"

"I'll tear out the throat of ye yet!" roared Winter, even under the blows. "I've saved ye up—till I could hang ye—"

He tried a kick. Ned parried it and drove out with his own booted foot. Winter gave a horrible grunt and doubled up, and Ned smote him full in the face, so that he jerked backward again and fell in the sand. He tried to rise, and could not.

"Up with ye, murderer!" cried Ned, kicking him. "Up, and take—"

Something flew over me, catching the last rays of the dying sunlight in its course; something that curved above me against the sky, like a blue flame. I heard Dickon's wild, shrill cry, and saw Ned Low stagger and throw out his arms. Then he set one hand to his side and pulled out the knife.

Ned plunged to his knees. Even then he tried to reach the figure of Winter, stabbed down at it with the crimsoned knife, but the blade only dabbled the sand. Ned fell to his hands, and then slowly rolled over and lay still.

Then there was a silence. Even Dickon stood aghast before his deed.

Upon that silence broke a storm of oaths and curses and orders from the ship. Gunner Basil stood on the rail, shaking his fist and trying to waken the staring men. "Aboard with ye! Aboard wi' the gold—aboard!" he yelled frantically. "Aboard, ye drunken fools, afore night comes!"

They awoke, stirred, broke into movement. I could say no word, for the tears that were blinding my eyes, until Dickon came and took the knife from Ned's relaxed hand. Then I cursed him, and cursed him so bitterly that he could not answer me, but ran to the boat.

Me they hove into the stern, and the groaning figure of Winter above me. Then the gold was stowed aboard, and, leaving poor Ned where he lay, they ran out the boat and set her for the ship.

So the day died, and the swift twilight of the tropics merged into night almost by the time I was carried over the rail and flung into the scuppers; and the buckets of sea-water that they flung over the quivering bulk of Winter came running down past me in reddened streams.

XIII

Lanterns were lighted above the deck, dimly lighting the planks and coiled ropes and sea-gear strewn about. Besides Winter, Gunner Basil, and Dickon, there remained four men, two of them wounded; I who lay bound in the scuppers; and cook Philip, who had been beaten into a mass of bruises and now went groaningly about his work in abject terror. Polly Langton had not appeared on deck, being still locked below.

Winter was a long time in being brought to life, for Ned had near killed him. I lay watching in bitterness of soul. So this man was Trunnel Toby! That explained much—his crafty dissimulation, his plotting, his venomous hatred of Ned Low, his anxiety to take Ned alive. Gunner Basil and he had shipped aboard us, with Dickon, with the twofold intent of pirating us and murdering Ned Low.

And they had won. Despite all, they had won. Pilcher was dead, and Russel, and Ned Low; they had the ship, the treasure—and at the thought of Polly Langton down below I kept back a groan.

Gunner Basil brought dry clothes, which Winter donned, his face all puffed and bruised out of shape. Dickon brought him a great flagon of rum, which he gulped down neat. With this to hearten him Winter was soon on his feet and ordering things. Gunner Basil, who knew what arrangements I had made with the black islanders, told him that he might look for a crew in the morning; but Winter was more interested in learning just what had happened ashore. He sent for Dickon, who faced him jauntily at first, but soon changed in demeanor.

"So it was you knifed Bloody Ned!" said Winter heavily. "I have a mind to hang 'ee, lad."

He meant the words, too. Dickon shivered under his baleful stare. "It was to save your life!" cried the boy. "He had 'ee down—"

An oath burst from Winter. "Stow yer jaw! I'd ha' broke his cursed neck in another moment, ye swab! Get out o' my sight afore I gut ye! Ho, gunner! Is the boat made fast?"

"Fast, but not hauled up," responded Gunner Basil. "I had thought to go ashore later and turn some turtle—"

"Turtle be damned!" growled Winter. "Where be the gold? Fetch it here, lads, on the deck. Fetch it here, my bullies!"

Dickon slunk into the background, stumbled over me and kicked me savagely, uttering a flood of curses whose malevolence was directed rather at Winter, I thought, than at me.

The roughly sacked gold was brought up and chunked down on the deck. Winter called for a knife and then stooped down—painfully, since he was bruised and sore from head to foot. With the knife he slit the canvas of each sack, and let all the gold come out into a ruddy yellow stream over the planks.

"There y'are!" he roared. "Dickon, more rum! There y'are, lads—fill yer pockets! That's what braw lads gets on the Account—gold! Take it, bullies!"

Though I was across the deck from them, I could see all that took place there beneath the lanterns. Everyone flung forward at the gold. Those four seamen, who a short fortnight previous had been exhorters to righteousness, and honest enough about it too, had now been turned completely to the rightabout. They matched the eager oaths of the gunner and Dickon in the scramble for the gold, until it dawned upon them that there was more gold here than they could well stuff into pockets, so that they all fell to laughing and jesting hideously.

The rum entered into it too, for a keg was brought up and broached, and all hands fell into a wild saturnalia. Each man decked himself to his fancy with plundered stuff from our after cabins; pistols and knives were brought forth and donned; in the midst came a flash and a roar as Dickon's pistol went off and came near to killing one of the men. The answer was a blow, and the two fell to fighting until Winter flung them apart with a bellowing laugh and made each of them down a mug of rum.

I soon saw where this would end. Presently Winter cocked one bunged eye at the main yard, and roared at the gunner. "Ha, Gunner Basil! Be that block an' tackle rigged to hang me?"

"Aye," hiccupped the gunner, who was reeling. "Master Roberts rigged un."

"Ho, ho!" laughed Winter, and flung a knife across the deck that passed over me and slapped into the bulwark. "Shalt hang at sunrise, Roberts, ye dog! Shalt go to Hell to join Bloody Ned, damn ye both! Dickon! Where are ye, Dickon? Go unlock the lass' door and bid her come hither, else I'll come down and fetch her!"

He added a jest to this that fetched a howl of lewd laughter from the other men. Dickon slipped away aft.

Just here I heard a faint sound, and twisted about to see the black cook Philip come crawling along the rail toward me cautiously. He was in mortal fear, and his teeth were chattering from terror; nonetheless, he reached up and took from the wood that knife Winter had flung, and then set it to my bound wrists.

"They'll murder us all," he whispered. "Swim for it, master! I'll wait."

Then he went crawling away again into the darkness, and I realized that my hands were free, and the knife left beside them. That was the act of a brave soul!

So numbed was I that it was some time ere any feeling crept into my fingers, and I was as helpless as if still bound, though my arms could move freely enough. While I lay trying to get some sense of touch into my hands, in order to take the knife and free my ankles, Polly Langton came quietly into the circle of lantern-light, followed by Dickon.

The men gaped at her in shamed silence. Winter was seated on the keg, and met her look with a bold stare. Then he spoke. "Dickon! Draw rum for the cap'n's lady!"

Dickon moved about the task. As for me, I found the knife with my fingers, and inch by inch moved it in front of me and toward my ankles, fearful lest some eye catch the motion. None did, however, and presently I was parting the hemp that bound me.

Not that this new freedom of mine gave me any hope. I lay at the starboard rail of the ship; across from me, near where Winter and the men were grouped, the ropes ran down to the longboat. Gain that boat I could not. All I could do would be to go over the rail and swim for the shore.

Help Polly Langton I could not, unless I attack and kill the whole band of those rogues; and that was an impossibility, even had I firearms. At best she might leap the rail and chance sharks in a swim for the shore. Even then Winter would pursue. And if we got away in the darkness, what remained? A lingering death from thirst and hunger and misery of the hot sun.

I had not forgotten Ned Low, however. As I felt the cords give under the blade, it came to me that I might at least finish Winter, give the lass a fighting chance to reach the shore and perhaps work damage on the other rogues ere they killed me. And this I resolved to do, for I was mad to get a blow at that devil Winter.

My ankles free, I began to rub them cautiously.

Dickon came with the pewter flagon, but Polly took no heed. He shoved it at her, and, grinning, laid his hand on her arm. At that she snatched the flagon and struck it over his head, so that he staggered from the blow and cursed as the rum went over his face.

Aye, and his hand went to the knife at his belt, whereat Winter came to life suddenly. Rising, he swept forward an open-handed blow that knocked Dickon sprawling. "None of that, ye spawn of Satan!" he roared. "Get up!"

Dickon rose with so black a look that I thought he would let fly at Winter. But the latter only broke into a laugh at the boy's aspect, in which the other men joined.

"Lay hand to the cap'n's lady again, and I'll hang ye!" he said, then turned to the lass with his bold regard. "Gi' me the cup, lass! I'll fill it again for 'ee. Shalt have silks and jewels, diamonds and pearls! Trunnel Toby's lass ye shall be—give it to me!"

She dropped the flagon on the deck. "Murderers!" she cried out. "Oh, I saw it all from the cabin window! What have ye done with Master Roberts?"

"We be going to hang un at dawn," said Winter, and grinned. "Come, lass, come! What wilt offer for his life, eh?"

"She be soft i' that quarter," spoke up Gunner Basil with a hiccup. "Main soft, I tell 'ee, Toby! Look out she don't knife ye, Toby. Dost remember the Spanish jade that slipped a knife into Cap'n Franklin, hey? Damn my eyes, but she split his weasand! Look out ye don't go the same way, Toby."

Winter laughed—broke into a hearty guffaw. He stooped for the pewter cup, bent it into shape again and held it to the spigot of the keg. When he had downed the rum he wiped his swollen lips and tossed away the flagon. "Come, lass!" he said in a maudlin jocularity that might turn any instant to a raging madness. "Come, lass! Wilt give a kiss to spare thy Roberts a day, eh? A kiss for a day—a day for a kiss, lass! Rot me, the rum ha' got my tongue.

"Bloody Ned be dead, and the bosun dead, and Trunnel Toby's loose. Here be a fine ship, and the *Rose Pink* yonder be waitin' for us, and Trunnel Toby be commodore. Aye! Ye shall be commodore's lady, sweet lass, wi' diamonds an' rubies from the Indies, and fine silk to wear! Come, lass—a day for a kiss!"

No one was watching me; all eyes were on the lass, standing there straight and slim and defiant before the brute who taunted her. I had no skill throwing the knife, or I might have sunk it into him then. I gathered myself together and waited, ready to shout to Polly and leap forward at them.

"I will ha' naught to do with you, ye murderers!" she spoke out bravely. "Aye, and if ye hang Master Roberts I'll never rest until I see each one of you brought to Tyburn Tree and laid there!"

At this, Winter guffawed again. "Sink me, but I like a lass o' spirit! So ye'll bring me to Tyburn, eh? Well, many another ha' said that, lass. Ned Low said it five year gone, when I pistoled the doddering old rogue who called him son, and when I put my knife into his lass! Aye, and where's Bloody Ned now, tell me? Call him up from Hell to help 'ee, lass! Here, give us a kiss and we'll leave Roberts' hanging until sunset instead o' sunrise!"

He lunged forward, his hand outstretched to grip the lass. She drew back a step, then, swift as light, threw her weight into a ringing blow. Her fist took Winter squarely in the mouth, where Ned Low had battered him sorely; and, no less from the pain than from the surprise, sent him staggering and stumbling sidewise until he tripped over a coiled rope and came to hands and knees.

A wild howl of laughter and mirthful oaths surged up from one and all. Winter recovered, swayed on his feet, then uttered a roar of anger. I gathered myself for the leap, and a shout to Polly was upon my very lips—when it was checked.

For the girl took a step backward, staring at the rail. So great was the fright painted in her face that the men turned to see what she was staring at; and so did Winter. And, over the rail, they saw the face of Ned Low rising.

Terror froze me, no less than them. Ned was dead in the sand, and Bosun Pilcher was dead—yet there rose the head and shoulders of Ned Low, and beside him those of Pilcher, whose earrings glittered yellow in the lantern-light. Ghastly and terrible were they, heads and faces streaming with water, and drew themselves over the rail to the deck. From the one side Winter gaped upon them, a frightful horror in his countenance; from the other, the group of men, sitting there paralyzed.

"Back from Hell to help the lass, Thomas Winter!" said Ned.

At the sound of his voice I ceased to shiver, for that voice of his was alive and no ghost. I rose and stepped forward to join them, but no man heeded me.

A sudden howl, an awful thing to hear, shrilled up from the men. They fell backward, rolled on the deck, stumbled over each other, trying to get away. Pilcher, empty-handed like Ned, grinned and started toward them.

But Ned Low stepped forward and faced Winter, who was trembling there as he stood. "Bloody Ned!" he gasped. "Back to Hell with 'ee; I'm done with 'ee!"

"You're not done with me till I see ye hung!" shot out Ned, and started forward.

"Ghost or no," rang out a thin, drunken scream, "I'll kill ye over again!"

It was Dickon. He darted out of the shadows, mad with fear and rum, and his arm swung in an arc. I shouted at Ned and, hearing the shout, Ned turned. The knife went past him, singing viciously— and thudded into another mark. The sound of it hitting was plain to all of us.

From Winter broke a furious, gasping shout. He put hand to belt, and a pistol broke the silence with its roar. Then he fired his second pistol. Through the smoke I saw Ned go plunging forward, bringing him down to the deck with naked hands. And through the smoke I saw the boy Dickon, rent and riddled by those bullets, fall across the rail and gasp out his life.

One of the seamen ran at me blindly and struck with his knife, and I loosed at him. We had it hot and thick for a moment, the man stark mad with fear, until the steel went into him and he sank blubbering away. Out of the shadows reeled two figures—Gunner Basil and the bosun, locked breast to breast and fighting like mad. Aye, and there was the black cook, Philip, swinging an empty musket and yelling as he ran after the frightened men.

Looking back to Ned, running to help him, I saw him swing an empty pistol and then come to his feet. I had him by the hand, and cried out at the good grip. "Man, man, I thought you dead there ashore—"

"Zounds, there's not much life left in me!" he said, and laughed out with so gay a note that I wondered. "Had not Dickon's knife spoiled Winter's aim, I'd be gone. But he's taken care of—see that he's bound fast, George—"

He staggered and would have fallen, but that I caught him. There was a bandage about his body, beneath his shirt, and the blood was seeping out afresh from his wound. Polly Langton ran to us, crying and laughing all at once, and as Ned sank down on the deck I turned to her. "Polly—take care of him, quickly!" I cried. "I must see to things—"

I left her kneeling over him and started forward, wild with eagerness to clinch this astounding turn that had flung the ship into our hands again. Bosun Pilcher rose up from the deck before me, a dripping knife in his hand, and I looked down to see Gunner Basil writhing out his life on the planks.

"Quick, bose! Go tie up Winter unless he's hurt to death. I'll see to all for'ard—"

I ran on, and in the bows found the three remaining seamen, partly recovered from their mad panic, roiled in a furious encounter with Philip, who had pursued them there. When I came up and the men knew my voice, they flung down knives and yelled for mercy. I shoved a coil of light line into Philip's hands and told him to bind them.

"You shall have what punishment Cap'n Low metes out," I told them. "Stay bound until morning, ye dogs, and if you're not hanged, thank your fortune. Philip, make 'em fast! Then haul each to a gun-carriage and lash 'em there. When you're done, report aft. We must have the ship cleaned up before those islanders come aboard in the morning, else they'll take us for pirates and not ship."

"Aye, sir," sang out Philip with a laugh.

I went back aft and found Bosun Pilcher just mounting to the main yard with a line. He grinned cheerfully and paused long enough to tell how he had been scraped by a bullet over the head but not greatly hurt, and how that evening he had found Ned Low crawling over the sand; and the rest was not hard to guess, though I shrank at thought of their swimming out to the ship through those shark-infested waters.

And so to where Polly Langton knelt weeping beside Ned, who sat up and caught at my hand with the shadow of his old gay laugh.

"Polly!" I exclaimed. "Why the tears, dear lass? Here Ned is hurt, but not badly, and the ship and the gold are ours, and yonder goes bose to reeve the line that hangs Trunnel Toby—why the tears?"

"That's why, George," she said, and laughed through her tears.

About Sidney Levett-Yeats

Sidney Levett-Yeats (1858-1916), whose family had traded around the globe for generations, was a true son of the British Empire who spent most of his life in India, in either the army or the civil service. He crossed paths with Rudyard Kipling when both were in the Punjab, and Kipling's success with adventure stories inspired Levett-Yeats to try his own hand at the form. But as Levett-Yeats noted in the preface to his first novel, *The Honour of Savelli* (1895), "the Author would say he has taken Dumas for his model," and set most of his stories in the Europe of the Renaissance.

Indeed, in plotting, pacing, and character, Levett-Yeats' best writing shows the influence of Dumas far more than of Kipling, though starting with his second novel, *The Chevalier d'Auriac* (1897), his work began to bear the more naturalistic hallmarks of the novels of Stanley J.

Weyman (whose work you'll meet later in this anthology).

His first two novels, written while he was still in India, were Levett-Yeats' most energetic work, which is probably why they were also his most successful. *The Honour of Savelli* was set in Italy under the Borgias, but *The Chevalier d'Auriac*, written shortly after the success of Weyman's *A Gentleman of France* and *Under the Red Robe*, was set like those two novels in late sixteenth-century France. For Levett-Yeats, it was a fruitful setting; he returned to it successfully in *The Traitor's Way* (1901), and in the story that follows, from *Cassell's Magazine* of December, 1899.

Levett-Yeats' hero in this story, Le Brusquet (that is, "The Brusque"), is a court jester who is also a romantic cavalier—a swashbuckler trope that is almost a subgenre of its own. As with so many swashbuckler traditions, its origin is with Alexandre Dumas, whose Chicot, main protagonist of *La Dame de Monsoreau* (1846), was so popular that English translations of the novel often bore the title *Chicot the Jester* rather than *The Lady of Monsoreau*. Chicot, like all the jester-cavaliers who followed him, is an aristocrat who has been forced to assume a *nom-de-geste* and become a court fool. The jester-cavalier is often confidant to a king, in the case of Chicot the doomed Henri III of France. Levett-Yeats' le Brusquet was undoubtedly inspired by Dumas' Chicot.

After Levett-Yeats' Brusquet, Rafael Sabatini took up the gage and created Boccadoro, the cavalier-fool of the court of the Borgias, in *The Shame of Motley* (1926). Sabatini was an expert on the Borgias, having written a biography of Cesare Borgia, so his setting and characters are thoroughly convincing. He was duly

followed by Jeffery Farnol, who in one of his last novels, *The Fool Beloved* (1949), gave us a romantic young nobleman wooing his lady-love under the assumed name of Bimbo the Jester.

The pinnacle of this subgenre was no novel at all, but a Hollywood movie, *The Court Jester*, Danny Kaye's delicious 1956 parody of medieval and Renaissance swashbucklers in general, and *The Adventures of Robin Hood* (1939) in particular. The film included numerous homages to the earlier film, including casting Basil Rathbone as the villain. It's easily the *funniest* of all swashbuckler movies.

The tradition continues today with Alan Gordon's "Fool's Guild" novels, a series of historical mysteries of a society of medieval jesters, starting with *Thirteenth Night* (1998). Keep an eye out for them.

The Queen's Rose

SIDNEY LEVETT-YEATS

CHAPTER I
HOW POMPON BECAME AN ORACLE

Perhaps it is because the tragedy of Fotheringay is still fresh in my mind that my eyes linger sadly on the faded roses I have taken from my cabinet, and placed with tender hands before me.

It is a week ago since Blancheforêt, on his way back from Paris, drew rein at Bèsme to give me the news of that deed of infamy, and left me stunned and bewildered, as he galloped off, red-spurred, to bear the tidings to Malézieux.

There are those who say she deserved her death; there are stories, I know, about her; but they lie in their throats who repeat them, and I blush with shame for my country that no sword was drawn to save her who was once Queen of France.

As I stare at the flowers before me, their delicate fragrance returns to them; they seem to bloom again in their rich, crimson splendor, and the memory of that night in June, when I received them from the hands of Mary of Scotland, comes back to me, so that my heart is full and my eyes grow dim.

She was of those women born to be queens over men; of those women who come once in a thousand years, who are in themselves the embodied spirits of romance, and for whose smile men would throw aside life, riches, empire, even honor, as lightly as a worn-out glove.

It was my fate to come within the range of her power, and I did as the rest. I, the poor gentleman of Quercy—the king's jester—dared to love her.

And yet I was not mad: the feeling in my heart was as if I had met in flesh and blood that vision of the perfect woman which lies in all men's souls. There was an immeasurable distance between us. I knew all that. I nursed no idle hopes. I looked upon her as a shepherd on the mountains might gaze upon the morning star—as some wandering angel of light that had come, to pass away, yet never to be forgotten.

And so, because a jester must have something of the poet in his spirit, I was accustomed to daydream a little, and used to slip out from the Louvre into that wilderness of a garden that stretched as far as the walls of Paris, between the Tour de Bois and the Porte St. Honoré, and lose myself there in enchanted dreams. The place exists no longer, I hear. It is all changed now, since the Médicis began the new palace of the Tuileries, near the tile-fields; and the sweet disorder of my garden has given place to sedate parterres, trimly-cut hedges, and walks that look like diagrams in the book of Euclid that Lorgnac used to pore over at college and I hated with a bitter hatred.

But at the time I speak of, when the sun was bright and the flowers were out, except my own home in far-off Quercy there was no spot more lovely to my mind than those neglected walks where the bind-weed and dog-rose starred the hedges, where the celandine and red campion made a gay border to the green rides, and, from amidst its spotted leaves, the cuckoo-pint lifted its purple wand, dripping with dew. Here, on a grassy bank, near an old oak, I would lie for hours, listening to the wind in the trees, listening to the hum of the city that was so near and yet so far, and building my castles in cloudland, whilst Pompon, my ape, gamboled in the branches above me. And here one morning in June I took my lute, and, with Pompon hobbling gravely at my heels, sought my retreat, to eat my lotus

and be happy in my dreams. I had almost come to the old rose pleasance, beyond which lay my oak, when I met Lorgnac face to face, as he stepped through a gap in the hedge and stood in the middle of the path. His drawn sword was in his hand, and for once the color was out of his cheek and his lips set and hard, making him look, though he was but five-and-twenty, a man touching on middle age.

"You cannot pass," he said stiffly, without any other greeting; and whilst I stopped for a moment in amaze, Pompon, who knew him well, ran up to him and began clutching at his cloak for a caress; but he shook the ape from him with a curse, saying again, "You cannot pass, de Bèsme. Go back!"

He called me by my own name, which he knew well, for we were next-door neighbors in the Quercy, and sworn friends at college and ever after. Only last night he had bidden me a laughing adieu, calling me le Brusquet, the nickname by which I was known to my intimates, and indeed to all the court; and now here he was, cold and stiff as a Spaniard, ordering me off the path as if I were a street-beggar.

But I took him quietly. Whistling Pompon back to me, I said, "Come, Lorgnac! I am only going to my oak—"

"You cannot pass," he interrupted, speaking like a machine.

"*Tu-dieu!*" I burst out, my temper rising. "If it is the king's order, I go back;

but if it is some grasshopper you have in your head, monsieur—" I clapped my hand to my side, forgetting that I wore but a gilded wooden sword, and as my fingers touched the hilt I stopped, disconcerted, and began to laugh. And whilst I laughed Lorgnac caught the humor of it and began smiling too. He stepped forwards and put his hand on my shoulder.

"No, old friend! There must be no quarrel between us, but I pray you go back!"

"Is the road then blocked?"

"Yes," he said in a hesitating voice, and I was about to shrug my shoulders and turn away when there was a rustling in the hedge, and a man leaped lightly through, saying in an alarmed voice, "Lorgnac, we are watched—spied upon!" And then he stopped and stared at me, and I, too, stared back in blank astonishment, for it was the Prince of Condé, the second prince of the blood, whom we all thought at the siege of Marienbourg.

His face was haggard and wan, and he was grey with dust, as one who had ridden fast and far. He struck nervously at his boot with his riding whip; and as we looked at each other, I noticed that in his clenched hand lay a woman's glove, small and white.

I took his words to apply to me, and, recovering myself, hastened to explain. "Monseigneur! Not spied upon by me. I came here—"

But Condé himself interrupted me. "It was not you I meant, Brusquet. It was someone else."

"No one has passed this way, monseigneur."

"Then someone was in hiding before we came, Lorgnac. Listen—I was just about to come for you, when I heard a laugh and a rustling in the hedges. I rushed forwards, but could see nothing. At last I heard voices and came here." Then, as if a sudden suspicion had struck him: "It was not you, le Brusquet?" And he cast a keen eye on me.

I shook my head and Condé went on, turning again to Lorgnac, whose eyes were bent reproachfully upon him: "Man, do not look at me like that! It was madness my coming here, I know, but I could not help it. And now—I suppose it will be all over Paris in an hour." And he looked at me once more.

I knew well enough that the king was boiling with wrath against Condé. Young as he was, his brilliant achievements, his personal grace and happy spirits, had won all hearts. Everything that a subject can hope for seemed within his grasp, and he was more than an ordinary subject, as the second prince of the blood. In a moment all this was changed. His commission as colonel-general was taken from him, his government of Picardy given to Coligny, and he who, in the morning, was in the full tide of court favor, had hurried off at dusk a simple volunteer for the defense of Marienbourg. What the secret of this was I did not know, but Condé's last words and the look he gave me pricked me; and I answered him coldly. "Monseigneur, so far as I am concerned, no one will know that I have seen you."

"I would put my honor on Monsieur de Bèsme's word," said Lorgnac, as he added: "And now, monseigneur, let us go at once, I pray you!"

"It is not for myself that I fear, but—" and the prince stopped, for Lorgnac made a warning gesture that stayed his words.

For a space we three young men looked at each other, and then monseigneur held out his hand to me. "Monsieur de Bèsme, I spoke in haste. I thank you for your promise. Adieu! Till better times!"

I took the hand he held out to me, and his grasp was firm and cordial. Then he went back as he had come, and Lorgnac with him; but, ere the latter left me, he bent forward, and said in a low voice, "Stay here for an hour or so! Let me know if anyone passes. There is life and death on this, old friend."

With that he followed the prince, leaving me with all my daydreams knocked out of my head, a prey to the most complete wonder and astonishment.

I made up my mind to do what Lorgnac wished. There was a council that day at which it was not necessary that le Brusquet should attend, and I should not be required until after the dinner-hour. Besides, my curiosity was stirred to its depths; and so I lingered, keeping a careful watch to the right and left of me, but saw nothing.

At last I began to weary of this, and on reflecting that there were three ways out of the garden—one by the wicket leading into the Louvre, the second near the Porte St. Honoré, and the third at the Tour de Bois—I came to the conclusion that if there was a spy about, he would have plenty of chance to escape. So I consulted the oracle. I picked Pompon up and let him drop on the sward, determined to follow the course he took. As he touched ground, the little beast gave a chuckle and scampered across the grass in the direction of the river. In brief, it was the riverbank near the Tour de Bois that the oracle pointed at. I followed Pompon across the hedge, and we went noiselessly through a tangled maze of bush and shrub and tree until we came to the old city wall that ended here on the river face. No sooner had we reached it than Pompon swarmed up the wall. With the aid of a friendly yew tree, I followed his example and, stretching myself on the flat surface, with the ape curled up close beside me, I waited and watched.

The day was perfect, and I basked like a lizard in the warm sunshine, listening to the buzzing of the wasps and the cheery whistle of a black-cap from a thorn-bush, not a bowshot from me. But my eyes were not idle. I had a good view from where I was, and I watched like a hawk from a cliff. I was beginning to despair, and was laughing to myself at my oracle, when a little skiff, that had been hugging the shore on my side, stole quietly up and grounded softly on the bank just beneath me. There was only one man within; but I saw at a glance he was not a regular boatman of our river. He was too tall and dark, and had a foreign air about him. With the aid of a tow-line he fastened the boat to a heavy stone, and then, throwing his coat on his arm—for he was in his shirt-sleeves—he stepped up the bank and sat contentedly down beneath the yew tree.

"Oh, ho!" I muttered to myself. "The oracle is working." Craning over, I took another look at my man; but I could see little except his shoulders and the top of his head. His coat, however, was on the grass beside him, and on its breast was embroidered the arms of Spain.

"From the Spanish Embassy!" I murmured again. "This grows interesting," and I stretched myself so that I could watch him without moving.

I had not long to wait, maybe a half-hour or so, when a shrill whistle rang out from amongst the trees, and my Spaniard, jumping up, whistled back as shrilly. Then there was a moment's silence, followed by the sound of hurrying feet as a man ran up, breathless with haste.

"*Caramba!*" exclaimed the Spaniard. "You are late!"

"'Twas not to be helped. I caught sight of the fool, le Brusquet, and his cursed ape moping about the gardens, and lay quiet to give the pair time to go. Have you seen anything of them?"

"No one has been here." And the Spaniard, lifting his coat, prepared to descend to the boat.

At first I could not recognize the voice; but as the two went down to the boat I got a glimpse of the newcomer's face. It was Aramon, or d'Aramon, as he called himself, a broken captain of the regiment of Aunis, and an utter scoundrel if ever there was one.

That there was villainy afoot I was sure now. I was hoping—nay, longing—that they would stay, and talk a little ere they went. But this was not to be. When they had stepped into the boat, however, and pushed off, d'Aramon threw himself back in the stern, and laughed long and loudly to himself.

I lay still for a few minutes, and then rising, shook Pompon by the neck.

"*Mon ami!*" I said. "The Delphic oracle was nothing to you!"

Whereat he scuffled with me; but I pacified him with a ginger-nut; and then we took our way slowly, but with great content, towards the palace.

CHAPTER II
THE AMBASSADOR'S WAGER

As I walked on, however, my mind was working like a clock. Lorgnac's agitated manner, his strange words at our parting, the presence of Condé in Paris, the fact of his being spied upon by the Spanish Embassy, and by such an agent as d'Aramon: all these pointed to some mystery. My curiosity was excited to the highest pitch. At that time no *badaud* of Paris was as eager as I to poke his nose into matters that did not concern him. And now that I am speaking of myself, I might as well describe myself as I was then. I was tall, and slightly built, but strong and active as a cat. My features were sharp and pointed, so that at college I got the unenviable nickname of La Fouine, or The Fitchet. The mention of this always led to trouble; sometimes for me, sometimes for my tormentors. But the name had dropped into oblivion since I had come to man's estate, although my sharp features remained.

In the meantime, there was this mystery to be solved, and I was determined to get at the bottom of the well. It was clear that it was a political matter, and then—I looked around me and saw that I was near a most inviting-looking seat, where the branches of a fallen tree spread out like an easy-chair. My companion, whose perception in matters of this nature was even keener than mine, was already there, and,

following Pompon's example, I settled myself down to unravel the skeins of the puzzle.

I had not been there above half an hour, during which I made but little progress, when I heard my name called out, and saw Lorgnac walking towards me with hasty steps.

"Well," he said, as he came up to me, "have you seen anyone?"

I did not exactly like to give away my nuts for nothing; but I swear that had I known how matters stood I would not have played with him as I did, but have spoken out at once. As it was, I answered, "Cabbage for cabbage, Lorgnac—tell me your secret and I'll tell you mine."

"My secret is not my own," he answered.

"Nor, I suppose, is mine; and I am growing old and wise. You remember the proverb—a close mouth catches no flies."

He stamped impatiently. "Look here, le Brusquet! If you have seen anyone let me know who it is. If the prince has been spied upon and seen, there will be a frightful disaster, unless we can prevent it. Not only disaster for him, but for—" He stopped, hesitating, and I lifted my hand.

"Do not give away your secret! Sit down and let us talk, and I'll tell you what I have seen."

He took a seat beside me, and I went on, "You see! I am going to tell you in my own way. But first I must ask you a question."

"And that is?"

"Why are you, a cadet of the regiment of Aunis, not with the army?"

He blushed a little and stammered, "The peace of Vaucelles still stands."

"And yet we are fortifying Marienbourg and Rocroy, and the admiral is levying forces openly in Picardy!"

"What has this to do with the matter in hand?"

"Wait and see. I will not be long now in coming to my point."

"Then come to it! I tell you every moment is of import!"

"Hasten slowly, Lorgnac! I have told you what we are doing; and now for the others. If there is war we shall have Spain and England against us, for Mary of England will side with her husband."

"Yes—yes."

"Well, *mon ami!* You are aware that England is open to attack from Scotland. You are aware, too, that the Cardinal Beaton and a large embassy are coming to France. You can see that an alliance between France and Scotland—say if the Dauphin were to wed the young Queen of Scots—would make us strong."

"Yes"—his voice was very grave.

My thoughts had run far beyond my speech by this, and I began to tremble at the end to which they were leading me. I, who had begun this talk in an idle spirit of mischief, was now being pricked by my own pins.

For a moment I remained silent, and Lorgnac's hand closed upon my arm like a vise. "Go on!" he said, his voice husky. He seemed to be moved powerfully by some inward feeling.

"Well! It would be a great thing for Spain to prevent such a marriage, would it not?"

He said nothing, but kept staring at me, and I went on, "And now, Lorgnac"—my own words came slowly and painfully— "suppose that the Spaniard could show there was truth in the story that was whispered here and there some weeks ago, there would be a scandal, and that marriage could not be."

"What do you mean?" His hand dropped from my arm as he spoke. He pretended not to understand, though he knew well enough. He rose from his seat and faced me, and I rose too, and bent towards him.

"You know what I mean, Blaise de Lorgnac. If it could be shown that Condé hurried back from Marienbourg, and had a secret meeting, say under my old oak tree, with the Queen of Scots—"

"You spy!" he said. "You have watched."

I could have struck him; but I held myself in, for he was my friend, and for the moment was mad.

"'Tis you who should wear the cap and bells, Lorgnac—not I. I am no spy. Yet I have watched the watcher. The secret is known, and d'Aramon is at this moment giving it to the Spanish ambassador."

"D'Aramon! That ruffian!"

"Yes."

"And you did not stay him? Made no effort to stop him?"

"I have only just found out the importance of the thing myself. Besides, I did exactly what you asked me to do. You made no mention of staying people."

He reflected a moment, a moment only, for if ever there was a man of action it was Lorgnac. Then he spoke. "De Bèsme, can I count on your old friendship? It is not for myself I ask, but for the fair fame of an innocent woman and a queen."

There was no need to mention names. I understood perfectly, and for her sake would have willingly given my life twice over. But as I looked at Lorgnac's burning, eager eyes, I read in them the same secret that I kept locked in my heart. He too! Ah! Was there a man who did not love her?

I answered him gravely. "My head and arm are with you—to the end. And now, do not waste time, or give me half-confidences. What am I to do?"

"I must get the prince from Paris at once; but he is penniless, and dare not go for money where he will be known, and I"—he laughed bitterly—"have but a brace of Henris."

"Where is the prince now?"

"In my house."

"In the Rue Tire Boudin?"

"Precisely. I have no other."

"I know that, and should not have asked. No one knows he is there?"

"I keep no servant, and you and I alone know this."

"So that if Condé can slip out of Paris, there will only be d'Aramon's word to say he was here."

"Exactly."

"Then, *mon cher*, things are not so black as they look."

With this I unfastened my purse from my belt and handed it to Lorgnac, saying, "There are forty fat crowns there. They will carry the prince to Marienbourg."

"De Bèsme, you are indeed a friend," and Lorgnac took the purse, as he added, "I shall get him off at once, and you must let her know he is gone."

"I!"

"Yes—manage it somehow. I have no chance of speaking to her, but you have a hundred. A word—a hint will suffice."

"Very well! And now hasten! I will do my best."

"It is a check to Spain, I think," he said with a laugh, and turned to go, but I stayed him.

"Is there anything else, le Brusquet?" And our eyes met.

Then I said slowly, "My friend! When this is over, you had better seek the war, and I shall go back to grow pears at Bèsme."

He made no answer; but our hands met in a warm clasp. If I had let him see that I knew his heart, I had also let him read mine.

I watched him until he was lost to view behind the hawthorns, and then, calling Pompon, took my way back to the Louvre. I made a little detour, passing my oak, and reached the ivy-grown wall, where a little wicket led to the Ladies' Terrace. I had a passkey given to me by the king himself, and, opening the gate, crossed the terrace and hastened towards the Pavillon du Roy, where the court was held. This faced the river, in all the elegance of its modern construction.

I went up the crowded stairway, Pompon at my heels, exchanging a word with one, a jest with another. At the archway leading into the audience-rooms the throng was so great that, for the moment, I could find no passage. I looked round and called out, "Way! Way! For the King of the Cap and Bells!"

There was a laugh, and a merry voice called out, "There is room for your majesty here—and for your prime minister too."

I looked at the smiling eyes and the curved, laughing lips, and Pompon and I were by the speaker's side in a moment. It was Mademoiselle de Foix, whom we used to call The Phoenix.

"So your majesty has not attended the council?" And she opened her silver bonbon box.

"No, mademoiselle; yet my most faithful subject and myself have been employed on high affairs of State."

"I am sure they will benefit from such united wisdom," and she gave a sweet to Pompon.

"*Hein!* And is there no tribute for me?" I grumbled.

"I always thought the honor went to the king, but the spoils to the minister; but if your majesty will accept an offering—" and Mademoiselle held out her box. With a bow, I helped myself to a dainty morsel, and at the same moment the strains of music floated towards us, and The Phoenix clapped her hands.

"'Tis the couranto!" she cried. "The Queen of Scots and the Princess Elisabeth dance in this. I wish I could see."

"Trust to your knight, mademoiselle," and she put a small hand in my arm. So, with laugh and jest, and sometimes an elbow in the ribs of a gay courtier, I at last succeeded in gaining a corner of vantage for my partner and myself.

There were many fair women and brilliant cavaliers in the dance. There was the Princess Elisabeth, afterwards the hapless wife of the tyrant of Spain; there were others I could name, but I had no eyes for them—nor, indeed, had anyone else. Every look, every glance, was bent on a tall, graceful figure, robed in white, with a cluster of red roses at her bosom. With a laugh in her eyes and a smile on her lips, she floated through the dance like a thing of air. Ay! I have lived long at courts. I have seen the fairest of my land, and women are fair in France; but never one to be the peer of my queen—of Mary of Scotland.

"Is she not lovely?" It was The Phoenix who cut in upon my thoughts, and I answered her:

"Mademoiselle! The Greeks are right. Nymph, and Dryad, and goddess have lived."

The Phoenix looked up, a little puzzled at my meaning; and then, someone addressing her, I took the opportunity to slip away and move up to my seat of privilege—a cushion near the still empty chair of the king. On my way I had to pass The Médicis. She was seated, watching the dance, surrounded by some ladies. At her side stood Diana of Valentinois, with that marvelous face on which time could leave no trace. The duchess smiled at me, as I bowed to her who was the real queen of France, and knelt to her who was queen but in name, to that wonderful woman whom we then thought to be but a mere stolid piece of humanity, whom we, because we were fools, looked upon with a sort of pitying contempt. But a day came when she dropped the mask that had covered her for five-and-twenty years—and then we found out.

As I rose from my knees before the queen—she had but given me a look from her dark, unfathomable eyes—Catherine turned to the duchess, saying with a slight sneer, "I see nothing to admire in her; but all your French heads have been turned by that little Scotch queenlet."

"French heads, your majesty, can but see with French eyes," answered Diana, and the queen bit her lip. But now the folding doors to our right were flung open by the ushers in violet and gold, and the king appeared. By his side was the constable, and around and behind him a brilliant group, amongst whom were de Vielleville and St. André, whilst towering above the others was the grim figure of the Cardinal of Lorraine. For a moment they stood watching the dance, and then came slowly forwards.

As Henri approached his seat the dancers stopped and bowed to him, and walking up to Mary of Scotland, the king kissed her on the cheek, saying kindly, "My daughter, the roses you carry here bear the palm from those you have gathered in that nosegay. *Pardieu!*" he continued, with a laugh, whilst Mary's face grew scarlet with pleasure, "is there no knight here who can turn a rondel to these roses? What say you, my cousin of the Kingdom of Folly?"

There was a general laugh; but I was tongue-tied, and could say nothing; but the constable, with the rough gallantry of a bear, was ready with a speech.

"I cannot use the pen," he cried, "but old as I am, I will try in the next war to write a verse with my sword on Spanish helmets."

A buzz arose at the words. There may perhaps have been a veiled threat concealed in them; I know not; but buzz and murmur were stilled by a voice, nasal, discordant, and harsh, which rang through the room.

"I protest, your majesty! I protest in the name of my master, the King of Spain! France and Spain are at peace."

It was Chantonnay, the Spanish ambassador, and tall, somber-robed, and thin, with the star of St. James at his neck, he stepped forwards from the group behind the king, and stood facing Montmorency, a sinister smile playing on his lips.

It was an awkward moment. From under his bushy white eyebrows the constable glared back at his adversary, and the king looked from one to another of them, annoyance and vexation stamped upon his features.

"I protest!" the ambassador repeated again, with his strange, nasal intonation, his white fingers playing with the star at his neck.

Montmorency's hand began to finger the glove he held—the stout old soldier knew but one answer to make at such a moment—when The Médicis spoke in her calm, passionless voice: "My lords! It seems but a light matter for all these frowns to lower—all about a rose! Put aside these dark looks, I pray you, and let us hear the song the king has commanded—will no one touch a lute?"

The constable's glove slipped back over his hand, and Chantonnay bowed low to the queen. Still there was no answer to her request, and there was a strained silence.

Suddenly a voice—it was that of The Phoenix—called out, "Le Brusquet!"

The cry was caught up at once, with a clapping of hands, and "Le Brusquet! Le Brusquet!" echoed through the hall.

I met my queen's eyes. She was smiling with the rest; and then the king's voice came to me: "You are named, my cousin."

It had to be; but as I slipped the broad yellow ribbon from my shoulders and took the lute in my hands, I felt my heart beat, my fingers tremble, and my voice fail me. Twice I struck the chords; but the song would not come—and then I met her eyes again and was strong. The jester's voice rang out full and clear, but it was the knight's heart that spoke.

"'Come! Choose me a flower from
    out thy bower!
    White blows the lily; but red
    the rose.
Come! Choose me a flower from
    out thy bower!'
    Belle Mabel she plucked him
    a red, red rose.

"'Lo! Here is a flower—the queen
    of my bower!

Pale white is the lily; but red
the rose.
I dub thee my knight. In the hour
of fight
Ride ever for right, and the
red, red rose.'

"'For God and my Lady, my
Queen of Arcady!
No shield will I bear but this
red, red rose.
In charge or in rally, in siege or
in sally,
The Paynim shall shrink at
the red, red rose.'

"'Lo! The night is unfolden, the
moonlight is golden.
Pure heart and strong arm,
let them go with the rose.
Lo! The night is unfolden, the
moonlight is golden.
Go! King of my Heart, and
my Knight of the Rose!'"

I brought my song to a close with a flourish on the lute-strings. For a little there was a hush, and then a low murmur arose that swelled to a tumult of applause. Kind faces pressed around me, there were kind voices in my ears; but I heard them not—the place had gone from me—and for a space I was in a dreamland of my own.

It was the king himself who put a gold chain round my neck, and as I rose from before him, Chantonnay held out to me a heavy purse, saying, "The king, my master, knows also how to reward a minstrel."

There was that in the tone that jarred upon me. I drew myself up and answered, "Monseigneur! The servants of the King of France take guerdon but from France."

Chantonnay shrugged his shoulders as he put back his purse, and, looking around him, said slowly to the king, "Your majesty has a faithful servant, and a great poet to celebrate the wedding."

"I fail to understand, monsieur!"

"I crave your majesty's pardon. I understood that the Prince of Condé had returned, and that your majesty's consent was given."

There were eager faces enough around us as the nasal tones of the ambassador drawled themselves out. I glanced around and saw that Mary was gone. Chantonnay spoke slowly and deliberately, and his meaning was not to be mistaken.

The king flushed with anger. "Monsieur!" he said. "Is this a jest?"

And Chantonnay went on, as a cat might with a mouse: "A jest, your majesty! A jest has never passed my lips in my life!"

"*Hein*!" I cut in, jingling the bells on my cap and approaching the king. "Monseigneur speaks the truth, my cousin. No word of jest has ever passed his lips. They have all come through his nose."

A half-suppressed titter followed the speech. The king frowned and Chantonnay's eyes looked death at me; but it was his turn now to be on the cross, and the constable seized the opportunity. "Be not offended, my lord! Le Brusquet but gave you his support. 'Tis not to be despised, I assure you!"

This was too much for the Spaniard. His face became pale, his lips blue, and then he said loudly, for his temper had mastered him: "The prince is in Paris! I wager a thousand pistoles with anyone that I prove my words by nine o'clock tonight!"

"And I take the wager!"

All eyes turned to the voice that came from the middle of the hall, and then the crowd parted as Lorgnac stepped forwards, and he and Chantonnay faced each other, their glances crossing like two rapiers.

CHAPTER III
THE WORD OF A PRINCE

The apartments assigned to me, in virtue of my office, lay in the wing of the Louvre looking towards the old chapels of St. Thomas, St. Nicaise and the Quinze Vingts. A balcony jutted out from my window, and sitting there one could see below the strange mass of grey and brown buildings that clung like wasps' nests to the walls of the palace, to be matched only in squalor by the high and tottering houses, crowding and jostling each other, on the opposite side of the narrow street.

It was to this refuge I had escaped from the stifling throng of the court. When Lorgnac had stepped forwards to accept the ambassador's wager, I felt as if a load was removed from my heart; he looked so calm and confident that I was sure he had performed his task—that the prince had quitted Paris, and that Chantonnay's scheme would miscarry.

Pompon sat on the balustrade and looked at me. The creature had an intelligence almost human; he understood voice and gesture perfectly, and I had taught him to do things that were scarcely credible. We two looked down into the yard beneath, where a little doorway led into the Rue St. Thomas du Louvre. The doorway and the yard were used as a passage to and from the street by the lower servants of the palace, and it was ordinarily open until close upon ten at night in summer. An archer was on guard there, and his tall figure caught my eye as he paced backwards and forwards at his post. I stood for a minute or so watching him, when I heard a step behind me and my name called out. I turned and saw Lorgnac.

"I knocked twice," he said, "but you did not answer; so I came in, as I guessed you would be cloud-gathering here."

"There is some wine in the flask there," I answered, pointing to a little table where a flagon of d'Arbois stood; but he shook his head and took a place beside me, running his hand gently over Pompon's fur.

"Well," I said, "has Chantonnay paid you?"

"Not yet," he laughed, "but he will tonight."

"So the prince has gone?"

"Yes; I found him in the house and told him how things were. All that was needed was a horse, and I gave him mine."

"You will be hard put to it for your equipment if there is war, and I fancy the peace was broken today."

"Oh, Monsieur de Chantonnay's pistoles will provide that!"

"*Hein*! But you were quick in coming back after seeing the prince off!"

"I did not see him off—be quiet, little beast!" And he put Pompon on one side.

"Not see him off!"

"No! I was on duty and could not. He gave me his word that he would start in an hour, and by this there should be a couple of leagues between him and Paris."

"If they pursue—"

"Who is to pursue? And they will be fleet hoofs that will overtake Cartouche."

"But if he has not gone?"

"Impossible! He knows the risk."

"Then," I said, "nothing remains, old friend, but the wars for you and my pears for me. I should like to see Bèsme once more."

He made no answer, and we both leaned together over the balustrade and looked down into the yard. It was dusk now, and the archer appeared like a grey shadow below us. Two women servants came through, and our sentinel levied a kiss from each ere he let them flutter past him into the palace, leaving him gazing wistfully after them.

"*Nom d'un gaillard*!" said Lorgnac. "The duty there is not so dull!"

"Hush!" I answered. "Here comes another."

In effect, as I spoke, another figure, wrapped in a light cloak, ran down the palace steps and tripped across the yard. We could not, of course, see properly; but there was a grace about her movements that struck us both.

"She is pretty, I wager," I said.

"Lucky archer!" exclaimed Lorgnac.

And at that moment our sentinel advanced for his toll; but the newcomer shrank back from him and kept him off.

"Ah! *Ma petite*!" said the archer. "I have not seen you before! Where have you dropped from? One kiss, and Perducas de Ponthieu will die for you."

He made a motion of his arm towards her; but recovering herself, she slipped nimbly aside, saying with a laugh, "*Bavard*! I may ask you to die for me someday without hope of reward." And in a moment she had flashed through the open gate and was gone.

But I knew—the voice was enough for me; and looking at Lorgnac, I saw his eyes blazing, and even through the dusk I could see the ivory pallor on his face. "My God!" I exclaimed. "Are we mad?"

But Lorgnac caught me by the arm. "Fool! There is no time to waste. By Heaven! Prince of the Blood though he be, if he has lied to me, he dies." Saying this, he fairly dragged me from the balcony. I stayed him for a moment to snatch up my rapier and fling aside my wooden sword, and then we two hurried down the winding stair, past the servants' quarters and out into the yard.

The archer saluted us as we came up. "Which way did—did mademoiselle go?" asked Lorgnac, his voice strange and husky.

"I know not, monsieur—she vanished like a spirit."

"Try your house," I suggested, plucking him by the sleeve. "Lose no time here!"

And as I uttered these words I saw Pompon beside me, and drove him back with a curse. But for once the ape disobeyed; and there was no help for it, I had to let him follow as best I could.

We dashed up the narrow Rue St. Thomas—fortunately there were not many people about—and just where the street opened out into the Rue St. Honoré we caught a glimpse of the graceful figure hesitating at a crossing. She had lifted her dress slightly, and though, to complete her disguise, she was wearing the flat-soled Spanish mules, not all their hideousness could conceal the perfect arch of her foot. For a moment she hesitated, as I have said, giving us time to gain well upon her, and then, drawing her hood closer together, she ran across the road and headed towards the labyrinth of streets around the Halles.

"Put not your trust in princes," I said bitterly; but Lorgnac made no answer, maintaining a grim silence.

We kept on the pavement opposite to her, never losing sight of her for an instant, although the streets were crowded here and the uncertain light made our task far from easy; but we had too much at stake to fail.

When she reached the *parvis* of St. Eustache, she crossed it slowly towards the portal of the still-unfinished church, though the first stone had been laid at the time I was born. As she approached the archway a man stepped forward from the shadow, and they met with outstretched hands. So they stood for a moment, talking earnestly together, and we halted too, and watched them with beating hearts.

"It is he," I whispered. "He has broken his word."

But still Lorgnac did not speak, though I could hear his labored breath. And as we watched, a man came over the flagged square, walking idly and carelessly towards them, humming as he did so the song called the "Three Cavaliers."

"D'Aramon!" exclaimed Lorgnac. "It is all over now, unless we can shut his mouth."

On his words, however, the two moved off arm-in-arm, swiftly together, and were lost in the unceasing crowd that was pouring from the Halles. I was for rushing after them at once; but Lorgnac held me by the arm. "Stay!" he said. "You must deal with d'Aramon. Stop him at all hazards. I look after the others. Meet me at my house."

And with these words he left me abruptly, crossing the pavement rapidly and mixing with the crowd.

I waited not a moment myself; I did not even answer Lorgnac, but pressed forward on the track of the spy, and overtook d'Aramon in the Rue Montorgueil. He was walking slowly, looking carefully about him, as if he had missed his prey, and was heading towards the Tiquetonne—the next turning to the right would bring him to the Tire Boudin.

I walked past him rapidly, brushing against him as I did so, and turned with an apology that broke into an exclamation of surprised recognition. "Your pardon, monsieur! *Hein*! Can I believe my eyes? Is it you, d'Aramon?"

"Yes—yes," he stammered uneasily. "I have business, Monsieur le Brusquet; another day," and he would have hastened on.

But I stood in his path, saying insolently, "And so have I; everybody's business is a jester's business. Come and drink!"

He thought I was in my cups, and still preserved his coolness. "Not now—*au revoir, au revoir*!" And he pressed on.

But I stuck like a fly to him, buzzing in his ear. "Tell me," I said loudly, "you appear to be on your feet again—does the Spanish ambassador pay well?"

He stopped short with a curse and turned on me, shaking with anger. "Begone, fool!" he shouted, his hand on the hilt of his poniard; but I slipped back nimbly, my drawn rapier pointed at him, and in a moment a crowd had gathered around us. He was no coward, and would certainly have not shrunk from an affair; but now it was absolutely necessary for him to have his hands free. He glanced around him, and then made a mistake. He attempted to dash across the road to the other side and escape me.

On the instant I had raised the cry, "*Au voleur*!" and the crowd was on his heels.

You all know the good people of Paris, and how hard it would go with a man behind whom the cry, "Stop, thief!" was raised. It fared so with d'Aramon. The spy had barely got across the Tiquetonne when he was surrounded by a shrieking, howling mob—and a mob, too, of the artisans and workers of the Halles. He drew his sword and swept it round him;

but they only gave way to form in closer behind him. And now stones and other missiles began to fly, and the rattles of the watch to be heard. I caught one glimpse of d'Aramon. He had backed up against the wall near a street lamp; his cheek was cut and bleeding, and his dress torn and soiled. He was trying to shout explanations, but he might as well have shouted to awaken the dead.

"*Au voleur! Au voleur!*" was shrieked and howled around him, and then someone brought him down with a blow from a staff, and he fell beneath a struggling heap of men.

I had no pity for the villain; he was one of the worst of his class, and deserved death at the lamppost. On the whole he got off easily enough, though he was marked for life, and it was many a long day ere the "captain's" limbs lost their soreness.

He was disposed of, at any rate. So leaving him to the tender mercies of the crowd—and of the watch, who had hurried up—I went rapidly on towards the Rue Tire Boudin, where Lorgnac's house stood. It was but a short way from the Tiquetonne, and on reaching the entrance to the street I halted for a moment, as if to examine the display in the window of a pastry-cook's shop, although my eyes were fixed anywhere but on his tartlets and cakes. The moon was out now, full and clear, and its light fell like a broad silver ribbon between the two rows of dark and silent houses that raised their grey and mottled walls on either side of the street. There were but a few passersby; but it seemed to me that there was an unwonted crowd near the door of the house where Lorgnac lived, for it lay about a third of the way down the street.

I took a step into the road and stopped again to get a better view, when I felt something plucking at my cloak. I looked down. It was Pompon, whose very existence I had forgotten, and he sat at my feet gazing wistfully up at my face, with eyes that told me he was wearied.

"Come, Pompon!" I said; and in a moment he was on my shoulder, where he sat light as a feather. I gave another look down the road and at the group near Lorgnac's house, and I was certain I caught the gleam of a cuirass. This augured ill; but it was no time to draw back, and singing a cheery catch, I stepped forwards. Coming boldly up to the door of the house I found myself stopped by Créquy, of the archer guard.

"*Diable!*" I exclaimed. "I have come to see my gossip, Lorgnac. What does all this mean?"

"I know no more than you, le Brusquet. If you want to see Lorgnac you will find him on the opposite side of the road with two of my men; but he is as sulky as a bear."

"What! Have you arrested him?"

"Yes."

"Then what are you doing here?"

"Obeying orders, my Lord of Folly; and if you will take my advice you will go home, for"—and he dropped his voice—"the king and the cardinal will be here in a few minutes. We have caged some birds within."

"Ah, well! That is their affair. I'll drop a consoling jest in Lorgnac's ear and be off."

In a few steps I was across the road and beside Lorgnac. He was standing, looking the picture of dejection, between two stalwart archers.

"Oh, ho, *mon ami!*" I exclaimed, as I embraced him. "So you have engaged pilots for the Châtelet!"

The archers laughed at this reference to them; but Lorgnac seized his chance and whispered quickly in my ear, "The horse is in the stables behind Barou's shop; there is a chance by the window." And he slipped a key into my hand.

"Never fear," I answered loudly, "you shall be free tonight. I shall see my gossip Henri, and we shall finish that d'Arbois of mine before tomorrow morning. Adieu, then, until we meet again!"

And waving my hand to Créquy, I turned back and walked off at a rapid pace, Pompon once more following at my heels.

CHAPTER IV
HOW POMPON SAVED A QUEEN

There are times when thought and action have to move together like lightning, when, if there is but a flicker of halt or hesitation, the result is disaster; and if ever such a moment had come to me, it had arrived now.

I thank God that, notwithstanding the tumult in my heart, I kept my head clear and my nerve steady in the crisis before me. It is true I held a great card. No one suspected me, except perhaps d'Aramon, and he was quieted. Not the most suspicious eye would turn on le Brusquet, the king's jester, as being in any way involved in a court intrigue, and I was safe from hindrance on that score; even Créquy, and he was no fool, had let me pass with a jest.

I could not help chuckling a little to myself at this, as, picking Pompon up, I crossed the road to the opposite side, where the shadows lay dark on the pavement. One look behind me—the archers were still at Lorgnac's door—and then I put myself to the run. A few steps brought me to a narrow side-street that went off at an angle from the road, heading back to the crossroads where Barou's shop lay, close to Lorgnac's house. Immediately behind the shop was Cartouche's stable, and from the stable there was a chance, a bare chance, to free my birds.

I knew the way perfectly, for I had used it as a short cut a hundred times on my visits to Lorgnac, when he lay ill, in the spring, of a tertian ague. I made all the haste I could, and at last reached Barou's shop. Two steps more and I was at the stable. If Lorgnac's ready wit had not thought of the key, all would have been lost; but as it was, the key was in my hand. In another moment I had opened the door and stepped in, shutting it carefully behind me.

A lantern, swinging to a chain attached to a crossbeam, was burning brightly in the stable, and in the stall before me was a magnificent grey horse, with a lofty crest and bright, full eyes that looked down upon me like two stars. It was Cartouche, and he was already saddled, though the girths hung loosely around him. He knew me, for we were old friends, and, tossing his head up and down, began to strike at the flooring with his forefoot and whinny.

I patted his sleek neck and looked around. Near me was some stable gear. To the right there was a loft, and above that a small window, which was open, for the night was warm. A ladder led to the loft, and up this I climbed, Pompon at my heels, and, passing through the window, found myself on the roof of Barou's store. On either hand the gables, with their lily-shaped finials, hid me from view, and I was, in short, on the backbone of the roof.

About twenty feet from me rose the back of Lorgnac's house, high and narrow. From a window in the second story there was a bright light, and I caught a glimpse of a shadow on the wall. I crept up beneath the window and looked. It was impossible to reach it, and I dare not raise my voice.

Every moment was precious, and with a groan I glanced about for some means of ascent. As I did so, Pompon began to clamber up the grooved brick drain-spout which terminated on a narrow ledge of ornamental stonework running around the house. Above this ledge a gargoyle, in the shape of a griffin's head, leered down at me.

A sudden thought struck me, and I seized the ape ere he could go further. Back I ran, with the quick, stealthy footsteps of a cat, and dropped down into the stable once more. Hastily, and with shaking hands, I examined the stable gear, throwing one thing after another aside, and at last I found what I was after: a spare halter. Oh, those seconds when I fumbled there in the stable! They were as hours. I snatched up the halter with an exclamation of joy, and in less time than I take to tell this, was once more beneath the window.

Here it was Pompon's turn, and I thanked my stars again and again for the months I had spent in teaching the ape to do almost anything I wished. I knotted one end of the halter into a noose and, giving it to Pompon, placed him where he had climbed to at first—and with a little wave of my hand said, "Up, Pompon! Up!"

Without a moment's hesitation he climbed to the ledge. I watched the small black figure looking down on me with little twinkling eyes, the halter, held by the noose, in its hands. I made a motion of my hand towards the gargoyle; but the ape only jabbered, and the cold sweat burst over me, for I was sure that I heard in the distance the sound of many horses trotting. Too late! After all this!

It could not be! Again and again I tried to make the ape understand; but he either could not or would not. In despair, I at last seized the end of the halter near me and looped it round my own neck—and imagine my utter disgust as Pompon did the same, and bobbed up and down on his hind legs. One might have laughed, if the issue at stake was not so serious. I took the loop off my neck—Pompon again followed my example—and then— it may have been God's mercy—he suddenly understood and slipped it over the gargoyle.

"Thank God!" I had tightened the noose in a moment, giving the ape no time to change his mind and remove it. In those days I was lithe and agile as a cat, and hand over hand I swarmed up the rope, at last gaining the narrow foothold of the ledge. The window was at least six feet from me, and I had to cross this space ere I came to it.

Holding on to the brickwork, I slipped the noose from the griffin's head, and then slowly and carefully made my perilous way to the window, the rope clutched in one hand, getting as much support as I could from the cracks between the bricks, where the cement had loosened and fallen away.

When, afterwards, I looked at what I had done, my blood ran cold at the very idea of it; but now I went without fear, without a single thought of anything but those whom I was striving to save. And yes, those were horses I had heard—I heard them again now, clear and distinct. I was not a moment too soon.

I boldly stood on the ledge and looked in at the window. It was a large room, and she, my queen, was sitting at the table; her hood had fallen back, showing the pale, clear-cut outlines of her face, and her eyes were full of tears. Condé stood by her, speaking earnestly, pleading as if for his life, and if ever there was love in a man's face it shone on his. Oh!—it was a mad thing to do; but she was a child, not eighteen, and he but five-and-twenty.

So earnestly were they talking that they did not hear me, though I stood boldly at the window, and it was only when I had sprung lightly into the room that they became aware of my presence. Mary rose to her feet with a little cry and her hands went up to her face; but Condé sprang at me without a word. But I seized his wrists like a vise, and said in a voice cracked with emotion, "You are betrayed; and there is only one chance—come with me!"

The fool struggled still, and, prince of the blood though he was, I cursed him to his face. "Will you lose all? Hark!" And the blare of a trumpet from the street came to us with discordant echoes.

He understood now, but his presence of mind had left him. "My God!" he cried, and he turned to Mary. "What can I do to save you?" To give him his due, he thought but of her, and he rushed to her side, where she stood staring at us, with a white face and large, frightened eyes.

The door of the room was open. As I ran to it I heard a battering below. "'Tis the king!" I cried. "Quick! To the window!"

His senses were coming back to him, and he half-dragged and half-carried Mary to the window. I closed and locked the heavy oaken door, and turning, saw Condé handling the rope I had thrown on the floor at my entrance. He had grasped at the chance of escape. But I would take no risk of failure. I was by his side in a moment, and snatched the halter from his hands.

"Put out the light," I said, and as he did so I ran a noose round the pillar of the balustrade across the window, and dropped the rope outside; then, turning to Condé, I said, "Descend, and hold the rope taut below."

The words were scarce out of my mouth when we heard the dull report of an arquebus. "They have blown in the lock—quick!"

But he needed no bidding. He was not good at climbing, but somehow he managed it, and I felt the rope tighten. He was safe below.

"Mademoiselle!" I said, turning to Mary. I pretended not to know her, but she shrunk back.

"I cannot! I cannot! Let them come!" Her words were followed by a crash, a hoarse shout, and the sound of many feet. Then I did what I have never done to woman before or after. The strength of ten possessed me. I took her in my arms like a child, and holding her round the waist with one hand began the descent.

She seemed to recover herself as I got out of the window, and clung on to the rope as well as I, else I had never succeeded; but we completed the descent as we heard them hammering at the door, and voice—it was the king's—called out, "An arquebus! An arquebus!"

Along the roof of the store we ran like hares, Pompon leading; and we had just gained the stable, and I had put out the light, when we heard the door of the room from which we had escaped being forced in. They would see the rope, I knew, and we were still not safe.

I whispered hastily to Condé, "Take the horse and ride for your life! Go by the Porte St. Honoré."

He was himself again, for the Bourbons never had the poltroon fever. He drew the girths, bent down and kissed Mary's hand, and mounted in the stable. As I held the door open for him, he turned to me, saying, "Monsieur, I swear—"

But the hot anger blazed within me at the man who could risk a woman's fair fame as he had done—at the man who had broken his word to his friend.

"Ride!" I said. "Waste no time in vows—'tis only a prince who thinks he can break his word without dishonor."

Following my words came yells and shouts from the window. They had found the rope. Condé made no answer, but bent his head and gave Cartouche the spur. We heard him clatter down the street, and I caught Mary's hand and we ran out together.

I took her northward, through passage and alley, until I felt her falter, and then I stopped, for she was breathless and almost fainting. But we were safe—no one would recognize a queen in the slight, grey-clad figure that clung to a jester's arm, as the two, followed by a small brown ape, picked their way along the narrow pavement of the Rue St. Sauveur.

It was then that she spoke for the first time, and as she did so she withdrew her hand from my arm. "Is—is he safe—do you think—monsieur?"

"Monseigneur is by now free of the Porte St. Honoré," I replied, still giving no sign that I knew her.

But the ice was broken now, and she went on, "Oh, it was folly! It was madness! Why ever did I come?"

"We will get back safely, thank God!" I said; but a great fear was in my heart, lest the king should send to order the Louvre gates to be shut. We went down the Rue Croix des Petits Champs, passed behind the *magasins* of the Louvre, and at last came to the gate below the riding-school. Once past that, we were safe indeed, for my little key would open the Terrace wicket, and then all would be well.

"Take my arm," I said. "Look as much like a servant woman of the palace as your highness can."

She did so without a word. As we came to the gate, the sentry looked at us narrowly. I stopped and addressed him. "My friend!" I said. "It is not yet ten, is it?"

"No, Monsieur le Brusquet"—But his eyes were on my companion, whose hood was drawn well over her face.

"Good!" I answered. "I shall be in time for the king's supper. Come, *mignonne!*"

I felt her shrink at the word; but she played her part bravely, and tripped by my side as we passed the gate. We were not a moment too soon, for as we turned the shrubberies, a horseman dashed up, and I heard him call out to the sentry.

It was Créquy. "Has anyone gone this way?"

We stopped in the shadow of the trees and listened. We dare not stir, for it would mean crossing a bright patch of moonlight where, for certain, we would be seen.

"Yes, monsieur—le Brusquet, his ape, and a girl—she looked pretty."

"And you did not stop them?"

"Monsieur! The gates are free until ten—and besides, le Brusquet has an evil sword, and he called her *mignonne.*"

"Three very good reasons; but the first is the best. Harkee! Close the gates at once. Let none pass in or out."

"Monsieur!"

And then Créquy, turning his horse's head, rode off at a canter.

As he did so, I drew the inference from his act. "The king is not back yet, your highness—we are safe."

Then we crossed the garden in silence, until we came to the little wicket leading to the Ladies' Terrace. I opened it with my key, and when we had gone up the steps and reached the platform of the terrace, she stopped, and we faced each other.

I shall never forget that night when we two stood there alone, the quiet moon looking down on us—the silver light, the shadowy trees, and the scent of the roses that came to us with the breeze. I saw my queen's eyes shining upon me, and I knelt at her feet.

"Your highness will forgive me—my freedom of speech, and all I have done; but there was no other way—and you are safe now."

She threw her hood back and looked down upon me with her glorious eyes, and then, stretching out her hand, raised me to my feet. "Monsieur de Bèsme," she said, "God has let me know today what a true gentleman is; keep these in memory of Mary of Scotland."

With these words she detached the two red roses she wore at the neck of her dress and placed them in my hands, and as I bowed low and in silence to receive them, she turned and ran up the stairway and into the palace—slipping from my sight like a ghost.

～

Late that night, as I sat in my chamber, thinking and staring at the roses I had placed in a vase on the table before me, I heard a step outside my door, and then a knock. I knew who it was.

"Enter!" I cried, and Lorgnac came in. His face was beaming, his eyes laughing. He shook me by the hand, and flinging himself into a chair, poured himself out a cup of d'Arbois, and drained it at a draught.

"See here!" he said, as he placed a small bag on the table. "A thousand pistoles in gold—and I owe you forty crowns." Saying this, he counted the money out on the table, and fell to laughing again.

"Come," he said, "tell me your story."

I told him all, omitting only the mention of the roses, and when I had done, he went to the little box where Pompon lay, wearied and asleep. He looked at the ape long and earnestly, and muttered, "You shall have a collar of gold, *mon ami*—for you have saved a queen."

Then he came back, and we spoke for a while gaily of many things, for our hearts were full of one thing, which we did not dare to speak of even to one another.

At last he rose to go. As he stood at the door, wishing me goodnight, he hesitated a little, and then went on, "It is goodnight and goodbye, le Brusquet. The king has forgiven me, and I leave tomorrow with despatches for Coligny."

"*Hein!*" I said. "The Treaty of Vaucelles is waste paper. Good luck and good fortune!"

I waited until his footsteps had died away. He was wearing his willow bravely, and like a gentleman. Then I went back to look at the Queen's Roses.

But six days later, Coligny had attacked Douai and stormed Lens, and the king had declared war against Spain.

Cheerly O and Cheerly O

JEFFERY FARNOL

Cheerly O and cheerly O,
Right cheerly I'll sing O,
Whiles at the mainyard to and fro
We watch a dead man swing O.
With a rumbelow and to and fro
He by the neck doth swing O!

Two on a knife did end their life
And three the bullet took O,
But three times three died plaguily
A-wriggling on a hook O.
A hook both strong and bright and long,
They died by gash o' hook O.

So cheerly O and cheerly O,
Come shake a leg, lads, all O.
Wi' a yo-ho-ho and a rumbelow
And main-haul, shipmates, haul O.

Some swam in rum to kingdom come,
Full many a lusty fellow.
And since they're dead I'll lay my head
They're flaming now in hell O.

From *Black Bartlemy's Treasure*, 1920.

About Johnston McCulley

Arthur Johnston McCulley (1883-1958) was born in Illinois, but spent his early years in New York City as a reporter writing for the *Police Gazette*, which specialized in sensational crime news. He began writing stories for the early pulp magazines, and by 1909 had given up journalism entirely for fiction. He moved to southern California, where he immersed himself in local history. One of the results was a novel called *The Curse of Capistrano*, serialized in *All-Story Weekly* in 1919.

Douglas Fairbanks, Sr., on his way to Europe on his honeymoon after marrying screen darling Mary Pickford, had brought a stack of *All-Story* with him to read during the crossing. He was struck by the hero of *The Curse of Capistrano*—Zorro, of course—and decided that he'd found the subject of his next movie. The next year Fairbanks played the starring role in the story he'd re-titled *The Mark of Zorro*; it was a gigantic hit, and Fairbanks was to spend the next ten years as a movie swashbuckler, appearing in lavish productions as Zorro, d'Artagnan, and Robin Hood.

McCulley recognized his debt to the actor, and when *Capistrano* appeared in book form in 1924 it bore the movie's title—*The Mark of Zorro*—and was dedicated to Fairbanks.

McCulley's idea of a swashbuckling hero with an aristocratic secret identity had most likely been borrowed from Baroness Orczy's Scarlet Pimpernel (who appears later in this volume). McCulley's brilliant innovation was to bedeck his hero in a mask and costume, thereby inventing the entire genre of costumed hero with a secret identity. McCulley himself must have been aware of the power of this concept as he repeated it over and over in the pulps, inventing other masked and costumed heroes such as the Green Ghost and the Crimson Clown. After them came the masked avengers of the hero pulps such as The Shadow and The Spider, radio heroes like the Green Hornet, and of course Bob Kane's Batman and the many superheroes of the comic books.

The story that follows is nothing less than the first four chapters of *The Curse of Capistrano*: the first appearance of Zorro, the greatest swashbuckler of the twentieth century. Enjoy!

Señor Zorro Pays a Visit

JOHNSTON McCULLEY

I

Again the sheet of rain beat against the roof of red Spanish tile, and the wind shrieked like a soul in torment, and smoke puffed from the big fireplace as the sparks were showered over the hard dirt floor.

"'Tis a night for evil deeds!" declared Sergeant Pedro Gonzales, stretching his great feet in their loose boots toward the roaring fire and grasping the hilt of his sword in one hand and a mug filled with thin wine in the other. "Devils howl in the wind, and demons are in the raindrops! 'Tis an evil night, indeed—eh, *señor?*"

"It is!" the fat landlord agreed hastily; and he made haste, also, to fill the wine mug again, for Sergeant Pedro Gonzales had a temper that was terrible when aroused, as it always was when wine was not forthcoming.

"An evil night," the big sergeant repeated, and drained the mug without stopping to draw breath, a feat that had attracted considerable attention in its time and had gained the sergeant a certain amount of notoriety up and down El Camino Real, as they called the highway that connected the missions in one long chain.

Gonzales sprawled closer to the fire and cared not that other men thus were robbed of some of its warmth. Sergeant Pedro Gonzales often had expressed his belief that a man should look out for his own comfort before considering others; and being of great size and strength, and having much skill with the blade, he found few who had the courage to declare that they believed otherwise.

Outside the wind shrieked, and the rain dashed against the ground in a solid sheet. It was a typical February storm for southern California. At the missions the *frailes*, the brothers, had cared for the stock and had closed the buildings for the night. At every great *hacienda* big fires were burning in the houses. The timid natives kept to their little adobe huts, glad for shelter.

And here in the little *pueblo* of Reina de Los Angeles, where, in years to come, a great city would grow, the tavern on one side of the plaza housed for the time being men who would sprawl before the fire until the dawn rather than face the beating rain.

Sergeant Pedro Gonzales, by virtue of his rank and size, hogged the fireplace, and a corporal and three soldiers from the *presidio* sat at table a little in rear of him, drinking their thin wine and playing at cards. An Indian servant crouched on his heels in one corner, no neophyte who had accepted the religion of the *frailes*, but a gentile and renegade.

For this was in the day of the decadence of the missions, and there was little peace between the robed Franciscans who followed in the footsteps of the sainted Junipero Serra, who had founded the first mission at San Diego de Alcalá, and thus made possible an empire, and those who followed the politicians and had high places in the army. The men who drank wine in the tavern at Reina de Los Angeles had no wish for a spying neophyte about them.

Just now the conversation had died out, a fact that annoyed the fat landlord and caused him some fear; for Sergeant Pedro Gonzales in an argument was Sergeant Gonzales at peace; and unless he could talk the big soldier might feel moved to action and start a brawl.

Twice before Gonzales had done so, to the great damage of furniture and men's faces; and the landlord had appealed to the *comandante* of the *presidio*, Captain Ramón, only to be informed that the captain had an abundance of troubles of his own, and that running an inn was not one of them.

So the landlord regarded Gonzales warily and edged closer to the long table and spoke in an attempt to start a general conversation and so avert trouble.

"They are saying in the *pueblo*," he announced, "that this Señor Zorro is abroad again."

His words had an effect that was both unexpected and terrible to witness. Sergeant Pedro Gonzales hurled his half-filled wine mug to the hard dirt floor, straightened suddenly on the bench, and crashed a ponderous fist down upon the table, causing wine mugs and cards and coins to scatter in all directions.

The corporal and the three soldiers retreated a few feet in sudden fright, and the red face of the landlord blanched; the native sitting in the corner started to creep toward the door, having determined that he preferred the storm outside to the big sergeant's anger.

"Señor Zorro, eh?" Gonzales cried in a terrible voice. "Is it my fate always to hear that name? Señor Zorro, eh? Mr. Fox, in other words! He imagines, I take it, that he is as cunning as one. By the saints, he raises as much stench!"

Gonzales gulped, turned to face them squarely, and continued his tirade.

"He runs up and down the length of El Camino Real like a goat of the high hills! He wears a mask, and he flashes a pretty blade, they tell me. He uses the point of it to carve his hated letter Z on the cheek of his foe! Ha! The mark of Zorro they are calling it! A pretty blade he has, in truth! But I cannot swear as to the blade—I never have seen it. He will not do me the honor of letting me see it! Señor Zorro's depredations never occur in the vicinity of Sergeant Pedro Gonzales! Perhaps this Señor Zorro can tell us the reason for that? Ha!"

He glared at the men before him, threw out his upper lip, and let the ends of his great black mustache bristle.

"They are calling him the Curse of Capistrano now," the fat landlord observed, stooping to pick up the wine mug and cards and hoping to filch a coin in the process.

"Curse of the entire highway and the whole mission chain!" Sergeant Gonzales roared. "A cutthroat, he is! A thief! Ha! A common fellow presuming to get him a reputation for bravery because he robs a *hacienda* or so and frightens a few women and natives! Señor Zorro, eh? Here is one fox it gives me pleasure to hunt! Curse of Capistrano, eh? I know I have led an evil life, but I only ask of the saints one thing now—that they forgive me my sins long enough to grant me the boon of standing face to face with this pretty highwayman!"

"There is a reward—" the landlord began.

"You snatch the very words from my lips!" Sergeant Gonzales protested. "There is a pretty reward for the fellow's capture, offered by his excellency the governor. And what good fortune has come to my blade? I am away on duty at San Juan Capistrano, and the fellow makes his play at Santa Barbara. I am at Reina de Los Angeles, and he takes a fat purse at San Luis Rey. I dine at San Gabriel, let us say, and he robs at San Diego de Alcalá! A pest, he is! Once I met him—"

Sergeant Gonzales choked on his wrath and reached for the wine mug, which the landlord had filled again and placed at his elbow. He gulped down the contents.

"Well, he never has visited us here," the landlord said with a sigh of thanksgiving.

"Good reason, fat one! Ample reason! We have a *presidio* here and a few soldiers. He rides far from any *presidio*, does this pretty Señor Zorro! He is like a fleeting sunbeam, I grant him that—and with about as much real courage!"

Sergeant Gonzales relaxed on the bench again, and the landlord gave him a glance that was full of relief, and began to hope that there would be no breakage of mugs and furniture and men's faces this rainy night.

"Yet this Señor Zorro must rest at times—he must eat and sleep," the landlord said. "It is certain that he must have some place for hiding and recuperation. Some fine day the soldiers will trail him to his den."

"Ha!" Gonzales replied. "Of course the man has to eat and sleep. And what is it that he claims now? He says that he is no real thief, by the saints! He is but punishing those who mistreat the men of the missions, he says. Friend of the oppressed, eh? He left a placard at Santa Barbara recently stating as much, did he not? Ha! And what may be the reply to that? The *frailes* of the missions are shielding him, hiding him, giving him his meat and drink! Shake down a robed *fray* and you'll find some trace of this pretty highwayman's whereabouts, else I am a lazy civilian!"

"I have no doubt that you speak the truth," the landlord replied. "I put it not past the *frailes* to do such a thing. But may this Señor Zorro never visit us here!"

"And why not, fat one?" Sergeant Gonzales cried in a voice of thunder. "Am I not here? Have I not a blade at my side? Are you an owl, and is this daylight that you cannot see as far as the end of your puny, crooked nose? By the saints—"

"I mean," said the landlord quickly and with some alarm, "that I have no wish to be robbed."

"To be—robbed of what, fat one? Of a jug of weak wine and a meal? Have you riches, fool? Ha! Let the fellow come! Let this bold and cunning Señor Zorro but enter that door and step before us! Let him make a bow, as they say he does, and let his eyes twinkle through his mask! Let me but face the fellow for an instant—and I claim the generous reward offered by his excellency!"

"He is perhaps afraid to venture so near the *presidio*," the landlord said.

"More wine!" Gonzales howled. "More wine, fat one, and place it to my account! When I have earned that reward, you shall be paid in full. I promise it on my word as a soldier! Ha! Were this brave and cunning Señor Zorro, this Curse of Capistrano, but to make entrance at that door now—"

The door suddenly was opened.

II

In came a gust of wind and rain and a man with it, and the candles flickered and one was extinguished. This sudden entrance in the midst of the sergeant's boast startled them all, and Gonzales drew his blade halfway from its scabbard as his words died in his throat. The native was quick to close the door again to keep out the wind.

The newcomer turned and faced them; the landlord gave another sigh of relief. It was not Señor Zorro, of course. It was Don Diego Vega, a fair youth of excellent blood and twenty-four years, noted the length of El Camino Real for his small interest in the really important things of life.

"Ha!" Gonzales cried, and slammed his blade home.

"Is it that I startled you somewhat, *señores*?" Don Diego asked politely and in a thin voice, glancing around the big room and nodding to the men before him.

"If you did, *señor*, it was because you entered on the heels of the storm," the sergeant retorted. "'Twould not be your own energy that would startle any man!"

"H-m!" grunted Don Diego, throwing aside his sombrero and flinging off his soaked serape. "Your remarks border on the perilous, my raucous friend."

"Can it be that you intend to take me to task?"

"It is true," continued Don Diego, "that I do not have a reputation for riding like a fool at the risk of my neck, fighting like an idiot with every newcomer, and playing the guitar under every woman's window like a simpleton. Yet I do not care to have these things you deem my shortcomings flaunted in my face!"

"Ha!" Gonzales cried, half in anger.

"We have an agreement, Sergeant Gonzales, that we can be friends, and I can forget the wide difference in birth and breeding that yawns between us only as long as you curb your tongue and stand my comrade. Your boasts amuse me, and I buy for you the wine that you crave— it is a pretty arrangement. But ridicule me again, *señor*, either in public or in private, and the agreement is at an end. I may mention that I have some small influence—"

"Your pardon, *caballero* and my very good friend!" the alarmed Sergeant Gonzales cried now. "You are storming worse that the tempest outside, and merely because my tongue happened to slip. Hereafter, if any man ask, you are nimble of wit and quick with a blade, always ready to fight or to make love. You are a man of action, *caballero*! Ha! Does any dare doubt it?"

He glared around the room, half drawing his blade again, and then he slammed the sword home and threw back his head and roared with laughter, and then clapped Don Diego between the shoulders; and the fat landlord hurried with more wine, knowing well that Don Diego would stand the score.

For this peculiar friendship between Don Diego and Sergeant Gonzales was the talk of El Camino Real. Don Diego came from a family of blood that ruled over thousands of broad acres, countless herds of horses and cattle, great fields of grain. Don Diego, in his own right, had a *hacienda* that was like a small empire, and a house in the *pueblo* also, and was destined to inherit from his father more than thrice what he had now.

But Don Diego was unlike the other full-blooded youths of the times. It appeared that he disliked action. He seldom wore his blade, except as a matter of style and apparel. He was damnably polite to all women and paid court to none.

He sat in the sun and listened to the wild tales of other men—and now and then he smiled. He was the opposite of Sergeant Pedro Gonzales in all things, and yet they were together frequently. It was as Don Diego had said—he enjoyed the sergeant's boasts, and the sergeant enjoyed the free wine. What more could either ask in the way of a fair arrangement?

Now Don Diego went to stand before the fire and dry himself, holding a mug of red wine in one hand. He was only medium in size, yet he possessed health and good looks, and it was the despair of proud *dueñas* that he would not glance a second time at the pretty *señoritas* they protected, and for whom they sought desirable husbands.

Gonzales, afraid that he had angered his friend and that the free wine would be at an end, now strove to make peace.

"*Caballero*, we have been speaking of this notorious Señor Zorro," he said. "We have been regarding in conversation this fine Curse of Capistrano, as some nimble-witted fool has seen fit to term the pest of the highway."

"What about him?" Don Diego asked, putting down his wine mug and hiding a yawn behind his hand. Those who knew Don Diego best declared he yawned ten score times a day.

"I have been remarking, *caballero*," said the sergeant, "that this fine Señor Zorro never appears in my vicinity, and that I am hoping the good saints will grant me the chance of facing him some fine day, that I may claim the reward offered by the governor. Señor Zorro, eh? Ha!"

"Let us not speak of him," Don Diego begged, turning from the fireplace and throwing out one hand as if in protest. "Shall it be that I never hear of anything except deeds of bloodshed and violence? Would it be possible in these turbulent times for a man to listen to words of wisdom regarding music or the poets?"

"Meal mush and goat's milk!" snorted Sergeant Gonzales in huge disgust. "If this Señor Zorro wishes to risk his neck, let him. It is his own neck, by the saints! A cutthroat! A thief! Ha!"

"I have been hearing considerable concerning his work," Don Diego went on to say. "The fellow, no doubt, is sincere in his purpose. He has robbed none except officials who have stolen from the missions and the poor, and punished none except brutes who mistreat natives. He has slain no man, I understand. Let him have his little day in the public eye, my sergeant."

"I would rather have the reward!"

"Earn it," Don Diego said. "Capture the man!"

"Ha! Dead or alive, the governor's proclamation says. I myself have read it."

"Then stand you up to him and run him through, if such a thing pleases you," Don Diego retorted. "And tell me all about it afterward—but spare me now."

"It will be a pretty story!" Gonzales cried. "And you shall have it entire, *caballero*, word by word! How I played with him, how I laughed at him as we fought, how I pressed him back after a time and ran him through—"

"Afterward—but not now!" Don Diego cried, exasperated. "Landlord, more wine! The only manner in which to stop this raucous boaster is to make his wide throat so slick with wine that the words cannot climb out of it!"

The landlord quickly filled the mugs. Don Diego sipped at his wine slowly, as a gentleman should, while Sergeant Gonzales took his in two great gulps. And then the scion of the house of Vega stepped across to the bench and reached for his sombrero and his serape.

"What?" the sergeant cried. "You are going to leave us at such an early hour, *caballero*? You are going to face the fury of that beating storm?"

"At least I am brave enough for that," Don Diego replied, smiling. "I but ran over from my house for a pot of honey. The fools feared the rain too much to fetch me some this day from the *hacienda*. Get me one, landlord."

"I shall escort you safely home through the rain!" Sergeant Gonzales cried, for he knew full well that Don Diego had excellent wine of age there.

"You shall remain here before the roaring fire," Don Diego told him firmly. "I do not need an escort of soldiers from the *presidio* to cross the plaza. I am going over accounts with my secretary, and possibly may return to the tavern after we have finished. I wanted the pot of honey that we might eat as we worked."

"Ha! And why did you not send that secretary of yours for the honey, *caballero*? Why be wealthy and have servants, if a man cannot send them on errands on such a stormy night?"

"He is an old man and feeble," Don Diego explained. "He also is secretary to my aged father. The storm would kill him. Landlord, serve all here with wine and put it to my account. I may return when my books have been straightened."

Don Diego Vega picked up the pot of honey, wrapped his serape around his head, opened the door, and plunged into the storm and darkness.

"There goes a man!" Gonzales cried, flourishing his arms. "He is my friend, that *caballero*, and I would have all men know it! He seldom wears a blade, and I doubt whether he can use one—but he is my friend! The flashing dark eyes of lovely *señoritas* do not disturb him, yet I swear he is a pattern of a man!

"Music and the poets, eh? Ha! Has he not the right, if such is his pleasure? Is he not Don Diego Vega? Has he not blue blood and broad acres and great storehouses filled with goods? Is he not liberal? He may stand on his head or wear petticoats, if it please him—yet I swear he is a pattern of a man!"

The soldiers echoed his sentiments since they were drinking Don Diego's wine and did not have the courage to combat the sergeant's statements anyway. The fat landlord served them with another round since Don Diego would pay. For it was beneath a Vega to look at his score in a public tavern, and the fat landlord many times had taken advantage of this fact.

"He cannot endure the thought of violence or bloodshed," Sergeant Gonzales continued. "He is as gentle as a breeze of spring. Yet he has a firm wrist and a deep eye. It merely is the *caballero*'s manner of seeing life. Did I but have his youth and good looks and riches—Ha! There would be a stream of broken hearts from San Diego de Alcalá to San Francisco de Asis!"

"And broken heads!" the corporal offered.

"Ha! And broken heads, comrade! I would rule the country! No youngster should stand long in my way. Out with blade and at them! Cross Pedro Gonzales, eh? Ha! Through the shoulder—neatly! Ha! Through a lung!"

Gonzales was upon his feet now, and his blade had leaped from its scabbard. He swept it back and forth through the air, thrust, parried, lunged, advanced, and retreated, shouted his oaths, and roared his laughter as he fought with shadows.

"That is the manner of it!" he screeched at the fireplace. "What have we here? Two of you against one? So much the better, *señores*! We love brave odds! Ha! Have at you, dog! Die, hound! One side, poltroon!"

He reeled against the wall, gasping, his breath almost gone, the point of his blade resting on the floor, his great face purple with the exertion and the wine he had consumed, while the corporal and the soldiers and the fat landlord laughed long and loudly at this bloodless battle from which Sergeant Pedro Gonzales had emerged the unquestioned victor.

"Were—were this fine Señor Zorro only before me here and now!" the sergeant gasped.

And again the door was opened suddenly, and a man entered the inn on a gust of the storm.

III

The native hurried forward to fasten the door against the forces of the wind, and then retreated to his corner again. The newcomer had his back toward those in the long room. They could see that his sombrero was pulled far down on his head, as if to prevent the wind from whisking it away, and that his body was enveloped in a long cloak that was wringing wet.

With his back still toward them, he opened the cloak and shook the raindrops from it and then folded it across his breast again as the fat landlord hurried forward, rubbing his hands together in expectation, for he deemed that here was some *caballero* off the highway who would pay good coin for food and bed and care for his horse.

When the landlord was within a few feet of him and the door the stranger whirled around. The landlord gave a little cry of fear and retreated with speed. The corporal gurgled deep down in his throat; the soldiers gasped; Sergeant Pedro Gonzales allowed his lower jaw to drop and let his eyes bulge.

For the man who stood straight before them had a black mask over his face that effectually concealed his features, and through the two slits in it his eyes glittered ominously.

"Ha! What have we here?" Gonzales gasped finally, some presence of mind returning to him.

The man before them bowed.

"Señor Zorro, at your service," he said.

"By the saints! Señor Zorro, eh?" Gonzales cried.

"Do you doubt it, *señor*?"

"If you are indeed Señor Zorro, then have you lost your wits!" the sergeant declared.

"What is the meaning of that speech?"

"You are here, are you not? You have entered the inn, have you not? By all the saints, you have walked into a trap, my pretty highwayman!"

"Will the *señor* please explain?" Señor Zorro asked. His voice was deep and held a peculiar ring.

"Are you blind? Are you without sense?" Gonzales demanded. "Am I not here?"

"And what has that to do with it?"

"Am I not a soldier?"

"At least you wear a soldier's garb, *señor*."

"By the saints, and cannot you see the good corporal and three of our comrades? Have you come to surrender your wicked sword, *señor*? Are you finished playing at rogue?"

Señor Zorro laughed, not unpleasantly, but he did not take his eyes from Gonzales.

"Most certainly I have not come to surrender," he said. "I am on business, *señor*."

"Business?" Gonzales queried.

"Four days ago, *señor*, you brutally beat a native who had won your dislike. The affair happened on the road between here and the mission at San Gabriel."

"He was a surly dog and got in my way! And how does it concern you, my pretty highwayman?"

"I am the friend of the oppressed, *señor*, and I have come to punish you."

"Come to—to punish me, fool? You punish me? I shall die of laughter before I can run you through! You are as good as dead, Señor Zorro! His excellency has offered a pretty price for your carcass! If you are a religious man, say your prayers! I would not have it said that I slew a man without giving him time to repent his crimes. I give you the space of a hundred heartbeats."

"You are generous, *señor*, but there is no need for me to say my prayers."

"Then I must do my duty," said Gonzales, and lifted the point of his blade. "Corporal, you will remain by the table, and the men also. This fellow and the reward he means are mine!"

He blew out the ends of his mustache and advanced carefully, not making the mistake of underestimating his antagonist, for there had been certain tales of the man's skill with a blade. And when he was within the proper distance he recoiled suddenly, as if a snake had warned of a strike.

For Señor Zorro had allowed one hand to come from beneath his cloak, and the hand held a pistol, most damnable of weapons to Sergeant Gonzales.

"Back, *señor*," Señor Zorro warned.

"Somebody told me you were a brave man," Gonzales taunted, retreating a few feet. "It has been whispered that you would meet any man foot to foot and cross blades with him. I have believed it of you. And now I find you resorting to a weapon fit for nothing except to use against red natives. Can it be, *señor*, that you lack the courage I have heard you possess?"

Señor Zorro laughed again.

"As to that we shall see presently," he said. "The use of this pistol is necessary at the present time. I find myself pitted against large odds in this tavern, *señor*. I shall cross blades with you gladly when I have made such a proceeding safe."

"I wait anxiously," Gonzales sneered.

"The corporal and the soldiers will retreat to that far corner," Señor Zorro directed. "Landlord, you will accompany them. The natives will go there also. Quickly, *señores*. Thank you. I do not wish to have any of you disturbing me while I am punishing this sergeant here."

"Ha!" Gonzales screeched in fury. "We shall soon see as to the punishing, my pretty fox!"

"I shall hold the pistol in my left hand," Señor Zorro continued. "I shall engage this sergeant with my right, in the proper manner, and as I fight I shall keep an eye on the corner. The first move from any of you, *señores*, means that I fire. I am expert with this you have termed the devil's weapon, and if I fire some men shall cease to exist on this earth of ours. It is understood?"

The corporal and the soldiers and land-lord did not take the trouble to answer. Señor Zorro looked Gonzales straight in the eyes again, and a chuckle came from behind his mask.

"Sergeant, you will turn your back until I can draw my blade," he directed. "I give you my word as a *caballero* that I shall not make a foul attack."

"As a *caballero*?" Gonzales sneered.

"I said it, *señor*!" Zorro replied, his voice ringing a threat.

Gonzales shrugged his shoulders and turned his back. In an instant he heard the voice of the highwayman again.

"On guard, *señor*!"

IV

Gonzales whirled at the word, and his blade came up. He saw that Señor Zorro had drawn his sword, and that he was holding the pistol in his left hand high above his head. Moreover, Señor Zorro was chuckling still, and the sergeant became infuriated. The blades clashed.

Sergeant Gonzales had been accustomed to battling with men who gave ground when they pleased and took it when they could, who went this way and that seeking an advantage, now advancing, now retreating, now swinging to left or right as their skill directed them.

But here he faced a man who fought in quite a different way. For Señor Zorro, it appeared, was as if rooted to one spot and unable to turn his face in any other direction. He did not give an inch, nor did he advance, nor step to either side.

Gonzales attacked furiously, as was his custom, and he found the point of his blade neatly parried. He used more caution then and tried what tricks he knew, but they seemed to avail him nothing. He attempted to pass around the man before him, and the other's blade drove him back. He tried a retreat, hoping to draw the other out, but Señor Zorro stood his ground and forced Gonzales to attack again. As for the highwayman, he did nought except put up a defense.

Anger got the better of Gonzales then, for he knew the corporal was jealous of him and that the tale of this fight would be told to all the *pueblo* tomorrow and so travel up and down the length of El Camino Real.

He attacked furiously, hoping to drive Señor Zorro off his feet and make an end of it. But he found that his attack ended as if against a stone wall, his blade was turned aside, his breast crashed against that of his antagonist, and Señor Zorro merely threw out his chest and hurled him back half a dozen steps.

"Fight, *señor*!" Señor Zorro said.

"Fight yourself, cutthroat and thief!" the exasperated sergeant cried. "Don't stand like a piece of the hills, fool! Is it against your religion to take a step?"

"You cannot taunt me into doing it," the highwayman replied, chuckling again.

Sergeant Gonzales realized then that he had been angry, and he knew that an angry man cannot fight with the blade as well as a man who controls his temper. So he became deadly cold now, and his eyes narrowed, and all boasting was gone from him.

He attacked again, but now he was alert, seeking an unguarded spot through which he could thrust without courting disaster himself. He fenced as he never had fenced in his life before. He cursed himself for having allowed wine and food to rob him of his wind. From the front, from either side, he attacked, only to be turned back again, all his tricks solved almost before he tried them.

He had been watching his antagonist's eyes, of course, and now he saw a change. They had seemed to be laughing through the mask, and now they had narrowed and seemed to send forth flakes of fire.

"We have had enough of playing," Señor Zorro said. "It is time for the punishment!"

And suddenly he began to press the fighting, taking step after step, slowly and methodically going forward and forcing Gonzales backward. The tip of his blade seemed to be a serpent's head with a thousand tongues. Gonzales felt himself at the other's mercy, but he gritted his teeth and tried to control himself and fought on.

Now he was with his back against the wall, but in such a position that Señor Zorro could give him battle and watch the men in the corner at the same time. He knew the highwayman was playing with him. He was ready to swallow his pride and call upon the corporal and soldiers to rush in and give him aid.

And then there came a sudden battering at the door, which the native had bolted. The heart of Gonzales gave a great leap. Somebody was there, wishing to enter. Whoever it was would think it peculiar that the door was not thrown open instantly by the fat landlord or his servant. Perhaps help was at hand.

"We are interrupted, *señor*," the highwayman said. "I regret it, for I will not have the time to give you the punishment you deserve, and will have to arrange to visit you another time. You scarcely are worth a double visit."

The pounding at the door was louder now. Gonzales raised his voice: "Ha! We have Señor Zorro here!"

"Poltroon!" the highwayman cried.

His blade seemed to take on new life. It darted in and out with a speed that was bewildering. It caught a thousand beams of light from the flickering candles and hurled them back.

And suddenly it darted in and hooked itself properly, and Sergeant Gonzales felt his sword torn from his grasp and saw it go flying through the air.

"So!" Señor Zorro cried.

Gonzales awaited the stroke. A sob came into his throat that this must be the end instead of on a field of battle where a soldier wishes it. But no steel entered his breast to bring forth his life's blood.

Instead, Señor Zorro swung his left hand down, passed the hilt of his blade to it and grasped it beside the pistol's butt, and with his right he slapped Pedro Gonzales once across the cheek.

"That for a man who mistreats helpless natives!" he cried.

Gonzales roared in rage and shame. Somebody was trying to smash the door in now. But Señor Zorro appeared to give it little thought. He sprang back, and sent his blade into its scabbard like a flash. He swept the pistol before him and thus threatened all in the long room. He darted to a window, sprang upon a bench.

"Until a later time, *señor!*" he cried.

And then he went through the window as a mountain goat jumps from a cliff, taking its covering with him. In rushed the wind and rain, and the candles went out.

"After him!" Gonzales screeched, springing across the room and grasping his blade again. "Unbar the door! Out and after him! Remember, there is a generous reward—"

The corporal reached the door first, and threw it open. In stumbled two men of the *pueblo*, eager for wine and an explanation of the fastened door. Sergeant Gonzales

and his comrades drove over them and left them sprawling, and dashed into the storm.

But there was little use in it. It was so dark a man could not see the distance of a horse's length. The beating rain was enough to obliterate tracks almost instantly. Señor Zorro was gone—and no man could tell in what direction.

There was a tumult, of course, in which the men of the *pueblo* joined. Sergeant Gonzales and the soldiers returned to the inn to find it full of men they knew. And Sergeant Gonzales knew, also, that his reputation was now at stake.

"Nobody but a highwayman, nobody but a cutthroat and thief would have done it!" he cried aloud.

"How is that, brave one?" cried a man in the throng near the doorway.

"This pretty Señor Zorro knew, of course! Some days ago I broke the thumb of my sword hand while fencing at San Juan Capistrano. No doubt the word was passed to this Señor Zorro. And he visits me at such a time that he may afterward say he had vanquished me."

The corporal and soldiers and landlord stared at him, but none was brave enough to say a word.

"Those who were here can tell you, *señores,*" Gonzales went on. "This Señor Zorro came in at the door and immediately drew a pistol—devil's weapon—from beneath his cloak. He presents it at us, and forces all except me to retire to that corner. I refused to retire.

"'Then you shall fight me,' says this pretty highwayman, and I draw my blade, thinking to make an end of the pest. And what does he tell me then?

"'We shall fight,' he says, 'and I will outpoint you, so that I may boast of it afterward. In my left hand I hold the pistol. If your attack is not to my liking, I shall fire, and afterward run you through, and so make an end of a certain sergeant.'"

The corporal gasped, and the fat landlord was almost ready to speak, but thought better of it when Sergeant Gonzales glared at him.

"Could anything be more devilish?" Gonzales asked. "I was to fight, and yet I would get a devil's chunk of lead in my carcass if I pressed the attack. Was there ever such a farce? It shows the stuff of which this pretty highwayman is made. Someday I shall meet him when he holds no pistol—and then—"

"But how did he get away?" someone in the crowd asked.

"He heard those at the door. He threatened me with the devil's pistol and forced me to toss my blade in yonder far corner. He threatened us all, ran to the window, and sprang through. And how could we find him in the darkness or track him through the sheets of rain? But I am determined now! In the morning I go to my Captain Ramón and ask permission to be absolved of all other duty, that I may take some comrades and run down this pretty Señor Zorro. Ha! We shall go fox hunting!"

The excited crowd about the door suddenly parted, and Don Diego Vega hurried into the tavern.

"What is this I hear?" he asked. "They are saying that Señor Zorro has paid a visit here."

"'Tis a true word, *caballero!*" Gonzales answered. "And we were speaking of the cutthroat here this evening. Had you remained instead of going home to work with your secretary, you should have seen the entire affair."

"Were you not here? Can you not tell me?" Don Diego asked. "But I pray you make not the tale too bloody. I cannot see why men must be violent. Where is the highwayman's dead body?"

Gonzales choked; the fat landlord turned away to hide his smile; the corporal and soldiers began picking up wine mugs to keep busy at this dangerous moment.

"He—that is, there is no body," Gonzales managed to say.

"Have done with your modesty, sergeant!" Don Diego cried. "Am I not your friend? Did you not promise to tell me the story if you met this cutthroat? I know you would spare my feelings, knowing that I do not love violence, yet I am eager for the facts because you, my friend, have been engaged with this fellow. How much was the reward?"

"By the saints!" Gonzales swore.

"Come, sergeant! Out with the tale! Landlord, give all of us wine, that we may celebrate this affair! Your tale, sergeant! Shall you leave the army, now that you have earned the reward, and purchase a *hacienda* and take a wife?"

Sergeant Gonzales choked again and reached gropingly for a wine mug.

"You promised me," Don Diego continued, "that you would tell me the whole thing, word by word. Did he not say as much, landlord? You declared that you would relate how you played with him; how you laughed at him while you fought; how you pressed him back after a time and ran him through—"

"By the saints!" Sergeant Gonzales roared, the words coming from between his lips like peals of thunder. "It is beyond the endurance of any man! You—Don Diego—my friend—"

"Your modesty ill becomes you at such a time," Don Diego said. "You promised me the tale, and I would have it. What does this Señor Zorro look like? Have you peered at the dead face beneath the mask? It is, perhaps, some man that we all know? Cannot some one of you tell me the facts? You stand here like so many speechless images of men—"

"Wine—or I choke!" Gonzales howled. "Don Diego, you are my good friend, and I will cross swords with any man who belittles you! But do not try me too far this night—"

"I fail to understand," Don Diego said. "I have but asked you to tell me the story of the fight—how you mocked him as you battled; how you pressed him back at will, and presently ended it by running him through—"

"Enough! Am I to be taunted?" the big sergeant cried. He gulped down the wine and hurled the mug far from him.

"Is it possible that you did not win the battle?" Don Diego asked. "But surely this pretty highwayman could not stand up before you, my sergeant. How was the outcome?"

"He had a pistol—"

"Why did you not take it away from him, then, and crowd it down his throat? But perhaps that is what you did. Here is more wine, my sergeant. Drink!"

But Sergeant Gonzales was thrusting his way through the throng at the door.

"I must not forget my duty!" he said. "I must hurry to the *presidio* and report this occurrence to the *comandante*!"

"But, sergeant—"

"And as to this Señor Zorro, he will be meat for my blade before I am done!" Gonzales promised.

And then, cursing horribly, he rushed away through the rain, the first time in his life he ever had allowed duty to interfere with his pleasure and had run from good wine. Don Diego Vega smiled as he turned toward the fireplace.

About Arthur Conan Doyle

Sir Arthur Conan Doyle (1859-1930) needs an introduction less than any other author in this collection: everybody knows the creator of Sherlock Holmes. Most readers have probably even heard how, tired of his greatest creation, Doyle tried to kill Holmes off in mid-career, having him plunge to the bottom of Reichenbach Falls with his nemesis, Professor Moriarty. Doyle felt confined writing mysteries, and wanted a larger canvas to paint upon.

In short, what Doyle really wanted to write were historical adventures.

He did it well, as you would expect, and his historicals were very popular in their day, especially his two novels of the knight Sir Nigel Loring set in the Hundred Years War, *The White Company* (1891) and *Sir Nigel* (1906). Now, knights are fine, but we're interested in swashbucklers, and there Doyle has gifted us with one of his greatest characters: the immortal Brigadier Gerard, the French Imperial hussar of the bristling moustache and the bold and roving eye, whose expectations of admiration for his bravery and good looks are met by his greatest admirer: himself.

If this characterization sounds somewhat familiar, it may be because Gerard's legacy lives on in the character of Harry Flashman, "hero" of a wonderful series of novels by the late George MacDonald Fraser. But where Flashman is a coward who hides behind the trappings of courage, Brigadier Gerard is the real goods. As you'll discover in this story from *The Exploits of Brigadier Gerard*, 1896.

How the Brigadier Played for a Kingdom

ARTHUR CONAN DOYLE

It has sometimes struck me that some of you, when you have heard me tell these little adventures of mine, may have gone away with the impression that I was conceited. There could not be a greater mistake than this, for I have always observed that really fine soldiers are free from this failing. It is true that I have had to depict myself sometimes as brave, sometimes as full of resource, always as interesting; but, then, it really was so, and I had to take the facts as I found them. It would be an unworthy affectation if I were to pretend that my career has been anything but a fine one. The incident which I will tell you tonight, however, is one which you will understand that only a modest man would describe. After all, when one has attained such a position as mine, one can afford to speak of what an ordinary man might be tempted to conceal.

You must know, then, that after the Russian campaign the remains of our poor army were quartered along the western bank of the Elbe, where they might thaw their frozen blood and try, with the help of good German beer, to put a little between their skin and their bones. There were some things which we could not hope to regain, for I daresay that three large commissariat fourgons would not have sufficed to carry the fingers and the toes which the army had shed during that retreat. Still, lean and crippled as we were, we had much to be thankful for when we thought of our poor comrades whom we had left behind, and of the snowfields—the horrible, horrible snowfields. To this day, my friends, I do not care to see red and white together. Even my red cap thrown down upon my white counterpane has given me dreams in which I have seen those monstrous plains, the reeling, tortured army, and the crimson smears which glared upon the snow behind them. You will coax no story out of me about that business, for the thought of it is enough to turn my wine to vinegar and my tobacco to straw.

Of the half-million who crossed the Elbe in the autumn of the year '12, about forty thousand infantry were left in the spring of '13. But they were terrible men, these forty thousand: men of iron, eaters of horses, and sleepers in the snow; filled, too, with rage and bitterness against the Russians. They would hold the Elbe until the great army of conscripts, which the Emperor was raising in France, should be ready to help them cross it once more.

But the cavalry was in a deplorable condition. My own hussars were at Borna, and when I paraded them first, I burst into tears at the sight of them. My fine men and my beautiful horses—it broke my heart to see the state to which they were reduced. "But, courage," I thought, "they have lost much, but their Colonel is still left to them." I set to work, therefore, to repair their disasters, and had already constructed two good squadrons, when an order came that all colonels of cavalry should repair instantly to the depots of the regiments in France to organize the recruits and the remounts for the coming campaign.

You will think, doubtless, that I was overjoyed at this chance of visiting home once more. I will not deny that it was a pleasure to me to know that I should see my mother again, and there were a few girls who would be very glad at the news; but there were others in the army who had a stronger claim. I would have given my place to any who had wives and children whom they might not see again.

However, there is no arguing when the blue paper with the little red seal arrives, so within an hour I was off upon my great ride from the Elbe to the Vosges.

At last, I was to have a period of quiet. War lay behind my mare's tail and peace in front of her nostrils. So I thought, as the sound of the bugles died in the distance, and the long, white road curled away in front of me through plain and forest and mountain, with France somewhere beyond the blue haze which lay upon the horizon.

It is interesting, but it is also fatiguing, to ride in the rear of an army. In the harvest time our soldiers could do without supplies, for they had been trained to pluck the grain in the fields as they passed, and to grind it for themselves in their bivouacs. It was at that time of year, therefore, that those swift marches were performed which were the wonder and the despair of Europe. But now the starving men had to be made robust once more, and I was forced to draw into the ditch continually as the Coburg sheep and the Bavarian bullocks came streaming past with wagon loads of Berlin beer and good French cognac. Sometimes, too, I would hear the dry rattle of the drums and the shrill whistle of the fifes, and long columns of our good little infantry men would swing past me with the white dust lying thick upon their blue tunics. These were old soldiers drawn from the garrisons of our German fortresses, for it was not until May that the new conscripts began to arrive from France.

Well, I was rather tired of this eternal stopping and dodging, so that I was not sorry when I came to Altenburg to find that the road divided, and that I could take the southern and quieter branch. There were few wayfarers between there and Greiz, and the road wound through groves of oaks and beeches, which shot their branches across the path. You will think it strange that a Colonel of hussars should again and again pull up his horse in order to admire the beauty of the feathery branches and the little, green, new-budded leaves, but if you had spent six months among the fir trees of Russia you would be able to understand me.

There was something, however, which pleased me very much less than the beauty of the forests, and that was the words and looks of the folk who lived in the woodland villages. We had always been excellent friends with the Germans, and during the last six years they had never seemed to bear us any malice for having made a little free with their country. We had shown kindnesses to the men and received them from the women, so that good, comfortable Germany was a second home to all of us. But now there was something which I could not understand in the behavior of the people. The travelers made no answer to my salute; the foresters turned their heads away to avoid seeing me; and in the villages the folk would gather into knots in the roadway and would scowl at me as I passed. Even women would do this, and it was something new for me in those days to see anything but a smile in a woman's eyes when they were turned upon me.

It was in the hamlet of Schmolin, just ten miles out of Altenburg, that the thing became most marked. I had stopped at the little inn there just to damp my moustache and to wash the dust out of poor Violette's throat. It was my way to give some little compliment, or possibly a kiss, to the maid who served me; but this one would have neither the one nor the other, but darted a glance at me like a bayonet-thrust. Then when I raised my glass to the folk who drank their beer by the door they turned their backs on me, save only one fellow, who cried, "Here's a toast for you, boys! Here's to the letter T!" At that they all emptied their beer mugs and laughed; but it was not a laugh that had good-fellowship in it.

I was turning this over in my head and wondering what their boorish conduct could mean, when I saw, as I rode from the village, a great T new carved upon a tree. I had already seen more than one in my morning's ride, but I had given no thought to them until the words of the beer-drinker gave them an importance.

It chanced that a respectable-looking person was riding past me at the moment, so I turned to him for information. "Can you tell me, sir," said I, "what this letter T is?"

He looked at it and then at me in the most singular fashion. "Young man," said he, "it is not the letter N." Then before I could ask further he clapped his spurs into his horse's ribs and rode, stomach to earth, upon his way.

At first his words had no particular significance in my mind, but as I trotted onwards Violette chanced to half turn her dainty head, and my eyes were caught by the gleam of the brazen N's at the end of the bridle-chain. It was the Emperor's mark. And those T's meant something which was opposite to it. Things had been happening in Germany, then, during our absence, and the giant sleeper had begun to stir. I thought of the mutinous faces that I had seen, and I felt that if I could only have looked into the hearts of these people I might have had some strange news to bring into France with me. It made me the more eager to get my remounts, and to see ten strong squadrons behind my kettledrums once more.

While these thoughts were passing through my head I had been alternately walking and trotting, as a man should who has a long journey before and a willing horse beneath him. The woods were very open at this point, and beside the road there lay a great heap of fagots. As I passed there came a sharp sound among them, and, glancing round, I saw a face looking out at me—a hot, red face, like that of a man who is beside himself with excitement and anxiety. A second glance told me that it was the very person with whom I had talked an hour before in the village.

"Come nearer!" he hissed. "Nearer still! Now dismount and pretend to be mending the stirrup leather. Spies may be watching us, and it means death to me if I am seen helping you."

"Death!" I whispered. "From whom?"

"From the Tugenbund. From Lutzow's night-riders. You Frenchmen are living on a powder-magazine, and the match has been struck which will fire it."

"But this is all strange to me," said I, still fumbling at the leathers of my horse. "What is this Tugenbund?"

"It is the secret society which has planned the great rising which is to drive you out of Germany, just as you have been driven out of Russia."

"And these T's stand for it?"

"They are the signal. I should have told you all this in the village, but I dared not be seen speaking to you. I galloped through the woods to cut you off, and concealed both my horse and myself."

"I am very much indebted to you," said I, "and the more so as you are the only German that I have met today from whom I have had common civility."

"All that I possess I have gained through contracting for the French armies," said he. "Your Emperor has been a good friend to me. But I beg you that you will ride on now, for we have talked long enough. Beware only of Lutzow's night-riders!"

"Banditti?" I asked.

"All that is best in Germany," said he. "But for God's sake ride forwards, for I have risked my life and exposed my good name in order to carry you this warning."

Well, if I had been heavy with thought before, you can think how I felt after my strange talk with the man among the fagots. What came home to me even more than his words was his shivering, broken voice, his twitching face, and his eyes glancing swiftly to right and left, and opening in horror whenever a branch cracked upon a tree. It was clear that he was in the last extremity of terror, and it is possible that after I had left him I heard a distant gunshot and a shouting from somewhere behind me. It may have been some sportsman halloaing to his dogs, but I never again heard or saw the man who had given me my warning.

I kept a good lookout after this, riding swiftly where the country was open, and slowly where there might be an ambuscade. It was serious for me, since 500 good miles of German soil lay in front of me; but somehow I did not take it very much to heart, for the Germans had always seemed to me to be a kindly, gentle people, whose hands closed more readily round a pipe-stem than a swordhilt—not out of want of valor, you understand, but because they are genial, open souls, who would rather be on good terms with all men. I did not know then that beneath that homely surface there lurks a devilry as fierce as, and far more persistent than, that of the Castilian or the Italian.

And it was not long before I had shown to me that there was something far more serious abroad than rough words and hard looks. I had come to a spot where the road runs upwards through a wild tract of heathland and vanishes into an oak wood. I may have been halfway up the hill when, looking forward, I saw something gleaming under the shadow of the tree-trunks, and a man came out with a coat which was so slashed and spangled with gold that he blazed like a fire in the sunlight. He appeared to be very drunk, for he reeled and staggered as he came towards me. One of his hands was held up to his ear and clutched a great red handkerchief, which was fixed to his neck.

I had reined up the mare and was looking at him with some disgust, for it seemed strange to me that one who wore so gorgeous a uniform should show himself in such a state in broad daylight. For his part, he looked hard in my direction and came slowly onwards, stopping from time to time and swaying about as he gazed at me. Suddenly, as I again advanced, he screamed out his thanks to Christ, and, lurching forwards, he fell with a crash upon the dusty road. His hands flew forward with the fall, and I saw that what I had taken for a red cloth was a monstrous wound, from which a dark blood-clot hung, like an epaulette upon his shoulder.

"My God!" I cried, as I spring to his aid. "And I thought you were drunk!"

"Not drunk, but dying," said he. "But thank Heaven that I have seen a French officer while I have still strength to speak."

I laid him among the heather and poured some brandy down his throat. All round us was the vast countryside, green and peaceful, with nothing living in sight save only the mutilated man beside me.

"Who has done this?" I asked, "and what are you? You are French, and yet the uniform is strange to me."

"It is that of the Emperor's new guard of honor. I am the Marquis of Château St. Arnaud, and I am the ninth of my blood who has died in the service of France. I have been pursued and wounded by the night-riders of Lutzow, but I hid among the brushwood yonder, and waited in the hope that a Frenchman might pass. I could not be sure at first if you were friend or foe, but I felt that death was very near, and that I must take the chance."

"Keep your heart up, comrade," said I. "I have seen a man with a worse wound who has lived to boast of it."

"No, no," he whispered; "I am going fast." He laid his hand upon mine as he spoke, and I saw that his fingernails were already blue. "But I have papers here in my tunic which you must carry at once to the Prince of Saxe-Felstein, at his Castle of Hof. He is still true to us, but the Princess is our deadly enemy. She is striving to make him declare against us. If he does so, it will determine all those who are wavering, for the King of Prussia is his uncle and the King of Bavaria his cousin. These papers will hold him to us if they can only reach him before he takes the last step. Place them in his hands tonight, and, perhaps, you will have saved all Germany for the Emperor. Had my horse not been shot I might, wounded as I am—" he choked, and the cold hand tightened into a grip which left mine as bloodless as itself. Then, with a groan, his head jerked back, and it was all over with him.

Here was a fine start for my journey home. I was left with a commission of which I knew little, which would lead me to delay the pressing needs of my hussars, and which at the same time was of such importance that it was impossible for me to avoid it. I opened the Marquis's tunic, the brilliance of which had been devised by the Emperor in order to attract those young aristocrats from whom he hoped to raise these new regiments of his Guard. It was a small packet of papers which I drew out, tied up with silk, and addressed to the Prince of Saxe-Felstein. In the corner, in a sprawling, untidy hand, which I knew to be the Emperor's own, was written: "Pressing and most important." It was an order to me, those four words—an order as clear as if it had come straight from the firm lips with the cold grey eyes looking into mine. My troopers might wait for their horses, the dead Marquis might lie where I had laid him amongst the heather, but if the mare and her rider had a breath left in them the papers should reach the Prince that night.

I should not have feared to ride by the road through the wood, for I have learned in Spain that the safest time to pass through a guerilla country is after an outrage, and that the moment of danger is when all is peaceful. When I came to look upon my map, however, I saw that Hof lay further to the south of me, and that I might reach it more directly by keeping to the moors. Off I set, therefore, and had not gone fifty yards before two carbine shots rang out of the brushwood and a bullet hummed past me like a bee. It was clear that the night-riders were bolder in their ways than the brigands of Spain, and that my mission would have ended where it had begun if I had kept to the road.

It was a mad ride, that—a ride with a loose rein, girth-deep in heather and in gorse, plunging through bushes, flying down hillsides, with my neck at the mercy of my dear little Violette. But she—she never slipped, she never faltered, as swift and as surefooted as if she knew that her rider carried the fate of all Germany beneath the buttons of his pelisse. And I—I had long borne the name of being the best horseman in the six brigades of light cavalry, but I never rode as I rode then. My friend the Bart has told me of how they hunt the fox in England, but the swiftest fox would have been captured by me that day. The wild pigeons which flew overhead did not take a straighter course than Violette and I below. As an officer, I have always been ready to sacrifice myself for my men, though the Emperor would not have thanked me for it, for he had many men, but only one—well, cavalry leaders of the first class are rare.

But here I had an object which was indeed worth a sacrifice, and I thought no more of my life than of the clods of earth that flew from my darling's heels.

We struck the road once more as the light was failing, and galloped into the little village of Lobenstein. But we had hardly got upon the cobblestones when off came one of the mare's shoes, and I had to lead her to the village smithy. His fire was low, and his day's work done, so that it would be an hour at the least before I could hope to push on to Hof. Cursing at the delay, I strode into the village inn and ordered a cold chicken and some wine to be served for my dinner. It was but a few more miles to Hof, and I had every hope that I might deliver my papers to the Prince on that very night, and be on my way for France next morning with despatches for the Emperor in my bosom. I will tell you now what befell me in the inn of Lobenstein.

The chicken had been served and the wine drawn, and I had turned upon both as a man may who has ridden such a ride, when I was aware of a murmur and a scuffling in the hall outside my door. At first I thought that it was some brawl between peasants in their cups, and I left them to settle their own affairs. But of a sudden there broke from among the low, sullen growl of the voices such a sound as would send Etienne Gerard leaping from his death-bed. It was the whimpering cry of a woman in pain. Down clattered my knife and fork, and in an instant I was in the thick of the crowd which had gathered outside my door.

The heavy-cheeked landlord was there and his flaxen-haired wife, the two men from the stables, a chambermaid, and two or three villagers. All of them, women and men, were flushed and angry, while there in the center of them, with pale cheeks and terror in her eyes, stood the loveliest woman that ever a soldier would wish to look upon. With her queenly head thrown back, and a touch of defiance mingled with her fear, she looked as she gazed round her like a creature of a different race from the vile, coarse-featured crew who surrounded her. I had not taken two steps from my door before she sprang to meet me, her hand resting upon my arm and her blue eyes sparkling with joy and triumph.

"A French soldier and a gentleman!" she cried. "Now at last I am safe."

"Yes, madam, you are safe," said I, and I could not resist taking her hand in mine in order that I might reassure her. "You have only to command me," I added, kissing the hand as a sign that I meant what I was saying.

"I am Polish," she cried; "the Countess Palotta is my name. They abuse me because I love the French. I do not know what they might have done to me had Heaven not sent you to my help."

I kissed her hand again lest she should doubt my intentions. Then I turned upon the crew with such an expression as I know how to assume. In an instant the hall was empty.

"Countess," said I, "you are now under my protection. You are faint, and a glass of wine is necessary to restore you." I offered her my arm and escorted her into my room, where she sat by my side at the table and took the refreshments which I offered her.

How she blossomed out in my presence, this woman, like a flower before the sun! She lit up the room with her beauty. She must have read my admiration in my eyes, and it seemed to me that I also could see something of the sort in her own. Ah! my friends, I was no ordinary-looking man when I was in my thirtieth year. In the whole light cavalry it would have been hard to find a finer pair of whiskers. Murat's may have been a shade longer, but the best judges are agreed that Murat's were a shade too long. And then I had a manner. Some women are to be approached in one way and some in another, just as a siege is an affair of fascines and gabions in hard weather and of trenches in soft. But the man who can mix daring with timidity, who can be outrageous with an air of humility and presumptuous with a tone of deference, that is the man whom mothers have to fear. For myself, I felt that I was the guardian of this lonely lady, and knowing what a dangerous man I had to deal with, I kept strict watch upon myself. Still, even a guardian has his privileges, and I did not neglect them.

But her talk was as charming as her face. In a few words she explained that she was traveling to Poland, and that her brother who had been her escort had fallen ill upon the way. She had more than once met with ill-treatment from the country folk because she could not conceal her goodwill towards the French. Then turning from her own affairs she questioned me about the army, and so came round to myself and my own exploits. They were familiar to her, she said, for she knew several of Poniatowski's officers, and they had spoken of my doings. Yet she would be glad to hear them from my own lips. Never have I had so delightful a conversation. Most women make the mistake of talking rather too much about their own affairs, but this one listened to my tales just as you are listening now, ever asking for more and more and more. The hours slipped rapidly by, and it was with horror that I heard the village clock strike eleven, and so learned that for four hours I had forgotten the Emperor's business.

"Pardon me, my dear lady," I cried, springing to my feet, "but I must be on instantly to Hof."

She rose also, and looked at me with a pale, reproachful face. "And me?" she said. "What is to become of me?"

"It is the Emperor's affair. I have already stayed far too long. My duty calls me, and I must go."

"You must go? And I must be abandoned alone to these savages? Oh, why did I ever meet you? Why did you ever teach me to rely upon your strength?" Her eyes glazed over, and in an instant she was sobbing upon my bosom.

Here was a trying moment for a guardian! Here was a time when he had to keep a watch upon a forward young officer. But I was equal to it. I smoothed her rich brown hair and whispered such consolations as I could think of in her ear, with one arm around her, it is true, but that was to hold her lest she should faint. She turned her tear-stained face to mine. "Water," she whispered. "For God's sake, water!"

I saw that in another moment she would be senseless. I laid the drooping head upon the sofa, and then rushed furiously from the room, hunting from chamber to chamber for a carafe. It was some minutes before I could get one and hurry back with it. You can imagine my feelings to find the room empty and the lady gone.

Not only was she gone, but her cap and silver-mounted riding switch which had lain upon the table were gone also. I rushed out and roared for the landlord. He knew nothing of the matter, had never seen the woman before, and did not care if he never saw her again. Had the peasants at the door seen anyone ride away? No, they had seen nobody. I searched here and searched there, until at last I chanced to find myself in front of a mirror, where I stood with my eyes staring and my jaw as far dropped as the chin-strap of my shako would allow.

Four buttons of my pelisse were open, and it did not need me to put my hand up to know that my precious papers were gone. Oh! the depth of cunning that lurks in a woman's heart. She had robbed me, this creature, robbed me as she clung to my breast. Even while I smoothed her hair and whispered kind words in her ear, her hands had been at work beneath my dolman. And here I was, at the very last step of my journey, without the power of carrying out this mission which had already deprived one good man of his life, and was likely to rob another one of his credit. What would the Emperor say when he heard that I had lost his despatches? Would the army believe it of Etienne Gerard? And when they heard that a woman's hand had coaxed them from me, what laughter there would be at mess-table and at campfire! I could have rolled upon the ground in my despair.

But one thing was certain—all this affair of the fracas in the hall and the persecution of the so-called Countess was a piece of acting from the beginning. This villainous innkeeper must be in the plot. From him I might learn who she was and where my papers had gone. I snatched my saber from the table and rushed out in search of him. But the scoundrel had guessed what I would do, and had made his preparations for me. It was in the corner of the yard that I found him, a blunderbuss in his hands and a mastiff held upon a leash by his son. The two stable-hands, with pitchforks, stood upon either side, and the wife held a great lantern behind him, so as to guide his aim.

"Ride away, sir, ride away!" he cried, with a crackling voice. "Your horse is ready, and no one will meddle with you if you go your way; but if you come against us, you are alone against three brave men."

I had only the dog to fear, for the two forks and the blunderbuss were shaking about like branches in a wind. Still, I considered that, though I might force an answer with my sword-point at the throat of this fat rascal, still I should have no means of knowing whether that answer was the truth. It would be a struggle, then, with much to lose and nothing certain to gain. I looked them up and down, therefore, in a way that set their foolish weapons shaking worse than ever, and then, throwing myself upon my mare, I galloped away with the shrill laughter of the landlady jarring upon my ears.

I had already formed my resolution. Although I had lost my papers, I could make a very good guess as to what their contents would be, and this I would say from my own lips to the Prince of Saxe-Felstein, as though the Emperor had commissioned me to convey it in that way. It was a bold stroke and a dangerous one, but if I went too far I could afterwards be disavowed. It was that or nothing, and when all Germany hung on the balance the game should not be lost if the nerve of one man could save it.

It was midnight when I rode into Hof, but every window was blazing, which was enough in itself, in that sleepy country, to tell the ferment of excitement in which the people were. There was hooting and jeering as I rode through the crowded streets, and once a stone sang past my head, but I kept upon my way, neither slowing nor quickening my pace, until I came to the palace. It was lit from base to battlement, and the dark shadows, coming and going against the yellow glare, spoke of the turmoil within. For my part, I handed my mare to a groom at the gate, and striding in I demanded, in such a voice as an ambassador should have, to see the Prince instantly, upon business which would brook no delay.

The hall was dark, but I was conscious as I entered of a buzz of innumerable voices, which hushed into silence as I loudly proclaimed my mission. Some great meeting was being held then—a meeting which, as my instincts told me, was to decide this very question of war and peace. It was possible that I might still be in time to turn the scale for the Emperor and for France. As to the major-domo, he looked blackly at me, and showing me into a small antechamber he left me. A minute later he returned to say that the Prince could not be disturbed at present, but that the Princess would take my message.

The Princess! What use was there in giving it to her? Had I not been warned that she was German in heart and soul, and that it was she who was turning her husband and her State against us?

"It is the Prince that I must see," said I.

"Nay, it is the Princess," said a voice at the door, and a woman swept into the chamber. "Von Rosen, you had best stay with us. Now, sir, what is it that you have to say to either Prince or Princess of Saxe-Felstein?"

At the first sound of the voice I had sprung to my feet. At the first glance I had thrilled with anger. Not twice in a lifetime does one meet that noble figure, that queenly head, those eyes as blue as the Garonne, and as chilling as her winter waters.

"Time presses, sir!" she cried, with an impatient tap of her foot. "What have you to say to me?"

"What have I to say to you?" I cried. "What can I say, save that you have taught me never to trust a woman more? You have ruined and dishonored me forever."

She looked with arched brows at her attendant.

"Is this the raving of fever, or does it come from some less innocent cause?" said she. "Perhaps a little blood-letting—"

"Ah, you can act!" I cried. "You have shown me that already."

"Do you mean that we have met before?"

"I mean that you have robbed me within the last two hours."

"This is past all bearing," she cried, with an admirable affectation of anger.

"You claim, as I understand, to be an ambassador, but there are limits to the privileges which such an office brings with it."

"You brazen it admirably," said I. "Your Highness will not make a fool of me twice in one night." I sprang forward and, stooping down, caught up the hem of her dress. "You would have done well to change it after you had ridden so far and so fast," said I.

It was like the dawn upon a snow-peak to see her ivory cheeks flush suddenly to crimson.

"Insolent!" she cried. "Call for the foresters and have him thrust from the palace!"

"I will see the Prince first."

"You will never see the Prince. Ah! Hold him, Von Rosen, hold him!"

She had forgotten the man with whom she had to deal—was it likely that I would wait until they could bring their rascals? She had shown me her cards too soon. Her game was to stand between me and her husband. Mine was to speak face to face with him at any cost. One spring took me out of the chamber. In another I had crossed the hall. An instant later I had burst into the great room from which the murmur of the meeting had come. At the far end I saw a figure upon a high chair under a dais. Beneath him was a line of high dignitaries, and then on every side I saw vaguely the heads of a vast assembly.

Into the center of the room I strode, my saber clanking, my shako under my arm. "I am the messenger of the Emperor," I shouted. "I bear his message to his Highness the Prince of Saxe-Felstein."

The man beneath the dais raised his head, and I saw that his face was thin and wan, and that his back was bowed as though some huge burden was balanced between his shoulders.

"Your name, sir?" he asked.

"Colonel Etienne Gerard, of the Third Hussars."

Every face in the gathering was turned upon me, and I heard the rustle of the innumerable necks and saw countless eyes without meeting one friendly one among them. The woman had swept past me, and was whispering, with many shakes of her head and dartings of her hands, into the Prince's ear. For my own part I threw out my chest and curled my moustache, glancing round in my own debonair fashion at the assembly. They were men, all of them, professors from the college, a sprinkling of their students, soldiers, gentlemen, artisans, all very silent and serious. In one corner there sat a group of men in black, with riding-coats drawn over their shoulders. They leaned their heads to each other, whispering under their breath, and with every movement I caught the clank of their sabers or the clink of their spurs.

"The Emperor's private letter to me informs that it is the Marquis Château St. Arnaud who is bearing his despatches," said the Prince.

"The Marquis has been foully murdered," I answered, and a buzz rose up from the people as I spoke. Many heads were turned, I noticed, towards the dark men in the cloaks.

"Where are your papers?" asked the Prince.

"I have none."

A fierce clamor rose instantly around me. "He is a spy! He plays a part!" they cried. "Hang him!" roared a deep voice from the corner, and a dozen others took up the shout. For my part, I drew out my handkerchief and flicked the dust from the fur of my pelisse.

The Prince held out his thin hands, and the tumult died away. "Where, then, are your credentials, and what is your message?"

"My uniform is my credential, and my message is for your private ear."

He passed his hand over his forehead with the gesture of a weak man who is at his wits' end what to do. The Princess stood beside him with her hand upon his throne, and again whispered in his ear.

"We are here in council together, some of my trusty subjects and myself," said he. "I have no secrets from them, and whatever message the Emperor may send to me at such a time concerns their interests no less than mine."

There was a hum of applause at this, and every eye was turned once more upon me. My faith, it was an awkward position in which I found myself, for it is one thing to address eight hundred hussars, and another to speak to such an audience on such a subject. But I fixed my eyes upon the Prince, and tried to say just what I should have said if we had been alone, shouting it out, too, as though I had my regiment on parade.

"You have often expressed friendship for the Emperor," I cried. "It is now at last that this friendship is about to be tried. If you will stand firm, he will reward you as only he can reward. It is an easy thing for him to turn a Prince into a King and a province into a power. His eyes are fixed upon you, and though you can do little to harm him, you can ruin yourself. At this moment he is crossing the Rhine with two hundred thousand men. Every fortress in this country is in his hands. He will be upon you in a week, and if you have played him false, God help both you and your people. You think that he is weakened because a few of us got the chilblains last winter. Look there!" I cried, pointing to a great star which blazed through the window. "That is the Emperor's star. When it wanes, he will wane—but not before."

You would have been proud of me, my friends, if you could have seen and heard me, for I clashed my saber as I spoke, and swung my dolman as though my regiment was picketed outside in the courtyard. They listened to me in silence, but the back of the Prince bowed more and more as though the burden which weighed upon it was greater than his strength.

He looked round with haggard eyes. "We have heard a Frenchman speak for France," said he. "Let us have a German speak for Germany."

The folk glanced at each other, and whispered to their neighbors. My speech, as I think, had its effect, and no man wished to be the first to commit himself in the eyes of the Emperor.

The Princess looked round her with blazing eyes, and her clear voice broke the silence. "Is a woman to give this Frenchman his answer?" she cried. "Is it possible, then, that among the night-riders of Lutzow there is none who can use his tongue as well as his saber?"

Over went a table with a crash, and a young man had bounded upon one of the chairs. He had the face of one inspired—pale, eager, with wild hawk eyes and tangled hair. His sword hung straight from his side, and his riding-boots were brown with mire.

"It is Körner!" the people cried. "It is young Körner, the poet! Ah, he will sing, he will sing."

And he sang! It was soft, at first, and dreamy, telling of old Germany, the mother of nations, of the rich, warm plains, and the grey cities, and the fame of dead heroes. But then verse after verse rang like a trumpet-call. It was of the Germany of now, the Germany which had been taken unawares and overthrown, but which was up again, and snapping the bonds upon her giant limbs. What was life that one should covet it? What was glorious death that one should shun it? The mother, the great mother, was calling. Her sigh was in the night wind. She was crying to her own children for help. Would they come? Would they come? Would they come?

Ah, that terrible song, the spirit face and the ringing voice! Where was I, and France, and the Emperor? They did not shout, these people, they howled. They were up on the chairs and tables. They were raving, sobbing, the tears running down their faces. Körner had sprung from the chair, and his comrades were round him with their sabers in the air.

A flush had come into the pale face of the Prince, and he rose from his throne. "Colonel Gerard," said he, "you have heard the answer which you are to carry to your Emperor. The die is cast, my children. Your Prince and you must stand or fall together."

He bowed to show that all was over, and the people with a shout made for the door to carry the tidings into the town. For my own part, I had done all that a brave man might, and so I was not sorry to be carried out amid the stream. Why should I linger in the palace? I had had my answer and must carry it, such as it was. I wished neither to see Hof nor its people again until I entered it at the head of a vanguard. I turned from the throng, then, and walked silently and sadly in the direction in which they had led the mare.

It was dark down there by the stables, and I was peering round for the ostler, when suddenly my two arms were seized from behind. There were hands at my wrists and at my throat, and I felt the cold muzzle of a pistol under my ear.

"Keep your lips closed, you French dog," whispered a fierce voice. "We have him, captain."

"Have you the bridle?"

"Here it is."

"Sling it over his head."

I felt the cold coil of leather tighten round my neck. An ostler with a stable lantern had come out and was gazing upon the scene. In its dim light I saw stern faces breaking everywhere through the gloom, with the black caps and dark cloaks of the night-riders.

"What would you do with him, captain?" cried a voice.

"Hang him at the Palace Gate."

"An ambassador?"

"An ambassador without papers."

"But the Prince?"

"Tut, man, do you not see that the Prince will then be committed to our side? He will be beyond all hope of forgiveness. At present he may swing round tomorrow as he has done before. He may eat his words, but a dead hussar is more than he can explain."

"No, no, Von Strelitz, we cannot do it," said another voice.

"Can we not? I shall show you that!" and there came a jerk on the bridle which nearly pulled me to the ground. At the same instant a sword flashed and the leather was cut through within two inches of my neck.

"By Heaven, Körner, this is rank mutiny," cried the captain. "You may hang yourself before you are through with it."

"I have drawn my sword as a soldier and not as a brigand," said the young poet. "Blood may dim its blade, but never dishonor. Comrades, will you stand by and see this French gentleman mishandled?"

A dozen sabers flew from their sheaths, and it was evident that my friends and my foes were about equally balanced. But the angry voices and the gleam of steel had brought the folk running from all parts.

"The Princess!" they cried. "The Princess is coming!"

And even as they spoke I saw her in front of us, her sweet face framed in the darkness. I had cause to hate her, for she had cheated and befooled me, and yet it thrilled me then and thrills me now to think that my arms have embraced her,

and that I have felt the scent of her hair in my nostrils. I know not whether she lies under the German earth, or whether she still lingers, a grey-haired woman in her Castle of Hof, but she lives ever, young and lovely, in the heart and the memory of Etienne Gerard.

"For shame!" she cried, sweeping up to me, and tearing with her own hands the noose from my neck. "You are fighting in God's own quarrel, and yet you would begin with such a devil's deed as this. This man is mine, and he who touches a hair of his head will answer for it to me."

They were glad enough to slink off into the darkness before those scornful eyes. Then she turned once more to me.

"You can follow me, Colonel Gerard," she said. "I have a word that I would speak to you."

I walked behind her to the chamber into which I had originally been shown. She closed the door, and then looked at me with the archest twinkle in her eyes.

"Is it not confiding of me to trust myself with you?" said she. "You will remember that it is the Princess of Saxe-Felstein and not the poor Countess Palotta of Poland."

"Be the name what it might," I answered, "I helped a lady whom I believed to be in distress, and I have been robbed of my papers and almost of my honor as a reward."

"Colonel Gerard," said she, "we have been playing a game, you and I, and the stake was a heavy one. You have shown by delivering a message which was never given to you that you would stand at nothing in the cause of your country. My heart is as German as yours is French, and I also would go all lengths, even to deceit and to theft, if at this crisis I can help my suffering fatherland. You see how frank I am."

"You tell me nothing that I have not seen."

"But now that the game is played and won, why should we bear malice? I will say this, that if ever I were in such a plight as that which I pretended in the inn of Lobenstein, I should never wish to meet a more gallant protector or a truer-hearted gentleman than Colonel Etienne Gerard. I had never thought that I could feel for a Frenchman as I felt for you when I slipped the papers from your breast."

"But you took them, nonetheless."

"They were necessary to me and to Germany. I knew the arguments which they contained and the effect which they would have upon the Prince. If they had reached him all would have been lost."

"Why should your Highness descend to such expedients when a score of these brigands, who wished to hang me at your castle gate, would have done the work as well?"

"They are not brigands, but the best blood of Germany!" she cried hotly. "If you have been roughly used you will remember the indignities to which every German has been subjected, from the Queen of Prussia downwards. As to why I did not have you waylaid upon the road, I may say that I had parties out on all sides, and that I was waiting at Lobenstein to hear of their success. When instead of their news you yourself arrived I was in despair, for there was only one weak woman betwixt you and my husband. You see the straits to which I was driven before I used the weapon of my sex."

"I confess that you have conquered me, your Highness, and it only remains for me to leave you in possession of the field."

"But you will take your papers with you." She held them out to me as she spoke. "The Prince has crossed the Rubicon now, and nothing can bring him back. You can return these to the Emperor and tell him that we refused to receive them. No one can accuse you then of having lost your despatches. Goodbye, Colonel Gerard, and the best I can wish you is that when you reach France you may remain there. In a year's time there will be no place for a Frenchman upon this side of the Rhine."

And thus it was that I played the Princess of Saxe-Felstein with all Germany for a stake, and lost my game to her. I had much to think of as I walked my poor, tired Violette along the highway which leads westward from Hof. But amid all the thoughts there came back to me always the proud, beautiful face of the German woman, and the voice of the soldier-poet as he sang from the chair. And I understood then that there was something terrible in this strong, patient Germany—this mother root of nations—and I saw that such a land, so old and so beloved, never could be conquered. And as I rode I saw that the dawn was breaking, and that the great star at which I had pointed through the palace window was dim and pale in the western sky.

About Pierce Egan

And now for the original swash-buckler: Robin Hood himself. Written tales of the outlaw archer extend as far back as the early 15th century, and probably existed as oral tradition long before that. But our modern idea of Robin Hood dates to the revival of the tales by Pierce Egan with the 1850 publication of *Robin Hood and Little John, or The Merry Men of Sherwood Forest*. Egan (1814-1880), known as Pierce Egan the Younger to distinguish him from his famous journalist father, was an author of popular serialized romance novels for English weeklies such as *Reynolds's Miscellany* and the *Illustrated London News*. In 1850 he decided to try his hand at a Sir Walter Scott-style historical romance, adapting and stringing together the known tales of Robin Hood and his men into an episodic novel. It was a huge success, inspiring both Howard Pyle's classic *The Merry Adventures of Robin Hood*, and an adaptation into French by no less than Alexandre Dumas *père*.

Egan's *Robin Hood and Little John* became a staple of Victorian libraries, despite—or perhaps because of—the faux-archaic style in which it's told. The book is organized as a biography of the noble outlaw, tracing his life from birth to death and including all his most famous exploits—including the following encounter between Robin and the villainous knight Sir Guy of Gisborne, one of the oldest of all the known tales of Robin Hood in Sherwood.

Robin Hood Meets Guy of Gisborne

PIERCE EGAN

It had been ascertained by the Sheriff of Nottingham that Robin Hood with half his men were away in Yorkshire, and he conceived with some shrewdness that it would be possible, with a sufficient number of men, to make an attack upon the merrie men who still remained—clear the wood of them, destroy the haunt, and lie in wait for Robin and the remainder of the men when they returned. He sent to London for a reinforcement of troops, making out a strong case of necessity for them, and they were sent to him; he organized them after his own fashion, and sent them out into the greenwood under the command of him who had brought the men from London.

The merrie men, from being connected with so many in Nottingham town, soon were aware of what was in store for them. They concerted measures accordingly, and disposed themselves to receive the troop, who marched on sanguine of success; but when they arrived at the spot where the men had prepared to meet them, they were welcomed with a shower of arrows, which committed dreadful slaughter; it was followed by a second and third, each arrow telling with a dreadful precision of aim, without the assailed knowing from whence the shafts came.

Then the merrie men rushed forth from their coverts with great shouts, and cut down all who offered resistance. A panic seized the troop at this sudden and terrible attack, and they fled without striking a blow in the greatest disorder into Nottingham, with the loss of nearly half their men. Not one of the merrie men received a hurt; they gathered together the bodies of those they had slain, and in the night bore them into the town. They laid them down at the castle gates, bidding that if the high sheriff paid them a visit in the greenwood, they would bring him home in the same fashion—an invitation which, had he received it, he would have had no hesitation in declining. He was horror-stricken at his ill success, and, while in the midst of his wailing at his misfortune, a Norman, whom he had known at Rouen, called to see him with a stout body of men. To him Sheriff Alwine detailed his disaster, and repeated a lying history of the way Robin Hood had treated him previously, and excused his own failures by swearing that Robin Hood and his men were invincible.

"Were he the devil himself," said his friend, who was called Sir Guy of Gisborne, from an estate he possessed there, "an' I took it into my head to pull his horns off, I would do it."

"Not if they were Robin Hood's," said the sheriff, who hoped to egg on Sir Guy to undertake an enterprise against the bold outlaw.

"Even if they were the devil's, I tell you," cried Sir Guy, "an' it pleased me to do it."

"Well," returned Sheriff Alwine, speaking in a careless tone, "I never knew the man who would not quail before Robin Hood."

"Then you never knew me," cried Sir Guy, with an expression of scorn.

"Oh, ho!" laughed Fitz Alwine. "He would make you quail like all the rest."

"Pshaw!" roared Sir Guy. "It is not in the power of mortal or devil to do it: I defy them both alike. Let me meet this Robin Hood, and I will cut off his ears, slit his nose, and hang him up like a swine by the feet."

"By the Mass, then," exclaimed the sheriff, "I wish you could meet with him; if you were able to do that it would serve me mightily."

"Tell me where he is to be found and I will undertake it—my head be the forfeit if I fail," cried Sir Guy.

"I have little doubt but it will," said Fitz Alwine, "for I think it is not in man's power to conquer him."

"You will see," said Sir Guy, contemptuously. "Where is this mighty man to be found?"

"He is in Barnsdale-wood, some two days' journey hence. I will accompany you, and join my men with yours. He has only half his crew there, and if we approach cautiously we shall have them all snugly."

"Be it so," returned Sir Guy, "but I will don a yeoman's garb and seek him single-handed, and then you shall find whether he or I am the most invincible."

Delighted that he had such an assistant, Sheriff Alwine set to work with alacrity; he got all his men ready, and with Sir Guy he started off to Barnsdale. It was agreed that he should lead his men to one part of the wood, and that Sir Guy, in the disguise of a yeoman, should take another, endeavor to find Robin Hood, and slay him if he could. In the event of success he was to blow a horn which had a peculiar tone to it, and thereupon the sheriff was to join him, and together they were to do the best they could to slay as many of the merrie men as they could, and take the others prisoners. With this intention, early one morning they quitted Nottingham.

Two days subsequent to this, Robin Hood, lying down beneath his trysting tree, fell into a slumber. Little John seated himself by his side and was conning over the merits of his pleasant wife, Winifred, when a woodwele—a kind of thrush—alighting on a bough above him, began singing with such extraordinary loudness that he could not but take note of it. Robin also awoke from sleep, and sprung suddenly to his feet.

"How now!" cried Little John, startled. "What is the matter, Robin?"

"Why, where am I? . . . Oh, I have been dreaming," he answered, rubbing his eyes. "I thought I was treated contumeliously by two yeomen; I threw back their scorn with interest, and we came to blows. They conquered me, beat me, bound me, and were about to slay me, when suddenly a bird alighted on a tree near me. It seemed like it was made of flame, and it spoke, bidding me be of good cheer. My bonds at that moment fell from me and I was free: then I awoke."

"It was odd," said Little John thoughtfully. "While you were sleeping, a woodwele sat itself on yon bough and sang so loud it waked you; it fled directly you moved."

"It may mean something," said Robin, scarcely allowing to himself that he was superstitious, and therefore chary of making the remark. "Warnings should never be despised, however slight; we will look about us and see what is going on."

The merrie men now drew nigh in answer to his summons, and bidding them away towards York, which was the only point from which he anticipated danger, he took Little John with him to reconnoiter one part of the wood, while Will Scarlet, with two others, went in the direction of Mansfeld.

As Robin Hood and Little John proceeded in somewhat the same direction that Will had taken, they saw a yeoman with a capul hide, or horse hide, about him as a species of cloak—not infrequently worn by Yorkshire yeomen of that day, especially those who had the charge of horses. He had a sword and dagger by his side, and looked as great a villain as he was in reality.

"Aha!" exclaimed Robin, on seeing him. "Here's a stranger. He looks a ruffian—I'll try if he be one. If he is, he has no business here, and unless he budges pretty quickly, he shall taste the quality of my weapons."

"He looks like a dog who will bite," said Little John, scanning the stranger from head to foot. "Stay, Robin, beneath this tree, and I will go ask him what he is doing here. Marry, I will make him troop quickly."

"No, Little John," uttered Robin hastily. "I have a fancy for this fellow. I have not had a bout in a long while, and by the

Holy Mother, I never would, if you had your way. You're always wishing me to send my men ahead, while I tarry behind. By St. Mary, some day I shall have to set to and beat you for mere lack of practice—except it would mean breaking a good staff, your head is of such especial thickness. No, Little John, I will trounce this knave myself, for I am sure he is one. You go to Will and bid him return; he is not far. When you hear my horn, I shall want you—but not before."

"Your will is my law," said Little John, turning away somewhat miffed because Robin would not let him fight.

Leaving Robin Hood to accost the stranger in his capul hide, we will follow Little John in his path to find Will Scarlet. He wandered on, annoyed that Robin should have taken into his own hands the task of fighting the stranger—for he easily guessed it would come to that—when he wished so much to have the pleasure himself. But a little reflection taught him that he was unjust in being offended where he had no right to take offense, so the fit passed away almost as quickly as it had come.

When he came to consider on what errand he was bound, he found he had wandered considerably out of his path; however, he bestirred himself, and was soon on the track of Will Scarlet. It was not long before he heard the clashing of weapons, as of men engaged in violent strife—he ran on in the direction of the sound, and soon came upon Will Scarlet and his two companions fighting desperately with eight or ten opponents, while the Sheriff of Nottingham advanced swiftly with a large body of men.

Little John rushed forward with a loud shout, and getting his bow ready, took aim at the sheriff in such an ecstasy of passion that the sudden force used in drawing his bow broke it. The arrow fell useless to the ground. "A curse on you and the worthless tree you came from," he cried bitterly, "to fail me at such a moment as this!"

He darted forward to help his companions. He saw one of them cut down, after opposing three most manfully without budging a foot. He seized the bow the unfortunate outlaw had dropped, took another aim at the sheriff, and exclaimed, "One shot will I shoot now that will quiet yonder rascally sheriff, who comes on so fast. He shall stop as suddenly as he advanced."

He drew the bow and loosed a shaft. The sheriff's quick eye detected the act, and he threw himself flat on his horse. A retainer close behind him, William-a-Trent, took it through his body and fell dead from his horse.

The troop pricked forward more quickly on perceiving one of their companions slain, and Little John threw himself among those who were sore pressing

Will Scarlet and his remaining comrade. He hurled one fellow to the ground like lightning, tore a spear from his grasp, and laid about him with tremendous energy and effect. Will Scarlet's companion was cut down—it was impossible to withstand so many opponents—and Will was himself hemmed in. Little John, however, who had seen the second outlaw fall, raged like a lion. He cleared Will in an instant from his assailants, and roared at him to fly.

"Never while I have breath," cried Will.

"Fly, Will, for the Holy Mother's sake!" urged Little John. "Seek Robin Hood and get together the merrie men, or there will be more true hearts this day on their backs than the green turf will be glad to receive."

Seeing the truth of Little John's words, Will made a desperate cut at one fellow who blocked his path, felling him, and then darted off to find Robin. Meanwhile Little John gave no ground and fought like a madman. But it was madness to contend with such numbers, and though his prodigious strength stood him in good stead, there were too many against him. A long staff was thrust between his legs and he was thrown; a body of men threw themselves upon him and bound him hand and foot.

There he lay until the sheriff came up. One fellow bared his sword to cut off his head, as he fully expected to receive an immediate command to that effect from Sheriff Alwine—but he did not give it. His eye lighted on Little John; with a grim smile he ordered him placed on his feet, and said to him with a chuckle, "I remember you, my forest pole—and you shall remember me before you are sent into the other world."

"I don't forget you," said Little John, gnawing his nether lip to conceal his rage and shame at being a prisoner. "I hung you like a thieving dog under your own roof. How did you relish your due? Robin Hood will be here anon—ask him if he recollects you, and note his reply."

"You mean his head will be here," said the sheriff, grinning. "His carcass will be left to rot in the greenwood—or else to make a meal for the wolves."

"It will never do that," said Little John. "You're only foretelling your own doom."

"You will find you are mistaken. I will let you live until his head is brought to me; then you shall speed after him with uncommon quickness."

"I fear your threats less than I fear you, and I fear you as I fear the miserable worm beneath my feet," returned Little John, with cool contempt.

"You shall—you shall—" The sheriff was at a loss for a simile, and wound up with, "You shall see! I will tell you your fate. You shall be wounded, but not to death, and then drawn at my horse's heels up hill and down dale, and then hung on the highest tree in these parts."

"But you may yet fail of your villainous purpose, if it pleases the Holy Son of God," said Little John quietly, "so I care not for what you say."

The sheriff intended to reply, but so many synonymous sentences rushed to his tongue, and each strove so hard to get out first, that he found himself spluttering, so he contented himself with saying nothing at all. He waved his hand for Little John to fall back among the troop, and quietly awaited the result of Sir Guy's undertaking.

We must now return to Robin Hood, who, advancing on the stranger wearing the capul hide, said to him blithely, "Good morrow, good fellow. Methinks, by the stout bow you bear in your hand, you should be a good archer."

"I have lost my way," said the stranger, not heeding Robin's question. "I know nought of this wood."

"I do, every turn," replied Robin. "I will lead you through it, if you tell me where you would go."

"I seek an outlaw whom men call Robin Hood," said the stranger. "I had rather meet with him than have the best—"

"What?" asked Robin Hood, seeing him hesitate.

"The best forty pounds that ever were coined," he replied hastily.

"If you come with me, my mighty yeoman, you shall soon see him," said Robin Hood, "but if you're in no exceeding haste, we will have some little pastime beneath the greenwood trees here. We may find this Robin Hood at some unlooked-for time, for I can tell you he is not always to be met when sought after. Let us try our skill at woodcraft."

Robin cut down the thin boughs of several shrubs, pared off the leaves, and then stuck them upright in the ground at some distance apart. "Now, yeoman," he said, "see if you can hit with your arrow, from sixty yards, either of those wands. Lead off, and I will follow your shot."

"Nay, good fellow," replied the stranger, "if you ask me to do what seems impossible, you had better lead off, and if it is to be done, show how you do it."

Robin shot without appearing to take aim, and his arrow went within an inch of one narrow wand—so close, indeed, that the stranger thought he had hit it. But Robin told him he had not, and made him go on. After several ineffectual essays, the stranger confessed that he could not come within a foot of the target.

Robin then made a small garland of wild flowers and hung it upon one of the wands, bidding the yeoman send his arrow through its center. He took a long aim at it, and the arrow went through the garland, just ruffling the inner edge. "Well shot!" said Robin. "But not well enough for a yeoman. You see the thin slip of wand which shows itself through the center of the garland? I will cleave it with my arrow."

"It cannot be done," said the stranger.

"Behold!" cried Robin, his arrow leaving his bow almost as soon as the words left his lips.

"Wonderfully done!" cried the stranger, decidedly astonished. "Why, good yeoman, if your heart be as stout as your hand, you are better than this same Robin Hood they talk so much of. What is your name, that I may remember who has so astonished me with his expertise at the bow?"

"Nay, by my faith," said Robin jovially, "let me know yours, and I will not withhold mine."

"I have a good estate to the west," replied the stranger, "and am called after it Sir Guy of Gisborne. You may marvel to see me in this unknightly apparel, but I have sworn to take Robin Hood, and I thought of this disguise as being likely to bring me into his presence. Now, what is your name, yeoman?"

"I have a good estate here," replied Robin. "I have one also in Nottinghamshire, and one in Huntingdonshire—though that one is kept from me. I am one who cares for or fears no man, especially one such as you. I am he you seek—my name is Robin Hood."

"Then here you shall die," cried Sir Guy, drawing his sword, "and this horn will convey news of your defeat to those near at hand who will be glad to hear of it. Say your prayers, Robin Hood; for come what may, I will not spare you. I have sworn to take back your head, and by Satan, I will!"

"When you have conquered me, you can do what you will with my body," said Robin coolly. "But mark my words, Sir Guy—you have sworn not to spare me, and if the Blessed Virgin gives me the victory, I will not spare you. For you are a Norman, and that seals your doom. Come on! No quarter: life for the victor, death to the vanquished!"

Not a word more passed between them, and they set to work in good earnest. Sir Guy of Gisborne, in addition to great personal strength, was an accomplished swordsman, and with these qualities he possessed a ruthless stony nature, which would induce him to take every advantage to draw blood, no matter how unknightly or unfair the act, or whether it gained him any advantage. Acting in this spirit, he attacked Robin before he had even drawn his sword. Robin leaped back to avoid him, and soon had his trusty blade opposed to the knight's; but he lost ground by it, and was forced close to the straggling roots of an oak tree. Sir Guy pressed him hard, for he well knew he had the advantage of the ground, and he determined to make the most of it. His blows rained hard and fast, delivered with such force, that Robin at each moment expected his own blade to shiver at the hilt—but it was a stout blade, and bore all the blows nobly.

Robin quickly found that, if he remained much longer in his present position, he was certain to be slain. He therefore resolved to use his best efforts to extricate himself, and in his turn attacked Sir Guy. But the knight stood like a rock, and budged not a foot, though Robin kept him well employed in defending himself.

Soon Robin saw that, without the most tremendous exertion, he could not gain his point—and as that might tell against him even if he were successful, he determined to leap lightly to one side, and then edge round and try to place Sir Guy in the same position he had just left. No sooner had he come to the conclusion than he determined to act upon it, and just as Sir Guy was delivering a heavy blow, he leaped aside—but his foot caught in a root of the tree and he fell to the ground.

Sir Guy was not the man to let such an opportunity pass, and with a shout he sprang on his prostrate opponent, with the intention of putting an end to the contest at once. Robin cried earnestly, "Holy Mother of God! Dear Lady! It is no man's destiny to die before the time allotted him in this world, and my hour has not yet come. Give me strength to win this fight, or die as becomes a man and a true Saxon."

As he uttered these words he felt a sudden vigor pass into his limbs, every sinew seemed strengthened, and dexterously avoiding the fierce blow Sir Guy made at him, he leaped upon his feet and took the position Sir Guy had previously possessed. He made the most of it, and the clashing of their weapons grew fiercer than ever.

At last Robin, making a powerful parry to a blow delivered by Sir Guy with terrific strength, succeeded in whirling his sword from his grasp, and of burying his own like lightning in his heart. Sir Guy clenched his hands convulsively and fell dead without a groan.

When Robin saw that he had slain his opponent, he offered up a prayer of thankfulness for his success. Then he bethought him of what Sir Guy had said about bearing his head to those who were near, and who would be glad to hear the tones of the horn which was to convey the news of his defeat.

"By the Mass!" he cried. "It will be as well to see who these folks are that are so near, and with that capul hide I may disguise myself well enough for my purpose. Now, Sir Guy, with your permission we will change clothes, and lose no time about it, for every moment wasted may be of consequence to those connected with me."

So saying, he stripped Sir Guy's body of such habiliments as he deemed necessary, and divesting himself of his own corresponding garments, he clothed himself in the dead man's garb, and threw the capul hide across his shoulders, as he had seen Sir Guy wear it. Then, for fear the strangers might come and discover the body of their friend while Robin was looking for them, he dressed Sir Guy in his clothes. He then cut off his head, which he gashed in the face so that it might not be recognized, and bore it with him in order to make his disguise more complete.

When he had made all his arrangements, he looked upon the body of Sir Guy and exclaimed, "Lie you there, Sir Guy, lie you there! You have nothing to complain of. I have done for you what you strove with all your might to do to me, so be not wrathful that I have prevailed. For, beshrew me, if you took the hardest knocks, you ended with the better garments—the best Lincoln cloth 'stead of your Yorkshire woolen. Now I will see what the effect of your little horn will be, for I will blow a lusty blast. I know not if there be any signal agreed upon, but I will take my chances."

He blew a loud blast, and the horn having a peculiar tone, he concluded there was nothing more needed to distinguish it from any others. It was heard and replied to, and no sooner did the return strike upon his ear than he hastened in the direction it came from. He was soon close to the sheriff and his party, and blew a second blast on Sir Guy's horn.

"Hark!" cried Sheriff Alwine joyfully. "That betokens good tidings! It is Sir Guy's horn; he has slain Robin Hood, the vile outlaw."

"A hundred Sir Guys could not do it, if he fought fairly and like a man!" roared Little John, with the horrible misgiving that the sheriff was speaking the truth—especially as he saw Robin coming down the glade, clad in the capul hide and imitating Sir Guy's bearing closely. "Give me a quarterstaff and let him take his blade, the best steel ever forged, and I will defeat him, if he has slain Robin. And if he has, there are as many hands as there are hairs on his head who will revenge it. He has used some vile means to gain his ends, which no honest man would stoop to."

"Say your prayers, dog!" cried the sheriff. "Your master is slain, and so shall you be. Better to spend your remaining moments in prayer than to rail at a noble-hearted knight who has slain your doughty leader as easily as cutting down a reed. Come hither, come hither, gallant Sir Guy!" he continued, addressing Robin Hood, whom he saw advancing quickly to him. "You have conquered the outlaw— you have delivered your country from the most monstrous villain the world e'er saw—you have slain Robin Hood! Ask what you will of me that I can grant, and it shall be yours."

Robin Hood, at a glance, had seen Little John's situation, and smiled as he encountered the fierce look of defiance and hatred which the latter threw at him, supposing him to be the slayer of his beloved friend and leader. The words of the sheriff, to Robin's ear, carried with them the means of extricating Little John from his situation. He said, "I have slain him who would have slain me, and since you give me the power of asking a boon of you, I ask but a blow at yonder knave, whom you have there bound. I have slain one; let me see if I cannot prevail over the other."

"If you wish to kill him with your own hand," answered the sheriff, not noticing the change of voice, because he never for an instant supposed that he could be deceived in this manner, "you can, if you like. But this is no boon; ask something else of me."

"I need no other," replied Robin.

"Then you shall have your will; his life is yours."

"I will shrive him first," said Robin. "Then I will loose his bonds and fight with him"

Little John, though he had not detected our hero in his disguise, knew him as soon as he heard his voice, and was in that moment relieved from the most terrible weight of anguish he had ever felt. He gave a long sigh, the effect of his relief, and waited patiently and quietly until Robin matured his plan, whatever it might be.

He was not long left in uncertainty, for Robin approached him with some haste; but on finding that the sheriff, with several of his followers, were close upon his heels, he stopped and said abruptly, "Stand back! Stand back, all of you! Did I not say I was going to hear his shrift before I fought with him? And you all know it is not the custom, nor right, that more than one should hear another's shrift. Stand back, I tell you, or I may trounce some of you, even as I have he whose headless carcass lies in yonder glade! There, dogs! Take it, and glut your eyes with the head of him who had a stouter heart than any hound among you!"

So saying, he threw the gashed head of Sir Guy into the sheriff's arms, who instantly threw it among his men as if it had been a ball of red-hot iron. None of them were more eager than their lord to possess it, and it fell to the ground to be kicked from one to the other.

Robin had no occasion to say another word; the men, accompanied by the sheriff, fell back to a more respectful distance, quite as much—possibly more—due to his promise to trounce them than out of respect for a man's shriving. Robin, as soon as he saw them as far as he considered essential for his purpose, approached Little John, and with a forest knife cut loose his bonds, placed in his hands the bow and quiver of arrows he had taken from Sir Guy (he still retained his own), and then blew a call on his own bugle— the one that summoned the merrie men.

He had scarce blown it when a loud shout rang in the air, and Will Scarlet, with a face like his name, came bounding into sight, sword in hand, followed by a body of the merrie men. The sight of this came upon the sheriff's vision like a horrible dream; but it quickly assumed the appearance of reality when Robin threw off the capul hide and declared his name, while Little John fitted an arrow to Sir Guy's bow and drew it to the head, awaiting only Robin's order to discharge it.

Then the sheriff "fettled him to be gone," and without stopping to give a command to his men, spurred his horse hard and dashed off at full gallop. The men were not long in following his example.

"May the foul fiend have a speedy grip of him!" cried Little John, gnashing his teeth. "But his cowardice shall not save him. I'll bring him down from here." And he prepared to discharge his arrow.

"Hold your hand!" exclaimed Robin. "Do not take his life—he has but a little while to live, according to nature; it is of little use to shorten his time here."

"Robin, I cannot let the old rogue escape scatheless," cried Little John. "I will not kill him, since you wish me not to, but I will give him something to remind him of us for some time to come."

As he concluded he discharged his arrow, and judging from the leap which Sheriff Alwine gave from the saddle, and the energetic speed with which he drew the arrow from where it had hit him, there is little doubt he would find either sitting or riding disagreeable for some time.

With congratulations upon the narrow escape which he had just had for his life, and at which he laughed almost contemptuously, Little John was led by the merrie men to the haunt in Barnsdale Wood, and the remainder of the day was passed in joyous festivity.

The Buccaneer's Last Shot

(STORMING OF FORT SAN LORENZO, AT THE MOUTH OF THE
CHAGRES RIVER, JANUARY, 1671) ·

FARNHAM BISHOP

Back fell the beaten buccaneers,
Back to the foot of the blood-stained hill.
Loud rang the Spanish garrison's cheers,
But a buccaneer was hard to kill!

A bow-string twanged on the castle wall;
In a pirate's breast the shaft sank home;
Prone on his face fell the rover tall,
Spitting curses and bloody foam.

He seized the arrow and plucked it out,
With never a wince at the fearful pain.
He wrapped the shaft in a cotton clout,
A vengeful thought in his dying brain.

Into his musket he rammed it tight,
And shot it back with a hunter's aim.
Lit by the flash and fanned by the flight,
The arrow flew in an arc of flame.

A thatch-roofed barrack, a well-hit mark,
A magazine with an open door;
A crackling blaze and a flying spark,
A blinding flash and a rending roar!

With no more strength than a little child
(The blood flowed fast and the end was near),
Patting his musket, he grimly smiled
And died the death of a buccaneer!

From *Adventure* magazine, June 18th, 1920.

About Alexandre Dumas

Alexandre Dumas, the 900-pound gorilla of historical adventure fiction, began his career as a playwright and poet. In 1839 he took up writing novels, and in 1844 he knocked it out of the park with *The Three Musketeers*, followed in the next year by *The Count of Monte Cristo*. Both books were worldwide sensations, and for the next fifteen years he could do no wrong; he wrote novel after successful novel, made multiple fortunes and threw them all away, being as much larger than life as his creations.

By 1865, his first fame past, Dumas was writing whatever would sell. Jules Noriac, editor of the weekly *Les Nouvelles*, needed a novel for serial publication, and asked Dumas if he would be willing to revisit the setting of his earliest success, *The Three Musketeers*. Dumas, who had not lost his fascination with the reign of Louis XIII and his prime minister, Cardinal Richelieu, was quick to accept. The result was *Le Comte de Moret*, a swashbuckling tale of King Louis, his adventurous half-brother Moret, and Cardinal Richelieu.

Especially Cardinal Richelieu; the novel is as much about Richelieu as it is about the Comte de Moret, and indeed its alternate title is *The Red Sphinx*. The focus on the Cardinal explains why Dumas refused to include appearances by d'Artagnan and his three Musketeer friends, as they would surely have walked away with the story. In any event, between *The Three Musketeers*, *Twenty Years Later*, *The Vicomte de Bragelonne*, and *The Man in the Iron Mask*, Dumas had already written over a million words about d'Artagnan and company. Why flog a dead horse?

That decision to leave out d'Artagnan and his famous friends probably accounts for how *Le Comte de Moret* fell between the cracks of history. It had but a single 19th-century translation into English that is now lost, and the novel wasn't even revived in France until 1946. For this volume, your editor has newly translated six chapters from the climax of the novel and distilled them into a short story, which I think displays a work that has been unfairly overlooked—till now.

Historically, Louis XIII's winter crossing of the Alps and the forcing of Susa Pass occurred very much as Dumas described it—with the exception of the critical involvement of the Comte de Moret. Was Moret, in fact, involved in King Louis' Alpine campaign? The historical record is a blank on this question. But you can't prove he *wasn't* there, and that was good enough for Dumas.

White Plume on the Mountain

ALEXANDRE DUMAS

TRANSLATED AND EDITED BY LAWRENCE ELLSWORTH

In Italy, the Duke of Mantua had died without an immediate heir. Related by marriage, the leading contender to rule the duchy was Charles de Gonzague, the French Duc de Nevers. King Louis XIII and Cardinal Richelieu supported him as new Duke of Mantua, but Spain championed another, and began to mobilize her troops in northern Italy. In Montferrat, an outlier of Mantua—and long coveted by the Duke of Savoy—the key fortification of Casale was placed under siege by Spanish forces.

Persuaded by Richelieu to act, Louis XIII decided to mobilize his forces to cross Savoy and come to the aid of Nevers in Mantua. After making this pact with the cardinal, the king left his eminence's study. In the antechamber he met Monsieur de Bassompierre, who had come to pay his respects to the cardinal. Seeing him, the king stopped and returned to Richelieu, who had escorted him to the door. "Hold, Monsieur le Cardinal," said the King, "here's one who will go with us and doubtless serve me well."

The cardinal smiled and gestured approvingly. "It is Monsieur le Maréchal's way," he said.

"Will your majesty excuse my ill manners in asking where I am to accompany you?" inquired Bassompierre.

"To Italy," said the king, "where I shall personally raise the siege of Casale. Prepare to depart, Monsieur Marshal. Take Créqui with you; he knows that country and hopefully will tell us all about it."

"Sire," replied Bassompierre with a bow, "I am your servant and will follow you to the end of the world—and even the moon, should it please you to ascend there."

"We will go neither so far nor so high, marshal. We rendezvous in Grenoble. If anything delays your joining the campaign, inform Monseigneur le Cardinal."

"Sire," said Bassompierre, "with God's aid, nothing will go amiss—especially if your majesty will order that old scoundrel de Vieuville to pay me what I'm owed as Colonel-General of the Swiss Guard."

The King laughed. "If Vieuville won't pay you," he said, "then Monsieur le Cardinal will."

"Indeed?" said the skeptical Bassompierre.

"Indeed, Monsieur le Maréchal. In fact, if you'd like to present me with your bill, you will leave here with your money. We depart in three or four days and have no time to lose."

"Monsieur le Cardinal," said Bassompierre, with that air of grand nobility unique to him, "when I go to play with the king I never carry cash with me. If you please, give me the honor to leave the bill with you, and I will send a lackey later to pick up the money."

The king departed. Bassompierre gave his bill to the Cardinal, and sent for the money the next day.

The king had previously bestowed on Monsieur, his younger brother, the title of Lieutenant General; but from the moment the cardinal rejoined the king, it was apparent that it would be Richelieu who would manage the conduct of the war, and that the Lieutenancy General was nothing but a sinecure. So, though Monsieur sent his train by way of Montargis and then followed it beyond Moulins, upon arrival at Chavagnes he changed his mind and announced to Bassompierre that, considering the insult he had been offered, he was withdrawing to his principality of Dombes where he would await the orders of the king. Bassompierre implored him to reconsider, but could get nothing from him.

No one was surprised by Monsieur's decision, most seeing in it cowardice rather than wounded pride.

As the Duke of Mantua learned through the ambassador, the cardinal and the king left Paris on January 4, and on Thursday the 15th had dined in Moulins and supped at Varenne. The King crossed Lyon quickly, but was stopped in Grenoble by an outbreak of the plague.

On Monday, February 19, he sent to the Marquis de Thoiras in Vienna to come join the army and oversee the passage of the artillery over the mountains.

The Duc de Montmorency had, on his part, informed the king that he would come by Nîmes, Sisteron, and Gap, joining the king at Briançon.

It was there that the real troubles began. Queen Anne and the queen mother both opposed war with Spain; on the pretext that they feared for the health of the king, but actually to subvert the influence of the cardinal, they had left Paris with the aim of joining the king in Grenoble. But he had ordered them to stop in Lyon, and they dared not disobey. However, in Lyon they made all the trouble they could, diverting Créqui's attention from preparing for the passage of the mountains, and delaying Guise from joining the fleet. But nothing discouraged the cardinal: so long as the king was his ally, the king was his strength. He hoped that the king, by taking the personal risk of crossing the Alpine passes in winter, would attract from the neighboring provinces the help they needed—and it had been working before the two queens began to interfere.

When they got to Briançon, it was clear that the two queens' meddling had been so successful that nothing that was supposed to be there had arrived: no food, no mules, almost no ammunition, and no more than a dozen cannon.

Worse, there were only 200,000 francs left of the million the cardinal had borrowed.

All this, while opposing the king was the Duke of Savoy, the most wily and deceitful prince of his time. He held Susa Pass, the way across the Alps to Casale and Mantua.

None of these obstacles stopped the cardinal for a moment. He convened their most skillful engineers and sought with them the means of doing everything men's arms could do. Charles VIII had been the first to carry cannon across the Alps, but that had been in good weather; it was hard enough to cross these almost inaccessible mountains in the summer, let alone the winter. They affixed cables to the artillery and attached them to pulleys and winches; some men cranked winches, others hauled cables by hand. The cannon balls were hoisted up in baskets; barrels containing ammunition, powder, and more balls were loaded onto mules, bought at a ruinous price.

In six days all this equipment was brought over Mont Genève and down to Oulx. The cardinal pushed on to Chaumont, where he hastily gathered what information he could and checked it against the intelligence gathered by the Comte de Moret.

It was there that, upon reckoning all the ammunition, he was told there were only seven cartridges per man. "What of that," Richelieu replied, "so long as Susa is taken with the fifth?"

Meanwhile rumors of these preparations reached the ears of Charles-Emmanuel, the Duke of Savoy; but the king and the cardinal were already in Briançon while Savoy thought them still in Lyon. Consequently he sent his son, Victor-Amadeus, to wait on King Louis XIII in Grenoble; but once in Grenoble, he learned that King Louis had already left and was at that hour crossing the mountains.

Victor-Amadeus set out at once in pursuit of the king and the cardinal. He caught up with Louis XIII at Oulx and asked for an audience, just as the last pieces of artillery were descending from the pass.

The king received him, but refused to listen to him and sent him on to the cardinal. Victor-Amadeus left immediately for Chaumont. There the Prince of Savoy, raised by a master of the ruse, hoped to use on the cardinal the methods familiar to himself and his father—but this time he was outfaced, a serpent against a lion.

The cardinal understood from the prince's first words that the Duke of Savoy had but one reason for sending his son, and that was to gain time. But where the king might have been taken in, the cardinal saw clearly the negotiator's intentions.

Victor-Amadeus came to ask for time so his father could find a way out of the promise he'd made to the Governor of Milan not to allow French troops to cross his domain. But even as he began to formulate his request, the cardinal forestalled him. "Your pardon, my prince," he said to him, "but His Highness the Duke of Savoy asks for time to repudiate a promise he was in no position to give."

"How is that?" asked the prince.

"Because, in his recent negotiations with France, he verbally agreed to allow my master the king passage through his domain, if needed to support his allies."

"But," said Victor-Amadeus, taken aback, "it's I who must beg pardon of your eminence, as I have seen this clause nowhere in the treaties between France and Savoy."

"And you are well aware why you have not seen it, prince. Because of the respect due the duke, your father, one is satisfied with his word of honor and does not

require his signature. According to him, the King of Spain had taken offense that he had granted such a privilege to France and gave him not a moment's rest until he'd obtained a similar right."

"But," ventured Victor-Amadeus, "the duke my father does not refuse passage to the king your master."

"Then," said the Cardinal, smiling as he recalled the details of the letter received from the Comte de Moret, "is it to honor the King of France that His Highness the Duke of Savoy has closed the pass of Susa with a demi-lune bastion large enough for three hundred, backed up by barricades with room for three hundred more, and on top of this the Fort of Montabon, built between two redoubts with outworks placed to create a crossfire? Is it to facilitate the passage of the king and the army of France that, beyond the difficulties presented by blocking the valley, boulders so large that no machine could move them have been rolled down into the road? Is it to plant trees and flowers along our path that for the last six weeks, three hundred workers have plied pickaxe and spade at work that has attracted visits from both you and your august father?

"No, prince, let us not mince words: speak frankly, as rulers should. You delay in order to give the Spanish enough time to take Casale, whose garrison is heroically dying of hunger. *Eh bien!* As it is in our interest, and is our duty, to rescue this garrison, we say to you: your father, Monseigneur le Duc, owes us this passage, and your father the duke will give it to us.

"We need two days for the rest of our materiel to arrive." The cardinal drew his watch. "It is eleven in the morning. Eleven in the morning, the day after tomorrow, will be on Tuesday; Wednesday at dawn we attack. You may take it as written. Now, whether you go to open the passage, or to prepare to defend it, you have no time to spare for reflection, so I will not keep you. A frank and open peace, monseigneur—or a good war."

"I fear it will be the good war, Monsieur le Cardinal," said Victor-Amadeus, rising.

"From the Christian point of view, and as a minister of the Lord, I hate war; but from the political point of view and as a minister of France, I think that sometimes war, though not a good thing, is a necessary thing.

"France is within its rights and will have them respected. When two states come to blows, bad luck comes to he who champions deceit and perfidy. God sees us; God will judge."

The cardinal saluted the prince, making it clear that further talk was futile. France would march on Casale, and no matter what obstacles arose, the path was irrevocably taken.

Victor-Amadeus had scarcely left when the cardinal approached a table and wrote the following letter:

Sire,

If your majesty, as God gives me to hope, has fortunately completed transport of our materiel over the mountains, I humbly beg you will order the artillery, caissons, and all machines of war brought immediately to Chaumont. We pray the king will have the kindness to proceed here without delay, as the day of hostilities is to be Wednesday—subject to the will of your majesty, though it were best not changed without good reason.

I eagerly await your majesty's response—or better still, your majesty himself.

I send a reliable man upon whom his majesty can depend for anything, even as an escort should his majesty choose to travel incognito by night.

I have the honor to be,
For your majesty,
Your most humble subject and most devoted servant,
Armand, Cardinal de RICHELIEU

Once the letter was written and folded, the cardinal called, "Étienne!"

At once the door of the room opened, and on the threshold appeared our old acquaintance Étienne Lathil, last seen entering the cardinal's study in Chaillot, pale, knees trembling, supporting himself against the wall, and sadly offering his devotion. But now with head high, bristling moustache, a spring in his step, hat in his right hand and the left on the pommel of his sword, he was once again that captain who might have stepped out of a sketch by Callot.

It had been fully four months since, struck at the same time by the Marquis Pisani and by Souscarrières, he had fallen unconscious to the floor of the *Maître Soleil* inn. However, if a wound isn't fatal, it's not long before a man put together like Étienne Lathil is back on his feet, hardier and heartier than ever.

The imminent hostilities lent a gaiety to his face that did not escape the cardinal. "Étienne," he said to him, "mount your horse this instant—unless you'd prefer, for your own reasons, to travel by foot—but however you will, this letter, which is of the highest importance, must reach the king before ten this evening."

"Would your eminence tell me what time it is?"

The cardinal drew his watch. "It is nearly noon."

"And the king is in Oulx?"

"Yes."

"Unless I plunge down the Doire, the king will have his letter by eight."

"Try not to plunge down the Doire, as that would cause me grief, whereas if the king receives his letter, I'll be pleased."

"I shall hope to satisfy your eminence on both points."

The cardinal knew Lathil for a man of his word, so judging that it was pointless to insist, he merely made a gesture of dismissal.

Lathil ran to the stable to choose a good horse, stopping at the smithy only long enough to have it shod with crampons; that business finished, he sprang on its back and launched himself down the road to Oulx.

He found the track in better condition than he'd expected. With the aim of making it passable for the cannons and other equipment, the pioneers had done everything feasible to improve it.

By four o'clock Étienne was at Saint-Laurent, and by half past seven he was at Oulx.

The king was at supper, served by Saint-Simon, who had succeeded Barabas in his favor. At the foot of the table was his fool and confidant, Angely. The message from the cardinal was announced, and immediately the king ordered that the messenger be brought before him.

Lathil was fully conversant with all forms of etiquette, having spent his time as a page of the Duc d'Épernon, and thus was no man to let himself be intimidated by royal majesty. He entered boldly into the room, advanced toward the king, placed one knee on the ground, and presented him his hat with the cardinal's letter balanced atop it.

Louis XIII watched this with a certain astonishment: Lathil had followed the rules of etiquette of the old-time court. *"Ouais!"* he said, taking the note. "Where do you come by these fine manners, my master?"

"Is not this the fashion, Sire, in which one presented letters to your illustrious father, of glorious memory?"

"Indeed! But the mode is a trifle passé."

"The respect is the same, Sire, so it seemed to me the etiquette should be the same."

"You seem well versed in etiquette for a soldier."

"I began as page to Monsieur le Duc d'Épernon, and in that time I more than once had the honor to present a letter to Henri IV in the manner I have now had the honor to present one to his son."

"Page to the Duc d'Épernon," repeated the King.

"And like him, Sire, I was on the running board of the carriage on May 14, 1610, in the Rue de la Ferronnerie, when Henri IV was slain; Your Majesty may have heard that it was a page that stopped the assassin by holding onto his cloak despite the knife-blows that slashed his hands."

"Yes. . . . This page, would he be you, by any chance?"

Lathil, still on one knee before the king, drew off his deerskin gloves, revealing hands furrowed by scars. "Sire, see my hands," he said.

The king looked at the man with visible emotion, and said, "These hands are the hands of loyalty. Give me your hands, *mon brave*." And taking Lathil's hands in his own, he gripped them. "Now, rise," he said.

Lathil rose. "A great king, Sire, was King Henri IV," he said.

"Yes, and God give me the grace to resemble him."

"The opportunity is here, Sire," replied Lathil, indicating the note he had brought him.

"Let us see," said the king, opening the letter.

"Ah!" he said, after reading it. "Monsieur le Cardinal says that he has engaged our honor, and that whether we disengage it or not, the matter will not wait. . . . Saint-Simon, inform Messieurs Créqui and Bassompierre that I must speak with them this very moment."

The two marshals were lodged in a house adjacent to that of the king, and were alerted within minutes; of the two other commanders, Monsieur de Schomberg was at Exilles, and Monsieur de Montmorency at Saint-Laurent.

The king conveyed the contents of Richelieu's letter to the two marshals, and ordered them to get the artillery and munitions to Chaumont as quickly as possible, declaring that everything must be at Chaumont by the end of the next day.

As for the marshals, he would expect them Tuesday evening so they could take part in a council of war, in which they would decide the mode of attack for the following day.

At ten o'clock that evening, in a murky night swirling with snow, without moon or stars, the king departed on horseback for Chaumont accompanied only by Lathil, Saint-Simon, and Angely. Having prepared his own horse for ice, Lathil now took the same precautions with the king's horse. Then he set out on that route for the third time, leading on foot and probing the road.

Never had the king displayed such a bold demeanor, nor been so satisfied with himself. If he didn't have the strength of character for actual grandeur, he at least had a sense of it. He wore his hat with the black plumes, and thought of the white plumes his father had worn during Henri IV's great victory at Ivry. If his son could change his black plume for a white plume, why couldn't Susa be his Ivry?

Lathil marched before the King's horse, sounding the road with an iron-shod staff, stopping from time to time to find better footing, taking the horse by the bridle and leading him over bad spots. At each guard post the king was recognized, and he gave the order to prepare the troops to march on Chaumont, enjoying in their obedience one of the sweetest prerogatives of power.

Just short of Saint-Laurent Lathil had an intimation, from the sharpness of the north wind, of the approach of one of those sudden whirlwinds that are dubbed in the mountains a "snowplow." He invited the king to dismount and shelter between Saint-Simon, Angely and himself, but the king wanted to stay on his horse, saying that if events called for him to be a soldier, he would act like a soldier. Consequently, he wrapped himself in his cloak and waited.

The whirlwind didn't keep them waiting long; it came on with a whine.

Angely and Saint-Simon pressed themselves in on either side of the king, who was wrapped in his cloak. Lathil seized the horse's bit with both hands and turned his back to the hurricane.

It arrived, terrible and howling.

The riders felt their horses tremble between their legs: in such cataclysms of nature, the animals share the fright of man. The silk ribbon which held on the king's hat parted, and the black felt with its black plumes disappeared into the darkness like a night-bird. In an instant, the road was covered with snow two feet deep.

Upon arrival at Saint-Laurent, the king inquired after the lodging of Monsieur de Montmorency. It was one o'clock in the morning; Monsieur de Montmorency had thrown himself fully clothed onto his bed. At the first word of the king's presence the duke sprang back up and stood in his doorway, awaiting the king's orders.

Such promptness pleased Louis XIII, and though not overly fond of Monsieur de Montmorency, who had at one time been enamored of the queen, he saluted him.

The duke offered to accompany the king and provide him with an escort. But Louis XIII replied that he was on the ground of France, and so long as he was on the ground of France he felt safe; the escort he had seemed sufficient, being entirely devoted. He merely invited Monsieur de Montmorency to make his way to Chaumont in time for the council of war to be held at nine o'clock the following evening.

The only thing he agreed to accept was another hat. When placing it on its head he realized that it had three white plumes, and once again he recalled Ivry. "It's a sign of good luck," he said.

Upon leaving Saint-Laurent, the snow was so deep that Lathil invited the king to come down from his horse. The king dismounted. Lathil led, taking the king's horse by the bridle; Angely came after, then Saint-Simon. Louis XIII thus had a path to follow leveled for him by three men and three horses.

Saint-Simon, who felt obliged to the cardinal for the favors he'd done him, praised to the king all the precautions Richelieu had taken and all the foresight he had shown. "Yes, yes," answered Louis XIII, "Monsieur le Cardinal is a good servant; I doubt that my brother, in his place, would have taken so many pains for me."

Two hours later the king arrived without incident at the door of the hôtel *Genèvrier d'Or* in Chaumont, as proud of his lost hat as of a wound, as proud of his night march as of a victory. He remarked that no one need awaken the cardinal.

"His eminence is not asleep," replied Maître Germain.

"And what is he doing at this hour?" asked the king.

"I work for the glory of your majesty," said the cardinal as he appeared, "and Monsieur de Pontis aids me with all his power in this glorious work."

And the cardinal invited the king into his room, where he found a large fire lit to heat it, and an immense map of the country, drawn up by Monsieur de Pontis, unrolled on a table.

One of the great strengths of the cardinal was not to believe King Louis XIII had virtues that he lacked, but nonetheless to make the king think he had them.

Lazy and languid, he made the king believe he was active; timid and distrustful, he made him believe he was brave; cruel and bloodthirsty, he made him believe he was just.

Richelieu said that, though the king's presence was not urgently required in

Chaumont at that hour of the night, still he had exalted his glory and that of France by having made the trek, in such times, on such roads and in the middle of such deep darkness, to answer the call of the nation. However, now the king must take to bed on the instant, as the day just beginning and the one to follow remained ahead of him.

By daybreak the orders had been given all along the route, so that the troops bivouacked in Saint-Laurent, in Exilles, and in Séhault were all under way toward Chaumont.

The four top commanders were the Duc de Montmorency and the three marshals: de Créqui, de Bassompierre, and de Schomberg.

The genius of the cardinal planned it all; he conceived, the king ordered.

As we have already told the story of the siege of La Rochelle, that glorious climax of the reign of Louis XIII, in our book *The Three Musketeers*, we are here permitted to dwell on some of the details of the famous forcing of the Pass of Susa, about which the official historians have made much ado.

Upon leaving Richelieu, Victor-Amadeus, to cover his exit, as they say in the theater, had announced that he was leaving for Rivoli where the duke, his father, awaited him, and that in twenty-four hours he would announce Charles-Emmanuel's decision; but when

he arrived in Rivoli the Duke of Savoy, whose one goal was to draw things out, had departed for Turin.

Thus around five in the evening, instead of Victor-Amadeus it was Savoy's prime minister, the Count of Verrue, who was announced in the house of the cardinal. At this, the cardinal turned to the king. "Would your majesty," he asked, "accept the honor of receiving him, or will you leave this burden to me?"

"If it was Prince Victor-Amadeus I'd receive him; but since the Duke of Savoy deems it appropriate to send me his prime minister, it is only right that my prime minister should answer him."

"Then does the king give me *carte blanche*?" asked the cardinal.

"Entirely."

"If the door is left open," continued Richelieu, "your majesty will hear the entire exchange, and if anything I say displeases him, he will be free to appear and contradict me."

Louis XIII gave a nod of assent. Richelieu, leaving the door open, went in the chamber where the Count of Verrue awaited.

This Count of Verrue, whom history barely mentions, was a man of forty years, acute, discerning, and of proven courage. Charged with a difficult mission, he brought an essential candor to the tortuous negotiations required of an emissary of Charles-Emmanuel.

Seeing the grave figure of the cardinal, with that eye that saw to the bottom of hearts, faced with this genius who alone held in check the other sovereigns of Europe, he bowed deeply and respectfully. "Monseigneur," he said, "I come in place of Prince Victor-Amadeus, who is needed at the side of the duke, his father, who has fallen seriously ill. When his son, after having left your eminence, arrived last night at Rivoli, he found his father had been taken to Turin."

"Then, Monsieur le Comte," said Richelieu, "you come charged with the full powers of the Duke of Savoy?"

"I come to announce that I precede his arrival, monseigneur; ill as he is, the Duke of Savoy wants to plead his case to his majesty in person. He is being carried here in a sedan chair."

"And when do you think he will arrive, Monsieur le Comte?"

"His Highness' state of weakness, and the slowness of his means of transport, means that, in my opinion, he can be here no sooner than the day after tomorrow."

"And about what hour?"

"I wouldn't dare to promise before noon."

"I am in despair, Monsieur le Comte: I told Prince Victor-Amadeus that on that day at daybreak we would attack the entrenchments of Susa—and at daybreak we shall attack."

"I hope your eminence will not be so inflexible," said the Count of Verrue, "since you know that the Duke of Savoy does not intend to deny passage."

"Ah, well, then," said Richelieu, "if we're in agreement, there's no need for further talk."

"It is true," said Verrue with some embarrassment, "that his highness has one condition . . . or rather, one hope," added the count.

"Ah ha!" said the cardinal, smiling. "And that is?"

"His Highness the Duke hopes that, due to the great sacrifice he is making, His Most Christian Majesty will cede from the Duchy of Mantua the same part of Montferrat that the King of Spain was allotting to Savoy in his division—or if he does not want to grant it to the duke, that he will make a gift of it to Madame, the king's sister and the prince's wife. On this condition, the pass will be open tomorrow."

The cardinal looked for a moment at the count, who could not sustain his regard and lowered his eyes. Then, as if that was what he awaited, he said, "Monsieur le Comte, all Europe has such a high opinion of my master the king's regard for justice, that I don't know how Monsieur the Duke of Savoy could imagine that his majesty would consent to such a proposition. Myself, I am certain he would never accept it. The King of Spain may well grant part of what does not belong to him, in order to engage Savoy to support an unjust usurpation; but God prevent that the king my master, who crosses the mountains to come to the aid of the oppressed Duke of Mantua, would treat his ally so. If Monsieur the Duke of Savoy forgets what a King of France is capable of, the day after tomorrow he will be reminded."

"But may I hope at least that these final proposals will be presented by your eminence to his majesty?"

"Useless, Monsieur le Comte," said a voice from behind the cardinal. "The king has heard, and is quite astonished that a man who must know better should make a proposal that would compromise France and stain its honor. If tomorrow the pass is not opened without condition, the next day, at daybreak, it will be attacked."

Then, drawing himself up and placing a foot before him with that majesty which he could sometimes assume, King Louis XIII added, "I will be there in person, and you will be able to recognize me by these white plumes, as my august father was recognized at Ivry. I hope that Monsieur the Duke will adopt a similar sign to identify him in the heat of battle. Take him my words, monsieur: they are the only response I can and must make."

And he saluted the count, who responded with a deep bow and withdrew.

All that evening and all that night, the army continued to assemble around Chaumont. By the following evening, the king commanded twenty-three thousand foot and four thousand horse.

Around ten at night, the artillery and all its materiel was lined up beyond Chaumont, the mouths of the guns turned toward enemy territory. The king ordered a check of the caissons and crates for a report on how much ammunition was available. At this time the bayonet had not yet been invented, so the cannon and the musket decided everything.

At midnight the council was convened. It was composed of the king, the cardinal, the Duc de Montmorency and the three marshals: Bassompierre, Schomberg and Créqui. Bassompierre, who was senior, took the floor. He cast his eyes over the map and studied the positions of the enemy—which they knew perfectly, thanks to the information sent by the Comte de Moret.

"Unless someone has a better idea," he said, "here is my proposal, Sire." And saluting the king and Monsieur le Cardinal to show that it was to them that he addressed himself, he said, "I propose that the regiments of the French and Swiss Guards take the lead; the Regiment of Navarre and the Regiment d'Estillac, the left and right. The two wings will each be led by two hundred musketeers who will gain the summit of the two peaks of Montmoron and Montabon. Once at the top of the two mountains, nothing will be easier than for them to get the drop on the guards at the barricades. At the first shot heard from the heights, we move; while the musketeers fire on the barricades from behind, we will make a frontal assault with the two Guard regiments. Approach the map, Messieurs, look at the position of the enemy, and if you have a better plan than mine, speak up."

Maréchal de Créqui and Maréchal de Schomberg studied the map and supported Bassompierre's proposal.

That left the Duc de Montmorency.

Montmorency was better known for his dauntless courage and audacity on the field of battle than as a strategist and man of discretion and foresight; moreover he spoke with a certain difficulty at first, with a stammer that he gradually lost as he went on. However, this time he found the courage to speak before the king.

"Sire," he said, "I respect the opinion of Monsieur le Maréchal de Bassompierre, and of Messieurs de Créqui and de Schomberg, and am well aware of their courage and experience; but while I don't doubt we can carry them, taking those barricades and the redoubts, especially the demi-lune that completely blocks the road, will be a difficult task indeed. Monsieur de Bassompierre has rightly said that we must take them; but is there no way to cut off these entrenchments? Can't we find, perhaps by a difficult mountain path, a way to turn the flank, to come down between the demi-lune and Susa and attack this position from behind? It would only be a question of finding a loyal guide and an intrepid officer, two things that don't seem impossible to me."

"You hear the proposal of Monsieur de Montmorency," said the king. "Do you agree?"

"Excellent!" replied the marshals. "But there's no time to lose in finding this guide and this officer."

At that moment Étienne Lathil spoke a few quiet words in the cardinal's ear, and Richelieu's face brightened. "Messieurs," he said, "I believe Providence sends us the loyal guide and intrepid officer in one and the same person."

And turning toward Lathil, who awaited his orders: "Captain Lathil," he said, "bring in Monsieur le Comte de Moret."

Lathil bowed.

Five minutes later the Comte de Moret entered, and despite his disguise as a humble mountaineer, everyone could see the resemblance to his august father—a resemblance that was the envy of King Louis XIII, illustrious son of Henri IV. He had just arrived from Mantua, sent by Providence, as the Duc de Richelieu had said.

The Comte de Moret, thanks to the route he had taken to cross Savoy in safety, could be at one and the same time a loyal guide and an intrepid officer.

Indeed, the question had scarcely been stated before, taking a pencil, he traced on Monsieur de Pontis' map the path that led from Chaumont to a smugglers' inn, and from the smugglers' inn to the bridge of Giacon; then he paused to recount how he had been forced to change his route to escape the Spanish bandits, and how this change of route had brought him to the path whereby one could slip past the ramparts that girdled the mountains above Susa.

He was ordered to take five hundred men with him, a larger troop being too awkward to maneuver on such a route.

The cardinal wanted the young prince to take a few hours of rest, but he refused, saying that if he was to arrive in time to create a diversion at the moment of the attack, he didn't have a minute to lose.

He requested the cardinal to give him, as second in command, Étienne Lathil, whose devotion and courage were beyond doubt.

They agreed to all his desires.

At three o'clock Moret's troop quietly departed; each man carried with him one day's rations.

Of the five hundred men who were to march under his orders the Comte de Moret knew only the young captain; but once they were told they were to have as leader the son of Henri IV, the soldiers crowded around him with cries of joy;

and it was necessary to bring two torches so as to see his face, whose resemblance to that of the *Béarnais* redoubled their enthusiasm.

Immediately after the Comte de Moret's five hundred men marched out, under cover of a night so dark it was impossible to see ten paces before oneself, the remainder of the army was put in motion. The timing was terrible, as the ground was covered with two feet of snow.

Fifty men remained to guard the artillery park. The rest of the troops marched to within five hundred paces of the Rock of Gélasse, just short of Susa Pass. Six pieces of cannon and six pallets of balls were brought up to force the barricade.

The troops chosen to attack were seven companies of Guards, six of Swiss, nineteen of Navarre, fourteen of Estissac and fifteen of Sault, plus the king's mounted musketeers.

Each unit was to throw out in front fifty storm troopers known as *"enfants perdus,"* supported by one hundred men, themselves supported by five hundred more.

Around six in the morning, the troops were marshaled into order. The king presided over these preparations, detailing a certain number of his musketeers to join the *enfants perdus*. Then he ordered the Sieur de Comminges, preceded by a trumpeter, to cross the border and ask the Duke of Savoy for passage for the army and the person of the king.

Monsieur de Comminges advanced, but a hundred paces from the barricade he was stopped by a challenge. He responded, "We wish to pass, monsieur."

"But," replied the Count of Verrue, "how do you wish to pass? As friends or as enemies?"

"As friends, if you open the pass to us; as enemies, if you close it. I am charged by the king my master to go to Susa and prepare lodgings for him, as he plans to sleep there tomorrow."

"Monsieur," answered the Count of Verrue, "the duke my master would hold it a great honor to host his majesty; but he comes with such a grand company that before I can respond, I must ask his highness for his orders."

"Well," said Comminges, "do you intend, by any chance, to dispute our passage?"

The Count of Verrue came forth and stood before him. "What would you have, monsieur?" asked the herald of the count.

"I have the honor to say to you, monsieur," replied Verrue coldly, "that on this subject I must first know the intentions of his highness, my master."

"Monsieur, I warn you," said Comminges, "that I must report this to the king."

"You may do what you please, monsieur," responded Verrue. "You are master of yourself."

And with this, each saluted the other. Monsieur de Verrue returned to his side of the barricades, and Comminges returned to the king.

"*Eh bien*, monsieur?" Louis XIII asked Comminges.

Comminges related his discussion with the Count of Verrue: Louis XIII listened without missing a word, and when Comminges had finished, the king stated, "The Count of Verrue answered not only as a trusty servant but as a man of spirit who knows his duty."

At that moment the king was on the farthest frontier of France, among the *enfants perdus* ready to charge, and the five hundred men who were to support them.

Bassompierre approached, smiling and with hat in hand. "Sire," he said, "the corps is ready, the violins are in tune, the masks are by the door; when it pleases your majesty, we may commence the ballet."

The king looked at him, brow furrowed. "Monsieur le Maréchal, did you know that I have just received a report that we have only five hundred rounds in the artillery park?"

"Well, Sire," answered Bassompierre, "this is certainly the right time to consider that; if the masque isn't ready, the ballet shouldn't be danced. But let us do it. All will be well."

"Is that your answer to me?" said the king, fixing the marshal with a look.

"Sire, it would be beyond bold to guarantee something as doubtful as a victory; but my answer to you is that we will return with our honor, or I will be dead or taken."

"Take care that if we are beaten, Monsieur de Bassompierre, that I am taken with you."

"Bah, what can happen to me worse than for your majesty to call me foolishly overconfident? But don't worry, Sire, I will try not to deserve such an insult. Let's just do it."

"Sire," said the cardinal, who held his horse close to the king's, "with an attitude like the marshal's, my hopes are high." Then, addressing Bassompierre: "Go, Monsieur le Maréchal, go—and do your utmost."

Bassompierre went to where the other commanders awaited, and dismounted with Messieurs de Créqui and de Montmorency for the frontal assault on the trenches. Only Monsieur de Schomberg remained mounted, due to the gout in his knee.

They marched past the base of the Rock of Gélasse; for some reason the enemy had abandoned that position, strong though it was, perhaps afraid that those who defended it would be cut off and obliged to surrender.

But as soon as the troops passed the rock they were exposed, and fire commenced from the mountain and the grand barricade. And at the first volley, Monsieur de Schomberg was hit in the lower back.

Bassompierre followed the valley floor and approached the demi-lune that blocked Susa Pass from the front, Monsieur de Créqui close beside him.

Monsieur de Montmorency, as if he were a simple musketeer, sprang up the mountain on the left toward the peak of Montmoron.

Monsieur de Schomberg was tied to his horse, which was led forward by its bridle due to the difficulty of the terrain; he made his way up the right-hand mountain in the midst of the *enfants perdus*.

One unit flanked the barricades, according to Bassompierre's plan, to shoot the defenders from behind, while the others attacked the front.

The Savoyards defended valiantly; Victor-Amadeus and his father commanded from the redoubt on the peak of Montmoron.

Montmorency, with his usual impetuosity, soon attacked and carried the first barricade on the left. As his armor had encumbered him while afoot, he had left its pieces all along his way, attacking the redoubt in his simple buff jerkin and velvet trunk-hose.

Bassompierre, for his part, remained on the valley floor, weathering the fire from the demi-lune.

Behind came the king, with his white plumes, and Monsieur le Cardinal in a gold-embroidered robe of russet velvet.

Three times the center charged the redoubt, and three times they were repulsed. Musket balls leaped and ricocheted down the valley from rock to rock, killing one of Monsieur de Créqui's esquires within a few feet of the king's horse.

Messieurs de Bassompierre and de Créqui then resolved to scale the slopes, each with five hundred men: Bassompierre the mountain on the left, to rejoin Monsieur de Montmorency, and Monsieur de Créqui the mountain on the right, to support Monsieur de Schomberg.

Two thousand five hundred men remained on the valley floor to keep pressure on the demi-lune.

Bassompierre, overweight and already fifty years old, had taken it on himself to climb the steepest slope; at every step he felt his footing would fail, and his aide beside him took a ball in the chest.

He arrived at the summit just as Monsieur de Montmorency was falling back from his third assault on the redoubt. They combined for the fourth.

Monsieur de Montmorency was lightly wounded in the arm, while Monsieur de Bassompierre's clothes were riddled with bullet-holes. But the redoubt on the left was carried, and the Savoyard defenders took refuge behind the demi-lune.

The two chiefs cast their eyes toward the redoubt on the right. The battle there was hotly contested.

Presently they saw two riders leave at a full gallop, making for a path that had apparently been prepared for their retreat down to the demi-lune. It was the Duke of Savoy, Charles-Emmanuel, and his son, Victor-Amadeus. A flood of fugitives followed them.

The redoubt on the right was taken. Only the demi-lune remained: the hardest nut to crack.

Louis XIII sent to congratulate the marshals and Monsieur de Montmorency on their success, while ordering them to take care of themselves. Bassompierre replied on behalf of himself and Messieurs de Schomberg, de Créqui, and de Montmorency:

Sire, we are grateful for the interest you take in us, but at times like these the blood of a prince or a marshal of France is not worth more than that of the meanest soldier.

We ask for ten minutes of rest for the men, after which the ball will start anew.

And, indeed, after ten minutes of rest the trumpets sounded, the drums beat again, and the two wings, in two tight columns, closed on the demi-lune.

The approaches had fallen to the French—but the last entrenchment remained, teeming with soldiers, bristling with cannons, and anchored by the fort of Montabon, built atop an inaccessible rock; the fort had but one approach, a staircase that could be climbed only in single file.

Left far behind were any guns that might bear on either the valley floor or the mountain summits. The soldiers advanced head down, not asking if they were being led to butchery; their commanders marched in the van, and that was enough.

His eminence was with the king on his horse, and the cardinal saw the sudden gaps the cannon plowed through the ranks; the king clapped his hands, applauding the soldiers' courage while at the same time his innate cruelty awoke like a tiger sensing blood.

The troops reached the wall; some carried ladders, and the escalade began.

Montmorency took a flag and was first upon the wall; Bassompierre, too old to follow, took a position halfway up the ramparts and exhorted the soldiers to do their utmost.

Some ladders broke beneath the weight of so many attackers, so keen were they to be the first to set foot on the rampart; others held back to allow time for their companions to go over, drawing up other ladders to mount the assault.

Suddenly they could see disarray among the defenders, while from beyond them came shouting and a fusillade.

"Courage, *amis*," cried Montmorency, mounting another assault, "it's the Comte de Moret to our rescue!" And he sprang forward anew, ragged and bloody though he was, carrying along with him, by this supreme effort, all who could see and hear him.

The duke was not mistaken: it was Moret who had produced the diversion.

The comte had left at three in the morning, as we have seen, with Lathil for captain and Galuar for aide-de-camp. They arrived at the bank of the torrent that had almost drowned Moret the first time he'd passed this way; but when the frost had come the water had dropped, and now one could cross by leaping from rock to rock.

Arriving on the other side of the torrent, the Comte de Moret and his men quickly crossed the field that separated them from the mountain. He found the rising path, and his men followed.

The night was dark, but the new-fallen snow lit the way.

The comte, aware of the difficulties ahead, had provided his troops with long ropes, one for each twenty-four men. Along the brink marched each twenty-four man unit; if one man slipped he was sustained by the other twenty-three. Twenty-four others marched behind them, acting as another stay or support.

As they approached the smugglers' inn, the comte enjoined silence. Though without knowing why, all remained quiet.

The comte gathered a dozen men about him, explained to them that the inn before them was their objective, and ordered them to instruct their comrades to quietly surround it. If but one man escaped this nest of villains and gave the alarm, their mission could be compromised.

Galuar, who knew this locale, took a score of men to surround the inn-yard; with twenty more Lathil guarded the gate, and the Comte de Moret led a similar number to the only window that let daylight into the house, and by which those inside might escape. The window glowed brightly, indicating the hosts were in residence.

The rest of the troop spread out along the road, in order to leave the bandits no route of escape.

The gate of the yard was closed; Galuar, with the lithe agility of a monkey, vaulted over, dropped into the yard and opened it.

In a moment the yard was full of soldiers, standing with muskets at the ready.

Lathil arranged his men in two rows opposite the door, ordering them to fire on anyone who attempted to flee.

The comte had slowly and quietly approached the window in order to see what went on inside; but the heat of the room had fogged the glass, preventing a view of the interior.

One of the window's four panes had been broken in some brawl and replaced by a sheet of paper affixed to the frame. The Comte de Moret got up on the windowsill, cut a slit in the paper with the point of his dagger, and could finally glimpse the strange scene passing within.

The smuggler who had warned Moret when he'd passed through before that Spanish bandits were after him was bound and gagged on a table; the bandits whom he had betrayed, gathered *en tribunal*, had just pronounced judgment. As the judgment could not be appealed, the only question was whether he should be hanged or shot.

Opinion was almost evenly divided. However, as is well known, the Spaniards are a thrifty people. One made the point that you could not execute a man with fewer than eight or ten musket shots, which would cost them eight or ten charges of lead and powder—while to hang a man, not only did you need only one rope, but afterwards that rope, having been used in an execution, multiplied its value by two, four, even ten times!

This sage advice, so economical, carried the day. As the bandits chose the rope by acclamation, the poor devil of a smuggler realized that his fate was sealed. His only recourse was the prayer of the dying: *My God, I place my soul within your hands!*

A rope never takes long to find, especially in an inn that caters to muleteers. In less than five minutes an actual muleteer—who didn't mind helping out, since it furthered the spectacle of a hanging—provided the required rope.

A ceiling lantern was suspended from a sort of hook as if it was, amidst seven or eight candles placed on the tables, the star at the center of a new planetary system. This lantern was taken down and put on the mantel; one of the Spaniards, the thrifty one who'd thought of the rope, passed it through the hook and tied a noose; the other end was put into the hands of four or five of his comrades. The condemned was marched to the table beneath the hook and, without the least resistance from the poor wretch, who believed himself completely lost, the noose was placed around his neck.

Then, amid the solemn silence that always precedes the terrible act of violent separation of body and soul, came the order: "Pull!"

But scarcely was this word pronounced when there came from the window the sound that paper or fabric makes as it tears, and into the room stretched an arm pointing a pistol. The pistol fired, and the man holding the noose around the neck of the condemned fell back dead.

At the same moment a vigorous kick broke the window latches, and in two more blows it was open, letting in the Comte de Moret, who leapt into the room followed by his men. At the gunshot, like a signal, the front door and the yard door also burst open, and all exits were visibly barred by armed soldiers.

Within moments the condemned was untied and passed from the agonies of anguish to the giddy joy of the man who had begun his march to the tomb, but leaps from the pit before the earth can cover him.

"Let no one attempt to leave here," said the Comte de Moret with that gesture of supreme authority that was his royal heritage. "Those who try to flee will be killed."

Nobody moved.

"Now," he said, addressing the smuggler whose life he'd saved, "I am the traveler whom you so generously warned, two months ago, of what dangers I was running, a warning for which you were just now about to die. It is only right that the roles be reversed, and that now the tragedy be followed to its end. Point out to me the wretches who hounded us; their trial will be short."

The smuggler didn't wait to be asked twice; he designated eight Spaniards—the ninth had died.

These eight bandits, seeing themselves condemned, and understanding that there would be no mercy, exchanged glances—and then with the energy of despair, daggers in hands, they fell on the soldiers who guarded the door to the road.

But they had bitten off too much. As you may recall, Lathil was in charge of guarding that door, and stood on the threshold with a gun in each hand. With two shots he killed two men.

The other six fought briefly with the men of the Comte de Moret and of Lathil. For a few seconds there was the clanging of iron, cries, oaths, two more gunshots, the thump of two bodies on the floor . . . and it was over.

Five were dead in their gore, and three others, still alive, were tied hand and foot and in the hands of the soldiers.

"Someone get that rope that was to be used to hang an honest man," said the Comte de Moret, "then find two more to hang these villains."

The muleteers, who were beginning to understand that they were not under suspicion, and that instead of seeing one man hang they were about to see three, a spectacle therefore three times as entertaining, offered up the ropes requested that very moment.

"Lathil," said the Comte de Moret, "I charge you with hanging these three gentlemen. I know you are efficient—don't let them linger. As for the rest of this honorable company, you will leave ten men to keep them here. Tomorrow, no sooner than midday, if the prisoners have caused no trouble, they may be set free."

"And where will I rejoin you?" asked Lathil.

"This brave man," answered the Comte de Moret, indicating the smuggler miraculously saved from the noose, "this brave man will lead you; but march double-time to catch up to us."

Then, addressing the smuggler himself, "Follow the same road you recall from before, my good man; when you arrive at Susa there will be twenty pistoles for you.

"Lathil, you have ten minutes."

Lathil bowed.

"Let's be on our way, messieurs," said the Comte de Moret. "We lost half an hour here, albeit in a good cause."

Ten minutes later, Lathil, guided by the smuggler, rejoined them; the task that the comte had left three quarters done was completed. The smuggler, who hadn't had time to thank him, threw himself at Moret's feet and kissed his hands.

"*C'est bien, mon ami*," said the Comte de Moret. "Now, we must be in Susa within the hour."

And the troop resumed their march. Strict silence was decreed, and no noise was heard but the sound of snow crunching under the soldiers' feet.

As they turned the shoulder of the mountain the town of Susa came into view, limned by the first light of morning.

The ramparts, this far up the mountain, were deserted. The road, if the narrow furrow they followed no more than two abreast could be called a road, passed about ten feet above the parapet. From there one could slip down to the ramparts.

The demi-lune which, after the barricades were carried and the redoubts had been taken, still held off the French army, was nearly three miles from Susa, and as no one could imagine an attack from the mountainside, no one was on guard there. However, by the light of dawn the sentinels in the town saw the small troop filing down the side of the mountain and raised the alarm.

The Comte de Moret heard their cries, saw their reaction, and knew there was no time to lose. Like a true mountaineer he leapt from rock to rock, and was the first to drop onto the ramparts.

Lathil was right by his side.

At the cries of the sentinels, the Savoyards in Susa gathered their guards and formed a troop of a hundred men, hoping to buy time for further reinforcements.

The soldiers of Charles-Emmanuel saw in the twilight a long dark file circling down the mountain, enemies who seemed to fall from the sky in what numbers they couldn't ascertain, so they didn't put up much of a fight; however, thinking it was critical that the duke and his son be informed, they dispatched a rider to Susa Pass to warn them of what was happening.

The Comte de Moret saw this man being detached and launched himself into the mêlée; he suspected to whom the courier was going at his fastest gallop, but had no way to stop him.

It was just one more reason to seize the Susa gateway, into which Louis XIII, after forcing the barricades, had made a partial entry. With what few men he had, he'd kicked the gate in upon those who defended it.

The diversion accomplished, the conclusion didn't take long. Surprised when they least expected it, ignorant of the number of their enemies, the Savoyards in Susa, good soldiers though they were, cried "Alarm!" and ran for it, some down the mountainside, others through the town.

The Comte de Moret seized the lower gateway, rallied his troops, turned four guns in case they needed to fire them, and with the four hundred fifty men who remained, advanced to the attack, cutting off the demi-lune from behind.

Cannon erupted from above, and smoke wreathed Montabon peak.

The two armies came to grips.

Moret doubled his men's pace; however, while still some distance from the demi-lune, he saw a corps of troops being detached from the Savoyard army and sent toward him. The unit was about equal in number to that of the Comte de Moret; at its head, mounted, was the colonel in command.

Lathil approached the comte. "I recognize the officer leading that troop," he said. "He's a gallant soldier named Colonel Belon."

"And so?" said the comte.

"I'd like monseigneur's permission to take him prisoner."

"I'll allow you to do that—*Ventre-saint-gris*, I could hardly ask for more! But how will you take him?"

"Nothing could be easier, monseigneur; when you see the colonel fall beneath his horse, charge his men furiously; they'll think he's dead and will scatter. Swoop in and take the flag, while I take the colonel; though you might rather have the colonel and I the flag, the colonel will pay a fine ransom of three or four hundred pistoles—while the flag, for all its glory, is nothing but a flag."

"To me then the flag," said the Comte de Moret, "and to you the colonel."

"*Là*, now . . . beat the drums and sound the trumpets!"

Moret raised his sword, the drums beat, and the trumpets sounded the charge.

Lathil took four men with him, each holding a musket, ready to pass a new weapon to him once he'd fired the first, the second, and even the third.

As for the enemy, at the sound of the French drums and bugles, the Savoyard troop seemed to quicken its step.

Soon the two troops were no more than fifty paces from each other.

The Savoyard unit stopped to fire a volley. "This is the moment," said Lathil. "Look out, monseigneur! Take their fire, shoot back, and then charge behind the flag."

Lathil had hardly finished when a hailstorm of balls passed like a hurricane—but mainly above the heads of the French soldiers, who held their ground.

"Aim low!" cried Lathil. And as an example, aiming at the colonel's horse, he fired just as the colonel loosened the reins to charge.

The horse took the ball just below the shoulder; carried forward by its charge, it drove to within twenty paces of the French ranks.

"To me the colonel, to you the flag, monseigneur," said Lathil, and he leapt, sword held high, upon the colonel.

The French soldiers had fired and, following Lathil's advice, aimed low, so that nearly all their shots struck home.

The comte took advantage of the chaos to hurl himself into the midst of the Savoyards.

In a few bounds, Lathil closed with Colonel Belon, pinned under his horse and stunned from his fall. Lathil put his sword to his throat and said to him, "Rescue or no rescue?"

The colonel slid a hand toward his holster.

"Just one movement, Colonel Belon," Lathil said, "and you are dead."

"I surrender," said the colonel, handing his sword to Lathil.

"Whether rescued or not rescued?"

"Whether rescued or not rescued."

"Then, colonel, keep your sword—one does not disarm a brave officer like you.

We'll come to terms after the battle; if I'm killed, you are free."

With these words he helped the colonel out from under his horse, and having set him on his feet, he sprang into the midst of the Savoyard ranks.

Thus what Lathil had predicted had happened.

The soldiers of Charles-Emmanuel, seeing the fall of the colonel, and ignorant as to whether it was he or his horse who was killed, had lost their nerve.

Lathil threw himself into the thickest part of the mêlée, shouting in a voice like thunder, "Moret! Moret to the rescue! Swing your sword for the son of Henri IV!"

This final onslaught broke the enemy troop. Cutting down the man who carried it, the Comte de Moret seized the Savoyard flag in his left hand. He raised it high and shouted, "Victory for France! Long live King Louis XIII!"

This cry was repeated by every Frenchman who was still upright. What followed was a rout. The troopers who had been sent to oppose the Comte de Moret, diminished by a third, took to their heels.

"Let's not lose a minute, monseigneur," said Lathil to the comte. "After them, firing as we go; we don't have to kill them, but it's important that our shooting be heard in the entrenchments."

And, indeed, their fire, heard in the demi-lune, spread chaos among the defenders.

Attacked from the front by Montmorency, Bassompierre and Créqui, attacked from behind by the Comte de Moret and Lathil, the Duke of Savoy and his son feared to be surrounded and captured; leaving the Count of Verrue to conduct a desperate defense, they went down to the stables, jumped into the saddle and flew from the entrenchments.

They found themselves in the middle of Colonel Belon's soldiers, who were fleeing pell-mell with the French in pursuit, firing at will.

These two riders trying to reach the mountainside attracted the attention of Lathil, who, thinking they looked important, sprang forward to cut them off; but just as he was about to grab the duke's horse by the bridle, he was dazed by a flash of light and a sharp pain in his left shoulder.

A Spanish officer in the service of the Duke of Savoy, seeing his master about to be taken, had jumped in and, with his long sword, gashed the shoulder of our swashbuckler.

Lathil let out a cry, less of pain than of anger at seeing his prey escape. With sword in hand, he threw himself on the Spaniard.

Though Lathil's sword was six inches shorter than that of his adversary, they'd barely met before Lathil, a master of arms, knew himself master of his enemy. Twice wounded, the Spaniard fell within ten seconds, shouting, "Save the duke!"

At these words, Lathil leapt over the wounded man and resumed his pursuit of the two riders, but thanks to their petite mountain horses they were already far enough down the road to be out of range.

Lathil returned, furious at having missed such glorious prey; but at least he still had the Spanish officer who, unable to defend himself, surrendered "rescue or no rescue."

Meanwhile the demi-lune was in turmoil. The Duc de Montmorency, first onto the ramparts, held his position, dispatching with blows of his axe all who tried to approach him, and opening a space for those who followed him.

Then, approaching one another across the walls and waving as a sign of victory, came the French flag that had first been planted on the walls of the demi-lune, and the Savoyard flag it had conquered. Saluting Louis XIII and lowering the two standards before him, all shouted together, *"Vive le Roi!"* It was over.

"No one is to enter the redoubt before the king," the cardinal said loudly.

Sentinels were placed at all entrances, and Montmorency and Moret went themselves to open the Gélasse postern for the king and the cardinal.

The two rode in, musketoon at the knee to signify that they entered as conquerors—and that the conquered, taken by storm, could expect only what was granted at the victors' good pleasure.

The king addressed the Duc de Montmorency first. "I know, Monsieur le Duc," he said, "that which is the object of your ambition. When the campaign ends, you shall be entitled to exchange your sword for one chased with golden *fleur de lis*, which will place you above all the Marshals of France."

Montmorency bowed. It was a formal promise, and the Sword of the Constable was his sole ambition in the world.

"Sire," said the Comte de Moret, presenting the king with the flag won from Colonel Belon's regiment, "allow me the honor of placing at your majesty's feet this standard I have taken."

"I accept it," said Louis XIII, "and in exchange, I hope you will be pleased to wear this white plume in your hat, in memory of the brother who gave it to you, and of our father who bore three of them at Ivry."

The Comte de Moret wanted to kiss the king's hand, but Louis XIII took him in his arms and cordially embraced him.

Then the king removed from his hat one of its three white plumes, along with the diamond clip that held it on, and gave it to the Comte de Moret.

And that same day, around five in the evening, King Louis XIII made his entry into Susa, after having received from its authorities, on a silver platter, the keys to the town.

About John Bloundelle-Burton

John Bloundelle-Burton (1850-1917) was an English naval officer and gentleman journalist turned novelist, publishing his first book in 1885. He put his naval experience to good use in a series of nautical adventures, but it's his historical swashbucklers that interest us, particularly *In the Day of Adversity* (1895), *The Clash of Arms* (1897), and *The Scourge of God* (1898), all set in France under Louis XIV. But if you're going to read just one Bloundelle-Burton novel, it has to be *The Hispaniola Plate* (1895), a cracking good tale of piracy, mutiny, and treasure in the late 17th-century Caribbean.

Bloundelle-Burton lived and wrote in Paris for many years, and was an aficionado of French history: all his historical tales are well researched and his settings always ring true. Like Weyman and Levett-Yeats, he didn't write very many short stories, preferring the novel, but it wasn't because he couldn't write a tight, compact tale when he wanted to—as you'll see, in this story from *Longman's Christmas Annual* of 1898.

The King of Spain's Will

JOHN BLOUNDELLE-BURTON

CHAPTER I

I can tell you there was a pretty bustle around Paris that night when the news came of the downfall of the old Fox—the fox being none other than Cardinal Alberoni, who had just been turned out of Spain for his intrigues, King Philip V having had enough of him. Not that the man, who had been a gardener's son, and a sort of buffoon to the Duke of Parma, was so wondrous old, since in this year of grace 1719 he was but fifty-five. Only, when a man is a scheming knave who has passed his full prime, and is also a fox— why, one generally calls him an old one.

Now, the news of Alberoni's disgrace at Madrid came first to Versailles, just about four of the afternoon, what time we of the Grey Musketeers were going off duty, our place till midnight being taken by those of the cavalry regiment of Vermandois, which had arrived a week ago from Blois—came at the hands of the Comte St. Denis de Pile, who had been sent off post-haste to Paris with the information, and also with another piece of intelligence,

at which, I protest, not one of us could help laughing, serious enough though the thing was. This news being none other than that the crafty old Italian, who was on his way to Marseilles, there to embark with all his wealth for his native land, had absolutely carried off in his possession the will of the late King of Spain, Charles II, in which he bequeathed his throne to the very man who now sat upon it.

"And," exclaimed St. Denis de Pile, as he drank down a flask of Florence wine which we produced for him in the guard-room, "I'll be sworn that he means to send that will to the Emperor of Austria, who, if he is not a fool, will at once destroy it. And then, poof! Poof! Poof!" And the Count blew out his moustache in front of his lip. "What becomes of all that we fought for in the War of the Succession? *Tête de mon chien*! It will have to begin all over again. Your countrymen, my boy," and he slapped me affectionately on the shoulder, for we had met often enough before, "your countrymen, the English, will want another war, King George may be willing enough to oblige them, and the Treaty of Utrecht may as well be used to light a fire."

Now here was what some of my countrymen call a pretty kettle of fish. Peace was expected to be proclaimed in Europe at this moment, since the war of the Pyrenees was over. France and England were sworn allies and bosom friends, otherwise be sure that I, an Englishman, young and enthusiastic, would not have been holding the commission of a cornet in the Musketeers, and serving the regent—or, rather, the boy king for whom he ruled. And all in a moment it was just as likely as not that war might break out again through the craftiness of the cardinal, who, since he had fallen, evidently did not mean to do so without pulling others down with him. For Austria had never willingly resigned her claims on the throne of Spain, remembering that the old French king had once formally waived all the claims of his own family to it, Will or no Will, and had then instantly asserted them on the death of Charles. As for my country—well! We English are not over-fond of retreating from anything we have undertaken, though, for widely known considerations not necessary to set down here, we had at last agreed to the peace of Utrecht, our having thoroughly beaten the French by sea and land before we did so, being, perhaps, the reason why we at last came in.

"What's to be done?" said old d'Hautefeuille, who was in command of the Grey Musketeers at this time.

"What? What? *Le Débonnaire*" (for so we called the regent) "is at the Palais Royal—he must know the news at once. De Pile, you must ride on to Paris."

"*Fichtre* for Paris!" exclaimed the count. "I am battered enough already with my long ride. Think on't—from Madrid! Through storms and burning suns, over mountains and through plains, over two hundred leagues and across half a score of horses' backs. Also, observe—the letter is inscribed to the Regent's Grace at Versailles. I have done my duty—"

"But—"

"No 'buts,' d'Hautefeuille. My work is done. Let the king's Lieutenant of Versailles, who commands in his and the regent's absence, take charge of the paper. For me a bottle and a meal, also a bed."

"Then take it to the lieutenant," said fiery d'Hautefeuille. "Hand it to him yourself, and bid him find a courier to Paris. *Peste!* You, a royal messenger who can ride from Madrid to here, and yet cannot finish the journey to Paris! Bah! Go and get your bottle and your bed—and much good may they do you."

Whereon the old fellow turned grumpily away, bidding some of the younger ones amongst us not to be loitering about the galleries endeavoring to catch the eyes of the maids of honor, but instead to get off to our quarters and be ready to relieve the officers of the Vermandois regiment at midnight.

Yet one amongst us, at least, was not to hear the chimes of midnight summoning us to the night guard, that one being myself, as you shall see. Nay, not one hour later was to ring out from the palace clock ere, as luck would have it, I was called forth from my own quarters—or rather from the little salon of Alison de Prie (who was a maid of honor, and who had invited me in to partake of a *pâté de bécasse* which her father had sent her from his property near Tours) by an order to attend on d'Hautefeuille in his quarters.

Whereon I proceeded thither and found him in a very bad temper—a thing he suffered much from lately, since he also suffered from a gout that teased him terribly. So immediately he burst out on my putting in an appearance, "Now, Adrian Trent, it is your month of special service, is it not?"

"It is, monsieur," I answered, wondering what was coming next.

"So! Very well. Here then is something for you to do—that is, if the turning of my officers into couriers and post-boys and lackeys constitutes 'special service.' However, three creatures have to obey orders in this world, soldiers, wives, and dogs, therefore I—and you—must do so. Here, take this," and he tossed to me across his table a mighty great letter on which was

a formidable red seal, "have your horse saddled and be off with you to Paris. Give it into the regent's hand. It is the account of Alberoni's disgrace which that *fainéant* de Pile could bring all this way, but no farther. Away with you! The king's lieutenant seems to think that de Pile is discharged of his duty here. Away with you! What are you stopping for? You know the road to Paris, I suppose? You ought to. It's hard enough to keep you boys out of it if I give you an afternoon's leave. Be off!"

So off I went, and five minutes afterwards my best grey, La Rose, was saddled, and I was riding swiftly towards where the regent was at the present moment.

Now, who'd have thought when I went clattering through Sèvres and Issy, on that fine winter afternoon, in all the bravery of my full costume—which was the handsomest of any regiment in France, not even excepting our comrades of the Black Musketeers—who'd have thought, I say, that I was really taking the first steps of a long, toilsome journey, which, ere it was ended, was to bring me pretty near to danger and death? However, no need to anticipate, since those who read will see.

An hour later I was in Paris, and then, even as I went swiftly along amidst the crowds that were in the streets, especially in those streets round about the Palais Royal, I found that one thing was very certain, namely, that though I might now be carrying on de Pile's message from the

Court of Spain to the Court of France, the purport of it was already known. Near the Palais Royal were numerous groups gathered, who cheered occasionally for France and England, which did me good to hear; then for Spain and France, which did not move me so much; while, at the same time, I distinctly heard Alberoni's name mentioned, with, attached to it, expressions and epithets that were anything but flattering. Also, as I made for the entrance opposite the Louvre, people called attention to me, saying, *"Voilà le beau Mousquetaire—chut!* Doubtless he rides from Versailles. Brings confirmation of the old trickster's downfall. *Ho! Le beau Mousquetaire!"* While a strident-voiced buffoon cried out to me, asking if all my gold galloon and feathers and lace did not sometimes get spoilt by the damp of the wintry weather, and another desired to know if my sweetheart did not adore me in my regimental fallals?

However, La Rose made her way through them all, shaking her bridle-chain angrily if any got before her, breathing out great gusts from her fiery nostrils, and casting now and again the wicked white of her eye around; she was a beauty who loved not to be pestered or interfered with. And at last I was off her back, at the door near the regent's apartments on the south side, and asking for the officer of the guard; and half-an-hour later I was in the presence of the regent himself, who sat writing in a little room about big enough to make a cage for a bird. Yet, in spite of the way in which his highness spent his evenings and nights, and also of his supper parties and other dissipations, he did as much work in that little cabinet as any other twelve men in France.

Because he was a very perfect gentleman—no matter what his faults were (he answered for them to his Maker but a little while after I met him)—he treated me exactly as though I were his equal, and bade me be seated while he read the letter calmly; then, looking up at me, he said, "I knew something of this before. Even my beloved Parisians know of it—how *they* have learnt it Heaven alone can say. Still it is known. Alberoni was to leave Madrid in forty-eight hours from the time of receiving notice. But—"

Here he paused, and seemed to be reflecting deeply. Then he said aloud, though more to himself than to me, "I wonder if he *has* got the will?"

It not being my place to speak, I said nothing, waiting to receive orders from him. And a moment later he again addressed me.

"You *mousquetaires* have always the best of horses and are proud of them. I know; I know. I have seen you riding races against each other at Versailles and Marly. And, for endurance, they will carry you far, both well and swiftly, in spite of your weight and trappings. Is it not so?"

"It is so, monseigneur," I answered, somewhat wonderingly, and not quite understanding what way this talk tended.

"How fast can you go? Say, a picked number of you—ten, twenty—for two days?"

"A long way, monseigneur. Perhaps, allowing for rest for the animals, nearer forty than thirty leagues."

"So! Nearer forty than thirty leagues. 'Tis well."

Here he rose from his chair (I, of course, rising also), turned himself round, and gazed at a map of France hanging on the wall; ran, too, his finger along it from the Pyrenees in the direction of Marseilles, while, as he did so, he muttered continually, yet loud enough to be quite audible to me.

"He would cross there—there, surely. Fifteen days to quit Spain, two to quit Madrid—seventeen altogether. From the fifth. The fifth! This is the twelfth. Ten days still."

Then he continued to run his finger along the coastline of the Mediterranean until it rested on Marseilles, at which he stood gazing for some time. But now he said nothing aloud for me to listen to, though it was evident enough that he was considering deeply; but at last he spoke again.

"His eminence must be met and escorted—yes, escorted, that is it—escorted in safety through the land.

Ay, in safety and safely. He must not be molested nor—" And then, though he turned his face away to gaze at the map again, I would have been sworn that I heard him mutter, "Nor allowed to depart quite yet." Then he suddenly said, "Do you know the house of the Chevalier de Marcieu? It is in the Rue des Mauvais Garçons."

"I know the street, monseigneur. I can find the house."

"Good! Therefore proceed there at once—the number is three—you are mounted, of course? Give my orders to him that he is to come here instantly; then return and I will give you some instructions for your commander."

Whereupon I bowed respectfully as I went to the door, the regent smiling pleasantly upon me. Yet, ere I left him, he said another word, asked a question.

"You *mousquetaires gris* have not had much exercise lately at Versailles, I think. Have you?"

"No, monseigneur, not our troop at least. The men have been but recently remounted."

"So. Very well. You shall have some exercise now. 'Twill do you good. You shall have a change of billet for a little while. In any case, Versailles is too luxurious a place for soldiers. Now, away with you to Marcieu's house and bid him come here. Return also yourself. Forget not that."

CHAPTER II
A GIRL CALLED DAMARIS

A week later, or, to be exact, six days, and the troop of Grey Musketeers, commanded by Captain the Vicomte de Pontgibaud—which was the one in which I rode as cornet—was making its way pleasantly enough along the great southern road that runs down from Paris to Toulouse. Indeed, we were very near that city now, and expected to be in it by the time that the wintry evening had fallen. In it, and safely housed for the night, not forgetting that the suppers of Southern France are most excellent and comforting meals, and that the Lunel and Roussillon are equally suited to the palate of a soldier, even though that soldier be but twenty years old; as I was in those days, now—alas!—long since vanished.

But, ere I go on with what I have to tell, perhaps you would care to hear in a few words how I, Adrian Trent, an Englishman, was riding as *cornette* or *porte drapeau* in a *corps d'élite* of our old hereditary enemies, the French. Well, this is how it was. The Trents have ever been Royalists, by which I mean that they and I, and all of our thinking, were followers of the House of Stuart. Now, you who read this may be one of those—or your father may have been one of those—who invited the Elector of Hanover to come over and ascend the English throne, or you may be what my family and I are

at the present moment, Jacobites. Never mind for that, however. You can keep your principles and we will keep ours, and need not quarrel about them. Suffice it, therefore, if I say that *our* principles have led us to quit England and to take up our abode in France. And if ever King James III sits on—however, no matter for that either; it concerns not this narrative.

My father was attached to the court of this king, who was just then in temporary residence in Rome—though, also, he sojourned some time in Spain—but, ere he followed his sovereign's errant fortunes, he obtained for me my guidon in the Musketeers, which service is most agreeable to me, who, from a boy, had sworn that I would be a soldier or nothing; and since I cannot be an English one, I must perforce be in the service of France. And, as I trust that never more will France and England be flying at each other's throats, I do hope that I may long wear the uniform of the regiment. If not—but of that, too, we will not speak.

To get on with what I have to tell, we rode into Toulouse just as the winter day was coming to an end, and a brave show we made, I can assure you, as we drew up in the great courtyard of the old "Taverne du Midi," a place that had been the leading hostelry ever since the dark ages. For in that tavern, pilgrims, knights on their road to Rome or even the Holy Land, men of different armies, wandering minstrels and troubadours, had all been accustomed to repose; even beggars and monks (who paid for nothing) could be here accommodated, if they chose to lie down in the straw amongst the horses and sing a good song in return for their supper.

And I do protest that, on this cold December night, when the icicles were hanging a foot long from the eaves, and bitter blasts were blowing all around the city—the northeast winds coming from away over the Lower Alps of Savoy—you might have thought that you were back again in those days, if you looked around the great *salle-à-manger* of the tavern. For in that vast room were gathered together a company which comprised as many different kinds of people as any company could have consisted of when met together in it in bygone ages. First, there was the nobleman who, because he was one, had had erected round his corner a great screen of arras by his domestics; such things being always carried in France by persons of much distinction, since they could neither endure to be seen by the commoner orders, nor, if they had private rooms, could they endure to look upon the bare whitewashed walls of the rooms, wherefore the arras was in that case hung on those walls. This great man we did not set eyes on, he being enshrouded in his haughty seclusion, but there was plenty else to be observed. Even now, in these modern days of which I write, there were

monks, travelers, a fantoccini troupe, some other soldiers besides ourselves, they being of the regiment of Perche, the *intendant* of the solitary lord, and ourselves. Our troopers alone numbered twenty, they having a table to themselves; while we, the officers, viz., the captain (de Pontgibaud), the lieutenant (whose name was Camier), and I (the cornet), had also a table to ourselves.

Yet, too, there was one other, and if only from her quaint garb, a very conspicuous person. This was a girl—and a mighty well-favored girl too—dark, with her hair tucked up all about her head; with superb full eyes, and with a color rich and brilliant as that of the Provence rose. She made good use of those eyes, I can tell you, and seemed nothing loth to let them encounter the glance of everyone else in the room. For the rest, she was a sort of wandering singer and juggler, clad in a short spangled robe, carrying a *tambour de basque* in her hand, while by her side hung a coarse canvas bag, in which, as we soon saw, she had about a dozen of conjuring balls.

"Who is that?" asked de Pontgibaud of the server, as he came near our table bearing in his hand a succulent *ragôut*, which was one of our courses. "Who and what? A traveler, or a girl belonging to Toulouse?"

"Oh!" said the man, with the true southern shrug of his shoulders.

"That—*elle!* She is a wandering singer, a girl called Damaris. On her road farther south. Pray heaven she steals nothing. She is as like to if she has the chance. A purse or even a spoon, I'll wager. If I were the master she should not be here. Yet, she amuses the company. Sings love ballads and such things, and juggles with those balls. Ha! Giglot," he exclaimed, seeing the girl jump off the table she had been sitting on, talking to a bagman, and come towards us, "away! The gentlemen of the *mousquetaires* require not your company."

"Ay, but they do though," the girl called Damaris said, as she drew close to where we sat. "Soldiers like amusement, and I can amuse them. Pretty gentlemen," she went on, "would you like a love song made in Touraine, or to see a trick or two? Or I have a snake in a box that can do quaint things. Shall I go fetch it—it will dance if I pipe—"

"To confusion with your snake!" exclaimed the waiting man. "We want no snakes here. Snakes, indeed—"

"Well, then, a love song. This pretty boy," and here she was forward enough to fix her eyes most boldly on me, "looks as if he would like a love song. How blue his eyes are!"

Alas! They are somewhat dim and old now, but then, because I was young and foolish, and because my eyes *were* blue, I felt flattered at this wandering creature's remark.

However, without waiting for an answer, she went on. "Come, we will have a trick first. Now," she said, pulling out three of the balls from her bag, "you hold that ball, *mon enfant*—thus," and she put the red one—the only red one—into my hand. "You have it?"

"Yes," I said, "I have it." And, because it was as big as a good-sized apple, I closed my two hands over it.

"You are sure?"

"Certain."

"Show it then." Whereon I opened my hands again, and lo! It was a gilt ball and not a red one that was in them.

"Show that trick to me," said a voice at my back, even as de Pontgibaud and Camier burst out a-laughing, and so, too, did some of the people in the great hall who were supping, while I felt like a fool. "Show that trick to me." And, looking round, I saw that it was the Chevalier de Marcieu who had spoken; the man to whom the regent had sent me, and who had ridden from Paris with us as a sort of civilian director, or guide; the man from whom we were to take our orders when acting as guard to Alberoni when he passed this way, presuming that we had the good fortune to encounter his eminence; he who was to be responsible for the safety of the cardinal.

Now, he knew well enough that we of the *mousquetaires gris* did not like him, that we regarded him as a spy—which in truth he was, more or less—and that his company was not absolutely welcome to us. Wherefore, all along the road from Paris he had kept himself very much apart from us, not taking his meals at our table—where he was not wanted!—and riding ever behind the troop, saying very little except when necessary. But now he had evidently left the table at which he ate alone and had come over to ours, drawn there, perhaps, by a desire to witness the girl's performances.

"No," she said, "I shall not show it to you. I do not do the same trick twice. But if you choose, I will fetch my little snake. Perhaps that would amuse *you*."

"I wish to see that trick with the red ball," said de Marcieu quietly, taking no notice of her emphasis on the word *you*. "Show it to me."

For answer, however, she dropped the balls into the bag, and drawing up a vacant chair which stood against our table—she was a free and easy young woman, this!—said she was tired, and should do no more tricks that night. Also, she asked for some of our Roussillon as a payment for what she had done. Whereupon Camier poured her out a gobletful and passed it over to her, which, with a pretty little bow and grimace, she took, drinking our healths saucily a moment later.

Meanwhile I was eyeing this stroller and thinking that she was a vastly well-favored one in spite of her brown skin, which, both on face and hands, was a strange color, it not being altogether that wholesome, healthy brown which the winds and sun bring to those who are always in the open, but instead a sort of muddy color, so that I thought, perhaps, she did not use to wash overmuch—which, maybe, was like enough. Also, I wondered at the shapeliness of her fingers and hands, the former being delicate and tapering, and the nails particularly well kept. Likewise, I observed something else that I thought strange. Her robe—for such it was—consisted of a coarse, russet-colored Nîmes serge, such as the poor ever wear in France, having in it several tears and jags that had been mended roughly, yet all the same, it looked new and fresh—too new, indeed, to have been thus torn and frayed. Then also, I noticed that at her neck, just above the collar of her dress, there peeped out a piece of lace of the finest quality, lace as good as that of my steinkirk or the ruffles of a dandy's frills. And all this set me a-musing, I know not why.

Meanwhile Marcieu was persistent about that red ball, asking her again and again to try the trick on him, and protesting in a kind of rude good-humor that she did not dare to let him inspect the ball, since she feared he would discover some cunning artifice in it which would show how she made it change from red to gilt.

"Bah!" she replied. "I can do it with anything else. Here, I will show you the trick with other balls." Whereon, as she spoke, she drew out two of the gilt ones and said, "Now, hold out your hands and observe. See, this one has a scratch on it; that one has none. Put the second in your hand; I will transfer the other in its place."

"Nay," said the chevalier, "you shall do it with the red or not at all."

"I will conjure no more," she said pettishly. Then she snatched up the goblet of wine, drank it down at a gulp, and went out of the room, saying, "Goodnight, *mousquetaires*. Goodnight, Blue Eyes," and, I protest, blew me a kiss with the tips of her fingers. The sauciness of these mountebanks is often beyond belief.

The chevalier took the vacant chair she had quitted, though no one invited him to do so, his company not being desired by any of us, and Pontgibaud, calling for a deck of cards, challenged Camier to a game of piquet. As for me, I sat with my elbows on the table watching them play, though at the same time my eye occasionally fell on the spy, and I wondered what he was musing upon so deeply. But presently, he called the drawer over to him and gave an order for some drink to be brought (since none of us had passed him over the flask, we aristocratic *mousquetaires* not deeming a *mouchard* fit bottle-companion for us). When it came he turned his back to the table at which

we sat and asked the man a question in a low voice; though not so low a one but that I caught what he said, and the reply too.

"Where is that vagrant disposed of?" he asked. "With those other vagabonds, I suppose," letting his eye fall on the members of the fantoccini troupe, "or in one of the stables."

"Nay, nay," the server said, "she is not here, but at the 'Red Glove' in the next street. She told me tonight that that was her headquarters until she had visited every inn and tavern in Toulouse and earned some money. Then she will go on to Narbonne."

"So! The 'Red Glove.' A poor inn that, is it not?"

Whereon the man said it was good enough for a wandering ballad-singer anyhow, and went off swiftly to attend to another order at the end of the room, while Marcieu sat there sipping his drink, but now and again casting his eye also over some tablets which he had drawn out of his pocket.

But at this time nine o'clock boomed forth from the tower of the cathedral hard by, which we had noticed as we rode in, and Pontgibaud gave the troopers their orders to betake themselves to their beds; also one to me to go to the stables and see that all the horses were carefully bestowed for the night, since, though the troop-sergeant had made his report that such was the case, he required confirmation of it. Wherefore I went to the end of the room, and taking my long grey *houppelande*, or horseman's cloak (which we *mousquetaires*, because we always had the best of everything, wore trimmed with costly grey fur), I donned it, and was about to go forth to the stables when I heard Pontgibaud's voice raised somewhat angrily as he spoke to the chevalier.

"*Fichtre* for such an arrest!" I heard him say, while the few strangers who had not gone to their beds—as most had done by now—cast their eyes in the direction where he and Marcieu were. "Not I! Body of my father! What do you take my gentlemen of the *mousquetaires* to be? Exempts? Police? Bah! Go to La Poste. Get one of their fellows to do it. We are soldiers, not—"

"I have the regent's orders, " Le Marcieu replied quietly, "to arrest him or anyone else I see fit. And, Monsieur le Vicomte, it is to assist me that your 'gentlemen of the *mousquetaires'* are here in Toulouse—have ridden with me from Paris. I must press it upon you to do as I desire."

Now, I could not wait any longer, since I had my orders from Pontgibaud to repair to the stables and see that the chargers were comfortable for the night, and as, also, I saw a glance shoot out of his eye over the other's head which seemed to bid me go on with my duty. Upon which I went out to the yard, noticing that the snow was falling heavily, and that it was like to be a hard winter night—went out accompanied by a stableman carrying a lantern.

"Give it me," I said, taking the lamp from him. "I will go the round myself. Also the key, so that I can lock the door when I have made inspection."

"Nay, monsieur," he answered, "the door cannot be locked. The inn is full; other travelers' horses are in the stable; they may be required at daybreak."

"Very well," I replied, "in that case one of our men must be roused and put as guard over the animals; they are too valuable to be left alone in an open stable," thinking as I spoke of my beautiful La Rose, for whom I had paid a hundred pistoles a year ago. Then I gave the fellow a silver piece and bade him go get a drink to warm himself with on this winter night, and entered the stable.

The whinny which La Rose gave as I went in showed me where all our horses were bestowed, and I proceeded down to the end of the stable, observing when I got there that they were all well housed for the night, and their straw clean and fresh; while, as the glimmer of the lamp proclaimed, they had been properly groomed and attended to. Everything was very well. Wherefore, giving my own mare the piece of sugar I had brought for her, I made for the door again, observing that Le Marcieu's red roan, a wiry but serviceable beast, was in a stall nearer to the entrance.

Then suddenly, as I raised the lantern to give a second glance at it, to my astonishment I saw the singing-girl, Damaris, dart out swiftly from near that stall and endeavor to push by me and escape through the door; which, however, I easily prevented her from doing, since I seized her at once by the arm and held her, while I exclaimed, "Not so fast, mademoiselle, not so fast. What are you doing here? You, who are at the 'Red Glove,' and have no business whatever in these stables."

CHAPTER III
"WHEN THE STEED HAS FLOWN"

At first she struggled a little, then all of a sudden she took a different tack and exclaimed, "How dare you touch me, fellow. You—a common *mousquetaire*—to lay your hands on me! You . . . you! Let go, or—"

However, I had let go of her by now through astonishment at her impertinence. A common *mousquetaire*, indeed! A common *mousquetaire*! When in all our regiment, there was scarce a trooper riding who was not of gentle blood—to say nothing of the officers.

"I may be 'a common *mousquetaire*,'" I replied, as calmly as I could, "yet, all the same, commit no rudeness to a wandering ballad-singer whom I find in the stable where our horses are; and—"

"Why," she exclaimed with a look (I could see it by the rays of the lantern) that was, I'll be sworn, as much a pretense as her words, "why, 'tis Blue Eyes. Forgive me; I thought it was one of your men. I . . . I did not know you in your great furred cloak. It becomes you vastly well, Blue Eyes," and the hussy smiled up approvingly at me.

"Does it?" I said. "No doubt. Yet nevertheless, I want an explanation of what you are doing in these stables at night, in the dark, when you are housed at the 'Red Glove.'" And I spoke all the more firmly because I felt certain that she had not taken me for one of the troopers at all.

"Imbecile!" she exclaimed petulantly, and for all the world as if she was speaking to an inferior. "Imbecile! Idiot! Since you know I am at the 'Red Glove,' don't you know too that they have no stabling for us who put up there, and that the travelers' livestock are installed here? Oh, Blue Eyes, you are only a simple boy!"

"No, I don't know it!" I exclaimed, a little dashed at this intelligence. "But, pardon me, I would not be ill-mannered, only . . . do ladies of your calling travel on horseback? I thought you wandered on foot from town to town giving your entertainments."

"I do not travel on horseback, but on muleback. There are such things as four-footed mules as well as two-footed ones, Blue Eyes. I assure you there are. And here is mine—look at it. Isn't it a sorry beast to be in company with the noble steeds of the aristocratic *mousquetaires*?"

"Oh, it's 'aristocratic' now, is it?" I thought to myself, "not 'common' *mousquetaires*," running my eye over the mule she pointed out, even as I held the lantern on high. Only as I did so, I saw it was not a sorry beast at all; instead, a wiry, clean-limbed Pyrenean mule, whose hind-legs looked as though they could spring forward mighty fast if wanted; in truth, an animal that looked as if it could show its heels to many of its nobler kin, namely horses. But also, I observed that its saddle was on, and that the halter was not fastened to the rack.

"Well, you see?" she said, looking at me with her mocking smile, and showing all her pretty white teeth as she did so. "You see? Now, Blue Eyes, let me go. I am tired and sleepy, and I want to go to bed."

This being sufficient explanation of her presence in the stables, there was no further reason why I should detain her and I said she might go, while even as I spoke, I fastened up the halter for her. After which we went out into the yard, where we bade each other a sort of goodnight, I doing so a little crossly since I was still sore at her banter, and she, on her part, speaking still in her mocking, gibing manner.

"And where do you go to," she asked, "after this? Eh, Blue Eyes? I should like to see you some day again, you know. I like you, Blue Eyes," and as she spoke I wondered what impish kind of thought was now in her mind, for she was standing close to me, and seemed to be emphasizing her remarks about her liking for me by clutching tight my *houppelande* in her hand.

"That," I said, "if you will excuse me, is our affair. Goodnight; I hope you will sleep well at the 'Red Glove.'" Then, because I did not want to part in anger from the volatile creature, and because I was a soldier to whom such license is permissible, I said, "Adieu, sweetheart."

"Sweetheart!" she exclaimed, turning round on me. "Sweetheart! You dare to speak to me thus—you—you—you base—" But, just as suddenly as she had flown out at me like a spitfire, she changed again, saying, "*Peste!* I forget—I am only a poor wandering vagrant. I did not mean that. I—I am sorry." And as she vanished round the corner of the yard into the street, I heard her laugh and say softly, though loud enough, "Goodnight, Blue Eyes; adieu—*sweetheart*," and again she laughed as she disappeared.

Now, all this had taken some little time, as you may well suppose, so that the great clock of the Cathedral of St. Etienne was striking ten as I re-entered the inn and went on to the large guests'-room, or *salle*. It was empty at this time of all the sojourners in the house except the captain, Pontgibaud, who was sitting in front of the huge fire, into which he stared meditatively while he drank some wine from a glass at his elbow.

"All well with the horses?" he asked as I went up to him. "I thought you were never coming back." Then, without waiting for any explanation from me as to my absence, he said, "We go toward the Pyrenees, by Foix, tomorrow, thereby to intercept Alberoni if we can. That fellow, that *mouchard*, Marcieu, says he is due to cross into France from Aragon. Meanwhile—" but there he paused, saying no more. Instead, he gazed into the embers of the fire; then suddenly, a moment or so after, spoke again. "Adrian," he said, "it is fitting I should tell you what Marcieu knows, or rather suspects, from information he has received from Dubois, who himself has received it from Madrid. Camier has been informed; so must you be."

"What is it now?" I asked, my anxiety aroused.

"This. Alberoni, as Marcieu says, has all the old Spanish aristocracy on his side, simply because the king, Philippe, is a Frenchman. They are helping him—especially the ladies. Now, it is thought one of them has carried off the will of the late King Charles, and not Alberoni himself."

"Who is she?"

"He, Marcieu, will not tell, though he knows her rank and title. But—" and now Pontgibaud looked round the room, which was, as I have said, quite empty but for us, then lowered his voice ere he replied—"but—he is going to arrest that girl called Damaris tomorrow morning," and as he spoke he delivered himself of a grave, solemn wink.

"Is he?" I said. "Is he?" and then fell a-musing. For this opened my eyes to much—opened them, too, in a moment. Now I understood her indignation at a *mousquetaire* seizing hold of her, a highborn damsel, probably of some old Castile or Aragon family, instead of a wandering stroller as we had thought her to be—understood, too, why I had seen that piece of rich lace peeping out at her throat; why her dress of Nîmes serge, which was a new one, was artfully torn and frayed. Also I understood, or thought I did, the strange color of her face and hands, which were, I now made no manner of doubt, dyed or stained to appear dirty and weather-beaten, and why the saddle was on her mule's back and the halter loose from the rack—understood, I felt sure, all about it.

Then, just as I was going to tell Pontgibaud this, we both started to our feet. For outside, where the stables were, we heard a horse's hoofs strike smartly on the cobblestones of the yard; we heard the animal break into a trot the moment it was in the street outside.

"Someone has stolen a horse from those stables," cried Pontgibaud, springing towards the door and rushing down the passage. "Pray Heaven 'tis not one of our chargers."

To which I answered calmly, "I think not. There are other animals there than ours, horses and *mules* belonging to people staying at other inns. It is a traveler setting forth before the city gates are closed at midnight."

And even as I spoke, I could not help laughing in my captain's face, as well as at the look upon it.

CHAPTER IV
ANA, PRINCESA DE CARBAJAL

We were riding through one of the innumerable valleys which are formed by the spurs of the Pyrenees running almost from where the Pic du Midi rises up to the city of Toulouse; a valley which was bordered on either side by shelving hills that were covered with woods nearly up to their summits. And now we were looking forward eagerly to meeting his eminence, the Cardinal Alberoni, of whose arrival in this neighborhood we had received certain intelligence from more than one of the innumerable spies whom both the regent and Cardinal Dubois maintained ever in this region—a region dividing Spain from France.

As for Marcieu, who, as usual, rode behind the troop, he had been in such a towering rage ever since the morning of our departure from Toulouse, and had used such violent language, that I for one had been obliged to tell him to keep a civil tongue in his head, while Pontgibaud, who was an aristocrat to the tips of his fingers as well as captain of a troop of *mousquetaires*, told him he must be more respectful in his language or altogether silent. For, as naturally you have understood, it was the girl who was pleased to call herself Damaris, and to assume the disguise of a wandering juggler and singer, who had ridden off that night on her mule, and was, no doubt, far enough away from us in the morning.

And she had got the late King of Spain's will in her pocket! Of that, Marcieu swore there could be no doubt—the will which, in truth, was the principal thing that brought the nations to agreeing that the Duke of Anjou should sit as King Philippe V on the throne of Spain—the will which, if it once fell into the hands of Austria, would instantly *disappear* forever and set all Europe alight with the flames of war again. She had got it, and when Alberoni was searched it would not be found. Perhaps, after all, it was not strange that Marcieu's expressions were writ in a good round hand. He had missed the chance of his life!

"I know her," he had stormed in the morning, when he found how abortive his attempts to arrest her had proved, "I know her. Dubois sent me intelligence of everything. She is the Princesa Ana de Carbajal, of an ancient and illustrious Catalonian house, a house faithful to all the interests of Austria since before the days of Charles V and of Philip. May the pest seize her! She came ahead of Alberoni disguised thus, and never thought she would encounter us. And I do believe she has the will in that accursed red ball. Such things have been used as hiding-places before. Even Alberoni once used his crook as a receptacle wherein to hide a slip of paper. And the late king's last will in favor of Philippe was itself but a slip of paper, signed when he was close to death." Then, again, he used strong language.

However, she was gone, and on the frail chance of his being misinformed after all, and because he also had orders to meet Alberoni in any circumstances, and to escort him to the Mediterranean coast without allowing him to hold converse with anyone, we set off to find him. For Dubois' spies had met us and said that Alberoni was on his way, that he was close at hand.

So we rode along, nearing rapidly the pass into Spain by which he was coming, and expecting at every moment to meet the cardinal's coach attended by all his servants and following. But suddenly, while we marched, there happened something which put all thoughts of the cardinal and his devoted friend, the Princess Ana, out of our heads—something terrible, awful, to behold.

A house, an inn, on fire, blazing fiercely, as we could see, even as we all struck spurs into our horses and galloped swiftly towards it—a house from the *upper* windows of which we could observe the faces of people looking. The upper windows, because all the lower part was in flames, and because they who were inside had all retreated up and up and up. Only, what could that avail them? Soon the house, the top floor—there were two above the ground—must fall in, and then—yes! Then!

We reached that burning *auberge*— 'twas terrible, ghastly, to see the flames bursting forth from it in the broad daylight and looking white in the glare of the warm southern sun, although 'twas winter—reached it, wondering what we could do to save those who were perishing; to save the screaming mother with her babe clasped to her breast, the white-faced man who called on God through the open window he was at to spare him and his, or, if not him, then his wife and child.

What could we do—what? Bid them leap down to us, fling themselves upon us—yes, at least we might do that. One thing at least we could undoubtedly do— bid them throw down the babe into our arms. And this was done. The troopers sat close upon their horses, their arms extended; a moment later the little thing was safe in the great strong arms of the men, and being caressed and folded to the breast of our great brawny sergeant. Then, even as I witnessed this, even, too, as I (dismounted now) hurried round with some *mousquetaires* to discover if, in God's mercy, there was any ladder behind in the outhouse or garden whereby the upper part might be reached, I myself almost screamed with horror; for at that moment, onto the roof there had sprung a woman shrieking; a woman down whose back fell coils of long black hair; a woman, handsome, beautiful, even in her agony and fear; a woman who was the girl called Damaris.

"Damaris!" I called out. "Damaris!" For by that name I had come to think of her, had known her for a short hour or so. "Damaris! Be calm, do nothing rash. We will save you; the walls will not fall in yet. Be cool."

But in answer to my words she could do nothing but wring her hands and shriek. "I cannot die like this—not like this. Oh, Blue Eyes, save me! Save me! Save me! You called me your sweetheart. Save me!"

Then, at that moment, I heard a calm, icy voice beside me say—it was the voice of Marcieu—"Does your highness intend to restore the late King of Spain's will? Answer that, or I swear, since I command here, that you shall not be saved."

In a moment I had sprung at him, would have pulled him off his horse, have struck him in the mouth, have killed him for his brutality, but that Camier and two of the troopers held me back. Even as they did so, I heard the girl's voice ring out, "Yes! Yes! Yes! 'Tis here!" And as she spoke, she put her hand in the bag by her side, drew out the red ball, and flung it down from the roof to where we all were.

But by now—Heaven in its mercy be praised!—some of the others had found a ladder and brought it round, and were placing it against the walls. Only it was too short! God help her! It but reached to the sill of the top-floor window.

And now I was distraught, was mad with grief and horror, when again that cold-blooded creature, Marcieu, spoke, saying, "What matter? Can she not descend from the roof to the room that window is in?" And at the same moment Pontgibaud called out to her to do that very thing, which she, at once understanding, prepared to accomplish.

Meanwhile, some of the men, who were all now dismounted, had sprung to the ladder, eager to save, first the girl, I think, then next the woman of the house, and then the man. But I ordered them back. I alone would save her, I said, I alone. Princess or stroller, noble or crafty adherent of a wronged monarchy—whichever she might be, I had taken a liking to this girl; she had called on me to save her, and I would do it. Wherefore, up the ladder I went as quickly as the weight of my great riding boots and trappings would permit me, while all the time the flames were shooting out from the lower windows— up, until I stood at the top and received her in my arms, telling the woman and the man they should be saved immediately. And so they were, the troopers fetching down the woman, and the man following directly after by himself; yet none too soon either, for even as he came down, the flames had set the lower part of the ladder afire, so that it fell down and he got singed as he came to earth. But nevertheless, all were now saved; and Damaris stood trembling by my side, and pouring out her thanks to, and blessing upon, me.

"I—I—did not mean what I said," stammered Marcieu. "I meant you should be saved. But I meant also to have that will, and I have got it." While, as his eye roved around us, he saw the disgust written upon all our faces, on the faces alike of officers and men.

"You have got it," she answered contemptuously. "You have! Much good may it do you, animal!" And again I saw the beautiful white teeth gleam between her lips.

"But why here, Dama . . . Señorita?" I whispered. "Why here? You came the wrong way if you wished to escape with the precious document."

She gave me somewhat of a nervous, tremulous smile, and was about to answer

me and give me some explanation, when lo! There came an interruption to all our talk. The long-expected cardinal was approaching. Alberoni had crossed the Pyrenees.

But in what a way to come! We could scarcely believe our eyes. There was no coach, nor heavily-laden mules to bear him and his followers and belongings. He was on foot; so, too, were his attendants. He, a cardinal; the arbiter of Spain, while ostensibly only the political agent of the Duke of Parma; a prince of the Church; a man who had intrigued for, and almost secured, one of the greatest prizes of that Church, the primacy of the land from which he had now been expelled—on foot! So that, if he had not had on his head his cardinal's hat—which he doubtless wore in his arrogance—none would have deemed him the great man he was, even in his downfall.

All doffed their own hats as he came near us, Marcieu doing so as respectfully as any, while, as we removed ours, I saw him steal a glance at her whom we had known as Damaris. Such a glance, such a sly, cunning one!

Then, as she sprang forward to take the cardinal's hand, meaning, I think, to kiss it, he prevented her from doing so by, instead, raising that hand above her head and muttering, as I supposed a blessing.

But now, even as he looked somewhat wonderingly at the still burning house, he turned to Marcieu and said, "You are the man, I imagine, and those your troopers, whom the regent has sent to intercept me. Ha! You are surprised that I know this," he went on, seeing the start that Marcieu gave when he heard those words. "Are you not? If you should ever know Alberoni better, you will learn that he is a match for most court spies in Europe."

Now the chevalier did seem so utterly taken aback at this (which caused Pontgibaud to give me a quaint look of satisfaction out of the tail of his eye—for every one of us hated that man mortally) that he could do nothing but bow, uttering no sound.

Whereon the cardinal proceeded, "Well! What do you expect to do with me? Your comrades of Spain—the knaves and brigands whom the king sent after me from Madrid—have pillaged me of all. Someday I will pay his majesty for the outrage—let him beware lest I place Austria back upon his throne. 'Twas a beggarly trick, to take my carriages and mules, my jewels and wealth—even the will of the late king, which was most lawfully and rightfully in my possession."

"What!" broke from several of our lips. "What!"

While from Marcieu's white and trembling ones came the words, "The late king's will! It is impossible. This girl—this lady—has handed it to me!"

For a moment the cardinal's sly glance rested on the princess, then on Marcieu, and then—then—he actually laughed, not loud, but long.

"Monsieur," he said at last, "you are a poor spy—easily to be tricked. You will never make a living at the calling. The will that lady gave you was a duplicate, a copy. It was meant that you should have *that*—that it should fall into your stupid hands. And, had I not been robbed on the other side of the mountains, you would not have seen me here."

"It is so," the princess said, striding up to where the chevalier stood. "It is so. You spy! You spy! You *mouchard!* If that worthless piece of paper in the red ball had been the real will, I would have perished in the burning house before letting it fall into your hands." Then, sinking her voice still lower, though not so low but that some of us could hear what she said, she went on: "Have a care for your future. The followers of Austria have still some power left, even at the Court of France. Your threat to let me burn on the roof was *not* unmeant. It will be remembered."

And now there is no more to tell, except that the princess knew that Marcieu meant to take the real will from the cardinal if he met him, and so it had been arranged that, through her, the paper which he would suppose was the real will was to fall into his hands, and Alberoni would thus have been enabled to retain the original and escape with it out of France. She had preceded us to the foot of the mountains from Toulouse, meaning, when we came up, to let Marcieu obtain the red ball and thus be hoodwinked; and the accident of the fire at the inn only anticipated what she intended doing. The unexpected following of, and attack upon, the cardinal, ere he quitted Spain and descended the Pyrenees into France, had, however, spoilt all their plans.

Here I should attempt that which most writers of narratives are in the habit of performing, namely, conclude by telling you what was the end of Ana de Carbajal's adventure, of how she won and broke hearts and eventually made a brilliant match. That is what Monsieur Marivaux or the fair Scuderi would have done, as well as some of the writers of my own native land. But I refrain, because this strange meeting between me and the beautiful and adventurous Spanish lady was but the commencement of a long friendship that eventually ripened—however, no matter. Someday when my hand is not weary and the spirit is upon me, I intend to write down more of the history of the high-bred young aristocrat who first appeared before me as a wandering stroller, and passed for "a girl called Damaris."

About Baroness Orczy

The Baroness Orczy (1865-1947)—but really, we must give her her full name: Emma Magdolna Rozália Mária Jozefa Borbála Orczy de Orczi—no wonder they called her "Emmuska" for short—was a Hungarian noble by birth, whose family left Hungary after her father's farm was burned by rioting peasantry. Which may have had something to do with her later decision to write about the persecution of aristocrats during the French Revolution.

Orczy's father was an amateur composer and good friend of Franz Liszt, and young Emma met the high and the interesting as her family moved about Europe for over a decade, finally settling in England in 1880. Emma attended art school in London, and there she met Montagu Barstow, an artist whom she eventually married in 1894. Barstow's income as an illustrator was unreliable, so to supplement it Emma began writing novels and detective stories in 1899, albeit at first with only modest success.

One day in 1903 the image of Sir Percy Blakeney appeared, fully formed, in Emma Orczy's mind's eye, and she knew she was seeing the protagonist of her next novel. She wrote *The Scarlet Pimpernel* in five weeks and sent it out with high hopes, but a dozen publishers turned it down. With her husband's collaboration she crafted a version of the story for the stage, and found a company willing to produce it. After a slow start the play took off and became a huge hit, after which selling the novel was suddenly easy.

Sequel followed sequel for the next thirty-plus years, and over more than a dozen novels and collections the dashing Scarlet Pimpernel probably saved more aristocrats from Mam'zelle Guillotine than were actually executed in the historically brief period of The Terror. But the Baroness wasn't a historian, she was a storyteller—and few storytellers have created a character as indelible as Sir Percy Blakeney, the Scarlet Pimpernel. All the classic hallmarks of that beloved swashbuckler can be found in the story that follows, drawn from the 1919 collection *The League of the Scarlet Pimpernel.*

Egregious aside: swashbucklers are gamblers; when they're not risking their lives in desperate exploits, they're risking their half-empty purses in games of chance. Your humble editor, in his day job, is a professional game designer, and keenly interested in the games the swashbucklers played: whether card games, like lansquenet and piquet, or dice games, like knucklebones and hazard.

At the beginning of "The Cabaret de la Liberté," the habitués of the eponymous *boite* are dicing, in a game the Baroness informs us is hazard. "Eight and eleven—nineteen!" they cry. Then: "Four and nine—thirteen!"

Nineteen? Thirteen?

Hazard, my eye.

Most of our readers are probably familiar with the modern dice game of craps. Hazard was its 17th-century predecessor, and like its descendant, was played with two six-sided dice. It's more interesting than craps, as the caster can specify any number between 5 and 9 as his "main," or target number, varying the odds and rewards— unlike craps, where the "main" is always 7, and the payout always the same.

But in no case can you roll 13 or 19. Not on two dice. Hrmpf.

As long as we're gambling, I'll lay you odds that Baroness Orczy, an aristocrat to her cuticles, was simply ignorant of the rules of hazard, a game of the low-born *canaille*—and frankly, didn't care. Do you doubt me? Come on, *mes amis*—I'll wager three-to-two on the Baroness' ignorance, in good red Spanish pistoles! Pass the box.

The Cabaret de la Liberté

BARONESS ORCZY

I

"Eight!"

"Twelve!"

"Four!"

A loud curse accompanied this last throw, and shouts of ribald laughter greeted it.

"No luck, Guidal!"

"Always at the tail end of the cart, eh, citizen?"

"Do not despair yet, good old Guidal! Bad beginnings oft make splendid ends!"

Then once again the dice rattled in the boxes; those who stood around pressed closer round the gamesters; hot, avid faces, covered with sweat and grime, peered eagerly down upon the table.

"Eight and eleven—nineteen!"

"Twelve and zero! By Satan! Curse him! Just my luck!"

"Four and nine—thirteen! Unlucky number!"

"Now then—once more! I'll back Merri! Ten assignats of the most worthless kind! Who'll take me that Merri gets the wench in the end?"

This from one of the lookers-on, a tall, cadaverous-looking creature, with sunken eyes and broad, hunched-up shoulders, which were perpetually shaken by a dry, rasping cough that proclaimed the ravages of some mortal disease, left him trembling as with ague and brought beads of perspiration to the roots of his lank hair. A recrudescence of excitement went the round of the spectators. The gamblers sitting round a narrow deal table, on which past libations had left marks of sticky rings, had scarce room to move their elbows.

"Nineteen and four—twenty-three!"

"You are out of it, Desmonts!"

"Not yet!"

"Twelve and twelve!"

"There! What did I tell you?"

"Wait! Wait! Now, Merri! Now! Remember, I have backed you for ten assignats, which I propose to steal from the nearest Jew this very night!"

"Thirteen and twelve! Twenty-five, by all the demons and the ghouls!" came a triumphant shout from the last thrower.

"Merri has it! *Vive* Merri!" was the unanimous and clamorous response.

Merri was evidently the most popular amongst the three gamblers. Now he sprawled upon the bench, leaning his back against the table, and surveyed the assembled company with the air of an Achilles having vanquished his Hector.

"Good luck to you and to your aristo!" began his backer lustily—would, no doubt, have continued his song of praise had not a violent fit of coughing smothered the words in his throat. The hand which he raised in order to slap his friend genially on the back now went with a convulsive clutch to his own chest.

But his obvious distress did not apparently disturb the equanimity of Merri, or arouse even passing interest in the lookers-on.

"May she have as much money as rumor avers," said one of the men sententiously.

Merri gave a careless wave of his grubby hand. "More, citizen; more!" he said loftily.

Only the two losers appeared inclined to skepticism. "Bah!" one of them said—it was Desmonts. "The whole matter of the woman's money may be a tissue of lies!"

"And England is a far cry!" added Guidal.

But Merri was not likely to be depressed by these dismal croakings. "'Tis simple enough," he said philosophically, "to disparage the goods if you are not able to buy."

Then a lusty voice broke in from the far corner of the room: "And now, Citizen Merri, 'tis time you remembered that the evening is hot and your friends thirsty!"

The man who spoke was a short, broad-shouldered creature, with crimson face surrounded by a shock of white hair, like a ripe tomato wrapped in cotton wool. "And let me tell you," he added complacently, "that I have a cask of rum down below which came straight from that accursed country, England, and is said to be the nectar whereon feeds that confounded Scarlet Pimpernel. It gives him the strength, so 'tis said, to intrigue successfully against the representatives of the people."

"Then by all means, citizen," concluded Merri's backer, still hoarse and spent after his fit of coughing, "let us have some of your nectar. My friend, Citizen Merri, will need strength and wits too, I'll warrant, for, after he has married the aristo, he will have to journey to England to pluck the rich dowry which is said to lie hidden there."

"Cast no doubt upon that dowry, Citizen Rateau, curse you!" broke in Merri, with a spiteful glance directed against his former rivals, "or Guidal and Desmonts will cease to look glum, and half my joy in the aristo will have gone."

After which, the conversation drifted to general subjects, became hilarious and ribald, while the celebrated rum from England filled the close atmosphere of the narrow room with its heady fumes.

II

Open to the street in front, the locality known under the pretentious title of "Cabaret de la Liberté" was a favored one among the flotsam and jetsam of the population of this corner of old Paris; men and sometimes women, with nothing particular to do, no special means of livelihood save the battening on the countless miseries and sorrows which this Revolution, which was to have been so glorious, was bringing in its train; idlers and loafers, who would crawl desultorily down the few worn and grimy steps which led into the cabaret from the level of the street. There was always good brandy or *eau de vie* to be had there, and no questions asked, no scares from the revolutionary guards or the secret agents of the Committee of Public Safety, who knew better than to interfere with the citizen host and his dubious *clientèle*. There was also good Rhine wine or rum to be had, smuggled across from England or Germany, and no interference from the spies of some of those countless committees, more autocratic than any *ci-devant* despot.

It was, in fact, an ideal place wherein to conduct those shady transactions which are unavoidable corollaries of an unfettered democracy. Projects of burglary, pillage, rapine, even murder, were hatched within this underground burrow, where, as soon as evening drew in, a solitary, smoky oil-lamp alone cast a dim light upon faces that liked to court the darkness, and whence no sound that was not meant for prying ears found its way to the street above. The walls were thick with grime and smoke, the floor mildewed and cracked; dirt vied with squalor to make the place a fitting abode for thieves and cutthroats, for some of those sinister night-birds, more vile even than those who shrieked with satisfied lust at sight of the tumbrel, with its daily load of unfortunates for the guillotine.

On this occasion that project that was being hatched was one of the most abject. A young girl, known by some to be possessed of a fortune, was the stake for which these workers of iniquity gambled across one of mine host's greasy tables. The latest decree of the Convention, encouraging, nay, commanding, the union of aristocrats with so-called patriots, had fired the imagination of this nest of jailbirds with thoughts of glorious possibilities. Some of them had collected the necessary information; and the report had been encouraging.

This self-indulgent aristo, the *ci-devant* banker Amédé Vincent, who had expiated his villainies upon the guillotine, was known to have been successful in abstracting the bulk of his ill-gotten wealth and concealing it somewhere—it was not exactly known where, but thought to be in England—out of the reach, at any rate, of deserving patriots.

Some three or four years ago, before the glorious principles of Liberty, Equality, and Fraternity had made short of all such pestilential aristocrats, the *ci-devant* banker, then a widower with an only daughter, Esther, had journeyed to England. He soon returned to Paris, however, and went on living there with his little girl in comparative retirement, until his many crimes found him out at last and he was made to suffer the punishment which he so justly deserved. Those crimes consisted for the most part in humiliating the aforesaid deserving patriots with his benevolence, shaming them with many kindnesses, and the simplicity of his home life, and, above all, in flouting the decrees of the Revolutionary Government, which made every connection with *ci-devant* churches and priests a penal offense against the security of the State.

Amédé Vincent was sent to the guillotine, and the representatives of the people confiscated his house and all his property on which they could lay their hands; but they never found the millions which he was supposed to have concealed. Certainly his daughter Esther—a young girl, not yet nineteen—had not found them either, for after her father's death she went to live in one of the poorer quarters of Paris, alone with an old and faithful servant named Lucienne. And while the Committee of Public Safety was deliberating whether it would be worthwhile to send Esther to the guillotine, to follow in her father's footsteps, a certain number of astute jailbirds plotted to obtain possession of her wealth.

The wealth existed, over in England; of that they were ready to take their oath, and the project which they had formed was as ingenious as it was diabolic; to feign a denunciation, to enact a pretended arrest, to place before the unfortunate girl the alternatives of death or marriage with one of the gang, were the chief incidents of this iniquitous project, and it was in the Cabaret de la Liberté that lots were thrown as to which among the herd of miscreants should be the favored one to play the chief *rôle* in the sinister drama.

The lot fell to Merri; but the whole gang was to have a share in the putative fortune—even Rateau, the wretched creature with the hacking cough, who looked as if he had one foot in the grave, and shivered as if he were stricken with ague, put in a word now and again to remind his good friend Merri that he, too, was looking forward to his share of the spoils.

Merri, however, was inclined to repudiate him altogether. "Why should I share with you?" he said roughly, when, a few hours later, he and Rateau parted in the street outside the Cabaret de la Liberté. "Who are you, I would like to know, to try and poke your ugly nose into my affairs? How do I know where you come from, and whether you are not some crapulent spy of one of those pestilential committees?"

From which eloquent flow of language we may infer that the friendship between these two worthies was not of very old duration. Rateau would, no doubt, have protested loudly, but the fresh outer air had evidently caught his wheezy lungs, and for a minute or two he could do nothing but cough and sputter and groan, and cling to his unresponsive comrade for support. Than at last, when he had succeeded in recovering his breath, he said dolefully and with a ludicrous attempt at dignified reproach:

"Do not force me to remind you, Citizen Merri, that if it had not been for my suggestion that we should all draw lots, and then play hazard as to who shall be the chosen one to woo the *ci-devant* millionaires, there would soon have been a free fight inside the *cabaret*, a number of broken heads, and no decision whatever arrived at; whilst you, who were never much of a fighter, would probably be lying now helpless, with a broken nose and deprived of some of your teeth, with no chance of entering the lists for the heiress. Instead of which, here you are, the victor by a stroke of good fortune, which you should at least have the good grace to ascribe to me."

Whether the poor wretch's argument had any weight with Citizen Merri, or whether that worthy patriot merely thought that procrastination would, for the nonce, prove the best policy, it were impossible to say. Certain it is that in response to his companion's tirade he contented himself with a dubious grunt, and without another word turned on his heel and went slouching down the street.

III

For the persistent and optimistic romanticist, there were still one or two idylls to be discovered flourishing under the shadow of the grim and relentless Revolution. One such was that which had Esther Vincent and Jack Kennard for hero and heroine. Esther, the orphaned daughter of one of the richest bankers of pre-Revolution days, now a daily governess and household drudge at ten francs a week in the house of a retired butcher in the Rue Richelieu, and Jack Kennard, formerly the representative of a big English firm of woolen manufacturers, who had thrown up his employment and prospects in England in order to watch over the girl whom he loved. He, himself an alien enemy an Englishman, in deadly danger of his life every hour that he remained in France; and she, unwilling at the time to leave the horrors of revolutionary Paris while her father was lingering at the Conciergerie awaiting condemnation, as such forbidden to leave the city. So Kennard stayed on, unable to tear himself away from her, and obtained an unlucrative post as accountant in a small wine shop over by Montmartre. His life, like hers, was hanging by a thread; any day, any hour now, some malevolent denunciation might, in the sight of the Committee of Public Safety, turn the eighteen-year-old "suspect" into a living peril to the State, or the alien enemy into a dangerous spy.

Some of the happiest hours these two spent in one another's company were embittered by that ever-present dread of the peremptory knock at the door, the portentous: "Open in the name of the Law!"— the perquisition, the arrest, to which the only issue, these days, was the guillotine.

But the girl was only just eighteen, and he not many years older, and at that age, in spite of misery, sorrow, and dread, life always has its compensations. Youth cries out to happiness so insistently that happiness is forced to hear, and for a few moments, at the least drives care and even the bitterest anxiety away.

For Esther Vincent and her English lover there were moments when they believed themselves to be almost happy.

It was in the evenings mostly, when she came home from her work and he was free to spend an hour or two with her. Then old Lucienne, who had been Esther's nurse in the happy, olden days, and was an unpaid maid-of-all-work and a loved and trusted friend now, would bring in the lamp and pull the well-darned curtains over the windows. She would spread a clean cloth upon the table and bring in a meager supper of coffee and black bread, perhaps a little butter or a tiny square of cheese. And the two young people would talk of the future, of the time when they would settle down in Kennard's old home, over in England, where his mother and sister even now were eating out their hearts with anxiety for him.

"Tell me all about the South Downs," Esther was very fond of saying, "and your village, and your house, and the rambler roses and the clematis arbor."

She never tired of hearing, nor he of telling. The old Manor House, bought with his father's savings; the garden which was his mother's hobby; the cricket pitch on the village green. Oh, the cricket! She thought that so funny—the men in high, sugarloaf hats, grownup men, spending hours and hours, day after day, in banging at a ball with a wooden bat!

"Oh, Jack! The English are a funny, nice, dear, kind lot of people. I remember—"

She remembered so well that happy summer which she had spent with her father in England four years before. It was after the Bastille had been stormed and taken, and the banker had journeyed to England with his daughter in something of a hurry. Then her father had talked of returning to France, and leaving her behind with friends in England. But Esther would not be left. Oh, no! Even now she glowed with pride at the thought of her firmness in the matter. If she had remained in England she would never have seen her dear father again.

Her remembrances grew bitter and sad, until Jack's hand reached soothingly, consolingly out to her, and she brushed away her tears, so as not to sadden him still more.

Then she would ask more questions about his home and his garden, about his mother and the dogs and the flowers; and once more they would forget that hatred and envy and death were already stalking their door.

IV

"Open, in the name of the Law!"

It had come at last. A bolt from out the serene blue of their happiness. A rough, dirty, angry, cursing crowd, who burst through the heavy door even before they had time to open it. Lucienne collapsed into a chair, weeping and lamenting, with her apron thrown over her head. But Esther and Kennard stood quite still and calm, holding one another by the hand, just to give one another courage.

Some half-dozen men stalked into the little room. Men? They looked like ravenous beasts, and were unspeakably dirty, wore soiled tricolor scarves above their tattered breeches in token of their official status. Two of them fell on the remnants of the meager supper and devoured everything that remained on the table—bread, cheese, a piece of homemade sausage. The others ransacked the two attic-rooms which had been home for Esther and Lucienne: the little living-room under the sloping roof, with the small hearth on which very scanty meals were wont to be cooked, and the bare, narrow room beyond, with the iron bedstead, and the palliasse on the floor for Lucienne.

The men poked about everywhere, struck great, spiked sticks through the poor bits of bedding, and ripped up the palliasse. They tore open the drawers of the rickety chest and of the broken-down wardrobe, and did not spare the unfortunate young girl a single humiliation or a single indignity.

Kennard, burning with wrath, tried to protest.

"Hold that cub!" commanded the leader of the party, almost as soon as the young Englishman's hot, indignant words had resounded above the din of overturned furniture. "And if he opens his mouth again throw him into the street!"

And Kennard, terrified lest he should be parted from Esther, thought it wiser to hold his peace.

They looked at one another, like two young trapped beasts—not despairing, but trying to infuse courage one into the other by a look of confidence and of love. Esther, in fact, kept her eyes fixed on her good-looking English lover, firmly keeping down the shudder of loathing which went right through her when she saw those awful men coming nigh her. There was one especially whom she abominated worse than the others, a bandy-legged ruffian, who regarded her with a leer that caused her an almost physical nausea. He did not take part in the perquisition, but sat down in the center of the room and sprawled over the table with the air of one who was in authority. The others addressed him as "Citizen Merri," and alternately ridiculed and deferred to him.

And there was another, equally hateful, a horrible, cadaverous creature, with huge bare feet thrust into sabots, and lank hair thick with grime. He did most of the talking, even though his loquacity occasionally broke down in a racking cough, which literally seemed to tear at his chest, and left him panting, hoarse, and with beads of moisture upon his low, pallid forehead.

Of course, the men found nothing that could even remotely be termed compromising. Esther had been very prudent in deference to Kennard's advice; she also had very few possessions. Nevertheless, when the wretches had turned every article of furniture inside out, one of them asked curtly, "What do we do next, Citizen Merri?"

"Do?" broke in the cadaverous creature, even before Merri had time to reply. "Do? Why, take the wench to—to—"

He got no further, became helpless with coughing. Esther, quite instinctively, pushed the carafe of water towards him.

"Nothing of the sort!" riposted Merri sententiously. "The wench stays here!"

Both Esther and Jack had much ado to suppress an involuntary cry of relief, which at this unexpected pronouncement had risen to their lips.

The man with the cough tried to protest. "But—" he began hoarsely.

"I said the wench stays here!" broke in Merri peremptorily. "*Ah, ça!*" he added, with a savage imprecation. "Do you command here, Citizen Rateau, or do I?"

The other at once became humble, even cringing. "You, of course, citizen," he rejoined in his hollow voice. "I would only remark—"

"Remark nothing," retorted the other curtly. "See to it that the cub is out of the house. And after that put a sentry outside the wench's door. No one to go in and out of here under any pretext whatever. Understand?"

Kennard this time uttered a cry of protest. The helplessness of his position exasperated him almost to madness. Two men were holding him tightly by his sinewy arms. With an Englishman's instinct for a fight, he would not only have tried, but also succeeded in knocking these two down, and taken the other four on after that, with quite a reasonable chance of success. That tuberculous creature, now! And that bandy-legged ruffian! Jack Kennard had been an amateur middleweight champion in his day, and these brutes had no more science than an enraged bull!

But even as he fought against that instinct he realized the futility of a struggle. The danger of it, too—not for himself, but for her. After all, they were not going to take her away to one of those awful places from which the only egress was the way to the guillotine; and if there was that amount of freedom there was bound to be some hope. At twenty there is always hope!

So when, in obedience to Merri's orders, the two ruffians began to drag him towards the door, he said firmly, "Leave me alone. I'll go without this unnecessary struggling."

Then, before the wretches realized his intention, he had jerked himself free from them and run to Esther. "Have no fear," he said to her in English, and in a rapid whisper. "I'll watch over you. The house opposite. I know the people. I'll manage it somehow. Be on the lookout."

They would not let him say more, and she only had the chance of responding firmly, "I am not afraid, and I'll be on the lookout." The next moment Merri's compeers seized him from behind—four of them this time.

Then, of course, prudence went to the winds. He hit out to the right and left. Knocked two of those recreants down, and already was prepared to seize Esther in his arms, make a wild dash for the door, and run with her, whither only God knew, when Rateau, that awful consumptive reprobate, crept slyly up behind him and dealt him a swift and heavy blow on the skull with his weighted stick.

Kennard staggered, and the bandits closed upon him. Those on the floor had time to regain their feet. To make assurance doubly sure, one of them emulated Rateau's tactics and hit the Englishman once more on the head from behind. After that, Kennard became inert; he had partly lost consciousness. His head ached furiously. Esther, numb with horror, saw him bundled out of the room. Rateau, coughing and spluttering, finally closed the door upon the unfortunate and the four brigands who had hold of him.

Only Merri and that awful Rateau had remained in the room. The latter, gasping for breath now, poured himself out a mugful of water and drank it down at one draught. Then he swore, because he wanted rum, or brandy, or even wine. Esther watched him and Merri, fascinated. Poor old Lucienne was quietly weeping behind her apron.

"Now then, my wench," Merri began abruptly, "suppose you sit down here and listen to what I have to say."

He pulled a chair close to him and with one of those hideous leers which had already caused her to shudder, he beckoned her to sit. Esther obeyed as if in a dream. Her eyes were dilated like those of one in a waking trance. She moved mechanically, like a bird attracted by a serpent, terrified yet unresisting. She felt utterly helpless between these two villainous brutes, and anxiety for her English lover seemed further to numb her senses. When she was sitting she turned her gaze, with an involuntary appeal for pity, upon the bandy-legged ruffian beside her.

He laughed. "No! I am not going to hurt you," he said with smooth condescension, which was far more loathsome to Esther's ears than his comrades' savage oaths had been. "You are pretty and you have pleased me. 'Tis no small matter, forsooth!" he added, with loud-voiced bombast, "to have earned the goodwill of citizen Merri. You, my wench, are in luck's way. You realize what has occurred just now. You are amenable to the law which has decreed you to be suspect. I

hold an order for your arrest. I can have you seized at once by my men, dragged to the Conciergerie, and from thence nothing can save you—neither your good looks nor the protection of Citizen Merri. It means the guillotine. You understand that, don't you?"

She sat quite still; only her hands were clutched convulsively together. But she contrived to say quite firmly, "I do, and I am not afraid."

Merri waved a huge and very dirty hand with a careless gesture. "I know," he said with a harsh laugh. "They all say that, don't they, Citizen Rateau?"

"Until the time comes," assented that worthy dryly.

"Until the time comes," reiterated the other. "Now, my wench," he added, once more turning to Esther, "I don't want that time to come. I don't want your pretty head to go rolling down into the basket, and to receive the slap on the face which the citizen executioner has of late taken to bestowing on those aristocratic cheeks which Madame la Guillotine has finally blanched forever. Like this, you see."

And the inhuman wretch took up one of the round cushions from the nearest chair, held it up at arm's length, as if it were a head which he held by the hair, and then slapped it twice with the palm of his left hand. The gesture was so horrible and withal so grotesque, that Esther closed her eyes with a shudder, and her pale cheeks took on a leaden hue.

Merri laughed aloud and threw the cushion down again. "Unpleasant, what? My pretty wench! Well, you know what to expect . . . unless," he added significantly, "you are reasonable and will listen to what I am about to tell you."

Esther was no fool, nor was she unsophisticated. These were not times when it was possible for any girl, however carefully nurtured and tenderly brought up, to remain ignorant of the realities and the brutalities of life. Even before Merri had put his abominable proposition before her, she knew what he was driving at. Marriage—marriage to him! That ignoble wretch, more vile than any dumb creature! In exchange for her life!

It was now her turn to laugh. The very thought of it was farcical in its very odiousness. Merri, who had embarked on his proposal with grandiloquent phraseology, suddenly paused, almost awed by that strange, hysterical laughter.

"By Satan and all his ghouls!" he cried, and jumped to his feet, his cheeks paling beneath the grime.

Then rage seized him at his own cowardice. His egregious vanity, wounded by that laughter, egged him on. He tried to seize Esther by the waist. But she, quick as some panther on the defense, had jumped up too, and pounced upon a knife—the very one she had been using for that

happy little supper with her lover a brief half-hour ago. Unguarded, unthinking, acting just with a blind instinct, she raised it and cried hoarsely, "If you dare touch me, I'll kill you!"

It was ludicrous, of course. A mouse threatening a tiger. The very next moment Rateau had seized her hand and quietly taken away the knife.

Merri shook himself like a frowsy dog. "Whew!" he exclaimed. "What a vixen! But," he added lightly, "I like her all the better for that—eh, Rateau? Give me a wench with a temperament, I say!"

But Esther, too, had recovered herself. She realized her helplessness, and gathered courage from the consciousness of it! Now she faced the infamous villain more calmly.

"I will never marry you," she said loudly and firmly. "Never! I am not afraid to die. I am not afraid of the guillotine. There is no shame attached to death. So now you may do as you please—denounce me, and send me to follow in the footsteps of my dear father, if you wish. But whilst I am alive you will never come nigh me. If ever you do but lay a finger upon me, it will be because I am dead and beyond the reach of your polluting touch. And now I have said all that I will ever say to you in this life. If you have a spark of humanity left in you, you will, at least, let me prepare for death in peace."

She went round to where poor old Lucienne still sat, like an insentient log, panic-stricken. She knelt down on the floor and rested her arm on the old woman's knees. The light of the lamp fell full upon her, her pale face and mass of chestnut-brown hair. There was nothing about her at that moment to inflame a man's desire. She looked pathetic in her helplessness, and nearly lifeless through the intensity of her pallor, whilst the look in her eyes was almost maniacal.

Merri cursed and swore, tried to hearten himself by turning on his friend. But Rateau had collapsed—whether with excitement or the ravages of disease, it were impossible to say. He sat upon a low chair, his long legs, his violet-circled eyes staring out with a look of hebetude and overwhelming fatigue. Merri looked around him and shuddered. The atmosphere of the place had become strangely weird and uncanny; even the tablecloth, dragged half across the table, looked somehow like a shroud.

"What shall we do, Rateau?" he asked tremulously at last.

"Get out of this infernal place," replied the other huskily. "I feel as if I were in my grave-clothes already."

"Hold your tongue, you miserable coward! You'll make the aristo think that we are afraid."

"Well?" queried Rateau blandly. "Aren't you?"

"No!" replied Merri fiercely. "I'll go now because . . . because . . . well! Because

I have had enough today. And the wench sickens me. I wish to serve the Republic by marrying her, but just now I feel as if I should never really want her. So I'll go! But, understand!" he added, and turned once more to Esther, even though he could not bring himself to go nigh her again. "Understand that tomorrow I'll come again for my answer. In the meanwhile, you may think matters over, and maybe you'll arrive at a more reasonable frame of mind. You will not leave these rooms until I set you free. My men will remain as sentinels at your door."

He beckoned to Rateau, and the two men went out of the room without another word.

V

The whole of that night Esther remained shut up in her apartment in the Petite Rue Taranne. All night she heard the measured tramp, the movements, the laughter and loud talking of men outside her door. Once or twice she tried to listen to what they said. But the doors and walls in these houses of old Paris were too stout to allow voices to filter through, save in the guise of a confused murmur. She would have felt horribly lonely and frightened but for the fact that in one window on the third floor in the house opposite the light of a lamp appeared like a glimmer of hope. Jack Kennard was there, on the watch.

He had the window open and sat beside it until a very late hour; and after that he kept the light in it, as a beacon to bid her be of good cheer.

In the middle of the night he made an attempt to see her, hoping to catch the sentinels asleep or absent. But, having climbed the five stories of the house wherein she dwelt, he arrived on the landing outside her door and found there half a dozen ruffians squatting on the stone floor and engaged in playing hazard with a pack of greasy cards. That wretched consumptive, Rateau, was with them, and made a facetious remark as Kennard, pale and haggard, almost ghostlike, with a white bandage around his head, appeared upon the landing.

"Go back to bed, citizen," the odious creature said, with a raucous laugh. "We are taking care of your sweetheart for you."

Never in all his life had Jack Kennard felt so abjectly wretched as he did then, so miserably helpless. There was nothing that he could do, save to return to the lodging which a kind friend had lent him for the occasion, and from whence he could, at any rate, see the windows behind which his beloved was watching and suffering.

When he went a few minutes before, he had left the *porte cochère* ajar. Now he pushed it open and stepped into the dark passage beyond. A tiny streak of light filtrated through a small curtained window in the *concierge*'s lodge; it served to guide Kennard to the foot of the narrow stone staircase which led to the floors above. Just at the foot of the stairs, on the mat, a white paper glimmered in the dim shaft of light. He paused, puzzled, quite certain that the paper was not there five minutes before when he went out. Oh! It may have fluttered in from the courtyard beyond, or from anywhere, driven by the draught. But, even so, with that mechanical action peculiar to most people under like circumstances, he stooped and picked up the paper, turned it over between his fingers, and saw that a few words were scribbled on it in pencil. The light was too dim to read by, so Kennard, still quite mechanically, kept the paper in his hand and went up to his room.

There, by the light of the lamp, he read the few words scribbled in pencil: "Wait in the street outside."

Nothing more. The message was obviously not intended for him, and yet. . . . A strange excitement possessed him. If it should be! If . . . !

He had heard—everyone had—of the mysterious agencies that were at work, under cover of darkness, to aid the unfortunate, the innocent, the helpless. He had heard of that legendary English gentleman who had before now defied the closest vigilance of the Committees, and snatched their intended victims out of their murderous clutches, at times under their eyes.

If this should be . . . ! He scarce dared put his hope into words. He could not bring himself really to believe. But he went. He ran downstairs and out into the street, took his stand under a projecting doorway nearly opposite the house which held the woman he loved, and leaning against the wall, he waited.

After many hours—it was then past three o'clock in the morning, and the sky of an inky blackness—he felt so numb that despite his will a kind of trance-like drowsiness overcame him. He could no longer stand on his feet; his knees were shaking; his head felt so heavy that he could not keep it up. It rolled round from shoulder to shoulder, as if his will no longer controlled it. And it ached furiously.

Everything around him was very still. Even "Paris-by-Night," that grim and lurid giant, was for the moment at rest. A warm summer rain was falling; its gentle, pattering murmur into the gutter helped to lull Kennard's senses into somnolence. He was on the point of dropping off to sleep when something suddenly roused him. A noise of men shouting and laughing—familiar sounds enough in these squalid Paris streets.

But Kennard was wide awake now; numbness had given place to intense quivering of all his muscles, and super-keenness of his every sense. He peered into the darkness and strained his ears to hear. The sound certainly appeared to come from the house opposite, and there, too, it seemed as if some thing or things were moving. Men! More than one or two, surely! Kennard thought that he could distinguish at least three distinct voices; and there was that weird, racking cough which proclaimed the presence of Rateau.

Now the men were quite close to where he—Kennard—still stood cowering. A minute or two later they had passed down the street. Their hoarse voices soon died away in the distance. Kennard crept cautiously out of his hiding-place. Message or mere coincidence, he now blessed that mysterious scrap of paper. Had he remained in his room, he might really have dropped off to sleep and not heard these men going away. There were three of them at least—Kennard thought four. But, anyway, the number of watchdogs outside the door of his beloved had considerably diminished. He felt that he had the strength to grapple with them, even if there were still three of them left. He, an athlete, English, and master of the art of self-defense; and they, a mere pack of drink-sodden brutes! Yes! He was quite sure he could do it. Quite sure that he could force his way into Esther's rooms and carry her off in his arms—whither? God alone knew. And God alone would provide.

Just for a moment he wondered if, while he was in that state of somnolence, other bandits had come to take the place of those that were going. But this thought he quickly dismissed. In any case, he felt a giant's strength in himself, and could not rest now till he had tried once more to see her.

He crept very cautiously along; was satisfied that the street was deserted. Already he had reached the house opposite, had pushed open the *porte cochère*, which was on the latch—when, without the slightest warning, he was suddenly attacked from behind, his arms seized and held behind his back with a vice-like grip, whilst a vigorous kick against the calves of his legs caused him to lose his footing, and suddenly brought him down, sprawling and helpless, in the gutter, while in his ear rang the hideous sound of the consumptive ruffian's racking cough.

"What shall we do with the cub now?" a raucous voice came out of the darkness.

"Let him lie there," was the quick response. "It'll teach him to interfere with the work of honest patriots."

Kennard, lying somewhat bruised and stunned, heard this decree with thankfulness. The bandits obviously thought him more hurt than he was, and if only they would leave him lying there, he would soon pick himself up and renew his attempt to go to Esther. He did not move, feigning unconsciousness, even though he felt rather than saw that hideous Rateau stooping over him, heard

his stertorous breathing, the wheezing in his throat.

"Run and fetch a bit of cord, Citizen Desmonts," the wretch said presently. "A trussed cub is safer than a loose one."

This dashed Kennard's hopes to a great extent. He felt that he must act quickly, before those brigands returned and rendered him completely helpless. He made a movement to rise—a movement so swift and sudden as only a trained athlete can make. But, quick as he was, that odious, wheezing creature was quicker still, and now, when Kennard had turned on his back, Rateau promptly sat on his chest, a dead weight, with long legs stretched out before him, coughing and spluttering, yet wholly at his ease.

Oh! The humiliating position for an amateur middleweight champion to find himself in, with that drink-sodden—Kennard was sure that he was drink-sodden—consumptive sprawling on top of him!

"Don't trouble, Citizen Desmonts," the wretch cried out after his retreating companions. "I have what I want by me."

Very leisurely he pulled a coil of rope out of the capacious pocket of his tattered coat. Kennard could not see what he was doing, but felt it with supersensitive instinct all the time. He lay quite still beneath the weight of that miscreant, feigning unconsciousness, yet hardly able to breathe, that tuberculous caitiff was such a towering weight. But he tried to keep his faculties on the alert, ready for that surprise spring which would turn the tables, at the slightest false move on the part of Rateau.

But, as luck would have it, Rateau did not make a single false move. It was amazing with what dexterity he kept Kennard down, even while he contrived to pinion him with cords. An old sailor, probably, he seemed so dexterous with knots.

My God! The humiliation of it all. And Esther a helpless prisoner, inside that house not five paces away! Kennard's heavy, wearied eyes could perceive the light in her window, five stories above where he lay, in the gutter, a helpless log. Even now he gave a last desperate shriek: "Esther!"

But in a second the abominable brigand's hand came down heavily upon his mouth, whilst a raucous voice spluttered rather than said, right through an awful fit of coughing, "Another sound, and I'll gag as well as bind you, you young fool!"

After which, Kennard remained quite still.

VI

Esther, up in her little attic, knew nothing of what her English lover was even then suffering for her sake. She herself had passed, during the night, through every stage of horror and of fear. Soon after midnight that execrable brigand Rateau had poked his ugly, cadaverous face in at the door and peremptorily called for Lucienne. The woman, more dead than alive now with terror, had answered with mechanical obedience.

"I and my friends are thirsty," the man had commanded. "Go and fetch us a liter of *eau-de-vie*."

Poor Lucienne stammered a pitiable, "Where shall I go?"

"To the house at the sign of '*Le fort Samson*,' in the Rue de Seine," replied Rateau curtly. "They'll serve you well if you mention my name."

Of course Lucienne protested. She was a decent woman who had never been inside a *cabaret* in her life.

"Then it's time you began," was Rateau's dry comment, which was greeted with much laughter from his abominable companions.

Lucienne was forced to go. It would, of course, have been futile and madness to resist. This had occurred three hours since. The Rue de Seine was not far, but the poor woman had not returned. Esther was left with this additional horror weighing upon her soul. What had happened to the unfortunate servant? Visions of outrage and murder floated before the poor girl's tortured brain. At best, Lucienne was being kept out of the way in order to make her—Esther—feel more lonely and desperate!

She remained at the window after that, watching that light in the house opposite and fingering her prayer-book, the only solace which she had. Her attic was so high up and the street so narrow that she could not see what went on in the street below. At one time she heard a great to-do outside her door. It seemed as if some of the bloodhounds who were set to watch her had gone, or that others came. She really hardly cared which it was. Then she heard a great commotion coming from the street immediately beneath her; men shouting and laughing, and that awful creature's rasping cough.

At one moment she felt sure that Kennard had called to her by name. She heard his voice distinctly, raised as if in a despairing cry.

After that, all was still. So still that she could hear her heart beating furiously, and then a tear falling from her eyes upon her open book. So still that the gentle patter of the rain sounded like a soothing lullaby. She was very young, and was very tired. Out, above the line of sloping roofs and chimney pots, the darkness of the sky was yielding to the first touch of dawn. The rain ceased. Everything became deathly still. Esther's head fell, wearied, upon her folded arms.

Then, suddenly, she was wide awake. Something had roused her—a noise. At first she could not tell what it was, but now she knew. It was the opening and shutting of the door behind her, and then a quick, stealthy footstep across the room. The horror of it all was unspeakable. Esther remained as she had been, on her knees, mechanically fingering her prayer-book, unable to move, unable to utter a sound, as if paralyzed. She knew that one of those abominable creatures had entered her room, was coming near her even now. She did not know who it was, only guessed it was Rateau, for she had heard a raucous, stertorous wheeze. Yet she could not have then turned to look if her life had depended upon her doing so.

The whole thing had occurred in less than half a dozen heartbeats. The next moment the wretch was close to her. Mercifully she felt that her senses were leaving her. Even so, she felt that a handkerchief was being bound over her mouth to prevent her screaming. Wholly unnecessary this, for she could not have uttered a sound. Then she was lifted off the ground and carried across the room, then over the threshold.

A vague, subconscious effort of will helped her to keep her head averted from that wheezing wretch who was carrying her. Thus she could see the landing, and two of those abominable watchdogs who had been set to guard her. The ghostly grey light of dawn came peeping in through the narrow dormer window in the sloping roof, and faintly illumined their sprawling forms, stretched out at full length, with their heads buried in their folded arms and their naked legs looking pallid and weird in the dim light. Their stertorous breathing woke the echoes of the bare, stone walls. Esther shuddered and closed her eyes. She was now like an insentient log, without power, or thought, or will—almost without feeling.

Then, all at once, the coolness of the morning air caught her full in the face. She opened her eyes and tried to move, but those powerful arms held her more closely than before. Now she could have shrieked with horror. With returning consciousness the sense of her desperate position came on her with its full and ghastly significance, its awe-inspiring details. The grey dawn, the abandoned wretch who held her, and the stillness of this early morning hour, when not one pitying soul would be astir to lend her a helping hand or give her the solace of mute sympathy. So great, indeed, was this stillness that the click of the man's sabots upon the uneven pavement reverberated, ghoul-like and weird.

And it was through that awesome stillness that a sound suddenly struck her ear, which, in the instant, made her feel that she was not really alive, or, if alive, was sleeping and dreaming strange and impossible dreams. It was the sound of a voice, clear and firm, and with a wonderful ring of merriment in its tones, calling out just above a whisper—and in English, if you please: "Look out, Ffoulkes! That young cub is as strong as a horse. He will give us all away if you are not careful."

A dream? Of course it was a dream, for the voice had sounded very close to her ear; so close, that . . . well! Esther was quite sure that her face still rested against the hideous, tattered, and grimy coat which that repulsive Rateau had been wearing all along. And there was the click of his sabots upon the pavement all the time. So, then, the voice and the merry, suppressed laughter which accompanied it, must all have been part of her dream.

How long this lasted she could not have told you. An hour and more, she thought, while the grey dawn yielded to the roseate hue of morning. Somehow, she no longer suffered either terror or foreboding. A subtle atmosphere of strength and of security seemed to encompass her. At one time she felt as if she were driven along in a cart that jolted horribly, and when she moved her face and hands they came in contact with things that were fresh and green and smelt of the country. She was in darkness then, and more than three parts unconscious, but the handkerchief had been removed from her mouth. It seemed to her as if she could hear the voice of her Jack, but far away and indistinct; also the tramp of horses' hoofs and the creaking of cart-wheels, and at times that awful, rasping cough, which reminded her of the presence of a loath-some wretch who should not have had a part in her soothing dream.

Thus many hours must have gone by.

Then, all at once, she was inside a house—a room, and she felt that she was being lowered very gently to the ground. She was on her feet, but she could not see where she was. There was furniture; a carpet; a ceiling; the man Rateau with the sabots and the dirty coat, and the merry English voice, and a pair of deep-set blue eyes, thoughtful and lazy and infinitely kind.

But before she could properly focus on what she saw, everything began to whirl and to spin around her, to dance a wild and idiotic saraband, which caused her to laugh, and to laugh, until her throat felt choked and her eyes hot; after which she remembered nothing more.

VII

The first thing of which Esther Vincent was conscious, when she returned to her senses, was of her English lover kneeling beside her. She was lying on some kind of couch, and she could see his face in profile, for he had turned and was speaking to someone at the far end of the room.

"And was it you who knocked me down," he was saying, "and sat on my chest, and trussed me like a fowl?"

"La! My dear sir," a lazy, pleasant voice riposted, "what else could I do? There was no time for explanations. You were half-crazed, and would not have understood. And you were ready to bring all the night-watchmen about our ears."

"I am sorry!" Kennard said simply. "But how could I guess?"

"You couldn't," rejoined the other. "That is why I had to deal so summarily with you and with Mademoiselle Esther, not to speak of good old Lucienne, who had never, in her life, been inside a cab-aret. You must all forgive me ere you start upon your journey. You are not out of the wood yet, remember. Though Paris is a long way behind, France itself is no longer a healthy place for any of you."

"But how did we ever get out of Paris? I was smothered under a pile of cabbages, with Lucienne on one side of me and Esther, unconscious, on the other. I could see nothing. I know we halted at the bar-rier. I thought we would be recognized, turned back! My God! How I trembled!"

"Bah!" broke in the other, with a careless laugh. "It is not so difficult as it seems. We have done it before—eh, Ffoulkes? A market-gardener's cart, a villainous wretch like myself to drive it, another hideous object like Sir Andrew Ffoulkes, Bart., to lead the scraggy nag, a couple of forged or stolen passports, plenty of English gold, and the deed is done!"

Esther's eyes were fixed upon the speaker. She marveled now how she could have been so blind. The cadaverous face was nothing but a splendid use of grease paint! The rags, the dirt, the whole assumption of a hideous character was masterly! But there were the eyes, deep-set and thoughtful and kind. How did she fail to guess?

"You are known as the Scarlet Pimpernel," she said suddenly. "Suzanne de Tournay was my friend. She told me. You saved her and her family, and now . . . oh, my God!" she exclaimed. "How shall we ever repay you?"

"By placing yourselves unreservedly in my friend Ffoulkes' hands," he replied gently. "He will lead you to safety and, if you wish it, to England."

"If we wish it!" Kennard sighed fervently.

"You are not coming with us, Blakeney?" queried Sir Andrew Ffoulkes, and it seemed to Esther's sensitive ears as if a tone of real anxiety and also of entreaty rang in the young man's voice.

"No, not this time," replied Sir Percy lightly. "I like my character of Rateau, and I don't want to give it up just yet. I have done nothing to arouse suspicion in the minds of my savory compeers up at the Cabaret de la Liberté. I can easily keep this up for some time to come, and frankly I admire myself as Citizen Rateau. I don't know when I have enjoyed a character so much!"

"You mean to return to the Cabaret de la Liberté!" exclaimed Sir Andrew.

"Why not?"

"You will be recognized!"

"Not before I have been of service to a good many unfortunates, I hope."

"But that awful cough of yours! Percy, you'll do yourself an injury with it one day."

"Not I! I like that cough. I practiced it for a long time before I did it to perfection. Such a splendid wheeze! I must teach Tony to do it someday. Would you like to hear it now?"

He laughed, that perfect, delightful, lazy laugh of his, which carried every hearer with it along the path of light-hearted merriment. Then he broke into the awful cough of the consumptive Rateau. And Esther Vincent instinctively closed her eyes and shuddered.

About Harold Lamb

Anyone reading this book is probably familiar with the works of author Robert E. Howard—at a minimum you know his most famous creation, Conan the Barbarian. Howard was one of the stars of the adventure and weird fiction pulps in the 1930s, but his tough-minded characters, fast-moving plots, and exotic settings didn't just appear out of nowhere. Before Howard began writing his tales, he read and studied the stories of Harold Lamb.

Lamb (1892-1962), son of an artist and a writer, became a writer himself in 1917 when *Adventure* magazine began publishing his series of tightly-plotted stories of Cossacks, Tatars, and Mongols. An expert on central Asia who traveled extensively there and knew six or seven languages, including ancient Persian and medieval Ukrainian, Lamb knew whereof he wrote; in every one of his stories this thorough grounding

in the time, place, and culture of its setting comes through and rings true.

Like many of the pulp writers, Lamb was extremely prolific. He began publishing novels in 1920 with *Marching Sands*, but ultimately fiction wasn't enough for him, and he commenced his successful transition to author of well-regarded historical biographies with *Genghis Khan: The Emperor of All Men* in 1927. His subsequent two-volume history of the Crusades brought him to the attention of Hollywood director Cecil B. DeMille, and in the 1930s he dabbled with screenwriting, but he is remembered most today for his biographies of the strong men of Asian history, such as Alexander, Suleiman, Tamerlane, and Cyrus the great.

Which is a shame, because he wrote fine historical adventure stories. Here's one of the best, from the August 3, 1920 issue of *Adventure*.

The Bride of Jagannath

HAROLD LAMB

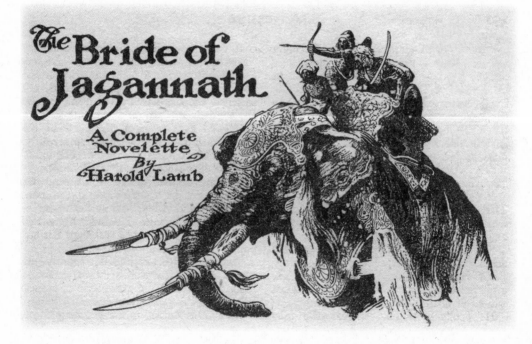

Down past the stone shrine of Kedar-nath, down and over the tall grass of the Dehra-Dun, marched the host of the older gods. The Pandas marched with feet that touched not the tall grass. Past the deva-prayag—the meeting-place of the waters—came the older gods bearing weapons in their hands.

In the deva-prayag they washed themselves clean. The gods were very angry. The wind came and went at their bidding.

Thus they came. And the snow-summits of Himal, the grass of the valley, and the meeting-place of the waters—all were as one to the gods.

The Vedas.

The heavy morning dew lay on the grass of the Land of the Five Rivers, the Punjab. The hot, dry monsoon was blowing up from the southern plains and cooling itself among the foot-hills of the Siwalik in the year of our Lord 1609 when two riders turned their horses from a hill-path into the main highway of the district of Kukushetra.

It was a fair day, and the thicket through which the trail ran was alive with the flutter of pigeons and heavy with the scent of wild thyme and jasmine and the mild odor of the fern-trees. The sun beat on them warmly, for the spring season was barely past and they were riding south in the eastern Punjab, by the edge of Rajasthan, toward the headwaters of the Ganges, in the empire of Jahangir, Ruler of the World and Mogul of India.

"A fair land," said one. "A land ripe with sun, with sweet fruits and much grain. Our horses will feed well. Here you may rest from your wounds—"

He pointed with a slender, muscular hand to where a gilt dome reared itself over the cypress-tops on a distant hill-summit.

"*Eh*, my Brother of Battles," he said, "yonder shines the dome of Kukushetra. Aye, the temple of Kukushetra wherein dwells an image of Jagannath—"

"*Jagannath!*"

It was a shrill cry that came from the roadside. A small figure leaped from the bushes at the word and seized the bridles of both horses. They reared back and he who had pointed to the temple muttered a round oath.

"Jagannath!" cried the newcomer solemnly.

He was a very slender man, half-naked, with a gray cloth twisted about his loins. The string hanging down his left chest indicated—as well as the caste-mark on his forehead—that he was a Brahman, of the lesser temple order.

"The holy name!" he chanted. "Lord of the World! Brother to Balabhadra and to Subhadra! Incarnation of the mighty Vishnu, and master of the Kali-*damana*! Even as ye have named Jagannath, so must ye come to the reception hall of the god—"

"What is this madness?" asked the elder of the two riders gruffly.

The Brahman glanced at him piercingly and resumed his arrogant harangue. "The festival of Jagannath is near at hand, warrior," he warned. "This is the land of the mighty god. Come, then, to the temple and bring your gift to lay at the shrine of Jagannath of Kukushetra, which is only less holy than the shrine of Puri itself, at blessed Orissa. Come—"

"By Allah!" laughed the first rider. "By the ninety-nine holy names of God!" He shook in his saddle with merriment. The Brahman dropped the reins as if they had been red hot and surveyed the two with angry disappointment.

"By the beard of the Prophet, and the ashes of my grandsire—this is a goodly jest," roared the tall warrior. "Behold, a pilgrim hunter come to solicit Abdul Dost and Khlit of the Curved Saber."

He spoke Mogholi, whereas the misguided Brahman had used his native Hindustani. Khlit understood Abdul Dost. Yet he did not laugh. He was looking curiously at the marked brow of the priest, which had darkened in anger at the gibe of the Moslem.

"*Eh*—this is verily a thing to warm the heart," went on Abdul Dost. "A Brahman, a follower of Jagannath, bids us twain come to the festival of his god. He knew not that I am a follower of the true Prophet, and you, Khlit, wear a Christian cross of gold under the shirt at your throat."

He turned to the unfortunate pilgrim hunter. "Nay, speaker-of-the-loud-tongue, here is an ill quarter to cry your wares. Would the wooden face of armless Jagannath smile upon a Moslem and a Christian, think you?"

"Nay," quoth the priest scornfully, "not so much as upon a toad, or a pariah who is an eater of filth."

In his zeal, he had not taken careful note of the persons of the two travelers. He scanned the warriors keenly, looking longest at Khlit. The other, an elegantly dressed Afghan, with his jeweled scimitar and his silver-mounted harness and small, tufted turban, was a familiar figure.

But the gaunt form of the Cossack was strange to the Brahman. Khlit's bearded cheeks were haggard with hardship and illness in the mountains during the long winter of Kashmir, and his wide, deep-set eyes were gray. His heavy sheepskin coat was thrown back, disclosing a sinewy throat and high, rugged shoulders.

In Khlit's scarred face was written the boldness of a fighting race, hardened, not softened by the wrinkles of age. It was an open face, lean and weather-stained. The deep eyes returned the stare of the priest with a steady, meditative scrutiny.

Abdul Dost was still smiling. His handsome countenance was that of a man in the prime of life, proud of his strength. He sat erect in a jeweled saddle, a born horseman and the finest swordsman of northern Hindustan. He rode a mettled Arab. Khlit's horse was a shaggy Kirghiz pony. "It is time," broke in Khlit bluntly—he was a man of few words—"that we found food for ourselves and grain for our horses. Where lies this peasant we seek?"

Abdul Dost turned to the watching priest, glancing at the sun. "Ho, hunter of pilgrims," he commanded, "since we are not birds for your snaring—and the enriching of your idol—tell us how many bowshots distant is the hut of Bhimal,

the catcher of birds. We have ridden since sunup, and our bellies yearn."

The Brahman folded his arms. He seemed inclined to return a sharp answer, then checked himself. His black eyes glinted shrewdly. He pointed down the dusty highway. "If the blind lead the blind, both will fall into the well," he chanted. "Nay, would you behold the power of the name of Jagannath whom you foolishly deride? Then come with me to the abode of this same Bhimal. I will guide you, for I am bound thither myself on a quest from the temple."

"So be it," nodded Abdul Dost carelessly and urged his horse forward, offering the pilgrim hunter a stirrup which the Brahman indignantly refused.

～

Abdul Dost was not the man to repent his own words, spoken freely. But he understood better than Khlit the absolute power of the Hindu priests in the Land of the Five Rivers.

The fertile province of Kukushetra was a favorite resort for the Hindu pilgrims of the highlands. Here were the ruins of an ancient temple, near which the new-gilded edifice—a replica of that at Puri at the Ganges' mouth—had been built. Here also were gathered the priests from the hill monasteries, to tend the shrine of the Kukushetra Jagannath.

Religious faith had not made a breach between Khlit and Abdul Dost. The Cossack was accustomed to keep his thoughts to himself, and to the *mansabdar* friendship was a weightier matter than the question of faith. He had eaten bread and salt with Khlit.

He had nearly slain the Cossack in their first meeting, and this had made the two boon companions. Khlit had treated his wounds with gunpowder and earth mixed with spittle—until Abdul Dost substituted clean bandages and ointment.

The two ate of the same food and slept often under the same robe. They were both veteran fighters in an age when a man's life was safeguarded only by a good sword-arm. Abdul Dost was pleased to lead his comrade through the splendid hill country of northern India perhaps influenced—for he was a man of simple ideas—by the interest which the tall figure of Khlit always aroused among the natives.

Khlit was well content to have the companionship of a man who liked to wander and who had much to say of India and the wars of the Mogul. Khlit himself was a wanderer who followed the path of battles. From this he had earned the surname of the "Curved Saber."

It was the first time that Khlit had set foot in Hindustan, which was the heart of the Mogul empire.

The priest, who had maintained a sullen silence, halted at a wheat-field bordering the road. Here a bare-legged, turbaned man was laboring, cutting the wheat with a heavy sickle and singing as he worked.

The Brahman called, and the man straightened, casting an anxious eye at the three in the road. Khlit saw his eyes widen as he recognized the priest. "Greetings, Kurral," spoke the man in the field. "May the blessing of divine Vishnu rest upon you."

"Come, Bhimal," commanded the Brahman sharply, "here be barbarian wayfarers who seek your hut. Lay aside your sickle. Your harvesting is done."

With a puzzled glance over his shoulders at the half-gathered grain Bhimal the *chiria mars*—Hindu of the bird-slaying caste—led the way to his cottage beside the field. It was a clay-walled hut with a roof of thatched roots, under the pleasant shade of a huge banyan.

On either side of the door within the shade grapevines were trained upon a lattice; in the rear an open shed housed two buffalo—the prized possessions of Bhimal and his brother.

At the threshold, however, the slayer of birds hesitated strangely and faced his companions as if unwilling for them to enter. Khlit and Abdul Dost dismounted, well content with the spot, where they had heard a good breakfast for a man and beast might be had from hospitable Bhimal. They had unsaddled and were about to request a jar of water from the cottage tank under the banyan when a word from Kurral arrested them.

"Stay," muttered the Brahman. Turning to Bhimal, he smiled, while the simple face of the old peasant grew anxious. "Is it not true, Bhimal, that this cottage belongs to you and your brother, who departed long ago on a pilgrimage to Puri?"

"It is true, Kurral," assented Bhimal.

"That you own two fields and a half of good wheat ready for the harvest? And two buffalo? This cottage?"

At each question the peasant nodded.

"And a few rare birds which you caught in snares?" Kurral drew a folded parchment from the robe at his waist and consulted it. Then he tossed it to Bhimal. "You cannot read, O slayer of birds," he smiled, "but this is a bond signed by your brother. You can make out his scrawl, over the endorsement of the holy priest of Puri, the unworthy slave of Jagannath. The bond is for the cottage and all the goods, animals, and tools of your brother and yourself. It was sent from the mighty temple of Puri to the lesser shrine at Kukushetra. And I am come to take payment."

Khlit, not understanding Hindustani, yet read sudden misery in the lined face of Bhimal. "How fares my brother?" cried the peasant.

"He brought fitting gifts of fruit, grain, and oatmeal to the shrine of Jagannath, Bhimal. His zeal was great. All the coins that he had, he gave. But mighty Jagannath was ill rewarded by your brother, for you came not with him on the pilgrimage."

"Nay, I am sorely lame." Bhimal pointed sadly to a partially withered leg.

"No matter," declared Kurral sternly. "Is Jagannath a pariah, to be cheated of his due—by miserable slayers of carrion birds? Your brother wrote the bond for this cottage and the fields. He offered it to the priest and it was taken. Thus he gained the blessing of all-powerful Jagannath."

"Then—he is ill?"

"Nay, I heard that he died upon the return journey, in the heat. By his death he is blessed—as are all those who perish on behalf of the All-Destroyer, whether under the wheels of the sacred car or upon the path of pilgrimage."

Bhimal hung his head in resignation. Abdul Dost, with a shrug of his slender shoulders, was about to take a jar of water from the tank when Kurral wheeled on him vindictively. "Stay, barbarian!" he warned. "This tank and the cottage and the food within are now the property of the temple of Kukushetra. No unclean hand may be laid upon it."

Abdul Dost stared at him grimly and glanced questioningly at Bhimal. "It is true," admitted the peasant sadly. "A bond given to the god by my brother is binding upon my unworthy self. Yet," he faced Kurral beseechingly, "the wheat and the rare birds are all that I have to live through the season of rains. Suffer me to stay in the cottage and work on behalf of the god. I shall render you a just tribute of all, keeping just enough for my own life. I would strew the ashes of grief upon my head in solitude—"

"Nay," retorted Kurral. "Would you mourn a life that has passed to the keeping of the gods? I have marked you as one of little faith. So you may not tend this property. Another will see to it."

A rebellious flicker appeared in the dim eyes of the peasant. "Has not Jagannath taken the things that are dearest to me, Kurral?" he cried shrilly. "My brother's life and these good buffaloes? Nay, then let me keep but one thing!"

"What?" demanded the priest, still enjoying his triumph over the two warriors.

"A peacock with a tail of many-colored beauty. I have tended it as a gift to my lord, the Rawul Matap Rao, upon his marriage. I have promised the gift."

Kurral considered. "Not so," he decided. "For the Rawul—so it is said— has not bent his head before the shrine of Kukushetra in many moons. It is rumored that he inclines to an unblessed sect, the worshipers of the sun-image of Vishnu— the followers of the *gosain* Chaitanya. He is unworthy of the name of Hindu. Better the peacock should adorn the temple garden than strut for the pleasure of the bride of Rawul Matap Rao."

Then Khlit saw a strange form appear from within the entrance of the hut. In the dim light under the great tree it appeared as a glittering child with a plumed head-dress. Kurral, too, saw it and started.

—

"Who names the Rawul with false breath?" cried the figure in a deep melodious voice. "Ho—it is Kurral, the pilgrim hunter. Methought I knew his barbed tongue."

By now Khlit saw that the figure was that of a warrior, standing scarce shoulder high to the Cossack and the tall Afghan. A slim, erect body was brightly clad, the legs bound by snowy white muslin, a shawl girdle of green silk falling over the loins, a shirt of finely-wrought silvered mail covering the small body, the brown arms bare, a helmet of thin bronze on the dark head.

The man's face was that of a Hindu of the warrior caste, the eyes dark and large, the nostrils thin. A pair of huge black mustaches were twisted up either cheek. A quiver full of arrows hung at the waist-girdle. In one hand the archer held a bow; under the other arm he clasped a beautiful peacock, whose tail had stirred Khlit's interest.

"Sawal Das!" muttered Kurral.

"Aye, Sawal Das," repeated the archer sharply, "servant and warrior of the excellent Rawul Matap Rao. I came to Bhimal's hut at sunup to claim the peacock, for my lord returns to his castle of Thaneswar tomorrow night. And now, O beguiler-of-men, you have wasted your breath; for I have already claimed the peacock on behalf of my lord."

"Too much of the evil juice of the grape has trickled down your gullet, Sawal Das," scowled the priest. "For that you came to the hut—under pretense of taking the bird. You are a dishonor to your caste—"

"Windbag! Framer of lies!" The archer laughed. "*Ohé*—are you one to question a warrior? When the very clients that come to your cell will not take food or water from the hand of a low *Barna* Brahman? *Oho*—well you know that my master would hold himself contaminated were your shadow to fall across his feet."

He paused to stare at Khlit and Abdul Dost, whom he had not observed before.

"So you would steal from Jagannath!" fumed the priest.

"Nay." The white teeth of the archer showed through his mustache. "Am I one of the godless Kukushetra brethren who gorge themselves with the food that is offered to Jagannath? I plunder none save my lawful foes—behold this Turkish mail and helmet as witness!"

"Skulker!" The hard face of the Brahman flushed darkly. "Eavesdropper!"

"At least," retorted the warrior, "I take not the roof from over the head of the man whose guest I am."

He turned to the mournful Bhimal. "Come, comrade, will you let this evil lizard crawl into your hut? A good kick will send him flying."

"Nay." The peasant shook his head. "It may not be. My brother gave a bond."

"But your brother is dead."

"He pledged his word. I would be dishonored were I not to fulfill it."

Sawal Das grimaced. "By Siva!" he cried. "A shame to give good grain and cattle to these scavengers. Half the farms of the countryside they have taken to themselves. Even the might of my lord the Rawul cannot safeguard the lands of his peasants. If this thing must be, then come to Thaneswar where you will be safe from the greed of such as Kurral."

"I thank you, Sawal Das." Bhimal looked up gratefully. "But I would be alone for a space to mourn my brother who is dead."

"So be it," rejoined the archer, "but forget not Thaneswar. Rawul Matap Rao has need of faithful house-servants."

"Aye," observed the priest, "the time will come when he who sits in Thaneswar will have need of—hirelings."

Khlit, indifferent to the discussion which he did not understand, had watered his horse and searched out a basket of fruit and cakes of jellied rice within the hut. Coming forth with his prize, he tossed a piece of silver money to Bhimal.

The peasant caught it and would have secreted it in his garments, but Kurral's sharp eye had seen the act. "Take not the silver that is Jagannath's!" He held out his hand. "Or you will be accursed."

Reluctantly the peasant was about to yield the money to the priest when Sawal Das intervened. "The bond said naught of money, Kurral," he pointed out. "Is your hunger for wealth like to a hyena's yearning for carrion? Is there no end of your greed? Touch not the dinar."

The priest turned upon the archer furiously. "Take care!" he cried. "Kukushetra has had its fill of the idolatry of the Rawul and the insolence of his servants. Take care lest you lose your life by lifting hand against mighty Jagannath!"

"I fear not the god," smiled Sawal Das. "Lo, I will send him a gift, even Jagannath himself, by the low-born Kurral."

So swiftly that the watching Abdul Dost barely caught his movements, the archer dropped the peacock and plucked an arrow from his quiver. In one motion he strung the short bow and fitted arrow to string.

Kurral backed away, his eyes widening in sudden fear. Evidently he had reason to respect the archer. A tree-trunk arrested his progress abruptly.

Sawal Das seemed not to take aim, yet the arrow flew and the bowstring twanged. The shaft buried itself deep into the tree-trunk. And the sacred cord which hung to Kurral's left shoulder was parted in twain.

Kurral gazed blankly at the severed string and the arrow embedded not two inches from his ear. Then he turned and fled into the thicket, glancing over his shoulder as he went.

"A good shot, that, archer," laughed Abdul Dost.

"It was nought," grinned Sawal Das. "On a clear day I have severed the head from a carrion bird in full flight. Nay, a good shaft was wasted where it will do little good."

He strutted from the hut, gathering up the peacock. "If you are strangers in Kukushetra," he advised, "you would do well to seek the door of my master, Rawul Matap Rao. He asks not what shrine you bow before, and he has ever an ear for a goodly song or tale, or—" Sawal Das noted the Afghan's lean figure appraisingly—"employment for a strong sword-arm. He is a just man, and within his gates you will be safe."

"So there is to be a marriage feast at Thaneswar?"

"Aye," nodded the archer, "and rare food and showers of silver for all who attend. This road leads to Thaneswar castle by the first turn uphill. Watch well the path you take, for there are evil bandits—servants of the death-loving Kali—afoot in the deeper jungle."

With that he raised a hand in farewell and struck off into a path through the brush, singing to himself, leaving Bhimal sitting grief-stricken on the threshold of the hut and Khlit and Abdul Dost quietly breakfasting.

II

On that day the young chieftain of Thaneswar had broken the *torun* over the gate of Rinthambur. The *torun* was a triangular emblem of wood hung over the portal of a woman who was to become a bride. Matap Rao, a clever horseman, rode under the stone arch, and while the women servants and the ladies of Rinthambur laughingly pelted him with flowers and plaited leaves he struck the *torun* with his lance until it fell to earth in fragments.

This done, as was customary, the mock defense of Rinthambur castle ceased; the fair garrison ended their pretty play and Rawul Matap Rao was welcomed by the men within the gate.

He was a man fit to be allied by blood even with the celebrated chiefs of the Rinthambur clan—a man barely beyond the limits of youth, who had many cares and who administered a wide province—Thaneswar—with the skill of an elder.

Perhaps the Rawul was not the fighting type beloved by the minstrels of the Rinthambur house. He was not prone to make wars upon his neighbors, choosing rather to study how the taxes of his peasants might be lightened and the heavy hand of the Kukushetra temple be kept from spoliation of the ignorant farmers.

The young Rawul, last of his line, was a breeder of fine horses, a student and a philosopher of high intelligence. He was the equal in birth to Retha of Rinthambur—the daughter of a warlike clan of the sun-born caste. She had smiled upon his wooing and the chieftains who were head of her house were not ill content to join the clans of Rinthambur and Thaneswar by blood.

War on behalf of the Mogul, and their own reckless extravagance with money and the blood of their followers, had weakened the clan. The remaining members had gathered at Rinthambur castle to pay fitting welcome to the Rawul.

"We yield to your care," they said, "her who is the gem in the diadem of Rajasthan—Retha of Rinthambur—who is called 'Lotus Face' in the Punjab. Guard her well. If need arise command our swords, for our clans are one."

So Matap Rao joined his hand to that of Retha, and the knot in their garments was tied in the hall of Rinthambur before the fire altar. Both Matap Rao and the Rinthambur chieftains were descendants of the fire family of the Hindus—devotees of the higher and milder form of Vishnu worship.

"Thaneswar," he said, "shall be another gate to Rinthambur and none shall be so welcome as the riders of Rinthambur."

But the chieftains, after bidding adieu to him and his bride, announced that they would remain and hold revelry in their own hall for two days, leaving the twain to seek Thaneswar, as was the custom.

Thus it happened that Matap Rao, flushed with exaltation and deep in love, rode beside his bride to the boundary of Rinthambur, where the last of the bride's clan turned back. His followers, clad and mounted to the utmost finery of their resources, fell behind the two.

The way seemed long to Matap Rao, even though a full moon peered through the soft glimmer of twilight and the minstrel of Thaneswar—the aged *Vina*, Perwan Singh—chanted as he rode behind them, and the scent of jasmine hung about their path.

In the Thaneswar jungle at the boundary of the two provinces a watch tower stood by the road, rearing its bulk against the moon. Here were lights and soft draperies and a banquet of sugared fruits, sweetened rice, jellies, cakes and curries, prepared by the skilled hands of the women slaves who waited here to welcome their new mistress. And here the party dismounted, the armed followers occupying tents about the tower.

While they feasted and Matap Rao described the banquet that was awaiting them on the following night at Thaneswar hall, Perwan Singh sang to them and the hours passed lightly, until the moon became clouded over and a sudden wind swept through the forest.

A drenching downpour came upon the heels of the wind; the lights in the tower were extinguished, and Retha laid a slim hand fearfully upon the arm of her lord. "It is an ill omen," she cried.

"Nay," he laughed, "no omen shall bring a cloud upon the heart of the queen of Thaneswar. Vishnu smiles upon us."

But Retha, although she laughed with her husband, was not altogether comforted. And, the next morning, when a band of horsemen and camels met them on the highway, she drew closer to Matap Rao.

A jangle of cymbals and kettle-drums proclaimed that this was the escort of a higher priest of Kukushetra. Numerous servants, gorgeously dressed, led a fine Kabul stallion forward to meet the Rawul, and its rider smiled upon him.

This was Nagir Jan, *gosain* of Kukushetra and abbot of the temple. He was a man past middle life, his thin face bearing the imprint of a dominant will, the chin strongly marked, the eyes piercing.

He bowed to Retha, whose face was half-veiled. "A boon," he cried, "to the lowly servant of Jagannath. Let him see but once the famed beauty of the Flower of Rinthambur."

Matap Rao hesitated. He had had reason more than once to feel the power of the master of the temple. Nagir Jan was reputed to be high in the mysteries of the nationwide worship of Jagannath.

Owing to the wealth of the priests of the god, and the authority centered in his temples, the followers of Jagannath were the only Hindus permitted by the Mogul to continue the worship of their divinity as they wished. The might of Jagannath was not lightly to be challenged.

But Nagir Jan was also a learned priest familiar with the Vedas and the secrets of the shrine of Puri itself. As such he could command the respect of Matap Rao, who was an ardent Vishnu worshiper. For Jagannath, by the doctrine of incarnation, embodied the worship of Vishnu. "If Retha consents," he responded, "it is my wish."

The girl realized that the priest had come far to greet her. She desired to please the man who was more powerful than the Rawul in Thaneswar. So she drew back the veil. But her delicate face wore no smile. The splendid, dark eyes looked once, steadily into the cold eyes of the priest.

"Truly," said Nagir Jan softly, "is she named the Lotus Face. The lord of Retha is favored of the gods."

While the twain rode past he continued to look after the girl. Glancing over his shoulder presently, the Rawul saw that Nagir Jan was still seated on his horse, looking at them. He put spurs to his horse, forcing a laugh.

But after the festival at Thaneswar Matap Rao would have given much, even half his lands, if he had not granted the wish of Nagir Jan.

⌐

The same thunderstorm that so disturbed the young bride of the Rawul caught Khlit and Abdul Dost on the open road. The warriors had lingered long at the hospitable hut of Bhimal to escape the midday heat. So the sun was slanting over the wheat-fields when they trotted toward the castle of Thaneswar. It was twilight when they came upon the crossroads described by the archer, Sawal Das.

Here was a grimy figure squatted upon a ragged carpet, the center of interest of a group of naked children who scampered into the bushes at the sight of the riders.

The man was a half-caste Portuguese, hatless and bootless. On the carpet before him were a mariner's compass, much the worse for wear, and one or two tattered books, evidently—as Khlit surmised—European prayer-books. He glanced up covertly at the warriors.

"What manner of man is this?" wondered Abdul Dost aloud in Hindustani.

"An unworthy astrologer, so please you, great sirs," bowed the half-caste. He closed both eyes and smiled. "My mystic instrument of divination"—he pointed to the compass—"and my signs of the Zodiac." He showed illuminated parchment pictures of the saints in the prayer-book. "It is a goodly trade, and the witless ones of this country pay well. My name is Merghu. What can I do for the great sirs?"

"*Jaisa des waisahi bhes!*" (For such a country, such a masquerade) responded the Afghan contemptuously. "Will not the priests of Kukushetra beat your back with bamboos if they find you here at the crossroads?"

Again the man's eyes closed slyly and his sullen face leered. He lifted a corner of his cloak, disclosing a huge, ulcerous sore. "Nay, noble travelers. They may not touch what is unclean. Besides the festival of *Janam* approaches, and the priests are busied within the temple—"

"Enough!" growled the Afghan at a sign from Khlit, who had marked a cloudbank creeping over the moon that was beginning to show between the treetops. "We are belated. We were told to take the upper hill trail to Thaneswar castle, but here be two trails. Which is the one we seek?"

"Yonder," muttered the astrologer, pointing. "The other leads to the temple."

Khlit and Abdul Dost spurred up the way he had indicated. Glancing back at the first turn in the trail, the Cossack noticed that the sham astrologer had vanished, with all his stock in trade.

But now the wind whipped the treetops that met over the trail. Rain poured down in one of the heavy deluges that precede the wet season in this country.

Khlit rode on unheeding, but Abdul Dost swore vehemently as his finery became soaked. He spurred his horse faster into the darkness without noticing where they went save that it was upward, trusting to the instinct of his mount to lead him safely.

So the two came at a round pace to a clearing in the trees. A high, blank wall emerged before them. This they circled until a gate opened and they trotted past a pool of water to a square structure with a high peaked roof whence came sounds of voices and the clang of cymbals.

"The wedding merriment has begun!" cried Abdul Dost. He swung down from his horse and beat at a bronze door with fist and sword-hilt. Khlit, from the caution of habit, kept to his saddle.

The door swung inward. A glare of light struck into their faces. "Who comes to the hall of offerings of Jagannath?" cried a voice.

Khlit saw a group of Brahmans at the door. Behind them candles and torches lighted a large room filled with an assemblage of peasants and soldiers who were watching a dance through a wide doorway that seemed to lead into a building beyond.

In this farther space a cluster of young girls moved in time to the music of drums and cymbals, tossing their bare arms and whirling upon their toes so that thin draperies swirled about their half-nude forms.

Abdul Dost, who was a man of single thought, stared at the spectacle in astonishment, his garments dripping and rain beating upon his back.

"Who comes armed to the outer hall of the Lord of the World?" cried a young priest zealously. "Know ye not this is the time of the *Janam*?"

"I seek Thaneswar castle," explained the Afghan. "Is it not here? Nay, I am a traveler, not a slave of your god—"

"Begone then from here," commanded the young priest. "This is no place for those of—Thaneswar. Begone, one-without-breeding—lowborn—"

"By Allah!" shouted Abdul Dost angrily. "Is this your courtesy to wayfarers in a storm?" He swung back into his saddle, drawing his sword swiftly. Khlit, lest he should ride his horse into the throng, laid firm hand on the arm of the irate Moslem. They caught a passing glimpse of the dancing women staring at them, and the crowd. Then the door swung to in their faces with a clang.

"Lowborn, they said in my teeth!" stormed the Afghan. "Base mouthers of indecency! Mockers of true men! Saw you the temple harlots offering their bodies to feast the eyes of the throng? Saw you the

faithless priest offering food to the sculptured images of their armless gods—"

"Peace," whispered Khlit. "Here is an ill place for such words."

"Why laid you hand on my rein?" fumed Abdul Dost. "If you had fear in your heart for such as these—offscourings of thrice-defiled dirt—why did you not flee? I would have barbered the head of yon shaven villain with my sword. *Eh—I* am not an old woman who shivers at hard words and sword-strokes—"

Khlit's grasp on his arm tightened. "The rain is ceasing," growled the Cossack. "I can see the lights of Kukushetra village through the farther gate in the temple wall. Many men are afoot. Come. Thaneswar is a better place than this."

While the Cossack eyed the surroundings of the temple enclosure curiously Abdul Dost shrugged his shoulders. "Age has sapped your courage, Khlit," muttered the *mansabdar*. "Verily, I heard tales of your daring from the Chinese merchants and the Tatars. Yet you draw back before the insult of a stripling priest."

Khlit wheeled his horse toward the gate, jerking the bridle of the Afghan's mount. "Aye, I am old," he said, half to himself. "And I have seen before this the loom of a man-trap. Come."

Sullenly the other trotted after him. Back on the trail the moon, breaking from the clouds by degrees, cast a network of shadows before them. The two rode in silence until Abdul Dost quickened his pace to take the lead. "Perchance," he observed grimly, "that miscreant astrologer abides yet at the crossroads. The flat of my sword laid to his belly will teach him not to guide better men than he astray."

Khlit lifted his head. "Aye, the astrologer," he meditated aloud. "Surely he must have known the way to Thaneswar, as well as the temple path. It would be well, Abdul Dost, to watch better our path. Why did he speak us false? That is a horse will need grooming."

"Aye, with a sword."

The *mansabdar* rode heedlessly forward until they had gained the main road. Khlit, looking shrewdly on all sides, thought that he saw a figure move in the thicket at the side of the path. He checked his horse with a low warning to his companion.

But Abdul Dost, lusting for reprisal, slipped down from his saddle and advanced weapon in hand to the edge of the brush, peering into the shadows under the trees, which were so dense that the rain could barely have penetrated beneath their branches. Standing so, he was clearly outlined in the moonlight. "Come forth, O skulker of the shadows!" he called. "Hither, false reader of the stars. I have a word for your ears—*Bismillah!*"

A dozen armed figures leaped from the bush in front of him. Something struck the mail on his chest with a ringing *clang*, and a spear dropped at his feet. Another whizzed past his head.

Abdul Dost gave back a pace, warding off the sword-blades that searched for his throat. Excellent swordsman that he was, he was hard pressed by the number of his assailants. A sweeping blow of his scimitar half-severed the head of the nearest man, but another weapon bit into his leg over the knee, and his startled horse reared back, making him half-lose his balance.

At this point Khlit spurred his horse at the foes of Abdul Dost, riding down one and forcing the others back. "Mount!" he cried over his shoulder to the Afghan.

Abdul Dost's high-strung Arab, however, had been grazed by a spear and was temporarily unmanageable. Khlit covered his companion, avoiding the blows of the attackers cleverly. They pressed their onset savagely.

Abdul Dost, cursing his injured leg, tossed aside the reins of his useless mount and stepped forward to Khlit's side, his sword poised.

Then, while the two faced the ten during one of those involuntary pauses that occur in hand-to-hand fights, a new element entered into the conflict at the crossroads.

There was a sharp twang, a whistling hum in the air, and one of the assailants flung up his arms with a grunt. In the half-light Khlit saw that an arrow had transfixed the man's head, its feathered end sticking grotesquely from his cheek.

A second shaft and a third sped swiftly, each finding its mark on their foes. One man dropped silently to earth, clutching his chest; a second turned and spun dizzily backward into the bush.

One of the surviving few flung up his shield fearfully in time to have an arrow pierce it cleanly and plant itself in his shoulder.

There was something inexorable and deadly in the silent flight of arrows. Those who could stand, in the group of raiders, turned and leaped into the protecting shadows.

Khlit and Abdul Dost heard them running, breaking through the vines. They stared curiously at the five forms outstretched in the road. On the forehead of one who faced the moon, a shaft through his breast, they saw the white caste-mark of Jagannath.

Already the five had ceased moving.

"Come into the shadow, O heedless riders of the north," called a stalwart voice.

Khlit turned his horse, and was followed by Abdul Dost, who by this time had recovered his mount.

Under the trees on the farther side of the road they found Sawal Das, chuckling. The archer surveyed them, his small head on one side. "Horses and sword-blades are an ill protection against the spears that fly in the dark," he remarked reprovingly.

"How came you here?" muttered Abdul Dost, who was in an ill humor, what with his hurt and the events of the night.

"Ohé—Oho!" Sawal Das laughed. "Am I not the right-hand man of my lord, the Rawul? Does he not ride hither with his bride tomorrow? Thus, I watch the road.

"A short space ago when the rain ceased I heard an ill-omened group talking at the crossroads. There was a half-caste *feringhi* who said that the two riders would return to seek the Thaneswar path—"

"The astrologer!" muttered Abdul Dost, binding his girdle over his thigh.

"Even so, my lord. Who is he but a spy of the temple? Ah, my bold swordsman, there be jewels in your turban and sword-hilt."

"Likewise—so Bhimal whispered—the lowborn followers of the temple have orders to keep armed men from Thaneswar gate. I know not. But I waited with bow strung, believing that there would be sport—"

"Bravely and well have you aided us," said Khlit shortly in his broken Mogholi. "I saw others moving in the bush—"

"Perchance the evil-faced Kurral and his friends," assented Sawal Das, who understood.

"I will not forget," grunted the Cossack.

"Nay." The archer took his rein in hand. "This is no spot for our talk. I will lead you to Thaneswar, where you may sleep in peace."

He led them forward, humming softly to himself. "Men of Jagannath have been slain," he murmured over his shoulder. "That will rouse the anger of the priests. Already the hot blood is in their foreheads at thought of the honor and wealth of my lord the Rawul. We will not speak of this, lest a cloud sully the bride-bringing of my lord.

"Verily," he said more softly, "did Perwan Singh, the chanter of epics, say that before long this place will be as it was in the days of the Pandas and the higher gods. Aye, Perwan Singh sang that blood would cover the mountains and bones will fill the valleys. Death will walk in the shadows of the men of Thaneswar."

After they had gone, a form scurried from the thicket down the muddy highway, a heavy pack on its back. It paused not, nor looked behind. Merghu, the astrologer, was leaving Kukushetra.

III

There is One who knows the place of the birds who fly through the sky; who perceives what has been and what will be; who knows the track of the wind—

He is named by many names; yet he is but one.

—Hymn to Vishnu

Khlit was disappointed in the sight of Thaneswar castle. On the day following the affray of the crossroads the Cossack was early afoot, and as the retainers were busied in preparing for the coming of their lord he was able to make the rounds of the place undisturbed save by a few curious glances.

The abode of Rawul Matap Rao was not a castle in the true sense of the word. In the midst of the wheat-fields of the province of Kukushetra a low wall of dried mud framed an enclosure of several buildings. The enclosure was beaten smooth by the feet of many animals, and against the wall were the stables, the elephant-stockade, the granaries and the quarters of the stable servants and the mahouts.

In the center of the site grew the garden of Thaneswar, a jumble of wildflowers, fern-trees and miniature deodars cleverly cultivated by gardeners whose hereditary task it was to tend the spot and keep clean the paths through the verdure, artfully designed to appear as if a haphazard growth of nature.

An open courtyard ornamented by a great pool of water shadowed by cypresses fronted the garden. At the rear of the courtyard, it was true, a solid granite building stood—the hall of the Rawul. Pillars of the same stone, however, supported a thatched roof, under which ran layers of cane. Numerous openings in the granite wall provided sleeping-terraces. The inner partitions were mainly lattice-work, and only one ceiling—that of the main hall—was of stronger material than the thatch. This was of cedar, inlaid with ivory and mosaic, and brightly painted.

To Khlit, accustomed to the rugged stone structures of Central Asia, the small palace was but a poor fortress. He had no eye for the throng of diligent servants who were spreading clean cotton cloths over the floor mattresses or placing flowers in the latticework. "The temple of the hill-god, yonder," he muttered to Sawal Das, who had joined him, "was stronger."

The archer fingered his mustache. "Aye," he admitted restlessly. "I would that the Rawul had kept the heavy taxes upon the peasants, so that the armed retainers of Thaneswar would be more numerous and better equipped. I have scarce two-score able men under me. And my lord has not many more men-at-arms to attend him. He would give the very gold of his treasury to the peasants, if need be.

"When I say that we should have more swords—when yonder eagle"—he pointed to the glittering dome of the temple—"cries out in greed—he laughs and swears that a word will rouse the peasantry and villagers of Kukushetra on our behalf. But I know not."

He shrugged his shoulders and dismissed his forebodings. "Ah, well, warrior, who would dare to lift hand against Rawul Matap Rao, the last of the Thaneswar clan? Come, here is the choicest defender of Thaneswar, with his companion." Sawal Das pointed to the stockade in one corner of the great enclosure. Here a half-dozen elephants were being groomed for the reception of the chieftain and his bride.

It was the first time that Khlit had seen the beasts nearby and he strode over to gaze at them. Seeing his absorption in the sight, the archer left to attend to his own affairs.

First the elephants were washed down well in a muddy pool outside the enclosure, reached by a wide gate through the wall. Then their heads, trunks and ears were painted a vivid orange, shaded off to green at the tips of the flapping ears and at the end of the trunk. Then crimson silk cloths were hung over their barrels, and a triangular piece of green velvet was placed over their heads between the eyes. This done, silk cords with silver bells attached were thrown about their massive necks.

The largest of the huge animals, however, was attired in full war panoply. Bhimal, who had come with several of the household to gaze at the sight, touched Khlit's elbow. "Behold Asil Rumi," he said in Mogholi. Khlit and Abdul Dost had treated the lame peasant kindly—something rare in his experience—and he was grateful. "The favorite elephant. He was a gift to the grandfather of the Rawul from a raja of Rinthambur. He has not his match for strength in this land. He is mightier than the storm-wind, which is the breath of the angry gods, for he can break down with his head a tree as big as my body."

The peasant sighed. "Oftentimes, when the Rawul hunted tiger toward Rinthambur, Asil Rumi has trod down my wheat. But always the Rawul flung me silver to pay for the damage. A just man."

Khlit glanced at the old peasant. "Have you left your farm?"

"Is it not Jagannath's? I would not dishonor the faith of my dead brother. See!" he cried.

Asil Rumi, with a thunderous internal rumbling, had planted his trunk against a post of the stockade a few yards from them. The elephant wore his battle armor—a bronze plate, heavily bossed, over his skull, stout leather sheets down either side, and twin sword-blades tied to his curving tusks.

Under the impact of the elephant's bulk the post creaked. Khlit saw it bend and heard it crack. The house servants ran back.

Asil Rumi leaned farther forward and the post—a good yard thick—gave as easily before him as an aspen. Then his mahout ran up. Khlit was surprised to hear the man talk to the beast urgently. The mahout held a silver prong, but this he did not use.

Asil Rumi drew back. At a second word from his master the elephant coiled his trunk about the post and straightened it. Then he stood tranquil, his huge ears shaking, muttering to himself.

"How is it," asked Khlit, "that a small man such as that can command a beast like Asil Rumi? The beast could slay him with a touch of the tusk."

"Aye," assented Bhimal gravely, "the father of this mahout was slain by Asil Rumi when he was angry. But today he only plays. So long as this man speaks to him Asil Rumi will obey because of his love for the man."

And Bhimal told how two generations ago the elephant had taken part in one of the battles of Rajasthan. The standard of the warlike Rinthambur clan had been placed on his back, and his mahout had led him well into the van of the Rajputs, ordering him to stand in a certain spot.

The battle had been closely fought about the beast, and the mahout slain. The elephant had been wounded in many places and the greater part of the Rinthambur Rajputs slain about him. Still Asil Rumi had remained standing where he was placed.

The Rajputs had won the battle, so Bhimal said. The soldiers had left the field during the pursuit, but Asil Rumi had stayed by the body of his mahout, refusing food or water for three days in his sorrow for the man who had been his master. Then they had brought the boy who was the son of the mahout. Him the elephant had recognized and obeyed.

"Asil Rumi will go to meet the bride of Rinthambur," concluded Bhimal. "She will mount his howdah, with her lord. It will be a goodly sight."

Presently came Abdul Dost, resplendent in a fresh tunic and girdle, to announce that it was time they should groom their horses for the ride to meet the Rawul.

But Khlit remained in the elephant-stockade watching the beasts until the household cavalcade had actually mounted, when he left the animals that had so stirred his interest. He washed his face hastily in the garden pool, drew his belt tighter about his *khalat*, pulled at his mustache and was ready to ride with the others.

⌒

Bhimal excused himself to Sawal Das from accompanying the leaders of the peasants, saying that he was too lame to walk with the rest. Khlit, however, noticed that Bhimal kept pace with them as far as the crossroads.

The bodies had been cleared away, and the feet of the men and beasts had obscured the imprint of blood here. Bhimal lingered. "So," said the Cossack grimly, "you go to Jagannath, not to your lord."

"Aye," said the peasant simply. "In the temple above is *he* who is greater than any lord. *He* is master of death and life. My brother died in his worship. Wherefore should I not go?"

Khlit lingered behind the other horsemen, scanning Bhimal curiously. As the elephants had been strange beasts to him, so Bhimal and his kind were a new race of men.

It was Khlit's habit to ponder what was new to him. In this he differed from Abdul Dost.

"Have many of the Thaneswar peasants gone to the temple festival?" he inquired, noticing that the foot retainers with the cavalcade were few.

"Aye."

"What is the festival?"

"It is the great festival of Jagannath. *Janam*, the holy priests call it. They say it is to honor the birth of the god. It has always been."

"Will the Rawul and his woman go?" Khlit did not care to revisit the temple after the episode of the night before.

"Nay. The Rawul has no love for the priests of the temple. He has said—so it is whispered through the fields—that they are not the true worshipers of Vishnu."

Down the breeze came the sound of the temple drums and cymbals. Khlit thought grimly that he also had no love for the servants of Vishnu. "What is this Jagannath?" he asked indifferently.

To Khlit the worship of an idol by dance or song was a manifestation of Satan. He was a Christian of simple faith. His tone, however, aroused the patient Hindu. "Jagannath!" he cried, and his faded eyes gleamed. "Jagannath is the god of the poor. All men stand equal before him. The raja draws his car beside the pariah. His festival lasts as many days as I have fingers, and every day there is food for his worshipers. It is the holy time when a bride is offered to Jagannath."

He pointed up to the temple. "A woman is chosen, and she is blessed. She is called the bride of Jagannath. Food and flowers are given her. She rides in the front of the great car which we build with our hands when Jagannath himself comes from his temple and is borne in the car to the ruins of the holy edifice which was once the home of the older gods themselves.

"The woman—so Kurral said—abides one night in the shrine of the god. Then Jagannath reveals himself to her. He tells the omens for the coming year, whether the crops will be good, the rains heavy and the cows healthy. Then this is told to us. It is verily the word of the god.

"Ah!" He glanced around. "I am late."

He hobbled off up the path, leaning on his stick, and Khlit spurred after the others, dismissing from his mind for a time what he had heard about the festival of *Janam*.

He soon forgot Bhimal in the confusion attending the arrival of the Rawul, and the banquet that night.

＊

There was good cheer in Thaneswar. The young Rawul with his bride and his companions feasted on the gallery overlooking the main hall. The soldiery and retainers shared the feast at the foot of the hall, or without on the garden terrace.

Khlit and Abdul Dost had discovered that wine was to be had by those who so desired, and seated themselves in a corner of the hall with a generous portion of the repast and silver cups of sherbet between them. "*Eh,*" cried the *mansabdar,* "these Hindus lack not a free hand. Did you mark how the Rawul scattered gold, silver and gems among the throng? The beauty of his bride has intoxicated him."

Khlit ate in silence. The music of Hindustan—a shrill clatter of instruments—held no charm for him. Abdul Dost, however, was accustomed to the melodies and nodded his head in time, his appreciation heightened by the wine. "Last night," he said bluntly, "I spoke in haste, for I was angry. You are my brother in arms. By Allah, I would cut the cheekbones from him who dared to say what I did."

He emptied his cup and cast a pleased glance over the merry crowd. "It was a good word you spoke when Sawal Das led you to the horse of the Rawul and spoke your name to Matap Rao. *Eh*, Matap Rao asked whether you had a rank as a chieftain." He smiled. "You responded that a chieftain's rank is like to the number of men who will follow his standard in battle. That was well said.

"I have heard tales that you once were leader of as many thousands as Matap Rao numbers tens among his men. Is that the truth? It was in Tartary, in the Horde."

"That time is past," said Khlit.

"Aye. Perchance, though, such things may arise again. Sawal Das says that there may be fighting. Yet I scent it not. What think you?"

Abdul Dost glanced at Khlit searchingly. Much he had heard of the Cossack's craft in war. Yet since their meeting Khlit had shown no desire to take up arms. Rather, he had seemed well content to be unmolested. This did not accord with the spirit of the fiery Afghan, to whom the rumor of battle was as the scent of life itself.

"I think," said Khlit, "that Matap Rao had done better to leave guards at the gate."

The Afghan shrugged his shoulders, then lifted his head at the sound of a ringing voice. It was aged Perwan Singh, and his song was the song of Arjun that begins:

As starlight in the Summer skies,
So is the brightness of a woman's eyes—
Unmatched is she!

Silence fell upon the hall and the outer corridors. All eyes were turned to the gallery where behind a curtain the young bride of Thaneswar sat beside the feast of Matap Rao and his companions, among them Perwan Singh.

The sunbeam of the morning shows
Within her path a withered lotus bud,
A dying rose.

Her footsteps wander in the sacred
place
Where stand her brethren, the ethe-
real race
For ages dead!

A young noble of the household parted the curtain at the song's end. He was a slender man, dark-faced, twin strings of pearls wound in his turban and about his throat—Serwal Jain, of Thaneswar. "Men of Thaneswar," he cried ringingly, "the Lotus Face is now our queen. Happy are we in the sight of the flower of Rinthambur. Look upon Retha, wife of your lord."

There was a murmur of delight as the woman stood beside him. She was of an even height with the boy, the olive face unveiled, the black eyes wide and tranquil, the dark hair empty of jewels except for pearls over the forehead. Her thin silk robe, bound about the waist and drawn up from feet to shoulder, showed the tight under-bodice over her breast and the outline of the splendid form that had been termed the "tiger-waisted."

"Verily," said Abdul Dost, "she is fair."

But Khlit had fallen asleep during the song. The minstrelsy of Hindustan held no charms for him, and he had eaten well.

A stir in the hall, followed by a sudden silence, aroused the Cossack. He was wide awake upon the instant, scenting something unwonted. Abdul Dost was on his feet, as indeed were all in the hall. Within the doorway stood a group of Brahmans, surrounded by representatives of the higher castes of Kukushetra.

The castle retainer stood at gaze, curious and expectant. Through the open gate a breath of air stirred the flames of the candles.

"What seek you?" asked Serwul Jain from the gallery.

"We have come from the temple of Kukushetra, from the holy shrine of the Lord of the World," responded the foremost priest. "Rawul Matap Rao we seek. We have a message for his ears."

By now the chieftain was beside Retha. The eyes of the throng went from him to the Brahman avidly. It was the first time the Brahmans had honored Thaneswar castle with their presence.

"I am here," said the Rawul briefly. "Speak."

The Brahman advanced a few paces, drawing his robe closer about him. The servants gave back respectfully. "This, O Rawul," he began, "is the festival of *Janam*. Pilgrims have come from every corner of the Punjab; aye, from the Siwalik hills and the border of Rajasthan to the temple of Jagannath. Yet you remain behind your castle wall."

He spoke sharply, clearly. No anger was apparent in his voice, but a stern reproach. Behind him Khlit saw the gaunt figure of Kurral.

"The day of my wedding is just past," responded Matap Rao quietly, "and I abide here to hold the feast. My place is in my own hall, not at the temple."

"So be it," said the priest. He flung his head back and his sonorous voice filled the chamber. "I bear a message from the shrine. Though you have forgotten the reverence due to the Lord of the World, though you have said harsh words concerning his temple, though you have neglected the holy rites and slandered the divine mysteries—even though you have forsworn the worship of Jagannath—the Lord of the World forgives and honors you."

He paused as if to give his words weight with the attentive throng. "For the space of years your path and that of the temple have divided. Aye, quarrels have been and blood shed. Last night five servants of the temple were slain on the highroad without your gate."

A surprised murmur greeted this. News of the fight had been kept secret by the priests until now, and Sawal Das had held his tongue.

"Yet Jagannath forgives. Matap Rao, your path will now lead to the temple. For tonight the bride of Jagannath is chosen. And the woman chosen is—as is the custom—fairest in the land of Kukushetra. Retha of Rinthambur."

Complete silence enveloped the crowd. Men gaped and started. Youthful Serwul Jain started and clutched at his sword. The lean hand of Perwan Singh arrested midway as he stroked his beard. The girl flashed a startled glance at her lord and drew the silk veil across her face.

A slow flush rose into the face of Matap Rao and departed, leaving him pale. He drew a deep breath and the muscles of his figure tightened until he was at his full height.

To be selected as the bride of the god on the *Janam* festival was held a high honor. It had been shared in the past by some of the most noted women of the land. The choice of the temple had never been denied.

But in the mild face of the Rawul was the shadow of fierce anger, swiftly mastered. He looked long into the eyes of the waiting priest while the crowd hung upon his word.

"Whose is the choice?" he asked slowly.

"Nagir Jan himself uttered the decree. The holy priest was inspired by the thought that Retha, wife of the Rawul, should hear the prophecy of the god for the coming year. Who but she should tell the omens to Kukushetra?"

Matap Rao lifted his hand. "Then let Nagir Jan come to Thaneswar," he responded. "Let him voice his request himself. I will not listen to those of lower caste."

IV

Upon the departure of the priests the curtain across the gallery was drawn. A tumult arose in the hall. Many peasants departed. The serving women fled back to their quarters, and the house retainers lingered, watching the gallery.

Abdul Dost leaned back against the wall, smiling at Khlit. "By the beard of my grandsire! If I had such a bride as Retha of Rinthambur I would yield her not to any muttering Hindu priest."

He explained briefly to Khlit what had happened. The Cossack shook his head moodily. "There will be ill sleeping in Thaneswar this night, Abdul Dost," he said grimly. "The quarrel between priest and chieftain cuts deeper than you think."

"It is fate. The Rawul may not refuse the honor."

Khlit stroked his gray mustache, making no response. The prime of his life he had spent in waging war with the reckless ardor for the Cossack against the enemies of the Cross. The wrong done to Bhimal had not escaped his attention. Nor had the one glimpse of the Kukushetra temple been agreeable to his narrow but heartfelt idea of a place of worship.

"When all is said," meditated the Afghan, "this is no bread of our eating."

"Nay, Abdul Dost. Yet we have eaten the salt of Matap Rao."

"Verily, that is so," grunted the Afghan. "Well, we shall soon see what is written. What is written, is written. Not otherwise."

Khlit seated himself beside his comrade and waited. Soon came Sawal Das through an opening in the wall behind them. Seeing them, he halted, breathing hard, for he had been running. "*Aie!*" he cried. "It was an ill thought that led Matap Rao to thin the ranks of his armed men. Nagir Jan has watched Thaneswar ripen like a citron in the sun. He has yearned after the wheat-fields and the tax paid by the peasants. Truly is he named the snake. See, how he strikes tonight.

"*Aie!* He is cunning. His power is like that of the furious *daevas*. His armor is hidden, yet he is more to be feared than if a thousand swords waved about him."

Abdul Dost laughed. "If that is the way the horse runs, archer, you could serve your master well by planting a feathered shaft under the ear of the priest."

Sawal Das shook his head. "Fool!" he cried. "The Rawul would lose caste and life itself were he to shed the blood of a higher priest of Jagannath. He would be left for the burial dogs to gnaw. The person of Nagir Jan and those with him is inviolate."

"Then must Matap Rao yield up his bride."

The archer's white teeth glinted under his mustache. "Never will a Rawul of Thaneswar do that."

Both men were surprised at the anger of the slender archer. They knew little of the true meaning of the festival of Jagannath.

"Perhaps he will flee, Sawal Das. Khlit and I will mount willingly to ride with him. Your shafts would keep pursuers at a distance."

"I have been the rounds of the castle enclosure," observed Sawal Das. "The watchers of the temple are posted at every gateway and even along the wall itself. Their spies are in the stables. Without the enclosure the peasants gather together. They have been told to arm."

"On behalf of their lord?"

"Vishnu alone knows their hearts."

Abdul Dost reached down and gripped the arm of Sawal Das. "Ho, little archer," he growled, "if it comes to sword-strokes—we have eaten the salt of your master, and we are in your debt. We will stand at your side."

"I thank you." The Hindu's eyes lighted. Then his face fell. "But what avail sword-strokes against Jagannath? How can steel cut the tendrils of his temple that coil about Thaneswar? Nay; unless my lord can overmaster him with fair words it will go ill with us."

He shook both fists over his head in impotent wrath. "May the curse of Siva and Vishnu fall upon the master of lies! He has waited until the people of the countryside are aflame with zeal. He has stayed his hand until the Lotus Face came to Thaneswar as bride. Did not he ask to look upon her when she rode hither? *Aie*, he is like a barbed shaft in our flesh."

Came Bhimal, limping, to their corner. "Nagir Jan is at the gate, Sawal Das," he muttered. "And behind him are the peasantry, soldiers and scholars of Kukushetra, many of them armed, to receive Retha as the chosen bride."

The archer departed. Bhimal squatted beside them, silent, his head hanging on his chest.

Abdul Dost glanced at Khlit. "Your pony is in the stable," he whispered. "Perchance if you ride not forth now the going will be ill."

"And so is yours, Abdul Dost," grunted Khlit. "Why do you not mount him?"

The Afghan smiled and they both settled back to await what was to come.

Nagir Jan entered the hall alone. Matap Rao advanced a few paces to meet him.

Neither made a salaam. Their eyes met and the priest spoke first, while those in the hall listened.

"I have come for the bride of the *Janam*. Even as you asked it, I have come. Tonight she must bathe and be cleansed of all impurity. The women of the wardrobe and the strewers of flowers will attend her, to prepare her to mount the sacred car on the morrow. Then will she sit beside the god himself. And on that night will she kneel before him in the chamber in the ruins and the god will speak to her and manifest himself in the holy mystery. Where is the woman Retha?"

Matap Rao smiled, although his face was tense and his fingers quivered. "Will you take the veil from your face? Will you withdraw the cloak from your words, Nagir Jan?"

The cold eyes of the priest flickered. His strong face showed no sign of the anger he must have felt.

"Nagir Jan, I will speak the truth. Will you answer me so?"

"Say on," assented the Brahman.

The young lord of Thaneswar raised his voice until it reached the far corners of the hall. "Why do you hold me in despite, Nagir Jan? You have said that I am without faith. Yet do I say that my faith is as great as yours. Speak!"

A murmur went through the watchers. The youths standing behind Matap Rao glanced at each other, surprised by the bold course the Rawul had taken.

"Does a servant of Jagannath speak lies?" Nagir Jan smiled. "Is the wisdom of the temple a house of straw, to break before the first wind? Nay."

He paused, meditating. He spoke clearly, forcibly in the manner of one who knew how to sway the hearts of his hearers. "Is not Jagannath Lord of the World, Matap Rao? In him is mighty Vishnu thrice incarnate; in him are the virtues of Siva, protector of the soul; and the virtues of Balabhadra and Subhadra. Since the birth of Ram, Jagannath has been. The power of Kali, the All-Destroyer, is the lightning in his hand. Is not this the truth?"

Nagir Jan bowed his head. Matap Rao made no sign.

"Surely you do not question the holiness of Jagannath, protector of the poor, guardian of the pilgrim and master of our souls?" continued the priest. "Nay, who am I but a lowly sweeper of the floor before the mighty god?"

He stretched out a thin hand. "Jagannath casts upon you the light of his mercy, Rawul. He ordains that your faithlessness be forgiven. Thus does Jagannath weld in one the twin rulers of Kukushetra.

"If you seek forgiveness, Kukushetra will prosper and the hearts of its men be uplifted. To this end has Jagannath claimed the beauty of Retha. Your wife will be the bond that will bind your soul to its forgotten faith."

He smiled and lowered his hand. Dignified and calm, he seemed as he said, the friend of the Rawul. "Is not this the truth, Matap Rao? Aye, it is so."

The priest ceased speaking and waited for the other to reply.

In his speech Nagir Jan had avoided the issue of Matap Rao's faith. He had spoken only of the claim of Jagannath. And a swift glance at his hearers showed him that his words had gone home. Many heads nodded approvingly.

The Rawul would not dare, so thought Nagir Jan, to attack the invisible might of Jagannath. By invoking the divinity of the god, Nagir Jan had made Matap Rao powerless to debate. And personal debate, he guessed, was the hope of Matap Rao. Something of triumph crept into his cold face.

Matap Rao was thoughtful, his eyes troubled. The chieftain was an ardent Hindu. How could he renounce his faith?

Abruptly his head lifted and he met the eyes of the priest. "What you have said of Jagannath, incarnation of Vishnu, is verily the truth, Nagir Jan," responded the Rawul. "Yet it is not all the truth. You have not said that the *priests* of Jagannath are false. They are false servants of Vishnu. They are not true followers of the One who is master of the gods."

He spoke brokenly, as a man torn by mingled feeling. "Aye. Wherefore do the priests of Kukushetra perform the rites in costly robes? Or anoint themselves with oil? With perfume, with camphor and sandal? Instead of the sacred Vedas, they chant the *prem sagar*—the ocean of love. The pictures and images of the temple are those of lust."

His voice was firmer now, with the ring of conviction. "Aye, you are faithless servants. The rich garments that are offered by the pilgrims to the gods, you drape once upon the sacred images. Then you wear them on your unclean bodies.

"What becomes of the stores of food yielded by peasants for the meals of Jagannath? Four times a day do you present food to the wooden face of the god; afterwards you feast well upon it."

Nagir Jan showed no change of expression; but he drew back as if from contamination.

"You have forgotten the wise teachings of Chaitanya, who declared that a priest is like to a warrior," continued the Rawul. "The *gosain* preached that sanctity is gained by inward warfare, by self-denial and privation.

"You of Kukushetra follow the doctrine of Vallabha Swami. He it was who said that gratified desire uplifts the soul. And so do you live. What are the handmaidens of Jagannath but the prostitutes of the temple and its people?"

An uneasy stir among the listeners greeted this. Many heads were shaken.

"It is the truth I speak," cried the Rawul, turning to them. "Nagir Jan claims to be the friend of the poverty-afflicted. Is it so? He seeks devotees among the merchants and masters of wealth.

"He takes the fields of the peasants by forfeiture, contrary to law. He has taken much of my land. He seeks all of Thaneswar."

The young chieftain spread out his arms. "My spirit has followed the way of Chaitanya. I believe that bloodshed is pollution. My household divinity is the image of the sun, which was the emblem of my oldest forebears, whose fields were made fertile by its light. Is it not the truth that a man may uplift his spirit even to the footstool of the One among the gods by *bahkti*—faith?"

While the watchers gazed, some frowning, some admiring, Abdul Dost touched the arm of Khlit and nodded approvingly. "An infidel," he whispered, "but—by the ninety-nine holy names—a man of faith."

Nagir Jan drew his robe closer about him, and spoke pityingly. "Blind!" he accused. "Does not the god dwell in the temple?"

"Then," responded Matap Rao, "whose dwelling is the world?"

He pointed at the priest. "What avails it to wash your mouth, to mutter prayers on the pilgrimage if there is no faith in your heart, Nagir Jan? For my faith, you seek to destroy me, to gain the lands of Thaneswar. And so, you have asked Retha as the bride of Jagannath."

The shaven head of the priest drew back with the swift motion of a snake about to strike. But Matap Rao spoke before him. "Well you know, Nagir Jan, that I will not yield Retha. If it means my death, Retha will not go to the temple."

"Thus you defy the choice of Jagannath?"

"Aye," said Matap Rao, and his voice shook. "For I know what few know. Among the ruins will the bride of Jagannath remain tomorrow night—where you and those who believe with you have said the god will appear as a man and foretell the omens, in the mystery of the *Janam*. But he who will come to the woman is no god but a man, chosen by lot among the priests—perhaps you, Nagir Jan."

His tense face flushed darkly. He lowered his voice, but in the silence it could be heard clearly. "The rite of *Janam* will be performed. But a *man* violates the body of the bride. It is a priest. And he prophesies the omens. That is why, O Nagir Jan, I have called the priests false.

"Never will the Lotus Face become the bride of Jagannath," he added quietly.

"Impious! Idolater!" The head of Nagir Jan shot forward with each word. "It is a lie, spoken in madness. But the madness will not save you." His eyes shone cruelly, and his teeth drew back from his lips. "You have blasphemed Jagannath, O Rawul. You have denied to Jagannath his bride."

He turned swiftly. "Thaneswar is accursed. Who among you will linger here? Who will come with me to serve Jagannath? The god will claim his bride. Woe to those who aid him not—"

He passed swiftly from the hall and a full half of the peasants as well as many of the house servants slipped after him. The soldiers around the Rawul stood where they were.

Rawul Matap Rao gazed after the fugitives with a wry smile. Old Perwan Singh laid down his *vina* and girded a sword-belt about his bony frame. Serwul Jain drew his scimitar and flung the scabbard away. "The battle-storm is at the gate of Thaneswar," he cried in his high voice. "Ho—who will shed his blood for the Lotus Face? You have heard the words of your lord."

A hearty shout from the companion nobles answered him, echoed by a gruffer acclaim from the soldiery, led by Sawal Das. Matap Rao's eyes lighted but his smile was sad. "Aye, blood will be shed," he murmured. "It is pollution—yet we who die will not bear the stain of the sin."

He laid an arm across the bent shoulder of the minstrel. "Even thus you foretold, old singer of epics. Will you sing also of the fate of Thaneswar?"

Abdul Dost spoke quickly to Khlit of what had passed. His face was alight with the excitement of conflict. But the shaggy face of Khlit showed no answering gleam.

"There will be good sword-blows, O wayfarer," cried the Moslem. "Come, here is a goodly company. We will scatter the rout of temple-scum! Eh— what say you?"

Khlit remained passive, wearing every indication of strong disgust. "Why did not yonder stripling chieftain prepare the castle for siege?" he growled. "Dog of the devil—he did naught but speak words."

He remained seated where he was while Abdul Dost ran to join the forces mustering under Serwul Jain at the castle gate. He shook his head moodily. But as the Rawul, armed and clad in mail, passed by, Khlit reached up and plucked his sleeve. "Where, O chieftain," he asked bluntly, "is Asil Rumi, defender of Thaneswar? He is yet armored—aye—the elephants are your true citadel—"

Not understanding Mogholi, and impatient of the strange warrior's delay, the Rawul shook him off and passed on.

Khlit looked after him aggrievedly. Then he shook his wide shoulders, yawned, girded his belt tighter and departed on a quest for good among the remnants of the banquet. It was Khlit's custom, whenever possible, to eat before embarking on any dangerous enterprise.

V

And they paused to hearken to a voice which said, "Hasten."

It was the voice of the assembler of men, of him who spies out a road for many, who goes alone to the mighty waters. It was Yama, the Lord of Death, and he said:

"Hasten to thy home, and to thy fathers."

Nagir Jan was not seen again at Thaneswar that night. But his followers heard his tidings and a multitude gathered on the road.

Those who accompanied the Brahman from the hall could give only an incoherent account of the words Matap Rao had spoken. The crowd, however, had been aroused by the priests in the temple.

It was enough for them that the Rawul had blasphemed against the name of Jagannath. They were stirred by religious zeal, at the festival of the god.

Moreover, as in all mobs, the lawless element coveted the chance to despoil the castle. Among the worshipers were many, well armed, who assembled merely for the prospect of plunder. They joined forces with the more numerous party.

The ranks of the pilgrims and worshipers who had been sent down from the temple by the Brahmans were swelled by an influx of villagers and peasants from the fields—ignorant men who followed blindly those of higher caste.

The higher priests absented themselves, but several of the lower orders such as Kurral directed the onset against the castle. Already the enclosure was surrounded. Torches blazed in the fields without the mud wall. The wall itself was easily surmounted at several points before the garrison could muster to defend it—even if they had been numerous enough to do so.

"Jagannath!" cried the pilgrims, running toward the central garden, barehanded and aflame with zeal, believing that they were about to avenge a mortal sin on the part of one who had scorned the gods.

"Jagannath!" echoed the vagrants and mercenary soldiers, fingering their weapons, eyes burning with the lust of spoil.

"The bride of Jagannath!" shouted the priests among the throng. "Harm her not, but slay all who defend her."

Torches flickered through the enclosure and in the garden. Frightened stable servants fled to the castle, or huddled among the beasts. The neighing of startled horses was drowned by the trumpeting of the elephants. A mahout who drew his weapon was cut down by the knives of the peasants.

But it was toward the palace that the assailants pressed through the pleasure garden; and the palace was ill designed for defense. Wide doorways and latticed arbors guided the mob to the entrances. The clash of steel sounded in the uproar, and the shrill scream of a wounded woman pierced it like a knife-blade.

The bright moon outlined the scene clearly. Khlit, standing passive within the main hall, could command at once a balcony overlooking the gardens and the front gate. He saw several of the rushing mob fall as the archers in the house launched their shafts.

A powerful blacksmith, half-naked, appeared on the balcony, whither he had yet climbed, dagger between his teeth. A loyal peasant rushed at him with a sickle, and paused at arm's reach.

"Jagannath!" shouted the giant, stepping forward.

The coolie shrank back and tossed away his makeshift weapon, crying loudly for mercy. He stilled his cry at a melodious voice.

"Chaitanya! Child of the sun!" It was old Perwan Singh, walking tranquilly along the tiles of the gallery in the full moonlight. The smith hesitated, then advanced to meet him, crouching. The minstrel struck down the dagger awkwardly with his sword. Meanwhile the recalcitrant peasant had crept behind him, and with a quick jerk wrested away the blade.

Perwan Singh lifted his arm, throwing back his head. He did not try to flee. The black giant surveyed him, teeth agrin, and, with a grunt, plunged his dagger into the old man's neck. Both he and the coolie gripped the minstrel's body before it could fall, stripping the rich gold bangles from arms and ankles of their victim and tearing the pearls from his turban-folds.

Before they could release the body an arrow whizzed through the air, followed swiftly by another. The giant coughed and flung up his arms, falling across the body of the coolie. The three forms lay on the tiles, their limbs moving weakly.

Sawal Das, fitting a fresh shaft to string, trotted by along the balcony, peering out into the garden.

The rush of the mob had by now resolved itself into a hand-to-hand struggle at every door to the castle. The bloodlust, once aroused, stilled all other feelings except that of fanatic zeal. Unarmed men grappled with each other, who had worked side by side in the fields the day before.

A woman slave caught up a javelin and thrust at the assailants, screaming the while. For the most part the house-servants had remained loyal to Matap Rao, whom they loved.

By now, however, all within the castle were struggling for their lives. A soldier slew the woman, first catching her ill-aimed weapon coolly on his shield. Khlit saw a second woman borne off by the peasants.

At the main gate the disciplined defenders under Matap Rao, aided well by that excellent swordsman, Abdul Dost, had beaten off the onset. Serwul Jain and several of the younger nobles had been ordered to safeguard Retha.

They stood in the rear of the main hall, the girl tranquil and proud, her face unveiled, her eyes following Matap Rao in the throng. The Rawul, by birth of the Kayasth or student caste, proved himself a brave man although unskilled.

It was when the first assault had been beaten off and the defenders were gaining courage that the crackle of flames was heard.

Agents of the priesthood among the mob had devoted their attentions to firing the thatch roof at the corners. Matap Rao sent bevies of house servants up to the terraces on the roof, but the flames gained.

A shout proclaimed the triumph of the mob. "Jagannath!" they cried. "The god claims his bride."

"Lo," screamed a pilgrim, "the fire spirits aid us. The *daevas* aid us."

Panic, that nemesis of ill-disciplined groups, seized on many slaves and peasants who were in the castle. "Thaneswar burns!" cried a woman, wringing her hands.

"The gods have doomed us!" muttered a stout coolie, fleeing down the hall.

Serwul Jain sprang aside to cut him down. "Back, dogs!" shouted the boy. "Death is without."

"*Aie!* We will yield our bodies to Jagannath," was the cry that greeted him.

"Jagannath!" Those outside caught up the cry. "Yield to the god."

The backbone of the defense was broken. Slaves threw down their arms. A frightened tide surged back and forth between the rooms. A Brahman appeared in the hall and ran toward Retha silently. A noble at her side stepped between, taking the rush of the priest on his shield. But the Brahman's fall only dispirited the slaves the more.

⌒

Khlit saw groups of half-naked coolies climbing into the windows—the wide windows that served to cool Thaneswar in the summer heat. He walked down the hall, looking for Abdul Dost.

He saw the thinned body of soldiers at the gate struggle and part before the press of attackers. Then Bhimal, who had remained crouched beside him during the earlier fight, started up and ran, limping, at Serwul Jain. "Jagannath!" cried the peasant hoarsely. "My brother's god."

He grappled with the noble from behind and flung him to the stone floor. Coolies darted upon the two and sank their knives into the youth. Bhimal stood erect, his eyes staring in frenzy. "Jagannath conquers!" he shouted.

Khlit caught a glimpse of Matap Rao in a press of men. He turned in time to see Retha's guards hemmed in by a rush of the mob, their swords wrested from their hands.

Retha was seized by many hands before she could lift a scimitar that she had caught up against herself. Seeing this and the agony in the girl's face, Khlit hesitated.

But those who held the wife of the Rawul were too many for one man to encounter. He turned aside, down a passage that led toward the main gate.

He had seen Abdul Dost and Matap Rao fight loose from the men who caught at them.

Then for a long space smoke descended upon the chambers of Thaneswar from the smoldering thatch. The cries of the hurt and the wailing of the women were drowned in a prolonged shout of triumph.

The Rawul and Abdul Dost, who kept at his side, sought fruitlessly through the passages for Retha. Those who met them stepped aside at the sight of their bloodied swords and stern faces. They followed the cries of a woman out upon the garden terrace, only to find that she was a slave in the hands of the coolies.

Matap Rao, white-faced, would have gone back into the house, but the Moslem held him by sheer strength. "It avails not, my lord," he said gruffly. "Let us to horse and then we may do something."

The chieftain, dazed by his misfortune, followed the tall Afghan toward the stables, which so far had escaped the notice of the mob, bent on the richer plunder of the castle. Here they met Khlit walking composedly toward them, leading his own pony and the Arab of Abdul Dost, fully saddled. "Tell the stripling," growled Khlit, "that his palace is lost. Retha I saw in the hands of the priests. They will guard her from the mob. Come."

He led them in the direction of the elephant-stockade. He had noted that morning that a gate offered access to the elephants' pool. Avoiding one or two of the great beasts who were trampling about the place, leaderless and uneasy, he came upon a man who ran along the stockade bearing a torch.

It was Sawal Das, bow in hand. The archer halted at sight of his lord. "I had a thought to seek for Asil Rumi," he cried. "But the largest of the elephants is gone with his mahout. *Aie*—heavy is my sorrow. My lord, my men are slain—"

"Come!" broke in Abdul Dost. "We can do naught in Thaneswar."

Even then, loath by hereditary custom to turn their backs on a foe, the chieftain and his archer would have lingered helplessly. But Abdul Dost took their arms and drew them forward. "Would you add to the triumph of Nagir Jan?" he advised coolly. "There be none yonder but the dead and those who have gone over to the side of the infidel priests. This old warrior is in the right. He has seen many battles. We be four men, armed, with two horses. Better that than dead."

A shout from the garden announced that they had been seen. This decided the archer, who tossed his torch to the ground and ran outward through the stockade and the outer wall.

Avoiding their pursuers in the shadows, they passed by the pool into the wood beyond the fields. Here a freshly beaten path opened before them. Sawal Das trotted ahead until all sounds of pursuit had dwindled. Then they halted, eying each other in silence.

Matap Rao leaned against a horse, the sweat streaming from his face. His slender shoulders shook. Khlit glanced at him, then fell to studying the ground under their feet.

Sawal Das unstrung his bow and counted the arrows in his quiver. "Enough," he remarked grimly, "to send as gifts into the gullets of the Snake and his Kurral. They will not live to see Retha placed upon the car of Jagannath. I swear it."

Abdul Dost grunted.

Matap Rao raised his head and they fell silent. "In the fall of my house and the loss of my wife," he said bitterly, "lies my honor. Fool that I was to bring Retha to Thaneswar when Nagir Jan had set his coils about it. I cannot face the men of Rinthambur."

"Rinthambur!" cried Abdul Dost. "Ho—that is a good word. The hard-fighting clan will aid us, nothing loath—aye, and swiftly. Look you, on these two horses we may ride there—"

"Peace!" said the Rawul calmly. "Think you, soldier, I would ride to Rinthambur when they still hold the wedding feast, and say that Retha has been taken from me?"

"What else?" demanded the blunt Afghan. "By Allah—would you see the Lotus Face fall to Jagannath? In a day and a night we may ride thither and back. With the good clan of Rinthambur at our heels. *Eh*—they wield the swords to teach these priests a lesson—"

"Nay, it would be too late."

"When does the procession of the god—?"

"Just before sunset the car of Jagannath is dragged to the ruins."

"Then," proposed the archer, "if Vishnu favors us we may attack—we four—and slay many. Twilight will cover our movements near the ruins. Aye, perchance we can muster some following among the nearby peasants.

"Then we will provide bodies in very truth for the car of Jagannath to roll upon. From this hour am I no longer a follower of the All-Destroyer—"

Matap Rao smiled wanly. "So have I not been for many years, Sawal Das. My faith is that of the Rinthambur clan, who are called children of the sun. I worship the One Highest. Yet what has it availed me?"

He turned as Khlit came up. The Cossack had lent an attentive ear to the speech of the archer. He had completed his study of the trail wherein they stood. He swaggered as he walked forward—a fresh alertness in his gaunt figure. "It is time," he said, "that we took counsel together as wise men and as warriors. The time for folly is past."

⌐

Abdul Dost and Sawal Das, nothing loath, seated themselves on their cloaks upon the ground already damp with the night dew. Matap Rao remained as he was, leaning against the horse in full moonlight notwithstanding the chance of discovery by a stray pursuer.

The mesh of cypress and fern branches overhead cast mottled shadows on the group. The moon was well in the west and the moist air of early morning hours chilled the perspiration with which the four were soaked. They drew their garments about them and waited, feeling the physical quietude that comes upon the heels of forcible exertion.

Khlit, deep in the shadows, called to Sawal Das softly. "What see you here in the trail?" he questioned. "This is not a path made by men, nor is it a buffalo-track leading to water."

The archer bent forward. "True," he acknowledged. "It is the trail of elephants. One at least has passed." He felt of the broad spoor. "Siva—none but Asil Rumi, largest of the Thaneswar herd, could have left these marks. They are fresh."

"Asil Rumi," continued Khlit from the darkness. "It is as I thought. Tell me, would the oldest elephant have fled without his rider?"

"Nay. Asil Rumi is schooled in war. He is not to be frightened. Only will he flee where his mahout leads. Without the man Asil Rumi would have stayed."

"This mahout—is he true man or traitor?"

"True man to the Rawul. It is his charge to safeguard the elephant. He must seek to lead Asil Rumi into hiding in the jungle."

"A good omen." Satisfaction for the first time was in the voice of the Cossack. "Now may we plan. Abdul Dost, have you a thought as to how we may act?"

The Moslem meditated. "We will abide with the Rawul. We have taken his quarrel upon us. He may have a thought to lead us into the temple this night, while the slaves of Jagannath sleep and the plundering engages the multitude—"

"Vain," broke in the archer. "The priests hold continued festival. The temple wall is too high to climb and the guards are alert. Retha will be kept within the sanctuary of the idols, under the gold dome where no man may come but a priest. The only door to the shrine is through the court of offerings, across the place of dancing, and through the audience hall—"

"Even so," approved Khlit. "Now is it the turn of Sawal Das. He has already spoken well."

"My thought is this," explained the archer. "There will be great shouting and confusion when the sacred car is led from the temple gate. A mixed throng will seek to draw the car by the ropes and to push at the many wheels. We may cover our armor with common robes and hide our weapons, disguising our faces. Men from the outlying districts will aid us, for they are least tainted by the poisonous breath of the Snake—"

"Not so," objected the Afghan, ill pleased at the archer's refusal of his own plan. "Time lacks for the gathering of an adequate force. Those who were most faithful to the Rawul have suffered their heads and hands cut off and other defects.

"Besides, the mastery of Thaneswar has passed to the Snake. When would peasants risk their lives in a desperate venture? *Eh*—when fate has decreed against them?"

"Justly spoken," said Khlit bluntly. "Sawal Das, you and the Rawul might perchance conceal your likeness, but the heavy bones of Abdul Dost and myself—they would reveal us to the throng. It may not be."

"What then?" questioned the archer fiercely. "Shall we watch like frightened women while this deed of shame is done?"

"Has the chieftain a plan?" asked Khlit.

Matap Rao lifted his head wearily. "Am I a warrior?" he said calmly. "The Rinthambur warriors have a saying that a sword has no honor until drawn in battle for a just cause. This night has brought me dishonor. There is no path for me except a death at the hands of the priests—"

"Not so," said Khlit.

The others peered into the shadows, trying to see his face.

"You have all spoken," continued the Cossack. "I have a plan that may gain us Retha. Will you hear it?"

"Speak," said Abdul Dost curiously.

"The temple may not be entered. The multitude of worshipers is too great for the assault of a few men. Then must the chieftain and Abdul Dost ride to Rinthambur as speedily as may be."

"And Retha?" questioned the Rawul.

"Sawal Das and I will fetch the woman from the priests and go to meet you, so that your swords may cover our flight."

Matap Rao laughed shortly. To him the rescue of Retha seemed a thing impossible. "Is my honor so debased that I would leave my bride to the chance of rescue at other hands?"

Whereupon Abdul Dost rose and went to his side respectfully. He laid a muscular hand on the shoulder of the youth. "My lord," he said slowly, "your misfortune has befallen because of the evil craft of men baser and shrewder than you. Allah—you are but a new-weaned boy in experience of combat. You are a reader of books.

"Yet this man called the Curved Saber is a planner of battles. He has had a rank higher than yours. He has led a hundred thousand swords. His hair is gray, and it was said to me not once but many times that he is very shrewd.

"It is no dishonor to follow his leadership. I have not yet seen him in battle, but I have heard what I have heard."

The Rawul was silent for a space. Then, "Speak," he said to Khlit.

While they listened Khlit told them what was in his mind, in few words. He liked not to talk of his purpose. He spoke to ease the trouble of the boy.

When he had done Sawal Das and Abdul Dost looked at each other. "Bismillah!" cried the Afghan. "It is a bold plan. What! Think you I would ride to Rinthambur and leave you—Khlit—to act thus?"

"Aye," said the Cossack dryly. "There is room for two men in my venture; no more. Likewise two should ride to the rajas, for one man might fail or be slain—"

Matap Rao peered close into Khlit's bearded face. "The greater danger lies here," he said. "You would take your life in your open hand. How can I ask this of you?"

Khlit grunted, for such words were ever to his distaste. "I would strike a blow for Retha," he responded, but he was thinking of Nagir Jan.

His words stirred the injured pride of the Hindu. "By the gods!" he cried. "Then shall I stay with you."

"Nay, my lord. Will the chieftains of Rinthambur raise their standard and mount their riders for war on the word of a stranger—a Moslem? So that they will believe, you must go," adding in his beard, "and be out of my way."

So it happened before moonset that Abdul Dost and the Rawul mounted and rode swiftly to the west through paths known to the chieftain.

At once Khlit and Sawal Das set forth upon the spoor of Asil Rumi, which led north toward the farm of Bhimal. Now as he went the little archer fell to humming under his breath. It was the first time he had sung in many hours.

VI

When the shadows lengthened in the courtyard of the temple of Kukushetra the next day a long cry went up from the multitude. From the door under the wheel and flag of Vishnu came a line of priests.

First came the strewers of flowers, shedding lotus-blossoms, jasmine and roses in the path that led to the car of Jagannath. The bevy of dancing women thronged after them, chattering excitedly. But their shrill voices were drowned in the steady, passionate roar that went up from the throng.

The temple prostitutes no longer drew the eyes of the pilgrims. Their task in arousing the desires of the men was done. Now it was the day of Jagannath, the festival of the *Janam*.

Bands of priests emerged from the gate, motioning back the people. A solid wall of human beings, straining for sight of the god, packed the temple enclosure and stretched without the gates. A deeply religious, almost frenzied mass, waiting for the great event of the year, which was the passage of the god to his country seat—as the older ruined temple was termed.

A louder acclaim greeted the appearance of the grotesque wooden form of the god, borne upon the shoulders of the Brahmans. The figure of Jagannath was followed by that of the small Balabhadra, brother to the god, and Subhadra, his sister.

Jagannath was carried to his car. This was a complicated wooden edifice, put together by reverent hands—a car some fifteen yards long and ten yards wide, and lofty. Sixteen broad wooden wheels, seven feet high, supported the mass. A series of platforms, occupied by the women of the temple, hung with garlands of flowers and with offerings to the god, led up to a wide seat wherein was placed Jagannath.

This done, those nearest the car laid hold of the wheels and the long ropes, ready to begin the famous journey. The smaller cars of Balabhadra and Suhadra received less attention and fewer adherents.

Was not Jagannath Lord of the World, chief among the gods, and divine bringer of prosperity during the coming year? So the Brahmans had preached, and the people believed. Had not their fathers believed before them?

The decorators of the idols had robed Jagannath in costly silk and fitted false arms to the wooden body so that it might be sightly in the eyes of the multitude.

The cries of the crowd grew louder and the ropes attached to the car tautened with a jerk. A flutter of excitement ran through the gathering. Had they not journeyed for many days to be with Jagannath on the *Janam*?

As always in a throng, the nearness of so many of their kind wrought upon them. Religious zeal was at a white heat. But the Brahmans raised their hands, cautioning the worshipers. "The bride of Jagannath comes!" they cried.

"Way for the bride of the god!" echoed the pilgrims.

The door of the temple opened again and Retha appeared, attended by some of the women of the wardrobe. The girl's slim form had been elaborately robed. Her cheeks were painted, her long hair allowed to fall upon her shoulders and back.

A brief silence paid tribute to the beauty of the woman. She glanced once anxiously about the enclosure; then her eyes fell, nor did she look up when she was led to a seat beside and slightly below the image of the god.

Once she was seated the guardians who had watched her throughout the night stepped aside. In the center of the crowd of worshipers Retha was cut off from her kind, as securely the property of the god as if she still stood in the shrine. For no one among the throng but was a follower of Jagannath, in the zenith of religious excitement.

The priests formed a cordon about the car. Hundreds of hands caught up the ropes. A blare of trumpets from the musicians on the car, and it lurched forward, the great wheels creaking.

"Honor to Jagannath!" screamed the voice of Bhimal. "The god is among us. Let me touch the wheels!"

The machine was moving forward more steadily now, the wheels churning deep into the sand. The pullers sweated and groaned, tasting keen delight in the toil; the throng crushed closer. A woman cried out and fainted.

But those near her did not give back. Instead they set their feet upon her body and pressed forward. Was it not true blessedness to die during the passage of Jagannath?

Contrary to many tales, they did not throw themselves under the wheels. Only one man did this, and he wracked with the pain of leprosy and sought a holy death, cleansed of his disease.

Perhaps in other days numbers had done this. But now many died in the throng, what with the heat and the pressure and the strain of the excitement, which had continued now for several days.

⁓

Slowly the car moved from the temple enclosure, into the streets of the village, out upon the highway that led to its destination. The sun by now was descending to the horizon.

But the ardor of the pilgrims waxed higher as the god continued its steady progress. For the car to halt would be a bad omen. And the dancing women, stimulated by *bhang*, shouted and postured on the car, flinging their thin garments to those below and gesturing with nude bodies in a species of frenetic exaltation.

Those pushing the car from behind shouted in response. The eyes of Nagir Jan, walking among the pilgrims, gleamed. Kurral, crouched on the car, had ceased to watch the quiet form of Retha. Rescue now, he thought, was impossible, as was any attempt on her part to escape. For the car was surrounded the space of a long bowshot on every side.

The wind which had fluttered the garlands on the car died down as the shadows lengthened. The leaders of the crowd were already within sight of the shrine whither they were bound.

Retha sat as one lifeless. Torn from the side of her husband and carried from the hall of Thaneswar, she had been helpless in the hands of the priests. A proud woman, accustomed to the deference shown to the clan of Rinthambur, the misfortune had numbed her at first.

Well knowing what Matap Rao knew of the evil rites of Jagannath, to be exhibited to the crowd of worshipers caused her to flush under the paint which stained her cheeks.

She would have cast herself down from the car if she had not known that the Brahmans would have forced her again into the seat. To be handled by such a mob was too great a shame.

She had heard that Matap had escaped alive the night before. One thought kept up her courage. Not without an effort to save her would the Rawul allow her to reach the shrine where the rites of that night were to take place.

This she knew, and she hugged the slight comfort of that hope to her heart. Rawul Matap Rao would not abandon her. But, seeing the number of the throng, even this hope dwindled.

How could the chieftain reach her side? But he would ride into the throng, she felt, and an arrow from his bow would free her from shame.

At a sudden silence which fell upon the worshipers she lifted her head for the first time.

Coming from the shrine of the elder gods she saw a massive elephant, appareled for war, an armored plate on his chest, sword-blades fastened to his tusks, his ears and trunk painted a bright orange and leather sheets strapped to his sides. And, seeing, she gave a low cry. "Asil Rumi!"

The elephant was advancing more swiftly than it seemed at first, his great ears stretched out, his small eyes shifting. On his back was the battle howdah. Behind his head perched the mahout wearing a shirt of mail. In the howdah were two figures that stared upon the crowd.

Asil Rumi advanced, interested, even excited, by the throng of men. Schooled to warfare, he followed obediently the instructions of his native master, scenting something unwonted before him. Those nearest gave back hastily.

For a space the throng believed that the elephant was running amuck. Never before had man or beast interfered with the progress of the god. But as Asil Rumi veered onward and the leading pullers at the ropes were forced to scramble aside an angry murmur went up.

Then the voice of Kurral rang out. "Infidels!" he cried. "Those upon the elephant are men of Matap Rao."

The murmur increased to a shout, in which the shrill cries of the women mingled. "Blasphemers! Profaners of Jagannath! Slay them!"

Nagir Jan raised his arms in anger. "Defend the god!" he shouted. "Turn the elephant aside."

Already some men had thrust at Asil Rumi with sticks and spears. The elephant rumbled deep within his bulk. His wrinkled head shook and tossed. His trunk lifted and his eyes became inflamed. He pushed on steadily.

A priest stepped into his path and slashed at his trunk with a dagger. Asil Rumi switched his trunk aside, and smote the man with it. The priest fell back, his skull shattered.

A soldier cast a javelin which clanged against the animal's breastplate. Angered, the elephant rushed the man, caught him in his trunk and cast him underfoot. A huge foot descended on the soldier, and the man lay where he had fallen, a broken mass of bones from which oozed blood.

Now Asil Rumi trumpeted fiercely. He had tasted battle and glanced around for a fresh foe. The bulk of the towering car caught his eye. With a quick rush the elephant pressed between the ropes, moving swiftly for all his size and weight.

The clamor increased. Men dashed at the beast, seeking to penetrate his armor with their weapons; but more hung back. For from on the howdah a helmeted archer had begun to discharge arrows that smote down the leaders of the crowd.

The mahout prodded Asil Rumi forward. The elephant, nothing loath, placed his armored head full against the car. For a moment the pressure of the crowd behind the wooden edifice impelled it against the animal. Asil Rumi uttered a harsh, grating cry and bent his legs into the ground.

He leaned his weight against the car. The wooden wheels of Jagannath creaked, then turned loosely in the sand. The car of the god had stopped. A shout of dismay went up.

Then the mahout tugged with his hook at the head of Asil Rumi. Obedient, even in his growing anger inflamed by minor wounds, the elephant placed one forefoot on the shelving front of the car. The rudely constructed wood gave way and the mass of the car sank with a jar upon the ground, broken loose from the support of the front wheels.

By now the mob was fully aroused. Arrows and javelins flew against the leather protection of the animal and his leather-like skin, wrinkled and aged to the hardness of rhinoceros hide.

A shaft struck the leg of the native mahout and a spear caught in his groin under the armor. He shivered, but retained his seat. Seeing this, Khlit clambered over the front of the howdah to the man's side. "Make the elephant kneel!" he cried.

Asil Rumi knelt, and the fore part of the car splintered under the weight of two massive knees. It fell lower. Now Asil Rumi was passive for a brief moment, and Sawal Das redoubled his efforts, seeking to prevent the priests with knives from hamstringing the beast.

"Come, Retha!" cried Khlit, kneeling and holding fast to the head-band beside the failing native.

The woman was now on a level with him. She understood not his words, but his meaning was plain. The shock to the car had dislodged many of the men upon it.

The temple women clutched at her, but she avoided them. She poised her slender body for the leap.

"Slay the woman!" cried Kurral, scrambling toward her.

A powerful Bhil perched beside the head of the elephant and slashed once with his scimitar. The blow half-severed the mahout's head from the body. Before he could strike again Khlit had knocked him backward.

Retha sprang forward, and the Cossack caught her with his free arm, drawing back as Kurral leaped, knife in hand. The priest missed the woman. The next instant his body slipped back, a feathered shaft from the bow of Sawal Das projecting from his chest.

"Ho—Kurral—your death is worthy of you," chanted the archer. "Gully jackal, scavenger dog—"

His voice trailed off in a gurgle. And Khlit and the girl were flung back against the howdah. Asim Rumi, maddened by his wounds and no longer hearing the voice of his master, started erect.

He tossed his great head, reddened with blood. His trumpeting changed to a hoarse scream. The knives of his assailants had hurt him sorely.

The sword-blades upon the tusks had been broken off against the car. The leather armor was cut and slashed. Spears, stuck in the flanks of the elephant, acted as irritants. His trunk—a most sensitive member—was injured, and his neck bleeding.

While Khlit and Retha clung beside the body of the mahout Asil Rumi shrilled his anger at the throng of his enemies. He broke crashing from the ruins of the car wherein lay the unattended figure of Jagannath, and plunged into the crowd. Weaving his head—its paint besmirched by blood—Asil Rumi raced forward.

He rushed onward until no more of his tormentors stood in his path. Then the elephant hesitated, and headed toward the trail up the hill which led down to his quarters at Thaneswar.

"Hearken," said a weak voice from the howdah.

Khlit peered up and saw the archer's face strangely pale.

"Asil Rumi will run," said Sawal Das, "until he sees the body of the native fall. Hold the mahout firmly."

A few foot soldiers had run after the elephant in a half-hearted fashion. There were no horsemen in the crowd, and few cared to follow the track of the great beast afoot. Asil Rumi had struck terror into the worshipers.

His appearance and the devastation he had wrought had been that of no ordinary elephant. Among the Hindus lingered the memory of the elder gods of the ruins from which Asil Rumi had so abruptly emerged. And some among them reflected that Vishnu, highest of the gods, bore an elephant head.

So had the deaths inflicted by Asil Rumi stirred their fears.

The sun had set, and the crimson of the western sky was fading to purple. The calm of twilight hung upon the forest through which Asil Rumi paced, following the trail. A flutter of night birds arose at his presence, and a prowling leopard slunk away at the angry mutter of the elephant, knowing that Asil Rumi was enraged and that an angry elephant was monarch of whatsoever path he chose to follow.

Again came the voice of Sawal Das, weaker now. "My heart is warm that the Lotus Face is saved for my lord," it said—neither Khlit nor the girl dared to look up from their precarious perch where the branches of overhanging cypresses swept. "An arrow"—the voice failed—"tell the Rawul how Sawal Das fought—for my spirit goes after the mahout—"

A moment later a branch caught the howdah and swept it to earth. Retha and Khlit clung tighter to the head-straps, pressing their bodies against the broad back of Asil Rumi. Khlit did not release his grasp on the dead native.

The wind of their passage swept past their ears; the labored breath of the old elephant smote their nostrils pungently. Ferns scraped their shoulders. They did not look up.

It was dark by now, and still Asil paced onward.

~

Dawn was breaking and a warm wind had sprung up when Matap Rao and Abdul Dost with the leaders of the Rinthambur clan passed the boundary tower of Thaneswar. A half-thousand armed men followed them, but few were abreast of them, for they had ridden steadily throughout the night, not sparing their horses.

Dawn showed the anxious chieftain the unbroken stretch of the Thaneswar forest through which he had passed on his bridal journey. He did not look at those with him, but pressed onward.

So it happened that Rawul Matap Rao and two of the best mounted of the Rinthambur riders were alone when they emerged into a glade where a path from Thaneswar crossed the main trail. And here they reined in their spent horses with a shout.

In the path lay the body of a native. Over the dead man stood the giant elephant, caked with mud and dried blood, his small eyes closed and his warlike finery stained and torn. And beside the elephant stood Khlit and Retha.

~

What followed was swift in coming to pass. After a brief embrace the Rawul left his bride to be escorted back to Rinthambur by Khlit and Abdul Dost at the head of a detail of horsemen while he and the Rinthambur men wrested Thaneswar from the priests.

It was a different matter this, from the assault upon the palace by Nagir Jan, and the followers of the temple were forced to give way before the onset of trained warriors.

The religious fervor of the Kukushetra men had suffered by the misfortune that befell their god before the ruins, and the fighting was soon at an end.

But it was not until Matap Rao was again in Thaneswar with Retha that Khlit and Abdul Dost turned their horses' heads from the palace. Peace had fallen upon the province again, for Matap Rao had sent a message to the shrine of Puri, and the high priests of Vishnu, among whom the ambitions of Nagir Jan had found no favor, had judged that Nagir Jan had made wrong use of his power and sent another to be head of the Kuku-shetra temple.

"Aye, and men whispered that there was a tale that the mad beast of the ruins was the incarnate spirit of an older god," laughed Abdul Dost, who wore new finery of armor and rode a fine horse—the Rawul had been generous. "Such are the fears of fools and infidels."

Khlit, who rode his old pony, tugged his beard, his eyes grave. "It was not the false gods," he said decidedly, "that saved Matap Rao his wife. It was verily a warrior—an old warrior. But how can the Rawul reward him?"

Abdul Dost glanced at Khlit curiously. "Nay," he smiled, "you are the one. You are a leader of men, even of the Rawul and his kind—as I said to them. Belittle not the gratitude of the chieftain. He would have kept you at his right hand, in honor. But you will not."

"Because I am not the one."

"Sawal Das?"

"Somewhat, perhaps." Khlit's voice roughened and his eyes became moody. "Asil Rumi is the one. Truly never have I seen a fighter such as he. Yet Asil Rumi is old. Soon he will die. Where is his reward?"

Whereupon Khlit shook his broad shoulders, tightened his rein and broke into a gallop. Abdul Dost frowned, pondering. He shook his handsome head. Then his brow cleared and he spurred after his friend.

The Pirate Sea

LILIAN NICHOLSON

I bear ships on my breast.
I turn them upside down—
Sometimes I right them up again
But let their inmates drown.

And then what glee is mine!
I stop their cries and groans,
And when they sleep a dreamless sleep
I strip them to their bones!

They come to me full-clothed,
They leave me bare—undone;
And be they duke or lord or knave
I treat them all as one.

Oh, sing the song of the Pirate Sea,
The rolling, storm-tossed, angry sea,
The staggering, swaggering, Pirate Sea
That strips men to their bones!

From *Argosy All-Story Weekly*, September 30, 1922.

About Rafael Sabatini (2)

We return now to Rafael Sabatini to sample his mature work with a story about his most famous and enduring character, Captain Peter Blood. In the twenty years after the publication of the story that leads off this anthology, Sabatini wrote constantly, honing his style and his storytelling skills, his characters becoming deeper, his settings richer and more evocative. And after the First World War (1914-1918), his novels developed an angry, indignant edge missing from his earlier work, his protagonists often fighting not only for themselves, but against greater injustice.

What happened? Certainly the horrors and atrocities of the Great War were enough to outrage and inspire cynicism in anyone. Sabatini, who had been born in Italy, became a British citizen when threatened with Italian conscription, and served his time in the war working for British Intelligence as a translator. After having worked for himself for two decades, fitting into a military hierarchy couldn't have been easy for the independent-minded Sabatini—and as an Intelligence translator, he would have had a window into the way that terrible war was conducted, in all its brutality and official bungling.

Whatever the reason, when he returned to writing after the war, his first novel was the angry and scathing *Scaramouche*—a worldwide bestseller in 1921. His follow-up was the even greater *Captain Blood: His Odyssey*, first published in the United States as a series of short stories in *Adventure* magazine. The story that follows, from the October 20, 1921 issue, is the climax of the novel.

Captain Blood's Dilemma

RAFAEL SABATINI

CHAPTER I
THE SERVICE OF KING LOUIS

Some three months before Colonel Bishop set out to reduce Tortuga, Captain Blood, bearing hell in his soul, had blown into its rockbound harbor ahead of the winter gales, and two days ahead of the frigate in which his pirate ally Wolverstone had sailed from Port Royal a day before him.

In that snug anchorage he found his fleet awaiting him—the four ships which had been separated in a gale off the Lesser Antilles, and some seven hundred men composing their crews. Because they had been beginning to grow anxious on his behalf, they gave him the greater welcome. Guns were fired in his honor and the ships made themselves gay with bunting. The town, aroused by all this noise in the harbor, emptied itself upon the jetty, and a vast crowd of men and women of all creeds and nationalities collected there to be present at the coming ashore of the great buccaneer.

Ashore he went, probably for no other reason than to obey the general expectation. His mood was taciturn; his face grim and sneering. Let Wolverstone arrive, as presently he would, and all this hero-worship would turn to execration.

His captains, Hagthorpe, Christian, and Yberville, were on the jetty to receive him, and with them were some hundreds of his buccaneers. He cut short their greetings, and when they plagued him with questions of where he had tarried, he bade them await the coming of Wolverstone, who would satisfy their curiosity to a surfeit. On that he shook them off, and shouldered his way through that heterogeneous throng that was composed of bustling traders of several nations—English, French, and Dutch—of planters and of seamen of various degrees, of buccaneers who were fruit-selling half-castes, negro slaves, some doll-tearsheets and dunghill-queans from the Old World, and all the other types of the human family that converted the quays of Cayona into a disreputable image of Babel.

Winning clear at last, and after difficulties, Captain Blood took his way alone to the fine house of M. d'Ogeron, there to pay his respects to his friends, the Governor and the Governor's family.

At first the buccaneers jumped to the conclusion that Wolverstone was following with some rare prize of war, but gradually from the reduced crew of the *Arabella* a very different tale leaked out to stem their satisfaction and convert it into perplexity. Partly out of loyalty to their captain, partly because they perceived that if he was guilty of defection they were guilty with him, and partly because being simple, sturdy men of their hands, they were themselves in the main a little confused as to what really had happened, the crew of the *Arabella* practiced reticence with their brethren in Tortuga during those two days before Wolverstone's arrival. But they were not reticent enough to prevent the circulation of certain uneasy rumors and extravagant stories of discreditable adventures—discreditable, that is, from the buccaneering point of view—of which Captain Blood had been guilty.

But that Wolverstone came when he did, it is possible that there would have been an explosion. When, however, the Old Wolf cast anchor in the bay two days later, it was to him all turned for the explanation they were about to demand of Blood.

Now Wolverstone had only one eye; but he saw a deal more with that one eye than do most men with two; and despite his grizzled head—so picturesquely swathed in a green and scarlet turban—he had the sound heart of a boy, and in that heart much love for Peter Blood.

The sight of the *Arabella* at anchor in the bay had at first amazed him as he sailed round the rocky headland that bore the fort. He rubbed his single eye clear of any deceiving film and looked again. Still he could not believe what it saw. And then a voice at his elbow—the voice of Dyke, who had elected to sail with him—assured him that he was not singular in his bewilderment.

"In the name of Heaven, is that the *Arabella* or is it the ghost of her?"

The Old Wolf rolled his single eye over Dyke, and opened his mouth to speak. Then he closed it again without having spoken; closed it tightly. He had a great gift of caution, especially in matters that he did not understand. That this was the *Arabella* he could no longer doubt. That being so, he must think before he spoke. What the devil should the *Arabella* be doing here, when he had left her in Jamaica? And was Captain Blood aboard and in command, or had the remainder of her hands made off with her, leaving the Captain in Port Royal?

Dyke repeated his question. This time Wolverstone answered him.

"Ye've two eyes to see with, and ye ask me, who's only got one, what it is ye see!"

"But I see the *Arabella*."

"Of course, since there she rides. What else was you expecting?"

"Expecting?" Dyke stared at him, open-mouthed. "Was you expecting to find the *Arabella* here?"

Wolverstone looked him over in contempt, then laughed and spoke loud enough to be heard by all around him. "Of course. What else?" And he laughed again, a laugh that seemed to Dyke to be calling him a fool. On that Wolverstone turned to give his attention to the operation of anchoring.

Anon when ashore he was beset by questioning buccaneers, it was from their very questions that he gathered exactly how matters stood, and perceived that either from lack of courage or other motive Blood, himself, had refused to render any account of his doings since the *Arabella* had separated from her sister ships. Wolverstone congratulated himself upon the discretion he had used with Dyke.

"The Captain was ever a modest man," he explained to Hagthorpe and those others who came crowding round him. "It's not his way to be sounding his own praises. Why, it was like this. We fell in with old Don Miguel, and when we'd scuttled him we took aboard a London pimp sent out by the Secretary of State to offer the Captain the King's commission if so be him'd quit piracy and be o' good behavior. The Captain damned his soul to hell for answer. And then we fell in wi' the Jamaica fleet and that grey old devil Bishop in command, and there was a sure end to Captain Blood and to every mother's son of us all. So I goes to him, and 'accept this poxy commission,' says I; 'turn King's man and save your neck and ours.' He took me at my word, and the London pimp gave him the King's commission on the spot, and Bishop all but choked hisself with rage when he was told of it. But happened it had, and he was forced to swallow it. We were King's men all, and so into Port Royal we sailed along o' Bishop. But Bishop didn't trust us. He knew too much. But for his lordship, the fellow from London, he'd ha' hanged the Captain, King's commission and all. Blood would ha' slipped out o' Port Royal again that same night. But that hound Bishop had passed the word, and the fort kept a sharp lookout. In the end, though it took a fortnight, Blood bubbled him. He sent me and most o' the men off in a frigate that I bought for the voyage. His game—as he'd secretly told me—was to follow and give chase. Whether that's the game he played or not I can't tell ye; but here he is afore me as I'd expected he would be."

There was a great historian lost in Wolverstone. He had the right imagination that knows just how far it is safe to stray from the truth and just how far to color it so as to change its shape for his own purposes.

Having delivered himself of his decoction of fact and falsehood, and thereby added one more to the exploits of Peter Blood, he enquired where the Captain might be found. Being informed that he kept his ship, Wolverstone stepped into a boat and went aboard, to report himself, as he put it.

In the great cabin of the *Arabella* he found Peter Blood alone and very far gone in drink—a condition in which no man ever before remembered to have seen him. As Wolverstone came in, the Captain raised bloodshot eyes to consider him. A moment they sharpened in their gaze as he brought his visitor into focus. Then he laughed, a loose, idiot laugh, that yet somehow was half a sneer.

"Ah! The Old Wolf!" said he. "Got here at last, eh? And whatcher gonnerdo wi' me, eh?" He hiccoughed resoundingly, and sagged back loosely in his chair.

Old Wolverstone stared at him in somber silence. He had looked with untroubled eye upon many a hell of devilment in his time, but the sight of Captain Blood in this condition filled him with sudden grief. To express it he loosed an oath. It was his only expression for emotion of all kinds. Then he rolled forward and dropped into a chair at the table, facing the Captain.

"My God, Peter, what's this?"

"Rum," said Peter. "Rum, from Jamaica." He pushed bottle and glass towards Wolverstone.

Wolverstone disregarded them.

"I'm asking you what ails you?" he bawled.

"Rum," said Captain Blood again, and smiled. "Jus' rum. I answer all your queshons. Why donjerr answer mine? Whatcher gonerdo wi' me?"

"I've done it," said Wolverstone. "Thank God, ye had the sense to hold your tongue till I came. Are ye sober enough to understand me?"

"Drunk or sober, allus 'derstand you."

"Then listen." And out came the tale that Wolverstone had told. The Captain steadied himself to grasp it.

"It'll do as well asertruth," said he when Wolverstone had finished. "And . . . oh, no marrer! Much obliged to ye, Old Wolf—faithful Old Wolf! But was it worthertrouble? I'm norrer pirate now; never a pirate again. 'S finished." He banged the table, his eyes suddenly fierce.

"I'll come and talk to you again when there's less rum in your wits," said Wolverstone, rising. "Meanwhile ye'll please to remember the tale I've told, and say nothing that'll make me out a liar. They all believes me, even the men as sailed wi' me from Port Royal. I've made 'em. If they thought as how you'd taken the King's commission in earnest, and for the purpose o' doing as Morgan did, ye guess what would follow."

"Hell would follow," said the Captain. "An' tha's all I'm fit for."

"Ye're maudlin," Wolverstone growled. "We'll talk again tomorrow."

They did; but to little purpose, either that day or on any day thereafter while the rains—which set in that night—endured. Soon the shrewd Wolverstone discovered that rum was not what ailed Blood. Rum was in itself an effect, and not by any means the cause of the Captain's listless apathy. There was a canker eating at his heart, and the Old Wolf knew enough to make a shrewd guess of its nature. He cursed all things that daggled petticoats, and, knowing his world, waited for the sickness to pass.

But it did not pass. When Blood was not dicing or drinking in the taverns of Tortuga, keeping company that in his saner days he had loathed, he was shut up in his cabin aboard the *Arabella*, alone and uncommunicative. His friends at Government House, bewildered at this change in him, sought to reclaim him. Mademoiselle d'Ogeron, particularly distressed, sent him almost daily invitations, to few of which he responded.

Later, as the rainy season approached its end, he was sought by his captains with proposals of remunerative raids on Spanish settlements. But to all he manifested an indifference which, as the weeks passed and the weather became settled, begot first impatience and then exasperation.

Christian, who commanded the *Clotho*, came storming to him one day, upbraiding him for his inaction, and demanding that he should take order about what was to do.

"Go to the devil!" Blood said, when he had heard him out. Christian departed fuming, and on the morrow the *Clotho* weighed anchor and sailed away, setting an example of desertion from which the loyalty of Blood's other captains would soon be unable to restrain their men.

Sometimes Blood asked himself why he had come back to Tortuga at all. Held fast in bondage by the thought of *Arabella* and her scorn of him for a thief and a pirate, he had sworn that he had done with buccaneering. Why, then, was he here? That question he would answer with another: Where else was he to go? Neither backward nor forward could he move, it seemed.

He was degenerating visibly, under the eyes of all. He had entirely lost the almost foppish concern for his appearance, and was grown careless and slovenly in his dress. He allowed a black beard to grow on cheeks that had ever been so carefully shaven; and the long, thick black hair, once so sedulously curled, hung now in a lank, untidy mane about a face that was changing from its vigorous swarthiness to an unhealthy sallow, whilst the blue eyes, that had been so vivid and compelling, were now dull and lackluster.

Wolverstone, the only one who held the clue to this degeneration, ventured once—and once only—to beard him frankly about it.

"Lord, Peter! Is there never to be no end to this?" the giant had growled. "Will you spend your days moping and swilling 'cause a white-faced ninny in Port Royal'll have none o' ye? 'Sblood and 'ounds! If ye wants the wench, why the plague doesn't ye go and fetch her?"

The blue eyes glared at him from under the jet-black eyebrows, and something of their old fire began to kindle in them. But Wolverstone went on heedlessly.

"I'll be nice wi' a wench as long as niceness be the key to her favor. But sink me now if I'd rot myself in rum on account of anything that wears a petticoat. That's not the Old Wolf's way. If there's no other expedition'll tempt you, why not Port Royal? What a plague do it matter if it is an English settlement? It's commanded by Colonel Bishop, and there's no lack of rascals in your company'd follow you to hell if it meant getting Colonel Bishop by the throat. It could be done, I tell you. We've but to spy the chance when the Jamaica fleet is away. There's enough plunder in the town to tempt the lads, and there's the wench for you. Shall I sound them on 't?"

Blood was on his feet, his eyes blazing, his livid face distorted. "Ye'll leave my cabin this minute, so ye will, or, by Heaven, it's your corpse'll be carried out of it. Ye mangy hound, d'ye dare come to me with such proposals?"

He fell to cursing his faithful officer with a virulence the like of which he had never yet been known to use. And Wolverstone, in terror before that fury, went out without another word. The subject was not raised again, and Captain Blood was left to his idle abstraction.

But at last, as his buccaneers were growing desperate, something happened, brought about by the Captain's friend M. d'Ogeron. One sunny morning the Governor of Tortuga came aboard the *Arabella*, accompanied by a chubby little gentleman, amiable of countenance, amiable and self-sufficient of manner.

"My Captain," M. d'Ogeron delivered himself, "I bring you M. de Cussy, the Governor of French Hispaniola, who desires a word with you."

Out of consideration for his friend, Captain Blood pulled the pipe from his mouth, shook some of the rum out of his wits, and rose and made a leg to M. de Cussy.

"*Serviteur!*" said he.

M. de Cussy returned the bow and accepted a seat on the locker under the stern windows.

"You have a good force here under your command, my Captain," said he.

"Some eight hundred men."

"And I understand they grow restive in idleness."

"They may go to the devil when they please."

M. de Cussy took snuff delicately. "I have something better than that to propose," said he.

"Propose it, then," said Blood, without interest.

M. de Cussy looked at M. d'Ogeron and raised his eyebrows a little. He did not find Captain Blood encouraging. But M. d'Ogeron nodded vigorously with pursed lips, and the Governor of Hispaniola propounded his business.

"News has reached us from France that there is war with Spain."

"That is news, is it?" growled Blood.

"I am speaking officially, my Captain. I am not alluding to unofficial skirmishes, and unofficial predatory measures which we have condoned out here. There is war—formally war—between France and Spain in Europe. It is the intention of France that this war shall be carried into the New World. A fleet is coming out from Brest under the command of M. le Baron de Rivarol for that purpose. I have letters from him desiring me to equip a supplementary squadron and raise a body of not less than a thousand men to reinforce him on his arrival. What I have come to propose to you, my Captain, at the suggestion of our good friend M. d'Ogeron,

is, in brief, that you enroll your ships and your force under M. de Rivarol's flag."

Blood looked at him with a faint kindling of interest. "You are offering to take us into the French service?" he asked. "On what terms, monsieur?"

"With the rank of *Capitaine de Vaisseau* for yourself, and suitable ranks for the officers serving under you. You will enjoy the pay of that rank, and you will be entitled, together with your men, to one-tenth share in all prizes taken."

"My men will hardly account it generous. They will tell you that they can sail out of here tomorrow, disembowel a Spanish settlement, and keep the whole of the plunder."

"Ah, yes, but with the risks attaching to acts of piracy. With us your position will be regular and official, and considering the powerful fleet by which M. de Rivarol is backed, the enterprises to be undertaken will be on a much vaster scale than anything you could attempt on your own account. So that the one-tenth in this case may be equal to more than the whole in the other."

Captain Blood considered. This, after all, was not piracy that was being proposed. It was honorable employment in the service of the King of France.

"I will consult my officers," he said; and he sent for them.

They came and the matter was laid before them by M. de Cussy himself.

Hagthorpe announced at once that the proposal was opportune. The men were grumbling at their protracted inaction, and would no doubt be ready to accept the service which M. de Cussy offered on behalf of France. Hagthorpe looked at Blood as he spoke. Blood nodded gloomy agreement. Emboldened by this, they went on to discuss the terms. Yberville, the young French filibuster, had the honor to point out to M. de Cussy that the share offered was too small. For one-fifth of the prizes, the officers would answer for their men; not for less.

M. de Cussy was distressed. He had his instructions. It was taking a deal upon himself to exceed them. The buccaneers were firm. Unless M. de Cussy could make it one-fifth there was no more to be said. M. de Cussy finally consenting to exceed his instructions, the articles were drawn up and signed that very day. The buccaneers were to be at Petit Goave by the end of January, when M. de Rivarol had announced that he might be expected.

After that followed days of activity in Tortuga, refitting the ships, boucanning meat, laying in stores. In these matters which once would have engaged all Captain Blood's attention, he now took no part. He continued listless and aloof. If he had given his consent to the undertaking, or, rather, allowed himself to be swept into it by the wishes of his officers—it was only because the service offered was

of a regular and honorable kind, nowise connected with piracy, with which he swore in his heart that he had done forever. But his consent remained passive. The service entered awoke no zeal in him. He was perfectly indifferent—as he told Hagthorpe, who ventured once to offer a remonstrance—whether they went to Petit Goave or to Hades, and whether they entered the service of Louis XIV or of Satan.

CHAPTER II
MONSIEUR DE RIVAROL

Captain Blood was still in that disgruntled mood when he sailed from Tortuga, and still in that mood when he came to his moorings in the bay of Petit Goave. In that same mood he greeted M. le Baron de Rivarol when this nobleman with his fleet of five men-of-war at last dropped anchor alongside the buccaneer ships, in the middle of February. The Frenchman had been six weeks on the voyage, he announced, delayed by unfavorable weather.

Summoned to wait on him, Captain Blood repaired to the Castle of Petit Goave, where the interview was to take place. The Baron, a tall, hawk-faced man of forty, very cold and distant of manner, measured Captain Blood with an eye of obvious disapproval. Of Hagthorpe, Yberville, and Wolverstone, who stood ranged behind their captain, he took no heed whatever. M. de Cussy offered Captain Blood a chair.

"A moment, M. de Cussy. I do not think M. le Baron has observed that I am not alone. Let me present to you, sir, my companions: Captain Hagthorpe of the *Elizabeth*, Captain Wolverstone of the *Atropos*, and Captain Yberville of the *Lachesis*."

The Baron stared hard and haughtily at Captain Blood, then very distantly and barely perceptibly inclined his head to each of the other three. His manner implied plainly that he despised them and that he desired them at once to understand it. It had a curious effect upon Captain Blood. It awoke the devil in him, and it awoke at the same time his self-respect which of late had been slumbering. A sudden shame of his disordered, ill-kempt appearance made him perhaps the more defiant. There was almost a significance in the way he hitched his sword-belt round, so that the wrought hilt of his very serviceable rapier was brought into fuller view.

He waved his captains to the chairs that stood about. "Draw up to the table, lads. We are keeping the Baron waiting."

They obeyed him, Wolverstone with a grin that was full of understanding. Haughtier grew the stare of M. de Rivarol. To sit at table with these bandits placed him upon what he accounted a dishonoring equality. It had been his notion that—with the possible exception of Captain Blood—they should take his instructions standing, as became men of their quality in the presence of a man of his. He did the only thing remaining to mark a distinction between himself and them. He put on his hat.

"Ye're very wise now," said Blood amiably. "I feel the draught myself." And he covered himself with his plumed castor.

M. de Rivarol changed color. He quivered visibly with anger, and was a moment controlling himself before venturing to speak. M. de Cussy was obviously very ill at ease.

"Sir," said the Baron frostily, "you compel me to remind you that the rank you hold is that of *Capitaine de Vaisseau*, and that you are in the presence of the General of the Armies of France by Sea and Land in America. You compel me to remind you further that there is a deference due from your rank to mine."

"I am happy to assure you," said Captain Blood, "that the reminder is unnecessary. I am by way of accounting myself a gentleman, little though I may look like one at present; and I should not account myself that were I capable of anything but deference to those whom nature or fortune may have placed above me, or to those who being placed beneath me in rank may labor under a disability to resent my lack of it." It was a neatly intangible rebuke. M. de Rivarol bit his lip.

Captain Blood swept on without giving him time to reply: "Thus much being clear, shall we come to business?"

M. de Rivarol's hard eyes considered him a moment. "Perhaps it will be best," said he. He took up a paper. "I have here a copy of the articles into which you entered with M. de Cussy. Before going further, I have to observe that M. de Cussy has exceeded his instructions in admitting you to one-fifth of the prizes taken. His authority did not warrant his going beyond one-tenth."

"That is a matter between yourself and M. de Cussy, my General."

"Oh, no. It is a matter between myself and you."

"Your pardon, my General. The articles are signed. So far as we are concerned, the matter is closed. Also out of regard for M. de Cussy, we should not desire to be witnesses of the rebukes you may consider that he deserves."

"What I may have to say to M. de Cussy is no concern of yours."

"That is what I am telling you, my General."

"But—*nom de Dieu!*—it is your concern, I suppose, that we cannot award you more than one-tenth share." M. de Rivarol smote the table in exasperation. This pirate was too infernally skillful a fencer.

"You are quite certain of that, M. le Baron—that you cannot?"

"I am quite certain that I will not."

Captain Blood shrugged, and looked down his nose. "In that case," said he, "it but remains for me to present my little account for our disbursement, and to fix the sum at which we should be compensated for our loss of time and derangement in coming hither. That settled, we can part friends, M. le Baron. No harm has been done."

"What the devil do you mean?" The Baron was on his feet, leaning forward across the table.

"Is it possible that I am obscure? My French, perhaps, is not of the purest, but. . . ."

"Oh, your French is fluent enough; too fluent at moments, if I may permit myself the observation. Now, look you here, M. *le Filibustier*, I am not a man with whom it is safe to play the fool, as you may very soon discover. You have accepted service of the King of France—you and your men; you hold the rank and draw the pay of a *Capitaine de Vaisseau*, and these your officers hold the rank of lieutenants. These ranks carry obligations which you would do well to study, and penalties for failing to discharge them which you might study at the same time. They are something severe. The first obligation of an officer is obedience. I commend it to your attention. You are not to conceive yourselves, as you appear to be doing, my allies in the enterprises I have in view, but my subordinates. In me you behold a commander to lead you, not a companion or an equal. You understand me, I hope."

"Oh, be sure that I understand," Captain Blood laughed. He was recovering his normal self amazingly under the inspiring stimulus of conflict. The only thing that marred his enjoyment was the reflection that he had not shaved. "I forget nothing, I assure you, my General. I do not forget, for instance, as you appear to be doing, that the articles we signed are the condition of our service; and the articles provide that we receive one-fifth share. Refuse us that, and you cancel the articles; cancel the articles, and you cancel our services with them. From that moment we cease to have the honor to hold rank in the navies of the King of France."

There was more than a murmur of approval from his three captains.

Rivarol glared at them, checkmated.

"In effect . . ." M. de Cussy was beginning timidly.

"In effect, monsieur, this is your doing," the Baron flashed on him, glad to have someone upon whom he could fasten the sharp fangs of his irritation. "You should be broken for it. You bring the King's service into disrepute; you force me, His Majesty's representative, into an impossible position."

"Is it impossible to award us the one-fifth share?" quoth Captain Blood silkily.

"In that case, there is no need for heat or for injuries to M. de Cussy. M. de Cussy knows that we would not have come for less. We depart again upon your assurance that you cannot award us more. And things are as they would have been if M. de Cussy had adhered rigidly to his instructions. I have proved, I hope, to your satisfaction, M. le Baron, that if you repudiate the articles you can neither claim our services nor hinder our departure—not in honor."

"Not in honor, sir? To the devil with your insolence! Do you imply that any course that were not in honor would be possible to me?"

"I do not imply it, because it would not be possible," said Captain Blood. "We should see to that. It is, my General, for you to say whether the articles are repudiated."

The Baron sat down. "I will consider the matter," he said sullenly. "You shall be advised of my resolve."

Captain Blood rose, and his officers rose with him. Captain Blood bowed. "M. le Baron!" said he. Then he and his buccaneers removed themselves from the august and irate presence of the General of the King's Armies by Land and Sea in America.

You conceive that there followed for M. de Cussy an extremely bad quarter of an hour. M. de Cussy, in fact, deserves your sympathy. His self-sufficiency was blown from him by the haughty M. de Rivarol, as down from a thistle by the winds of autumn. The General of the King's Armies abused him—this man who was Governor of Hispaniola—as if he were a lackey. M. de Cussy defended himself by urging the thing that Captain Blood had so admirably urged already on his behalf—that if the terms he had made with the buccaneers were not confirmed there was no harm done. M. de Rivarol bullied and browbeat him into silence.

Having exhausted abuse, the Baron proceeded to indignities. Since he accounted that M. de Cussy had proved himself unworthy of the post he held, M. de Rivarol took over the responsibilities of that post for as long as he might remain in Hispaniola, and to give effect to this he began by bringing soldiers from his ships, and setting his own guard in M. de Cussy's castle.

Out of this, trouble followed quickly. Wolverstone coming ashore next morning in the picturesque garb that he affected, his head swathed in a colored handkerchief, was jeered at by an officer of the newly landed French troops. Not accustomed to derision, Wolverstone replied in kind and with interest. The officer passed to insult, and Wolverstone struck him a blow that felled him, and left him only the half of his poor senses. Within the hour the matter was reported to M. de Rivarol, and before noon, by M. de Rivarol's orders, Wolverstone was under arrest in the castle.

The Baron had just sat down to dinner with M. de Cussy when the negro who waited on them announced Captain Blood. Peevishly M. de Rivarol bade him be admitted, and there entered now into his presence a spruce and modish gentleman, dressed with care and somber richness in black and silver, his swarthy, clear-cut face scrupulously shaven, his long black hair in ringlets that fell to a collar of fine point. In his right hand the gentleman carried a broad black hat with a scarlet ostrich-plume, in his left hand an ebony cane. His stockings were of silk, a bunch of ribbons masked his garters, and the black rosettes on his shoes were finely edged with gold.

For a moment M. de Rivarol did not recognize him. For Blood looked younger by ten years than yesterday. But the vivid blue eyes under their level black brows were not to be forgotten, and they proclaimed him for the man announced even before he had spoken. His resurrected pride had demanded that he should put himself on an equality with the baron and advertise that equality by his exterior.

"I come inopportunely," he courteously excused himself. "My apologies. My business could not wait. It concerns, M. de Cussy, Captain Wolverstone of the *Lachesis*, whom you have placed under arrest."

"It was I who placed him under arrest," said M. de Rivarol.

"Indeed! But I thought that M. de Cussy was Governor of Hispaniola."

"Whilst I am here, monsieur, I am the supreme authority. It is as well that you should understand it."

"Perfectly. But it is not possible that you are aware of the mistake that has been made."

"Mistake, do you say?"

"I say mistake. On the whole, it is polite of me to use that word. Also it is expedient. It will save discussions. Your people have arrested the wrong man, M. de Rivarol. Instead of the French officer, who used the grossest provocation, they have arrested Captain Wolverstone. It is a matter which I beg you to reverse without delay."

M. de Rivarol's hawk-face flamed scarlet. His dark eyes bulged. "Sir, you . . . you are insolent! But of an insolence that is intolerable!" Normally a man of the utmost self-possession, he was so rudely shaken now that he actually stammered.

"M. le Baron, you waste words. This is the New World. It is not merely new; it is novel to one reared amid the superstitions of the Old. That novelty you have not yet had time, perhaps, to realize; therefore I overlook the offensive epithet you have used. But justice is justice in the New World as in the Old, and injustice as intolerable here as there. Now justice demands the enlargement of my officer and the arrest and punishment of yours. That justice I invite you, with submission, to administer."

"With submission?" snorted the Baron in furious scorn.

"With the utmost submission, monsieur. But at the same time I will remind M. le Baron that my buccaneers number eight hundred; your troops five hundred; and M. de Cussy will inform you of the interesting fact that any one buccaneer is equal in action to at least three soldiers of the line. I am perfectly frank with you, monsieur, to save time and hard words. Either Captain Wolverstone is instantly set at liberty, or we must take measures to set him at liberty ourselves. The consequences may be appalling. But it is as you please, M. le Baron. You are the supreme authority. It is for you to say."

M. de Rivarol was white to the lips. In all his life he had never been so bearded and defied. But he controlled himself. "You will do me the favor to wait in the anteroom, *M. le Capitaine.* I desire a word with M. de Cussy. You shall presently be informed of my decision."

When the door had closed, the baron loosed his fury upon the head of M. de Cussy. "So, these are the men you have enlisted in the King's service, the men who are to serve under me—men who do not serve, but dictate, and this before the enterprise that has brought me from France is even under way! What explanations do you offer me, M. de Cussy? I warn you that I am not pleased with you. I am, in fact, as you may perceive, exceedingly angry."

The Governor seemed to shed his chubbiness. He drew himself stiffly erect. "Your rank, monsieur, does not give you the right to rebuke me; nor do the facts. I have enlisted for you the men that you desired me to enlist. It is not my fault if you do not know how to handle them better. As Captain Blood has told you, this is the New World."

"So, so!" M. de Rivarol smiled malignantly. "Not only do you offer no explanation, but you venture to put me in the wrong. Almost I admire your temerity. But there!" he waved the matter aside. He was supremely sardonic. "It is, you tell me, the New World, and—new worlds, new manners, I suppose. In time I may conform my ideas to this new world, or I may conform this new world to my ideas." He was menacing on that. "For the moment I must accept what I find. It remains for you, monsieur, who have experience of these savage byways, to advise me out of that experience how to act."

"M. le Baron, it was a folly to have arrested the buccaneer captain. It would be madness to persist. We have not the forces to meet force."

"In that case, monsieur, perhaps you will tell me what we are to do with regard to the future. Am I to submit at every turn to the dictates of this man Blood? Is the enterprise upon which we are embarked to be conducted as he decrees? Am I, in short, the King's representative in America, to be at the mercy of these rascals?"

"Oh, by no means. I am enrolling volunteers here in Hispaniola, and I am raising a corps of negroes. I compute that when this is done we shall have a force of a thousand men, the buccaneers apart."

"But in that case why not dispense with them?"

"Because they will always remain the sharp edge of any weapon that we forge. In the class of warfare that lies before us they are so skilled that what Captain Blood has just said is not an overstatement. A buccaneer is equal to three soldiers of the line. At the same time we shall have a sufficient force to keep them in control. For the rest, monsieur, they have certain notions of honor. They will stand by their articles, and so that we deal justly with them, they will deal justly with us, and give no trouble. I have experience of them, and I pledge you my word for that."

M. de Rivarol condescended to be mollified. It was necessary that he should save his face, and in a degree the Governor afforded him the means to do so, as well as a certain guarantee for the future in the further force he was raising. "Very well," he said. "Be so good as to recall this Captain Blood."

The Captain came in, assured and very dignified. M. de Rivarol found him detestable; but dissembled it. "*M. le Capitaine*, I have taken counsel with *M. le Gouverneur*. From what he tells me, it is possible that a mistake has been committed. Justice, you may be sure, shall be done. To ensure it, I shall myself preside over a council to be composed of two of my senior officers, yourself and an officer of yours. This council shall hold at once an impartial investigation into the affair, and the offender, the man guilty of having given provocation, shall be punished."

Captain Blood bowed. It was not his wish to be extreme. "Perfectly, M. le Baron. And now, sir, you have had the night for reflection in this matter of the articles. Am I to understand that you confirm or that you repudiate them?"

M. de Rivarol's eyes narrowed. His mind was full of what M. de Cussy had said—that these buccaneers must prove the sharp edge of any weapon he might forge. He could not dispense with them. He perceived that he had blundered tactically in attempting to reduce the agreed share. Withdrawal from a position of that kind is ever fraught with loss of dignity. But there were those volunteers that M. de Cussy was enrolling to strengthen the hand of the King's General. Their presence might admit anon of the reopening of this question. Meanwhile he must retire in the best order possible.

"I have considered that, too," he announced. "And whilst my opinion remains unaltered, I must confess that since M. de Cussy has pledged us, it is for us to fulfill the pledges. The articles are confirmed, sir."

Captain Blood bowed again. In vain M. de Rivarol looked searchingly for the least trace of a smile of triumph on those firm lips. The buccaneer's face remained of the utmost gravity.

Wolverstone was set at liberty that afternoon, and his assailant sentenced to two months' detention. Thus harmony was restored. But it had been an unpromising beginning, and there was more to follow shortly of a similar discordant kind.

Blood and his officers were summoned a week later to a council which sat to determine their operations against Spain. M. de Rivarol laid before them a project for a raid upon the wealthy Spanish town of Cartagena. Captain Blood professed astonishment. Sourly invited by M. de Rivarol to state his grounds for it, he did so with the utmost frankness.

"Were I General of the King's Armies in America," said he, "I should have no doubt or hesitation as to the best way in which to serve my Royal master and the French nation. That which I think will be obvious to M. de Cussy, as it is to me, is that we should at once invade Spanish Hispaniola and reduce the whole of this fruitful and splendid island into the possession of the King of France."

"That may follow," said M. de Rivarol. "It is my wish that we begin with Cartagena."

"You mean, sir, that we are to sail across the Caribbean on an adventurous expedition, neglecting that which lies here at our very door. In our absence, a Spanish invasion of French Hispaniola is possible. If we begin by reducing the Spaniards here, that possibility will be removed. We shall have added to the Crown of France the most coveted possession in the West Indies. The enterprise offers no particular difficulty; it may be speedily accomplished, and once accomplished, it would be time to look farther afield. That would seem the logical order in which this campaign should proceed."

He ceased, and there was silence. M. de Rivarol sat back in his chair, the feathered end of a quill between his teeth. Presently he cleared his throat and asked a question. "Is there anybody else who shares Captain Blood's opinion?"

None answered him. His own officers were overawed by him; Blood's followers naturally preferred Cartagena, because offering the greater chance of loot. Loyalty to their leader kept them silent.

"You seem to be alone in your opinion," said the Baron with his vinegary smile.

Captain Blood laughed outright. He had suddenly read the Baron's mind. His airs and graces and haughtiness had so imposed upon Blood that it was only now that at last he saw through them, into the fellow's peddling spirit. Therefore he laughed; there was really nothing else to do. But his laughter was charged with more anger even than contempt. He had been deluding himself that he had done with piracy. The conviction that this French service was free of any taint of that was the only consideration that had induced him to accept it. Yet here was this haughty, supercilious gentleman, who dubbed himself General of the Armies of France, proposing a plundering, thieving raid which, when stripped of its mean, transparent mask of legitimate warfare, was revealed as piracy of the most flagrant.

M. de Rivarol, intrigued by his mirth, scowled upon him disapprovingly. "Why do you laugh, monsieur?"

"Because I discover here an irony that is supremely droll. You, M. le Baron, General of the King's Armies by Land and Sea in America, propose an enterprise of a purely buccaneering character; whilst I, the buccaneer, am urging one that is more concerned with upholding the honor of France. You perceive how droll it is."

M. de Rivarol perceived nothing of the kind. M. de Rivarol in fact was extremely angry. He bounded to his feet, and every man in the room rose with him—save only M. de Cussy, who sat on with a grim smile on his lips. He, too, now read the

Baron like an open book, and reading him despised him.

"*M. le filibustier,*" cried Rivarol in a thick voice, "it seems that I must again remind you that I am your superior officer."

"My superior officer! You! Lord of the World! Why, you are just a common pirate! But you shall hear the truth for once, and that before all these gentlemen who have the honor to serve the King of France. It is for me, a buccaneer, a sea-robber, to stand here and tell you what is in the interest of French honor and the French Crown. Whilst you, the French King's appointed General, neglecting this, are for spending the King's resources against an outlying settlement of no account, shedding French blood in seizing a place that cannot be held, only because it has been reported to you that there is much gold in Cartagena, and that the plunder of it will enrich you. It is worthy of the huckster who sought to haggle with us about our share, and to beat us down after the articles pledging you were already signed. If I am wrong—let M. de Cussy say so. If I am wrong, let me be proven wrong, and I will beg your pardon. Meanwhile, monsieur, I withdraw from this council. I will have no further part in your deliberations. I accepted the service of the King of France with intent to honor that service. I cannot honor that service by lending countenance to a waste of life and resources in raids upon unimportant settlements, with plunder for their only object. The responsibility for such decisions must rest with you, and with you alone. I desire M. de Cussy to report me to the Ministers of France. For the rest, monsieur, it merely remains for you to give me your orders. I await them aboard my ship—and anything else, of a personal nature, that you may feel I have provoked by the terms I have felt compelled to use in this council. M. le Baron, I have the honor to wish you good-day."

He stalked out, and his three captains—although they thought him mad—rolled after him in loyal silence.

M. de Rivarol was gasping like a landed fish. The stark truth had robbed him of speech. When he recovered, it was to thank Heaven vigorously that the council was relieved by Captain Blood's own act of that gentleman's further participation in its deliberations. Inwardly M. de Rivarol burned with shame and rage. The mask had been plucked from him, and he had been held up to scorn—he, the General of the King's Armies by Sea and Land in America.

Nevertheless, it was to Cartagena that they sailed in the middle of March. Volunteers and negroes had brought up the forces directly under M. de Rivarol to twelve hundred men. With these he thought he could keep the buccaneer contingent in order and submissive.

They made up an imposing fleet, led by M. de Rivarol's flagship, the *Victorieuse,* a mighty vessel of eighty guns. Each of the four other French ships was at least as powerful as Blood's *Arabella*, which was of forty guns. Followed the lesser buccaneer vessels, the *Elizabeth*, *Lachesis*, and *Atropos*, and a dozen frigates laden with stores, besides canoes and small craft in tow.

Narrowly they missed the Jamaica fleet with Colonel Bishop, which sailed north for Tortuga two days after the Baron de Rivarol's southward passage.

CHAPTER III
CARTAGENA

Having crossed the Caribbean in the teeth of contrary winds, it was not until the early days of April that the French fleet hove in sight of Cartagena, and M. de Rivarol summoned a council aboard his flagship to determine the method of assault.

"It is of importance, messieurs," he told them, "that we take the city by surprise, not only before it can put itself into a state of defense; but before it can remove its treasures inland. I propose to land a force sufficient to achieve this to the north of the city tonight after dark." And he explained in detail the scheme upon which his wits had labored.

He was heard respectfully and approvingly by his officers, scornfully by Captain Blood, and indifferently by the other buccaneer captains present. For it must be understood that Blood's refusal to attend councils had related only to those concerned with determining the nature of the enterprise to be undertaken.

Captain Blood was the only one amongst them who knew exactly what lay ahead. Two years ago he had himself considered a raid upon the place, and he had actually made a survey of it in circumstances which he was presently to disclose.

The Baron's proposal was one to be expected from a commander whose knowledge of Cartagena was only such as might be derived from maps.

Geographically and strategically considered, it is a curious place. It stands almost four-square, screened east and north by hills, and it may be said to face south upon the inner of two harbors by which it is normally approached. The entrance to the outer harbor, which is in reality a lagoon some three miles across, lies through a neck known as the Boca Chica—or Little Mouth—and defended by a fort. A long strip of densely wooded land to westward acts here as a natural breakwater, and as the inner harbor is approached, another strip of land thrusts across at right angles from the first, towards the mainland on the east. Just short of this it ceases, leaving a deep but very narrow channel, a veritable gateway, into the secure and sheltered inner harbor.

Another fort defends this second passage. East and north of Cartagena lies the mainland, which may be left out of account. But to the west and northwest this city, so well guarded on every other side, lies directly open to the sea. It stands back beyond a half-mile of beach, and besides this and the stout walls which fortify it, would appear to have no other defenses. But those appearances are deceptive, and they had utterly deceived M. de Rivarol, when he devised his plan.

It remained for Captain Blood to explain the difficulties when M. de Rivarol informed him that the honor of opening the assault in the manner which he prescribed was to be accorded to the buccaneers.

Captain Blood smiled sardonic appreciation of the honor reserved for his men. It was precisely what he would have expected. For the buccaneers the dangers; for M. de Rivarol the honor, glory and profit of the enterprise.

"It is an honor which I must decline," said he quite coldly.

Wolverstone grunted approval and Hagthorpe nodded. Yberville, who as much as any of them resented the superciliousness of his noble compatriot, never wavered in loyalty to Captain Blood. The French officers—there were six of them present—stared their haughty surprise at the buccaneer leader, whilst the Baron challengingly fired a question at him.

"How? You decline it, 'sir'? You decline to obey orders, do you say?"

"I understood, M. le Baron, that you summoned us to deliberate upon the means to be adopted."

"Then you understood amiss, M. le Capitaine. You are here to receive my commands. I have already deliberated, and I have decided. I hope you understand."

"Oh, I understand," laughed Blood. "But, I ask myself, do you?" And without giving the Baron time to set the angry question that was bubbling to his lips, he swept on: "You have deliberated, you say, and you have decided. But unless your decision rests upon a wish to destroy my buccaneers, you will alter it when I tell you something of which I have knowledge. This city of Cartagena looks very vulnerable on the northern side, all open to the sea as it apparently stands. Ask yourself, M. le Baron, how came the Spaniards who built it where it is to have been at such trouble to fortify it to the south, if from the north it is so easily assailable."

That gave M. de Rivarol pause.

"The Spaniards," Blood pursued, "are not quite the fools you are supposing them. Let me tell you, messieurs, that two years ago I made a survey of Cartagena as a preliminary to raiding it. I came hither with some friendly trading Indians, myself disguised as an Indian, and in that guise I spent a week in the city and studied carefully all its approaches. On the side of the sea where it looks so temptingly open to assault, there is shoal water for over half a mile out—far enough out, I assure you, to ensure that no ship shall come within bombarding range of it. It is not safe to venture nearer land than three-quarters of a mile."

"But our landing will be effected in canoes and piraguas and open boats," cried an officer impatiently.

"In the calmest season of the year, the surf will hinder any such operation. And you will also bear in mind that if landing were possible as you are suggesting, that landing could not be covered by the ships' guns. In fact, it is the landing parties would be in danger from their own artillery."

"If the attack is made by night, as I propose, covering will be unnecessary. You should be ashore in force before the Spaniards are aware of the intent."

"You are assuming that Cartagena is a city of the blind, that at this very moment they are not conning our sails and asking themselves who we are and what we intend."

"But if they feel themselves secure from the north, as you suggest," cried the Baron impatiently, "that very security will lull them."

"Perhaps. But, then, they are secure. Any attempt to land on this side is doomed to failure at the hands of Nature."

"Nevertheless, we make the attempt," said the obstinate Baron, whose haughtiness would not allow him to yield before his officers.

"If you still choose to do so after what I have said, you are, of course, the person to decide. But I do not lead my men into fruitless danger."

"If I command you . . ." the Baron was beginning.

But Blood unceremoniously interrupted him. "M. le Baron, when M. de Cussy engaged us on your behalf, it was as much on account of our knowledge and experience of this class of warfare as on account of our strength. I have placed my own knowledge and experience in this particular matter at your disposal. I will add that I abandoned my own project of raiding Cartagena, not being in sufficient strength at the time to force the entrance of the harbor, which is the only way into the city. The strength which you now command is ample for that purpose."

"But whilst we are doing that, the Spaniards will have time to remove great part of the wealth this city holds. We must take them by surprise."

Captain Blood shrugged. "If this is a mere pirating raid, that, of course, is a prime consideration. It was with me. But if you are concerned to abate the pride of Spain and plant the Lilies of France on the forts of this settlement, the loss of some treasure should not really weigh for much."

M. de Rivarol bit his lip in chagrin. His gloomy eye smoldered as it considered the self-contained buccaneer. "But if I command you to go—to make the attempt?" he asked. "Answer me, monsieur, let us know once and for all where we stand, and who commands this expedition."

"Positively, I find you tiresome," said Captain Blood, and he swung to M. de Cussy, who sat there gnawing his lip, intensely uncomfortable. "I appeal to you, monsieur, to justify me to the General."

M. de Cussy started out of his gloomy abstraction. He cleared his throat. He was extremely nervous. "In view of what Captain Blood has submitted. . . ."

"Oh, to the devil with that!" snapped Rivarol. "It seems that I am followed by poltroons. Look you, M. le Capitaine, since you are afraid to undertake this thing, I will myself undertake it. The weather is calm, and I count upon making good my landing. If I do so, I shall have proved you wrong, and I shall have a word to say to you tomorrow which you may not like. I am being very generous with you, sir." He waved his hand regally. "You have leave to go."

It was sheer obstinacy and empty pride that drove him, and he received the lesson he deserved. The fleet stood in during the afternoon to within a mile of the coast, and under cover of darkness three hundred men, of whom two hundred were negroes—the whole of the negro contingent having been pressed into the undertaking—were pulled away for the shore in the canoes, piraguas, and ships' boats. Rivarol's pride compelled him, however much he may have disliked the venture, to lead them in person.

The first six boats were caught in the surf, and pounded into fragments before their occupants could extricate themselves. The thunder of the breakers and the cries of the shipwrecked warned those who followed, and thereby saved them from sharing the same fate. By the Baron's urgent orders they pulled away again out of danger, and stood about to pick up such survivors as contrived to battle towards them. Close upon fifty lives were lost in the adventure, together with half-a-dozen boats stored with ammunition and light guns.

The Baron went back to his flagship an infuriated, but by no means a wiser man. Wisdom—not even the pungent wisdom experience thrusts upon us—is not for such as M. de Rivarol. His anger embraced all things, but focused chiefly upon Captain Blood. In some warped process of reasoning he held the buccaneer chiefly responsible for this misadventure. He went to bed considering furiously what he should say to Captain Blood upon the morrow.

He was awakened at dawn by the rolling thunder of guns. Emerging upon the poop in nightcap and slippers, he beheld a sight that increased his unreasonable and unreasoning fury. The four buccaneer ships under canvas were going through extraordinary maneuver half a mile off the Boca Chica and little more than half a mile away from the remainder of the fleet, and from their flanks flame and smoke were belching each time they swung broadside to the great round fort that guarded that narrow entrance. The fort was returning the fire vigorously and viciously. But the buccaneers timed their broadsides with extraordinary judgment to catch the defending ordnance reloading; then as they drew the Spaniards' fire, they swung away again not only taking care to be ever moving targets, but, further, to present no more than bow or stern to the fort, their masts in line, when the heaviest cannonades were to be expected.

Gibbering and cursing, M. de Rivarol stood there and watched this action, so presumptuously undertaken by Blood on his own responsibility. The officers of the *Victorieuse* crowded round him, but it was not until M. de Cussy came to join the group that he opened the sluices of his rage. And M. de Cussy himself invited the deluge that now caught him. He had come up rubbing his hands and taking a proper satisfaction in the energy of the men whom he had enlisted.

"Aha, M. de Rivarol!" he laughed. "He understands his business, eh, this Captain Blood. He'll plant the Lilies of France on that fort before breakfast."

The Baron swung upon him snarling. "He understands his business, eh? His business, let me tell you, M. de Cussy, is to obey my orders, and I have not ordered this. *Par la Mordieu!* When this is over I'll deal with him for his damned insubordination."

"Surely, M. le Baron, he will have justified it if he succeeds."

"Justified it! Ah, *parbleu!* Can a soldier ever justify acting without orders?" He raved on furiously, his officers supporting him out of their detestation of Captain Blood.

Meanwhile the fight went merrily on. The fort was suffering badly. Yet for all their maneuvering the buccaneers were not escaping punishment. The starboard gunwale of the *Atropos* had been hammered into splinters, and a shot had caught her astern in the coach. The *Elizabeth* was badly battered about the forecastle, and the *Arabella*'s maintop had been shot away, whilst towards the end of that engagement the *Lachesis* came reeling out of the fight with a shattered rudder, steering herself by sweeps.

The absurd Baron's fierce eyes positively gleamed with satisfaction.

"I pray Heaven they may sink all his infernal ships!" he cried in his frenzy.

But Heaven didn't hear him. Scarcely had he spoken than there was a terrific explosion, and half the fort went up in fragments. A lucky shot from the buccaneers had found the powder magazine.

It may have been a couple of hours later, when Captain Blood, as spruce and cool as if he had just come from a levee, stepped upon the quarter-deck of the *Victorieuse*, to confront M. de Rivarol, still in bedgown and nightcap.

"I have to report, M. le Baron, that we are in possession of the fort on Boca Chica. The standard of France is flying from what remains of its tower, and the way into the outer harbor is open to your fleet."

M. de Rivarol was compelled to swallow his fury, though it choked him. The jubilation among his officers had been such that he could not continue as he had begun. Yet his eyes were malevolent, his face pale with anger.

"You are fortunate, M. Blood, that you succeeded," he said. "It would have gone very ill with you had you failed. Another time be so good as to await my orders, lest you should afterwards lack the justification which your good fortune has procured you this morning."

Blood smiled with a flash of white teeth, and bowed. "I shall be glad of your orders now, General, for pursuing our advantage. You realize that speed in striking is the first essential."

Rivarol was left gaping a moment. Absorbed in his ridiculous anger, he had considered nothing. But he made a quick recovery. "To my cabin, if you please," he commanded peremptorily, and was turning to lead the way, when Blood arrested him.

"With submission, my General, we shall be better here. You behold there the scene of our coming action. It is spread before you like a map." He waved his hand towards the lagoon, the country flanking it and the considerable city standing back from the beach. "If it is not a presumption in me to offer a suggestion. . . ." He paused. M. de Rivarol looked at him sharply, suspecting irony. But the swarthy face was bland, the keen eyes steady.

"Let us hear your suggestion," he consented.

Blood pointed out the fort at the mouth of the inner harbor, which was just barely visible above the waving palms on the intervening tongue of land. He announced that its armament was less formidable than that of the outer fort, which they had reduced; but on the other hand, the passage was very much narrower than the Boca Chica, and before they could attempt to make it in any case, they must dispose of those defenses. He proposed that the French ships should enter the outer harbor and proceed at once to bombardment. Meanwhile, he would land three hundred buccaneers and some artillery on the eastern side of the lagoon, beyond the fragrant garden islands dense with richly bearing fruit-trees, and proceed simultaneously to storm the fort in the rear. Thus beset on both sides at once, and demoralized by the fate of the much stronger outer fort, he did not think the Spaniards would offer a very long resistance. Then it would be for M. de Rivarol to garrison the fort, whilst Captain Blood would sweep on with his men, and seize the Church of Nuestra Señora de la Poupa, plainly visible on its hill immediately eastward of the town. Not only did that eminence afford them a valuable and obvious strategic advantage, but it commanded the only road that led from Cartagena to the interior, and once it were held there would be no further question of the Spaniards attempting to remove the wealth of the city.

That to M. de Rivarol was—as Captain Blood had judged that it would be—the crowning argument. Supercilious until that moment, and disposed for his own pride's sake to treat the buccaneer's suggestions with cavalier criticism, M. de Rivarol's manner suddenly changed. He became alert and brisk, went so far as tolerantly to commend Captain Blood's plan, and issued orders that action might be taken upon it at once.

It is not necessary to follow that action step by step. Blunders on the part of the French marred its smooth execution, and the indifferent handling of their ships led to the sinking of two of them in the course of the afternoon by the fort's gunfire. But by evening, owing largely to the irresistible fury with which the buccaneers stormed the place from the landward side, the fort had surrendered, and before dusk Blood and his men with some ordnance hauled thither by mules dominated the city from the heights of Nuestra Señora de la Poupa.

At noon on the morrow, shorn of defenses and threatened with bombardment, Cartagena sent offers of surrender to M. de Rivarol.

Swollen with pride by a victory for which he took the entire credit to himself, the Baron dictated his terms. He demanded that all public effects and office accounts be delivered up; that the merchants surrender all moneys and goods held by them for their correspondents; the inhabitants could choose whether they would remain in the city or depart; but those who went must first deliver up all their property, and those who elected to remain must surrender half, and become the subjects of France; religious houses and churches should be spared, but they must render accounts of all moneys and valuables in their possession.

Cartagena agreed, having no choice in the matter, and on the next day, which was the 5th of April, M. de Rivarol entered the city and proclaimed it now a French colony, appointing M. de Cussy its Governor. Thereafter he proceeded to the Cathedral, where very properly a *Te Deum* was sung in honor of the conquest. This by way of grace, whereafter M. de Rivarol proceeded to devour the city. The only detail in which the French conquest of Cartagena differed from an ordinary buccaneering raid was that under the severest penalties no soldier was to enter the house of any inhabitant. But this apparent respect for the persons and property of the conquered was based in reality upon M. de Rivarol's anxiety lest a doubloon should be abstracted from all the wealth that was pouring into the treasury opened by the Baron in the name of the King of France. Once the golden stream had ceased, he removed all restrictions and left the city in prey to his men, who proceeded further to pillage it of that part of their property which the inhabitants who became French subjects had been assured should remain inviolate. The plunder was enormous. In the course of four days over a hundred mules laden with gold went out of the city and down to the boats waiting at the beach to convey the treasure aboard the ships.

CHAPTER IV
THE HONOR OF M. DE RIVAROL

During the capitulation and for some time after, Captain Blood and the greater portion of his buccaneers had been at their post on the heights of Nuestra Señora de la Poupa, utterly in ignorance of what was taking place. Blood, although the man chiefly, if not solely, responsible for the swift reduction of the city, which was proving a veritable treasure-house, was not even shown the consideration of being called to the council of officers which with M. de Rivarol determined the terms of the capitulation.

This was a slight that at another time Captain Blood would not have borne for a moment. But at present, in his odd frame of mind, and its divorcement from piracy, he was content to smile his utter contempt of the French General. Not so, however, his captains, and still less his men. Resentment smoldered amongst them for a while, to flame out violently at the end of that week in Cartagena. It was only by undertaking to voice their grievance to the Baron that their captain was able for the moment to pacify them. That done, he went at once in quest of M. de Rivarol.

He found him in the offices which the Baron had set up in the town, with a staff of clerks to register the treasure brought in and to cast up the surrendered account-books, with a view to ascertaining precisely what were the sums yet to be delivered up. The Baron sat there scrutinizing ledgers, like a city merchant, and checking figures to make sure that all was correct to the last *peso*. A choice occupation this for the General of the King's Armies by Sea and Land. He looked up irritated by the interruption which Captain Blood's advent occasioned.

"M. le Baron," the latter greeted him. "I must speak frankly; and you must suffer it. My men are on the point of mutiny."

M. de Rivarol considered him with a faint lift of the eyebrows. "Captain Blood, I, too, will speak frankly; and you, too, must suffer it. If there is a mutiny, you and your captains shall be held personally responsible. The mistake you make is in assuming with me the tone of an ally, whereas I have given you clearly to understand from the first that you are simply in the position of having accepted service under me. Your proper apprehension of that fact will save the waste of a deal of words."

Blood contained himself with difficulty. One of these fine days, he felt, that for the sake of humanity he must slit the comb of this supercilious, arrogant cockerel.

"You may define our positions as you please," said he. "But I'll remind you that the nature of a thing is not changed by the name you give it. I am concerned with facts; chiefly with the fact that we entered into definite articles with you. Those articles provide for a certain distribution of the spoil. My men demand it. They are not satisfied."

"Of what are they not satisfied?" demanded the Baron.

"Of your honesty, M. de Rivarol."

A blow in the face could scarcely have taken the Frenchman more aback. He stiffened, and drew himself up, his eyes blazing, his face of a deathly pallor. The clerks at the tables laid down their pens and awaited the explosion in a sort of terror.

For a long moment there was silence. Then the great gentleman delivered himself in a voice of concentrated anger. "Do you really dare so much, you and the dirty thieves that follow you? God's blood! You shall answer to me for that word, though it entail a yet worse dishonor to meet you. Faugh!"

"I will remind you," said Blood, "that I am speaking not for myself, but for my men. It is they who are not satisfied, they who threaten that unless satisfaction is afforded them, and promptly, they will take it."

"Take it?" said Rivarol, trembling in his rage. "Let them attempt it, and. . . ."

"Now don't be rash. My men are within their rights, as you are aware. They demand to know when this sharing of the spoil is to take place, and when they are to receive the fifth for which their articles provide."

"God give me patience! How can we share the spoil before it has been completely gathered?"

"My men have reason to believe that it is gathered; and, anyway, they view with mistrust that it should all be housed aboard your ships, and remain in your possession. They say that hereafter there will be no ascertaining what the spoil really amounts to."

"But—name of Heaven!—I have kept books. They are there for all to see."

"They do not wish to see account-books. Few of them can read. They want to view the treasure itself. They know— you compel me to be blunt—that the accounts have been falsified. Your books show the spoil of Cartagena to amount to some ten million *livres*. The men know— and they are very skilled in these computations—that it exceeds the enormous total of forty millions. They insist that the treasure itself be produced and weighed in their presence, as is the custom among the Brethren of the Coast."

"I know nothing of filibuster customs." The gentleman was disdainful.

"But you are learning quickly."

"What do you mean, you rogue? I am a leader of armies, not of plundering thieves."

"Oh, but of course!" Blood's irony laughed in his eyes. "Yet, whatever you may be, I warn you that unless you yield to a demand that I consider just and therefore uphold, you may look for trouble, and it would not surprise me if you never leave Cartagena at all, nor convey a single gold piece home to France."

"Ah, *pardieu*! Am I to understand that you are threatening me?"

"Come, come, M. le Baron! I warn you of the trouble that a little prudence may avert. You do not know on what a volcano you are sitting. You do not know the ways of buccaneers. If you persist, Cartagena will be drenched in blood, and whatever the outcome the King of France will not have been well served."

That shifted the basis of the argument to less hostile ground. Awhile yet it continued, to be concluded at last by an ungracious undertaking from M. de Rivarol to submit to the demands of the buccaneers. He gave it with an extreme ill-grace, and only because Blood made him realize at last that to withhold it longer would be dangerous. In an engagement, he might conceivably defeat Blood's followers. But conceivably he might not. And even if he succeeded, the effort would be so costly to him in men that he might not thereafter find himself in sufficient strength to maintain his hold of what he had seized.

The end of it all was that he gave a promise at once to make the necessary preparations, and if Captain Blood and his officers would wait upon him on board the *Victorieuse* tomorrow morning, the treasure should be produced, weighed in their presence, and their fifth share surrendered there and then into their own keeping.

Among the buccaneers that night there was hilarity over the sudden abatement of M. de Rivarol's monstrous pride. But when the next dawn broke over Cartagena, they had the explanation of it. The only ships to be seen in the harbor were the *Arabella* and the *Elizabeth* riding at anchor, and the *Atropos* and the *Lachesis* careened on the beach for repair of the damage sustained in the bombardment. The French ships were gone. They had been quietly and secretly warped out of the harbor under cover of night, and three sails, faint and small, on the horizon to westward was all that remained to be seen of them. The absconding M. de Rivarol had gone off with the treasure, taking with him the troops and mariners he had brought from France. He had left behind him at Cartagena not only the empty-handed buccaneers, whom he had swindled, but also M. de Cussy and the volunteers and negroes from Hispaniola, whom he had swindled no less.

The two parties were fused into one by their common fury, and before the exhibition of it the inhabitants of that ill-fated town were stricken with deeper terror than they had yet known since the coming of this expedition.

Captain Blood alone kept his head, setting a curb upon his deep chagrin. He had promised himself that before parting from M. de Rivarol he would present a reckoning for all the petty affronts and insults to which that unspeakable fellow—now proved a scoundrel—had subjected him.

"We must follow," he declared. "Follow and punish."

At first that was the general cry. Then came the consideration that only two of the buccaneer ships were seaworthy—and these could not accommodate the whole force, particularly being at the moment indifferently victualed for a long voyage. The crews of the *Lachesis* and *Atropos* and with them their captains, Wolverstone and Yberville, renounced the intention. After all, there would be a deal of treasure still hidden in Cartagena. They would remain behind to extort it whilst fitting their ships for sea. Let Blood and Hagthorpe and those who sailed with them do as they pleased.

Then only did Blood realize the rashness of his proposal, and in attempting to draw back he almost precipitated a battle between the two parties into which that same proposal had now divided the buccaneers. And meanwhile those French sails on the horizon were growing less and less. Blood was reduced to despair. If he went off now, Heaven knew what would happen to the town, the temper of those whom he was leaving being what it was. Yet if he remained, it would simply mean that his own and Hagthorpe's crews would join in the saturnalia and increase the hideousness of events now inevitable. Unable to reach a decision, his own men and Hagthorpe's took the matter off his hands, eager to give chase to Rivarol. Not only was a dastardly cheat to be punished but an enormous treasure to be won by treating as an enemy this French commander who, himself, had so villainously broken the alliance.

When Blood, torn as he was between conflicting considerations, still hesitated, they bore him almost by main force aboard the *Arabella*.

Within an hour, the water-casks at least replenished and stowed aboard, the *Arabella* and the *Elizabeth* put to sea upon that angry chase.

"When we were well at sea, and the *Arabella*'s course was laid," writes Pitt, in his log, "I went to seek the Captain, knowing him to be in great trouble of mind over these events. I found him sitting alone in his cabin, his head in his hands, torment in the eyes that stared straight before him, seeing nothing."

"What now, Peter?" cried the young Somerset mariner. "Lord, man, what is there here to fret you? Surely 't isn't the thought of Rivarol!"

"No," said Blood thickly. And for once he was communicative. It may well be that he must vent the thing that oppressed him or be driven mad by it. And Pitt, after all, was his friend and loved him, and so a proper man for confidences. "But if she knew! If she knew! O God! I had thought to have done with piracy; thought to have done with it forever. Yet here have I been committed by this scoundrel to the worst

piracy that ever I was guilty of. Think of Cartagena! Think of the hell those devils will be making of it now! And I must have that on my soul!"

"Nay, Peter—'t isn't on your soul; but on Rivarol's. It is that dirty thief who has brought all this about. What could you have done to prevent it?"

"I would have stayed if it could have availed."

"It could not, and you know it. So why repine?"

"There is more than that to it," groaned Blood. "What now? What remains? Loyal service with the English was made impossible for me. Loyal service with France has led to this; and that is equally impossible hereafter. What remains then? Piracy? I have done with it. Egad, if I am to live clean, I believe the only thing is to go and offer my sword to the King of Spain."

But something remained—the last thing that he could have expected—something towards which they were rapidly sailing over the tropical, sunlit sea. All this against which he now inveighed so bitterly was but a necessary stage in the shaping of his odd destiny.

Setting a course for Hispaniola, since they judged that thither must Rivarol go to refit before attempting to cross to France, the *Arabella* and the *Elizabeth* ploughed briskly northward with a moderately favorable wind for two days and nights without ever catching a glimpse of their quarry. The third dawn brought with it a haze which circumscribed their range of vision to something between two and three miles, and deepened their growing vexation and their apprehension that M. de Rivarol might escape them altogether.

Their position then—according to Pitt's log—was approximately 75° deg. 30′ W. Long. by 17° deg. 45′ N. Lat., so that they had Jamaica on their larboard beam some thirty miles to westward, and, indeed, away to the northwest, faintly visible as a bank of clouds, appeared the great ridge of the Blue Mountains whose peaks were thrust into the clear upper air above the low-lying haze. The wind, to which they were sailing very close, was westerly, and it bore to their ears a booming sound which in less experienced ears might have passed for the breaking of surf upon a lee shore.

"Guns!" said Pitt, who stood with Blood upon the quarterdeck. Blood nodded, listening. "Ten miles away, perhaps fifteen—somewhere off Port Royal, I should judge," Pitt added. Then he looked at his captain. "Does it concern us?" he asked.

"Guns off Port Royal . . . that should argue Colonel Bishop at work. And against whom should he be in action but against friends of ours? I think it may concern us. Anyway, we'll stand in to investigate. Bid them put the helm over."

Close-hauled they tacked aweather, guided by the sound of combat, which grew in volume and definition as they approached it. Thus for an hour, perhaps. Then, as, telescope to his eye, Blood raked the haze, expecting at any moment to behold the battling ships, the guns abruptly ceased.

They held to their course, nevertheless, with all hands on deck, eagerly, anxiously scanning the sea ahead. And presently an object loomed into view, which soon defined itself for a great ship on fire. As the *Arabella* with the *Elizabeth* following closely raced nearer on their northwesterly tack, the outlines of the blazing vessel grew clearer. Presently her masts stood out sharp and black above the smoke and flames, and through his telescope Blood made out plainly the pennon of St. George fluttering from her maintop.

"An English ship!" he cried.

He scanned the seas for the conqueror in the battle of which this grim evidence was added to that of the sounds they had heard, and when at last, as they drew closer to the doomed vessel, they made out the shadowy outlines of three tall ships, some three or four miles away, standing in toward Port Royal, the first and natural assumption was that these ships must belong to the Jamaica fleet, and that the burning vessel was a defeated buccaneer, and because of this they sped on to pick up the three boats that were standing away from the blazing hulk. But Pitt, who through the telescope was examining the receding squadron, observed things apparent only to the eye of the trained mariner, and made the incredible announcement that the largest of these three vessels was Rivarol's *Victorieuse*.

They took in sail and hove to as they came up with the drifting boats, laden to capacity with survivors. And there were others adrift on some of the spars and wreckage with which the sea was strewn, who must be rescued.

CHAPTER V
THE SERVICE OF KING WILLIAM

One of the boats bumped alongside the *Arabella*, and up the entrance ladder came first a slight, spruce little gentleman in a coat of mulberry satin laced with gold, whose wizened, yellow, rather peevish face was framed in a heavy black periwig. His modish and costly apparel had nowise suffered by the adventure through which he had passed, and he carried himself with the easy assurance of a man of rank. Here, quite clearly, was no buccaneer. He was closely followed by one who in every particular, save that of age, was his physical opposite, corpulent in a brawny, vigorous way, with a full, round, weatherbeaten face whose mouth was humorous and whose eyes were blue and twinkling. He was well dressed without fripperies, and bore with him an air of vigorous authority.

As the little man stepped from the ladder into the waist, whither Captain Blood had gone to receive him, his sharp, ferrety dark eyes swept the uncouth ranks of the assembled crew of the *Arabella*.

"And where the devil may I be now?" he demanded irritably. "Are you English, or what the devil are you?"

"Myself, I have the honor to be Irish, sir. My name is Blood—Captain Peter Blood, and this is my ship the *Arabella*, all very much at your service."

"Blood!" shrilled the little man. "O 'Sblood! A pirate!" He swung to the Colossus who followed him—"A damned pirate, van der Kuylen. Rend my vitals, but we're come from Scylla to Charybdis."

"So?" said the other gutturally, and again, "So?" Then the humor of it took him, and he yielded to it.

"Damme! What's to laugh at, you porpoise?" spluttered mulberry-coat. "A fine tale this'll make at home! Admiral van der Kuylen first loses his fleet in the night, then has his flagship fired under him by a French squadron, and ends all by being captured by a pirate. I'm glad you find it matter for laughter. Since for my sins I happen to be with you, I'm damned if I do."

"There's a misapprehension, if I may make so bold as to point it out," put in Blood quietly. "You are not captured, gentlemen; you are rescued. When you realize it, perhaps it will occur to you to acknowledge the hospitality I am offering you. It may be poor, but it is the best at my disposal."

The fierce little gentleman stared at him. "Damme! Do you permit yourself to be ironical?" he disapproved him, and possibly with a view to correcting any such tendency, proceeded to introduce himself. "I am Lord Willoughby, King William's Governor-General of the West Indies, and this is Admiral van der Kuylen, commander of His Majesty's West Indian fleet, at present mislaid somewhere in this damned Caribbean Sea."

"King William?" quoth Blood, and he was conscious that Pitt and Dyke, who were behind him, now came edging nearer, sharing his own wonder. "And who may be King William, and of what may he be King?"

"What's that?" In a wonder greater than his own, Lord Willoughby stared back at him. At last: "I am alluding to His Majesty King William III—William of Orange—who, with Queen Mary, has been ruling England for two months and more."

There was a moment's silence, until Blood realized what he was being told.

"D'ye mean, sir, that they've roused themselves at home, and kicked out that scoundrel James and his gang of ruffians?"

Admiral van der Kuylen nudged his lordship, a humorous twinkle in his blue eyes.

"His bolitics are fery sound, I dink," he growled.

His lordship's smile brought lines like gashes into his leathery cheeks. "'Slife! Hadn't you heard? Where the devil have you been at all?"

"Out of touch with the world for the last three months," said Blood.

"Stab me! You must have been. And in that three months the world has undergone some changes." Briefly he added an account of them. King James was fled to France, and living under the protection of King Louis, wherefore, and for other reasons, England had joined the league against her, and was now at war with France. That was how it happened that the Dutch Admiral's flagship had been attacked by M. de Rivarol's fleet that morning, from which it clearly followed that in his voyage from Cartagena, the Frenchman must have spoken some ship that gave him the news.

After that, with renewed assurances that aboard his ship they should be honorably entreated, Captain Blood led the Governor-General and the Admiral to his cabin, what time the work of rescue went on. The news he had received had set Blood's mind in a turmoil. If King James was dethroned and banished, there was an end to his own outlawry for his alleged share in an earlier attempt to drive out that tyrant. It became possible for him to return home and take up his life again at the point where it was so unfortunately interrupted four years ago. He was dazzled by the prospect so abruptly opened out to him. The thing so filled his mind, moved him so deeply, that he must afford it expression. In doing so, he revealed of himself more than he knew or intended to the astute little gentleman who watched him so keenly the while.

"Go home, if you will," said his lordship, when Blood paused. "You may be sure that none will harass you on the score of your piracy, considering what it was that drove you to it. But why be in haste? We have heard of you, to be sure, and we know of what you are capable upon the seas. Here is a great chance for you, since you declare yourself sick of piracy. Should you choose to serve King William out here during this war, your knowledge of the West Indies should render you a very valuable servant to His Majesty's Government, which you would not find ungrateful. You should consider it. Damme, sir, I repeat: it is a great chance you are given."

"That your lordship gives me," Blood amended, "I am very grateful. But at the moment, I confess, I can consider nothing but this great news. It alters the shape of the world. I must accustom myself to view it as it now is, before I can determine my own place in it."

Pitt came in to report that the work of rescue was at an end, and the men picked up—some forty-five in all—safe aboard the two buccaneer ships. He asked for orders.

Blood rose. "I am negligent of your lordship's concerns in my consideration of my own. You'll be wishing me to land you at Port Royal."

"At Port Royal?" The little man squirmed wrathfully on his seat. Wrathfully and at length he informed Blood that they had put into Port Royal last evening to find its Deputy-Governor absent. "He had gone on some wild-goose chase to Tortuga after buccaneers, taking the whole of the fleet with him."

Blood stared in surprise a moment; then yielded to laughter. "He went, I suppose, before news reached him of the change of government at home, and the war with France?"

"He did not," snapped Willoughby. "He was informed of both, and also of my coming before he set out."

"Oh, impossible!"

"So I should have thought. But I have the information from a Major Mallard whom I found in Port Royal, apparently governing in this fool's absence."

"But is he mad, to leave his post at such a time?" Blood was amazed.

"Taking the whole fleet with him, pray remember, and leaving the place open to French attack. That is the sort of Deputy-Governor that the late Government thought fit to appoint: an epitome of its misrule, damme! He leaves Port Royal unguarded save by a ramshackle fort that can be reduced to rubble in an hour. Stab me! It's unbelievable!"

The lingering smile faded from Blood's face. "Is Rivarol aware of this?" he cried sharply.

It was the Dutch Admiral who answered him. "Vould he go dere if he were not? M. de Rivarol he take some of our men prisoners. Berhabs dey dell him. Berhabs he make dem tell. Id is a great obbordunidy."

His lordship snarled like a mountain-cat. "That rascal Bishop shall answer for it with his head if there's any mischief done through this desertion of his post. What if it were deliberate, eh? What if he is more knave than fool? What if this is his way of serving King James, from whom he held his office?"

Captain Blood was generous. "Hardly so much. It was just vindictiveness that urged him. It's myself he's hunting at Tortuga, my lord. But I'm thinking that while he's about it, I'd best be looking after Jamaica for King William."

He laughed, with more mirth than he had used in the last two months. "Set a course for Port Royal, Jeremy, and make all speed. We'll be level yet with M. de Rivarol, and wipe off some other scores at the same time."

Both Lord Willoughby and the Admiral were on their feet. "But you are not equal to it, damme!" cried his lordship. "Any one of the Frenchman's three ships is a match for both yours, my man."

"In guns—aye," said Blood, and he smiled. "But there's more than guns that matter in these affairs. If your lordship would like to see an action fought at sea as an action should be fought, this is your opportunity."

Both stared at him. "But the odds!" his lordship insisted.

"Id is imbossible," said van der Kuylen, shaking his great head. "Seamanship is imbordand. Bud guns is guns."

"If I can't defeat him, I can sink my own ships in the channel, and block him in until Bishop gets back from his wild-goose chase with his squadron, or until your own fleet turns up."

"And what good will that be, pray?" demanded Willoughby.

"I'll be after telling you. Rivarol is a fool to take this chance, considering what he's got aboard. He carried in his hold the treasure plundered from Cartagena, amounting to forty million *livres*." They jumped at the mention of that colossal sum. "He has gone into Port Royal with it. Whether he defeats me or not, he doesn't come out of Port Royal with it again, and sooner or later that treasure shall find its way into King William's coffers—after, say, one fifth share shall have been paid to my buccaneers. Is that agreed, Lord Willoughby?"

His lordship stood up, and shaking back the cloud of lace from his wrist, held out a delicate white hand. "Captain Blood, I discover greatness in you," said he.

"Sure it's your lordship has the fine sight to perceive it," laughed the Captain.

"Yes, yes! Bud how vill you do id?" growled van der Kuylen.

"Come on deck, and it's a demonstration I'll be giving you before the day's much older."

CHAPTER VI
THE LAST FIGHT OF THE *ARABELLA*

"Vhy do you vait, my friend?" growled van der Kuylen.

"Aye—in God's name!" snapped Willoughby.

It was the afternoon of that same day, and the two buccaneer ships rocked gently with idly flapping sails under the lee of the long spit of land forming the great natural harbor of Port Royal, and less than a mile from the straits leading into it, which the fort commanded. It was two hours and more since they had brought up thereabouts, having crept thither unobserved by the city and by M. de Rivarol's ships, and all the time the air had been aquiver with the roar of guns from sea and land, announcing that battle was joined between the French and the defenders of Port Royal.

That long, inactive waiting was straining the nerves of both Lord Willoughby and van der Kuylen. "You said you vould show us zome vine dings. Vhere are dese vine dings?"

Blood faced them, smiling confidently. He was arrayed for battle, in back-and-breast of black steel. "I'll not be trying your patience much longer. Indeed, I notice already a slackening in the fire. But it's this way, now: there's nothing at all to be gained by precipitancy, and a deal to be gained by delaying, as I shall show you, I hope."

Lord Willoughby eyed him suspiciously. "Ye think that in the meantime Bishop may come back or Admiral van der Kuylen's fleet appear?"

"Sure, now, I'm thinking nothing of the kind. What I'm thinking is that in this engagement with the fort M. de Rivarol, who's a lubberly fellow, as I've reason to know, will be taking some damage that may make the odds a trifle more even. Sure, it'll be time enough to go forward when the fort has shot its bolt."

"Aye, aye!" The sharp approval came like a cough from the little Governor-General. "I perceive your object, and I believe ye're entirely right. Ye have the qualities of a great commander, Captain Blood. I beg your pardon for having misunderstood you."

"And that's very handsome of your lordship. Ye see, I have some experience of this kind of action, and whilst I'll take any risk that I must, I'll take none that I needn't. But. . . ." He broke off to listen. "Aye, I was right. The fire's slackening. It'll mean the end of Mallard's resistance in the fort. Ho there, Jeremy!"

He leaned on the carved rail and issued orders crisply. The bo'sun's pipe shrilled out, and in a moment the ship that had seemed to slumber there, awoke to life. Came the padding of feet along the decks, the creaking of blocks and the hoisting of sail. The helm was put over hard, and in a moment they were moving, the *Elizabeth* following, ever in obedience to the signals from the *Arabella*, whilst Ogle the gunner, whom he had summoned, was receiving Blood's final instructions before plunging down to his station on the main deck.

Within a quarter of an hour they had rounded the head, and stood in to the harbor mouth, within saker shot of Rivarol's three ships, to which they now abruptly disclosed themselves.

Where the fort had stood they now beheld a smoking rubbish heap, and the victorious Frenchman with the lily standard trailing from his mastheads was sweeping forward to snatch the rich prize whose defenses he had shattered.

Blood scanned the French ships, and chuckled. The *Victorieuse* and the *Medusa* appeared to have taken no more than a few scars; but the third ship, the *Baleine*, listing heavily to larboard so as to keep the great gash in her starboard well above water, was out of account.

"You see!" he cried to van der Kuylen, and without waiting for the Dutchman's approving grunt, he shouted an order: "Helm, hard-a-port!"

The sight of that great red ship with her gilt beak-head and open ports swinging broadside on must have given check to Rivarol's soaring exultation. Yet before he could move to give an order, before he could well resolve what order to give, a volcano of fire and metal burst upon him from the buccaneers, and his decks were swept by the murderous scythe of the broadside. The *Arabella* held to her course, giving place to the *Elizabeth*, which, following closely, executed the same maneuver. And then whilst still the Frenchmen were confused, panic-stricken by an attack that took them so utterly by surprise, the *Arabella* had gone about and was returning in her tracks, presenting now her larboard guns, and loosing her second broadside in the wake of the first. Came yet another broadside from the *Elizabeth* and then the *Arabella's* trumpeter sent a call across the water, which Hagthorpe perfectly understood.

"On now, Jeremy!" cried Blood. "Straight into them before they recover their wits. Stand by, there! Prepare to board! Hayton . . . the grapnels! And pass the word to the gunner in the prow to fire as fast as he can load."

He discarded his feathered hat and covered himself with a steel head-piece, which a negro lad brought him. He meant to lead this boarding-party in person. Briskly he explained himself to his two guests. "Boarding is our only chance here. We are too heavily outgunned."

Of this the fullest demonstration followed quickly. The Frenchmen having recovered their wits at last, both ships swung broadside on, and concentrating upon the *Arabella* as the nearer and heavier and therefore more immediately dangerous of their two opponents, volleyed upon her jointly at almost the same moment.

Unlike the buccaneers, who had fired high to cripple their enemies above decks, the French fired low to smash the hull of their assailant. The *Arabella* rocked and staggered under that terrific hammering, although Pitt kept her headed towards the French so that she should offer the narrowest target. For a moment she seemed to hesitate, then she plunged forward again, her beak-head in splinters, her forecastle smashed, and a gaping hole forward that was only just above the water-line. Indeed, to make her safe from bilging, Blood ordered a prompt jettisoning of the forward guns, anchors, and water-casks and whatever else was moveable.

Meanwhile, the Frenchmen going about gave the like reception to the *Elizabeth*. The *Arabella*, indifferently served by the wind, pressed forward to come to grips. But before she could accomplish her object, the *Victorieuse* had loaded her starboard guns again and pounded her advancing enemy with a second broadside at close quarters. Amid the thunder of cannon, the rending of timbers, and the screams of maimed men, the half-necked *Arabella* plunged and reeled into the cloud of smoke that concealed her prey, and then from Hayton went up the cry that she was going down by the head.

Blood's heart stood still. And then in that very moment of his despair, the blue and gold flank of the *Victorieuse* loomed through the smoke. But even as he caught that enheartening glimpse he perceived, too, how sluggish now was their advance, and how with every second it grew more sluggish. They must sink before they reached her.

Thus, with an oath, opined the Dutch Admiral, and from Lord Willoughby there was a word of blame for Blood's seamanship in having risked all upon this gambler's throw of boarding.

"There was no other chance!" cried Blood, in broken-hearted frenzy. "If ye say it was desperate and foolhardy, why, so it was; but the occasion and the means demanded nothing less. I fail within an ace of victory."

But they had not yet completely failed. Hayton himself, and a score of sturdy rogues whom his whistle had summoned, were crouching for shelter amid the wreckage of the forecastle with grapnels ready. Within seven or eight yards of the *Victorieuse*, when their way seemed spent and their forward deck already awash under the eyes of the jeering, cheering Frenchmen, those men leapt up and forward and hurled their grapnels across the chasm. Of the four they flung, two reached the Frenchman's decks and fastened there. Swift as thought itself was then the action of those sturdy, experienced buccaneers. Unhesitatingly all threw themselves upon the chain of one of those grapnels, neglecting the other, and heaved upon it with all their might to warp the ships together. Blood, watching from his own quarterdeck, sent out his voice in a clarion call: "Musketeers to the prow!"

The musketeers, at their station at the waist, obeyed him with the speed of men who know that in obedience is the only hope of life. Fifty of them dashed forward instantly, and from the ruins of the forecastle they blazed over the heads of Hayton's men, mowing down the French soldiers who, unable to dislodge the irons, firmly held where they had deeply bitten into the timbers of the *Victorieuse*, were themselves preparing to fire upon the grapnel crew.

Starboard to starboard the two ships swung against each other with a jarring thud. By then Blood was down in the waist, judging and acting with the hurricane speed the occasion demanded. Sail had been lowered by slashing away the ropes that held the yards. The advance guard of boarders, a hundred strong, was ordered to the poop, and his grapnel-men were posted and prompt to obey his command at the very moment of impact. As a result, the foundering *Arabella* was literally kept afloat by the half-dozen grapnels that in an instant moored her firmly to the *Victorieuse*.

Willoughby and van der Kuylen on the poop had watched in breathless amazement the speed and precision with which Blood and his desperate crew had gone to work. And now he came racing up, his bugler sounding the charge, the main host of the buccaneers following him, whilst the vanguard, led by the gunner Ogle, who had been driven from his guns by water in the gun-deck, leapt shouting to the prow of the *Victorieuse*, to whose level the high poop of the water-logged *Arabella* had sunk. Led now by Blood himself, they launched themselves upon the French like hounds upon the stag they have brought to bay. After them went others, until all had gone, and none but Willoughby and the Dutchman were left to watch the fight from the quarterdeck of the abandoned *Arabella*.

For fully half-an-hour that battle raged aboard the Frenchman. Beginning in the prow, it surged through the forecastle to the waist, where it reached a climax of fury. The French resisted stubbornly, and they had the advantage of numbers to encourage them. But for all their stubborn valor they ended by being pressed back and back across the decks that were dangerously canted to starboard by the pull of the water-logged *Arabella*. The buccaneers fought with the desperate fury of men who know that retreat is impossible, for there was no ship to which they could retreat, and here they must prevail and make the *Victorieuse* their own, or perish.

And their own they made her in the end, and at a cost of nearly half their numbers. Driven to the quarterdeck, the surviving defenders, urged on by the infuriated Rivarol, maintained awhile their desperate resistance. But in the end, Rivarol went down with a bullet in his head, and the French remnant, numbering scarcely a score of whole men, called for quarter.

Even then the labors of Blood's men were not at an end. The *Elizabeth* and the *Medusa* were tight-locked, and Hagthorpe's followers were being driven back aboard their own ship for the second time. Prompt measures were demanded. Whilst Pitt and his seamen bore their part with the sails, and Ogle went below with a gun-crew, Blood ordered the grapnels to be loosed at once. Lord Willoughby and the Admiral were already aboard the

Victorieuse. As they swung off to the rescue of Hagthorpe, Blood, from the quarterdeck of the conquered vessel, looked his last upon the ship that had served him so well, the ship that had become to him almost as a part of himself. A moment she rocked after her release, then slowly and gradually settled down, the water gurgling and eddying about her topmasts, all that remained visible to mark the spot where she had met her death.

As he stood there, above the ghastly shambles in the waist of the *Victorieuse*, someone spoke behind him. "I think, Captain Blood, that it is necessary I should beg your pardon for the second time. Never before have I seen the impossible made possible by resource and valor, or victory so gallantly snatched from defeat."

He turned, and presented to Lord Willoughby a formidable front. His headpiece was gone, his breastplate dinted, his right sleeve a rag hanging from his shoulder about a naked arm. He was splashed from head to foot with blood, and there was blood from a scalp-wound that he had taken matting his hair and mixing with the grime of powder on his face to render him unrecognizable.

But from that horrible mask two vivid eyes looked out preternaturally bright, and from those eyes two tears had ploughed each a furrow through the filth of his cheeks.

CHAPTER VII
HIS EXCELLENCY THE GOVERNOR

When the cost of that victory came to be counted, it was found that of three hundred and twenty buccaneers who had left Cartagena with Captain Blood, a bare hundred remained sound and whole. The *Elizabeth* had suffered so seriously that it was doubtful if she could ever again be rendered seaworthy, and Hagthorpe, who had so gallantly commanded her in that last action, was dead. Against this, on the other side of the account, stood the facts that, with a far inferior force and by sheer skill and desperate valor, Blood's buccaneers had saved Jamaica from bombardment and pillage, and they had captured the fleet of M. de Rivarol, and seized for the benefit of King William the splendid treasure which she carried.

It was not until the evening of the following day that van der Kuylen's truant fleet of nine ships came to anchor in the harbor of Port Royal, and its officers, Dutch and English, were made acquainted with their Admiral's true opinion of their worth.

Six ships of that fleet were instantly refitted for sea. There were other West Indian settlements demanding the visit of inspection of the new Governor-General, and Lord Willoughby was in haste to sail for the Antilles.

"And meanwhile," he complained to his Admiral, "I am detained here by the absence of this fool of a Deputy-Governor."

"So?" said van der Kuylen. "But vhy should dad dedain you?"

"That I may break the dog as he deserves, and appoint his successor in some man gifted with a sense of where his duty lies, and with the ability to perform it."

"Aha! But id is not necessary you remain for dat. And he vill require no insdrucshons, dis one. He vill know how to make Port Royal safe, bedder nor you or me."

"You mean Blood?"

"Of gourse. Could any man be bedder? You haf seen vhad he can do."

"You think so, too, eh? Egad! I had thought of it; and, rip me, why not? He's a better man than Morgan, and Morgan was made Governor."

Blood was sent for. He came, spruce and debonair once more, having exploited the resources of Port Royal so to render himself. He was a trifle dazzled by the honor proposed to him, when Lord Willoughby made it known. It was so far beyond anything that he had dreamed, and he was assailed by doubts of his capacity to undertake so onerous a charge.

"Damme!" snapped Willoughby, "Should I offer it unless I were satisfied of your capacity? If that's your only objection. . . ."

"It is not, my lord. I had counted upon going home, so I had. I am hungry for the green lanes of England." He sighed.

"There will be apple-blossoms in the orchards of Somerset."

"Apple-blossoms!" His lordship's voice shot up like a rocket, and cracked on the word. "What the devil . . . ? Apple-blossoms!" He looked at van der Kuylen.

The Admiral raised his brows and pursed his heavy lips. His eyes twinkled humourosly in his great face. "So!" he said. "Fery boedical!"

My lord wheeled fiercely upon Captain Blood. "You've a past score to wipe out, my man!" he admonished him. "You've done something towards it, I confess; and you've shown your quality in doing it. That's why I offer you the governorship of Jamaica in His Majesty's name—because I account you the fittest man for the office that I have seen."

Blood bowed low. "Your lordship is very good. But. . . ."

"Tchah! There's no 'but' to it. If you want your past forgotten, and your future assured, this is your chance. And you are not to treat it lightly on account of apple-blossoms or any other damned sentimental nonsense. Your duty lies here, at least for as long as the war lasts. When the war's over, you may get back to Somerset and cider or your native Ireland and its potheen; but until then you'll make the best of Jamaica and rum."

Van der Kuylen exploded into laughter. But from Blood the pleasantry elicited no smile. He remained solemn to the point of glumness. His thoughts were on Miss Bishop, who was somewhere here in this very house in which they stood, but whom he had not seen since his arrival. Had she but shown him some compassion. . . .

And then the rasping voice of Willoughby cut in again, upbraiding him for his hesitation, pointing out to him his incredible stupidity in trifling with such a golden opportunity as this.

He stiffened and bowed. "My lord, you are in the right. I am a fool. But don't be accounting me an ingrate as well. If I have hesitated, it is because there are considerations with which I will not trouble your lordship."

"Apple-blossoms, I suppose?" sniffed his lordship.

This time Blood laughed, but there was still a lingering wistfulness in his eyes. "It shall be as you wish—and very gratefully, let me assure your lordship. I shall know how to earn His Majesty's approbation. You may depend upon my loyal service."

"If I didn't, I shouldn't offer you this governorship."

Thus it was settled. Blood's commission was made out and sealed in the presence of Mallard, the Commandant, and the other officers of the garrison, who looked on in round-eyed astonishment, but kept their thoughts to themselves.

"Now ve can aboud our business go," said van der Kuylen.

"We sail tomorrow morning," his lordship announced.

Blood was startled. "And Colonel Bishop?" he asked.

"He becomes your affair. You are now the Governor. You will deal with him as you think proper on his return. Hang him from his own yardarm. He deserves it."

"Isn't the task a trifle invidious?" wondered Blood.

"Very well. I'll leave a letter for him. I hope he'll like it."

Captain Blood took up his duties at once. There was much to be done to place Port Royal in a proper state of defense after what had happened there. He made an inspection of the ruined fort and issued instructions for the work upon it, which was to be started immediately. Next he ordered the careening of the three French vessels that they might be rendered seaworthy once more. Finally, with the sanction of Lord Willoughby, he marshaled his buccaneers and surrendered to them one fifth of the captured treasure, leaving it to their choice thereafter either to depart or to enroll themselves in the service of King William.

A score of them elected to remain, and amongst these were Jeremy Pitt, Ogle, and Dyke, whose outlawry, like Blood's, had come to an end with the downfall of King James. They were—saving old Wolverstone, who had been left behind at Cartagena—the only survivors of that band of rebels-convict who had left Barbados over three years ago in the *Cinco Llagas*.

On the following morning, whilst van der Kuylen's fleet was making finally ready for sea, Blood sat in the spacious whitewashed room that was the Governor's office, when Major Mallard brought him word that Bishop's homing squadron was in sight.

"That is very well," said Blood. "I am glad he comes before Lord Willoughby's departure. The orders, Major, are that you place him under arrest the moment he steps ashore. Then bring him here to me. A moment." He wrote a hurried note. "That to Lord Willoughby aboard Admiral van der Kuylen's flagship."

Major Mallard saluted and departed. Peter Blood sat back in his chair and stared at the ceiling, frowning. Time moved on. Came a tap at the door, and an elderly negro slave presented himself. Would his excellency receive Miss Bishop?

His excellency changed color. He sat quite still, staring at the negro a moment, conscious that his pulses were drumming in a manner wholly unusual to them. Then quietly he assented.

He rose when she entered, and if he was not as pale as she was, it was because his tan dissembled it. For a moment there was silence between them as they stood looking each at the other. Then she moved forward and began at last to speak, haltingly, in an unsteady voice, amazing in one usually so calm and deliberate.

"I . . . I . . . Major Mallard has just told me. . . ."

"Major Mallard exceeded his duty," said Blood, and because of the effort he made to steady his voice it sounded harsh and unduly loud.

He saw her start, and stop, and instantly made amends. "You alarm yourself without reason, Miss Bishop. Whatever may lie between me and your uncle, you may be sure that I shall not follow the example he has set me. I shall not abuse my position to prosecute a private vengeance. On the contrary, I shall abuse it to protect him. Lord Willoughby's recommendation to me is that I shall treat him without mercy. My own intention is to send him back to his plantation in Barbados."

She came slowly forward now. "I . . . I am glad that you will do that. Glad, above all, for your own sake." She held out her hand to him.

He considered it critically. Then he bowed over it. "I'll not presume to take it in the hand of a thief and a pirate," said he bitterly.

"You are no longer that," she said, and strove to smile.

"Yet I owe no thanks to you that I am not," he answered. "I think there's no more to be said, unless it be to add the assurance that Lord Julian Wade has also nothing to apprehend from me. That, no doubt, will be the assurance that your peace of mind requires?"

"For your own sake—yes. But for your own sake only. I would not have you do anything mean or dishonoring."

"Thief and pirate though I be?"

She clenched her hand, and made a little gesture of despair and impatience. "Will you never forgive me those words?"

"I'm finding it a trifle hard, I confess. But what does it matter, when all is said?"

Her clear hazel eyes considered him a moment wistfully. Then she put out her hand again. "I am going, Captain Blood. Since you are so generous to my uncle, I shall be returning to Barbados with him. We are not like to meet again—ever. Is it impossible that we should part friends? Once I wronged you, I know. And I have said that I am sorry. Won't you . . . won't you say 'goodbye'?"

He seemed to rouse himself, to shake off a mantle of deliberate harshness. He took the hand she proffered. Retaining it, he spoke, his eyes somberly, wistfully considering her. "You are returning to Barbados?" he said slowly. "Will Lord Julian be going with you?"

"Why do you ask me that?" she confronted him quite fearlessly.

"Sure, now, didn't he give you my message, or did he bungle it?"

"No. He didn't bungle it. He gave it me in your own words. It touched me very deeply. It made me see clearly my error and my injustice. I owe it to you that I should say this by way of amend. I judged too harshly where it was a presumption to judge at all."

He was still holding her hand. "And Lord Julian, then?" he asked, his eyes watching her, bright as sapphires in that copper-colored face.

"Lord Julian will no doubt be going home to England. There is nothing more for him to do out here."

"But didn't he ask you to go with him?"

"He did. I forgive you the impertinence."

A wild hope leapt to life within him. "And you? Glory be, ye'll not be telling me ye refused to become my lady, when. . . ."

"Oh! You are insufferable!" She tore her hand free and backed away from him. "I should not have come. Goodbye!" She was speeding to the door.

He sprang after her and caught her. Her face flamed, and her eyes stabbed him like daggers. "These are pirate's ways, I think! Release me!"

"Arabella!" he cried on a note of pleading. "Are ye meaning it? Must I release ye? Must I let ye go and never set eyes on ye again? Or will ye stay and make this exile endurable until we can go home together? Och, ye're crying now! What have I said to make ye cry, my dear?"

"I . . . I thought you'd never say it," she mocked him through her tears.

"Well, now, ye see there was Lord Julian, a fine figure of a. . . ."

"There was never, never anybody but you, Peter."

They had, of course, a deal to say thereafter, so much, indeed, that they sat down to say it, whilst time sped on, and Governor Blood forgot the duties of his office. He had reached home at last. His odyssey was ended.

And meanwhile Colonel Bishop's fleet had come to anchor, and the Colonel had landed on the mole, a disgruntled man to be disgruntled further yet. He was accompanied ashore by Lord Julian Wade.

A corporal's guard was drawn up to receive him, and in advance of this stood Major Mallard and two others who were unknown to the Deputy-Governor: one slight and elegant, the other big and brawny.

Major Mallard advanced. "Colonel Bishop, I have orders to arrest you. Your sword, sir!"

"By order of the Governor of Jamaica," said the elegant little man behind Major Mallard.

Bishop swung to him. "The Governor? Ye're mad!" He looked from one to the other. "I am the Governor."

"You were," said the little man dryly. "But we've changed that in your absence. You're broke for abandoning your post without due cause, and thereby imperiling the settlement over which you had charge. It's a serious matter, Colonel Bishop, as you may find. Considering that you held your office from the Government of King James, it is even possible that a charge of treason might lie against you. It rests with your successor entirely whether ye're hanged or not."

Bishop rapped out an oath, and then, shaken by a sudden fear: "Who the devil may you be?" he asked.

"I am Lord Willoughby, Governor General of His Majesty's colonies in the West Indies. You were informed, I think, of my coming."

The remains of Bishop's anger fell from him like a cloak. He broke into a sweat of fear. Behind him Lord Julian looked on, his handsome face suddenly white and drawn. "But, my lord . . ." began the Colonel.

"Sir, I am not concerned to hear your reasons," his lordship interrupted him harshly. "I am on the point of sailing and I have not the time. The Governor will hear you, and no doubt deal justly by you." He waved to Major Mallard, and Bishop, a crumpled, broken man, allowed himself to be led away.

To Lord Julian, who went with him, since none deterred him, Bishop expressed himself when presently he had sufficiently recovered. "This is one more item to the account of that scoundrel Blood," he said through his teeth. "My God, what a reckoning there will be when we meet!"

Major Mallard turned away his face that he might conceal his smile, and without further words led him a prisoner to the Governor's house, the house that so long had been Colonel Bishop's own residence. He was left to wait under guard in the hall, whilst Major Mallard went ahead to announce him.

Miss Bishop was still with Peter Blood when Major Mallard entered. His announcement startled them back to realities. "You will be merciful with him. You will spare him all you can for my sake, Peter," she pleaded.

"To be sure I will," said Blood. "But I'm afraid the circumstances won't."

She effaced herself, escaping into the garden, and Major Mallard fetched the Colonel.

"His excellency the Governor will see you now," said he, and threw wide the door.

Colonel Bishop staggered in and stood waiting.

At the table sat a man of whom nothing was visible but the top of a carefully curled black head. Then this head was raised, and a pair of blue eyes solemnly regarded the prisoner. Colonel Bishop made a noise in his throat, and, paralyzed by amazement, stared into the face of his excellency the Deputy-Governor of Jamaica, which was the face of the man he had been hunting in Tortuga to his present undoing.

The situation was best expressed to Lord Willoughby by van der Kuylen as the pair stepped aboard the Admiral's flagship.

"Id is fery boedigal!" he said, his blue eyes twinkling. "Cabdain Blood is fond of boedry—you remember de abble-blossoms. So? Ha, ha!"

About Stanley J. Weyman

During the half-century between the death of Alexandre Dumas *père* in 1870 and Rafael Sabatini's popularity in the 1920s, the leading writer of historical adventure fiction in English was Robert Louis Stevenson. Right behind him in popularity and influence was a man you in all probability have never heard of: Stanley J. Weyman. Swashbuckler authority Jessica Amanda Salmonson has called him the "greatest of the Yellow Nineties swashbuckling romancers," and his admirers included Stevenson himself and Oscar Wilde. Rafael Sabatini acknowledged Weyman as one of his most important influences.

Like Anthony Hope, Weyman was an English lawyer with no enthusiasm for the law who turned to writing for fulfillment. His first novel was *House of the Wolf* in 1890, but his breakthrough books were *A Gentleman of France* and *From the Memoirs of a Minister of France*, both in 1893. For the next fifteen years he published about a book a year, mostly novels but some collections, and was well received both critically and by the reading public, who gave him a number of bestsellers.

Weyman's novels are not only strong on action and romance, they are intelligent and thoughtful, with complex characters caught up in the challenges and moral dilemmas that accompany profound historical changes. His firm grasp of period setting and society reflect his depth of research and personal travel, but Weyman never veers off into historical digressions like Dumas: every detail is in support of story and character.

Weyman wrote relatively few short stories, which is a shame because his short stories are every bit as good as his novels. The one that follows is drawn from *In King's Byways*, published in 1902.

Crillon's Stake

STANLEY J. WEYMAN

On a certain wet night, in the spring of the year 1587, the rain was doing its utmost to sweeten the streets of old Paris: the kennels were aflood with it, and the March wind, which caused the crowded signboards to creak and groan on their bearings, and ever and anon closed a shutter with the sound of a pistol-shot, blew the downpour in sheets into exposed doorways, and drenched to the skin the few wayfarers who were abroad. Here and there a stray dog, bent over a bone, slunk away at the approach of a roisterer's footstep; more rarely a passenger, whose sober or stealthy gait whispered of business rather than pleasure, moved cowering from street to street, under such shelter as came in his way.

About two hours before midnight, a man issued somewhat suddenly from the darkness about the head of the Pont du Change and turned the corner into the Rue de St. Jacques la Boucherie, a street which ran parallel with the Quays, about half a mile east of the Louvre. His heavy cloak concealed his figure, but he made his way in the teeth of the wind with the spring and vigor of youth; and arriving presently at a doorway, which had the air of retiring modestly under a couple of steep dark gables, and yet was rendered conspicuous by the light which shone through the unglazed grating above it, he knocked sharply on the oak. After a short delay the door slid open of itself and the man entered. He showed none of a stranger's surprise at the invisibility of the porter, but after staying to shut the door, he advanced along a short passage, which was only partially closed at the further end by a high wooden screen. Coasting round this he entered a large low-roofed room, lighted in part by a dozen candles, in part by a fire which burned on a raised iron plate in the corner.

The air was thick with wood smoke, but the occupants of the room, a dozen men, seated, some at a long table, and some here and there in pairs, seemed able to recognize the newcomer through it, and hailed his appearance with a cry of welcome—a cry that had in it a ring of derision. One man who stood near the fire, impatiently kicking the logs with his spurred boots, turned, and seeing who it was moved towards him. "Welcome, M. de Bazan," he said briskly; "so you have come to resume our duel! I had given up hope of you."

"I am here," the newcomer answered. He spoke curtly, and as he did so he took off his horseman's cloak and laid it aside. The action disclosed a man scarcely twenty, moderately well dressed, and of slight though supple figure. His face wore an air of determination singular in one so young, and at variance with the quick suspicious glances with which he took in the scene. He did not waste time in staring, however, but quickly and with a business-like air he seated himself at a small wooden table which stood in a warm corner of the hearth, and directly under a brace of candles. Calling for a bottle of wine, he threw a bag of coin on the table; at the same time he hitched forward his sword until the pommel of the weapon lay across his left thigh; a sinister movement which the debauched and reckless looks of some of his companions seemed to justify. The man who had addressed him took his seat opposite, and the two, making choice of a pair of dice-boxes, began to play.

They did not use the modern game of hazard, but simply cast the dice, each taking it in turn to throw, and a nick counting as a drawn battle. The two staked sums higher than were usual in the company about them, and one by one, the other gamblers forsook their tables, and came and stood round. As the game proceeded, the young stranger's face grew more and more pale, his eyes more feverish. But he played in silence. Not so his backers. A volley of oaths and exclamations almost as thick as the wood smoke that in part shrouded the game, began to follow each cast of the dice. The air, one moment still and broken only by the hollow rattle of the dice in the box, rang the next instant with the fierce outburst of a score of voices.

The place, known as Simon's, was a gaming-house of the second class: frequented, as the shabby finery of some and the tarnished arms of others seemed to prove, by the poorer courtiers and the dubious adventurers who live upon the great. It was used in particular by the Guise faction, at this time in power; for though Henry of Valois was legal and nominal King of France, Henry of Guise, the head of the League, and the darling of Paris, imposed his will alike upon the King and the favorites. He enjoyed the substance of power; the King had no choice but to submit to his policy. In secret Henry the Third resented the position, and between his immediate servants and the arrogant followers of the Guises there was bitter enmity.

As the game proceeded, a trifle showed that the young player was either ignorant of politics, or belonged to a party rarely represented at Simon's. For some time he and his opponent had enjoyed equal luck. Then they doubled the stakes, and fortune immediately declared herself against him; with wondrous quickness his bag grew lank and thin, the pile at the other's elbow a swollen sliding heap. The perspiration began to stand on the young man's face. His hand trembled as he took out the last coins left in the bag and shoved them forward amid a murmur half of derision half of sympathy; for if he was a stranger from the country—that was plain, and they had recognized it at his first appearance among them three days before—at least he played bravely. His opponent, whose sallow face betrayed neither joy nor triumph, counted out an equal sum, and pushed it forward without a word. The young man took up the box, and for the first time seemed to hesitate; it could be seen that he had bitten his lip until it bled. "After you," he muttered at last, withdrawing his hand. He shrank from throwing his last throw.

"It is your turn," the other replied impassively, "but as you will." He shook the box, brought it down sharply on the table and raised it. "The Duke!" he said with an oath—he had thrown the highest possible. "Twelve is the game."

With a shiver the lad—he was little more than a lad, though in his heart, perhaps, the greatest gambler present—dashed down his box. He raised it. "The King!" he cried; "long life to him!" He had also thrown twelve. His cheek flushed a rosy red, and with a player's superstitious belief in his luck he regarded the check given to his opponent in the light of a presage of victory. They threw again, and he won by two points—nine to seven. Hurrah!

"King or Duke," the tall man answered, restraining by a look the interruption which more than one of the bystanders seemed about to offer, "the money is yours; take it."

"Let it lie," the young man answered joyously. His eyes sparkled. When the other had pushed an equal amount into the middle of the table, he threw again, and with confidence.

Alas! His throw was a deuce and an ace. The elder player threw four and two. He swept up the pile. "Better late than never," he said. And leaning back he looked about him with a grin of satisfaction.

The young man rose. The words which had betrayed that he was not of the Duke's faction, had cost him the sympathy the spectators had before felt for him; and no one spoke. It was something that they kept silence, that they did not interfere with him. His face, pale in the light of the candles which burned beside him, was a picture of despair. Suddenly, as if he bethought him of something, he sat down again, and with a shaking hand took from his neck a slender gold chain with a pendant ornament. "Will you stake against this?" he murmured with dry lips.

"Against that, or your sword, or your body, or anything but your soul!" the other answered with a reckless laugh. He took up the chain and examined it. "I will set you thirty crowns against it!" he said.

They threw and the young man lost.

"I will stake ten crowns against your sword if you like," the victor continued, eyeing the curiously chased pommel.

"No," the young man replied, stung by something in the elder's tone. "That I may want. But I will set my life against yours!"

A chuckle went round. "Bravo!" cried half a dozen voices. One man in the rear, whose business it was to enlist men in the Duke's guard, pressed forward, scenting a recruit.

"Your life against mine! With these?" the winner answered, holding up the dice.

"Yes, or as you please." He had not indeed meant with those; he had spoken in the soreness of defeat, intending a challenge.

The other shook his head. "No," he said, "no. No man can say that Michel Berthaud ever balked his player, but it is not a fair offer. You have lost all, my friend, and I have won all. I am rich, you are poor. 'Tis no fair stake. But I will tell you what I will do. I will set you your gold chain and seventy crowns—against your life if you like."

A roar of laughter hailed the proposal. "A hundred!" cried several, "a hundred!"

"Very well. The gold chain and a hundred. Be it so!"

"But my life?" the young man muttered, gazing at him in bewilderment. "Of what use will it be to you, M. Berthaud?"

"That is my business," was the dry answer. "If you lose, it is forfeit to me. That is all, and the long and the short of it. To be frank, I have a service which I wish you to perform for me."

"And if I will not perform it?"

"Then I will take your word as a gentleman that you will kill yourself. Observe, however, that if I win I shall allow you a choice, my friend."

He leaned back with that, meeting with a faint smile and half-lowered eyelids the various looks bent on him. Some stared, some nodded secret comprehension, some laughed outright, or nudged one another and whispered. For four evenings they, the habitués of the place, had watched this play duel go on, but they had not looked for an end so abnormal as this. They had known men stake wives and mistresses, love and honor, ay, their very clothes, and go home naked through the streets; for the streets of Paris saw strange things in those days. But life? Well, even that they had seen men stake in effect, once, twice, a hundred times; but never in so many words, never on a wager as novel as this. So with an amazement which no duel, fought as was the custom in that day, three to three, or six to six, would have evoked, they gathered round the little table under the candles and waited for the issue.

The young man shivered. Then, "I accept," he said slowly. In effect he was desperate, driven to his last straits. He had lost his all, the all of a young man sent up to Paris to make his fortune, with a horse, his sword, and a bag of crowns—the latter saved for him by a father's stern frugality, a mother's tender self-denial. A week ago he had never seen a game of chance. Then he had seen; the dice had fallen in his way, the devil of play, cursed legacy of some long-forgotten ancestor, had awoke within him, and this was the end. "I accept," he said slowly.

His opponent, still with his secretive smile, took up the caster. But a short, sturdy man, who was standing at his elbow, and who wore the colors of the Duke of Guise, intervened. "No, Michel," he said, with a good-natured glance at the young player. "Let the lad choose his bones, and throw first or last as he pleases."

"Right," said Berthaud, yawning. "It is no matter. My star is in the ascendant tonight. He will not win."

The young man took up the box, shook it, hesitated, swallowed, and threw seven!

Berthaud threw carelessly—seven!

Some shouted, some drew a sharp breath, or whispered an oath. These wild spirits, who had faced death often in one form or another, were still children, and still in a new thing found a new pleasure.

"Your star may be in the ascendant," the man muttered who had intervened before, "but it—well, it twinkles, Michel."

Berthaud did not answer. The young man made him a sign to throw. He threw again—eight.

The young man threw with a hand that scarcely dared to let the dice go. Seven! He had lost.

An outburst might have been expected, some cry of violence, of despair. It did not come. And a murmur passed round the circle. "Berthaud will recruit him," growled one. "A queer game," muttered another, and thought hard. Nor did the men go back to their tables. They waited to see what would follow, what would come of it. For the young man who had lost sat staring at the table like one in a dream; until presently his opponent reaching out a hand touched his sleeve. "Courage!" Berthaud said, a flicker of triumph in his eye, "a word with you aside. No need of despair, man. You have but to do as I ask, and you will see sixty yet."

Obedient to his gesture the young man rose, and the other drawing him aside began to talk to him in a low voice. The remaining players loitering about the deserted table could not hear what was said; but one or two by feigning to strike a sudden blow, seemed to pass on their surmises to those round them. One thing was clear. The lad objected to the proposal made, objected fiercely and with vehemence; and at last submitted only with reluctance. Submit in the end, however, he did, for after some minutes of this private talk he went to his cloak, and avoiding, as it seemed, his fellows' eyes, put it on. Berthaud accompanied him to the door, and the winner's last words were audible. "That is all," he said; "succeed in what I impose, M. de Bazan, and I cry quits, and you shall have fifty crowns for your pains. Fail, and you will but be paying your debt. But you will not fail. Remember, half an hour after midnight. And courage!"

The young man nodded sullenly, and drawing his cloak about his throat, went through the passage to the street. The night was a little older than when he had entered, otherwise it was unchanged. The rain was still falling; the wind still buffeted the creaking shutters and the swinging sign-boards. But the man? He had entered, thinking nothing of rain or wind, thinking little even of the horse and furniture, and the good clothes made under his mother's eye, which he had sacrificed to refill his purse. The warmth of the play fever coursing through his veins had clad him in proof against cold and damp and the depression of the gloomy streets, even against the thought of home. And for the good horse, and the laced shirts and the gold braid, the luck could not run against him again! He would win all back, and the crowns to boot.

So he had thought as he went in. And now? He stood a moment in the dark, narrow chasm of a street, and looked up, letting the rain cool his brow; looked up, and, seeing a wrack of clouds moving swiftly across the slit of stormy sky visible between the overhanging roofs, faced in a dull amazement the fact that he who now stood in the darkness, bankrupt even in life, was the same man who had entered Paris so rich in hope and youth and life a week—only a week—before. He remembered—it was an odd thing to occur to him when his thoughts should have been full of the events of the last hour—a fault of which he had been guilty down there in the country; and of which, taking advantage of a wrathful father's offer to start him in Paris, he had left the weaker sinner to bear the brunt. And it seemed to him that here was his punishment. The old grey house at home, quaint and weather-beaten, rose before him. He saw his mother's herb-garden, the great stackyard, and the dry moat, half filled with blackberry bushes, in which he had played as a boy. And on him fell a strange calm, between apathy and resignation. This, then, was his punishment. He would bear it like a man. There should be no flinching a second time, no putting the burden on others' shoulders, no self-sparing at another's cost.

He started to walk briskly in the direction of the Louvre. But when he had gained the corner of the open space in front of the palace, whence he had a view of the main gate between the two tennis courts, he halted and looked up and down as if he hesitated. A watch-fire smoldering and sputtering in the rain was burning dully before the drawbridge; the forms of one or two men, apparently sentinels, were dimly visible about it. After standing in doubt more than a minute, Bazan glided quickly to the porch of the church of St. Germain l'Auxerrois, and disappeared in the angle between it and the cloisters.

He had been stationary in this position for some half-hour—in what bitterness of spirit, combating what regrets and painful thoughts it is possible only to imagine—when a slight commotion took place at the gate which faced him. Two men came out in close converse, and stood a moment looking up as if speaking of the weather. They separated then, and one who even by that uncertain light could be seen to be a man of tall, spare presence, came across the open space towards the end of the Rue des Fosses, which passed beside the cloisters. He had just entered the street, when Bazan, who had been closely watching his movements, stepped from the shadow of the houses and touched his sleeve.

The tall man recoiled sharply as he turned. He laid his hand on his sword and partly drew it. "Who are you?" he said, trying in the darkness to make out the other's features.

"M. de Crillon, is it not?" the young man asked.

"Yes. And you, young sir?"

"My name is Claude de Bazan, but you do not know me. I have a word to say to you."

"You have chosen an odd time, my friend."

"Some things are always timely," the young fellow answered, the excitement under which he labored and the occasion imparting a spice of flippancy to his tone. "I come to warn you that your life is in danger. Do not go alone, M. de Crillon, or pass this way at night! And whatever you do, walk for the future in the middle of the street!"

"For the warning I am obliged to you," the tall man answered, his voice cool and satirical, while his eyes continued to scan the other's features. "But, I say again, you have chosen a strange time to give it, young sir. Moreover, your name is new to me, and I do not know your face."

"Nor need you," said Bazan.

"Ay, but I think I need, craving your pardon," replied the tall, spare man with some sternness. "I am not wont to be scared by little things, nor will I give any man the right to say that he has frightened me with a lighted turnip."

"Will it convince you if I tell you that I came hither to kill you?" the young man cried impetuously.

"Yes, if you will say also why you did not—at least try?" Crillon answered drily.

Bazan had not meant to explain himself; he had proposed to give his warning, and to go. But on the impulse of the moment, carried away by his excitement, he spoke, and told the story, and Crillon, after leading him aside, so that a building sheltered them from the rain, listened. He listened, who knew all the dark plans, all the scandals, all the jealousies, all the vile or frantic schemings of a court, that, half French, half Italian, mingled so grimly force and fraud. Nay, when all was told, when Bazan, passing lightly over the resolution he had formed to warn the victim instead of attacking him, came suddenly and lamely to a stop, he still for a time stood silent. At last, "And what will you do now, my friend?" he asked.

"Go back," the young man answered.

"And then?"

"Pay my debt."

The courtier swore a great oath—it was his failing—and with sudden violence he seized his companion by the arm, and hurried him into the roadway, and along the street. "To Simon's!" he muttered.

"To Simon's, my friend. I know the place. I will cut that villain Berthaud's throat."

"But what shall I be the better of that?" the young man answered, somewhat bitterly. "I have none the less lost, and must pay."

Crillon stopped short, the darkness hiding alike his face and his feelings. "So!" he said slowly, "I did not think of that! No, I did not think of that. But do you mean it? What, if I kill him?"

"I have played for my life, and lost," Bazan answered proudly. "I promised, and I am a gentleman."

"Pheugh!" Crillon whistled. He swore again, and stood. He was a great man, and full of expedients, but the position was novel. Yet, after a minute's thought, he had an idea. He started off again, taking Bazan's arm, and impelling him onwards, with the same haste and violence. "To Simon's! to Simon's!" he cried as before. "Courage, my friend, I will play him for you and win you; I will redeem you. After all, it is simple, absolutely simple."

"He will not play for me," the young man answered despondently. Nevertheless he suffered himself to be borne onwards. "What will you set against me?"

"Anything, everything!" his new friend cried recklessly. "Myself, if necessary. Courage, M. de Bazan, courage! What Crillon wills, Crillon does. You do not know me yet, but I have taken a fancy to you, I have!" He swore a grisly oath. "And I will make you mine."

He gave the young man no time for further objection, but, holding him firmly by the arm, he hurried him through the streets to the door below the two gables. On this he knocked with the air of one who had been there before and to whom all doors opened. In the momentary pause before it yielded Bazan spoke. "Will you not be in danger here?" he asked, wondering much.

"It is a Guise house? True, it is. But there is danger everywhere. No man dies more than once or before God wills it! And I am Crillon!"

The superb air with which he said this last prepared Bazan for what followed. The moment the door was opened, Crillon pushed through the doorway, and with an assured step strode down the passage. He turned the corner of the screen and stood in the room; and, calmly smiling at the group of startled, astonished faces which were turned on him, he drew off his cloak and flung it over his left arm. His height at all times made him a conspicuous figure; this night he was fresh from court. He wore black and silver, the hilt of his long sword was jeweled, the Order of the Holy Ghost glittered on his breast; and this fine array seemed to render more shabby the pretentious finery of the third-rate adventurers before him. He saluted them coolly. "It is a wet night, gentlemen," he said.

Some of those who sat farthest off had risen, and all had drawn together as sheep club at sight of the wolf. One of them answered sullenly that it was.

"You think I intrude, gentlemen?" he returned, smiling pleasantly, drinking in as homage the stir his entrance had caused. For he was vain. "I want only an old friend, M. Michel Berthaud, who is here, I think?"

"And for what do you want him?" the tall dark player answered defiantly; he alone of those present seemed in a degree a match for the newcomer, though even his gloomy eyes fell before Crillon's easy stare. "For what do you want me?"

"To propose a little game to you," Crillon answered; and he moved down the room, apparently at his ease. "My friend here has told me of his ill luck. He is resolved to perform his bargain. But first, M. Berthaud, I have a proposal to make to you. His life is yours. You have won it. Well, I will set you five hundred crowns against it."

The scowl on Berthaud's face did not relax. "No," he said contemptuously. "I will not play with you, M. de Crillon. Let the fool die. What is he to you?"

"Nothing, and yet I have a fancy to win him," Crillon replied lightly. "Come, I will stake a thousand crowns against him! A thousand crowns for a life! *Mon Dieu*," he added, with a whimsical glance at Bazan, "but you are dear, my friend!"

Indeed, half a score of faces shown with cupidity, and twice as many bearded lips watered. A thousand crowns! A whole thousand crowns! But to the surprise of most—a few knew their man—Berthaud shook his head.

"No," he said, "I will not play! I won his life, and I will have it."

"Fifteen hundred crowns. I will set that! Fifteen—"

"No!"

"Two thousand, then! Two thousand, man! And I will throw in my chain. It is worth five hundred more."

"No! No! No!"

"Then, say what you will play for!" the great man roared, his face swelling with rage. "Thousand devils and all tonsured! I have a mind to win his life. What will you have against it?"

"Against it?"

"Ay!"

"Yours!" said M. Berthaud, very softly.

Bazan drew in his breath—sharply; otherwise the silence was so intense that the fall of the wood-ashes from the dying fire could be heard. The immense, the boundless audacity of the proposal made some smile and some start. But none smiled so grimly as M. Michel Berthaud the challenger and none started so little as M. de Crillon, the challenged.

"A high bid!" he said, lifting his chin with something almost of humor; and then glancing round him, as a wolf might glance if the sheep turned on him. "You ask much, M. Berthaud."

"I will ask less, then," replied Berthaud, with irony. "If I win, I will give you his life. He shall go free whether you win or lose, M. de Crillon."

"That is much!" with answering irony.

"Much or little—"

"It is understood?"

"It is," Berthaud rejoined with a sarcastic bow.

"Then I accept!" Crillon cried: and with a movement so brisk that some recoiled, he sat down at the table. "I accept. Silence!" he continued, turning sharply upon Bazan, whose cry of remonstrance rang above the astonished murmur of the bystanders. "Silence, fool!" He struck the table. "It is my will. Fear nothing! I am Crillon, and I do not lose."

There was a superb self-confidence in the man, an arrogance, a courage, which more than anything else persuaded his hearers that he was in earnest, that he was not jesting with them.

"The terms are quite understood," he proceeded grimly. "If I win, we go free, M. Berthaud. If I lose, M. de Bazan goes free, and I undertake on the honor of a nobleman to kill myself before daylight. Shall I say within six hours? I have affairs to settle!"

Probably no one in the room felt astonishment equal to that of Berthaud. A faint color tinged his sallow cheeks; a fierce gleam of joy flashed in his eyes. But all he said was, "Yes, I am satisfied."

"Then throw!" said Crillon, and leaning forward he took a candle from a neighboring table and placed it beside him. "My friend," he added, speaking to Bazan with earnest gravity, "I advise you to be quiet. If you do not we shall quarrel."

His smile was as easy, his manner as unembarrassed, his voice as steady, as when he had entered the room. The old gamesters who stood round the table, and had seen, with interest indeed and some pity, but with no great emotion, a man play his last stake, saw this, saw a man stake his life for a whim, with very different feelings; with astonishment, with admiration, with a sense of inferiority that did not so much gall their pride as awaken their interest. For the moment, the man who was above death, who risked it for a fancy, a trifle, a momentary gratification, was a demigod. "Throw!" repeated Crillon, heedless and apparently unconscious of the stir round him: "Throw! But beware of that candle! Your sleeve is in it."

It was; it was singeing. Berthaud moved the candle, and as if his enemy's *sang froid* wounded him, he threw savagely, dashing down the dice on the table and lifting the box with a gesture of defiance. He had thrown aces only.

"So!" murmured his opponent quietly. "Is that all? A thousand crowns to a hundred that I better that! Five hundred to a hundred that I double it! Will no one take me? Then I throw. Courage, my friend. I am Crillon!"

He threw: an ace and a deuce.

"I waste nothing," he said.

But few heard the words—his opponent perhaps and one or two others—for from end to end the room rang and the oaken rafters shook with a great cry of "Long live Crillon! The brave Crillon!"— A cry which rose from a score of throats. Then and onwards till the day of his death, many years later, he was known throughout France by no other name. "Hang yourself, brave Crillon. We have fought today, and you were not there!" is not yet forgotten—nay, never will be forgotten—in a land where, more than in any other, the memories of the past have been swept away.

He rose from the table, bowing grandly, superbly, arrogantly. "Adieu, M. Berthaud—for the present," he said; and had he not seemed too proud to threaten, a threat might have underlain his words. "Adieu, gentlemen," he continued, throwing on his cloak. "A good night to you, and equal fortune. M. de Bazan, I will trouble you to accompany me? You have exchanged, let me tell you, one taskmaster for another."

The young man's heart was too full for words, and making no attempt to speak, or to thank his benefactor, before those who had seen the deed, he followed him from the room. Crillon did not speak or halt until they stood in the Rue des Fosses; nor even there, for after a momentary hesitation he passed through it, and led the way to the middle of the open space before the Louvre. Here he stopped and touched his companion on the breast. "Now," he said, "we can speak with freedom, my friend. You wish to thank me? Do not. Listen to me instead. I have saved your life, ay, that have I; but I hold it at my will? Say, is it not so? Well, I too, in my turn wish you to do something for me."

"Anything!" said the young man, passionately. The sight of the other's strange daring had stirred his untried nature to its depths. "You have but to ask and have."

"Very well," Crillon answered gravely, "be it so. I take you at your word. Though, mind you, M. de Bazan, 'tis no light thing I ask. It is something," pausing, "from which I shrink myself."

"Then it is nothing you ask me to do," Bazan answered.

"Not so," the courtier replied, though he looked far from ill-pleased by the compliment. "Listen. Tomorrow the king sups at the house of Madame de Sauves. I shall be with him. Her house is in the Rue de l'Arbre Sec, two doors from the convent. Here are a hundred crowns. Dress yourself so that you may appear as one of my gentlemen, and wait near the gates till I

come. Then follow me in, and at supper stand behind my chair, as the others of my suite will stand."

"And is that all?" Bazan asked in astonishment.

"No, not quite," Crillon answered dryly. "The rest I will whisper in your ear as I pass. Only do what I bid you boldly and faithfully, my friend, and afterwards, if all be well, I will not forget you."

"I am yours! Do with me as you will!" Bazan protested.

But to mortals the unknown is ever terrible; and for twenty-four hours Bazan had the unknown before him. What could that be from which Crillon himself said that he shrank—a man so brave? It could not be death, for that he had risked on the lightest, the flimsiest, the most fantastic provocation. Then what could it be? Bazan turned the question in his mind, turned it a hundred times that night, turned it a hundred times as he went about his preparations next day. Turned it and turned it, but instinctively, though no injunctions to that effect had been given him, took care to show himself as little in possible in public, and especially to shun all places where he might meet those who had been present at that strange game at Simon's.

A quarter before nine on the next evening saw him waiting with a beating heart outside the house in the Rue de l'Arbre Sec. He formed one of a crowd of lackeys and linkboys, citizens, apprentices, and chance passers who had been attracted to the spot by the lights and by the guards in the royal livery, who already, though the king was not yet come, kept the entrance to the courtyard. Bazan pushed himself with some difficulty into the front rank and there waited, scanning with feverish eagerness everyone who entered.

Time passed and no Crillon appeared, though presently a great shouting along the street proclaimed the approach of the Duke of Guise, and that nobleman passed slowly in, noting with a falcon's eye the faces of the bowing throng. He was a man of grand height and imperial front—a great scar seeming to make the latter more formidable—his smile a trifle supercilious, his eyes somewhat near one another; and under his glance Bazan felt for the moment small and mean. A little later, from the talk of those about him, the young man learned that the king was drawing near, and Henry's coach, surrounded by a dozen of the Forty-five, lumbered along the street. It was greeted with comparative coldness, only those who stood under the guards' eyes performing a careless salute.

Bazan was no Parisian, though for the present in Paris, and no Leaguer, though a Roman Catholic; and he forgot his present errand in the excitement of his rustic loyalty. Raising his bonnet, he cried loudly *"Vive le Roi!"*—cried it more than once.

There were six in the coach, but Henry, whose pale meager face with its almond eyes and scanty beard permitted no mistake, remarked the salutation and the giver, and his look cast the young man into a confusion which nearly cost him dearly; for it was only as the guards closed round the coach that he perceived Crillon sitting in the nearer boot. The moment he did see him he pushed forward among the running footmen who followed the coach, and succeeded in entering with it.

The courtyard, crowded with gentlemen, lackeys and torch-bearers, was a scene of great confusion, and Bazan had no difficulty in approaching Crillon and exchanging a sentence with him. That effected, so completely was he confounded by the order whispered in his ear, that he observed nothing more until he found himself in a long gallery, waiting with many others attached to the great men's suites, while the magnificoes themselves talked together at the upper end. By listening to the gossip round him he learned that one dark handsome man among the latter was Alphonso d'Ornano, often called the Corsican Captain. A second was M. d'O, the Governor of Paris; a third, the Count of Soissons. But he had scarcely time to note these, or the novel and splendid scene in which he stood, before the double doors at the end of the gallery were thrown widely open, and amid a sudden hush the great courtiers passed into the supper room in which the king, the Duke of Guise, and several ladies, already stood or sat in their places, having entered by another door. Bazan pressed in with the flock of attendant gentlemen, and seeing Crillon preparing to sit down not far from the dais and canopy which marked the king's chair, he took his stand against the wall behind him.

If the words which Crillon had dropped into his ear had not occupied three-fourths of his thoughts, Bazan would have felt a keener admiration of the scene before him; which, as was natural, surpassed in luxury anything the country lad had ever imagined. The room, paneled and ceiled with cedar, was hung with blue velvet and lighted by a hundred tapers. The table gleamed with fine napery and gold plate, with Palissy ware and Cellini vases; and these, with the rich dresses and jewels and fair shoulders of the ladies, combined to form a beautiful interior which resounded with the babble of talk and laughter. It was hard to detect danger lurking under these things, under the silk, within the flashing, gleaming cups, behind smiling eyes; still harder to discern below these fair appearances a peril from which a Crillon shrank.

But to Bazan, as he waited with tortured nerves, these things were nothing. They were no more than fair flowers to the man who espies the coils of a snake among the blossoms. Crillon's whisper had revealed all to him—all, in one brief sentence; so that when he presently recognized Michel Berthaud standing near the upper end of the table and on the farther side of it, in attendance upon the Duke of Guise, he felt no astonishment, but only a shrewd suspicion of the quarter from which the danger might be expected.

The king, a man of thirty-seven, so effeminate in appearance that it was hard to believe he had seen famous fields and had once bidden fair to be a great Captain, was nursing a dog on his lap, the while he listened with a weary air to the whispers of the beautiful woman who sat next him. Apparently he had a niggard ear even for her witcheries, and little appetite save for the wine flask. Lassitude lived in his eyes, his long thin fingers trembled. Bazan watched him drain his goblet of wine almost as soon as he sat down, and watched him, too, hold out the gold cup to be filled again. The task was performed by an assiduous hand, and for a moment the king poised the cup in his fingers, speaking to his neighbor the while. Then he laid it down, but his hand did not quit its neighborhood.

The next moment the room rang with a cry of alarm and indignation, and every face was turned one way. Bazan with unparalleled audacity had stepped forward, had seized the sacred cup almost from the royal hand, and drained it!

While some sprang from their seats, two or three seized the culprit and held him fast. One more enthusiastic than the others or more keenly sensitive to the outrage of which he had been guilty, aimed a fierce blow at his breast with a poniard. The stroke was well meant, nay, was well directed; but it was adroitly intercepted by M. de Crillon, who had been among the first to rise. With a blow of his sheathed sword he sent the dagger spinning towards the ceiling.

"Back!" he cried, in a voice of thunder, placing himself before the culprit. "Stand back, I say! I will answer to the king for all!"

He cleared a space before him with his scabbard, and a quick signal brought to his side the two guards at the nearest door, who were men of his command. These, crossing their pikes before the prisoner, secured him from immediate attack. By this time all in the room had risen save the king, who appeared less moved than any by the incident. At this point he raised a hand to procure silence.

"Is he mad?" he asked calmly. "What is it, Crillon?"

"I will satisfy your Grace," the courtier answered. But the next moment, with a sudden change of tone, he cried loudly and rapidly, "Stop that man, I beg you, d'Ornano! Stop him!"

The warning came too late. The Corsican sprang indeed to the door, but the crowd impeded him; and the man to whom Crillon referred—the same who had struck at Bazan, and who was no other than Berthaud—got to it first, slipped out and was gone from sight before those near the entrance had recovered from their surprise.

"Follow him," Crillon cried loudly. "Seize him at all hazards! *Mort de Dieu!* He has outwitted us at last."

"His Majesty has asked, M. de Crillon," said one at the table, speaking in the haughty, imperious tone of a man who never spoke unheeded, "what is the meaning of all this? Perhaps you will kindly satisfy him."

"I will satisfy him," Crillon answered, grimly fixing his eyes on the other's handsome face. "And you, too, M. de Guise. An attempt has been made to poison my master. This young man, observing that a strange hand poured the king's wine, has saved his Majesty's life by taking the poison himself!"

Henry of Guise laughed scornfully. "A likely story!" he said.

"And in my house!" Madame de Sauves cried in the same tone. "His Majesty will not believe that I—"

"I said nothing against Madame de Sauves," Crillon answered, with firmness. "For the rest, let the king be judge. The issue is simple. If the lad go scatheless, there was no poison in that cup and I am a liar. If he suffer, then let the king say who lies!"

A close observer might have seen an uneasy expression flit across more than one face, darken more than one pair of eyes. Crillon remained on his guard facing the table, his eyes keenly vigilant. The Count of Soissons, one of the younger Bourbons, had already stepped to the king's side and taken place by his chair, his hand on his hilt. D'Ornano, who had despatched two guards after Berthaud, openly drew his long sword and placed himself on the other side of the dais. Nor was suspicion confined to their party. Half a dozen gentlemen had risen to their feet about the Duke of Guise, who continued to sit with folded arms, content to smile. He was aware that at the worst here in Paris he was safe; perhaps he was innocent of harm or intent.

The main effect, however, of Crillon's last words was to draw many eyes, and amongst them the king's, to the prisoner's face. Bazan was leaning against the wall, the cup still in his grasp. As they turned with a single movement towards him, his face began to grow a shade paler, a spasm moved his lips, and after the interval of a moment the cup fell from his hand to the ground. Thrusting himself with a convulsive movement from the wall, he put out his hands and groped with them as if he could no longer see; until, one of them meeting the pike of the nearest guard, he tried to support himself by this. At the same time he muttered hoarsely,

"M. de Crillon, you saw it! We are—we are quits!"

He would have fallen on that, but the men caught him in their arms and held him up, amid a murmur of horror; to many brave men death in this special form is appalling. Here and there a woman shrieked; one fainted. Meanwhile, the young man's face was becoming livid; his neck seemed to stiffen, his eyes to protrude. The king looked at him and shuddered. "Saint Denis!" he muttered, the perspiration standing on his brow. "What an escape! What an escape! Can nothing be done for him?"

"I will try, Sire," Crillon answered, abandoning for the first time his attitude of watchfulness. Drawing a small phial from his pocket, he directed one of the guards to force open the lad's teeth, and then himself poured the contents of the bottle between them.

"Good lad," he muttered to himself, "he has drained the cup. I bade him drink only half. It would have been enough. But he is young and strong. He may surmount it."

The rest looked on, some in curiosity, some in pity, some in secret apprehension. It was the Duke of Guise who put into words the thoughts of many. "Those," he said scornfully, "who find the antidote, may know the poison, M. de Crillon."

"What do you mean, duke?" Crillon replied passionately, as he sprang to his feet. "That I was in this? That I know more than I have told of it? If so, you lie, sir; and you know it!"

"I know it?" the duke cried, his eyes aflame, his cheeks reddening. Never had he heard such words. "Do you dare to insinuate—that I know more of this plot than yourself—if plot there be?"

"Enough!" said the king, rising in great haste, and with a face which betrayed his emotion. "Silence, gentlemen! Silence! And you, my cousin, not another word, I command you! Who poured out the wine?"

"A villain called Berthaud," Crillon answered promptly and fiercely, "who was in attendance upon the Duke of Guise!"

"He was not in attendance on me!" the duke answered, with spirit.

"Then on Madame de Sauves."

"I know nothing of him!" cried that lady, hysterically. "I never spoke to the man in my life. I do not know him!"

"Enough!" the king said with decision; but the gloom on his brow grew darker. "Enough. Until Berthaud is found, let no more be said. Cousin," he continued to the Count of Soissons, "you will see us home. D'Ornano, we return at once, and you will accompany us. For M. de Crillon, we commit to him the care of this young man, to whom we appear to be indebted, and whose thought for us we shall not forget. Madame, I kiss your hand."

Guise's salutation he acknowledged only by a grave bow. The last of the Valois could at times exert himself, could at times play again the hero of Jarnac and Montcontour, could even assume a dignity no whit less than that of Guise. As he retired all bowed low to him, and the greater part of the assemblage—even those who had not attended him to the house—left in his train. In three minutes Crillon, a couple of inferior officers, and a handful of guards alone remained around the young man.

"He will recover," Crillon said, speaking to the officer next to him. "He is young, and they did not dare to make the dose too strong. We shall not, however, convict anyone now, unless Berthaud speaks."

"Berthaud is dead."

"What?"

"As dead as Clovis," the lieutenant repeated calmly. "He is lying in the passage, M. de Crillon."

"Who killed him?" cried Crillon, leaping up in a rage. "Who dared to kill him? Not those fools of guards when they knew it was his evidence we wanted."

"No, no," said the other man coolly. "They found him dead not twenty paces from the house. He was a doomed man when he passed through the door. You understand, M. de Crillon? He knew too much to live."

"*Mort de Dieu!*" cried Crillon, raising his hands in admiration. "How clever they are! Not a thing forgotten! Well, I will to the king and tell him. It will put him on his guard. If I had not contrived to try the draught there and then, I could not have convinced him; and if I had not by a lucky hazard won this young man last night, I might have whistled for one to try it! But I must go."

Yet he lingered a minute to see how the lad progressed. The convulsions which had for a time wracked Bazan's vigorous frame had ceased, and a profuse perspiration was breaking out on his brow.

"Yes, he will recover," said Crillon again, and with greater confidence.

As if the words had reached Bazan's brain, he opened his eyes.

"I did it!" he muttered. "I did it. We are quits, M. de Crillon."

"Not so!" cried the other, stooping impetuously and embracing him. "Not quits! The balance is against me now, but I will redress it. Be easy; your fortune is made, M. de Bazan. While James Berthon de Crillon lives you shall not lack a friend!"

He kept his word. There can be little doubt that the Laurence de Bazan who held high office under the Minister Sully, and in particular rose to be Deputy Superintendant of the Finances in Guienne, was our young Bazan. This being so, it is clear that he outlived by many years his patron: for Crillon, *"le brave Crillon,"* whose whim it was to dare greatly, and on small occasion, died early in the seventeenth century—in his bed— and lies under a famous stone in the Cathedral of Avignon. Whereas we find Bazan still flourishing, and a person of consequence at Court, when Richelieu came to the height of his power. Nevertheless on him there remains no stone; only some sketch of the above, and a crabbed note at the foot of a dusty page in a dark library.

About Marion Polk Angellotti

Marion Polk Angellotti (1887-1979) was the daughter of a California judge who took up writing historical adventures in her early twenties, and very successfully so: her first major sale was a novel about the Renaissance mercenary captain Sir John Hawkwood to the prestigious *Adventure* magazine. It received book publication in 1911 as *Sir John Hawkwood: A Tale of the White Company,* followed by two novels of medieval France, *The Burgundian* (1912), and *Harlette* (1913).

Angellotti then took a break from writing to travel in Europe, and was there through most of the First World War, eventually volunteering to work for the Red Cross in France. She assisted at a hospital for severely wounded soldiers, and then was herself injured when the military truck she was riding in overturned. After she returned to the United States her writing took a darker, more serious turn, as she wrote novels about the war and its aftermath. However, she is remembered today mainly for her series of Hawkwood stories—of which this is the last and most telling, from *Adventure* magazine of July, 1915.

The Black Death

MARION POLK ANGELLOTTI

It is the law of life that none of us can work on forever without rest. Even the stormy petrel dozes in fair weather, and the best hunting dog when the chase is ended, will stretch himself before the fire, drop his head on his paws and snore away the night. So it is with soldiers, too; for at the very worst of a siege there will often come a lull, and then the odds are that the combatants, instead of using the breathing-space to recommend their souls to heaven, will fall to earth like so many logs and be fast asleep within the instant.

For my part, I am as well pleased with my trade as the next man, let him be who he may, and if you care to ask questions about me in Italy you can soon learn that I am not called a do-nothing. But for all that, being human like other folk, I have my lazy moments, and I recall—with good reason, as you shall hear—a certain day some five years past, when I felt that unless I could banish wars, plots, and treaties from my thoughts for a bit, I should shortly go mad.

No doubt I experienced this perverse desire, as it seems a man's nature to do, simply because there appeared to be no chance of gratifying it. I had just ended a three-months' campaign against a veritable hornet's nest of foes.

The fighting had been desperate, and to crown all, the plague—or the Black Death, to give it the name by which it goes hereabouts—had been afoot in the neighborhood and had cost me more men than I could spare. Now, with a safe conduct and a score of troopers, I was on my way back to Florence through the conquered, sullen territory, to settle with the Signoria what peace terms should be granted, and to return hot-foot to enforce them.

Altogether, the future bade fair to prove sufficiently lively, and when on the heels of my wish for rest I saw my own little lordship of Montecchio rise before me, I promptly told myself that it was a pity indeed if I might not spend a night now and again about my own affairs, and that, if the heavens fell thereafter, I meant to forget for a few hours all things in the world save good food and wine.

It was scarce a place where most men would have cared to take their leisure, this Montecchio, for it perched on a hill in the very heart of the Arezzo, between Cortona and Castiglione, with Siena to westward—nestled in, you perceive, among the cities which I had just been fighting, and which at intervals I had fought for years. But to me at least its disadvantages had proved a godsend, and I was wont to regard them with a most indulgent eye, since the prudent Florentines had been moved to offer me the stronghold for the very reason that the game of defending it against its hostile neighbors seemed to them not worth the candle.

Well, I had taken the gift with a sober face, rebuilt its walls, and put a castellan in charge to hold it in the teeth of whoever might attack.

Never yet, as I watched my revenues fatten, had I regretted my decision, but never had I recalled it with such complacency as on the present night, when I ate a hearty meal before my own castle hearthstone and for the nonce consigned all Italian squabbles to the deuce.

Having taken my last mouthful, I was in a mood for some cheery talk over my wine, so it put me in the best possible humor when steps sounded outside and the door opened to reveal my castellan, one Roger Thornbury, who had been an officer of my White Company until I sent him to rule Montecchio.

We had been acquainted in England, he and I, in the days when we were a pair of lads with our heads full of John-o'-dreams visions of soldiering; and as he was the only man in Italy of whom I could say as much, I had for him a certain fondness which he returned by a real devotion. So I greeted him now with a good deal of cordiality. "Ha, Roger!" I cried. "Draw your chair to the fire and fill your cup! Well, and how have affairs marched since my last visit, eh? If you have not squeezed the last *soldo* of rents and cattle tolls from my tenants, you had best tremble! Come, hand them over, man," and I pointed at the fat bag in his hold, which clinked most comfortably as he advanced.

I had thought he would pay my words the tribute of a chuckle, since it was an old jest between us that I should pick flaws in his reckoning and accuse him of filling his pockets at my expense. But to my discomfiture, he looked as solemn as a man who attends a funeral. "It has been a good year," he informed me sepulchrally, rather as if he were announcing that everyone in Montecchio was dead.

From past experience I knew only too well what this half grim, half desperate manner meant. No doubt because I was his one link with a world of splendor and success which he could never hope to touch in person, Roger paid me the compliment to make me his chief interest in life, and at risk of seeming ungrateful I must say that he showed his solicitude in such a fashion as I would have endured for nothing on earth save old time's sake.

For example, although he was, to do him justice, perfectly indifferent to danger on his own account, he took any peril of mine with a seriousness little short of maddening, and whenever he learned that in my war-making I had run some risk which seemed to him a trifle too daring, he thought it his part as my oldest friend to rate me for it like any schoolboy. Something of the sort was in the wind now. My visions of a cheerful evening began to go a-glimmering, together with my temper.

"Well, what is amiss?" I snapped irritably. "Do you take me for the plague in person, that you look so glum? And can you not sit down, as I bade you? The saints grant me patience, for I need it when I get a welcome like this!"

My castellan raised both hands and shook them like a man beside himself. "Why did you come here, Sir John? What ill wind blew you to us now, of all times?" he stormed at me by way of a hospitable greeting. "I tell you I would give Montecchio, yes gladly, to have you safe in Florence—"

"Upon my word!" I exclaimed, staring at him. "Then perhaps you will do me the favor to recall, my friend, that Montecchio is mine and not yours, and that I have a fancy to keep it a while longer!"

His response was mystifying: "Are you mad, Sir John, to take your ease before the fire at a time like this?" he cried. "Come out with me, follow me for one half-hour with a shut mouth and open eyes—then tell me, if you can, that some black mischief is not brewing hereabouts!"

The hall was warm, the wine good, and my chair comfortable; so his request was by no means welcome, and I told him flatly that if I did any such thing, the fiends had my leave to fly away with me immediately thereafter. At this he subsided into the chimney corner, a picture of gloom.

But if I thought he had given up the battle, I was doomed to be disappointed. "I expected as much," he croaked like a raven. "Never yet, Sir John, did I see you turn a hand to guard your life. It is plain you want to die. And her ladyship? It matters nothing, eh, that she should be left a widow and rue the day when she gave up so much to wed a soldier who will not even try to foil his foes?"

The wretch had an almost diabolical gift for piercing my armor, and that last thrust of his worked on me as nothing else would have done. I held out for some five minutes more out of pure stubbornness and then rose sulkily, picked up my cloak from the nearby settle, and stalked stiffly and wearily out of the hall in my castellan's triumphant wake.

Night had fallen three hours since, and the moon was up. Passing through the courtyard—where I sighed enviously to see my troopers, a deal luckier than their master, contentedly doing justice to the wine I had sent out—we entered the town by the castle gate.

Montecchio is a small place, and its people are for the most part sheep-tenders or field-tillers who cannot stop abed after cock-crow. So all things appeared wrapped in slumber as my castellan, with a manner which reminded me forcibly of a night thief, led me down a narrow street and into a yet narrower one, and finally, always imploring me fervently to move without noise, drew me into a tiny dark doorway, from which a winding staircase led up into blackness.

"Sit down, Sir John," said he in an impressive whisper. "It will be but for a moment. The hour is nearly come!"

To this cryptic utterance I returned no answer save a shrug, for I was thoroughly out of patience with him and his fool's errand. Never did I enter these walls, I told myself, but he had some such mare's nest to regale me with. He made a greater fuss over governing Montecchio than the Signoria made over ruling Florence; the time had come when I must read him such a lesson as would put an end, once and for all, to his foolery.

However, for the time being I seated myself on the lowest step of the staircase and, though I had no idea that this mummery portended anything serious, peered about me from a soldier's instinct to learn how the land lay.

There was very little to see. The street was one in the poorer part of the town. It was lined with dark, low, half-ruined buildings, little more than huts, which doubtless sheltered the folk who made a scanty living out of my fields. Altogether, it seemed a remarkably unlikely place for any important secret to lurk, and when not only Roger's minute, but full five minutes or ten, had dragged by, I came to the conclusion that I had spent time enough in the humoring of even the oldest comrade.

"If you keep this vigil any longer, you will keep it alone!" I announced, getting to my feet. "For my part, I am going back to the castle like a sane man!"

On the last word I felt Thornbury's fingers seize my arm in a convulsive grasp, and simultaneously it was borne in upon me that the door just across the street was opening. I must say it gave me a bit of a thrill, the way that door swung out! It was too slow, too noiseless. It looked furtive—for if some honest man were inside, why in heaven's name did he not stumble into the street and be done with it?

The door swung wider. I caught a glimpse of a narrow little room, with earthen pots and the like scattered around it, and a fire winking at the farther end. Then the sight was blotted out, and by— of all things—a woman's figure.

What on earth did this mean, I asked myself? To be sure, it might be a harmless occurrence enough, but for all that I felt sufficient interest in the woman to stare hard at her as she stood in the moonlight. She was a peasant; so much was plain from her dress of some coarse blue stuff and the gay-colored handkerchief on her head, though her thick black hair and keen eyes and strong-hard features might have belonged to any great lady of the virile sort that Italy breeds. She looked shrewd, and obviously had all her wits about her.

For a full minute she stood still, darting sharp glances to right and left. Then she stepped over the threshold, drew the door shut after her, and passing close beside us where we crouched in the dark, was off down the street as swiftly and noiselessly as a shadow.

"Aha, Sir John! What do you say now?" hissed Roger triumphantly, as she vanished.

~

If I had thought that the pursuit would be easy, I was soon undeceived. Never in my life, before or since, have I tracked a quarry so wary, and had we not been two old soldiers used to reconnoitering, we would have been detected ignominiously within a hundred feet. The woman turned this way, that way; she halted just around corners; she pause to look behind her—a dozen times we slipped into a dark doorway or the shadow of a buttress with not a second to spare.

The chase led us twice around the town, doubling, turning, passing the castle, the little church of San Biagio, the arsenal; and frankly, by this time I was as absorbed in the affair as Roger himself could have wished, for having seen something of life I was by no means so guileless as to think that anyone would take precautions like these for pure amusement.

Now the houses were growing fewer and more scattered, the oak trees and chestnuts more numerous. We were heading straight for the eastern wall and the gate that faces the valley which stretches off toward Castiglione.

"Stop here, Sir John," breathed Roger, drawing me behind a great oak trunk.

And if you will believe it, hardly were we snugly settled in our new place of vantage when he chose this time, of all others, to exult over me. "Ha, ha!" he whispered with the ghost of a cackle. "I am not such a fool after all, eh? At times I have my glimmers of reason, like another man?"

And by way of conclusion he sniggered to himself in a subdued fashion that made

my fingers itch. There have been occa-
sions when I have praised heaven for its
mercy in giving me but a single old friend
in Italy, and I cannot deny that I offered
up such a thanksgiving now.

Turning my back on him and peering
out, I saw the one spot in Montecchio
where the earth overtopped the walls—a
steep little hill, covered with nettles and
climbing vines. The woman climbed the
slope, paused at the summit, and stood
for a moment sharply outlined in the
moonlight. Then she bent down and I
caught the scraping of flint, followed by
a brief flash.

"She lights a torch, Sir John!" breathed
Roger in my ear.

Above us, the woman was raising her
flaming torch over her head. Holding it
at arm's length, she turned it in a circle,
once, twice, three times. At the third
revolution I heard Roger's chuckle end
abruptly in a hoarse gasp. But I was no
longer paying him the least heed, for
the zest of the adventure had now taken
full hold on me and I was watching the
woman as if my life hung on her next
act.

It appeared, however, that the play
was ended. Even as I looked she dropped
her hissing torch to earth, set her foot on
it and ground out the flames. Then she
came back down the hill and went swiftly
back toward the village, walking with the
air of one whose work is well done.

II

Being by this time a good deal excited
over the night's doings, I was annoyed
to find, when we had regained the castle,
that Roger had very little more to divulge.
All he could tell me was that this woman
had appeared in Montecchio some two
weeks earlier, poorly dressed and carrying
a bag of copper coins, and had asked leave
to rent a hut inside the walls and a plot
of land without. As to her own affairs she
was close-mouthed, saying only that she
had lived in the Chiana valley, had lost
her husband by a fever, and now, being
alone, wanted to live in the shelter of a
walled town. It was a likely enough story
and had aroused no suspicion.

Since then she had lived a life that
jibed perfectly with her account of herself, mixing seldom with her neighbors
and working hard in her field outside the
walls. Whatever her aim, she had been in
a fair way to succeed when, as luck would
have it, Roger one night rode home late
from a day afield, caught the flash of her
torch on the hill, and by hiding there
next night had touched the hem of the
mystery. With all my heart I wished he
had accomplished a trifle more, but he
gave me small chance to say so. That
third revolution of the torch, had, for
some reason, plunged him into a state
of absolute terror, and after giving me
the facts of the case he seemed to lose
all sanity.

"I tell you, Sir John," he raved, "there is some plot against you! She signals to Castiglione, this woman; that is plain as day. Always before she has waved her torch but twice, and tonight she waved it three times. What can the change mean, save the news that you have come to Montecchio?

"Ah, what madness, your visit! Siena, Castiglione and the rest are mad with hate of you because you ride to make peace terms against them. Do you think they would not rejoice to have your life on the journey? And then, her face—so hard, so resolute! It comes into my dreams! As I am a living man, Sir John, I believe that if ever you enter Florence again, it will be on your bier!"

At this point I cut his encouraging predictions short, for I was beginning to feel that if I heard many more of them, I would turn as crazy as he. "Have the woman here in the castle hall at noon tomorrow," I said. "I will have speech with her and get at the truth of the affair in short order. Now, as it appears I might as well hope for peace in Siena itself as in this castle, I am going to bed!"

And to bed I went in spite of his protests.

It was my custom when at Montecchio to give myself more sleep than I was lucky enough to get as a common thing, and to lie abed till noon. I had promised myself such a holiday on this occasion too, so I was anything but pleased, as you may imagine, to be aroused at dawn by sounds in the courtyard under my window—the whistling of a lash in the air, and the groans of some wretch unfortunate enough to be receiving its weight on his back.

Evidently Roger was evening scores with a sentry who had dozed at his post, or some such delinquent, and while I wished him joy of his task it struck me that he might have done me the favor to perform the ceremony at a rather more distant spot. My plan for enjoying a brief interval of rest and peace had undeniably proved a complete failure, and as I turned on my couch I determined to make no further effort at seeking blessings which plainly were not for me.

The worst of the affair was, however, yet in store. When at a little after noon I descended to the castle hall, in fairly good spirits at the prospect of matching wits with my mysterious tenant, I found the place occupied only by Roger who at sound of my step looked up at me with such a face of anguish as must have moved a heart of stone.

"Sir John, Sir John! She is gone, that woman!" was his greeting.

Here was pleasant news indeed. Staring at him blankly, I sank into a chair and he gave me the rest of his tidings in a sort of desperate outburst.

"Aye, gone!" he moaned. "And what is the more, she went last night, straight from the hill, the moment her work was done! At nine of the clock she was at the east gate, telling the sentry some tale of having left her tools in the field and wanting to fetch them lest they should be stolen overnight. He believed her, the fool! He let her pass out, in spite of the law that closes the gates at sunset, and she has not come back."

"Ah!" I commented, remembering the sounds that had broken my rest. "And you have had a word with this clever sentry, eh?"

Roger nodded. "Another time he will know better than to let spies go skirmishing in and out of Montecchio at their pleasure, I think!" he said grimly, and then relapsed into his former despair. "But when all is said," he groaned with tears in his eyes, "if justice were done, it is my own back should suffer! Of all fools in the world, surely I am the greatest, that I did not send last night to seize her!

"Oh, I make a botch of all I touch; I love you more than any man on earth, and behold how I serve you! I know well, Sir John, you could never bear with me save for old time's sake. It is plain I lack wits to be a simple soldier, let alone a castellan!"

For an instant, in my exasperation, I felt inclined to say that I agreed with him, for when on the previous night I had told him that I wanted speech with the woman, I had certainly credited him with sense enough to send at once to secure her. But his despair was so obvious that it roused all my old kindness for him, and, concealing my irritation with an effort, I put an encouraging hand on his shoulder. "It matters nothing, Roger," I said with an assurance I was far from feeling. "Never fret over it. The saints know we all cut a foolish figure now and again."

He fixed imploring eyes on me. "In the name of Heaven, Sir John," he cried, "do me one grace! Not a moment's peace shall I have till you are safe in Florence. Ride at once, then, and never draw rein till you are there."

To tell the truth, though I affected to laugh at his speech, I was not sure that it was not the most sensible counsel I had ever heard him utter.

"Well, you have no need to put yourself in a flurry about that," said I, "for I had intended departing at noon, and had bidden my troopers be ready. Come, pluck up spirit. You and I will laugh over this business when I stop here next month!"

And hastily draining a cup of wine, I strode out of the hall and into the castle courtyard.

⌐

The sight that met my eyes was an extraordinary one. Instead of awaiting me in proper order, sitting motionless in their saddles, my troopers had left their horses near the gate and were gathered together in the center of the court, whispering with their heads close.

It was plain that something out of the ordinary had happened to disturb them, for as they turned at sound of my step I saw that one and all of them looked pale and shaken, and that their eyes held such a look of anxiety as I had never known the prospect of the bloodiest battle to bring there. But at present I was less concerned with their emotions than with the amount of respect they were deigning to show me.

"Well, what does this mean, pray?" I asked sharply, as I strode forward. "Am I the Captain-General of Florence, or some rogue of a trooper like yourselves, that you laze about my court without a by-your-leave?"

Though they gave back from me at my question, it was evident they had some excuse which they thought more or less serviceable, for they promptly began to nudge their leader. After an instant that worthy, a fellow named Andrea, advanced a step. "Your pardon, Sir John," he stammered, "but this accursed tale has robbed us all of our wits."

"What tale?" I demanded. "It should be something alarming indeed, to make your legs shake like two straws."

He moistened dry lips before proceeding. "Your pardon again for the question, my General," he began, "but was it not your will to ride to Florence by the highroad, passing through Montevaroni?"

"It was," I answered grimly. "Are you going to tell me that you prefer another route?"

A little choking gasp ran about among my troopers, and as for their spokesman, he turned whiter yet, if that could be. "Sir John," he cried, "if we go that way, we are all dead men! The Black Death is traveling eastward from Siena. The countryside is rife with it, and the rumor runs that Montevaroni is already doomed!"

Here indeed was a pretty imbroglio. On the spot I granted my troop a mental absolution for their scared faces; for the Black Death is, with good reason, the terror of Italy, and I fancy there lives no soldier who would not rather take his chances with twenty swordsmen than with this horrible sickness. To ride through the infested country was impossible, yet we must win through somehow to Florence, and in short order too. Undeniably my visit to Montecchio had been ill-starred. From the moment I had entered the gates, nothing had chanced but a series of disasters.

"Where did you get this news?" I asked shortly, in the end.

As is usual in such cases, no one could oblige me with a clear answer. Each man referred me to a different source, and even Andrea, the most intelligent of the party, could only tell me that the story had been whispered about the town on the previous night, and with the coming of morning had run riot.

For a moment there was silence. Then, as I stood scowling and racking my brains for a way out of the difficulty, Andrea ventured to make a suggestion. "There is the bypath through the Chiana Valley, Sir John," said he, "the path that leads by the Stone Ford. If you would be pleased to go that way, we could sleep below Vallombrosa and reach Florence tomorrow. And here is Gilberto who knows the route."

"As well as my pocket, Sir John. I have traveled it a hundred times," volunteered Gilberto himself.

Well, if this was what they had been mustering up courage to ask of me I was ready enough to oblige them, for while I flattered myself that it was not in my nature to grow pasty-faced and weak-kneed at the sight of danger, still I was not much fonder of the Black Death than they were.

"In Heaven's name, then, let us be about it!" I cried and got hastily to horse.

But I was not done with Montecchio yet. As I settled into my saddle I chanced to glance back over my shoulder, and there, riding at the very end of my line of troopers, with his face half hidden and a bearing so unostentatious that it might well-nigh have been described as slinking, whom should I see but Roger Thornbury!

"The saints pity us!" I exclaimed, drawing rein to stare at him. "What new foolery is this?"

Seeing himself discovered, he pushed his hat off his eyes and faced me sulkily. "Well," he growled, "and did you think I meant to let you go without me, to meet who knows what danger? Not I, Sir John! I mean to ride with you to Florence and see for myself that you run no risks you need not run!"

At this announcement I distinctly heard Andrea chuckle, though when I wheeled on him with a glare he skillfully turned his ill-timed mirth into a violent fit of coughing; and I must confess I did not greatly blame him, for the idea of John Hawkwood junketing over Italy in charge of a species of duenna, who should decide what risks were to be taken and which avoided, was enough to make a graven image smile. If any such story got abroad I would never hear the last of it, and many as were the allowances I was prepared to make for the sake of an ancient friendship, I felt that this was the last straw.

"Roger, you old fool," I said sternly, "off of that horse with you and back into the castle! You will not ride to Florence; you will stop here and watch my holdings.

Not a word more will I hear, do you understand? Now goodbye to you, and may you practice more sense against my return!"

Obstinate as he was, he had wit to know when he had gone far enough. With a noisy sigh of resignation he wheeled his horse aside and sat dejectedly watching us depart.

"You ride off very gaily, Sir John!" he gloomed, evidently hoping to the last that I might be moved to relent. "Heaven grant you may not change your tune before you see the Arno! In your place I would not be so scornful of a comrade's aid—for mark my words, you have not seen the last of her yet—that woman whom we tracked last night!"

With this cheerful prophecy still ringing in my ears I rode out of Montecchio.

III

It was near dusk when our little *cortège* wound through the Chiana Valley and approached the ford, and as the river came in sight I for one felt inclined to offer up thanks, for, truth to tell, the journey had proved anything but agreeable. Though my troopers had set out in fairly good spirits at avoiding Montevaroni and the Black Death, this self-congratulation had not endured long. Before we had ridden a mile their fears were stirring again, reminding them how near was the terrible sickness, and turning them little by little into as pitiful a set of figures, for seasoned soldiers, as ever I saw.

A little thing might have put them in an uncontrollable panic, and while I knew better than to encourage them by taking the least notice of their terror, I dared not let them exchange ideas either. So I announced that until we were safely out of the hostile country not a tongue in the troop was to wag, and we jogged along in sepulchral silence, like a train of mourners.

All things considered, I could not find it in my heart to blame the poor wretches overmuch, for the road we were traveling was not an enlivening one, and I soon registered a vow that my first experience of it should also be my last. Our path, a mere thread, wound through a veritable maze of fever-swamps.

I suppose it occurred to everyone present, as it did to me, that even Montevaroni could not have been much worse than this poisonous air, full of evil vapors and reeking with deadly midsummer heat. The leafless trees to right and left of us looked unpleasantly like specters; and as for our horses, during most of the trip they were knee deep in the soft marshy bogs.

Whether or no it was the scenery that worked on me I cannot say, but my spirits fell lower and lower, and though I do not commonly yield to foolish fancies I began to feel as if some catastrophe were hanging over us. Roger's final words, to which I had paid scant heed as he uttered them, now beat themselves in my brain like witch's music, and despite all my efforts to think of other matters, I found myself forever harking back to the affair of the previous night.

It had been a strange business, no doubt about that, for when all is said and done a woman does not commonly pop out of a hut, circle a town three times, signal from the walls, and vanish from the place she has chosen as a home, all within an hour. And then, her face—strong, hard, resolute! She had been working for some definite purpose, and though I had not an idea what it was, I felt uneasily convinced that she was likely to succeed.

It appeared, however, that my fears were unwarranted, for we pursued our journey without encountering a soul, friendly or otherwise, and toward dusk approached the river without even so trivial a misadventure as a broken girth or lamed horse. At sight of the water my spirits went up with such a bound that not even the landscape, now more depressing than ever—the thunderous yellow clouds in the west and the sickly mist in the air were creating an effect no less than grisly—could dampen them by a jot; for once across, we would be on Florentine soil, with nothing to fear from either foes or plague. My troopers knew this full as well as I did, as their lightening faces showed, and it was with a very respectable pretense at good cheer that we followed Gilberto, at a gallop, to the river's brink.

—

"But how does this happen, eh?" I demanded in surprise, as we halted. "You talked of bringing me to a ford, and certainly I see none hereabouts!"

"Oh, that will be because of the storms we had last week, Sir John," Gilberto explained readily. "The water is running high, you perceive, and since the ford is but a rude one of stones, it is hidden. I know the spot well. Do but enter here, in a line with the great charred oak."

So assured was his tone that I never dreamed of doubting him. Urging my horse forward, I splashed into the water at the precise spot he indicated—and came as near meeting my death as ever I did yet.

Stone ford in that river there was none. In less time than it takes to tell it I was up to my neck in ice-cold water, and under me my terrified horse was battling wildly with the fierce Chiana current, which was doing its best to sweep us off to perdition. You can picture for yourself, if you choose, the minutes that followed. Though they did not last long, they were lively while they did endure, and it gives me no pleasure to recall them even now; so suffice it to say that in the end I somehow won back to shore, and, dripping from head to foot, stood again among my petrified troopers.

"Saints of mercy!" cried Gilberto at last, with eyes as round as plates. "The stones are gone!"

A cold bath of the sort I had just enjoyed is not a soothing experience. My intention was that someone should pay for it, and here undoubtedly was the proper person. Striding up to him, I caught him by the back of the neck. "Gone, you villain!" I cried in a rage. "They were never here! You have offered to guide me to a place of which you know no more than a babe unborn. But I will teach you to crack jests at my expense!"

Before my arm could descend, however, Andrea took up the word. "But, Sir John, it is true, what Gilberto says!" he exclaimed, staring wide-eyed at the river. "I also have ridden this way, though less often than he, and I can swear that the ford was at that very spot!"

Now I was well aware that Gilberto was as arrant a liar as walked the earth, and no protestation of his would have had a feather's weight with me. But Andrea, to the best of my knowledge, had never deceived me yet, nor was there any reason why he should try to do so now. Moreover, at this instant another trooper volunteered the information that he too had once made the journey, and

recalled distinctly that the stones had been, as Gilberto asserted, in a line with the burned tree.

"By your leave, Sir John, someone has destroyed the ford!" was his solution of the puzzle.

The words gave me a colder chill than had the water. For a moment I stood staring at the man who had uttered them. Then, all dripping as I was, I strode over to a fallen tree-trunk, seated myself upon it, and, propping my elbows on my knees, began to think. My wits, which had apparently been woolgathering during the greater part of the last four and twenty hours, now returned to me in full force, and I saw a good many things which I might well have glimpsed earlier.

Suppose, I reasoned, that Roger had been right. Suppose the conquered cities, whose fate I was on my way to settle at Florence, had determined to get rid of me by foul means in the course of my journey. What would their first step be? Divining that I would doubtless halt at Montecchio, they would despatch there some shrewd emissary like my mysterious woman, who would signal them in a certain fashion on the nights when the town went unhonored by my presence, and in another fashion on the night when I arrived. She had flashed the news to them with her torch the previous evening; and I fancied that a troop of men had instantly left Castiglione on a night jaunt to the Chiana Ford, and that by dawn every vestige of the stones had been hewn away.

I could find but one missing link in the chain—the fact that unless the tale of the plague had reached Montecchio in the very nick of time, a circumstance they could not possibly have foreseen, I would never on earth have traveled by the lonely river-path instead of by the high-road. After puzzling over this for a little, I began to have a shrewd suspicion that the Black Death was not raging in Montevaroni at all. It was more than likely that the whole story was a lying rumor, set afloat last night by the woman of the torch, and palmed off by her on the folk of Montecchio as a true tale from a trust-worthy source.

Well, if that were the case, the trap had been prettily baited, and I had fallen into it with a readiness that must have proved gratifying to my foes. Surely I had proved myself the king of fools, and so I admitted between teeth that still chattered from my impromptu bath.

And finally, what had been the end and aim of so much plotting? Again I reflected; and since I knew that to try to swim the strong currents of the river in the dusk would probably mean death, and there was no habitation within miles of me on this side of the water, I thought it fairly plain that my foes had been working for the purpose of forcing me to spend the night where I was. But why, then? There seemed to be but one answer. No doubt they intended to set a band of cutthroats upon me in this lonely spot, and to make an end of both me and my troopers.

With this pleasant thought for company, I began to study the ghastly yellowish landscape, which I must say looked as appropriate a spot for a murder as fancy could paint. There was no living soul in sight, but that fact reassured me very little since the attack would be all the more deadly if made later, under cover of darkness.

Of course, the sole thing to do was, as any soldier worth his salt will guess, to find some place in which to barricade ourselves; and scarcely had I begun to look about when I saw, not two hundred feet away on the crest of a hill, a small half-ruined hut which struck me as a very promising spot for the purpose.

I got to my feet briskly. "My friends," said I to the gaping circle about me, "it is my belief that we have been decoyed here for a purpose, and that we will be attacked before morning. Well, since to go forward is impossible and to go back is to court an ambush, we will stop where we are.

"Do you see that hut yonder? Let us go quarter ourselves in it, kindle a fire, and sup on what food we have in our pouches. After that we will take turns at watching out the night—and if there is killing to be done, at least we will do what we can to give as good as we get!"

One tribute I must, in common honesty, pay these fellows of mine—if they were afraid of the Black Death, they were not afraid of cold steel. Indeed, the prospect of facing a flesh-and-blood enemy seemed to have a steadying effect on their nerves, and it was with perfect good temper that they followed me as I got to horse and started up the hill. The ascent was steep and the dusk was rapidly deepening, so we had need to go with care; and we were no more than halfway to the top when Andrea touched my arm. "Look yonder, Sir John! Who is coming?" he muttered under his breath.

For an instant I thought, and so I will warrant did the others, that our foes were upon us, but a brief use of my eyes acquainted me with the reassuring fact that it was but a single horseman who approached. Moreover, he was not coming in any stealthy fashion. He was spurring frantically, shouting to us inarticulately at the top of his voice, and waving his arms like a madman.

"Saints, Sir John!" cried Gilberto, with a sort of wild snigger. "It is Messer Roger Thornbury!"

And so, of all men, it was. He reached the river, wheeled his horse and dashed up the hill; fell, rather than clambered, to earth; dropped in a nerveless heap on the ground in front of me; and finally, even in his exhaustion, found strength to beat the air madly with his arms, as if warning me back.

"Not that hut, Sir John! Not that hut!" he gasped with all the force he could muster.

The man was near a swoon. Seeing it, I took my flask from my saddlebag and poured its contents, none too gently, down his throat, after which I pulled him unceremoniously to his feet.

"Now then, my friend," I said grimly, "we will hear what this means, if you please! Do you dare tell me that you followed me here after the commands I gave you?"

Roger had by now recovered his breath, and with it his assurance. "Aye, I did!" he said defiantly. "I thought, Sir John, that what you did not know would not hurt you! And you would never have known of my presence five hundred feet behind you, had I not needed to appear to save your life—"

"My life? I have not seen you save it yet!" I retorted with small gratitude.

Roger struck an attitude and swelled visibly with importance. "You think so?" he exulted. "Then listen, Sir John! I fancy you have not traveled this way before, eh? And perhaps none of your troopers have passed here within a twelvemonth? Then you are all ignorant who dwelt lately in that little hut you were approaching so gaily?

"But I know! It was the home of two wretched peasants who begged alms of such few folk as used this river-road; and three months since they had guests overnight—a poor peasant family fleeing from Siena and the plague.

"But as it chanced, these guests had not fled quite soon enough. Unknown to themselves, they brought the Black Death with them. They died in that hut, and their hosts died too! And if you had slept within those walls, Sir John, mark me well, not all the doctors in Italy could have saved your life!"

If he wanted his revenge, he had it. For a long minute there was no sound save the sharp, hoarse breathing of my men. Their faces showed through the dusk as white as paper, and I do not doubt that I looked a bit shaken myself, for it seemed to me that, as the saying has it, someone was walking over my grave.

Now at last I knew why I had been stranded hereabouts for the night, with no visible shelter save the little hut. To have killed the Florentine Captain-General by cutthroats' daggers would have been plain murder, and might have brought terrible vengeance from the Republic; but since the broken ford, the sole piece of proof of the black affair, might be rebuilt tomorrow, who could be blamed if I were carried off by the plague?

Yes, but for Roger's timely advent I would have died, not as soldiers die, but horribly, as men go when the Black Death takes them. Ah, of all the schemes that had been woven around me in my life, surely there had been none so shrewd, so certain, so devilish as this.

To pull myself together was something of a task, but I did it and turned my back with a shudder on that grisly hut. "Well, my good friends," I remarked to my men, "I think you will agree with me that even if we must ride until midnight before reaching our beds, it will be more pleasant to sleep at Montecchio than here. Let us be off, then.

"As for you, Roger, you are a jewel of a castellan, and I will grant you anything on earth that lies in my power, save only my leave to trail me in secret, which is an experiment you had better not try twice. And since you have proved yourself so clever, I wish you might do me one more favor. It is a thousand pities you cannot tell me the name of the woman whom I have to thank for this cheerful jaunt!"

"As to that, Sir John," said Roger, with a shudder, "you are like never to learn it, for I think she was some fiend from below!"

⌒

For my part, I looked on this idea with some skepticism, being of the opinion that she was as mortal as Roger or myself, though perhaps rather more dangerous than either of us; but I had little more hope than he of arriving at the truth of the matter. However, time, which clears up a good many mysteries, was fated to solve this one too.

A month after my experience in the Chiana Valley I returned from Florence with my peace terms and halted at Castiglione to let the Podesta of that place know what he must do if he did not want to see his city in ruins. Being perfectly aware that I had the whip-hand of him, he made the best of the matter. He welcomed me with a splendid banquet. Just before the beginning of this festivity he came to me where I stood talking with his officers and my own, in the center of his castle hall.

"By your leave, Sir John," said he, "I will now present to you my lady, whom doubtless you know already by report."

To be sure I had heard often enough of Madonna Donnina. Indeed, though I did not tell him as much, I had heard things of her that would have made her lord scowl could he have listened to them, since the common rumor was that without her to aid him he would never have climbed where he now stood. It was her brain that planned for him, men said, her will that guided him. She had a soldier's heart, and once in his absence had held the city against a besieging army.

"Her acquaintance will honor me, my lord," I said.

Together we crossed the hall and paused before his lady. She was very proud, very splendid; she was dressed in silks and glittered with jewels. I looked at her, and on the instant the gay scene about us seemed to vanish. I was back in a dark street, looking at a low, mean hut, an open door; and, on the threshold in the moonlight, a woman in a coarse blue dress, with a peasant's handkerchief on her black hair!

"There is no need that you should present me to your wife, my lord!" I announced. "We are old friends, she and I. A full month ago we met in my town of Montecchio!"

The Podesta fell back with a low gasp. As for me, my vision had changed. Now I was looking at a yellowish landscape, a river, and a tiny desolate hut perched on a hill. All the horror of that night swept back on me, and I was opening my lips to say something very much to the purpose when a look at the woman halted me.

She was as pale as death. She was staring at me in speechless terror—the Podesta's wife, mark you, who was said to have never known fear! The triumph was sufficient, and since a man does not deal with women as he deals with men, I determined to be content with the revenge my dramatic remark had brought me.

"Madonna Donnina," said I, saluting her airily, "I have lived through such perils as you would never believe, I have escaped such clever plots as you would scarce credit, only for the pleasure of this minute!"

Then I bent above the fingers which had held the torch to signal for my death; and we all went to supper. But both the Podesta and his lady made a very poor meal.

About Jeffery Farnol

By now you know the pattern: author of swashbucklers, phenomenally popular in his day, now virtually forgotten. All of that applies to Jeffery Farnol, but in every other way he was . . . different.

For one thing, he didn't learn the craft of writing studying for the bar or at Oxford or Cambridge. He was educated at home, and as a writer was entirely self-taught. He always told his parents that he intended to be a writer when he grew up, and nothing but.

They sent him to work in a foundry.

It didn't work out very well; he was fired, with the comment, "No good for work, always writing." Farnol also had some talent as an artist, so his parents, allowing as how he might be able to make a living as an illustrator, sent him to the Westminster School of Art in London.

. . . Where he continued to spend most of his time writing. He also fell in love with and married Blanche Hawley, daughter of an English artist who had found success in New York. Though penniless, the couple moved to New York, where Farnol found work as a theater scene painter.

Meanwhile, he wrote—and began to sell a story here, a story there. In 1907 he sold his first novel, a wry and fanciful romance titled *My Lady Caprice*. It didn't exactly set the world on fire.

His second novel did. Published in 1910, *The Broad Highway* is a 200,000-word historical romance with a two-fisted hero that established the genre we know today as the "Regency romance." It was also one of the best-selling novels of its decade, a genuine sensation.

Farnol and family moved back to England, and he settled down to writing in earnest, publishing nearly fifty books over the next thirty-five years: Regency romances and thrillers, historical mysteries, modern-day love stories, medieval adventures, and a round dozen swashbucklers, including some excellent tales of piracy.

Though little-read nowadays, Farnol was an influence on George MacDonald Fraser, author of the *Flashman* novels, and on the American fantasist Jack Vance. However, Farnol's style, it must be admitted, is not for everyone. His writing is mannered, wry, and playful, and employs antiquated language and grammar in a fashion that most readers either love or hate. Personally, I find it delightful—but if it's not for you, well, at least the story we've chosen here is the last, and you can put down the book without guilt. It first appeared as the concluding chapters of *Black Bartlemy's Treasure*, 1920, Farnol's greatest novel o' bloody piracy, d'ye see.

The Fight for
Black Bartlemy's Treasure

JEFFERY FARNOL

What has gone before: Martin Conisby, a young man of the rural English gentry, had run afoul of an old feud between his family and the neighboring Brandons, and been betrayed into slavery on a Spanish galley. After five years chained to an oar, he escaped and returned to England, seeking mad vengeance on his betrayer, Abner Brandon—only to encounter kindness and succor from the daughter of the family, Lady Joan Brandon. At war with himself over his feelings for Joan, Martin fell in with the buccaneer Adam Penfeather, who was in pursuit of his own nemesis, be-hooked villain Roger Tressady. Nautical adventure ensued, culminating with Martin Conisby and Joan Brandon shipwrecked together on a desert Caribbean island—a sometime lair of pirates! Martin and Joan availed themselves of the pirates' stores, while striving to prepare for their inevitable return.

CHAPTER I
OF THE VOICE THAT SANG ON DELIVERANCE SANDS

If clothes be the outward and visible (albeit silent) expression of a man, his tastes and certain attitudes of his mind, yet have they of themselves a mighty influence on their wearer, being, as it were, an inspiration to him in degree more or less.

And this is truth I will maintain let say who will to the contrary, since 'tis so my experience teacheth me.

Hitherto my ragged shirt, my rough leathern jerkin and open-kneed sailor's breeches had been a constant reminder of the poor, desperate rogue I had become, my wild hair and shaggy beard evidences of slavedom. Thus I had been indeed what I had seemed in looks, a rude, ungentle creature expectant of scorns and ill-usage and therefore very prone to fight and quarrel, harsh-tongued, bitter of speech, and in all circumstances sullen, ungoverned and very desperate.

But now, seeing myself thus gently dight, my wild hair tamed by comb and scissors, there grew within me a new respect for my manhood, so that, little by little, those evils that slavery had wrought slipped from me. Thus, though I still labored at my carpentry and such business as was to do, yet the fine linen rolled high above my scarred and knotted arm put me to the thought that I was no longer the poor, wild wretch full of despairing rage against Fate her cruel dealings, but rather a man gently born and therefore one who must endure all things as uncomplainingly as might be, and one moreover who, to greater or less degree, was master of his own fate.

And now came Hope, that most blessed and beneficent spirit that lifteth the fallen from the slough, that bindeth up the broken heart, that cheereth the sad and downcast and maketh the oft-defeated bold and courageous to attempt Fortune yet again.

O thou that we call Hope, thou sweet, bright angel of God! Without thee life were an evil unendurable, with thee for companion gloomy Doubt, sullen Fear and dark Despair flee utterly away, and we, bold-hearted, patient and undismayed by any dangers or difficulties, may realize our dreams at last. O sweet, strong angel of God, with thee to companion us all things are possible!

Thus every morning came Hope to greet me on my waking, and I, forgetting the futile past, began to look forward to a future more glorious than I had ever dreamed; so I, from a sullen rogue full of black humors, grew to know again the joy of laughter and put off my ungracious speech and ways with my rough attire. Though how much the change thus wrought in me was the work of my sweet comrade these pages, I do think, will show.

As for my lady she, very quick to mark this change, grew ever the more kind and trusting, sharing with me all her doubts and perplexities; thus, did some problem vex her, she must come to me, biting her pretty lips and her slender brows wrinkled, to ask my advice.

At this time (and at her suggestion) I built a fireplace and oven within our third or inmost cave (that was by turns her larder, stillroom, dairy and kitchen) and with a chimney to carry off the smoke the which I formed of clay and large pebbles, and found it answer very well. Thus, what with those things I contrived and others she brought from her treasure-house (the secret whereof she kept mighty close) we lacked for nothing to our comfort, even as Adam had promised in his letter. Moreover, I was very well armed both for offense and defense, for, one by one, she brought me the following pieces, viz., a Spanish helmet, inlaid with gold and very cumbersome; a back and breast of fine steel of proof; four wheel-lock arquebuses, curiously chased and gilded, with shot and powder for the same; three brace of pistols, gold-mounted and very accurate; and what with these, my sword, axe, and trusty knife, I felt myself capable to drive away any should dare molest us, be he Indian, buccaneer, or pirate, as I told her.

"Aye, but," says she, "whiles you fought for our lives what must I be doing?"

"Lying secure within your secret treasure-house."

"Never!" says she, setting her chin at me, "O never, Martin; since I am your comrade my place must be beside you."

"'Twould but distress me and spoil my shooting."

"Why then, my aim should be truer, Martin. Come now, teach me how to use gun and pistol."

So then and there I fetched a pistol and one of the arquebuses and showed her their manage, namely—how to hold them, to level, sight, etc. Next I taught her how to charge them, how to wad powder and then shot lest the ball roll out of the barrel; how having primed she must be careful ever to close the pan against the priming being blown away. All of the which she was mighty quick to apprehend. Moreover, I took care to keep all my firearms cleaned and loaded, that I might be ready for any disturbers of our peace.

So the days sped, each with its meed of work, but each full-charged of joy. And dear to me beyond expressing is the memory of those days whenas I, laboring with my new tools, had but to lift my head to behold my dear comrade (herself busy as I). Truly how dear, how thrice-blessed the memory of it all! A memory this, indeed, that was to become for me sacred beyond all others; for now came Happiness with arms outstretched to me and I (poor, blind wretch) suffered it to plead in vain and pass me by, as you shall hear.

It was a night of splendor with a full moon uprising in majesty to fill the world with her soft radiance; a night very warm and still and we silent, I think because of the tender beauty of the night.

"Martin," says my companion softly at last, "here is another day sped—"

"Alas, and more's the pity!" quoth I.

"O?" says she, looking at me askance.

"Our days fly all too fast, Damaris. Here is a time I fain would linger upon, an' I might."

"It hath been a very wonderful time truly, Martin, and hath taught me very much. We are both the better for it, I think, and you—"

"What of me, comrade?" I questioned as she paused.

"You are grown so much gentler since your sickness, so much more my dear friend and companion."

"Why, 'tis all your doing, Damaris."

"I am glad—O very glad!" says she almost in a whisper.

"Why, 'tis you who have taught me to—to love all good, sweet things, to rule myself that I—I may someday, mayhap, be a little more worthy of—of—" Here, beginning to flounder, I came to sudden halt, and casting about in my mind for a likely phrase, saw her regarding me, the dimple in her cheek, but her eyes all compassionate and ineffably tender.

"Dear man!" says she, and reached me her hand.

"Damaris," says I heavily and looking down at these slender fingers, yet not daring to kiss them lest my passion sweep me away, "you know that I do love you?"

"Yes, Martin."

"And that, my love, be it what it may, is yet an honest love?"

"Yes, dear Martin."

Here was silence a while, she looking up at the moon, and I at her.

"I broke my oath to you once," says I, "nor will I swear again, but, dear my lady, know this: though I do hunger and thirst for you, yet mine is such reverent love that should we live thus together long years—aye, until the end of our lives, I will school myself to patience and wait ever upon your will. Though 'twill be hard!" says I 'twixt my teeth, thrilling to the sudden clasp of her fingers.

"But, Martin," says she softly, "how if our days together here should all suddenly end—"

"End?" cries I, starting, "Wherefore end? When? Why end?" And I trembled in a sick panic at the mere possibility. "End?" quoth I again. "Would you have an end?"

"No—ah, no!" says she, leaning to me that I could look down into her eyes.

"Doth this—O Damaris, can this mean that you are happy with me in this solitude—content—?"

"So happy, Martin, so content that I do fear lest it may all suddenly end and vanish like some loved dream."

"Damaris—O Damaris!" says I, kissing her sweet fingers. "Look now, there is question hath oft been on my lips yet one I have not dared to ask."

"Ask me now, Martin."

"'Tis this . . . could it . . . might it perchance be possible you should learn with time . . . mayhap . . . to love me a little? Nay, not a little, not gently nor with reason, but fiercely, mightily, beyond the cramping bounds of all reason?"

Now here she laughed, a small, sad laugh with no mirth in it, and leaned her brow against my arm as one very weary.

"O foolish Martin!" she sighed. "How little you have seen, how little guessed—how little you know the real me! For I am a woman, Martin, as you are a man and joy in it. All these months I have watched you growing back to your nobler self, I have seen you strive with yourself for my sake and gloried in your victories, though . . . sometimes I have . . . tempted you . . . just a little, Martin. Nay, wait, dear Martin. Oft-times at night I have known you steal forth, and hearkened to your step going to and fro out in the dark, and getting to my knees have thanked God for you, Martin."

"'Twas not all in vain, then!" says I, hoarsely, bethinking me of the agony of those sleepless nights.

"Vain?" she cried, "Vain? 'Tis for this I do honor you—"

"Honor—me?" says I, wincing.

"Above all men, Martin. 'Tis for this I—"

"Wait!" says I, fronting her all shame-faced. "I do love you so greatly I would not have you dream me better than I am! So now must I tell you this . . . I stole to you once . . . at midnight . . . you were asleep, the moonlight all about you and looked like an angel of God."

And now it was my turn to stare up at the moon whiles I waited miserably enough for her answer.

"And when you went away, Martin," says she at last, "when I heard you striding to and fro, out here beneath God's stars, I knew that yours was the greatest, noblest love in all the world."

"You—saw me?"

"Yes, Martin!"

"Yet your eyes were fast shut."

"Yes, but not—not all the time. And, O Martin, dear, dear Martin, I saw your

great, strong arms reach out to take me— but they didn't, they didn't because true love is ever greatly merciful! And your triumph was mine also, Martin! And so it is I love you—worship you, and needs must all my days."

And now we were on our feet, her hands in mine, eyes staring into eyes and never a word to speak.

"Is it true?" says I at last. "God, Damaris—is it true?"

"Seems it so wonderful, dear Martin? Why, this love of mine reacheth back through the years to Sir Martin, my little knight-errant, and hath grown with the years till now it filleth me and the universe about me. Have you forgot 'twas your picture hung opposite my bed at home, your sword I kept bright because it had been yours? And often, Martin, here on our dear island I have wept sometimes for love of you because it pained me so! Nay, wait, beloved, first let me speak, though I do yearn for your kisses! But this night is the greatest ever was or mayhap ever shall be, and we, alone here in the wild, do lie beyond all human laws soever save those of our great love—and, O Martin, you—you do love me?"

Now when I would have answered I could not, so I sank to my knees and stooping ere she knew, clasped and kissed the pretty feet of her.

"No, Martin—beloved, ah, no!" cries she as it were pain to her, and kneeling before me, set her soft arms about my neck. "Martin," says she, "as we kneel thus in this wilderness alone with God, here and now, before your lips touch mine, before your dear strong hands take me to have and hold forever, so great and trusting is my love I ask of you no pledge but this: Swear now in God's sight to renounce and put away all thought of vengeance now and forever, swear this, Martin!"

Now I, all bemused by words so unexpected, all dazzled as it were by the pleading, passionate beauty of her, closed my eyes that I might think:

"Give me until tomorrow—" I groaned.

"'Twill be too late! Choose now, Martin."

"Let me think—"

"'Tis no time for thought! Choose, Martin! This hour shall never come again, so, Martin—speak now or—"

The words died on her lip, her eyes opened in sudden dreadful amaze, and thus we remained, kneeling rigid in one another's arms, for, away across Deliverance beach, deep and full and clear a voice was singing:

"There are two at the fore,
At the main are three more,
Dead men that swing all in a row;
Here's fine dainty meat
For the fishes to eat:
Black Bartlemy—Bartlemy ho!"

CHAPTER II
CONCERNING THE SONG OF A DEAD MAN

Long after the singing was died away I (like one dazed) could think of nought but this accursed song, these words the which had haunted my sick-bed and methought no more than the outcome of my own fevered imagination; thus my mind running on this and very full of troubled perplexity, I suffered my lady to bring me within our refuge, but with my ears on the stretch as expectant to hear again that strange, deep voice sing these words I had heard chanted by a dead man in my dreams.

Being come within our third cave (or kitchen) my lady shows me a small cord that dangled in certain shadowy corner, and pulling on this cord, down falls a rope-ladder and hangs suspended; and I knew this for Adam's "ladder of cords" whereby he had been wont to mount into his fourth (and secret) cavern, as mentioned in his chronicle.

"Here lieth safety, Martin," says my lady, "for as Master Penfeather writes in his journal, 'One resolute man lying upon the hidden ledge' (up yonder) 'may withstand a whole army so long as his shot last.' And you are very resolute and so am I!"

"True!" says I, "True!" Yet, even as I spake, I stood all tense and rigid, straining my ears to catch again the words of this hateful song. But now my dear lady catches my hand and, peering up at me in the dimness, presently draws me into the outer cave where the moon made a glory.

"O Martin!" says she, looking up at me with troubled eyes. "Dear Martin, what is it?"

"Aye—what?" quoth I, wiping sweat from me. "God knoweth. But you heard? That song? The words—"

"I heard a man singing, Martin. But what of it—we are safe here! Ah—why are you so strange?"

"Damaris," says I, joying in the comfort of her soft, strong arms about me, "dear love of mine, here is thing beyond my understanding, for these were words I dreamed sung to me by a dead man—the man Humphrey—out beyond the reef—"

"Nay, but dear Martin, this was a real voice. 'Tis some shipwrecked mariner belike, some castaway—"

"Aye, but did you—mark these words, Damaris?"

"Nay! O my dear, how should I—at such a moment!"

"They were all—of Black Bartlemy! And what should this mean, think you?"

"Nay, dear love, never heed!" says she, clasping me the closer.

"Aye, but I must, Damaris, for—in a while this singing shall come again mayhap and—if it doth—I know what 'twill be!"

"O Martin—Martin, what do you mean?"

"I mean 'twill be about the poor Spanish lady," says I, and catching up my belt where it hung, I buckled it about me.

"Ah—what would you do, Martin?"

"I'm for Deliverance Beach."

"Then will I come also."

"No!" says I, catching her in fierce arms. "No! You are mine henceforth and more precious than life to me. So must you bide here—I charge you by our love. For look now, 'tis in my mind Tressady and his pirates are upon us at last, those same rogues that dogged the *Faithful Friend* over seas. Howbeit I must find out who or what is it is that sings this hateful—"

I stopped all at once, for the voice was come again, nearer, louder than before, and singing the very words I had been hearkening for and dreading to hear:

"There's a fine Spanish dame,
And Joanna's her name,
Shall follow wherever ye go:
'Til your black heart shall feel
Your own cursed steel:
Black Bartlemy—Bartlemy ho!"

"You heard!" says I, clapping hand on knife. "You heard?"

"Yes—yes," she whispered, her embrace tightening until I might feel her soft body all a-tremble against mine. "But you are safe here, Martin!"

"So safe," says I, "that needs must I go and find out this thing—nay, never fear, beloved, life hath become so infinite precious that I shall be a very coward—a craven for your sake. Here shall be no fighting, Damaris, but go I must. Meanwhile do you wait me in the secret cave and let down the ladder only to my whistle."

But now, and lying all trembling in my embrace, she brake into passionate weeping, and I powerless to comfort her. "Farewell happiness!" she sobbed. "Only, Martin, dear Martin, whatsoever may chance, know and remember always that I loved and shall love you to the end of time."

Then (and all suddenly) she was her sweet, calm self again, and bringing me my chain-shirt, insisted I must don it there and then beneath my fine doublet, the which (to please her) I did. Then she brought me one of the arquebuses, but this I put by as too cumbersome, taking one of the pistols in its stead. So, armed with this together with my hatchet and trusty knife, I stepped from the cave and she beside me. And now I saw she had dried her tears and the hand clasping mine was firm and resolute, so that my love and wonder grew.

"Damaris," I cried, casting me on my knees before her, "O God, how I do love thee!" And kneeling thus, I clasped her slender loveliness, kissing the robes that covered her; and so, rising to my feet I hasted away. Yet in a little I turned to see her watching me but with hands clasped as one in prayer. Now, beholding her thus, I was seized of a sudden great desire to go back to give her that promise and swear that oath she sought of me, viz., that I would forego my vengeance and all thought thereof, forgetting past wrongs in the wonder of her love. But, even as I stood hesitating, she waved her hand in farewell and was gone into the cave.

CHAPTER III
OF THE DEATH-DANCE OF THE SILVER WOMAN

A small wind had sprung up that came in fitful gusts and with sound very mournful and desolate, but the moon was wonderfully bright and, though I went cautiously, my hand on the butt of the pistol in my girdle, yet ever and always at the back of my mind was an infinitude of joy by reason of my dear lady's love for me and the wonder of it.

I chose me a devious course, avoiding the white sands of Deliverance Beach, trending towards that fatal cleft hard by Bartlemy's tree (the which we had come to call Skeleton Cove) though why I must go hither I knew no more then than I do now.

Thus went I (my eyes and ears on the stretch) pondering what manner of man this should be who sang words the which had so haunted my sick dreams; more than once I stopped to stare round about me upon the wide expanse of ocean, dreading and half expecting to behold the loom of that black craft had dogged us over seas.

Full of these disquieting thoughts I reached the cove and began to descend the steep side, following goat-tracks long grown familiar. The place hereabouts was honeycombed with small caves and with ledges screened by bushes and tangled vines; and here, well hid from observation, I paused to look about me. But (and all in a moment) I was down on my knees, for from somewhere close by came the sharp snapping of a dried stick beneath a stealthy foot.

Very still I waited, every nerve a-tingle, and then, forth into the moonlight, sudden and silent as death, a man crept; and verily if ever murderous death stood in human shape it was before me now. The man stood half-crouching, his head twisted back over his shoulder as watching one who followed; beneath the vivid scarf that swathed his temples was a shock of red hair and upon his cheek the sweat was glittering; then he turned his head and I knew him for the man Red Andy, that same I had fought aboard ship. For a long moment he stood thus, staring back ever and anon across Deliverance, and so comes creeping into the shadow of the cliff, and I saw the moon glint on the barrel of the long pistol he clutched, as, sinking down behind a great boulder, he waited there upon his knees.

Now suddenly as I lay there watching Red Andy's murderous figure and strung for swift action, I started and (albeit the night was very warm) felt a chill pass over me, as, loud and clear upon the stilly air, rose again that full, deep voice singing hard by upon Deliverance:

"Go seek ye women everywhere,
North, South, lads, East or West,
Let 'em be dark, let 'em be fair,
My Silver Woman's best,
Blow high, blow low,
Where e'er ye go
The Silver Woman's best.
Aha!
My Silver Woman's best!"

Thus sang the unknown who, all unwitting, was coming to his death; sudden as it came the voice was hushed and nought to hear save the hiss and murmur of the surge, and I saw the man Andy stir restlessly as minute after minute dragged by.

The rock where he crouched lay at the mouth of this cove towards Deliverance, it being one of many that lay piled thereabout. Now chancing to look towards these scattered rocks (and for no reason in the world) I saw a thing that held me as it were spellbound, and this a small enough thing in itself, a sharp, glittering thing that seemed fast caught in a fissure of one of those rocks, and I knew it for a steel hook; but even as I stared at it, the thing was gone and so noiselessly that I half-doubted if I had seen it or no. But, out from the shadow of this rock flashed something that whirled, glittering as it flew, and Red Andy, starting up from his knees was shaken by a fit of strange and awful coughing and came stumbling forward so that I could see his chin and breast bedabbled with the blood that spurted from his gaping mouth. All at once he sank to his knees and thence to his face, spreading his arms wide like one very weary, but with the moonlight flashing back from that which stood upright betwixt his shoulder-blades. And thus I saw again the silver haft of the dagger that was shaped like to a woman, saw this silver woman dance and leap, glittering, ere it grew terribly still.

Then came Roger Tressady from the shadows and stooping, turned up the dead face to the moon, and tapped it gently with his shining hook. And now, whipping out his dagger, he bent to wipe it on the dead man's shirt, but checked suddenly as a pebble started beneath my foot, and, stooped thus, he glared up beneath thick brows as I rose up with pistol leveled and the moon bright upon my face, whereupon he leaped backwards, uttering a choking cry:

"Black Bartlemy—by God!" he gasped and let fall his reeking dagger upon the sand; and so we stood staring on each other and with the dead man sprawling betwixt us.

CHAPTER IV
HOW I HAD SPEECH WITH ROGER TRESSADY TO MY UNDOING

For maybe a full minute we fronted each other unmoving and with never a word; and thus at last I beheld this man Tressady.

A tall, lusty fellow, square of face and with pale eyes beneath a jut of shaggy brow. A vivid neckerchief was twisted about his head and in his hairy ears swung great gold rings; his powerful right hand was clenched to knotted fist, in place of his left glittered the deadly hook.

"Sink me!" says he at last, drawing clenched fist across his brow. "Sink me, but ye gave me a turn, my lord! Took ye for a ghost, I did, the ghost of a shipmate o' mine, one as do lie buried yonder, nought but poor bones—aye, rotten bones—as this will be soon!" Here he spurned the dead man with his foot. "'Tis black rogue this, my lord, one as would ha' made worm's-meat o' poor Tressady—aye, a lump o' murdered clay like my shipmate Bartlemy yonder—but for this Silver Woman o' mine!" Here he stooped for the dagger, and having cleaned it in the sand, held it towards me upon his open palm: "Aha, here's woman hath never failed me yet! She's faithful and true, friend, faithful and true, this Silver Woman o' mine. But 'tis an ill world, my master, and full o' bloody rogues like this sly dog as stole ashore to murder me—the fool! O 'tis a black and bloody world."

"So it is!" quoth I, 'twixt shut teeth, "And all the worse for the likes o' you, Roger Tressady!"

"So ho—he knoweth my name, then!" says Tressady, rubbing shaven chin with silver dagger-hilt and viewing me with his pale, keen gaze. "But do I know him now—do I?"

"I know you for pirate and damned murderer, Roger Tressady, so shall you quit this island this very hour or stay here to rot along with Bartlemy and Red Andy!"

Now at this (and all careless of my pistol) he drew a slow pace nearer, great head out-thrust, peering.

"Why," says he at last, "why—bleed me! If—if it aren't—aye, 'tis Martin! Why for sure 'tis my bonny Marty as saved my skin time and again aboard the *Faithful Friend*! Though ye go mighty fine, lad, mighty fine! But good luck t'ye and a fair wind, say I!" And thrusting the dagger into his girdle he nodded mighty affable. "But look'ee now, Marty, here's me wishing ye well and you wi' a barker in your fist, 'tis no fashion to greet a shipmate, I'm thinking."

"Enough words!" says I, stepping up to him. "Do you go alive, or stay here dead—which?"

"Split me!" says he, never stirring. "But 'tis small choice you offer, Marty—"

"My name's Martin!"

"And a curst good name too, Marty. But I've no mind to be worm's-meat yet awhile—no! Come, what's your quarrel wi' me? First Andy would murder me and now 'tis you—why for? Here's me wi' a heart of gold t' cherish a friend and never a friend t' cherish! What's your quarrel, lad, what?"

"Quarrel enough, what with your drugging me and murder aboard ship—"

"Avast, lad! Here's unchancy talk, ill and unmannered!"

"You murdered divers men aboard the *Faithful Friend*."

"Only three, Marty, only three—poor souls! Though yours is a foul word for 't. I took 'em off, lad, took 'em off as a matter of policy. I've never took off any yet as I wasn't forced to by circumstances. Look'ee, there's men in this world born to be took off by someone or other, and they always come a-drifting across my hawse and get took off accordingly, but don't blame me, lad, don't.

"And as for a-drugging of ye, Marty, true again! But love me! What was I to do? But I didn't take you off, lad, no, nor never shall unless you and policy force me so to do. I'm no murderer born—like

Adam—curse him! Clap me alongside Adam and I'm a turtle-dove, a babe for innocence and a lamb for meekness! There never was such a murderer born into this wicked world as Adam Penfeather, with a curse! 'Twas he as murdered Black Bartlemy and nine sweet, bright lads arter him, murdered 'em here one by one, and wi' a parchment rove about the neck of each poor corpse, Marty. 'Twas he as drove their mates out to sea to perish in a leaky boat—ask Abnegation Mings! 'Twas him nigh murdered me more than once, aye me, lad, as can't *be* killed according to the prophecy of the poor mad soul aboard the old *Delight*. Why Adam, curse him, has murdered more men than you have years. And talking of him, how cometh it you aren't blown t' hell along wi' him and the rest?"

"Do you tell me Adam is dead?"

"Blown up aboard the *Faithful Friend*, lad. Just after we run her aboard and grappled, aye, blew up she did and nigh took us wi' her. Aha, but Adam's dead at last, curse him! Unless he can't be killed either, unless he is—"

Here, and all at once, he turned to stare away across Deliverance, then shrinking, cowered towards me as in sudden terror stabbing at the empty air with his glittering hook:

"Ha—what's yon!" cried he in awful voice; and I turning whither his glaring eyes stared (and half-dreading to behold my lady) had the pistol wrenched from my hold and the muzzle under my ear all in a moment; and stood scowling and defenseless like the vast fool I was.

"Split me!" says he, tapping me gently with his hook. "O blind me if I thought ye such a lubberly fool! So old a trick, Marty! Now look'ee, were I a murderer and loved it—like Adam, curse him—I should pull trigger! But being Roger Tressady wi' a heart o' gold, I say sit down, lad, sit down and let us talk, friend, let us talk. Come—sit down! Never mind Andy, he shan't trouble us!"

So with the pistol at my ear we sat down side by side, and the dead man sprawling at our feet. "Now first, Marty lad, how come ye here alone on Bartlemy's island—how?"

But sitting thus chin on fist I stared down at Red Andy's stiffening body silent as he, I being too full of fierce anger and bitter scorn of my folly for speech.

"Come, come, Marty, be sociable!" says Tressady, tapping my cheek with the pistol-muzzle. "Was it Penfeather sent ye hither t' give an eye to—the treasure? Was it?"

"Aye!"

"'Twould be the night he made the crew drunk and spoiled my plans. Ha, 'twas like him—a cunning rogue! But for this I'd have had the ship and him and the treasure. O a right cunning, fierce rogue was Adam, and none to match him but me."

"But he nearly did for you once!" says I bitterly. "And he such a small, timid man!"

"Look'ee, Martin, when Adam grows timid 'tis time for your bold, desperate fellows to beware! But he's dead at last, though I'd ha' felt more comfort, aye, I'd ha' took it kinder had he been took off by my Silver Woman—or this!" Here he thrust his hook before my eyes. "It ain't a pretty thing, Martin, not pretty, no—but 'tis useful at all times and serves to shepherd my lambs wi' now and then, 'tis likewise a mighty persuading argument, but, and best of all—'tis sure, lad, sure. So I'd ha' took it kinder had I watched him go off on this, lad, this. My hook for my enemies and for my friends a heart o' gold! And, talking o' gold, Marty, what—what o' Bartlemy's Treasure?"

"You are happily welcome to it for all of me."

"Why, that's spoke manly and like a friend, rot me but it is! And now where might it lie, Marty, where?"

"I've no idea."

"What, ha'n't ye found it, lad?"

"No!"

"Not even—seen it, then?"

"No!"

"Why, think o' that now, think of that! And you wi' a fortune o' pearls on you, Marty. These pearl studs and buttons, lad. Pearls—ha, pearls was meat and drink to Bartlemy. And here's you wi' pearls I've seen on Bartlemy many a time. And yet you ha'n't found the treasure, says you. If I was a passionate man, Marty, I should call ye liar, says I. Howsoever what I do say is—that you've forgot, and very right and proper. But we'm friends, you and me, so far, and so, 'twixt friends, I ask you to think again until you remember, and to think hard, lad, hard."

Now as I sat (and miserably enough) staring down at my jeweled buttons that seemed to leer up at me like so many small, malevolent eyes, upon the air rose a distant stir that grew and grew to sound of voices with the creak and rumble of oars.

"Here come my lambs at last, Marty, and among 'em some o' the lads as sailed wi' Bartlemy aboard the *Delight*. There's Sam Spraggons for one—Smiling Sam as you'll mind aboard the *Faithful Friend*. Now the Smiler knoweth many and divers methods of persuasion, Marty lad, tricks learned of the Indians as shall persuade a man to anything in this world. But first, seeing 'tis you, Martin, as saved my life aboard ship, though all unknowing, here's my offer: show me how to come by Bartlemy's Treasure as is mine—mine by rights, let me get my hands on to it and none the wiser, and there shall be share for you, Marty lad, share for you. Otherwise I must let Sam try to persuade you to remember where it lieth—come, what d'ye say?"

"What—you'll torture me, then?"

"If I must, friend, if I must. 'Tis for you to say."

"Why, then, 'twill be labor in vain, Tressady, for I swear I know nought of this treasure—"

"Sit still, lad, sit still!" says he, clapping the pistol to my ear again. "Though a fool in many ways, Marty, you're proper enough man to look at and 'twill be pity to cripple ye! Aye, there won't be much left when Sam is done wi' you, more's the pity."

Hereupon he hailed loudly and was answered from the lagoon, and glancing thither, I saw two boats crowded with men pulling for the beach.

"A wildish company, Martin, desperate fellows as ever roved the Main, as I do love no more than they love me. So say the word and we'll share Black Bartlemy's treasure betwixt us, just you and me, lad, me and you! Come, what's your will?" But shaking my head (and hopelessly enough) I set my teeth and watched the coming of my tormentors.

And foremost was a short, plump, bright-eyed man who lacked an ear, and at his elbows two others, the one a lank rogue with a patch over one eye, the third a tall, hairy fellow.

And observing them as they came I knew them for those same three rogues I had fought with in the hedge-tavern beside Pembury Hill on that night I had first seen my dear lady. Hard upon their heels came a riotous company variously armed and accoutered, who forthwith thronged upon me pushing and jostling for sight of me, desecrating the quiet night with their hoarse and clamorous ribaldry. Unlovely fellows indeed and clad in garments of every shape and cut, from stained home spun and tattered shirts to velvet coats be-laced and gold-braided; and beholding this tarnished and sordid finery, these clothes looted from sinking ships and blazing towns, I wondered vaguely what had become of their late owners.

At a gesture from Tressady I was dragged to my feet and my arms jerked, twisted and bound before me crosswise, and so stood I helpless and in much painful discomfort whiles Tressady harangued his fellows, tapping me gently with his hook:

"Look'ee, my bullies," quoth he, "I promised ye gold aplenty and here, somewhere on this island, it lieth waiting to be found. It needeth but for this fool Martin here, as some o' you will mind for Adam Penfeather's comrade, with a curse, it needeth but for him to speak, I say, and in that same hour each one o' you may fill your clutch wi' more treasure than ever came out o' Eldorado or Manoa—so speak he must and shall—eh, bullies, eh?"

"Aye, aye, Cap'n!" they roared, pressing upon me with a shaking of fists and glitter of eager steel.

"Twist his thumbs, Cap'n!" cried one.

"Slit his nose!" roared another.

"Trim his yeres!" cried a third.

But Tressady silenced them with a flourish of his hook. "Hark'ee, lads!" says he. "You all mean well, but you're bunglers, here's a little delicate matter as none can handle like the Smiler. There's none like Sam can make a man give tongue! Pass the word for Smiling Sam! Step forward, Sammy."

Hereupon cometh the great, fat fellow Spraggons who had been bo'sun's mate aboard the *Faithful Friend*, forcing his way with vicious elbows and mighty anxious to come at me.

"O love my limbs!" says he in his high-pitched voice and blinking his hairless lids at me, "O cherish my guts—leave him to me, Cap'n! Sam's the lad to make this yer cock crow. See now—a good, sharp knife 'neath the finger or toenails—drew slow, mates, slow! Or a hot iron close agen his eyes is good. Or boiling water poured in his yeres might serve. Then—aha, Cap'n! I know a dainty little trick, a small cord, d'ye see, twisted athwart his head just a-low the brows, twisted and twisted—as shall start his eyes out right pretty to behold. I mind too as Lollonais had a trick o' bursting a man's guts wi' water—"

"Bring him to the beach yonder!" says Tressady, watching me ever with his pale eyes. "There shall be more room for't yonder!"

So they haled me along betwixt them, and with huge merriment; but scarce were we out of the cove and hard beside Bartlemy's tree than I started to the vicious prick of a knife, and whirling about despite the fierce hands that sought to hold me, I saw Smiling Sam about to stab me again. But now, as I strove with my reeling captors, was a flicker of vicious steel as Tressady sprang and, whipping his hook beneath the great fellow's belt, whirled Smiling Sam from his feet despite his prodigious weight and forthwith trampled upon him.

"So-ho, my merry lad!" quoth Tressady, glaring down into Smiling Sam's convulsed face. "And must ye be at it afore I give the word? Who's captain here—who? Come, speak up, my roaring boy!" And he thrust his hook beneath the Smiler's great, flabby chin.

"Mercy, Cap'n—mercy!" cried Spraggons, his high-pitched voice rising to a pitiful squeal. "Not the hook, Cap'n—O Lord love me—not the hook!"

"Hook? And why not, Sam, why not? 'Tis sharp and clean and quick, and hath done the business o' nicer rogues than you, bully, aye and better, Sam, better—"

"O Cap'n—for God's sake—"

"Who're you to call on God so glib, Sammy? 'Tis marvel He don't strike ye blind, lad. Or there's your innards, Sam, here's that may whip out your liver, lad—So!" I saw the glitter of the hook, heard Smiling Sam's gasping scream as the steel bit into him, and then Tressady was on his feet smiling round upon his awed and silent company.

"Look'ee, bullies!" says he, pointing to the Smiler's inanimate form. "Here's poor Sam all swooned away at touch o' my hook like any woman—and him my bo'sun! Pshaw! I want a man!" Here he stooped, and wrenching the silver pipe from Smiling Sam's fat throat stared from one shuffling rogue to another. "Step forward, Abner," says he at last. "Come, you'll do—you're a prime sailor-man, you're my bo'sun henceforth."

But now Smiling Sam awaking from his swoon moaned feebly and sat up. "Not the hook, Cap'n!" he wailed. "O not that—"

"No, Smiler, no, I keep it for better men. Disobey me again and I'll drown ye in a puddle. And now up wi' you, Sammy, up wi' you and stand by to teach Martin here how to talk."

"Aye, aye, Cap'n—aye, aye!" says the gross fellow, rising nimbly enough, whiles his comrades closed about us expectant, and glancing from me to Tressady where he had seated himself on a boulder.

"Here will do!" says he, pointing to a brilliant strip of moonlit sand midway betwixt the shadows of the cliff and Bartlemy's tree. "On his back, hearties, and grapple him fast, he's strong well-nigh as I am. Now his hand, Smiler, his right hand—"

"Aye, aye, Cap'n!" quoth the fellow, kneeling above me where I lay helpless. "Will I cut it adrift—slow like?" And as he flourished his knife I saw a trickle of saliva at the corners of his great, loose mouth. "Off at the wrist, Cap'n, or fingers first?"

"No, fool! His thumbnail first—try that!"

Sweating and with every nerve a-quiver I watched that cruel knife, holding my breath in expectation of the coming agony, and then—from the black gloom of the cliff beyond burst a sudden echoing roar, I heard the whine of a bullet and immediately all was confusion and uproar, shouts of dismay and a wild rush for shelter from this sudden attack. But as I struggled to my knees Tressady's great hand gripped my throat, and dragging me behind a boulder he pinned me there.

"Stand by, lads!" he roared. "Level at the cliff yonder, but let no man pull trigger! Wait till they fire again and mark the flash!"

Helpless in my bonds and crushed beneath Tressady's knee I heard a stir and rustle to right and left of me, the click of cocking triggers and thereafter—silence. And, marking the gleam of pistol and musket-barrel, I fell to an agony of dread, well knowing whence that merciful shot had come.

For mayhap five minutes nought was to hear save the rustle of stealthy arm or leg and the sound of heavy breathing, until at length one spoke, loud-voiced: "What now, Captain? Us can't bide here all night."

"How many are we, Purdy?"

"Thirty and nine, Captain."

"Then do you take ten and scale the starboard cliff and you, Abner, with another ten take the cliff to larboard. I'll bide here wi' the rest and so we'll have 'em—"

"Them cliffs be perilous high, Cap'n!"

"My hook is more perilous, Tom Purdy! Off wi' you, ye dogs, or I'll show ye a liver yet and be—"

He stopped all at once as, faint at first yet most dreadful to hear, there rose a man's cry, chilling the flesh with horror, a cry that waxed and swelled louder and louder to a hideous screaming that shrilled upon the night and, sinking to an awful bubbling murmur, was gone.

Up sprang Tressady to stare away across Deliverance whence this dreadful cry had come, and I saw his hook tap-tapping at his great chin; then beyond these shining sands was the thunderous roar of a great gun, a furious rattle of small-arms that echoed and re-echoed near and far, and thereafter single shots in rapid succession.

Hereupon rose shouts and cries of dismay: "Lord love us we'm beset! O Cap'n, we be took fore and aft. What shall us do, Cap'n? Yon was a gun. What o' the ship, Cap'n—what o' the ship?"

"Yonder—look yonder! Who comes?" cried Tressady, pointing towards Deliverance Beach with his glittering hook.

Twisting my head as I lay, I looked whither he pointed, and saw one that ran towards us, yet in mighty strange fashion, reeling in wide zigzags like a drunken man; and sometimes he checked, only to come on again, and sometimes he fell, only to struggle up.

"By God—it's Abnegation!" cries Tressady. "'Tis my comrade, Abnegation Mings! Look to the prisoner, ye dogs—you, Tom Purdy! I'm for Abnegation!" And off he went at a run. At his going was mighty talk and discussion what they should do, some men being for stealing away in the boats, others for taking to the woods, and all clean forgetting me where I lay.

But suddenly they fell silent all for Abnegation was hailing feebly, and was come so nigh that we might see him, his face all bloody, his knees bending under him with weakness as he stumbled on. Suddenly, beholding Tressady, he stopped and hailed him in wild, gasping voice: "Roger—O Roger! The devil's aboard us, Roger—Penfeather's on us—Penfeather's took the ship—I'm all that's left alive! They killed Sol first—did ye . . . hear him die, Roger? O did ye hear—"

I saw him fall and Tressady run to lift him, and watched these pirate rogues as, with oaths and cries of dismay, they hasted hither to throng about the two;

then, rolling into the nearest shadow I struggled to my feet and found myself beneath the spreading branches of Bartlemy's tree. And now, as I strove desperately against the rope that bit into the flesh of me, I felt the rope fall away, felt two soft arms close about me and a soft breath on my cheek: "Martin—O thank God!"

Turning, I caught my dear, brave lady to my heart. Heedless of aught else in the world beside I clasped her in my aching arms, and kissed her until she stayed me and showing me where stood our enemies, a wild disordered company, took my hand and began to run. Reaching the cliff we climbed together nor stayed until she had brought me to a little cave where lay an arquebus together with bandoliers. "I tried to reload it, dear Martin, but 'twas vain—my poor, silly hands shook so. For, O my dear, I—heard them—saw them and—thought I should run mad—O Martin my love!"

So now whiles I loaded the arquebus I told her as well as I might something of what I thought concerning her brave spirit, of my undying love for her, though in fashion very lame and halting. Thereafter, the weapon being ready I placed it near and, sitting within the gloom of this little cave, I took my love into my arms, her dear head pillowed on my breast, and kissed the tremors from her sweet mouth and the horror from her eyes. And thus with her arms about my neck and her soft, smooth cheek against mine, we waited for what was to be.

CHAPTER V
OF THE COMING OF ADAM PENFEATHER

In the shadow of the cliff below our hiding-place crept divers of these pirate rogues, and, crouching there cheek by jowl fell to a hoarse mutter of talk yet all too low for us to catch; but presently there brake out a voice high-pitched, the which I knew for that of Smiling Sam. "We'm done, lads, I tell ye. O love my lights—we'm done! 'Tis the end o' we since Penfeather hath took the ship—and here's us shall lie marooned to perish o' plagues, or Indian-savages, or hunger unless, lads, unless—"

"Unless what, Smiler?" questioned one eagerly.

"Unless we'm up and doing. Penfeather do lack for men—Mings says he counted but ten at most when they boarded him! Well, mates—what d'ye say?"

"Ha, d'ye mean fight, Smiler? Fall on 'em by surprise and recapture the ship—ha?"

"O bless my guts, no! Penfeather aren't to be caught so—not him! He'll ha' warped out from the anchorage by this! But he be shorthanded to work the vessel overseas, 'tis a-seekin' o' likely lads and prime sailor-men is Penfeather, and we sits on these yere sands. Well, mates, on these yere sands we be but what's took up us on these yere sands? The boats lie yonder! Well?"

"Where be you heading of now, Smiler? Where's the wind? Talk plain!"

"Why look'ee all, if Penfeather wants men, as wants 'em he doth, what's to stay or let us from rowing out to Penfeather soft and quiet and 'listing ourselves along of Penfeather, and watch our chance t' heave Penfeather overboard and go a-roving on our own account? Well?"

At this was sudden silence and thereafter a fierce mutter of whispering lost all at once in the clatter of arms and breathless scuffling as they scrambled to their feet; for there, within a yard of them, stood Tressady, hand grasping the dagger in his belt, his glittering hook tapping softly at his great chin as he stared from one to other of them.

"Ha, my pretty lambs!" says he, coming a pace nearer. "Will ye skulk then, will ye skulk with your fools' heads together? What now, mutiny is it, mutiny? And what's come o' my prisoner Martin, I don't spy him hereabouts?"

Now at this they shuffled, staring about and upon each other and (as I think) missed me for the first time.

"You, Tom Purdy, step forward—so! Now where's the prisoner as I set i' your charge, where, my merry bird, where?"

The fellow shrank away, muttering some sullen rejoinder that ended in a choking scream as Tressady sprang. Then I (knowing what was toward) clasped my lady to me, covering her ears that she might not hear those ghastly bubbling groans, yet felt her sweet body shaking with the horror that shook me.

"So, there's an end o' Tom Purdy, my bullies!" gasped Tressady, stooping to clean his hook in the sand. "And I did it, look'ee, because he failed me once, d'ye see! Who'll be next? Who's for mutiny— you, Sammy, you—ha?"

"No—no, Cap'n!" piped Smiling Sam. "Us do be but contriving o' ways and means seein' as Penfeather do ha' took our ship, curse him!"

"And what though he has? 'Tis we have the island and 'tis on this island lieth Black Bartlemy's Treasure, and 'tis the treasure we're after! As to ways and means, here we be thirty and eight to Penfeather's fourteen, and in a little 'twill be dark and the guns shan't serve 'em and then—aha, look yonder! The fools be coming into our very clutches! To cover, lads, and look to your primings and wait my word."

Now glancing whither he pointed, I saw, above the adjacent headland, the tapering spars of a ship. Slowly she hove into view, boltsprit, forecastle, waist and poop, until she was plain to view, and I knew her for that same black ship that fouled us in Deptford Pool. She was standing in for the island under her lower

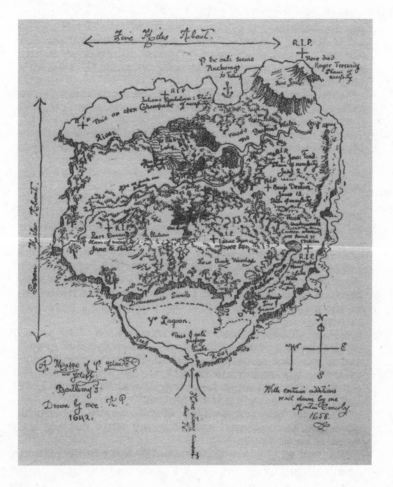

courses only, although the wind was very light, but on she came, and very slowly, until she was so near that I might see the very muzzles of her guns. Suddenly with a cheery yo-ho-ing her yards were braced round, her anchor was let go and she brought to opposite Skeleton Cove and within fair pistol-shot.

Now glancing below I saw Tressady stand alone and with Abnegation Mings huddled at his feet, but in the gloom of the cave and to right and left, in every patch of shadow and behind every bush and rock, was the glimmer of pistol or musket-barrel, and all leveled in the one direction.

Presently up to the lofty poop of the ship clambered a short, squat man in marvelous wide breeches and a great cutlass on hip, who clapping speaking-trumpet to mouth, roared amain: "Ahoy the shore! We be shorthanded. Now what rogues o' ye will turn honest mariners and 'list aboard us for England? Who's for a free pardon and Old England?"

Hereupon, from bush and shadow and rock, I heard a whisper, a murmur, and the word "England" oft repeated.

Tressady heard it also, and stepping forward he drew a long furrow in the sand with the toe of his shoe. "Look'ee my hearty boys," says he, pointing to this furrow with his hook. "The first man as setteth foot athwart this line I send to hell-fire along o' Tom Purdy yonder!"

"Ahoy the shore!" roared Godby louder than ever. "Who's for an honest life, a free pardon and a share in Black Bartlemy's Treasure—or shall it be a broadside? Here be every gun full charged wi' musket-balls—and 'tis point-blank range! Which shall it be?"

Once again rose a murmur that swelled to an angry muttering, and I saw Smiling Sam come creeping from the shadow of the cave. "O Cap'n," he piped, "'tis plaguy desperate business, here's some on us like to be bloody corpses—but I'm wi' you, Cap'n Roger, whether or no, 'tis me to your back!"

"To my back, Sammy? Why so you shall, lad, so you shall, but I'll ha' your pistols first, Smiler—so!" And whipping the weapons from the great fellow's belt, Tressady gave them to Abnegation Mings where he lay in the shelter of a rock, and sitting down, crossed long legs and cocked an eye at the heavens.

"Hearties all," quoth Tressady, "the moon sinketh apace and 'twill be ill shooting for 'em in the dark, so with dark 'tis us for the boats—muffled oars—we clap 'em aboard by the forechains larboard and starboard, and the ship is ours, bullies—ours!"

"Well and good, Cap'n!" piped Smiling Sam. "But how if she slip her cable and stand from us?"

"And how shall she, my fool lad, and the wind dropped? The wind's failed 'em and they lie helpless—"

"And that's gospel true, Cap'n. Aye, aye, we'm wi' you! Gi'e us the word, Cap'n!" quoth divers voices in fierce answer.

"O sink me!" groaned Mings. "Here lies poor Abnegation shattered alow and aloft—O burn me, here's luck! But you'll take me along, Roger? If Death boards me tonight I'd rayther go in honest fight than lying here like a sick dog—so you'll have me along, Roger?"

"Aye that will I, lad, that will I and—"

"Ahoy the shore!" roared Godby's great voice again. "Let them rogue-dogs as'll turn honest mariners, them as is for England and a free pardon, stand by to come aboard and lively! In ten minutes we open fire wi' every gun as bears!"

Now here there brake forth a clamor of oaths, cries and dismayed questioning: "Lord love us, what now, Cap'n? Is us to be murdered, look'ee? Doomed men we be, lads! Shall us wait to be shot, mates? What shall us do, Cap'n, what shall us do?"

"Lie low!" quoth Tressady, rising. "Bide still all and let no man stir till I give word. In half an hour or less 'twill be black dark—very well, for half an hour I'll hold 'em in parley, I'll speak 'em smooth and mighty friendly, here shall be no shooting. I'll hold 'em till the moon be down—and Smiler shall come wi' me. Come, Sammy lad—come!"

So saying he turned and I watched him stride out upon that spit of sand hard by Bartlemy's tree and this great fat fellow trotting at his heels. Upon the edge of the tide Tressady paused and hailed loud and cheerily, "Penfeather ahoy! O Adam Penfeather here come I Roger Tressady for word wi' you. Look'ee, Adam, we've fought and run foul of each other this many a year—aye, half round the world and all for sake o' Black Bartlemy's Treasure as is mine by rights, Adam, mine by rights. Well now tonight let's, you and me, make an end once and for all one way or t'other. There's you wi' my ship—true, Adam, true! But here's me wi' the island and the treasure, Adam, and the treasure. And what then? Why then, says I, let's you and me, either come to some composition or fight it out man to man, Adam, man to man. So come ashore, Captain Penfeather— you as do be blacker pirate than ever was Bartlemy—come out yonder on the reef alone wi' me and end it one way or t'other. Come ashore, Adam, come ashore if ye dare adventure!"

"Ahoy you, Tressady!" roared Godby in reply. "Cap'n Adam is ashore wi' ye this moment—look astarn o' you, ye rogue!"

Round sprang Tressady as out from the dense shadow of Bartlemy's tree stepped Adam Penfeather himself. He stood there in the moonlight very still and viewing Tressady with head grimly outthrust, his arms crossed upon his breast, a pistol in the fist and deadly menace in every line of his small, spare figure.

"I'm here, Tressady!" says he, his voice ringing loud and clear. "And I am come to make an end o' you this night. It hath been long a-doing—but I have ye at last, Roger."

"Be ye sure, Adam, so sure?"

"As death, Tressady, for I have ye secure at last."

"Bleed me but you're out there, Adam, you're out there! The boot's on t'other leg, for hereabouts do lie thirty and eight o' my lads watching of ye this moment and wi' finger on trigger."

"I know it!" says Adam nodding. "But there's never a one dare shoot me, for the first shot fired ashore shall bring a whole broadside in answer, d'ye see. But as for you, Tressady, pray if you can, for this hour you hang."

"Hang is it, Adam?" says Tressady, and with swift glance towards the sinking moon, "And who's to do it—who?"

"There be thirty and eight shall swing ye aloft so soon as I give 'em the word, Tressady."

"You do talk rank folly, Adam, folly, and ye know it!" says he smiling and stealing furtive hand to the dagger in his girdle. "But and I should die this night I take you along wi' me and you can lay to—" But he got no further, for Smiling Sam (and marvelous nimble) whipped up a stone, and leaping on him from behind smote him two murderous blows and, staggering helplessly, Tressady pitched forward upon his face and lay upon the verge of the incoming tide.

Beholding his handiwork, Smiling Sam uttered a thin, high-shrilling laugh, and spitting upon that still form kicked it viciously.

"Oho, Cap'n Penfeather," cries he, "'tis the Smiler hath saved ye the labor, look'ee! 'Tis Sam hath finished Tressady at last and be damned t' him! And now 'tis the Smiler as do be first to 'list wi' ye!" And he began to shamble across the sands; but passing that rock where crouched Abnegation Mings he tripped and fell, and I saw the flash of Abnegation's knife as they rolled and twisted in the shadow of this rock, whiles, from this shadow, rose a shrill crying like the wail of a hurt child, and into the moonlight came a great, fat hand that clutched and tore at the sand then grew suddenly still, and with crooked fingers plunged deep into the sand like a white claw. Then, tossing aside his bloody knife, Abnegation Mings struggled to his feet and came staggering to kneel above his comrade Tressady and to turn up the pallid face of him to the moon.

And now Adam thrust away his pistols and with hands clasped behind him, turned to face the gloomy shadows of Skeleton Cove: "Come out, sons o' dogs!" says he. "Step forward and show yourselves—and lively it is!" Ensued a moment's breathless pause, then, from bush and shadow and rocks, they stole forth these thirty and eight and, at Adam's harsh command, lined up before him shoulder and shoulder. "Well," says Adam, pacing slowly along their rank to peer into every sullen, hangdog face. "Am I captain here? Aye or no?"

"Aye—aye!" they cried in eager chorus.

"And us was promised a free pardon, Cap'n!" quoth one.

"And a share of the treasure, Cap'n!" says another.

"And England, Cap'n!" cried a third. "There's some on us as do be honest sailor-men and forced to turn pirate in spite o' we—"

"Avast!" says Adam. "What I promise I stand by. But mark this! Let any man fail of his duty to me but once and I shoot that man or hang him out o' hand—is't understood?"

"Aye, aye, Cap'n—'tis agreed! We'll serve ye faithful and true," they cried.

"Why then, bring ropes!" says Adam, and with his new 'listed men at his heels, goes whither lay Tressady and with Abnegation Mings yet crouched above him.

What now was doing I might not see by reason of the crowd, but I heard the voice of Mings upraised in fierce invective, and the throng presently parting, beheld him trussed hand and foot and dragged along with Tressady towards Bartlemy's tree. There a noose was set about the neck of each, and the rope's ends cast over a branch.

But as at Adam's command these miserable wretches were hauled aloft to their deaths, my lady uttered a cry of horror and grasped my arm in desperate hands. "Martin!" she panted. "O Martin, 'tis horrible! Save them, this must not—shall not be—"

"'Tis but justice," says I. "These men are pirates and murderers—"

"This is no justice!" cries she breathlessly, her face all pale and drawn. "And these men are sore hurt beside—ah, God—look! Stop them, Martin—O stop them! Nay, then I will!"

And here, or ever I could let or stay her, she begins to clamber down into the cove. Howbeit, quick and sure-footed though she was, I was presently before her and so came running, knife in hand. Nor was I any too soon, for as I reached the tree Tressady and Mings were dragged, choking, from their feet; but with a couple of strokes my keen knife had cut those deadly ropes asunder, and as the two fell gasping on the sand I turned to stare into the scowling eyes of Adam Penfeather.

Now as I stood thus someone spoke 'twixt sigh and groan: "Bartlemy—'tis Bartlemy!" And the word was taken up by others, "Bartlemy—Black Bartlemy!" and all men fell back from me whiles Adam scowled at me above leveled pistol.

"Hold off, Adam!" I panted. "Let be, Adam Penfeather—let be!"

"What?" says he, peering. "And is it—Martin? Lord love me, now what fool's ploy is this?"

"What you will," quoth I, "only here has been enough of death for one night—"

"'Tis but you do think so, Martin, and you was ever a fool! I came ashore to see these two rogues hang, and hang they shall!"

"Now look you, Adam Penfeather," says I, scowling in turn, "you have cozened and tricked me since first you crossed my path—well, let that go! But mark this: according to your letter three-quarters of this treasure is mine. Very well—take it back. I'll buy these rogues' lives of you—"

"Lord love me!" says he, staring in blank amaze. "What new fool craze is this? Will ye save this bloody murderer Tressady that drugged ye aboard ship, the man that was our bane and plague all along? The rogue hath been my deadliest enemy seeking my destruction these fifteen years, and you would save him alive! It seemeth my pistol-butt must ha' harmed what little brain you have and you be run stark, staring mad, Martin!"

"Howbeit," says I, mighty determined, "you don't hang these men whiles I live!"

"Why, there's no difficulty either, Martin, for what's to stay me from hanging you along with 'em, or shooting you for the fool you are?"

"I!" cried a voice, and there betwixt us was my lady, she all stately dignity despite her hurried breathing, at sight of whom these lawless fellows gave back one and all, even Adam himself retreated a step, staring upon her round-eyed. Then, very slowly he thrust pistols into belt and uncovering his head bowed full low, and I fancied his thin lips twitched as he did so.

"So be it, my lady," says he. "I call on your ladyship to witness that I sell two bundles of very unseemly merchandise," and he pointed towards the two helpless forms at his feet. "And now, with your fair leave, madam, I'll see these fellows safe aboard and warn my Lord Dering and gentlemen of your welfare and presence here."

"Wait!" says I as he turned to go. "First I would have these my purchases set aboard a boat, with such stores needful, and cast adrift."

"Why, this was not in the bargain, Martin!" says he, shaking his head. "But it shall be done for sake of our one-time comradeship." And away he goes and his fellows with him. True to his word he orders the pinnace launched and sends divers men to bear these two rogues aboard. Hereupon I cut away their bonds, doing the which I found Tressady still unconscious, but Mings for all his wounds seemed lively enough.

"Master," says he, staring hard at me, "your name's Martin, as I think?"

"And what then?" says I, mighty short.

"'Tis a name I shall mind as long as I do my own, and that is Mings—Abnegation Mings."

"Aye," says I. "You told me this when you sang of dead men in a wood at midnight—"

"Ha, 'twas you, was it, master? Well, here lieth poor Roger dead or dying and me little better, and 'tis far to the Main and an ill journey, but should we come there and live, there be two men shall wonder at ye, master, nor ever forget the name o' the man as saved our necks. Howsoever, come life or death, here's Abnegation doth wish ye a fair wind ever and always, master."

So they bore him, together with Tressady, to the pinnace, and setting them aboard, shoved them adrift, and I watched Abnegation ply feeble oars until the boat was through the passage in the reef and out in the open sea beyond.

CHAPTER VI
HOW I DOUBTED MYSELF

Now as I stood thus, staring out to sea, the moon sank and with it my heart also, for as the dark came about me so came darkness within me and sudden sorrow with great fear of the future; wherefore, beholding the loom of the ship where lights twinkled, I would gladly have seen her a shattered wreck, and hearing the hoarse laughter and voices of these lawless fellows waking the echoes of Deliverance Beach, I hated them one and all, and to my fear and sorrow anger was added.

But now cometh my dear lady to stand beside me, to steal her hand into mine, and never a word betwixt us for a while. At last: "So endeth our solitude, Martin!"

"Aye!"

"Our deliverance is come!" says she. And then, very softly, "Doth not this rejoice you?"

Here answer found I none, since now at last I knew this the very thing I had come most to dread. So was silence again save for these hoarse unlovely voices where they launched and boarded the longboat. "Master Adam would have me go on board, Martin, but 'tis near dawn so will I bide with you to welcome this new day."

"I'm glad you stayed, Damaris." At this I felt her clasp tighten on my fingers, and so she brings me to a rock hard by and, sinking on the warm sand, would have me sit by her; thus, side by side, we watched the boat pull away to the ship, and presently all about us was hushed and still save for the never-ceasing murmur of the surge.

"Martin," says she in a while, "with this new day beginneth for us a new life! In a few short hours we sail for England."

"England! Aye, to be sure!" says I, mighty doleful, but, conscious of her regard, strove to look happy yet made such a botch of it that, getting to her knees, she takes my hangdog face betwixt her two hands.

"O but you are glad?" she questions, a little breathlessly. "Glad to come with me to England—to leave this wilderness?"

"Aye!" I nodded, well-nigh choking on the word.

"Dear Martin, look at me!" she commanded. "Now speak me plain. Whence is your grief?"

"O, my lady," quoth I, "'tis the knowledge of my unworthiness, my unloveliness, my rude and graceless ways; England is no place for like of me. I am well enough here in the wild—to work for you, fight for you an' need be, but how may I compare with your fine gallants and courtly gentlemen?"

Now at this she clasps me all sudden in her arms and setting soft cheek to mine falls a-chiding me, yet kissing me full oft, calling me "silly," "dear," "foolish," and "beloved."

"How shall you compare?" cries she. "Thus and thus, dear Martin—so infinitely above and beyond all other men that unless you wed me needs must I die a maid!"

Thus did she comfort me, soothing my fears, and thus the dawn found us.

"O 'tis day!" she sighed. "'Tis day already!" And now 'twas her voice was doleful whiles her eyes gazed regretful round about the white sands of Deliverance and the tree-clad highlands beyond.

"O indeed I do love this dear island of ours, Martin!"

Sudden upon the stilly air was the beat of oars, and we beheld a boat rowed by a couple of mariners and in the stern-sheets Sir Rupert Dering and the three gentlemen, his companions. Hereupon my lady would have me go with her to meet them then and there, but I shook my head. "Do you go, Damaris, I'll not speak them before I must. And should you have cause to mention me I pray you will not tell my name."

"As you will, dear Martin," says she and, pressing my hand, goes her way. From the shadow of the rock I watched these gentlemen leap gaily ashore to bow before her with many and divers elegant posturings, flourishes and flauntings of hats, kissing of her hands and the like gallantries until I must needs scowl otherwhere; yet even so, was conscious of their merry laughter where they paced to and fro and the new risen sun making a glory about her.

At last she curtseys, and staying them with a gesture, comes hasting back to me. "Martin," says she, "it seems there be men wounded and dying on board ship, so must I go to them. Will you not come with me?"

"Nay," I answered, "I'll to the caves for such things as you would bring away."

"Why then, my spoon, Martin, and three-legged stool, bring these—nay, wait, 'tis there I would bid farewell to this our dear island. Wait me there, Martin."

So away she goes on her errand of mercy, leaving me to my thoughts and these all of England and my future life there. I was fain to picture myself married and happy in my lady's love, my life thenceforth a succession of peaceful days amid the ordered quiet of that Kentish countryside I knew and loved so well. With the eye of my mind I seemed to see a road winding 'twixt bloomy hedgerows, past chattering brooks and pleasant meadows, past sleepy hamlet bowered 'mid trees and so, 'neath a leafy shade, to where rose tall gates, their pillars crowned by couchant leopards wrought in the stone, and beyond these a broad avenue, its green shadow splashed with sunlight, leading away to the house of Conisby Shene with its wide terrace where stood my lady waiting and expectant; yet nowhere could I vision myself. And now I must needs bethink me of Godby's "long, dark road with the beckoning light and the waiting arms of love," and in my heart the old doubt waked and a fear that such peace, such tender meetings and welcomes sweet, were not for such as I, nor ever could be.

From these gloomy reflections I was roused by a giggling laugh, and glancing about, espied Sir Rupert and his three fellows, their finery somewhat the worse for their late hardship yet themselves very gay and debonair nonetheless as they stood viewing me and mighty interested. Presently Sir Rupert steps up to me with his haughtiest fine-gentlemanly air and no civility of bowing.

"Let me perish but here's notable change!" says he, surveying my rich attire, so that I yearned for my rags again. "Here is strange metamorphosis! The sullen and rustic Cymon bloometh at Beauty's mandate, and Caliban is tamed!" At the which sally his companions giggled again.

"Sir," quoth I, and awkwardly enough, "I am in no mood for your pleasantries. If therefore you have aught else to say of me, pray remove out o' my hearing."

This protest Sir Rupert fanned airily aside with be-ringed hand. "I gather," says he, "that you have been at some pains of service to my Lady Brandon in her late dolorous situation here—receive my thanks!"

"I wish none o' your thanks, sir—"

"Nonetheless I bestow 'em—on my Lady Brandon's behalf. Furthermore—"

"Enough, sir, I would be alone."

"Furthermore," he continued and with another airy motion of his white fingers, "I would have you particularly remark that if my Lady Brandon, lacking better company, hath stooped to any small familiarities with you, these must be forgot and—"

"Ha!" I cried, springing to my feet. "Begone, paltry fool, lest I kick you harder than I did last time at Conisby Shene."

"Insolent gallows'-rogue!" he panted, reaching for his sword-hilt, but as he freed it from scabbard I closed with him and, wrenching it from his hold, belabored him soundly with the flat of it, and such of his companions as chanced within my reach, until hearing shouts, I espied Adam approaching with divers of his grinning fellows; whereupon I snapped the blade across my knee and hasted from the place.

I strode on haphazard in a blind fury, but reaching the woods at last and safe from all observation, I cast myself down therein, and gradually my anger grew to a great bitterness. For (thinks I) "gallows'-rogue" am I in very truth an outcast from my kind, a creature shamed by pillory and lash, a poor wretch for spiteful Fortune's buffets. Hereupon (being a blind fool ever) I cursed the world and all men in it saving only my unworthy self. And next, bethinking me of my dear lady who of her infinite mercy had stooped to love such as I, it seemed that my shame must smirch her also, that rather than lifting me to her level I must needs drag her down to mine. She, wedding me, gave all, whiles I, taking all, had nought to offer in return save my unworthiness. Verily it seemed that my hopes of life with her in England were but empty dreams, that I had been living in the very Paradise of Fools unless—

Here I raised bowed head, and clenching my fists stared blindly before me.

How if the ship should sail without us?

CHAPTER VIII
HOW MY DOUBTING WAS RESOLVED FOR ME

The sun being high-risen and myself famished with hunger, I set off for our habitation by paths well-hid from observation and yearning mightily to find my lady there. Having scaled the cliff I reached the little plateau, and parting the bushes, recoiled from the muzzle of a piece leveled at me by a squat, grim fellow.

"What, Godby!" says I, frowning. "D'ye take me for murderer still, then?"

At this he let fall his musket in blank amaze, and then came running and with hands outstretched. "O pal!" cries he. "O pal—have I found ye at last? Ha, many's the time I've grieved for ye and my fool's doubts o' you, Martin, choke me else! I'm sorry, pal, burn me but I've repented my suspecting o' you ever since, though to be sure you was mighty strange aboard the *Faithful Friend* and small wonder. But here's me full o' repentance, Martin, so— if you can forgive poor Godby—?"

"Full and freely!" says I, whereupon he hugs me and the tears running down his sunburned cheeks.

"Then we'm pals again, Martin, and all's bowmon!"

"And what o' me?" Turning about I beheld Adam on the threshold of the cave. "What o' me, shipmate?"

"Aye—what?" says I, folding my arms.

"Ha, doth the tap o' my pistol-butt smart yet, Martin?"

"I know you beyond all doubt for pirate and buccaneer—"

"All past and done, Martin."

"I know you planned from the first to seize the *Faithful Friend*."

"Aye, but where's your proof? The *Faithful Friend* is blown up—"

"And by your hand, like as not."

"True again, so it was, Martin, and thereby did I outwit Tressady and saved the lives of my own people."

"You have been at great pains to befool me to your evil ends."

"At no pains, Martin, 'twas purely simple matter!"

"You have been the death of divers men on this island."

"But always in fair fight!" says he, glancing at me in his furtive fashion. "'Twas them or me, comrade, and black rogues all."

"So you say!"

"And who's to deny it, shipmate?"

"Aye, who indeed? It seems you've killed 'em all."

"Ha, d'ye doubt my word, Martin?"

"Aye, I do so, and judging from what I know, I do take ye for a very rogue and so I'm done with you henceforth."

"Rogue?" says he. "'Tis an ill word! And yet I had rather be rogue than fool, and you are the fool of the world, Martin, for here are you seeking quarrel with your best friend."

"Friend?" quoth I. "O God protect me from such!"

"Now, look'ee, you have named me rogue and good as called me liar, which is great folly seeing you do lie in my power. So here will I prove my friendship and the depth of your folly."

"Nay—I'll hear no more!"

"Aye—but you will! Cover him, Godby, and fire if I say so!"

"O Lord love me!" groaned Godby, but obeyed nevertheless, and looking where he stood, his piece leveled at me, I knew he would obey Adam's word despite his anguished looks.

"And now," says Adam, crossing his arms, "here's the truth on't. I found a poor wretch bent on vengeance, murder, and a rogue's death, which was pure folly. I offered you riches, the which you refused, and this was arrant folly. I took you for comrade, brought you aboard ship with offer of honest employ which you like-wise refused and here was more folly. Your conduct on board ship was all folly. So, despite yourself, I set you on a fair island with the right noble and handsome lady that you, by love, might perchance learn some little wisdom. Well, you fall in love—"

"Stop!" cried I, clenching my fists.

"Not I!" says he, uncrossing his arms, and I saw he had leveled a pistol at me in the crook of his arm. "I'm no fine gentleman for ye to bruise, so haul your wind and listen! You fall in love with my lady, as how could you help, and she with you, which is a matter of some wonder. So here are you full o' love, but doth this teach ye wisdom? Never a whit! For now must you fall foul and belabor our four gallants, and from mere fine gentlemen transform 'em into your deadly enemies, and here was folly stupendous! And now you must quarrel with me, the which is folly absolute. Thus do I find ye fool persistent and consistent ever, and I, being so infinitely the opposite, do contemn you therefore—"

"And now ha' you done?" I demanded, raging.

"Not quite, Martin. You balked me i' the hanging o' these two rogues Tressady and Mings, and here was pitiful folly, since to hang such were a wise and prudent measure. Thus have you loosed murder on my heels again—well, let that go. But you doubted my word, you named me rogue, and for this you shall fight me!" So saying he stepped into the cave and brought thence that same bejeweled Spanish rapier.

"I've no mind to fight with you," says I, turning away.

"An excellent blade!" says he, making a pass in the air, then he tendered it to me hilt foremost and with the little bow.

"'Tis right you should know I am wearing the chain-shirt."

"No matter," quoth he, drawing, "there is your throat or your eye—come!"

So point to point we fell to it. I had been somewhat esteemed at the art once and now I matched his vicious thrusts with cunning parades, with volts and passes, pushing at him when I might, so that twice I was very near. But suddenly as he retreated before my attack, his blade darted and flashed and he called out: "One!" And now he pressed me in turn with quick thrusts and bewildering feints, and presently called out again: "Two! Three! Four!" Then I saw he was cutting the buttons from my sleeve, how and when he would; therefore I cast away my sword in petulant anger and folded my arms.

"Lord love me! Are ye done, Martin?"

"O make an end one way or t'other. I'll not be played with!"

"Verily, you were more dangerous with the club!" says he, and sheathed his rapier. As for me, espying the three-legged stool, I sat me down mighty dejected and full of bitter thoughts until, feeling a touch on my bowed shoulder, I looked up and found him beside me.

"Martin," says he, "'tis true you are a fool but your folly harmeth none but yourself! And thou'rt such honest fool that I must needs love thee, which is strange, yet so it is. Look 'ee, we have quarreled and fought, very well—what's to let us from being friends again?"

"But if I doubt you, Adam?"

"Why, as to that," says he with his whimsical look, "I verily do think myself a something doubtful being at times."

Now at this, up I rose and gripped his hand right heartily; which done he brought me into the cave whiles Godby posted himself on the threshold, leaning on his musket.

"What now, Adam?" I questioned.

"Now let us divide our treasure, Martin—"

"But I bartered my share for the lives of—"

"Tush!" says he, and reaching a valise from shadowy corner he opened it and I beheld such a glory of flashing gems as nigh dazzled me with their splendor. "Look at 'em, Martin, look at 'em!" he whispered. "Here's love and hate, life and death, every good and all the sins— look at 'em!" And catching up a handful he let them fall, glittering, through his fingers. "Lord love me, Martin," he whispered, "'tis enough to turn a man's brain! Have ye counted 'em over, comrade?"

"I never saw them until this moment, Adam." And I confessed how in my folly I had cast his letter of instruction into the sea, and of how my lady had found the secret at her dire peril.

"And she never showed you, Martin?"

"I was always too busy!"

"Busy!" says he, sitting back on his heels to stare up at me. "Busy? O Lord love me! Sure there's not your like i' the whole world, Martin!"

"Which is mighty well for the world!" says I bitterly.

"'Tis vasty treasure, Martin and worth some little risk. And in the cave lie yet fifty and four bars of gold and others of silver, with store of rix-dollars, dou-bloons, moidores and pieces of eight— gold coins of all countries. There let 'em rot—here's more wealth than we shall ever spend. Shall we divide it here or aboard ship?"

"Wait rather until we reach England."

"So be it, comrade. Then I'm minded to apportion a share to Godby here—what d'ye say?"

"With all my heart!"

"Why then, 'tis time we got it safe on board."

"But how to do it—what of Tressady's rogues, Adam?"

"Having buried such of themselves as needed it, Martin, you shall see 'em playing leap-frog on the sands down yonder happy as any innocent school-lads, and never a firearm amongst 'em."

"Hist, Cap'n!" says Godby, suddenly alert. "The man Abner and his two mates a-peeping and a-prying!"

"Where away, Godby man?"

"Hove to in the lee o' them bushes yonder."

"'Tis sly, skulking rogue, Abner!" says Adam, closing and strapping the valise. "'Tis in my mind, Godby, this Abner will never live to see England. Summon 'em hither, all three."

This Godby did forthwith, and presently the three fellows appeared who, knuckling their foreheads, made us their several reverences.

"What now, lads?" says Adam, viewing them with his keen eyes. "I seem to mind your looks—you sailed with Black Bartlemy aboard the *Delight*, I think? Nay, 'tis no matter, we'll let bygones be bygones, and we be all marvelous honest these days, the which is well. Meantime take this dunnage down to the boat," and he pointed to the valise. Hereupon one of the fellows took it up, and knuckled an eyebrow to us in turn. "We sail at sundown," says Adam, "so, Godby, you may as well go aboard and see that all be ready."

"Aye, aye!" says Godby, tightening the belt where swung his great cutlass and, shouldering his musket, set off after the three.

"So there goeth our fortune aboard, comrade."

"And in desperate risky fashion, Adam."

"In safe, straightforward fashion rather, and in broad daylight, the which is surer than stealing it aboard in the dark."

"But should these rogues guess what they carry—"

"They won't, Martin—and if they should they have but their knives 'gainst Godby's musket and pistols."

"Ha—murder, Adam?"

"Would you call this murder, comrade?"

"What other? . . . I wonder what manner of man you'll be, away there in England?"

"A worthy, right worshipful justice o' the peace, Martin, if Providence seeth fit, in laced coat and great peruke, to see that my tenants' cottages be sound and wholesome, to pat the tousled heads o' the children, bless 'em! And to have word with every soul i' the village. To snooze i' my great pew o' Sundays and, dying at last, snug abed, to leave behind me a kindly memory. And what for you, Martin? What see you in the ship yonder?"

"God knoweth!" says I, gloomily.

"Why not a woman's love, comrade, why not good works, rank and belike—children to honor your memory?"

"Were I but worthy all this, Adam."

"Zounds, but here's humility! Yet your true lover is ever humble, I've heard, so 'tis very well, Martin. And this doth mind me I bear you a message from my lady—"

"A message—from her?" I cried, gripping his arm. "Out with it, man, out with it and God forgive you this delay! What says my lady?"

"This, Martin: she would have you shave according to late custom."

"Why, so I will! But said she no more?"

"Aye, something of meeting you here. So get to your shaving and cheerily, comrade, cheerily. I'll to the ship, for at sunset 'tis up anchor and hey for England! I'll fire two guns to warn you aboard, and tarry not, for the ship lieth within a sunken reef and we must catch the flood." Here he turned to go, then paused to glance round the horizon with a seaman's eye. "The wind is fair to serve us, Martin," says he, pinching his chin, "yet I could wish for a tempest out o' the north and a rising sea!"

"And why, Adam, in Heaven's name?"

"'Twould be the sure and certain end of Tressady and Mings, comrade. Howbeit what's done is done and all things do lie in the hands of Providence, so do I cherish hope. Go and shave, Martin, go and shave!"

Left alone I betook me to my razors and shaved me with unwonted care, yet hearkening for her quick, light step the while.

Scarce was my labor ended that I thought to hear the rustle of leaves and hasted from the cave, calling on her name and mighty joyous and eager: "Damaris! Art here at last, dear my lady!"

And so came face to face with Sir Rupert.

He stood smiling at my discomfiture, yet his black brows were close—but he halted and folded his arms and I could see the betraying bulge of the pistol on his great side-pocket. For a while he measured me with his eye, at last he spoke: "Within the hour my Lady Brandon sails for England, and from this hour you will forget my Lady Brandon ever existed or—"

"Tush, man!" says I. "Begone, you weary me."

"Or," he went on with an airy gesture of his hand, "I shall cure your weariness for good—"

"Shoot me?"

"Most joyfully! Whatsoever hath chanced betwixt you in this wilderness, my Lady Brandon's honor must and—"

Warned by my look he clapped hand to his pocket, but as he freed the weapon I was upon him, grasping his pistol-hand. For a moment we swayed together, he striving frantically to break my hold, I to wrest the weapon from him, then it exploded, and uttering a sudden, long-drawn gasp he sank to the grass at my feet and lay very mute and still. Whilst I yet stared from his pallid face to the pistol where it had fallen, I heard shouts, a running of feet, and glancing up saw the three gentlemen, his companions, standing at gaze, motionless; then suddenly, they turned and hasted away, crying "Murder" on me as they ran.

Like one in a dream I stared down at Sir Rupert's motionless form, until I was aware of my lady beside him on her knees and of the pallor of her face as she looked from him to me, her eyes wide with horror: "If you have killed him,

Martin—if you have killed him, here is an end of our happiness—God forgive you!"

Now would I have spoken but found no words, for in this moment I knew that Sir Rupert was surely dead. Dumbly I watched the passionate labor of her dexterous hands, saw them pause at last to clasp and wring themselves in helpless despair, saw the three gentlemen, obedient to her word, stoop and lift that limp form and bear it slowly away towards Deliverance Sands and she going beside them.

Now as I stood watching her leave me, I heard the sudden roar of a gun, and glancing towards the ship saw they were already making sail. Roused by this I came beside my lady, and found my voice at last. "Here was the work of chance—not I, Damaris, not I!"

But she, gazing ever on that piteous, limp form, sought to silence me with a gesture. "God, Damaris, you'll never doubt my word? Speak—will you not speak to me? He threatened me—we strove together and the pistol went off in his grasp—"

"Damned murderer!" cried one of the gentlemen.

After this I held my peace, despairing, and thus we went in silence until before us was Deliverance Beach. All at once I caught her up in my arms and, despite her struggles, began to bear her back up the ascent. For a moment only she strove,

uttering no word, then hiding her face against me, suffered me to bear her where I would.

But now I heard shouts and cries that told me I was pursued. "You are mine, Damaris!" I cried. "Mine henceforth, and no man shall take you from me whiles I live!"

Despite my haste the noise of pursuit waxed louder, spurring me to greater effort. And now it became the end and aim of my existence to reach the cave in time, wherefore I began to run, on and up, until my breath came in great, panting sobs; my heart seemed bursting, and in my throbbing brain a confusion of wild thoughts:

"Better die thus, my love upon my heart. . . . The ship shall sail without us. . . . The door of the cave is stout, God be thanked and, firing from the loophole, I may withstand them all."

Breathless and reeling I gained the plateau at last, but as I staggered towards the cave I tripped and fell heavily, crushing her beneath me. But I struggled up, and bearing her within the cave, laid her upon my bed and closing the door, barred it; then I reached my muskets from their rack and set them in readiness. This done, and finding my lady so still and silent, I came to view her where she lay and, peering in the dimness, uttered a great cry to see the pale oval of cheek horribly bedabbled with blood. Trembling in a sickness of fear I sank beside her on my knees, then, seeing she yet breathed, I parted the silky hair above her temple and so came on a cruel gash. Now as I strove to staunch this precious blood I heard again the echoing thunder of a gun.

"Damaris!" says I, clasping her to me and kissing her pallid lips. "O Damaris, they are summoning us to England, d'ye hear, beloved, d'ye hear? Well, they shall call in vain—they shall sail without us. Love hath found us and here with Love will we abide. Wake, beloved, wake and tell me you would have it so!"

But, save for her breathing, and despite all my pleading and caresses, she lay like one dead. So I brought water and bathed her face and throat and wrists, yet all to no purpose, so that fear grew to agony. How if she die thus (thinks I)? Why then I can die likewise. But again, how if she wake, and finding the ship gone, despise me and, in place of her lover, look on me as her gaoler? For a long while I crouched there, my head bowed on my fists, since well I knew that England might shelter me nevermore. And yet to part with her that was become my very life—

As I knelt thus, in an agony of indecision, was sudden tumult of knocking upon the door and the sound of fierce voices: "Come forth, murderer! Open to us, rogue—open!"

But still I knelt there heeding only the hurry of my thoughts: "How if the ship sail without us? How if she wake and know me for her gaoler? How might I endure loneliness? How part with her that was become my life? Belike she might not hate me—"

"Open, murderer, open!" roared the voices.

"A murderer! How if she believe this? Better loneliness and death than to read horror of me in her every look!"

And now beyond the door was silence, and then I heard Adam hailing me "Oho, shipmate—unbar! Tide's on the turn and we must aboard. And trust me, Martin, for your comrade as will see justice done ye. So come, Martin, you and my lady and let's aboard!"

"Aye, aye, Adam!" quoth I. "Better die o' solitude than live with a breaking heart. So cheerily it is, Adam!"

Then rising, I took my dear lady in my arms, and holding her against my heart, I kissed her hair, her closed eyes, her pale, unresponsive lips, and bearing her to the door, contrived to open it and stepped forth of the cave. And here I found Adam, pistol in hand, with divers of his fellows and the three gentlemen who scowled amain, yet, eyeing Adam's weapon, did no more than clench their fists and mutter of gibbets and the like.

"Look you, Adam," says I, "my lady is stunned of a fall, but 'twill be no great matter once we come aboard—let us go."

"Why then, Lord love you, Martin—hasten!" says he. "For tide's falling and it's all we shall do to clear the reef."

Reaching Deliverance Sands I saw the boat already launched and manned and, wading into the water, laid my lady in the stern sheets.

"Come!" cried Adam, reaching me his hand. "In with ye, man—"

"Not I, Adam."

"Why, what now, comrade?" says he, staring.

"Now—my hand, Adam, and a prosperous voyage!"

"How, comrade, will ye stay marooned in this desolation?" And he stooped to peer down at me. "Martin," says he, gripping my hand and staring into my eyes, "doth this mean you are safer here by reason of the mystery of Sir Rupert's sudden end?"

"Mayhap!" says I, and loosed his hand. "What think you?"

"That you are no murderer, comrade, nor ever will be!"

"My lady said as much once! Farewell, Adam!" And I waded back to the beach.

"Give way, lads!" cries he. "Give way!" I heard the splash and beat of their oars, and when I turned to look I saw them halfway across the lagoon.

Then I turned and wandered aimlessly along these white sands that had known so often the light tread of her pretty feet. Very slowly I went, with eyes that saw not, ears that heard not and my mind a confusion of bitter thoughts.

At last I reached the little plateau, and from this eminence beheld the ship standing away under a press of sail, and saw that night was at hand. Suddenly as I watched, the ship, her lofty masts and gleaming canvas swam all blurred and misty on my sight, and sinking to my knees I bowed my head.

"Almighty God!" says I. "Thou hast shown unto me the wonder of love and the heaven it might have been, but since love is not for me, teach me how I may be avenged."

But now, even as I prayed thus, my voice brake upon a great sob insomuch that I might pray no more. Therefore I cast myself upon my face, forgetting all things but my great and bitter loneliness.

And so came night and shut me in.

Here then I make an end of this narrative of Black Bartlemy's Treasure—but how and in what manner I came to my vengeance is yet to tell.

EDITOR'S NOTE: *Martin Conisby's Vengeance*, by Jeffery Farnol, will be included in *The Even Bigger Book of Swashbuckling Adventure*.

Illustration Credits

Sword and Mitre—Maurice Leloir

The Sin of the Bishop of Modenstein—H. C. Edwards

Map by Howard Ince

Pirates' Gold—A. L. Ripley

The Queen's Rose—W. B. Gilbert

Señor Zorro Pays a Visit—Unknown

How the Brigadier Played for a Kingdom—William Barnes Wollen

Robin Hood Meets Guy of Gisborne—Louis Rhead

Map by Louis Rhead

White Plume on the Mountain—Alphonse de Neuville

The King of Spain's Will—Fred Money

The Cabaret de la Liberté—R. Caton Woodville

The Bride of Jagannath—Unknown

Captain Blood's Dilemma—Howard Pyle

Crillon's Stake—H. C. Edwards

The Black Death—Unknown

The Fight for Black Bartlemy's Treasure—Howard Pyle

Map—Unknown

If you enjoyed this anthology you should check out Lawrence Ellsworth's website, SwashbucklingAdventure.net, where you will find news, reviews, and additional content that will interest you. Trust me on this.